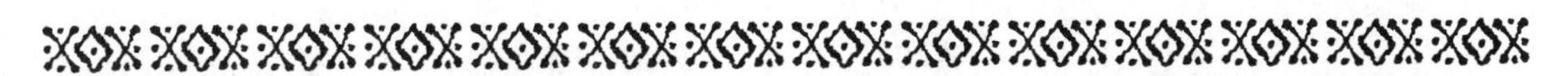

The African Storyteller

Stories from African Oral Traditions

Harold Scheub
University of Wisconsin-Madison

KENDALL/HUNT PUBLISHING COMPANY
4050 Westmark Drive Dubuque, Iowa 52002

ISBN 0-7872-5538-6

Library of Congress Catalog Card Number: 98-67966

Printed in the United States of America

10 9 8 7 6 5 4 3 2

≋ CONTENTS ≋

≋ Preface ≋

The stories in this collection range geographically from northern Africa to the south, from the east to the west. There are fifty-six stories; forty-three societies in thirty African countries are represented. Theme, genre, and performance style were considerations when tales were selected for inclusion in this volume.

The stories, taken from various collections, including those of nineteenth century travelers and those of contemporary folklorists, were gathered in diverse ways and under very different circumstances, depending on the period and on the resources of the collectors.

The materials have not been altered in any appreciable way, although language has sometimes been changed to assure consistency of verb tense, clarity, etc., and appropriate paragraphing has been provided. In certain cases, literal translations were rendered, it is hoped, more readable.

A collection such as this can give but a glimpse into the artistry and accomplishment of African oral performers. As is noted a number of times by those observers of African tradition quoted here, the full beauty and force of the performances are inevitably diminished when the stories are written down and divorced from their contexts, from the bodies and voices of the artists, from the audiences. Even so, the narratives as presented here do suggest the authority and splendor of storytelling in Africa, from earlier times to the present.

Map of Africa

The Art of the Storyteller

A Xhosa storyteller (photo by Harold Scheub)

The Language of Storytelling

Oral stories are not simply tales with obvious morals. One should not assume that thousands of years of humanity, of great civilizations and sophisticated artistic, religious and philosophical systems, would have resulted in a tradition containing the essence of the world's thought that is composed of a mere set of elementary fables.

We should attend to the works of the world's storytellers without leveling their works of art to the level of trivial moralizing. The stories of any given society encapsulate the deepest fears and hopes, dreams and nightmares of the people; within these emotional images, thinkers pass on to those of us who care to listen the thoughts and ideals of our forebears. Hear the storytellers, and do not patronize them.

The storytellers can enchant us and give us the wisdom of the ages. If we want to experience their stories in their fullest dimension, then we must not force the tales into stereotyped views of the oral tradition. We have to master the language of storytelling. We have to understand how patterns work, what motifs are and how they hold within them ancient emotions that have the capacity to elicit deep responses from contemporary audiences.

It is the storytellers who provide continuity between the generations, who maintain in a seemingly eternal flow the essential images of a society. Storytellers keep alive images of humanity that take audiences to the core of society. Tale, epic, myth: each deals with change, albeit on different levels, and each suggests the means for a recapturing of a mythic original, when humans were next to the gods. So it is that storytellers touch the face of God, and bring their audiences along with them.

Storytellers do not memorize stories: they remember the ancient images, or motifs, that contain the essential experiences of a people, and they place these within contemporary contexts, and so shape our conception of the real. Without the contemporary framework, the images would be of historical value but of no immediate benefit to the members of the audience. Storytellers always remember, always extemporize.

If change is a preoccupation of the storytelling tradition, then it is understandable that the great rites of passage are common themes. These are birth, puberty, marriage, and death. All humans experience these dramatic shifts in their lives, these crises, and, as with all of life's vicissitudes, storytellers are present to provide explanations, emotional cushioning, insight: the stories become our means of making corrections in our life cycles.

Myths, with gods as central characters, deal with change on a cosmological, universal scale. Epics, having heroes as central characters, describe change on a national or cultural plane. And the most common of the storytelling genres, tales, with central characters who are everyman and everywoman, celebrate change or transformation on an individual level. During the period that these transformations occur, great and unpredictable energies are unleashed, represented in the oral tradition by a character who cannot be categorized, the trickster, in both his divine and profane manifestations.

Some Definitions

Tradition is the handing down of information, beliefs, and customs by word of mouth or by example from one generation to another without written instruction.

Storytelling is not simply spoken narrative; it is *performance.* It includes the spoken word, but the performer's entire body is involved: it is a kind of restrained dance. The poetic qualities of oral languages are exploited during the telling of a tale, so that music is also an integral part of storytelling performance. Audience-performer relations are also important aspects of storytelling.

The language of the tales is not a language of realism; it is a language of art. One image or set of images frequently comes to stand for something else. *Fantasy* should not be interpreted in a literal way. It is a means of getting beyond reality, to explain the essence of real-life crises and rituals. "The Gamboler of the Plain" (story 8), for example, is not about a real-life buffalo. That buffalo comes to stand for something else: it becomes a symbol. A symbol is something that stands for or represents another thing, especially an object used to represent something abstract. This buffalo is a symbol of tradition, that which holds a society together.

One of the most complex devices used by storytellers is a *mirroring* process, during which images become metaphorical replications of other images. Here is where fantasy and reality are most vividly bonded.

The Storyteller's Tools

The *motif* is the basis of oral performance; it is an ancient image around which the patterns of the story are constructed, the persistent pursuer in "The Unborn Child" (story 2), for example. Motifs have to do with the gods, animals, magic, transformation, the dead, marvels, ogres, tests, identity, quests, and the like.

A motif is an image that is often fantastic, usually ancient, that, because of its value to the storyteller, persists in the tradition. The motif evokes emotional responses from members of audiences. Storytellers build patterns around motifs or clusters of motifs. Typical motifs: least likely hero, impossible tasks, bride/groom quests, swallowing monsters.

Repetition, *patterning,* with the motif at the core, is the essence of storytelling. Meaning, theme, message grow out of the combination of motif and pattern. All stories have patterns. Patterns are the chief organizing devices of storytelling. Images, which are sensed actions, are organized into patterns, and theme, or meaning, grows out of these patterns.

Storytellers typically work motifs into patterns, thereby linking the ancient motifs with contemporary images. It is this combination of ancient and modern images that provides generational continuity. But there is more than the word involved: storytelling is performance, an artistic blending of the body and voice of the performer, the music of the language, movements of the human body elevated into dance; it involves the performer's relations with the audience, a bonding of past and present, of the real and the fantastic.

Storytelling makes a community of us, enabling us to experience ourselves at our best . . . and at our worst. It is an art form that richly remembers and celebrates our finest impulses, as it recalls and commemorates our cruelest proclivities. Storytellers remember the past, and use that past to shape the present and the future. For better or for worse, storytellers forget nothing; they scrutinize our history, they plumb the most ancient depths of our human experience. Storytellers remind us that we continue to be motivated by emotions as deep as humanity itself. It is profoundly true that, as far as our emotional lives and histories are concerned, there is nothing new under the sun.

Finally, this admonition: Do not read the stories literally; they are works of art, and are not meant to be realistic appraisals of societies.

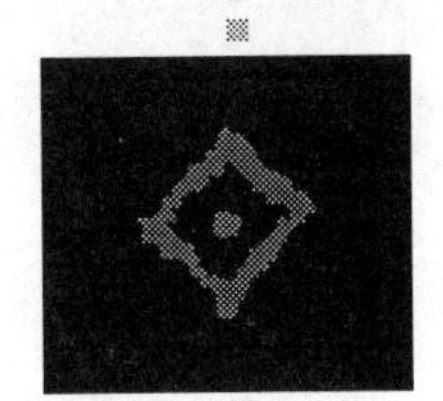

Mouse goes everywhere. Through rich men's houses she creeps, and visits even the poorest. At night, with her little bright eyes, she watches the doings of secret things, and no treasure-chamber is so safe but she can tunnel through and see what is hidden there.

In old days she wove a story-child from all that she saw, and to each of these she gave a gown of different colors—white, red, blue, or black. The stories became her children, and lived in her house and served her, because she had no children of her own.

Agra of Mbeban, an Ekoi storyteller

From P. Amaury Talbot, *In the Shadow of the Bush* (London: William Heinemann, 1912), p. 337.

Kabyle

The Beauty of the Partridge

The Kabyle live in Algeria.

A partridge rolled about on a forest floor, it rolled on the forest floor, rolled on the forest floor until its feathers took on a beautiful sheen.

It climbed halfway up a mountain and beat its beak against a rock, it beat its beak, it beat its beak until its beak became a glowing red hue.

Then it climbed to the top of the mountain and stared at the sky until its eyes became blue.

The partridge came down from the mountain, and it met a donkey, who said, "You are so beautiful, you must ride on my back."

The partridge got on the back of the donkey and rode across a plain.

As the partridge moved along on the back of the donkey, they met a jackal. When the jackal saw the partridge, he asked, "How did you become so beautiful?"

The partridge said, "I rolled on the forest floor until my feathers became as you see them, I beat my beak against a rock until my beak became the red that you see, and I stared into the sky until my eyes became the blue that you see."

The jackal said, "I must do that too."

The jackal rolled about on the forest floor, and its hair fell out.

It beat its nose against a rock, and broke its teeth.

The jackal climbed to the top of a mountain and stared at the sky. It became blind, and, as it came down from the mountain, it tripped, and plunged over a precipice. Its entrails fell out.

From Leo Frobenius, *Volksmärchen der Kabylen*, Vol. 3, *Das Fabelhafte* (Jena: Eugen Diederichs, 1921), p. 33.

Commentary

The storyteller frequently sets up a model, then repeats it with a significant variation. It is in the contrast between the model and its repetition that meaning is communicated.

In this story, the Kabyle storyteller establishes the model with the movements of the partridge into the forest, its rolling on the forest floor, the beating of its beak against the rock, staring into the sky. The resulting beauty of the partridge sets the jackal, and the second part of the story, into motion: the attempted replication of the model created by the partridge. The point of the story is in the contrast: the jackal does precisely what the partridge did, but with ruinous results.

The storyteller establishes a pattern, then manipulates the pattern to produce meaning: one should, like the partridge, fulfill oneself to the fullest, but one should not, like the jackal, attempt to be something that one is not. But the force of the story is not to be found in that obvious moral. It is in the emotions generated by the friction produced by the orchestration of the pattern.

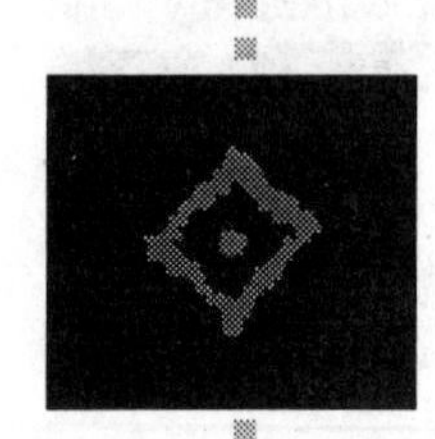

You have never known real, earthy, satisfying drama, the kind that gets into the blood and stays there, until you have been a part of these storytelling marathons.

Jessie Alford Nunn, *African Folk Tales* (New York: Funk and Wagnalls, 1969), p. 11.

Lenje

The Unborn Child

by Cibuta

The Lenje live in Zambia

A man had taken a wife, and now she had the joy of being with child. But there was an acute famine.

One day, when hunger was particularly severe and the man, accompanied by his wife, was dragging himself along in the direction of her mother's home in the hope of getting a little food there, they happened to find on the road a tree with abundant wild fruit on the top.

"Wife," he said, "get up there and get some fruit!"

She refused, saying, "I am with child! How can I climb a tree?"

He said, "Well then, don't climb!"

And he himself climbed the tree. He shook the branches, and his wife picked up had fallen down.

But he said, "Don't pick up my fruit! You just refused to climb!"

She said, "But I was only picking them up."

Thinking about his fruit, the man hurried down from the top of the tree, and said, "You have eaten some of it!"

She said, "Why, I have not!"

From J. Torrend, *Specimens of Bantu Folk-lore from Northern Rhodesia* (London: Kegan Paul, French, Trübner, 1921), pp. 14–17.

And he came at her with his spear, and he stabbed his wife. And there, on that spot, she died.

Then the man gathered his fruit with both hands. There he is, eating the fruit, remaining there where his wife was stretched out dead.

Then, all of a sudden, he started to run! Run! Run! Run! Without stopping once, until he reached a rise.

There he slept, out of sight of the place where he had left the woman.

Meanwhile, the child that was in the womb rushed out of it, dragging its umbilical cord. First, it looked around for the direction that its father had taken, then it started singing a song:

"Father, wait for me!
Father, wait for me,
The little wombless.
Who is it who has eaten my mother?
The little wombless!
How swollen are those eyes!
Wait till the little wombless comes."

That gave him a fright.

"There," he said, "there comes a thing that is speaking." He listened, he stared in that direction. "This is the child coming to follow me after all that, after I have killed its mother. It was left in the womb." Then rage took his wit away, and he killed the little child!

And there the man is, starting anew, moving on.

And here, where the little bone of the child had been left: "Little bone, gather yourself up! Little bone, gather yourself up!"

Soon it was up again, and then came the song:

"Father, wait for me!
Father, wait for me,
The little wombless.
Who is it who has eaten my mother?
The little wombless!
How swollen are those eyes!
Wait till the little wombless comes."

The father stopped. "Again, the child that I have killed! It has risen and is coming, I'll wait for him."

So he hid and waited for the child, and he had a spear in his hand. The child came, he could be seen a short distance away. And as soon as the child came—quick with the spear! Stab it! Then the man looked for a hole, he shoveled the little body into it and heaped branches up at the entrance.

Then he ran with all speed! With all speed!

At last he reached the kraal where lived the mother of his dead wife, the grandmother of the child.

When he arrived, he sat down.

Then his brothers and sisters-in-law came with smiling faces.

"Well! Well! You have come to see us!"

"We have," he said, "come to see you."

And a house was prepared for him and his wife—she was expected.

Then his mother-in-law was heard asking from afar, "Well! And my daughter, where has she been detained?"

He said, "I have left her at home. I came alone to beg for a little food. Hunger is roaring!"

"Sit down inside there, Father."

Food was brought to him. And he began to eat. And when he had finished eating, he even went to sleep.

Meanwhile, the child had squeezed itself out of the hole it had been put into, and again, with its umbilical cord trailing behind:

> "Father, wait for me!
> Father, wait for me,
> The little wombless!
> Who is it who has eaten my mother?
> The little wombless!
> How swollen are those eyes!
> Wait till the little wombless comes!"

The people listened to the song coming from the direction of the path.

"That thing coming along there, speaking indistinctly—what is it?"

"It seems to be a person."

"What is it?"

"It looks, man, like a child killed by you on the road!"

"And now, as we look at the way you're sitting—you seem to be only half-seated!"

"We cannot see him very well."

"It cannot be the child, Mother. It remained at home."

The man got up to shake himself a little.

And his little child, too, was coming with all speed! It was quite near now, with its mouth wide open:

> "Father, wait for me!
> Father, wait for me,
> The little wombless!
> Who is it who has killed my mother?

The little wombless!
How swollen are those eyes!
Wait till the little wombless comes!"

Everyone was staring. They said, "There comes a little red thing. It still has the umbilical cord hanging on."

Inside the house there, where the man was, there was complete silence.

Meanwhile, the child was coming on feet and buttocks, with its mouth wide open—but still at a distance from its grandmother's house.

"Just over there!" everyone said.

The grandmother looked towards the road, and noticed that the little thing was perspiring, and what speed!

Then the song:

"Father, wait for me!
Father, wait for me,
The little wombless.
Who is it who has eaten my mother?
The little wombless!
How swollen are those eyes!
Wait till the little wombless comes!"

Great Lord! It scarcely reached its grandmother's house when it jumped into it. And on the bed:

"Father, wait for me!
Father, have you come?
Yes, you have killed my mother.
How swollen are those eyes!
Wait till the little wombless comes."

Then the grandmother put this question to the man: "Now what sort of song is this child singing? Have you not killed our daughter?"

She had scarcely added, "Surround him," and he was already in their hands. His very brothers-in-law tied him. And then, all the spears were poised together in direction, everyone saying, "You are the man who killed our sister. . . ."

Then they just threw the body away there to the west.

And the grandmother picked up her little grandchild.

Commentary

There is a single pattern in this story: an unborn child becomes representative of a father's guilty conscience.

The conflict has to do with the father's murder of his wife. In the pattern, the unborn child, a manifestation of a venerable motif, that of the persistent pursuer, stalks the murdering husband. The child cannot be killed. The murderer attempts to destroy it again and again, but it reconstitutes itself, until it has identified the murderer in the presence of his in-laws.

The child is both an extension of the mother and a representation of the father's guilt-ridden conscience. The father, agonized because of what he has done, moves to his own doom. The meaning is obvious; the power of the story is in the motif of the persistent pursuer and in the emotions that it generates.

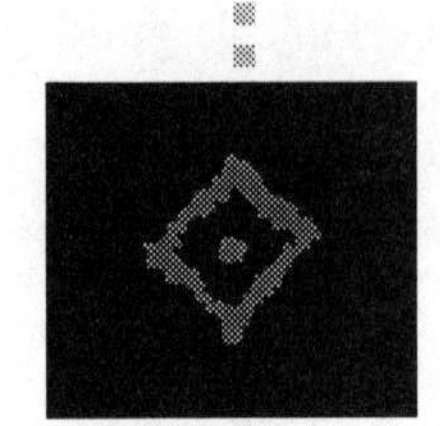

The narrator commences the story with the formal beginning of the story. This said in a slightly high-pitched voice. It appears to be done in order to prepare the audience: it proves to be an effective way of drawing their attention and arousing their interest. . . . Then the narrator enters upon his narrative by tackling the first episode which is in actual fact the introduction. This usually includes mention of indirectly introduced characters whose part will become clear as the story develops or as they participate in the story. Then the narrator explains or unfolds the story: thus the story is developed. . . . When the events of the story have all thus been narrated, the relater closes the "scene" by saying the formal ending. This, like the beginning, is said in a slightly high-pitched voice. . . .

Garvey Nkonki, "The Traditional Prose Literature of the Ngqika," M.A. (African Studies), University of South Africa, n.d., pp. 91–93.

San

The Blue Crane

The San once lived throughout southern Africa. They now live in the Kalahari Desert and in Namibia

The blue crane's friend was the frog.

The frog was a person, her husband was a person, the blue crane was a person. They were people of the early race.

The frog's husband sat and sulked because the frog would not speak to him. As he sat there, the beetle came flying; it flew past his nose, and he jumped up and ran away.

Then the blue crane also jumped up; she ran after the frog's husband to catch him. She went along, snatching at him, and he went into a stone, a flat stone.

The blue crane was searching for him. She went on and on. She found his spoor, and followed it.

She said, "This is the place where I trod. I was trying to catch my friend's husband here. I snatched at him, but missed him, because he went in just here."

Then she went back and found her own footprints.

She said, "This is the place along which I ran. I was trying to grab my friend's husband here."

She grew lean while she was searching there. Grief made her grow lean, she became bones.

Two lions, Belt and Mat, heard her as she was searching there. The lions followed the sound to where she was. They saw her, they stole up to her. The lions killed her, and ate her.

From Dorothea F. Bleek, ed., *The Mantis and His Friends* (Cape Town: T. Maskew Miller, [1923]), pp. 26–27.

Mat said, "Belt, I don't want this person's bone to spring out of your mouth."

They were eating the blue crane. Then the blue crane's merrythought sprang out of Belt's mouth, and went and lay nearby. They tried to find it, but they could not see it, so they went away.

Then the mantis sought the blue crane. He saw the lions' spoor. He searched, and found the place where they had killed the blue crane. He went along searching, until he caught sight of the merrythought lying there, for it was big. He picked it up, and went and put it into the water. The mantis went home, and stayed at the houses there.

Then the mantis came out and went to look.

The blue crane jumped up and splashed into the water.

So the mantis turned back and returned to the houses. He stayed there.

Once more, he went out to look. As he came up, he saw the blue crane sitting in the sun. She had grown. He turned back without startling her. While the blue crane sat basking, he went to make things, clothes which he meant to give to the blue crane when she grew up.

He went out again, and again saw the blue crane sitting in the sun. He turned back and left her in peace, for he wished her to sit quietly. He did not startle her. He returned home.

Then he took the clothes, because he thought that the blue crane had grown up; she seemed to be a girl. He went out, he saw the blue crane sitting, basking. He put down the things and stole up to her. He caught hold of her. When she tried to get into the water, he held her fast and rubbed her face with his perspiration; he made her smell his scent. He told the blue crane that he was her brother. It was he, the tinderbox, who was holding her; he was her elder brother. She should stop struggling and sit down.

Then the blue crane sat down.

He covered her with a cap that he had made for her, he gave her a cape and a skin petticoat. The blue crane put on the cape and tied on the petticoat.

Then the mantis took the blue crane with him.

They returned home.

Commentary

This is a myth, explaining the origin and differentiation of living beings and heavenly bodies. Mantis (lkággen—see stories 13 and 14) is God. The story takes place at the beginning of time, during myth time, the time of creation. This is not simply a story of mythic origins, nor is it merely the story of a domestic conflict. It is a heavenly comment on peace and harmonious human relations. God emphasizes domestic consonance, and blesses the acts of those who would assist in this peaceful endeavor. The gods do not just create life, they generate life that is meant to be ordered, serene, agreeable.

The story begins as a domestic drama, a tale, in which the blue crane attempts to reconcile the frogs. When the blue crane is killed, the story becomes a creation myth. In the main pattern, a pattern of the creation of life, Mantis creates the blue crane. It is an etiological or mythic ending: God creates the blue crane, and the lions move into the heaven as stars.

Part one is a tale. In the opening segment, a brief domestic drama, the frog will not speak to her husband. This establishes the conflict that sets the story into motion and will lead to the mythic ending. The husband, annoyed, runs off. Blue Crane, Frog's friend, goes after him, to reconcile husband and wife. But the frog has disappeared. A pattern ensues: as Blue Crane continues her quest for Frog, she grows lean.

Part two is a myth. The domestic dispute now assumes cosmological proportions: the blue crane is destroyed by representations of the universe—the lions, who will become stars, a part of the cosmos, of God. The eat her, all but her merrythought. Then God, in the main pattern of the story, recreates Blue Crane from her merrythought, her soul, and life has been created. This is the mythic part of the story, the creation, the act of God.

This is the relationship between myth and tale: By creating life from the merrythought of Blue Crane, God is celebrating her life-giving qualities and thereby approving what she was doing in the part one of the story, her efforts to help the frogs. It is a storyteller's way of saying that this kind of activity is proper, that it is life-producing, that it is blessed by the gods.

The main mythic part of the story has to do with differentiation, creation—the making of the universe (the lions become stars), of the animals (the blue crane). And this is a moral universe, so goodness is enshrined at this earliest of periods. In giving life to Blue Crane, God is touching her acts with immortality.

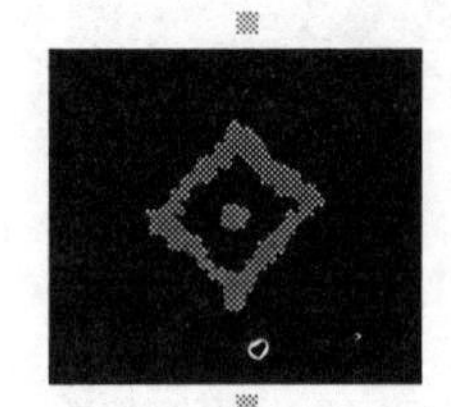

Africans gave artistic utterance to their deepest thoughts and feelings about those abstract and concrete things that came within their existence; to their speculation about the origin of things, including man himself and the universe; to their interpretation of the struggle between man and the mysterious forces that surrounded him, and to their admiration for those individuals of the human race to whom legend gave credit for the triumph of man over such forces; to their traditional wisdom concerning conduct. Lastly, they gave "concrete and artistic expression . . . in emotional and rhythmical language" to their admiration for collective and individual courage and achievement. . . .

A. C. Jordan, a Xhosa writer *Towards an African Literature* (Berkeley: University of California Press, 1973), p. 3.

Ekoi

The Python's Shining Stone

by Okun Asere

The Ekoi live in southern Nigeria.

Sheep lived in a certain town. He became a close friend of Antelope, whose home was in the bushes. When the two animals had grown up, they went out and cleared farm land. Sheep planted plantains in his, while Antelope set his with coco-yams.

When the time came for the fruits to ripen, Sheep went to his farm and cut a bunch of plantains, while Antelope dug up some of his coco-yams.

Each cleaned his food and put it in the pot to cook. When all was ready, they sat down and ate.

Next morning, Antelope said, "Let's trade. I saw a bunch of plantains on your farm that I would like to have. Will you go to mine and take some coco-yams?"

That was arranged, and Antelope said to Sheep, "Try to beat up some fufu."

Sheep tried, and found that it was very good. He gave some to Antelope, who ate all he wanted. Then he took the bunch of plantains and hung it up in his house.

Next morning, he found that the fruit had grown soft, so he did not care to eat it. He took the plantains and threw them away in the bushes.

During the day, Mbui Sheep came along and smelled the plantains. He looked around until he found them, then picked one up and began to eat. They were very

From P. Amaury Talbot, *In the Shadow of the Bush* (London: William Heinemann, 1912), p. 344–349.

sweet. He ate his fill, then went on, and later met a crowd of apes. To them he said, "Today I found a very sweet thing in the bushes."

In time, Antelope grew hungry again, and Sheep said to him, "If you're hungry, why don't you tell me?"

He went back to his farm and got four bunches of plantains. As he came back, he met the monkey people. They begged for some of his fruit, so he gave it to them.

After they had eaten all there was, they in their turn went on and met a herd of wild boars. To these they said, "There is very fine food to be got from Sheep and Antelope."

The wild boars therefore came and questioned Antelope: "Where is coco-yam to be had?"

Antelope answered, "The coco-yams belong to me."

The boars begged for some, so Antelope took a basket, filled it at his farm, and gave it to them.

After they were satisfied, they went on their way, and next morning they met Elephant. To him they said, "Greetings, Lord! Last night, we got very good food from the farms over there."

Elephant at once ran and asked the two friends, "Where do you get so much food?"

They said, "Wait a little."

Sheep took his long machete and went to his farm. He cut five great bunches of plantains, and carried them back. Antelope got five baskets of coco-yams, which he brought to Elephant. After Elephant had eaten all this, he thanked them and went away.

All the beasts of the field came in their turn and begged for food, and to each the two friends gave willingly of all that they had.

Bush-cow was the last to come.

Now, not far from the two farms there was a great river called Akarram. In the midst of the river, deep down, dwelt Crocodile.

One day, Bush-cow went down into the water to drink, and from him Crocodile learned that much food was to be had nearby.

Crocodile came out of the water and began walking towards the farms. He went to Sheep and Antelope, and said, "I am dying of hunger. Please give me food."

Antelope said, "To the beasts who are my friends, I shall give all that I have. But to you I shall give nothing, for you are no friend of mine."

But Sheep said, "I do not like you very much, but I shall give you one bunch of plantains."

Crocodile took them and said, "Do not close your door tonight when you lie down to sleep. I'll come back and buy more food from you at a great price."

Crocodile then went back to the water and sought out a python that dwelt there. To him he said, "I have found two men on land who have much food."

Python said, "I too am hungry. Will you give me something to eat?"

So Crocodile gave Python some of the plantains that he had brought. When Python had tasted one of them, he said, "How sweet it is! Will you go back and bring more?"

Crocodile said, "Will you give me something with which to buy?"

Python answered, "Yes, I'll give you something with which you can buy the whole farm!"

Then he took from within his head a shining stone, and gave it to the crocodile, who began his journey back to the farm. As he went, night fell, and all the road grew dark. But he held in his jaws the shining stone, and it made a light on his path so that all the way was bright. When he neared the dwelling of the two friends, he hid the stone, and called out, "Come out and I will show you something that I have brought."

It was very dark when they came to speak with him. Slowly the crocodile opened his claws in which he held up the stone, and it began to glimmer between them. When he held it right out, the entire place became so bright that one could see to pick up a needle or any small thing.

He said, "The price of this object that I bring to you is one whole farm."

Antelope said, "I cannot buy. If I give up my farm, nothing remains to me. What is the use of this great shining stone if I starve to death?"

But Sheep said, "I shall buy—oh, I shall buy, I shall give my farm full of plantains, for what you bring fills the whole earth with light. Come, let us go. I shall show you my farm. From here to the water-side, all round is my farm. Take it all, do what you choose with it. Only give me the great shining stone so that when darkness falls the entire earth may still be light."

Crocodile said, "I agree."

Then Sheep went to his house with the stone, and Antelope went to his. Sheep placed the stone above the lintel, so that it might shine for all the world, but Antelope closed his door and lay down to sleep.

In the morning, Sheep was very hungry, but he had nothing to eat because he had sold all his farm for the great white stone.

Next night and the night after, he slept filled with hunger. But on the third morning, he went to Antelope, and asked, "Will you give me a single coco-yam?"

Antelope answered, "I can give you nothing, for now you have nothing to give in exchange. It was not I who told you to buy the shining thing. To give something when plenty remains is good, but no one but a fool would give his all so that a light may shine in the dark!"

Sheep was very sad. He said, "I have done nothing bad. Formerly, no one could see in the night. Now the python stone shines so that everyone can see to go wherever he chooses."

All that day, Sheep still endured, though nearly dying of hunger, and at night he crept down to the water, very weak and faint.

By the side of the river he saw a palm tree, and on it a man trying to cut down clusters of ripe kernels, but this was hard to do because it had grown very dark.

Sheep said, "Who is there?"

The man answered, "I am Effion Obassi."

Sheep called, "What are you doing?"

Effion Obassi replied, "I am trying to gather palm kernels, but I cannot do so because it is so dark among these great leaves."

Sheep said to him, "It is useless to try to do such a thing in the dark. Are you blind?"

Effion Obassi answered, "I am not blind. Why do you ask?"

Then Sheep said, "Good. If you are not blind, I beg you to throw me down only one or two palm kernels, and in return I shall show you a thing brighter and more glorious than anything you have seen before."

Effion Obassi replied, "Wait a minute, and I will try to throw a few kernels down to you. Afterwards, you can show me the shining thing, as you said."

He threw down three palm kernels, which Sheep took. They stayed his hunger a little.

Then he called, "Please try to climb down. We'll go together to my house."

Effion Obassi tried very hard, and after some time he stood safely at the foot of the tree by the side of Sheep.

When they got to his house, Sheep said, "Will you wait here a little while I go to question the townspeople?"

First, he went to Antelope, and asked, "Will you not give me a single coco-yam to eat? See, the thing that I bought at the price of all that I had turns darkness to light for you. But as for me, I shall die of hunger."

Antelope said, "I shall give you nothing. Take back the thing for which you sold everything, and we'll stay in our darkness as before."

Then Sheep begged all the townsfolk to give him a little food in return for the light that he had bought for them. But they all refused.

So Sheep went back to his house, and he took the shining stone and gave it to Effion Obassi, saying, "I love the earth-folk, but they do not love me. Now take the shining thing for which I gave all my possessions. Go back to the place from which you came, because I know that you belong to the sky-people. And when you reach your home in the heavens, hang my stone in a place where all the earth-folk may see its shining and be glad."

Effion Obassi took the stone, and went back by the road on which he had come. He climbed up the palm tree, and the great leaves raised themselves upwards, pointing to the sky, and they lifted him up until, from their points, he could climb into heaven.

When he reached his home, he called all the lords of the sky, and said, "I have brought back a thing today that can shine so that all the earth will be light. From now on, everyone on earth or in heaven will be able to see at the darkest hour of the night."

The lords looked at the stone and wondered. Then they consulted together, and made a box.

Effion Obassi said, "Make it so that the stone can shine out only from one side."

When the box was finished, he set the globe of fire within it, and said, "This stone is mine. From this time, all the people must bring me food. I shall no longer go to seek any for myself."

For some time, they brought him plenty of food, but after a while they grew tired. Then Effion Obassi covered the side of the box, so that the stone would not shine until they brought him more food.

That is the reason the moon is sometimes dark, and people on earth say, "It is the end of the month. The people have grown weary of bringing food to him, and he will not let his stone shine out until they bring him a fresh supply."

Commentary

This is a myth, an etiological story: it explains how the moon came into being. In the etiological or mythic ending, Sheep gives the stone to the godly Effion Obassi, who takes it into the heavens where it becomes the moon.

◇ **Images and patterns**—The images in the story are organized primarily by two patterns: In pattern one, animals of the field come to Sheep and Antelope, asking for food. In pattern two, Sheep, having traded his farm for the shining stone, begs for food and gets none.

There is a pattern of generosity followed by a pattern of want. The patterns emphasize generosity and selfishness, and the story becomes a heavenly comment on generosity. The gods stress a society of giving: the moon symbolizes this, and the sacrifices demanded by the gods (or there will be no moon) assure it. Stories often speak to themselves in this way, one part explaining the other. This might involve a domestic tale and a cosmological myth: the origin of the moon and of sacrifices to the gods grows out of a domestic situation having to do with neighbors and farming. The story parallels Effion Obassi (God) and Sheep (a mortal): human behavior finds reflection and correction in godly acts

Pattern one is a pattern of generosity of Sheep and Antelope. They feed all the animals of the field (Mbui sheep, apes, boars, elephant, all beasts, bushcow). The pattern is broken when Antelope refuses to feed Crocodile, and the theme is revealed when Sheep returns to the pattern, and gives Crocodile food.

Crocodile buys the farm of Sheep for a shining stone given to him by Python. Crocodile and Python are the most despised of the animals, yet they provide the moon and the test of generosity, symbol of the gods. And Sheep, who seems to have learned the lesson of generosity well, puts the moon on the lintel "that it might shine for all the world."

Pattern two is a pattern of selfishness. The generosity earlier displayed now ceases. Sheep has no food, and begins to waste away. Antelope and other townspeople will not help him.

Other animals, whom he has helped, now turn against him because he bartered his farm for a stone. Now there is no generosity.

Meaning grows out of the patterns. Out of the contrast between the two patterns emerges the theme of the tale. The etiological ending stresses the gods' reaction to the second pattern. The sheep and the stone are equated to the gods and the moon: if the moon is to glow, the people must give sacrifices to the gods; if humans are to prosper, they must be generous to each other.

Sheep gets food from Effion Obassi, a god. Because no one on earth will help him (a return to the second pattern), he gives the shining stone to God who carries it to the heavens. The gods put it into a box, so that the light can be denied to the people until they provide sacrifices to the gods of food—that is, until they learn the lesson of Sheep. God is thereby giving immortality to Sheep's generous acts.

There is another etiological element here: the story explains the moon's phases, tying these to human traits. The moon and its waning and waxing are a constant reminder to humans of Sheep's generosity.

This is a story about creation, but it is also about generosity and selfishness.

A Xhosa storyteller (photo by Harold Scheub)

Tata Manga, regardless of the size of his audience, entered fully into the spirit of each tale he told, dramatizing the dialogues, varying his tone and his speed, utilizing the full range of Lonkundo locutions, and employing every opportunity for the increasing of suspense. . . . His mastery of both content and style was borne out by his unflawed handling of the cumulative songs; his flexibility and his awareness of his audience were shown by his sharing of their merriment and his alteration of pacing to make room for their laughter and still not lose the narrative thread.

Mable H. Ross and Barbara K. Walker, *"On Another Day . . ." Tales Told among the Nkundo of Zaire* (Hamden, Conn.: Archon Books, 1979), p. 50.

Arabic

The Weight before the Door

This story was collected in Morocco.

There lived once a man so rich that he measured his money by the bushel, as we poverty-stricken ones measure barley or bran.

One day, he fell very ill, and, feeling that his last hour had come, he called his son, and gave over to him all his wealth and property. He said to him, "My son, I leave your welfare in the hands of the Almighty, and to the care of such-and-such a one, a Jew, who is my friend. Listen to his words, as if they were mine. I have instructed him to find a bride for you when you are ready to marry."

Having blessed his son, the man died.

After a time, the young man desired to marry, so, according to his father's last words, he went to the Jew and informed him.

The Jew said, "It is well," and he set out and found a young woman. He made all necessary preparations, and caused a suitable feast to be prepared. The morning before the carrying of the bride to the groom, he called the young man and said to him, "Son of my friend, I have found you a bride. But before we may know that she is the one destined for you by Allah, it is necessary that you should do this. Tonight, after the bride has been brought to your house and she is seated in your room awaiting you, and before you go to her, I shall cause a heavy weight to be placed before the door of the room. You are to attempt to remove the weight. If she is the fitting wife for you, you will succeed; if you do not succeed, you will know that she is not for you, and you should divorce her tomorrow without so much as seeing her face."

The young man wondered about this, but said, "It is well."

From Feridah Kirby Green, "Folklore from Tangier," *Folklore*, XIX (1908), 453–455.

That night, the bride was brought with much pomp and rejoicing, and the bride was taken to the man's apartment and seated there in a rich robe to await him. Her eyes were closed, and a veil covered her face.

The bridegroom, after tarrying a while in the mosque with young men of his acquaintance, came up to the door of the room. The door was ajar, so that he could see the shrouded figure. Before the door lay the weight, of which the Jew had spoken. The weight was round like a ball, and not large.

The youth thought, "I shall lift it with ease, and won't wait to go in to my wife."

But when he tried to lift the weight, he could not move it—no, not the breadth of a finger nail. He tried with all his strength to move it by lifting and pushing and rolling it, but in vain.

He did not enter the room.

The next morning, he went into the Jew, and told him what had happened.

The Jew said, "You must divorce this woman, my son, and I shall seek another for you."

This was done.

The Jew, after he had found a second woman, caused a yet finer feast to be prepared. The bride was brought, as had happened the first time, and the bride was seated in the young man's room.

When he came to enter, the weight again lay before the slightly open door. Though he saw the veiled woman, and though he tried with all his strength to remove the obstacle and go to her, he could not—no, though he struggled until dawn.

When the Jew heard that the young man had failed once more, he sighed, and said, "Nor is this wife destined for you by the All-wise. Let us send her back to her father, and I shall seek again."

All was done as he said.

When the young man came for the third time to try to enter the bridal chamber, for the third time he saw that the way was blocked.

He said, "This time, I shall remove the weight, or, if I cannot do it, I shall try no more. If I do not succeed this time, I shall know that it is decreed that I should die unmarried."

He bent his back and seized the ball with his two hands, and he pulled at it until he groaned with weariness, but in vain.

The young woman within heard his groans, and she said to herself, "Shall I let this man who is my husband kill himself without striving to help him?"

She arose, put aside her veil and her outer robe of gold, and pushed herself through the half-open door. She approached the young man who was wrestling with the heavy weight, and she said, "Let me help, my lord."

The two placed their hands together on the ball, and pushed with all their force. The weight rolled on one side of the door, so that the entrance was free.

The young man looked on the fair face of the woman who had come to his aid, and saw that she was in truth the bride destined for him. He embraced her, and the two entered the room together.

Commentary

This is a realistic story, with no discernible fantasy images in it. But the Jew plays the role of god here, and so moves the story into the realm of the supernatural. In the process, he reveals what marriage is all about.

There is a single pattern in the tale. The Jew becomes the means whereby the significance of the marriage bond is revealed. Taking on the role of God, he sets things up, knowing that the perfect marriage will be one in which husband and wife together struggle with life's problems, problems that are here represented by the weight before the door.

Motifs include bride quest and impossible tasks. The pattern has to do with the several attempts to remove the weight from the door. After failing twice, the young man is able to remove the weight with the assistance of his bride-to-be.

Meaning, as always, grows out of the pattern. The wise Jew, who sets up the meetings, knows that the best bride will be the woman who assists the man in removing the weight. The suggestion is that marriage is a partnership.

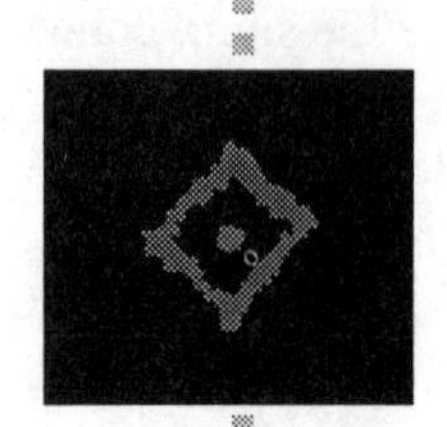

When the day's toil is over, the dura pounded, the two meals cooked, the water carried, the children cared for, the mother sits there in the light of the smudge fire which is made to keep mosquitoes away. She has had a busy day. Now they all sit around in the firelight, visiting, or telling tales of long ago. . . .

Ray Huffman, *Nuer Customs and Folklore* (Oxford: Oxford University Press, 1931), p. 24.

Tswana

Salamone the Orphan

The Tswana live in Botswana and South Africa.

Once, there was a boy, Salamone, whose father was dead. The boy mourned for him day after day, until at last his mother went to the chief and asked that the boy be put to death.

The chief agreed to this request. He sent the boy out with a hunting party so that he might be killed while hunting.

But the servant of his father told Salamone what had been decided with regard to him, and warned him to be wary as they intended to kill him during the hunt.

The hunters spread themselves in such a manner that it seemed impossible for Salamone to escape, but he managed to evade them. He ran to the chief, but as no man had laid hands on him, he could not substantiate his complaint.

He ran away then, and during his flight he met an ant.

The ant asked him where he was going.

He told the ant what had happened, and said that he did not know where to go.

Then the ant pulled out one of its antennae, and gave it to him, saying, "If you have difficulty, think of me."

The lad went on his way, and after a time he met a dove.

The dove asked him where he was going.

His reply was, "I don't know."

The dove gave him a feather from its wing, saying, like the ant, "If you have difficulty, think of me."

From J. Tom Brown, *Among the Bantu Nomads* (Philadelphia: Seeley, Service, 1926), pp. 178–181.

Salamone proceeded on his journey, and after a time he came to a house that had no door or opening except at the pinnacle of the roof.

He did not know what to do.

Then he remembered the words of the ant, and, taking its little antenna, he put it into his hair. He was instantly transformed into an ant, and was able to enter the house by means of the little cracks through which the ants went in.

He found a woman inside who was surprised to see him.

She asked him where he was going.

Salamone also found inside the house a large flower. He asked what it was.

The woman said, "I live here with an ogre, and this flower is his strength. If you can sever it, you will have conquered him."

After a time, the ogre, who had ten heads, came home, and Salamone changed himself into an ant once more.

But the ogre, as it entered the house, said, "Where does the scent of a human being come from?"

The woman denied that anyone had entered the house.

Then the ogre slept.

When the ogre was asleep, Salamone broke off the flower.

Immediately, the ogre awoke. As they started to fight, Salamone cut off one of the ogre's heads.

But the ogre only said, "Nine heads remain! You shall not cut off another!"

Then Salamone cut off the second head, but the ogre said, "You shall not cut off any of the remaining heads!"

The fight went on in that way until all the heads were cut off. With each cut, the ogre said, "You shall not cut off another!"

When all the heads had been cut off and the ogre was dead, Salamone took the woman and the cattle, and they departed from that place and built a house in another part of the country.

Now, war had scattered the society from which Salamone had fled. Among the refugees was the servant who had warned Salamone of the plot of his enemies. In his flight, the servant came to the house of Salamone, who asked him where he had come from.

The servant told the story of the war and how the people had fled. He said, "Your mother and some other people are just behind me, quite near!"

Salamone sent the servant to call his mother.

When she arrived, he slaughtered a beast for her. While the meat was still in the pot on the hearth, he told someone to get a bowl and give her some of the soup. But while his mother was still drinking the soup, he pushed the bowl into her face. The hot soup was forced into her mouth and nostrils, and she died.

Then Salamone took the people back to their deserted town and became their chief, for their former chief had been killed in the war.

Commentary

This story has to do with a boy moving away from a tainted society; away from home, with the assistance of nature, he is reborn. All of the deaths in the tale suggest loss, but out of death comes new life. It is a story of transition.

This is the conflict: Salamone's efforts to escape death at the hands of his mother and chief. These activities raise questions about the morality of this community.

◇ **Patterns and meaning**—Three patterns are relevant to the theme of this story. The first pattern runs through the story, and has to do with various efforts to kill, whether at the hands of the mother, the chief, warriors in battle. The motif: death-dealers. The second pattern involves assistance from nature in the form of an ant and a dove. This is a common motif of the storytelling tradition: the helpful animal. The third pattern is a fantasy mirror of the first: destruction by a fantastic ogre. The pattern involves the cutting off of its ten heads. The motif, another common one, is that of the swallowing monster. The relationship of the patterns: the third pattern is a fantasy mirroring of the realistic first pattern. The second pattern, a harmony with nature pattern, makes possible the third, a harmony with culture pattern.

The theme that grows out of these three patterns has to do with the war that occurs in Salamone's land. This is a mirror of the efforts to destroy Salamone, efforts that are destructive of human society. With the help of nature, the ant and dove, Salamone destroys the evil in his society, that is, his mother, his origins, and sets things right, restoring order and peace, appropriately becoming the leader. A boy is cutting himself off from his tainted past, represented here by his mother, undergoing an ordeal (he could die), and is reborn a man.

A mother and a political leader conspire to kill the youth: it is a society that is out of joint, and the war mirrors this. Salamone is assisted by an ant and, potentially, a dove. With this help, he cuts off the ten heads of an ogre. The ogre is representative of death, a fantasy replication, a mirroring, of the deaths in the real world (war), of the tainted society (the death-dealing mother and chief). As Salamone, with the help of nature, sets things right in fantasy, so in reality, the mother is destroyed: she represents death, Salamone's past. And Salamone, representing life and nature, becomes the leader of the people, the chief having appropriately been destroyed in the war. When Salamone moves into the world of fantasy, his wretched experiences in the real world are duplicated.

Fantasy becomes a storyteller's means of commenting on reality.

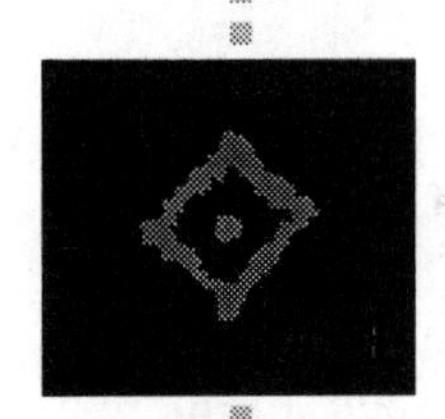

The stories are told round the fire on nights that are too dark for dancing. The various groups will arrange themselves round the blazing hearths, and after the news of the day has been exhausted, one will tell a story suggested by some item of news, or the actions of a friend, or the saying of an enemy.

The story is told with dramatic power and forcible eloquence, the narrator acting the various parts and imitating the sounds of the different animals. In some of the stories there are choruses, and these are taken up and sung heartily by the clapping of their hands.

There is no greater treat than to listen to a Congo story told in the original by one of these born storytellers—the lights and shadows caused by the flickering fire, the swaying body of the narrator, the fixed attention and grunts of approval by the listeners, the great dark beyond, the many mystic sounds issuing from the surrounding bush and forest lend a peculiar weirdness to the story and its teller.

John H. Weeks, *Congo Life and Folklore* (London: Religious Tract Society, 1911), pp. 369–370.

Kikuyu

The Head of a Masai Woman

The Kikuyu live in Kenya in eastern Africa.

One day, many years ago, three Kikuyu warriors went off to steal some cattle from a hostile people. With them, they took a bullock for food, because the enemy's villages were many days away.

After traveling for a long distance, they came to an open space, and while they were crossing it they heard a voice calling out to them to stop. They turned around, but the only thing they could see anywhere near them was the head of a Masai woman, with large ornaments fixed in her ears, lying on the ground close by.

At first, they were afraid, and said, "Is it a god, or what is it?"

One of them, however, laughed, and the others joined in, saying, "It is impossible for this object to have called us."

Then all three proceeded to go on their way.

The head, however, immediately said, "Stop! I am speaking to you, but you leave me!"

Hearing this, the warriors became terrified and ran off, taking the bullock with them.

The head, however, outstripped them, and, standing in front of the animal, stopped it.

When they saw this, the warriors fled, leaving the bullock where it was.

But the head called out to them, to be afraid of nothing and to stop running, for she wished them no harm; all that she wanted was a little blood from their animal, as she was hungry.

From W. E. H. Barrett, "A'Kikuyu Fairy Tales (Rogano)," *Man* 12 (1912): 112–114.

Recovering somewhat from their fright, the warriors stopped at a little distance, and told her to kill the animal and drink its blood, as they had no bowl into which to put the blood.

She, however, said, "I do not want to kill the beast." She took off a belt that she was wearing, and tied it around the bullock's head. Then she produced a small knife and made a slit in the animal's neck, so that blood flowed. Sitting underneath the beast, she opened her mouth, and caught the blood as it fell. She drank until she was satisfied.

Then she told the warriors, who were standing a short way off, to go home and take their property with them, but that on no account were they to mention to anyone else what they had seen. Before they left, she warned them that she would follow them and hear if any of them disobeyed her.

The warriors went towards their home, and on the journey they remained silent.

On the evening of the day that they arrived at their village, they all sat around the fire in one of their houses and ate food with several of their woman friends and some other warriors. Their friends pressed them to tell of the adventures they had on their recent journey. Two of them refused.

The third, however, thinking it was safe to do so, and in spite of the entreaties of his two companions, related the whole story. He did not know that the head, who had followed them, was hiding in the bushes and heard every word he said.

That night, as the warrior slept, the head crept softly up to his house, pushed the door open, and, having entered, killed him. She cut out his liver and kidneys, and took them with her into the forest close by. She lit a fire and cooked them over it. When the liver and kidneys were well done, she took them to the house of his mother and left them inside, near the fire stones. Then she went off to her hiding place.

The next morning, the old woman woke early and, seeing some well-cooked liver and kidneys lying in the house, she ate them, thinking that her son had placed them there during the night as a gift to her.

Shortly afterwards, she heard shrieks coming from her son's house. She went there, and found her son's loved one wringing her hands with grief. Several other people assembled outside. When she entered, the old woman found her son's dead body lying on his bed. Everyone discussed this strange occurrence, but no one could say how it happened. Some said that God had killed him, and others, that a man had done the deed.

Because the warrior was dead, his body was taken out and thrown into the bushes.

That night, the head, who had been hiding in the forest, took the corpse, and carried it back to the house and laid it on the bed.

The next morning, some men passing by, noticing that the door of this house was open, looked in, and to their astonishment they saw the body of the dead warrior lying inside. Everyone in the village tried to solve the problem as to how the corpse had come to be laid in the house from which they had carried it the previous day, but no one was able to say how it had returned. They again took the body and threw it into the forest.

That night, several warriors kept watch near the house, determined to find out what was happening. Towards midnight, they heard a voice singing in the Masai language,

> "I am tired of carrying this dead man.
> He has not given me water, food, blood, or milk.
> I killed him and left him on his bed.
> His mother and father had thrown him away.
> Why do I not leave him to be eaten by the hyenas?
> Never mind, I shall take him and leave him in his house."

They then saw the head of a Masai woman come out of the forest and enter the house. Looking through the door, they saw her place the corpse on the bed. When she had done this, she came out and was at once seized by them.

They cried out to her, "Now, you shall die!" and they started pulling at her ear ornaments.

She became very angry, and told them to kill her if they wished to do so, but she would not tolerate them pulling her ornaments about.

At this moment, the deceased warrior's mother arrived on the scene, and she commenced weeping bitterly.

The head, when she saw her, laughed at her, and said, "Why do you weep, you who have eaten your son's liver and kidneys?"

When she heard this, the wretched woman wept more than ever, but some of those standing nearby laughed.

The head said to them, "Bring me a gift of cattle, and all will be well."

Two warriors at once went and brought her a number of cattle as a gift. When she received the cattle, she entered the dead man's house, applied medicine to his wounds, then sewed them up. In a short time, her medicine had the desired effect, and the warrior came to life.

The pair of them then came out, the warrior as strong and healthy as he had ever been.

The head then asked his father and mother why they had taken him out into the forest and then wept. She said it was evident that, as they had left him as food for the hyenas, they had not much affection for him. She added, "I have brought your son to life, and if you or any of the others mention a word of what has happened to a single soul, I shall punish you all. In the future, when you are told not to mention a certain thing to anyone, take care that you do not do so."

When she said these words, she herded up her cattle and drove them off.

She has not again made her appearance among the Kikuyu.

Commentary

This is another story of life and death. As in "Salamone the Orphan" (story 6), a society is tainted: the youth's family is unfeeling—the mother eats his liver and kidneys, the family throws his body into the forest. The meaning of the story is suggested, as always, by the relationship between fantasy and reality, by the head of the Masai woman, in this case, and what that head represents. Its presence suggests a society gone wrong: (a) a sacred interdiction is broken, (b) a mother eats her own son, (c) a society does not respect the dead. This can only be alleviated when proper attention is paid to the head, meaning that the people understand that death characterizes their world. When they have realized this, life can return. The youth dies, then is reborn. The head of the Masai woman orchestrates this activity. She cleanses the society (it must acknowledge its wrongdoing by sacrificing cattle to her), and then life can return to the community, life in the form of the reborn youth, now a man.

Motifs in this story include a talking head, a persistent pursuer, a returning corpse, and magic resuscitation. The initial conflict involves the breaking of an interdiction given by a mysterious, supernatural being: Do not tell anyone of the head of the Masai woman. The main pattern has to do with the returning corpse (the relatives throw the corpse into the forest, the head of the Masai woman returns it). The resolution of the story occurs when the head of the Masai woman, having destroyed the youth, gives him life. The youth's family is unfeeling; the youth died because he broke the Masai woman's interdiction. He is given life when his family follows her instructions.

◇ **The symbolism of the Masai woman's head**—She represents the adventure of the three Kikuyu warriors, a forbidden adventure: they are not to speak of it. The adventure and the accompanying interdiction set up the main part of the tale. In the strange world of fantasy, what does the head come to represent? God? as the warriors think when they first see her. A diabolical force? Death? Whatever it is, it must be appeased, it must not be disobeyed, its force is greater than that of humans. The head represents a kind of mystical, godly vengeance when humans go against the strictures of the heavens, when they treat humans in inhuman ways. But there is something else here: there is the fear of this awful and not wholly understood pursuit. This is unlike "The Unborn Child" (story 2) in which a rational purpose for the pursuit can be found. In this tale, the very lack of a clear reason for the pursuit is a part of its power. The oral tradition touches on irrational fears as well as those to which clear morals can be attached.

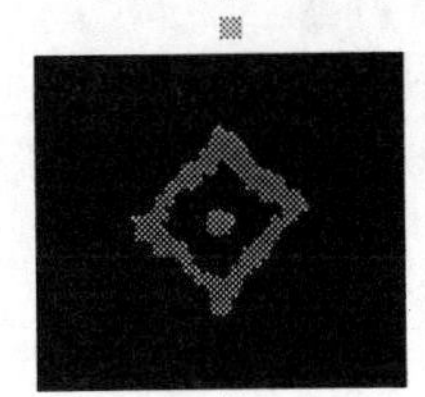

While the Bura People had no written language, we found that they had an unusually full system of culture embodied in their folk tales. It was a surprise to learn that quite small boys and girls had a rather clear idea of the socially desirable ends which had been set up by the Bura. These ends had been taught and emphasized through the folk tales which had been passed on by word of mouth. The most respected women of each community had assumed the responsibility of passing on the culture of the Bura by telling stories to the younger children in the evening time. The older children carried on by reciting the stories to one another.

Albert D. Helser, *African Stories* (New York: Fleming H. Revell, 1930), p. 9.

Ronga

The Gamboler of the Plain

The Ronga live in Mozambique.

1

A man and a woman first had a son and then a daughter. When the daughter was married, and the dowry was provided, the parents said to their son, "Now we have a herd of cattle at your disposal. It is time now for you to take a wife. We shall select an attractive bride, one whose parents are worthy people."

But the son firmly refused. "No!" he said. "Do not trouble yourselves. I do not like the girls who are here. If I must marry, I shall find myself the bride I want."

"Do as you wish," said his parents, "but if, later on, you're unhappy, it will not be any fault of ours."

He parted, the boy left the country, he traveled a great distance, very far, into an unknown country. He came to a village, he saw some young women who were grinding corn, others were cooking. He silently made his choice, and said to himself, "That one there suits me!" Then he went to the men of the village, and said to them, "Greetings, my fathers."

"Greetings, young man. What do you want?"

"I have come to look at your daughters, because I wish to take a wife."

"Well, well!" they said. "We shall show them to you, and you shall choose."

They brought all of them before him, and he indicated the one he desired, and she consented.

From Henri A. Junod, *Les Ba-Rongas* (Neuchâtel: Paul Attinger, 1898), pp. 353–360.

"Your parents will visit us and bring the dowry, not so?" the parents of the young woman said.

"Not at all," he responded. "I have the dowry with me. Take it, here it is."

They said, "Then, they will visit us later, to meet your wife and to conduct her to your place?"

"No, no! I'm afraid that they will insult you with harsh exhortations of the young woman. Allow me to take her at once."

The parents of the newly married woman consented, but they took her aside in the house to instruct her: "Behave properly to your parents-in-law, and take good care of your husband."

They offered them a young girl to help them in their domestic work. But the wife refused. They offered them two, ten, twenty girls from whom to choose, all the girls passed in review and were then offered to her.

"No," she said. "Give me the buffalo of the country, our buffalo, the Gamboler-of-the-Plain. Let it serve me."

"How can that be?" they said. "You know that our life depends on the buffalo. Here, it is well cared for, it is well attended to. What will you do with it in an alien country? It will starve, it will die and all of us will die with it."

"But no," she said. "I'll take care of it."

Before she left her parents, she took with her a small cooking pot containing a package of medicinal roots, along with a horn for bleeding, a little knife for incisions, and a calabash full of fat.

She parted with her husband. The buffalo followed them, but it was visible only to her. The man did not see it. He had no idea that the Gamboler-of-the-Plain was the servant who was accompanying his wife.

2

When they arrived in the husband's village, all the family welcomed them with exclamations of joy: "Hoyo! Hoyo! Hoyo!"

"So," said the old people, "you have found a wife! You did not want one of those women whom we proposed to you, but that is unimportant. It is well! You have done what you wanted. But if you have problems, you'll have nothing to complain about."

The husband accompanied his wife to the fields, and showed her his fields and those of his mother. She observed everything, and returned with him to the village. But along the way, she said, "I dropped my beads in the field, I shall go and get them." But she was going to see the buffalo.

She said to the buffalo, "You see the boundary of the fields. Remain here. There's a forest too, in which you can hide."

It responded, "All right."

When the wife wanted water, she went to the cultivated fields, and put the pitcher there before the buffalo. Then it ran with the pitcher to the lake, drew the water, and returned with the filled pitcher to its mistress. When she wanted wood, it went into the bushes, broke the trees with its horns, and brought her what she needed.

In the village, the people were amazed. "What strength she has!" they said. "She always returns from the well at once. In the wink of an eye, she has gathered a bundle of dry wood." No one suspected that she was helped by a buffalo that was her servant.

But she did not bring it any food to eat, because she had only one plate for herself and her husband. Over there at her home, they had a plate especially for the Gamboler-of-the-Plain, and they fed it with care. But now, the buffalo was hungry. She brought it her pitcher and sent it to get water. It parted, but it suffered distress because of hunger.

She showed the buffalo a corner of the bushes where it was to work. During the night, the buffalo took a hoe and prepared an enormous field.

Everyone said, "How capable she is. How fast she works."

But in the evening, it said to its mistress, "I am hungry, and you give me nothing to eat. I shall not be able to work."

"What shall I do?" she said. "We have just one plate in the house. The people at my home were right when they said that you would have to steal. Well, steal then! Go into my field, take a bean here, a bean there. Then go further: if you don't take beans from the same place, perhaps the owners will not know what's going on, will not be shocked by what's going on."

That night, the buffalo went to the fields, and it snatched a bean here, it snatched a bean there. It leapt from one corner to another, and finally went and concealed itself.

In the morning, when the women went to the fields, they were surprised by what they saw: "What's happened here? Never have we seen anything like this! A wild beast has ravaged our fields, and one cannot follow its tracks. Ho, the land is diseased!"

They returned to report the news in the village.

In the evening, the young woman said to the buffalo, "They were shocked, all right, but not much. They did not fall and break their backs. Continue to steal tonight."

So it went on. The owners of the ravaged fields cried loudly, they turned to the men and told them to call the guards with their guns.

The husband of the young woman was a good marksman. He stationed himself in his field, and waited.

The buffalo thought that someone might be lying in wait at the place where it had stolen beans the night before, so it went to eat the beans of its mistress, the field where it had grazed the first time.

"Well," said the man, "it's a buffalo. Its like has never been seen here. This is a strange thing!"

He fired. The bullet entered the temple of the beast, near its ear, and it came out on the other side. The Gamboler-of-the-Plain tumbled and fell dead.

"I've made a good hit!" cried the hunter, and he went to announce it to the village.

Immediately the woman began to moan and writhe, "Oh! Oh, I have a stomach-ache!"

Someone said, "Calm yourself."

She seemed to be sick, but in reality it was to explain her cries and her terror when she heard of the death of the buffalo. She was given medicine, but when no one was looking she poured it out.

3

Now everyone set out, the women with their baskets, the men with their weapons, going to cut up the buffalo.

The wife remained alone in the village. But she soon followed them, holding her middle, whining and crying.

"Why do you come here?" said her husband. "If you're sick, stay at home."

"No, I don't want to stay by myself in the village."

Her mother-in-law scolded her, she told her that she could not understand what she was doing. She said that she would kill herself if she went on like this.

When they had filled the baskets with meat, the young wife said, "Let me carry the head."

"No, you're sick. It is too heavy for you!"

"No," she said, "allow me." She took it and carried it away.

When they arrived in the village, instead of going into the house, she went into the house where the pots were stored, and put down the buffalo's head. She obstinately remained there. Her husband looked for her to bring her into the house, saying that she would be better off there.

"Don't trouble me!" she said sharply.

Her mother-in-law came to her and spoke to her gently.

"Why do you vex me?" she said angrily. "Won't you let me sleep a little?"

They brought her some food, she pushed it aside.

Night came. Her husband went to bed, but she did not sleep. She listened.

She went and brought a fire, she heated water in her little pot, and she poured it into the package of medicine that she had brought with her from her home. She took the head of the buffalo and made incisions with the knife in front of the ear, at the temple, where the bullet had hit the animal. Then she took the bleeding horn, and she sucked, sucked with all her might. She drew out some clots of blood, then liquid blood. Then she exposed the place in question to the vapor that steamed from the pot, having anointed it with the fat that she had conserved in the calabash. Then she chanted as follows:

"Ah, my father, Gamboler-of-the-Plain!
They told me, they told me, Gamboler-of-the-Plain,
They told me: You would go through profound darkness,
You would wander through the night in all directions,
Gamboler-of-the-Plain!
You are the young plant that grows out of the ruins,
That dies before its time,
Consumed by a gnawing worm.
You made flowers and fruit fall on your path,
Gamboler-of-the-Plain!"

When she had finished her incantations, the head stirred. The limbs grew again. The buffalo began to revive, it shook its ears and its horns, it raised itself and stretched its limbs.

But then the husband, who could not sleep in the house, came out and said, "Why is my wife crying for such a long time? I must go and find out why she utters these sighs."

He entered the house where pots were stored and called her.

She responded to him in a tone fraught with anger, "Leave me alone!"

But the head of the buffalo fell to the ground, dead, pierced as before.

The husband returned to the house, having understood nothing at all and having seen nothing.

Again, the wife took the pot, prepared the medicine, made the incisions, placed the horn, exposed the wound to the vapor, and chanted as before:

"Ah, my father, Gamboler-of-the-Plain!
They told me, they told me, Gamboler-of-the-Plain,
They told me: You would go through profound darkness,
You would wander through the night in all directions,
Gamboler-of-the-Plain!
You are the young plant that grows out of the ruins,
That dies before its time,
Consumed by a gnawing worm.
You made flowers and fruit fall on your path,
Gamboler-of-the-Plain!"

The buffalo again arose. Its limbs were restored. It started to revive, it shook its ears and its horns, it stretched.

But the husband came again, uneasy, to see what his wife was doing. She was vexed with him. He settled down in the shed to watch what was happening.

She took her fire, her pot, and all of her utensils, and went out. She pulled up grass to make the fire, and she began for the third time to revive the buffalo.

Morning had appeared when her mother-in-law arrived, and again the head fell.

Day came, and the buffalo's wound began to be tainted.

She said to them, "Let me go to the lake and bathe alone."

They responded to her, "Sick as you are, how will you get there?"

Nevertheless she went, then returned and said, "Along the way, I encountered someone from my home. He told me that my mother is very, very sick. I told him to come to the village. He refused, saying, 'They would offer me food, and would delay me.' He went on his way, and told me to hurry lest my mother die before I arrive. Now goodbye, I must go!"

Well, it was all a lie. She had thought of the idea of going to the lake so that she could create this story and have a reason for taking to her family the news of the buffalo's death.

4

Carrying the basket on her head, she parted, chanting along the road the song of the Gamboler-of-the-Plain. After she had passed, the people assembled behind her and accompanied her to the village. When she got there, she told them that the buffalo was no longer alive.

They sent out in all directions messengers to gather all the people of the country. They reproached the young woman, saying, "You see, it is as we told you. You refused all the young girls whom we offered you, and insisted on having the buffalo. Now you have killed us all."

That is the way things were when the woman's husband, who had followed his wife to the village, arrived. He put his gun against the trunk of a tree, and sat.

Then they greeted him, saying, "Hail, criminal! Hail! You have killed us all!"

He did not understand, and wanted to know how he could be called a murderer, a criminal. "Indeed, I have killed a buffalo," he said, "but that is all."

"Yes, but this buffalo was your wife's servant. It drew water for her, it cut her wood, it worked her field."

The husband, thoroughly astonished, said, "Why did you not tell me that? I would not have killed it!"

"That is the way it is," they said. "Our lives depended on the buffalo."

Then the people began to cut their throats. The young wife cut her throat first, singing,

> "Ah, my father, Gamboler-of-the-Plain. . . ."

Then it was the turn of her parents, her brothers, her sisters, one after the other. One of them sang:

"You shall go through profound darkness!"

Another sang:

"You shall wander through the night in all directions!"

And another:

"You are the young plant that grows out of the ruins
That dies before its time."

And another:

"You make flowers and fruit fall on your path. . . ."

They all cut their throats, they also killed the little children who were carried in skins on their backs, "because," they said, "why should we let them live, because they would go mad."

The husband returned to his home, and he told his people how he had killed them all because he had shot the buffalo.

His parents said to him, "You see, did we not tell you that you would be visited by misfortune? When we offered you a fine and sagacious woman, you insisted on following your own desires. Now you have lost everything. Who will return your fortune, now that the parents of your wife, those to whom you gave your money, are all dead?"

That is the end.

Commentary

The intent of the storyteller is made clear by an initial situation: A stubborn son insists that he marry whom he please, against the better judgement of his society. And a stubborn bride insists that she do as she pleases when she marries, even if it is against the tradition of her society. The motif in both instances is a bride quest. Marriage customs are broken at the outset, and the remainder of the story explains the significance of this breach of tradition in fantasy terms. It is a story that emphasizes the necessity of adhering to tradition.

There are five major patterns in the story: In pattern one, the Gamboler does the work of the bride. This is a fantasy view of the bride's work in the household, what would have happened if tradition had been followed. In pattern two, the Gamboler begins to die. This is a fantasy summary of what has already happened: the Gamboler cannot live when tradition is broken; it comes to stand for, to symbolize, traditions which hold a society together. In pattern three, the Gamboler, to survive, does anti-social things. The society is thereby endangered, its fabric weakened. The pattern is actually broken earlier, when the husband kills the buffalo; this parallels the husband's earlier breaking of tradition. The wife, in pattern four, tries to bring the Gamboler to life. She cannot do so. She and the husband are both guilty—the husband keeps interrupting this process, but she is guilty, too. This is a fantasy way of showing what has happened. The Gamboler is dead, killed by the husband (he shot it) and wife (she cannot bring it back to life) when they broke tradition. In pattern five, all die. "Now you have killed us all." The people kill themselves, while singing the buffalo-song.

◇ **Meaning grows out of the patterns**—The emphasis is on tradition, on the custom of marriage. The young man's parents tell him: ". . . if you are unhappy later on, it will not be our fault." Later: "So you have found a wife. You did not want one of those women proposed to you, but that is unimportant. It is well. You have done what you wanted. But if you have problems, you will have nothing to complain about." And, at the end: "Do you see now? Did we not tell you that you would be visited by misfortune? When we offered you a fine and sagacious woman, you insisted on following your own desires. Now you have lost everything."

As for the wife: ". . . they offered them a young girl to help them in their domestic work. But the wife refused. They offered them two, ten, twenty girls from whom to choose. [She refused them all.]" She insisted on breaking tradition: "Give me instead the buffalo of the country, our buffalo, the Gamboler-of-the-Plain. Let it serve me." They emphasized the import of her act: "You know that our lives depend on the buffalo. Here, it is well cared for, it is well attended to. What will you do with it in an alien country? It will starve, it will die, and all of us will die with it."

Later: "You see, it is as we told you. You refused all the young girls whom we offered you and insisted on having the buffalo. Now you have killed us all."

◇ **Symbolism**—The song sung by the wife is significant. She calls the Gamboler "My father," her progenitor, protector, source of life. I was taught by my people, she sings, that the buffalo would get them through difficulties, bring them through the night. The buffalo is vitality, youth, a promise among the ruins. It is dying too early, eaten up by the worm of death. Everywhere the Gamboler went, it caused fertility. Now, it is gone.

Origins

A Zulu storyteller (photo by Harold Scheub)

Myth

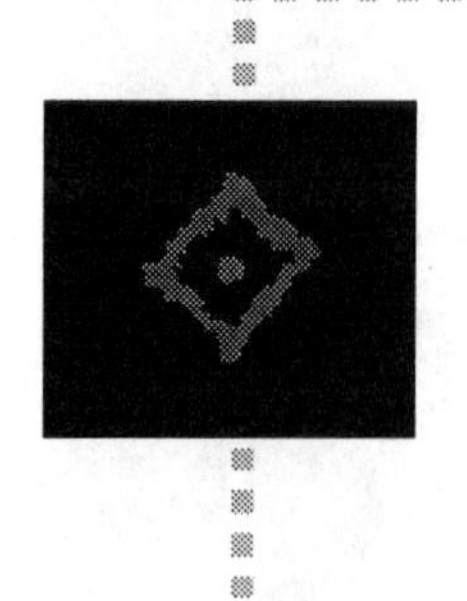

Mircea Eliade: Myth narrates a sacred history; it relates an event that took place in primordial time, the fabled time of the "beginnings." In other words, myth tells how, through the deeds of supernatural beings, a reality came into existence, be it the whole reality, the cosmos, or only a fragment of reality—an island, a species of plant, a particular kind of human behavior, an institution. Myth, then, is always an account of a "creation"; it relates how something was produced, began to be.

Notes on Myth

There are many African religions, each as complex as Christianity, Judaism, and Islam, so it is not always productive to make generalizations about those faiths. But there are some characteristics that a number of these belief systems have in common.

◇ **The Three Ages**—Some believe that, in the history of the cosmos, there were three ages: These include a perfect time, a golden age when god, human, and animal existed in a perfect harmony. Then, during the second of these three periods, the age of creation, the creator god brought into existence the earth, along with humans and animals. It was a period of differentiation, as God originated life by using him- or herself as material and model, an attempt to re-create the golden age on earth. But something happened during this period to assume that the perfect age was gone forever, that it could not be transferred to the earth: death came into the world, and the earth and humankind were flawed. It was a period of chaos and order, of fear and hope, of the diminishing of the past and the promise of a new future. The chaos-order dualism was seen as the nature of the creator god. In some religious systems, this creator was a divine trickster, both a benevolent and creative god, and an unpredictable and frequently destructive being. He was a god who had within him both life and death. He was an ambiguous figure who had within him both the sublime and the outrageous. This same dualistic mixture persists in the creation of humans: they have within them both life and death, sublime and outrageous conduct. That is the result of the flaw of the age of creation, a period of transformation, a rite of passage on a cosmological level. As time went on, the godly, creative part of the divine trickster and the dualistic god repaired to heaven, moved further away from humans and earth, and the destructive part of the divine trickster and dualistic god went to the earth, with the echo of perfection and the potential for good remaining: the divine trickster had become the profane trickster. This third age was the contemporary age, the world of today, a realm in which humans and gods have become remote from each other, in which humans through their rituals and traditions seek to duplicate that long lost perfect age, only a dimly perceived echo now.

In the movement from the perfect age to the contemporary age, humans or animals express their free will, and thereby separate themselves from God. This is a part of the differentiation process that is characteristic of the creation period. As humans and animals separate themselves from God, they retain certain qualities of that original oneness (theirs during the perfect age), but they lose an essential godly quality, everlasting life. For a variety of reasons, as they separate themselves from God, they become mortal. Death comes into the world. Death is often the result of an act of free will on the part of the human or animal; this act is at the center of the age of creation. Were humans and animals to remain like plants, they would retain that essential unity with nature and God. But they go another way.

◇ **The Divine Trickster**—In African religions, the creator god may take varied forms. There may be a single god or a pantheon of gods. God may be a wholly positive being, or a dualistic force composed of both good and evil, order and chaos. God may be a divine trickster, both sublime and outrageously debased, a spirit of order and a spirit of disorder, by turns creative and destructive. The divine trickster is a symbol of the betwixt and between period of transformation that characterizes the age of creation: as he moves from the perfect or golden age to the contemporary age, he embodies the changes—the move is from the perfection of God (the creative side of the divine trickster) to the flawed human (the destructive side of the divine trickster). In the contemporary age, the divine part of this trickster is gone, and what remains is the profane trickster, an unpredictable character whose residual creativeness is seen in the illusions that he establishes, whose amorality is witnessed in his outrageous conduct, often anti-social.

Why is the creation so important to us? Why are the gods and their activities so significant to us? Why do we keep reliving the creation myths? Because these are the prototypes of our own movement to fulfillment and maturity, of our own triumph over chaos as we move through the rites of passage into adulthood. From chaos comes order, the struggle between order and chaos, between creativity and destructiveness. That primal cosmological struggle is our conflict writ large. The dualistic god is everyman and everywoman, grappling with the two sides of their nature. The overcoming of chaos and the ordering of the world become our promise and our hope, but the divine trickster and the profane trickster, ever amoral and ever ready to obscure order with chaos, are a part of us as well. The myths are the tales on a vast cosmological scale, with gods taking the roles of humans. Myth becomes a constant metaphor for what we can become, moving from the chaos of our lives to a kind of eternal order. It becomes a ritualizing of our everyday lives, a linkage to our gods. But while we long for that sense of order, there is danger in yearning for a oneness with God, for the golden age, if that means a loss of our free will. The myths often begin with a familiar domestic scene, something the audience can at once relate to—an outrageous sexual affair, a bride quest, someone attacking a child. From out of these often anti-social events comes new life. The outrage is purposeful because it represents chaos; the contrasting creation that emerges represents order.

◇ **The Argument**—We move reluctantly away from the oneness, the perfect age. The origin of death usually results from our first act of free will. God is punishing us, as we separate ourselves from him and go our own way. The plants of the earth remain our constant contrast; they are one with God, the perfect age, in total harmony, in bondage to the eternal. We have lost that oneness in our independence, our free will, and we are terrified. So are animals. We long for that completeness. Within us, a battle rages—between the desire for oneness and the demand for independence. This battle we see as we move closer to the contemporary age . . . and we see it especially in the divine trickster, where the struggle between free-willed humanity and God-related unity goes on. That unity is lost as we move closer to our world, and the profane trickster becomes the specter of what we could become if we move away from god, toward amorality, from the morality of perfection to the amorality of indifference. Free will and unity—that is the great enigma for humans. The stories, conservative, looking back to that perfection, provide a means for solace: remain in harmony with nature, remain in harmony with culture, and free will or not, we have that union, if only in shadow. Free will is fine, but it is frightening. We need God. The tales show us how to find God and comfort. The myths explain what happened to create the gulf between free will and unity.

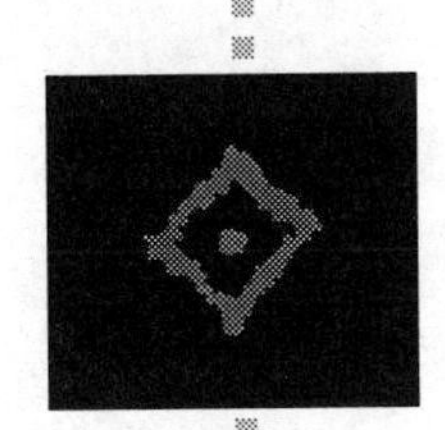

[Death's] occurrence must be explained, and the explanation can only be given in the form of myth.

Hans Abrahamsson, *The Origin of Death, Studies in African Mythology* (Uppsala: Studia Ethnographica Upsaliensia, 1951), p. 1.

Ganda

The Creation

The Ganda live in Uganda.

Kintu was the first man.

When he came from the unknown, he found nothing in Uganda—no food, no water, no animals, nothing but a void.

He had a cow with him, and when he was hungry he drank her milk.

One day, as he roamed about searching for things, he saw two girls just dropped down from heaven. He stopped. The girls also stopped a long way off. They were Mugulu's daughters, Nambi and her sister. The girls were surprised.

Nambi said, "Sister, look at the two things over there. What can they be?"

The sister looked, but said nothing.

Nambi continued, "We have never seen anything like them! Just go down and see what brings things like this to such a place as the earth."

"How can I?" asked the sister. "Look at those horns!"

"I don't mean that one. Try the other."

The sister then advanced a little way. When Kintu saw her coming, he advanced to meet her. Then the sister ran back to Nambi, and they both prepared to flee. Kintu, however, did not continue the pursuit, but returned to the cow.

After some time, Nambi and her sister decided to come close to Kintu.

When only one hundred paces separated them, Nambi spoke to him: "Who are you?"

"I am Kintu."

"And what is that?" pointing to the cow.

From Harry Johnston, *The Uganda Protectorate* (London: Hutchinson, 1904), vol. 2, pp. 700–705.

"That is my cow."

Nambi and her sister withdrew to consider whether this could possibly be true. Then they returned, and said, "We have never seen anything like you. Where did you come from?"

"I do not know."

Then Kintu milked the cow, and put milk on the palm of his left hand, and he drank it.

"What did you do that for?" asked Nambi.

"That is my food," said Kintu.

"We see no water here. What do you drink?"

"I drink milk."

Then the girls retired for another conference, and Nambi confided to her sister that she believed that this was a man. Nothing else could do such extraordinary things. They returned to Kintu and submitted their decision.

Kintu said, "Yes, I am a man."

Nambi then told him all about themselves, and suggested that he should accompany them to heaven.

Kintu agreed, on condition that they also took his cow.

They declined to do this, and they disappeared.

As soon as they arrived in heaven, they told Mugulu that they had found a man and a cow.

"Where?" asked Mugulu.

"On the earth."

"Not a real man, surely?" Mugulu smiled as if he did not believe them, but they suspected that he knew all the time.

"Yes, a real man! We know he is a real man because he wants food, and when he is hungry he drags the udder of his cow, and squeezes out white juice, which he drinks."

"I shall make inquiries."

"He is very nice," said Nambi, "and I wanted to bring him up here. May I go and fetch him?"

"Leave the matter to me," said Mugulu, and the girls withdrew.

When they had gone, Mugulu called his sons, and said, "Go to the earth and test this story about a real man being there. Nambi says that she saw a wild man and a cow, and that the man drank the cow's juice. Fetch the cow."

The boys prepared to start at once.

"Wait a bit," said Mugulu. "I don't want the man. He will probably die when he sees you. Just bring the cow."

The boys arrived near Kintu's resting place, and he was asleep. They took the cow, and carried her off.

When Kintu awoke, he did not see the cow, but he did not start in search of her just then, because he supposed that she had only wandered a short distance.

Presently, he got hungry, and he tried to find the cow, but in vain. He ultimately decided that the girls must have returned and stolen her, and he was very angry and hungry. He used many words not of peace. He sat down and pointed his nails and sharpened his teeth, but there was no one with whom to fight. Then he peeled the bark off a tree and sucked it, and thus he fed himself.

Next day, Nambi saw Kintu's cow as the boys arrived, and she exclaimed, "You have stolen Kintu's cow! That cow was his food and drink, and now what has he to eat? I like Kintu, if you do not. I shall go down tomorrow, and if he is not dead I shall bring him up here."

And she went and found Kintu.

"So they have taken away your cow?"

"Yes."

"What have you been eating since?"

"I have been sucking the bark of a tree."

"Have you really been doing that?"

"What else is there to do?"

"Come with me to Mugulu, and your cow shall be returned to you."

They went, and Kintu, when he arrived, saw a vast multitude of people and plenty of bananas and fowls and goats and sheep—in fact, everything was there in plenty.

The boys, when they saw Nambi arrive with Kintu, said, "Let us tell our father, Mugulu."

And they went and told him.

Mugulu said, "Go, and tell my chiefs to build a big house without a door for the stranger, Kintu."

The house was built, and Kintu went into it.

Mugulu then gave an order: "My people, go and cook ten thousand dishes of food, and roast ten thousand cows, and fill ten thousand vessels with beer. Give it to the stranger. If he is a real man, he will eat it. If not—the penalty is death."

The food was prepared and taken to Kintu's house. As there was no door, the members of the crowd put their shoulders to one side of the house and raised it off the ground, and put the food inside. They told Kintu that, if he did not finish it all at a meal, the result would be death. Then they dropped the side of the house down again, and waited outside.

Kintu surveyed the mass of food with dismay, and then started to walk around it, muttering his feelings to himself. As he went around the heap, his foot slipped into a hole. On examination, he found that it was the opening of a cavern. "Aha!" he said. "This cave has a good appetite. Let me feed it!" And he took the ten thousand measures of beer, and spilled them in, putting the empty vessels to one side. Then the ten thousand carcases of roast cows were pitched into the cavern, and lastly the food from the ten thousand baskets. Then, after he had closed the hole, he called to the people outside: "Haven't you got a little more food out there?"

"No," they replied. "Did we not give you enough?"

"Well, I suppose I must do with it, if you have nothing more cooked."

"Have you finished it all?"

"Yes, yes! Come, and take away the empty dishes."

The crowd raised the side wall of the house, came inside, and asked Kintu whether he had really disposed of the food.

He assured them that he had.

Then, with one accord, they cried out, "Then this is a man indeed!"

They went directly to Mugulu, and told him that the stranger had finished his meal, and had asked for more.

Mugulu at first branded this statement as a falsehood, but on consideration he believed it. He pondered for a moment, then, taking up a copper axe, he said to his chiefs, "Take this to Kintu. Tell him that I want material to make a fire. Tell him that Mugulu is old and cold, and that Mugulu does not burn wood for a fire. Tell him that I want stones, and tell him that he must cut up rocks with this copper axe and fetch the pieces and light me a fire. If he does so, then he may claim his cow. He may also have Nambi, and he can return to the earth."

The chiefs went to Kintu, and told him that Mugulu wanted a fire made of stones, and that he must chop a rock with the copper axe.

Kintu suspected that there was something wrong, but he spoke no words to that effect. He put the axe on his shoulder and went out before they allowed the wall to drop to the ground. He walked straight to a big rock, stood in front of it, placed the head of the axe on the rock, and rested his chin on the tip of the handle.

"It does not seem easy to cut," he said to the axe.

"It is easy enough to me," replied the axe. "Just strike and see."

Kintu struck the rock, and it splintered in all directions. He picked up the pieces of rock, and went straight to Mugulu, and said, "Here is your firewood, Mugulu. Do you want any more?"

Mugulu said, "This is marvelous! Go back to your home. It only remains now for you to find your cow."

And Kintu went away.

Next morning, the chiefs were called before Mugulu.

He said, "Take this bucket to Kintu, and tell him to fetch water. Tell him that Mugulu does not drink anything but dew, and if he is a man he is to fetch it quickly."

Kintu received the bucket and the message, and again he suspected that there was something wrong. But he did not utter his suspicions. He took the bucket and went out. He put it down on the grass, and he said to it, "This does not seem very easy."

The bucket replied, "It is easy enough to me," and when Kintu looked down he saw that the bucket was full of dew.

He took it to Mugulu, and said, "Here is your drinking water, Mugulu. Do you want any more?"

Mugulu said, "This is marvelous! Kintu, you are a prodigy. I am now satisfied that you are a man indeed, and it only remains for you to get your cow. Whoever took Kintu's cow, let him restore it."

"Your own sons stole my cow," said Kintu.

"If so," replied Mugulu, "drive all the cows here, and let Kintu pick out his cow if she is among them."

Ten thousand cows were brought in a herd.

Kintu stood near the herd in great perplexity, lost in thought. A hornet came and sat on Kintu's shoulder, and, as Kintu gave no heed, the hornet prepared its sting and drove it home.

Kintu struck at the hornet and missed it, and the hornet said, "Don't strike! I'm your friend."

"You have just bit me," replied Kintu.

"It wasn't a bite. Listen. You'll never be able to identify your cow in all that herd. Just wait, I'll fly out among the herd. The cow whose shoulder I sit on is yours. Mark her."

The herd of ten thousand cows was driven past, but the hornet did not move.

Kintu said aloud, "My cow is not among them."

Mugulu then ordered another herd to be brought, numbering twice as many cows as the last herd. But the hornet did not move.

Kintu said aloud, "My cow is not among them."

The herdsmen drove the cows away, and another herd was brought. The hornet flew off and sat on the shoulder of a cow. Kintu went forward and marked her.

"That's mine," he said to Mugulu.

The hornet then flew to another, a young cow, and Kintu went forward and marked her.

He said, "That cow is also mine."

The hornet flew to a third cow, and Kintu went forward and marked this one also.

He said, "That cow is mine also."

Mugulu said, "Quite correct. Your cow has had two calves since she arrived in heaven. You are a prodigy, Kintu. Take your cows, and take Nambi also, and go back to the earth." Then Mugulu said, "Wait a bit," and he called his servants and said to them, "Go to my store, and fetch one banana plant, one potato, one bean, one Indian corn, one ground-nut, and one hen." These things were brought, and Mugulu addressed Kintu and Nambi: "Take these things with you, you may want them." Then, addressing Kintu, he said, "I must tell you that Nambi has a brother named Warumbe [meaning "disease" or "death"]. He is mad and ruthless. At the moment, he is not here, so you had better start quickly, before he returns. If he sees you, he may want to go with you, but you are certain to quarrel." Mugulu said to Nambi, "Here is some millet to feed the hen on the road down. If you forget anything, do not come back to fetch it." Then he said, "That is all. You may go."

Kintu and Nambi started, and when they were some distance on the journey, Nambi suddenly remembered that it was time to feed the hen. She asked Kintu for the millet, but it was nowhere to be found. It was clear that they had forgotten it in the hurry of departure.

"I shall return and fetch it," said Kintu.

"No, no, you must not! Warumbe will have returned, and he will probably wish to accompany us. I don't want him, and you had better not return."

"But the hen is hungry, and we must feed it."

"Yes, it is," said Nambi.

Nambi remained where she was, and Kintu returned to Mugulu, and explained that he had forgotten the millet.

Mugulu was angry that Kintu had returned, and Warumbe, who had just arrived, asked, "Where is Nambi?"

"She has gone to the earth with Kintu."

"Then I must come, too," said Warumbe.

After some hesitation, Kintu agreed to this, and they returned together to Nambi.

Nambi and Kintu greeted each other, and Nambi objected to Warumbe accompanying them. But he insisted, and finally it was agreed that he should come for a time and stay with Nambi and Kintu.

The three proceeded, and reached the earth at a place called Magongo in Uganda, and they rested.

Then the woman planted the banana and the Indian corn, the bean and the ground-nut, and there was a plentiful crop.

In the course of time, three children were born, and Warumbe claimed one of them.

"Let me have this one," he said to Kintu. "You still have two children remaining."

"I cannot spare one of these," Kintu said, "but later on, perhaps, I may be able to spare one."

Years passed, and many more children were born.

Warumbe again begged Kintu to give him one.

Kintu went round to all the children with the object of selecting one for Warumbe, but he finally returned, and said, "Warumbe, I cannot spare you one just yet. But later on, perhaps, I may be able to do so."

"When you had three, you said the same thing. Now you have many, and still you refuse to give me one. Now I shall kill them all. Not today, not tomorrow, not this year, not next year, but one by one I shall claim them all."

Next day, one child died.

Kintu charged Warumbe with the deed.

The following day, another died, and the next day, another.

At last, Kintu proposed to return to Mugulu and tell him how Warumbe was killing all his children. He went to Mugulu, and explained matters.

Mugulu replied that he had expected it. His original plan was that Kintu and Warumbe should not have met. He told Kintu that Warumbe was a mad man, and that trouble would come of it. Yet, Kintu had returned for the millet against the orders of Mugulu, and this was the consequence. "However," continued Mugulu, "I shall see what can be done." And with that, he called Kaikuzi [literally, "the digger"], and said to him, "Go down and try to bring Warumbe back to me."

Kintu and Kaikuzi started off together, and when they arrived were greeted by Nambi. She explained that in his absence Warumbe had killed several more of her sons.

Kaikuzi called up Warumbe, and said, "Why are you killing all these children?"

"I wanted one child badly to help me cook my food. I begged Kintu to give me one. He refused. Now I shall kill them, every one."

"Mugulu is angry. He sent me down to recall you."

"I shall not leave here."

"You are only a small man in comparison to me. I shall take you by force."

They grappled then, and a severe contest ensued. After a while, Warumbe slipped from Kaikuzi's grasp, and he ran into a hole in the ground. Kaikuzi started to dig him out with his fingers, and he succeeded in reaching him. But Warumbe dived still deeper into the earth. Kaikuzi tried to dig him out again, and had almost caught him when Warumbe sank still further into the ground.

"I'm tired now," said Kaikuzi to Kintu. "I shall remain for a few days, and have another try to catch him."

Kaikuzi then issued an order that there was to be two days' silence on the earth, and that Warumbe would come out of the ground to see what it meant. The people were ordered to lay in two days' provisions, and firewood and water, and not to go out of doors to feed goats or cattle. This having been done, Kaikuzi went into the ground to catch Warumbe, and pursued him for two days. He forced Warumbe out at a place called Tanda. At this place, there were some children feeding goats, and when they saw Warumbe they cried out, and the spell was broken. Warumbe returned again into the earth.

Directly afterwards, Kaikuzi appeared at the same place, and asked why the children had broken the silence. He was angry and disappointed; he said to Kintu that the people had broken his order, and that he would concern himself no further with the recalling of Warumbe.

"I am tired now," said Kaikuzi.

"Never mind him," said Kintu. "Let Warumbe remain, since you cannot expel him. You may go back to Mugulu now, and thank you."

Kaikuzi returned to Mugulu, and explained what had happened.

"Very well," said Mugulu. "Let Warumbe stay there."

And Warumbe remained.

Commentary

In the Ganda pantheon of gods, Mugulu (Gulu) is a sky deity. Kintu, an ancestral hero, is the first man. Mugulu, God, has three children—Nambi, a daughter; Warumbe ("Death"), a son; and Kaikuzi ("Digger"), another son.

The movements of the characters are important: (1) from earth to heaven: Nambi takes Kintu to heaven for it is still possible for mortals to touch God; (2) from heaven to earth: Nambi and Kintu go to earth, and heaven is closed off to mortals forever.

The first pattern is built on a set of motifs, including impossible tasks, bride quest, and reluctant in-law. The pattern consists of the tasks set by Mugulu, the reluctant father-in-law: the eating of prodigious amounts of food, cutting a rock with a copper axe, filling a bucket with dew, selecting his cow from various huge herds. Kintu, with the assistance of nature, proves himself to be equal to God, and therefore worthy of marrying God's daughter.

Now, the domestic tale of a bride quest moves into myth. The young couple, with God's blessing, makes the trip to earth, taking with them domesticated animals, grains, and plants. God is bringing the earth and its inhabitants into existence. But there is also an interdiction: Access to heaven is now denied to humans. If they seek to return, death with be the result. Now the story moves into the second pattern: Death comes into the world. God's son, Warumbe, follows the newly weds to earth, demands the children of the humans, and begins to destroy them. Nothing can be done to dislodge death from the earth.

In this myth, God's dual nature is dramatized. His paradoxical life-giving and death-dealing characteristics are manifested, in the language of storytelling, by his children: Nambi, his life-giving side, and Warumbe, his death-dealing side.

As in such myths as "The Blue Crane" (story 3), this story begins as a domestic tale, a bride quest with a reluctant in-law who sets impossible tasks, and ends as a myth, the origin of life and death.

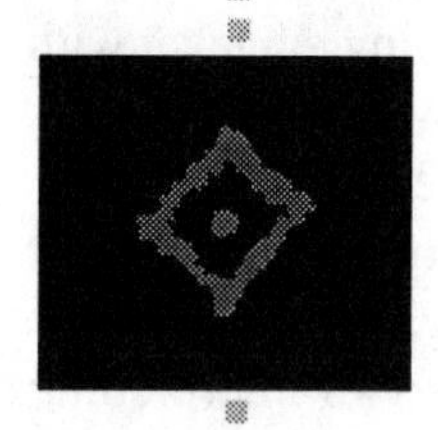

. . . at night the people gather round the flickering fire, within the dark circle of the house, to hear the grandmother, as she leans against the house pole, telling how the animals live and talk. Her imagination and her personality illuminate the ancient stories with her own turns and phrases. The story is the same, but its telling is ever changing, for the long grass whispers its secrets anew to each hearer.

Margaret Read, in the "Foreword," Geraldine Elliot, *The Long Grass Whispers* (New York: Schocken Books, 1968), p. vii.

Anuak

God Creates Man and Woman

by Sheikh Oterie of Dimma

The Anuak live in Sudan.

Jwok [an androgynous god] had sons—first, an elephant; then, a buffalo, a lion, a crocodile; after that, a little dog; and, finally, man and woman.

Upon seeing the humans, God said, "What are these things without hair? All my other offspring have hair or scales, but what are these things?"

God said to the little dog, "Take them away, throw them away on the plain!"

The dog took the man, departed, and after a short time found a tree with a big hole in it—like a house. The dog put the children in this. Then it took a cow from among God's flocks and brought it to the tree. The dog milked it night and morning, putting the milk into a gourd. It gave the milk to the children. This was done without God's knowledge.

The boy grew and with him his twin sister, and they soon got too big for their hole in the tree. The dog then took them away into the country. They built a straw house, and the boy and girl went in, and they lived there.

Then the dog returned to God who, upon seeing the dog, said, "What have you been doing all this time? Where have you been?"

The dog said, "I have been away on the plain herding the cows. There is no good grazing here, so I went to a far place."

From A. G. Cummins, "Annuak Fable," *Man* 15 (1915): 34–35.

Time passed, and the boy and girl became man and woman.

At length, the dog brought them before God.

God said, "What is this? Where have you brought them from?"

The dog answered, "These are the ones you told me long ago to take and leave on the plain."

God said, "Bring them here, I shall kill them!"

The dog answered, "Not so. These are people whose eyes look about and see things and understand. They are not like your other children. Let them stay with me, let them live as my brother and sister."

So they all settled down together with God.

Presently, God looked around and found that the land was getting too crowded. "I must now allot land to all of my people, I must send them to their countries. Let the elephant, the buffalo, and the lion come first, and let the man and woman come last."

The dog heard this, and at once went in and told the man, "This is not good. If you go in last, you shall get nothing. You must go first, and say that you are the elephant, the buffalo, and the lion."

The man at once agreed, and he walked first to the house of God.

God heard the man approaching, and called out, "Who are you?"

The man replied, "I am the elephant, the buffalo, and the lion."

"Very well." God threw him all the spears. "Take these, go on your way."

The man took the spears and departed.

Then up marched the elephant, the buffalo, and the lion.

God heard them approaching, and called out, "Who are you?"

"The elephant!"

"The buffalo!"

"The lion!"

"What!" cried God. "Who then were those who have just gone?"

They answered, "Perhaps the man and the dog."

"Ah!" said God. "And I have given them all the spears. What am I to do for you? Here, take these," and God handed the elephant its tusks.

"And you, take these," and God handed the buffalo its horns.

"Take these," and God handed the lion its claws.

To the crocodile, God gave teeth.

All was finished, and they departed.

But whenever the man saw the elephant, the buffalo, the lion, or the crocodile, he would kill them with his spear. So the elephant, the buffalo, and the lion departed onto the plains, and the crocodile, finding the sun too hot, went down into the river. And man took the best place.

All this took place in a far country.

The name of the first man was Otino.

The name of the first woman was Akongo.

Commentary

God in this story is, like Mugulu in "The Creation" (story 9), a dualistic god; in this case, the dualism is indicated by androgyny: God is both male and female in one, hermaphroditic.

This myth describes the creation of humans and animals, the differentiation that occurs during the Age of Creation, as God, humans, animals, and plants are evolved into separate species. The Anuak myth-maker clothes the story in irony: God sees humans as throw-aways, as creative failures. The lowly dog saves the humans from god, brings them up, then presents them to God as adults, which is the real creation of humans. The pattern has to do with the distribution of traits. The motif: cheating God. Humans pretend to be the great animals, elephant, buffalo, lion, so God gives them the means whereby they can subdue the earth: spears. Then, when the elephant, buffalo, and lion come to him, he has no weapons left to give them, so he gives the elephant tusks, the buffalo horns, the lion claws, the crocodile teeth. It is a story of creation and differentiation. An etiological ending explains why these animals and humans are at enmity.

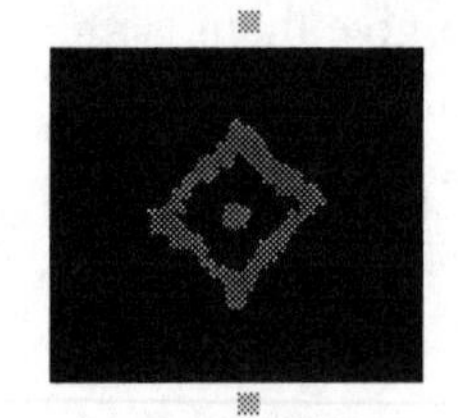

One listens to a clever storyteller, as was our old friend Mungalo. . . . Speak of eloquence! . . . [E]very muscle of face and body spoke, a swift gesture often supplying the place of a whole sentence. He would have made a fortune as a raconteur upon the English stage.

Edwin E. Smith and Andrew Murray Dale, *The Ila-speaking Peoples of Northern Rhodesia* (London: Macmillan, 1920), vol. 2, p. 336.

Egyptian

Isis and Osiris

Thea, having stealthily accompanied Kronos, was discovered by Helios, who pronounced a curse on her, "that she should not be delivered in any month or year."

Hermes, however, in love with the same goddess, in recompense for the favors that he had received from her, played at tables with Selene, and won from her the seventieth part of each of her illuminations. These several parts, making in the whole five new days, he afterwards joined together, and added to the three hundred and sixty, of which the year formerly consisted. Those days are still called by the Egyptians the "superadded," and observed by them as the birthdays of the gods.

On the first of those days, Osiris was born. When he entered the world, a voice was heard saying, "The lord of all the earth is born."

On the second of these days, Aroueris was born. On the third day, Set came into the world, born neither at the proper time nor by the right place, but forcing his way through a wound that he had made in his mother's side. Isis was born on the fourth day, in the marshes of Egypt. Nephthys was born on the last day. Isis and Osiris, having a mutual affection, enjoyed each other in their mother's womb before they were born; from this commerce sprang Horus.

Osiris, having become king of Egypt, applied himself to civilizing his countrymen, turning them from their former indigent and barbarous course of life. He taught them how to cultivate and improve the fruits of the earth. He gave them a body of laws by which to regulate their conduct, and instructed them in that reverence and worship which they were to pay to the gods. With the same good disposition, he afterwards traveled over the rest of the world, inducing the people everywhere to submit to his

Adapted from *Plutarch's Lives,* ed. S. Squire (Cambridge: Cambridge University Press, 1744), pp. 15 ff. Translated from Greek.

discipline, not compelling them by force of arms but persuading them to yield to the strength of his reasons, which were conveyed to them in the most agreeable manner, in hymns and songs accompanied by instruments of music.

During Osiris's absence from his kingdom, Set had no opportunity to make any innovations in the state, Isis being extremely vigilant in the government and always on her guard. After Osiris's return, however, having first persuaded seventy-two other persons to join with him in the conspiracy, Set contrived a stratagem to execute his base designs.

Having secretly taken the measure of Osiris's body, he caused a chest to be made of exactly the same size, a beautiful chest set off with all the ornaments of art. He brought it into his banquet room. After it had been much admired by all who were present, Set, as if in jest, promised to give it to anyone of them whose body, upon trial, might be found to fit. Upon hearing this, all the members of the company, one after another, went into it, but it did not fit any of them. Finally, Osiris lay down in it. When he did so, the conspirators clapped the cover on the chest, then fastened it down on the outside with nails, pouring melted lead over it. Then they carried it to the river side, and conveyed it to the sea by the Tanaitic mouth of the Nile. These matters were executed, they say, on the seventeenth day of the month, when the sun was in Scorpio. Osiris was no more than twenty-eight years old at this time.

The first who learned about what had befallen their king were the pans and satyrs who inhabited the country. They immediately acquainted the people with the news.

As soon as the report reached Isis, she immediately cut off one of the locks of her hair, and put on mourning apparel on the very spot where she then happened to be.

Then she wandered everywhere about the country, full of disquietude and perplexity, in search of the chest, inquiring of every person she met, even of some children whom she chanced to see, whether they knew what had become of it. It so happened that these children had seen what Set's accomplices had done with the body, and they told her by what mouth of the Nile it had been conveyed into the sea.

During this interval, Isis, having been informed that Osiris, deceived by her sister, Nephthys, who was in love with him, had unwittingly enjoyed her instead of herself, as she concluded from the melilot garland that he had left with her, made it her business to seek out the child, the fruit of this unlawful commerce (for her sister, dreading the anger of her husband, Set, had exposed it as soon as it was born). After much difficulty, by means of some dogs that conducted her to the place where the child was, she found him and brought him up. In time, the child became her constant guide and attendant, and had therefore obtained the name, Anubis, being thought to watch and guard the gods, as dogs do mankind.

Finally, she received more news of the chest, that it had been carried by the waves of the sea to the coast of Byblos, and there gently lodged in the branches of a tamarisk bush. In a short time, this shot up into a large and beautiful tree, growing around the chest and enclosing it on every side, so that it was not to be seen. The king of the country, amazed at the tree's unusual size, cut it down, and made that part of the trunk in which the chest was concealed into a pillar to support the roof of his house. These matters were made known to Isis in an extraordinary manner, by the report of demons. She immediately went to Byblos where, setting herself down by the side of a fountain, she refused to speak to anybody except the queen's women who happened to be there. She saluted them and caressed them in the kindest manner possible, plaiting their hair for them, transmitting into them part of the wonderful odor that issued from her own body. This aroused a great desire in the queen, their mistress, to see the stranger who had this admirable faculty of transfusing so fragrant a smell from herself into the hair and skin of other people. She sent for her to come to the court, and, after a further acquaintance with her, made her nurse to one of her sons.

The name of the king who reigned at this time at Byblos, a city in the papyrus swamps of the delta, was Melcarthus; the name of his queen was Astarte.

Isis fed the child by giving it her finger to suck instead of the breast. Every night, she put him into the fire in order to consume his mortal part, each time transforming herself into a swallow and hovering round the pillar and bemoaning her sad fate. She continued to do this for some time, until, one day, the queen saw her, saw the child in the flame. She cried out, and thereby deprived the child of that immortality that would otherwise have been conferred on him. Then the goddess, revealing herself, requested that the pillar that supported the roof be given to her.

She took the pillar down, and then, easily cutting it open, took out what she wanted. She wrapped up the remainder of the trunk in fine linen, and, pouring perfumed oil on it, delivered it again into the hands of the king and queen. When this was done, she threw herself on the chest, at the same time making such a loud and terrible lamentation over it that it frightened the younger of the king's sons, who heard her, out of his life.

The elder of the king's sons Isis took with her, and she set sail with the chest for Egypt. It was then about morning, and the river Phaedrus sent forth a rough and sharp air, but Isis, in her anger, dried up its current.

No sooner had she arrived at a desert place, where she imagined herself to be alone, than she opened the chest, and, laying her face on her dead husband's, she embraced his corpse and wept bitterly. Perceiving that the little boy had silently stolen behind her and found out the reason for her grief, she turned around suddenly and, in her anger, gave him so fierce and stern a look that he immediately died of fright.

Isis, intending to pay a visit to her son, Horus, who was brought up at Butos, deposited the chest, in the meanwhile, into a remote, unfrequented place.

Set, however, as he was hunting one night by the light of the moon, accidentally met with it, and, knowing the body that was enclosed in it, tore it into several pieces, fourteen in all, dispersing them up and down in different parts of the country.

When she learned of this event, Isis set out in search of the scattered fragments of her husband's body, making use of a boat made of the papyrus reed in order to pass more easily through the lower and fenny parts of the country.

It was because of this event that there are so many different sepulchers of Osiris in Egypt, for we are told that wherever Isis met with any of the scattered limbs of her husband, she buried it there. Others tell us that this variety of sepulcher was owing rather to the policy of the queen, who, instead of the real body, as was pretended, presented these several cities with the image only of her husband, and that she did this not only to render the honors, which would be by this means paid to his memory, more extensive, but likewise that she might thereby elude the malicious search of Set. If Set got the better of Horus in the war in which they were going to be engaged, distracted by this multiplicity of sepulchers, he might despair of being able to find the true one. We are told, moreover, that, notwithstanding all her searching, Isis was never able to recover the privy member of Osiris, which, having been thrown into the Nile immediately upon its separation from the rest of the body, had been devoured by the lepidotus, the phagrus, and the oxyrynchus, fish which, of all others and for this reason, the Egyptians especially avoid. In order, however, to make amends for the loss, Isis consecrated the phallus made in imitation of it, and instituted a solemn festival to its memory, which is even to this day observed by the Egyptians.

After these events, Osiris, returning from the other world, appeared to his son, Horus, encouraged him to battle, and at the same time instructed him in the exercise of arms.

He then asked him what animal he thought most serviceable to a soldier.

Horus answered, "A horse."

This raised the wonder of Osiris, so that he further questioned him, why he preferred a horse before a lion.

"Because," said Horus, "though the lion is the more serviceable creature to one who stands in need of help, the horse is more useful in overtaking and cutting off a flying adversary."

These replies delighted Osiris, as they showed him that his son was sufficiently prepared for his enemy.

Among the great numbers who were continually deserting from Set's party was his concubine, Ta-urt. A serpent pursuing her as she was coming over to Horus was killed by his soldiers—the memory of which action, they say, is still preserved in that cord that is thrown into the midst of their assemblies, and then chopped into pieces. Afterwards, it came to a battle between them; it lasted many days. But victory, at length, inclined to Horus, and Set himself was taken prisoner.

Isis, however, to whose custody he was committed, was so far from putting him to death that she even loosed his bonds and set him at liberty. This action of his mother so incensed Horus that he laid hands on her and pulled off the ensign of royalty that she wore on her head. In its stead, Hermes clapped on a helmet made in the shape of an ox's head.

After this, Set publicly accused Horus of being a bastard, but with the assistance of Hermes, Horus's legitimacy was fully established by the judgment of the gods themselves.

After this, there were two other battles fought between them, in both of which Set had the worst.

Isis is said to have accompanied Osiris after his death, and in consequence to have brought forth Harpocrates, who came into the world before his time and was lame in his lower limbs.

Commentary

Plutarch's biography of Osiris was taken by him from the oral tradition. The story has been in existence for over five thousand years. It is a love story, having to do with betrayal and loyalty, death and rebirth, forgetting and memory, evil and righteousness, duty and compassion. It deals with the manifestation of the forces of nature, the meaning of sisterhood and fatherhood, and the mysteries of the body, the soul, and the spirit.

In the *Pyramid Texts,* the poet addressed Osiris as the god who departed but returned, who slept but awakened, who died but lived again. In a hymn to Osiris, he was designated as the Nile River, praised because gods and humans endured "from your overflow."

These are the Egyptian Gods in this myth: Osiris, King of Egypt, was originally a vegetation god, closely linked to corn; later, he was god of the dead, the supreme funerary deity. He taught Egyptians the arts and crafts of civilization. Isis, the sister-wife of Osiris, was the greatest of Egyptian divinities, the embodiment of ideal motherhood and womanhood. Set, Osiris' brother, was God of thunder and storm, the personification of evil in the battle against good. Nephthys was Goddess of the dead, the wife of Set. Anubis was the funerary god of embalming and of tombs, son of Osiris and Nephthys. Horus was the son of Osiris and Isis.

In ancient Egypt, the god whose death and resurrection were annually celebrated with alternate sorrow and joy was Osiris, the most popular of all Egyptian deities. He was a personification of the yearly transformations of nature. In the beginning, Osiris, whose presence was manifested in the sprouting grain and the rising waters of the Nile, invented agriculture, writing, and the arts, and transformed humanity from barbarism to civilization. He was murdered and cut into fourteen pieces by his jealous brother, Set, and he was put back together by his devoted sister/wife. When he was physically resurrected for a night, Osiris fertilized the seed of eternity within the womb of Isis, who magically conceived a son named Horus. When he grew to manhood, Horus eventually challenged and overthrew his uncle and father's murderer.

This story is remembered because it is the passionate account of the love of two soul mates, the betrayal but not the destruction of that love, the longing and searching for the body of the beloved, and the reuniting of that body. Significant patterns are (1) the attempts of Set to kill Osiris, (2) Isis seeking her husband's body, gathering the pieces, giving them life, (3) the regular death and resurrection of Osiris, reflected in the fall and rise of the life-giving Nile. Presiding motifs include death and resurrection, and transformation.

◇ **Notes:** (a) With the assistance of other gods and goddesses, Isis embalmed the body, and Osiris was revived into eternal life. He retired to the Underworld. (b) Osiris was the corn and the vine, born every year and slain every year; he was the Nile which rises and falls, the rising and setting sun, the fertile land about the Nile threatened by the desert, Set. (c) The struggle is between Osiris and Set, good and evil, with Isis protecting and nourishing Osiris, giving him life.

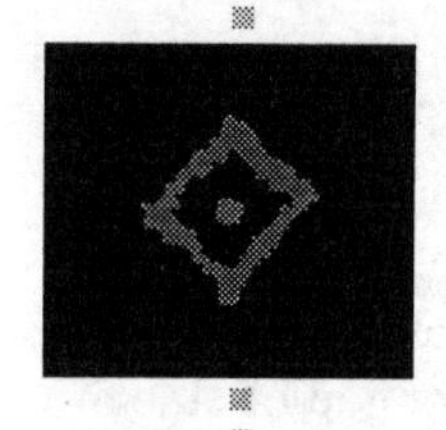

I wish I could give my readers an idea of the entranced attention with which these stories, and a hundred like them, are received by African audiences—and these not of tender years, but grown men and women, who listen to the well-worn recitals open-mouthed, punctuating them with wonder-stricken ejaculations of "Eh-yah," "Eh-bo-o-o-o," "Wah-h-h-h," the palm of the right hand dropped helplessly into that of the left, to signify that the last conceivable condition of wonder has been reached

Reginald Charles F. Maugham, *Zambezia* (London: J. Murray, 1910), pp. 380–381.

Khoi

The Parting of the Waters

The Khoi lived in southern Africa.

1. Heitsi Eibip

Heitsi Eibip was a great and celebrated sorcerer among the Namaqua people. He could tell secret things, and prophesy what would happen.

One day, he was traveling with a great number of people, and an enemy pursued them.

They came to some water, and Heitsi Eibip said, "My grandfather's father, open yourself, so that I may pass through. Then close yourself afterwards."

It happened as he had said, and Heitsi Eibip and his people went through safely.

Then their enemies tried to pass through the opening also, but when they were in the midst of it, it closed on them, and they perished.

Heitsi Kabip died several times, and came to life again.

When the Khoi pass one of his graves, they throw a stone on it for good luck.

Heitsi Eibip could take many different forms. Sometimes he appeared handsome, very handsome. Or his hair grew long, down to his shoulders; at other times, it was short.

W. H. I. Bleek, *Reynard the Fox in South Africa* (London: Trübner, 1864), pp. 75–76, 61–64.

2. A Nama Woman Outwits Elephants

An elephant, it was said, was married to a Nama woman, whose two brothers came to her secretly because they were afraid of her husband.

She went out, as if to fetch wood, then hid her two brothers within the wood, and laid them in the house.

Then she said, "Since I married into this homestead, has a sheep been slaughtered for me?"

Her blind mother-in-law said, "Things are being uttered by the wife of my eldest brother that she has never said before."

Then the elephant, who had been in the field, arrived, and, smelling something, rubbed against the house.

The wife said, "I do now what I should not have done in the past. When did you slaughter a sheep for me?"

The mother-in-law said to him, "As she is saying things that she has not said before, do it now."

So a sheep was slaughtered for her. She roasted it whole.

That same night, after supper, she asked her mother-in-law, "How do you breathe when you sleep the sleep of life [i.e., a light sleep]? And how do you breathe when you sleep the sleep of death [i.e., a deep sleep]?"

Then the mother-in-law said, "Well, this is an evening full of conversation! When we sleep the sleep of death, we breathe like this: Sui sui. And when we sleep the sleep of life, we breathe like this: Xou! awaba! Xou! awaba!"

The wife prepared everything while they were asleep.

She listened to their snoring, and while they were sleeping sui sui, she rose and said to her two brothers, "The sleep of death is upon them. Let us make ready."

They arose and went out, and she broke up the house in order that she might carry away everything that was possible, she took the necessary things, and said, "Whoever makes noise wills my death." They were all quiet.

When her two brothers had packed up, she went with them among the cattle. But she left at home one cow, one ewe, and one goat. She gave instructions to these three animals, saying to the cow, "If you do not wish for my death, you must not low as if you were by yourself alone." And she taught the ewe and the goat the same.

Then she and her brothers departed with all the other livestock. Those three animals they left behind made sounds during the night as if they were many, and the elephant thought, "They are all there."

But when he got up in the morning, he saw that his wife and all his livestock were gone.

He took his stick, and said to his mother, "If I fall, the earth will tremble!"

With these words, the elephant followed them.

When they saw him approaching, they ran fast to one side, at a narrow spot against a rock.

She said, "We are people behind whom a large traveling party comes. Stone of my ancestors, divide yourself for us!"

Then the rock divided itself, and, when they had passed through it, it closed again behind them.

Then the elephant came along, and said to the rock, "Stone of my ancestors, divide yourself for me also!"

The rock divided itself again, but when the elephant entered, the rock closed on him. So the elephant died, and the earth trembled.

The mother, at her home, said, "As my eldest son said, so it has happened. The earth shakes."

Commentary

"Heitsi Eibip"

Heitsi Eibip is a mythical ancestral hero and a god. He refers to the water as "My grandfather's father . . . ," a reference to the time before differentiation, when all beings were the same, when all were in harmony. In the myth's sole pattern, the water opens, then closes on the enemy, as good and evil continue their struggle, as evil is vanquished and good is reborn.

This is also the story of a dying and resurrected god: Heitsi Eibip, a god, dies and comes to life again. A renowned shape-shifter, he takes different forms. He is not a creator god, but he gives humans and animals their special characteristics.

"A Nama Woman Outwits Elephants"

It is the age of creation, a time of differentiation. Change is occurring, as the main pattern suggests: the mother-in-law comments that the things that the daughter-in-law is asking for have never before been requested.

A Nama woman is married to an elephant. She learns the secret of the sleeping patterns of the elephant and his mother. When they are asleep, she and her two brothers—humans—flee with everything that provide the basis for Khoi civilization. The world is being created, and the forces that would stand in the way of that creation, the forces that claim the human woman as their own, are destroyed when the rock opens and closes on the elephant. "The earth shakes."

The story begins as a tale, a domestic situation, and ends as a myth, the creation of Khoi civilization.

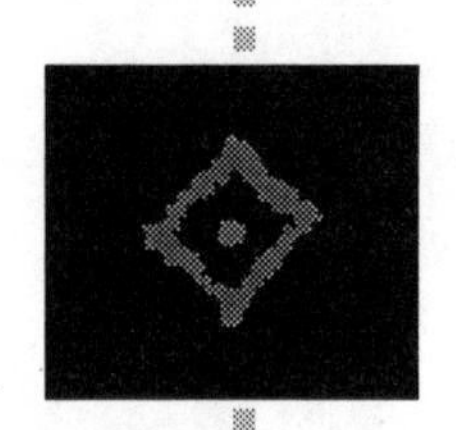

A story is like the wind. It comes from a far-off place, and we feel it.

I am waiting for the moon to turn back for me, so that I may return to my home and listen to all the people's stories when I visit them. When the weather gets a little warmer, I sit in the sun, sitting and listening to the stories that come from out there, stories that come from a distance. Then I catch hold of a story that floats out from the distant place—when the sun feels warm and when I feel that I must visit and talk with my fellows.

||kábbo, a San storyteller

From W. H. I. Bleek and Lucy C. Lloyd, *Specimens of Bushman Folklore* (London: George Allen, 1911), pp. 298–301.

San

|kággen and the All-devourer

by ||kábbo

The San live in southern Africa.

|kággen, the mantis, went to the ticks' house. They saw him, and said to each other, "What man is coming here?"

Another said, "|kággen is coming. We'll creep into the sheep's wool, and let him come into the house. Let the little child remain here, he can look after the pots on the fire. Then the old man will come into the house as the child sits here alone. Now, you must all carry knobkerries. We'll listen to |kággen, when he approaches the child. He'll question the child, because he'll see that we're not in the house."

The ticks then went into the sheep's wool.

|kággen went up to the child. "Am I like a fighting man, that the people have fled in fear of me? But I'm just a quiet man. There's no one here but this black child. The others have gone, leaving him sitting alone in the house tasting the contents of this pot. The houses have no people!"

But the people were listening in the sheep's wool.

|kággen said, "Let me just put my quiver down and take out this fat and eat it—because the people have fled in fear. As for this child, I'll first eat until I am satisfied, then I'll knock him down because he has no sense."

A tick fell down from the sheep's wool.

From D. F. Bleek, ed., *The Mantis and His Friends* (Cape Town: T. Maskew Miller, [1923]), pp. 30–40.

|kággen saw him, and asked, "Where did you come from?"

But the young man tick was silent. He lifted the pot and placed it carefully on the fire.

Then his sister fell down, his older brother fell down and snatched the pot. Other ticks fell down at other fires.

The other ticks that were still in the sheep's wool whispered to each other, "You must fall down one by one!"

A big young man tick slipped down beside |kággen, and he sat there holding |kággen by his cape.

His older brother slipped down on the other side of |kággen, and he held him by the other side of the cape.

Another tick made a rustling sound as he dropped down—vvv.

Their father, an old tick, was still up in the sheep's wool. He said to another, "You must wait! Hold the stick, ready to strike. Many people are down there, sitting about on the ground. They'll beat him while we knock him down, as he sits among the people."

|kággen drew back. He said to himself, "Let me move a little further away." He pulled at the cape that was fast to the ground.

Then the old tick fell upon him, and knocked him down. Another tick fell on the mantis, he beat |kággen's shoulders, he struck with the knobkerrie. Another tick sprang out here, on one side, and he beat |kággen's side. Another tick leapt down on him, he beat his other side until |kággen screamed.

Then |kággen slipped out of the cape. The ticks rushed together and struck at him. He called out as the ticks beat him.

|kággen was going. He called to his hartebeest-skin bag, and the bag came to him. The quiver arose by itself, and came to him. The stick came, the bag came. |kággen went away first, his things followed him. He went flying into the water, he swam across, he walked up the water's bank.

He said to the hartebeest's children, "Wait for me over there, so that I can come to you slowly to carry you. The people have beaten me badly, and I must go home slowly."

The ichneumon saw him, and said, "|kággen comes, he's coming over there. He's coming slowly. The ticks seem to have beaten him, as they're accustomed to do because they're angry people. |kággen remembered that he has wings, that's why we see him returning. He'll not sleep well tonight."

|kággen sat down, and said, "The people to whom I went must have been hidden. I didn't see them. They kept coming out from above, they kept sliding down. They beat me while the sheep were in the kraal."

The ichneumon said to |kággen, "You went to the house to which people do not go, at which they merely look in passing when the sheep are in the kraal, and go to their own homes. For those people are black, they are accustomed to beating a man to death because of those sheep. They go into the sheep's wool, and we cannot see them. They keep a lookout, they see a man first, while he's still far off. They hide their bodies in the sheep's capes hanging up there. Then they keep falling down, and they beat a man from all sides."

|kággen agreed with him: "That's just what they did. One man knocked me down, others dropped down and struck me. I didn't pick up my stick and strike back, I got up and left my stick. My things were still lying on a bush. The quiver came after me to the water where I went to wash off the blood, the other things followed me."

The ichneumon said, "You're sitting there shivering because you went into cold water to cleanse your wounds. You might have died without our knowing. You had to go into the water because of your tricks, because you went to play tricks on the people you did not know! Nobody goes to them, because they drink blood! They are black people, they are bloody-handed. Their houses are always black, because they are angry folk."

|kággen said to him, "Ichneumon, don't teach me, I'm an old man! I feel as if I would like to sit listening to stories, that's what I would like to hear. You always scold me. But I think that I'm the one who should be angry. Now I'm not going to talk any more, I'm going to lie down. My head aches. And don't say that you don't sleep well, because I really ache! I shall writhe in pain!"

|kággen lay down to sleep, he covered his head.

The ichneumon said, "You always act like this."

|kággen lies there, he moans, he dreams that all the ticks' houses arise and come. The sheep rise up, the sheep come and stand in front of his house, and the ticks' houses are at the side of his houses, while the ichneumon is still asleep. The ichneumon will see when he awakens—the capes of the ticks are here, all their things are here, their knobkerries with which they beat him are here. Those ticks will soon feel the cold, even though they are asleep. They shall sleep very heavily, they'll feel as if they were wrapped up even though they are not, as they lie in the cold. They'll feel as if they are lying inside houses, but they'll wake up and miss them. And they shall not see the spoor of their sheep, for the spoor will have gone into the air, the kraal will have mounted upwards with the sheep in it.

Then they'll first miss their fire early, for their fire will have gone with the house, the pots will have entirely disappeared. Those people will not cook for their knives will have gone. I shall be cutting up sheep with them, while the ticks are walking about in their bare flesh, no longer possessing the things they once possessed. Now they will have to drink blood, because they will no longer have a fire as they used to have. Real people will henceforth cook, while the ticks walk entirely in the dark. They will have to continue biting the bodies of things, they will have to drink the blood of things and no longer eat cooked meat.

The ichneumon awoke.

|kággen said, "Icheumon, are you sufficiently awake to look out at the thing that's bleating like a sheep outside? It seems to have come to us early while we were asleep here." The mantis lay there, he questioned the ichneumon while he still had his head covered.

The ichneumon got up and came out. He saw the sheep, and said, "People, get up! Get up, and see the sheep standing in this kraal that my grandfather |kággen has brought! Sheep are here, and the houses have come with them! And look at these pots that he has brought! Look at the ticks' capes, in which we shall lie wrapped up! Now I can keep warm from this cold in which I have always lain uncomfortably. The knobkerries with which they beat my grandfather are here—I shall possess them, so that I can beat the people! My grandfather |kággen will take the old fellow's knobkerries, and I'll take my fellow-children's knobkerries, because they helped their parents to strike my grandfather |kággen when he was alone."

The rock-badger got up. She said to |kággen, "|kággen, why did you take away the people's sheep?"

|kággen answered her as he lay there, "It seemed right to me, because those people attacked me, they wanted to kill me in their anger. Then, because they fought me at their fire, I felt that I wished those angry folk over there should no longer warm themselves at a fire. They shall now drink raw blood because they lack a fire, they cannot make a fire. They cannot cook, they also cannot roast meat to feed themselves. Now they shall walk about in their flesh. In these pots here the San shall some day cook, because they shall have a fire. We who are here will then also be as the ticks now are. We'll eat different things, because we too shall lack fire. You, the ichneumon, will then go to dwell in the hills with your mother. She will truly become a porcupine, she will live in a hole, while Grandmother Rock-badger will live in a mountain den, for her name is really 'Rock-badger.' I shall have wings, I shall fly when I am green, I'll be a little green thing. You, the ichneumon, will eat honey because you will be living on the hill. Then you will marry a she-ichneumon."

The porcupine called to Kwammanga: "Oh Kwa! Look at the sheep standing here, |kággen has brought them! We don't have to eat them, because the tick-people did not see them go, they'll not know where the sheep have gone. The sheep went straight up into the air as they stood in the kraal. The other things went up with the sheep. The sheep came out of the sky, they stood here. The things also came out of the sky and sat down here, while the people were asleep over there."

The ichneumon said, "|kággen! Now leave these people's things alone, let them keep their houses."

|kággen replied, "Do you not see why I thought it right? These people did bad things to me, they wished me to tremble with the pain of my skin. I want those people to see what I can do and recognize it. They would not give me food, so that I could eat and then return to my home. Had I been able to return comfortably, I would not have done this to them. Now they must truly suck blood, for they lack a fire altogether. They must walk about in their flesh which is black, because they cannot find capes. They'll walk about at night with their naked bodies. They must sit in the cold, because they have no houses. They'll continue to bite the hare's ears to drink its blood. The old tick will always bite men's skins, he'll suck out blood because he lacks a knife altogether. They'll suck blood with their mouths, when they have bitten through the

skin. They'll fill themselves with blood, they shall truly be blood-bellies. And they will continue to bite the sheep. Men will search through the sheep's wool, dividing the wool, throwing the ticks down on the ground and crushing them, because they are sheep's ticks." |kággen said, "Now I want you, the ichneumon, to catch some fat sheep for Father to cut up for us and hang up to dry near the house. For I don't feel like cutting up, because I'm still writhing in pain. The swelling must first be over, then I can cut up, then I shall hang meat to dry at my house—because I want the sheep's fat to be dry, so that the women can render it, so that we can moisten the dry meat that we've been crunching, the quagga's meat that was white with age and not tender. So now, I want you to cut up the old sheep—let the young ones wait a little, because we'll not finish these sheep, there are so many. I want the porcupine to go out tomorrow, when she has cooked and put aside the meat that she has dried, and invite the man over there to come and eat these sheep with me, because I've counted them and see that they are plentiful."

The porcupine said, "Do you really want me to go to the man who eats bushes? He'll come and swallow all the sheep as they stand in the kraal! And don't think that these bushes will be left, because we'll all be swallowed with the sheep. He is a man who devours things! He walks along eating up the bushes as he passes, the bushes among which he walks."

|kággen said to her, "You must go to your older father, the All-devourer, so that he can help me to eat up these sheep and drink this soup—because I've poured some of the soup away because I feel that my heart is upset. Fat has taken hold of my heart, I don't want to drink more soup. So I want the old man over there to come, he'll drink up the soup and then I can talk, for I don't talk now. So fill the sack there with cooked meat and take it, then he'll come. Otherwise he might refuse."

The porcupine said, "People do not live with that man, he is alone. People cannot hand him food, for his tongue is like fire. He burns people's hands with it. Don't think that we can hand food to him, because we'll have to dodge away to the sheep over there! The pots will be swallowed with the soup in them! Those sheep will be swallowed up in the same way, for the man over there always does so. He doesn't often travel, because he feels the weight of his stomach which is heavy. I, the porcupine, live with you, even though <u>he</u> is my real father, because I fear that he may devour me and I know that you will not devour me. Nevertheless, I'll bring him tomorrow. Then you'll see him with your own eyes."

The next day the porcupine went, she carried cooked meat. She arrived at her father's place, the place of the All-devourer. She stood there, and took off the sack of meat.

She said to her father, "Go! Cousin there invites you to come and eat the sheep over there, for his heart is troubling him. He wants you to come. I have told you, now I'll go on in front because I don't walk fast."

She shook out the meat from the bag onto the bushes. The All-devourer licked up the meat and the bushes with it, he gulped down the bushes too. The porcupine slung on the bag. She went forward quickly, she walked on giving directions: "You must climb up to that place from which I came, you'll see the sheep standing there." She felt that she was going in fear of the All-devourer. She was the first to reach the house.

|kággen asked her, "Where is Father?"

The porcupine answered him, "He's still coming. Look at the bush standing up there, watch for a shadow that will come gliding from above. Watch for the bush to break off. Then look for the shadow when you see that the bushes up there have disappeared. For his tongue will take away the bushes beforehand, while he is still approaching behind the hill. Then his body will come up and the bushes will be finished off right up to where we are, when he arrives. We'll no longer sit hidden here. Now I want the ichneumon to eat plenty, for of that meat he will never eat. For the man who comes yonder, the bushes are finished, the sheep will likewise be swallowed up."

The All-devourer followed the spoor of the porcupine. As he went, he ate up the bushes. He climbed up the hill, finishing off the bushes, while his shadow glided up to |kággen's house. It fell upon |kággen. He looked at the sun, he asked where the clouds were, for the sun seemed to be in the clouds.

The porcupine said to him, "There are no clouds there! But I want the ichneumon to go and hide this pot away for me, for he truly feels the shadow of the man coming over there, it altogether shuts us in, the sun will seem to have set when he reaches us. His mouth sits black along there—it is not a shadow, it is what the trees go into."

|kággen saw the All-devourer's tongue. He asked the porcupine, "Is Father holding fire in his hand? for a fire is waxing red over there!"

The porcupine answered him, "It is the man coming there, his tongue is red. He is near, that's why you see his tongue. We'll get out of the way here. We'll not hand him anything ourselves, just put down something for him, because his tongue would singe our hands if we held anything out to him. I want the rock-badger to hide the other pot so that she can still have soup. Now she herself can see the stomach, it truly extends to either side of us! We do not hear the wind, because he is coming. The wind does not blow, because he always makes a shelter when he stands. He does not sit down, he stands. He'll first eat the things up, for they are still plentiful. He has put in a layer of bushes at the bottom of his stomach, he has partly filled it, but he has not filled it up yet. That's why he is still seeking food. For he is a man who fills himself to his trunk. If he looks around and finds no food, he'll swallow these folk, because they invited him to come to eat food that was not enough."

The All-devourer arrived, |kággen placed food for him. The All-devourer gulped it down quickly. |kággen took soup and poured it into a bucket. The All-devourer swallowed the bucket. A pot was still keeping warm. |kággen took meat that had been put away in a bag, he put it into a bucket; he pushed the bucket towards the All-devourer. The All-devourer put out his tongue, he licked and scorched the mantis's hands.

|kággen pulled his arms quickly away, he sprang aside, knocking against the rock-badger.

The rock-badger said, "Why does |kággen spring aside from the man whom he invited to come? The porcupine told him not to give anything to the All-devourer with his hands, but to put meat on the bushes."

|kággen took meat and put it in the pot.

He said to the young mantis, "Child, make a good fire for the pot. My hands are burning, keeping me sitting where Grandfather scorched me. For you can feel his hot breath! His tongue feels like that too!"

The rock-badger said to him, "You ought to ladle out sheep's meat and put it on the bushes."

|kággen did not hear, he sat spitting on his hands to cool them. He ladled out another bucketful. He again pushed the bucket to the All-devourer. The All-devourer licked |kággen's hands. |kággen sprang aside, losing his balance, and tumbled into the house. He got up, he sat licking, cooling his hands.

He said to the ichneumon, "Ichneumon, give me meat to cook, for you see it is as Mother told us—the buckets seem to have vanished."

The ichneumon said to |kággen, "Mother told you that it would be like this. You would not listen, you invited the big cousin whom people know, whom no one invites, because his tongue is like fire."

|kággen called to the young mantis, "Go and fetch me the meat that the porcupine hid, for you see this bucket of meat has been devoured. You must look at the stomach."

|kággen brought two buckets, he ladled out meat. The rock-badger nudged him, he winked at her. He slung a bucket forward with meat in it, then he slung another bucket forward alongside of it. The All-devourer's tongue licked his ear, he tumbled into the house. The rock-badger spoke to him, he winked at her.

She said, "|kággen, leave off winking at me! You must feed Cousin, whom you invited here. You must give him plenty to eat, for the porcupine told you that she did not want to fetch him because his tongue is always like this!"

The All-devourer gobbled up both buckets, he licked up the meat that was on the bushes of the house, he devoured it together with the bushes.

|kággen said to the ichneumon, "Ichneumon, you must cook at that place, and bring the meat that is on the bushes, because the buckets are all finished. I'll give the old man a pot that is hot to swallow, for you see that the bushes are swallowed up. I shall no longer sit and cook in the bushes when the wind blows."

The All-devourer stepped backwards, he licked up Kwammanga's home-bushes, he devoured them quickly with the meat on them.

|kággen said to the ichneumon, "Ichneumon, quickly bring a sheep, you must cut up a sheep quickly, for you see that the bushes have been swallowed with the meat!"

The All-devourer asked for water. |kággen lifted a whole water-bag, and placed it before him. The All-devourer's tongue took up the water-bag, he swallowed it with the water in it. He licked up a thorn bush.

|kággen said to the young mantis, "You see, we shall not eat, for that thorn bush has been devoured, although it has thorns." |kággen said to the ichneumon, "Ichneumon, fetch that water there that is in the water-bag, for you see that this water-bag has been swallowed. Grandfather turns his head seeking more water. He himself has devoured everything else, he still seems likely to gobble up our beds! I'll truly sit upon the ground if Grandfather eats up all the things in my house!"

The All-devourer licked up the porcupine's things, he swallowed them quickly. |kággen said to his son, the young mantis, "See, Sister's things there have been devoured, Sister sits there on a bare place. The sheep will soon be devoured."

The All-devourer looked towards the sheep, his tongue took up all the sheep, he swallowed them quickly while they were still alive.

|kággen said, "Haven't the sheep been quickly swallowed? before I had cut them up as I had meant to do! And the bushes have vanished, swallowed up! We're sitting on a bare place. Now I no longer have those things that I brought here so that I might possess them!"

The porcupine winked at the ichneumon. "Ichneumon, I tell you, your younger brother must spring away. Father will be swallowed if he goes on acting bravely like this, and Grandfather |kággen is the one who takes—he'll certainly be swallowed!"

The All-devourer called his name, he who is a devourer of things whom |kággen called to come to him.

He said to |kággen, "|kággen, bring out the things you invited me to eat, the real things that I, a devourer of things, should eat!"

He advanced, he burned the mantis with his tongue.

|kággen said, "I who am |kággen invited you who devour things to my home. You came and finished off my things. You should not now ask for the real food for which I invited you—those sheep that you've devoured, that was the food that I invited you to eat. There is no other food."

The All-devourer quickly devoured |kággen, and |kággen shut up. The young mantis sprang away, he took up the bow. The All-devourer looked towards Kwammanga. Young Kwammanga sprang aside, he ran away. |kággen was quite silent because he was in the stomach. The All-devourer stood opposite Kwammanga, he said that he was really going to swallow his daughter's husband. Although he was handsome, still he would swallow him for he felt inclined to do so. He advanced, and he quickly swallowed his daughter's husband with the bed on which he was sitting. The stomach of the All-devourer now hung down almost to the earth.

The porcupine wept, she stood sighing. The children came from afar.

The porcupine asked the young mantis, "Are you a fierce man?"

He was silent.

She asked him, "Are you angry?"

The young mantis was silent, because he felt angry.

She also questioned her son, young Kwammanga. She turned as she sat, she heated a spear, she asked her son, "Are you angry? You must remember that Grandfather's tongue resembles fire. I don't want you to flinch if your heart is like Father's heart."

Young Kwammanga sat still, they agreed to cut his grandfather open. She took the spear out of the fire, she drew it burning along her younger brother's temple. The fire burnt his ear, he sat still. She reheated the spear, it became red hot. She put the spear burning hot into her younger brother's nose. Tears slowly gathered and stood in his eyes.

She said to him, "A mild person is his, whose tears slowly gather."

She heated the spear, she placed it burning hot to her son's ear-root, her son sat still. She heated the spear again, she said to her son, "Grandfather's tongue is like this. I don't want you to flinch from him, if your heart is like your father's heart." She took the spear out when it was red, and put it into her son's nose. She looked at his eyes, they were dry.

She said to herself, "Yes, a fierce man is this. That one is a mild man. This one is fierce, he resembles his father. That one is mild, he resembles his father |kággen, he is a runaway." She said to her son, "Remember, Grandfather's tongue is like this. You must sit firmly when you go to Grandfather."

The children went in wrath to their grandfather, they approached him as he lay in the sun. He arose, he stood up, and waited.

Young Kwammanga said to the other, "Mother wished me to sit on one side of Grandfather, and you to sit on the other side. Because you cut with the left hand like your father, you must sit with your left arm outwards, the arm in which you hold your spear. I will sit opposite on this side, so that I may have my right arm outside, the arm in which I hold the spear."

The All-devourer scorched the young mantis's temple with his tongue. He walked forward, he scorched with his tongue the root of his grandson young Kwammanga's ear. He said that this little child seemed very angry. He walked forward, he scorched the root of the young mantis's ear with his tongue, the young mantis sat still. He went forward again, he again scorched the young mantis's other ear with his tongue. Young Kwammanga looked hard at the other, he signed to him to hold his spear fast, and he held his own well. The other held his spear well, because he had said beforehand, "You must cut one side, while I cut the other side. Then we must run away, while the people pour out."

He sprang forward, and cut. And the other cut too. They ran away, while their fathers poured forth. The sheep also poured out, the buckets poured out. His father sat on the bed. The pots poured out, the things poured out. His grandfather doubled up and died.

The children said, "Bushes, we have cut you out! You should truly become bushes, you'll grow at your place, you'll be what you were before. The place will be right again, and these sheep will wander over it, they'll graze over it and again return to the kraal which will be as it was before. For that man who now lies here, who ate up the bushes, he shall utterly die and go away, so that the people may gather dry bushes and be able to warm themselves."

The young mantis spoke, he felt that he truly resembled his father, his speech resembled his father's speech—it came true.

The rock-badger gave |kággen water, she said to him, "|kággen, you must only drink a little."

|kággen said, "I'm dying of thirst, I must drink up the eggshellful!"

He gulped all the water down, and he fell. Kwammanga still waited.

The porcupine said to the rock-badger, "Take that long stick lying there. You must beat your husband on the shin-bone with it until he gets up, you must hold his face fast and rub it."

The rock-badger took the long stick and hit |kággen on the shin. He started up quickly, he sat there shivering.

The rock-badger reproved him: "I told you to drink only a little, because you would be like this if you gulped down all the water. But you would drink! nearly killing yourself, so that you fell down!"

The porcupine gave Kwammanga water, she said to him, "Kwammanga you must only drink a little, you must soon put the water down—when you have just wet your mouth. You must sit down and wash yourself a little, for you have just come out of the stomach. After a while you can drink plentifully, when you feel that your body is warm."

Kwammanga drank a little, he put the water down and did not gulp it all. He washed himself, he drank, and then he drank plentifully.

His wife cooked meat for him which she had kept hidden away, for she had told the ichneumon to hide some for her so that they could eat it when the children had dealt with the man who was devouring them and he lay dead.

"We must eat here, for he lies over there where the children have killed him. Then we'll travel away, leaving him lying outside that house. We'll move away, seeking a new home, because the man lies in front of this home. We'll live in a different house, which we'll make our home."

They traveled to a new home, and left the house at which the man who had devoured the people was lying.

At this new home, they always lived in peace.

Commentary

This is a Xhosa view of the origin of the mantis (from Garvey Nkonki, "The Traditional Prose Literature of the Ngqika," M. A. [African Studies], University of South Africa, n.d., pp. 52–53): One day, there was a big thunderstorm in a certain village. A big house in one homestead was struck by lightning. People were asked to come and extinguish the blaze. They tried and tried, but gave up. Suddenly, there appeared a thin, weak, green insect. It perched on the burning house, and the fire immediately subsided. The people at once called that insect the Child of Heaven.

And this is Dorothea Bleek's view: "The mantis is the favorite hero of (San) folklore. He is gifted with supernatural powers, yet shows great foolishness. He is sometimes mischievous, sometimes kind, at all times very human. His wife is the dasse [rock-badger], also called Kauru, as the mantis too has several other names. . . . Besides his own children the mantis has an adopted daughter, the porcupine, who is really a child of the All-devourer; but fear of her own father has led her to leave him and live with her adopted father. The porcupine is married to Kwammanga, a mythical person not identified with any animal, but seen in the rainbow. . . . This strange couple have two children, young Kwammanga, who is brave and quiet like his father, and the young ichneumon, who is a great talker, always lecturing his grandfather the mantis on his foolish doings. . . . Although the mantis has creative powers and can bring people to life again, [San] did not worship him, yet they prayed to his creation, the moon, and to other heavenly bodies. He seems to me to be just a sort of dream [San]." (Notes by Dorothea Bleek, in the introduction to *The Mantis and His Friends.*)

This myth occurs at the end of the golden age, the beginning of the age of creation. The enmity that is beginning between lkággen and the ticks suggests the differentiation characteristic of this period.

The San are about to be created. lkággen will take the things of civilization from heaven, where they belong to the ticks, and transfer them to the earth, where they will become the materials of San culture. The audience is present at the birth of San civilization.

The myth operates on the premise that God dreams, and so things happen: God dreams, and San civilization is born. And now, God orders the world, putting all beings and things into their proper places.

But humans do not yet know how to make use of the things that God has given them, as is suggested when all things are destroyed, when God's creation is swallowed up. Humans must learn how to deal with the great forces that God has given them; those forces are here suggested by the unrestrained fire of the All-devourer. Such energy can be creative, but destructive, too. So it is that young Mantis and young Kwammanga are taught by Porcupine, and they learn to withstand the fearsome force of All-devourer, untamed fire, and thereby bring about a second creation, demonstrating that humans have learned to deal with God's creations.

The first pattern is introductory: it establishes the conflict, the provocation that will move God, lkággen, into action, motivating succeeding events: ticks fall down from the thatch and beat him.

The second pattern is the main pattern; it has to do with creation and re-creation. Creation is the result of |kággen's dream, a dream that grows out of the ticks' behavior.

When God awakens, all around is the fulfillment of the dream: differentiation has occurred. But the pattern is broken when the creation is undone by the destructiveness of All-devourer. In a subsidiary pattern, young Mantis and young Kwammanga, the new generation, are educated, and this results in the re-creation.

◇ **Notes**: (a) The primal wresting of fire and the things of civilization from the ticks, the ordering of the creatures of the earth and of the society of humans: these are what the first part of the story is about. (b) For humans to be civilized, nature (the ticks) must be properly ordered, must be put into its place. |kággen prophesies the way all creatures, including himself, will find their proper place in the San scheme of things. (c) For humans to be civilized, fire (All-devourer) must be brought under control. They are the same: the stealing of fire from the ticks, the controlling of fire which is All-devourer; the destruction of the power of the ticks, the destruction of the power of All-devourer.

A Xhosa storyteller (photo by Harold Scheub)

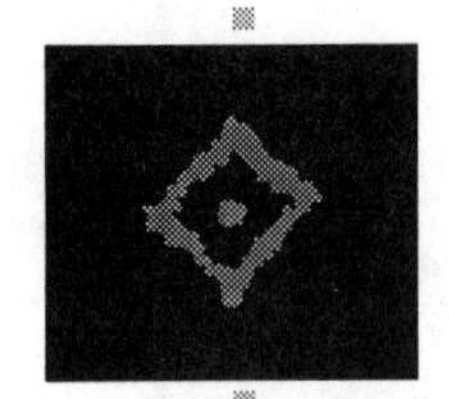

Narrators, while preserving the original plot and characters of a tale, vary it, and make it graphic by introducing objects known and familiar to their audience. . . .

Only a few . . . are noted as skilled narrators. . . .

The occasions selected for the renditions are nights, after the day's work is done, especially if there are visitors to be entertained. The places chosen are the open village street, or, in forest camps where almost all the population of a village go for a week's work on their cutting of new plantations. . . . At night, all gather around the camp fire; and the tales are told with, at intervals, accompaniment of a drum; and parts of the plot are illustrated by an appropriate song, or short dance, the platform being only the earth, and the scenery the forest shadows and the moon or stars.

Robert Hamill Nassau, *Where Animals Talk, West African Folk Lore Tales* (Boston: Gorham Press, 1912), pp. 4–5.

San

|kággen Creates an Eland

by ||kábbo

The San live in southern Africa.

|kággen, the mantis, once did this:

Kwammanga, his son, had taken off a part of his shoe and thrown it away. |kággen picked it up, and went and soaked it in the water at a place where reeds stand.

He went away, then came back again, came and looked. He returned home again when he saw that the eland was still small.

Again he came to the water, he found the eland's spoor at the place where the eland had come out of the water to graze. |kággen went to the water while the eland was seeking the grass that it eats. |kággen waited, sitting by the water. He was on the water's bank, opposite the eland's spear. The eland came to drink there. He saw the eland as it came to drink.

He said, "Kwammanga's shoe-piece."

The person walked up while his father trilled to him.

Then |kággen went to get some honey, he went to cut it. He came and put the bag of honey down near the water. He returned home.

Before the sun was up, he came back, came to pick up the bag. He approached while the eland was in the reeds.

From Dorothea F. Bleek, ed., *The Mantis and His Friends* (Cape Town: T. Maskew Miller, [1923]), pp. 5–9.

He called to it: "Kwammanga's shoe-piece."

The eland got up from the reeds and walked to his father. His father put down the bag of honey. He took out the honeycomb and laid it down. He kept picking up pieces of it and rubbing it on the eland's ribs, at the same time splashing the ribs, making them very nice.

Then |kággen went away, he took the bag to seek more honey which he cut. Then he came back and laid the bag down near the water. He returned home.

Once more he came and picked up the bag; once more he went up to that place and called the eland out of the water, saying, "Kwammanga's shoe-piece."

The person stood shyly in the water. Then he walked up to his father. He had grown. His father wept, fondling him.

|kággen again worked, making the eland nice with honeycomb. Then he went away, while the eland walked back into the water, went to bask in the water.

|kággen did not come back for a time, and for three nights the eland grew, becoming like an ox.

Then |kággen went out early. The sun rose as he walked up to the water. He called the eland, and the eland rose up and came forth. The ground resounded as he came.

|kággen sang for joy about the eland. He sang,

> "Ah, here is a person!
> Kwammanga's shoe-piece!
> My eldest son's shoe-piece!
> Kwammanga's shoe-piece!
> My eldest son's shoe-piece!"

Meanwhile, he rubbed the person down nicely, rubbed down the male eland. Then he went away, he returned home.

Next morning, he called young Ichneumon, his grandson, saying that young Icheumon should go with him, they would be only two. He was going to deceive young Ichneumon.

They went out and reached the water while the eland was grazing. They sat down in the shade of the bush by which the eland's spear stood, where he kept coming to take it.

|kággen said, "Young Ichneumon, go to sleep," for he meant to deceive him.

Young Ichneumon lay down as the eland came to drink—the sun stood at noon, and it was getting hot. Young Ichneumon had covered his head because the mantis wished him to cover it. But young Ichneumon did not sleep, he lay awake.

Then the eland walked away, and young Ichneumon said, "Hi, stand! Stand! Stand!"

|kággen said, "What does my brother think he has seen over there?"

Young Ichneumon said, "A person is standing over there, standing there."

|kággen said, "You think it is magic, but it is a very small thing, it is a bit of your father's shoe that he dropped. It is not magic."

They went home.

Then young Ichneumon told his father, Kwammanga, about it, and Kwammanga said that young Ichneumon must guide him and show him the eland. He would see whether the eland was so very handsome after |kággen had rubbed him down.

Young Ichneumon guided his father while |kággen was at another place—he meant to go to the water later on. Meantime, they went up to the eland at the water while |kággen was not there. Kwammanga knocked the eland down and was cutting it up before |kággen came. When |kággen arrived, he saw Kwammanga and the others standing there, cutting up the eland.

|kággen said, "Why could you not first let me come?" And he wept for the eland, he scolded Kwammanga's people because Kwammanga had not let him come first and let him be the one to tell them to kill the eland.

Kwammanga said, "Tell Grandfather to leave off! He must come and gather wood for us so that we may eat, for this is meat."

Then |kággen came, he said he had wanted Kwammanga to let him come while the eland was still alive, he should not have killed the eland when |kággen was not watching. They might have waited to kill the eland until he was looking on, then he would have told them to kill the eland, then his heart would have been comfortable—for his heart did not feel satisfied about his eland, whom he alone had made.

As he went to gather wood, |kággen caught sight of a gall there, it was the eland's gall. He said he would pierce the gall open, he would jump on it.

The gall said, "If you do, I shall burst and cover you."

Young Ichneumon said, "What are you looking at there? Why are you not gathering wood?"

|kággen left the gall, he brought wood and put it down.

Then he again looked at the place where the gall had been. He went to the gall, he again said he would pierce the gall open, he would jump on it.

The gall said that it would burst and cover him.

|kággen said he would jump on it, the gall must burst when he stepped on it, when he jumped on it.

Young Ichneumon scolded |kággen again. He said, "What is it over there that you keep going to see? You do not gather wood, you just keep going to that bush. You're going to play tricks instead of gathering wood."

Kwammanga said, "You must hurry. When you have called Grandfather, let's go. The gall lies over there, and Grandfather has seen it. So you must hurry. When Grandfather behaves like this about anything, he is not acting straightly, he is playing tricks. So, when you have called Grandfather, we should start to leave the place where the gall is."

They packed the meat in a net while |kággen untied his shoe, he put the shoe into his bag. It was an arrow bag that he had slung on, next to the quiver. They carried the things, and headed for home.

On the way, |kággen said, "This shoe string has broken."

Young Ichneumon said, "You must have put the shoe in your bag."

|kággen said, "No, no, the shoe must be lying back there, where we cut up the eland. I must go back and get the shoe."

Young Ichneumon said, "You must have put the shoe in your bag. Feel in the bag, feel in the middle of the bag, to see if the shoe is there."

|kággen felt in his bag, he kept feeling above the shoe. He said, "See, the shoe is not in the bag. I must go back and pick it up, the shoe is truly over there."

Young Ichneumon said, "We must go home! We really must go home!"

|kággen said, "You can go home, but I must go back and get the shoe."

Then Kwammanga said, "Let Grandfather be! Let him turn back and do as he says."

Young Ichneumon said, "I just wish that |kággen would listen for once when we speak."

|kággen said, "You always go on like this! I really must go and get the shoe."

Then |kággen turned back. He ran up to the gall, he reached it. Then he pierced the gall, he made the gall burst. And the gall broke, covering the head of |kággen. His eyes became big, he could not see. He groped about, feeling his way. As he groped about, he found an ostrich feather. |kággen picked up the feather and sucked it. Then he brushed the gall from his eyes with the feather.

He threw the feather up, and said, "You must now lie up in the sky, you must from now on be the moon. You shall shine at night. By your shining, you shall light the darkness for men, until the sun rises to light up all things for men. It is the sun under which men hunt. You, the moon, glow for men, while the sun shines for men. Under the sun, men walk about, they go hunting, they return home. You are the moon, you give light for men, and then you fall away, you return to life when you have fallen away, and you give light to all people."

That is what the moon does: the moon falls away and returns to life, and he lights up all the flat places.

Commentary

The first pattern in this myth involves the creation, by God, Ikággen, of an eland. It is a pattern revealing the joy of creation. Ikággen, the father of the eland, anoints a piece of his son Kwammanga's shoe, and so brings the creature to life. As the eland grows, it becomes more and more splendid, and God sings a song of rejoicing. That pattern of creation is then broken by a destructive act, by the coming into existence of death. God's children, in the sense that all humans are God's children, destroy the eland and cut it up for food, saddening God because he rejoiced in his creation, angering God because the humans did not seek his permission before committing their deed.

|kággen, because he is a divine trickster, plays a silly trick in the second pattern, when he returns to the eland's gall to puncture it. The gall keeps warning him of the results of such an action: this is the early time, even the gall can speak. Trickster nevertheless returns to the gall and pierces it, and, on the premise that what happens to God happens to all of us, darkness is created when the gall splatters its bile into God's eyes, blinding him. Night has come into being. This darkness is the punishment God gives to humans for killing his creatures. That is the vengeful, destructive part of this dualistic God.

But he is also life-giving and benevolent: he takes an ostrich feather and cleans the gall from his eyes, and he can see again, albeit dimly. When he throws the feather into the heavens, it becomes the moon, another creation resulting from the idea that what happens to God happens to all. By creating night, darkness, God punishes humans for destroying his creation. But he knows that humans must live, and to live they must hunt. So he now provides hunters with the wherewithal to guide them during the night.

This points to the ambiguity of God and of existence: humans must kill animals to live, but in killing them they upset the balance of nature and must therefore be punished. God punishes, but simultaneously gives humans the means to continue to kill and so to live.

The story raises a major theme in myth, a question that is asked but never really answered: it has to do with the situation that humans find themselves in. They are instructed not to destroy God's creations; to do so is to upset the delicate ecological balance, inviting the wrath of God and nature. But they cannot survive without doing just that. This paradox is built into the final part of this myth.

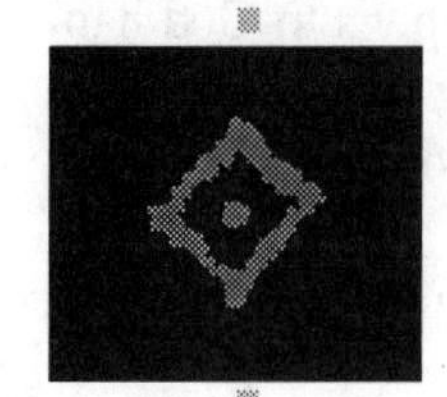

Tension is a key to understanding the aesthetic principles that underlie the production of [an oral tale]: (1) the tension of conflict to resolution, (2) the tension of developing form and the consequent aesthetic suspense, (3) the tension between performer and audience, and (4) the tension of developing inner emotions and ideas by means of traditional core-images. Form in a [tale] production is "form in suspense," until the end of the performance an unfulfilled illusion. It is also a series of interconnected elements—language, character, action, conflict, resolution; body movement, song, gesture, vocal dramatics. Considered together, these combine to give depth and color to the developing form.

Harold Scheub, *The Xhosa Ntsomi* (Oxford: Clarendon Press, 1975), p. 169.

How Death Came into the World: Five Myths

Kamba

God's Message Is Garbled

The Kamba live in Kenya

There was once a frog, Chua, a chameleon, Kimbu, and a bird called Itoroko. These three were sent by Enkai, God, to search for human beings who died one day and came to life again the next day.

The chameleon was in those days a very important person, and he led the way. They went on their mission, and presently the chameleon saw some people lying apparently dead, so as they approached the corpses he called out to them softly, "Niwe, niwe, niwe."

Itoroko was vexed with the chameleon, and asked what he was making that noise for.

The chameleon replied, "I am only calling the people who have gone forward to come back."

From Charles William Hobley, *Ethnology of A-Kamba and Other East African Tribes* (Cambridge: Cambridge University Press, 1910), pp. 107–108.

Itoroko decisively declared that it was an impossible task to find people who ever came back to life.

The chameleon, however, maintained that it was possible, and jokingly said, "Do I not go forward and come back?" (referring to the unique way a chameleon swings or lurches backwards and forwards before taking a step).

The three then reached the spot where the dead people were lying, and in response to the calling of the chameleon they opened their eyes and listened to him.

But Itoroko called out and said, "You are dead to this world and must stay where you are. You cannot rise to life again."

Itoroko then flew away, and the frog and chameleon stayed behind.

The chameleon spoke again to the dead, "I was sent by Enkai to wake you up. Do not believe the words of Itoroko, he only tells you lies."

The spell of his power was, however, broken, and his entreaties of no avail.

They then returned to Enkai, and he questioned the chameleon as to the result of his mission. He said, "Did you go?"

The chameleon said, "Yes."

Enkai said, "Did you find the people?"

The chameleon said, "Yes."

He asked, "What did you say?"

The chameleon said, "I called out, 'Niwe, niwe, niwe.' I spoke very gently, but Itoroko interrupted me and drowned my voice, so the dead people only listened to what he said."

Enkai then asked Itoroko if this was so, and Itoroko stated that the chameleon was making such a mess of his errand that he felt obliged to interrupt him.

Enkai believed the story of Itoroko, and, being very vexed with the way the chameleon had executed his commands, he reduced him from his high estate and ordained that ever after he should only be able to walk very, very slowly, and he should never have any teeth.

Itoroko came into high favor, and Enkai delegated to him the work of waking up the inhabitants of the world. The itoroko bird therefore to this day wakes up and calls out at about 2 a.m., whereas the other birds only awaken at about 4 a.m.

Yao

The Chameleon Is Late

The Yao live in Malawi, Mozambique, and Tanzania

The chameleon was sent to the graves to say, "When people die, they may return to their homes."

He went off and was passing along the road.

Later, the salamander was called and told to go to the graves and say, "When people die, they must not return."

The salamander ran and arrived quickly, while the chameleon was still on the way, and said, "When people die, they must not return."

Next morning, the chameleon appeared. He said, "When people die, they may return to life."

Those at the grave said, "No, the salamander came and told us the truth."

The chameleon went back to report at the village from which he had been sent, and said, "The salamander got there first. He gave the order, 'When people die, they must not return.'"

The people at the village said, "Chameleon, you should have made haste."

From Duff Macdonald, *Africana* (London: Simkin Marshall, 1882), vol. 1, p. 288.

Zande

The Dead Man and the Moon

The Zande live in southern Sudan.

The moon was shining on a corpse.

An old man saw this, and called together a large number of animals. He said to them, "Which of you will carry this body to the opposite side of the river. And which of you will carry the dead moon?"

Two toads said that they would do it.

The toad with long legs took the moon, and the short-legged toad carried the dead man.

The toad who carried the moon succeeded in crossing the river, but the toad bearing the corpse of the man was drowned because its legs were short.

The moon, when it dies, returns again.

When a man perishes, he does not come back at all.

From Gaetano Casati, *Ten Years in Equatoria,* Vol. I (New York: F. Warne and Co., 1891), p. 221.

Boloki

Sleep and Death

The Boloki live in the Central African Republic.

Nkengo was the son of Libuta, and he noticed that the people were dying daily in great numbers. So one day, he called out loudly, "You Cloud-folk, throw me down a rope!"

The Cloud-folk heard and threw him a rope. Nkengo held on to it, and was pulled up into Cloud-land.

When he arrived there, Nkengo had to wait one day, and in the morning the Cloud-folk said to him, "You have come here to receive lasting life and escape from death. You cannot make your request for seven days, and in the meantime you must not go to sleep."

Nkengo was able to keep awake for six days, but on the seventh day he nodded and went to sleep.

The Cloud-folk woke him up, saying, "You came here to receive lasting life and escape from death. You were able to keep awake six days. Why did you abandon your purpose on the seventh day?"

They were so angry with him that they drove him out of Cloud-land and lowered him to the earth.

The people on the earth asked him what had happened up above, and Nkengo replied, "When I reached Cloud-land they told me that in order to gain lasting life I must keep awake for seven days. I did not sleep for six days and six nights, but on the seventh day I nodded in sleep, whereupon they drove me out, saying, 'Get away with your dying. You shall not receive lasting life, for every day there shall be death among you!'"

His friends laughed at him because he went to receive lasting life and lost it through sleeping. That is the reason death continues in the world.

From John H. Weeks, *Among Congo Cannibals* (London: Seeley, Service, 1913), pp. 217–218.

Kono

The First War on Earth

The Kono live in Liberia and Sierra Leone.

Once, long ago, there was no war in the land. No one ever killed another, and peace was everywhere.

A time came when there were many more men than women in the world, and then the first trouble began.

Now, there was a certain man called Tamba. His wife was dead, but his son, Samba, lived with him, and grew up a strong man.

When Tamba was old, he took a young wife to himself. Then Samba did wrong: he courted his father's wife. And his father beat him. Samba begged his father to get him a wife, but his father refused. At last, Samba said, "I will go and beg God to give me a wife."

After many days, Samba came to the place where God lived, and begged God to give him a wife.

God told him to go and cut wood for him and to light his fire, and in the evening God slept at the fireside. This went on for many days, and each day Samba begged God to give him a wife.

One night, God told Samba to go into the house and lie down; God covered him with a cloth, and charged him not to move or speak until he called him in the morning. While Samba slept, God went out and cut a banana tree, the height of his chin, and came and put this beside the sleeping Samba. God covered the tree with a cloth also.

Early the next morning, God came to the door and knocked. He called, "Lango! Lango, get up and open the door!"

And from where the banana tree had been, a woman arose, so beautiful that no man had ever seen her like, and she opened the door.

Samba wanted to speak to her, but feared to do so until God spoke to him.

Then God came and told Samba to go and get wood.

But Samba pleaded with God for the woman, Lango.

From R. H. K. Williams, "The Konnoh People," *Journal of the African Society* 8 (1909): 136–137.

Finally, God said that he would give her to him when he had got more wood.

Samba then brought Lango home to his father's house.

When his father, Tamba, saw Lango, he sought to drive Samba away and keep the woman, Lango, for himself. Trouble arose then, and something occurred for the first time in the world: Samba threatened to kill his father, Tamba, if he interfered with his wife.

The father drove his son away, and Lango lived with Tamba.

Samba could not forget Lango, he loved her still. He went to a chief called Momodu, and persuaded him to take up his cause and send messengers to Tamba, asking for his son's wife.

When the messengers came to Tamba, he would not give up the woman and killed them. The killing of the messengers was the first murder in this world.

Momodu was very angry, and began war on Tamba because of the death of his messengers. Momodu was victorious, and Tamba was killed.

But when Momodu saw Lango, he loved her at once, and took her as his wife. He drove Samba away with threats.

Samba then went to a chief, Fabamba, and persuaded him to take up his case.

Momodu was defeated, and when Fabamba saw Lango, he loved her, and he knew that there would be no peace while Samba lived, because Samba loved Lango. So Momodu enticed Samba away, and murdered him.

But there was no peace for Fabamba, for other chiefs saw Lango and loved her, and Fabamba was himself killed.

As long as Lango lived, there was continual war.

So it was that the first war and the first murder came into this world, for the sake of a woman, and it has been so ever since.

Commentary

In a number of African traditions, a message of eternal life is sent by a messenger to humans on earth. But somehow, that message gets intercepted or garbled, and the word that humans get is that they will die. The Kamba and Yao stories are examples of this theme.

In "The Dead Man and the Moon," an old man tells toads to carry the body of a corpse and the moon across a river. The toad carrying the moon succeeds, the toad carrying the corpse does not succeed. Therefore, the moon, when it dies, returns; but when a human perishes, he does not return at all. The pattern involves the carrying of bodies across a river. From the pattern emerges the etiological meaning of the myth, why humans do not live forever, and why the moon is forever dying and being reborn. The myth tells of the origin of death, the loss of everlasting life. It describes what might have been. Had the toad not failed, humans would have been like the moon, ever waxing and waning, dying and being reborn.

In "Sleep and Death," the relationship between sleeping and dying is the subject. "Sleep," says a Pare proverb (the Pare live in Tanzania), "is the messenger of death." And the Yao in

Mozambique argue that "Death and sleep are one word, they are of one family." The San in southern Africa say that "Death is only a sleep." In some myths, humans are sleeping when immortality comes into the world. In Rwanda, Imana (God) called man and a snake to his presence. Imana told them to remain and during the night they would be called three times, and they must reply. Both replied when Imana called the first time. But when, at midnight, he called a second time, only the snake replied. The man had fallen asleep. When the cock crowed, God called again, and once more only the snake replied. The snake would therefore live forever, but man would die. Among the Lunda in the Democratic Republic of Congo, Nzambi (God) came to earth on a rainbow. He created animals and plants, and then created a man and a woman. But there was a prohibition: they must not sleep when the moon is in the sky. If they did not obey, they would die. The first man became old and his sight was no longer good, and once when the moon was behind a cloud he could not see it, and he went to sleep. He died, and since then all men have died. It was because they were unable to stay awake when the moon was up.

God creates a woman, Lango, in "The First War on Earth." The pattern: various men fight for her, including Samba; his father, Tamba; messengers; various chiefs, including Momodu and Fabamba. The result is continual war. "So it was that the first war and the first murder came into this world, for the sake of a woman, and it has been so ever since." The myth is built on acquisitiveness, with woman as chattel. The etiological elements in this myth are woven into the first murder, the beginning of war, the struggle for a woman.

A Xhosa storyteller (photo by Harold Scheub)

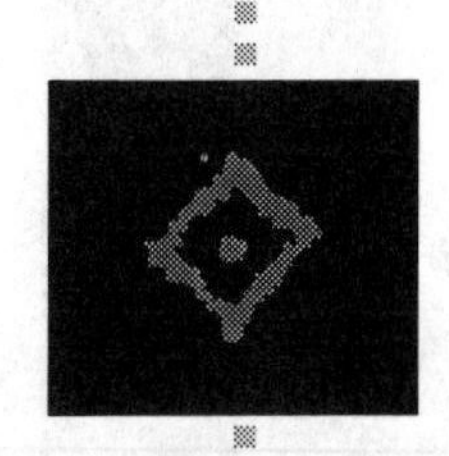

[W]e are in the . . . market place which lies within the casbah of a Moroccan town. Blind Mahjoub, the storyteller, is in the center of a circle of spellbound listeners who are eagerly drinking in his tales of caliphs, jinns and saints, of enchanted gardens and alabaster palaces. . . .

Elisa Chimenti, *Tales and Legends from Morocco* (New York: Ivan Obolensky, 1965), p. 1.

Two Stories about Primal Choices

Boloki

The Two Bundles

The Boloki live in Central African Republic.

While a man was working one day in the forest, a little man with two bundles, one large and one small, went to him.

The little man asked, "Which of these two bundles will you have? This one," he said, taking up the large bundle, "contains looking-glasses, knives, beads, and cloth. And this one," he took up the little bundle, "contains lasting life."

The man said, "I cannot choose by myself. I must go and ask the other people in town."

While he was gone to ask the other people which bundle to choose, some women came along, and the choice was put to them.

The women tried the edges of the knives, bedecked themselves in the cloth, admired themselves in the looking-glasses, and, without more ado, they selected the big bundle, and took it away.

The little man picked up the small bundle, and vanished.

From John H. Weeks, *Among Congo Cannibals* (London: Seeley, Service, 1913), p. 218.

When the man returned from town, both the little man and his bundle had disappeared.

The women exhibited and shared the things, but death continued on the earth.

The people say, "If those women had only chosen the small bundle, we folk would not be dying like this."

Asante

The Crow and the Vulture

The Asante live in Ghana.

In the beginning, Crow and Vulture served the same master.

At that time, Vulture was remarkable for his graceful form and handsome plumage, in which he greatly surpassed his fellow slave, Crow, and, perhaps for this reason, his master regarded him with special favor and treated him with greater indulgence than any of his other slaves.

But in spite of his advantages, Vulture regarded Crow with a jealous eye, and lost no opportunity of carrying to his master such tales and reports as might tend to his disparagement.

It happened one day that Crow and Vulture were journeying together to a neighboring market to buy plantains for their master, and they had nearly reached their destination when they suddenly came upon two boxes lying on the ground by the roadside.

One of these boxes was quite small, but it was very handsome in appearance and was richly ornamented. The other was larger, but was merely a plain wooden box without any embellishment.

As soon as the two birds came in sight of the boxes, Vulture rushed forward and seized the smaller, more handsome one, and, when he had secured it, pointed out the other one to his companion, with the remark, "See, brother Crow, there is a box for you also. It is true it is not a very handsome one, but it will at least be as beautiful as its possessor."

From Richard Austin Freeman, *Travels and Life in Ashanti and Jaman* (New York: Frederick A. Stokes, 1898), pp. 284–286.

At these insolent words, Crow, who was of humble disposition and was, moreover, quite sensible of his unattractive appearance, was by no means offended, but quietly picked up the box that his greedy companion had allotted to him.

Both now sat down to examine the contents of their boxes.

First, Vulture opened his, but no sooner had he raised the lid than he was filled with disappointment and disgust, because it contained nothing but filth and rubbish.

But when Crow looked into his box, he saw that it was filled with fine clothing and glossy silks and a snow-white sash.

At this sight, Vulture became inflamed with jealous anger, and he overwhelmed his companion with reproaches and abuse, not ceasing to revile him until they came to the market.

Here, they put their case before the old men of the village, who, when they had listened to the story of each, gave judgement in favor of Crow, saying to Vulture, "Why do you complain of your fortune? You made your choice and have that which you chose. Be satisfied, therefore, and hold your peace."

But Vulture refused to be appeased, and he continued to abuse Crow until they reached home, when they decided to appeal to their master. But when he had heard them, he said to Vulture, "You have made your choice and it is now too late to repent. Filth and garbage you have chosen, and filth and garbage shall henceforth be your inheritance."

Then, turning to Crow, he directed him to clothe himself in the silks and fine clothing.

Commentary

These are stories of choice, and each has a mythic echo: The first tells how death came into the world; the second, how two birds came to be as they are. And, as frequently happens in myth, these contemporary realities of the way we are have their origins in stories that touch on human frailties, vanity in these cases.

A little man with two bundles gives a working man a choice—a large bundle, containing looking-glasses, knives, beads, and cloth; a small bundle, containing lasting life. When the working man goes to get advice, some women come along and select the large bundle. The little man takes the small bundle, and vanishes. So death persists. The etiological meaning of the story: How death came into the world, a fate resulting from vanity. The pattern: The little man presents the bundles—first, to the men; then, to the women. The myth depends on a stereotyped view of women as vain, of men as practical.

The second story, "The Crow and the Vulture," is also mythic, in the sense that it is an etiological story, telling how it is that crows and vultures have their present characteristics. The story is the same, a choice made because of vanity.

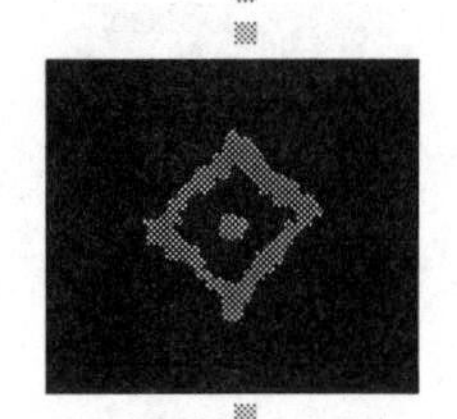

Sometimes these persons are the elders of the village, sometimes the telling of the tales is left to the young men, who amuse themselves and their friends by relating fables of the Aesop variety, or by describing with a wealth of pantomime and gesture some event round which a mass of legendary detail has arisen. The narrative holds the audience enthralled, though most of the tales will be familiar, and the eloquence of the teller receives instant appreciation. The various actions described are imitated, and onomatopoeic sounds are freely used.

H. L. M. Butcher, "Four Edo Fables," *Africa* 10 (1937): 342.

Lozi

God Moves to the Heavens

The Lozi live in Zambia

Long ago, Nyambe made the world and his wife, Nasilele. It was he who made the forests, the river, and the plain, and it was he who made all the animals, birds, and fishes. He also made Kamunu and his wife.

Kamunu made haste to separate himself from the animals. If Nyambe carved wood, he carved his also. If Nyambe made a wooden dish, he made his also. If Nyambe forged iron, so did he. Nyambe was surprised and began to be afraid of him.

Later, Kamunu made a spear and one day killed a lechwe ram besides other animals, and ate them. Nyambe reprimanded him saying, "Man, you have fallen into evil ways. What have you killed them for? They are your kin."

Nyambe then drove the man a distance away.

Kamunu stayed away for a year and when he returned he went down to a place where there was water to drink, and was seen there by Kang'omba, a lechwe ram. Kang'omba went and told Sasisho, Nyambe's messenger, "He whom I have seen over there carrying a small pot of medicine and a knobkerrie, is it not Kamunu who used to kill us?"

Sasisho went and told Nyambe, saying, "Kamunu has returned!"

Nyambe said, "I hear. Let him be."

Upon one occasion, Kamunu went to Nyambe having gone first to Kang'omba who took him to Sasisho, Nyambe's messenger, who then took him into Nyambe's presence. Kamunu begged from Nyambe a place to cultivate, and he was given a garden, which he cultivated.

From Ad. Jalla, *History, Traditions and Legends of Barotseland* (London: Colonial Office, 1921), pp. 1–2.

One night, buffaloes got into Kamunu's garden. He stabbed a buffalo, killing it. At dawn, he went and found it was dead, so he went to Nyambe and said, "I have killed a buffalo."

Nyambe said, "You may eat it."

The little pot in which Kamunu brewed his medicine broke.

Kamunu went to Kang'omba and said, "My things also finish in that way." Kamunu went to his village.

One night, an eland got into his garden, and Kamunu killed a bull and took the tail to Kang'omba, saying, "I have killed an eland."

Kang'omba went to Nyambe with this news with this news, and Nyambe said, "Let him eat it, it is my present of food to him."

Kamunu returned.

His dog was dying, so he went to Kang'omba, and said, "My dog is dead."

Nyambe said, "All right, I hear."

Kamunu returned to his home and said to his wife, "Nyambe has got my dog and also my little pot."

But his wife replied: "It is not so."

At sunset, elephants came into Kamunu's garden. His wife woke him up, and he went and killed one with his spear.

At dawn, finding it dead, he went to Kang'omba and said, "Tell Nyambe I have killed an elephant."

Nyambe replied, "Eat it. I have not given you a present of food since you came back."

Kamunu returned to his wife and said, "Nyambe says we are to eat the elephant."

Kamunu's child died and Kamunu went to Kang'omba and said, "Tell Nyambe my child is dead."

They both went to Nyambe and found Kamunu's child there sitting with Nyambe.

Nyambe said, "My things finish in this way also."

Kamunu then went back to his wife and told her that he had found their child with Nyambe.

Kamunu asked Nyambe for medicine that would save his things but Nyambe said that his things also finish in that way.

Nyambe reassembled the animals and men, and said, "If there is a man born, he is very soft, he is only water and cannot be taken by Nyambe nor even any other man except the one who gave him birth." Then Nyambe said, "If there is an animal born today, let it come here." An animal appeared quickly. Nyambe said, "An animal walks at birth, man waits a year before walking."

Some of the animals agreed to go with Nyambe, and those are the kinds unknown to us.

Nyambe and Nasilele went away with Sasisho, and crossed the river to Litooma, Nyambe's village, being taken there by spiders. Nyambe went to heaven on the spiders' web, and said, "Let the spiders return to earth." But he added, "The spiders must have their eyes put out, so that they may be powerless to find the way again, because they must not take Kamunu to Nyambe."

Nyambe went up to heaven thus, alone.

When Nyambe had gone to heaven, Kamunu assembled the people and told them to build a tall platform so that they could go to Nyambe. They stuck poles in the ground, they put other poles on top of them, and tied them with cord, making it grow until it reached the sky. But because of its weight, the rope at the bottom broke, the platform fell, and those who were at the top were killed.

So Kamunu gave up trying to find Nyambe.

Commentary

A pattern is initiated and sustained by the mortal Kamunu, a pattern that begins to suffocate Nyambe, the creator. First, Kamunu attempts to do everything that Nyambe does, having the temerity to be equal to God. Second, he begins to kill God's creatures, something that God seems to tolerate until another pattern becomes evident, and Kamunu's own home and possessions begin to suffer as a consequence. In the end, God moves into the heavens on a web constructed by spiders. When Kamunu returns to his initial pattern of regularly importuning God, his efforts, the tower to heaven, fail.

Tricksters

A Xhosa storyteller (photos by Harold Scheub)

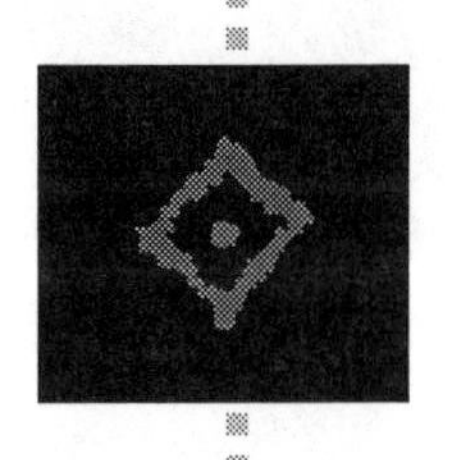

Carl Jung: This phantom of the trickster haunts the mythologies of all ages, sometimes in unmistakable form, sometimes in strange guise.

Notes on the Trickster

The trickster is an indifferent, amoral, undifferentiated force, as if God the creator had never got around to ordering this part of the universe. He is always on the boundaries, the periphery: Trickster is a liminal being. In the heavens, he is called a divine trickster; on the earth, a profane trickster.

Disguise, deception, illusion are his tools and weapons. He is an ambiguous character: usually a male, he is often androgynous. Trickster moves through the universe undertaking to satisfy his basic appetites. This is largely the case with both profane and divine tricksters. If the divine trickster also creates something permanent along the way, so much the better, but that is not always his aim. The trickster is outrageous, obscene, death-dealing, uncaring, ignoble. This does not mean that he is incapable of socially acceptable practices and activities, but these are usually by-products of his acts rather than conscious efforts on his part. He remains forever an undifferentiated force: he is never tamed, never domesticated, although he may appear to be so at times, usually as a part of a sly plan to gain something for himself.

The profane or earth-bound trickster is, like the divine trickster, ribald, aggressive, selfish, without moral compass. In this, he is the closest to the basest of humans. He lacks the sublime connection with the gods; this is what distinguishes the profane from the divine trickster. Yet, in a way, the profane trickster does retain an echo of the divine connection, if tenuously: he also creates in the sense that he establishes a world of illusion; he imposes his own corrupt sense of order on the real world. An agent of chaos, he disrupts harmony; in those instances when he produces harmony, it is according to his own whim, his own capricious and self-serving sense of order. Trickster combines horror and glee: his is the comedy of the absurd. With his enormous penis, his diminutive size, his love of dance, his amorality, his clownishness, he is a grotesque. He is a rootless, unattached being who seeks to secure his own survival and psychological well-being in a society that espouses traditional values while actually sanctioning dehumanizing modes of behavior. Trickster inherits no place he can call home; he is forever an outsider. To impose his will on a hostile world, he uses trickery, invents ruses, wears masks. The profane trickster stories reveal the undifferentiated energy, represent the period of betwixt and between: they are the enormous energy that is released during the period of transition . . . sometimes good, sometimes bad, but amoral, actually, and self-serving. The trickster, profane and divine, always represents the combination of chaos and order.

◇ **Trickster and hero**—While the hero's plan is for a return to wholeness, the trickster represents the fragmentation of humanity. Both hero and trickster are possessed of enormous energy. The hero's energy is always carefully directed, visionary, socially revolutionary but also socially responsible. The trickster's energy is by contrast undifferentiated, moving in ways understood only to himself, for the fulfillment of his unending appetites. These are the two antithetical forces unleashed during the age of creation, the two forces at work in the dualistic god and the divine trickster, and they are forces at work in the contemporary age. The profane trickster and the hero represent humankind's two possibilities.

The trickster and the hero are trying the limits of their societies and their own natures. If the hero pushes back the frontiers of his culture, Trickster pushes back the frontiers of human nature. He is the new human, filled with the excitement of his own strength and wit. He moves into the world like a child freshly born, trying out his considerable powers on everyone and everything he meets. He is a human walking the earth on the morning of creation—naming things, creating things, fine-tuning the creation, at the same time that he is becoming aware of his own limitations. He is the eternally youthful, and we like that in him. He is forever trying things out. When he sees someone doing something, he must do it too. He wants to be everything. He is a renaissance man gone wild. He is the force that occurs when change is taking place. He is the divine trickster present at the greatest change of all, the creation. Trickster is a clown, a master of disguise, of deception. He is often menacing. And he is present at the beginning of things.

Trickster energy is abroad during the interstices of human and natural existence. The dauntless echoes of the trickster are found in these cracks of human existence, when nature changes, when humans change, when societies change. These are periods of upheaval, when unusual forces are unleashed. These are periods between sets of rules, when no rules operate. It is the perfect climate for the trickster: he embodies this liminal period. He is not heroic. When he does begin to follow the path of the hero, then we are no longer in the presence of the trickster, we have shifted to the tale character or the epic hero (both of whom have trickster in them). Trickster may set out, and he may struggle, but there is never any chance that he will bring back an elixir for all humankind. In a rite of passage, a person stands in the unusual situation of being both outside and inside: he is outside the adult world at the same time that he is inside. He is in the transitional phase, the trickster phase.

He is characterized, then, by trickery and indifference. Sometimes, the indifference becomes acceptable conduct, as in the story, "Mohammed with the Magic Finger" (story 26), but remember that, even in his case, his behavior towards his parents is marked by acts of studied and murderous indifference. The trickster is an eternal force that may or may not be molded for socially acceptable ends, but whatever the current ordering of that force may be, in the end, it again reverts to undifferentiated force. Trickster may be tamed for a time, but not forever. He remains the undifferentiated part of ourselves, that part that requires social forming and education. This is his defining character: trickery is at the base of his nature. He is on the boundaries, and in this he is like the hero. But, unlike the hero, he does not have a moral regard for his society. Like the hero, he may move a part of a society into a new dispensation, but it is always for his own self-interests. He never rises above himself and his own needs and desires. Trickster establishes an upside-down world, he thrives in a world of chaos. There is much energy there. Trickster breaks rules for their own sake. The hero breaks rules to bring new rules into existence. This breaking of the rules is the period of chaos.

In all tales, there is a trickster period, a period when things are in turmoil. The tale character experiences periodic states of alienation, he is cyclically on the boundary as he moves from outside the society to inside. For a time, that character behaves according to natural instinct; that is the trickster in him or her. But that must be brought under control, must be concealed. It never is veiled in the trickster, it must be masked in everyperson. He becomes a trickster during the betwixt and between stage, then reverts to proper behavior. The trickster in us is that part of us that cannot be tamed by society. It is always there, but it is effectively masked by cultural tradition. It becomes evident whenever culture breaks down, as during the liminal periods of rites of passage.

Trickster characterizes those moments, when we are on the boundaries, when we are on the outside, when we are our true selves. The hero moves an entire society into a state of alienation, on the boundary. His life may itself reflect this state of alienation, this liminality. The hero moves from outside the current society to the inside of a new society. He is the model for the new society, he is revolutionary. The hero goes through a liminal phase, but because he is in the process of bringing a new tradition into existence, he is not humorous, except, perhaps at an early period in his life. The hero suffers as he brings the new world into existence, and we do not find his suffering comic; we find it noble, even tragic. If the hero errs, we suffer with him, we do not laugh at him.

The epic is the liminal period, and the epic hero is the embodiment of social change. It is not an easy period. This period of chaos is not comic, as it is in the trickster tales. It is a different world here. The same forces of chaos are unleashed here, but we perceive them differently. The reason for this is that we identify fully with the hero, we claim no identification with the trickster . . . except from a safe distance. There is no distance between us and the hero, and, for that matter, the tale character. But the trickster is forever liminal, the hero only for a time. They are both marginal characters for a time, and in that they are one with the tale character.

The trickster is outrageous. He embodies a liminal state, the state of betwixt and between. As we move from one state to another, we are in that liminal state, that state of betwixt and between, that trickster state. Trickster is undifferentiated energy, ungovernable. He may appear tame, but in the next instant he shows that he is not. In the trickster and hero, all is change, transformation. Enormous untamed energy is in the process of being controlled, funneled.

He is always re-inventing the world, testing boundaries, re-learning the possibilities. This does not justify his acts: in fact, it is difficult to see Trickster in a moral framework. And as we curse and revile him, we understand that he is the representative of us, of our emotions and urges, of our inner world. He is our id, unvarnished, untempered. He is stupid at times, he is brilliant at others. He is small and he is large, but most of the time small, and therefore dependent on his wiles rather than his brawn. We never give him up, because he represents something within us. We can laugh at him because he is, we insist, so inane, so unlike us, at the same time that we understand his likeness to us.

It is not enough to say that he is a safety valve for us, though he is that, doing things to leaders that we dare not do, saying things that we dare not say. Trickster is congenial at times, and brutal at others. He is unpredictable. The cuddly spider and hare may also be deadly. That is the power of the trickster. He is the clown who makes one laugh . . . but nervously, because, in his stupidity and witless humor, we see ourselves.

There are many divine and profane trickster stories in which nothing is accomplished but a trick. This is the energy-potential that the trickster represents, the energy released during the betwixt and between stage when no laws are operating, when destructive and creative forces contend with each other, and when, out of these forces, a change frequently occurs. But that change does not affect the amorality of the divine and profane tricksters: they can be just as infuriating the next moment. But when their energies are joined to rites of passage, to transformations, then that force is muted, tamed, re-directed. In the end, the trickster continues unaffected, but something has happened, something has been left behind of a positive and moral nature. The divine trickster leaves a permanent residue, and so, at times, does the profane trickster. In some of the tales having to do with the puberty ritual, the trickster actually appears, revealing that betwixt and between amoral energy. In most puberty rite tales, however, the trickster is not himself present: only the energy is. The trickster stories embody that energy in a character.

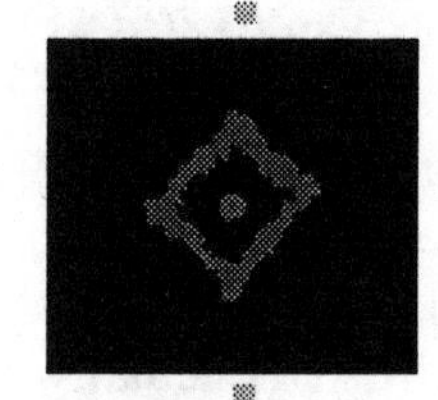

Ture [Trickster] tales are told after sunset, when the man of the home sits with his children, round the family fire in their courtyard. . . . In the absence of tape recorders [the tales] had to be taken down laboriously by long hand, and this in itself affects the narrative, leading sometimes to curtailed or garbled versions. . . . [T]he vivacity is lost: the tone of voice, the singsong of the chants, and the gestures and mimicry which give emphasis to what is being said and are sometimes a good part of its meaning. But perhaps most serious in the bare setting down of a tale in writing is the loss of the audience.

E.E. Evans-Pritchard, *The Zande Trickster* (Oxford: Clarendon Press, 1967), pp. 18–19.

Tigre

Abunawas and the Goat's Horns

The Tigre live in Ethiopia.

Abunawas had a well and also a young goat. Around his well he had stuck goat's horns in the ground, but the points of the horns were above ground. Now there was a man traveling who was leading a loaded camel, and he turned aside to the well of Abunawas to drink water. When Abunawas saw the man coming to him with his camel, he put the goat in the well. When the camel-driver arrived, he and Abunawas greeted each other.

The stranger said to Abunawas, "Let me drink!"

Abunawas said, "Very well," and went down into the well to draw water. First, he pulled up the goat and brought it out. After that he let the stranger drink.

When the stranger had drunk, he asked Abunawas, "This goat which you have brought out of the well, where did you find it?"

Abunawas replied, "These horns that you see around the well, they are goats, all of them. And every day, if I pull out two of them, a goat comes out of this well."

The man was astonished. He entreated Abunawas, "Give me this well of yours, and you take this camel of mine with its load."

Abunawas answered, "This place of mine is of great profit to me; but for your sake—what shall I do? Take it then!"

The man said to Abunawas, "What is your name?"

Abunawas answered, "My name is Nargus-fen [lit., Where shall we dance?]." Then Abunawas said to the man, "Now then, pull out two of these horns every day, and at

From Enno Littmann, *Publications of the Princeton Expedition to Abyssinia* (Leyden: E. J. Brill, 1910), pp. 32–33.

once a goat will come out to you. Today, however, do not pull out any horns, because I have already pulled out two of them and brought out this goat."

The man said, "All right."

Abunawas took the loaded camel went to his village.

The next morning the man pulled out two of the horns, but the horns came out by themselves. Nor, when he looked into the well, did he find anything.

He said, "What is this?" He pondered a great deal. Every day, he said, "Today, I shall find it."

And he pulled out all the horns.

Then he thought in his heart. "Nargus-fen has cheated me. Now I must go and seek him."

So he set out to find Nargus-fen.

When he came to a village, he asked the people, "Do you know Nargus-fen [where shall we dance]?"

The people of the village replied, "Dance here."

Gathering around him, they clapped their hands for him.

But the man was terrified because they made fun of him.

When he went into another village and inquired, these people did the same to him as the first, and the man was about to go crazy.

Later, the chief of the village asked him, "What kind of man are you? And what do you wish to say?"

Then the man told him of all that had happened to him.

The chief sent word and asked, "Who is it who cheated this man?"

All the people said, "We do not know."

Then the chief took an oath, saying, "I shall give money to the one who has done this, if he says to me, 'It is I.'"

Abunawas said to him, "It is I who have done this."

The chief gave him money, but the camel with its load he took from Abunawas and gave it to its owner.

And all the people were astonished at the doings of Abunawas.

Commentary

Abunawas was a famous poet in the second half of the eighth century AD. Later, he became known as a trickster.

This trickster story is constructed around a pattern of deception. The trickster establishes his illusion, in this case, that pulling the horns from the ground will result in a goat emerging from a well. And the trickster builds into his deceit another pattern, another illusion, this one having to do with his name: He tells his dupe that he is Nargus-fen, a name that means "Where shall we dance?" This creates confusion later when the defrauded man seeks the trickster.

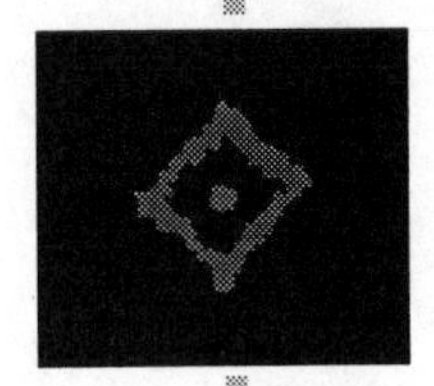

Now the sky-god called his elders, the Kontire and Akwam chiefs, the Adonten, leader of the main body of the army, the Gyase, the Oyoko, Ankobea, and Kyidom, leader of the rear guard. And he put the matter before them, saying, "Very great kings have come, and were not able to buy the sky-god's stories, but Kwaku Ananse, the spider, has been able to pay the price. I have received from him Mmoboro, the hornets; I have received from him Mmoatia, the fairy; I have received from him Osebo, the leopard; I have received from him Onini, the python; and, of his own accord, Ananse has added his mother to the lot. All these things lie here." He said, "Sing his praise."

"Eee!" they shouted.

The sky-god said, "Kwaku Ananse, from today and going on forever, I take my sky-god's stories and I present them to you. Kose! Kose! Kose! My blessing, blessing, blessing. No more shall we call them the stories of the sky-god, but we shall call them Spider Stories."

R. R. Rattray, *Akan-Ashanti Folk-tales* (Oxford: Clarendon Press, 1930), p. 59.

Zulu

The Story of Chakijana

by Sondoda Ngcobo

The Zulu live in southeastern Africa

It happened. . . .

There was a woman who had a child, a small child. She had had another child in her maidenhood, before she had married.

Now this boy grew up, the one she had given birth to when she was still unmarried. And he became a fine young fellow. When he was already a young man, the one she had borne in her maidenhood, she gave birth to a small child. Then her husband died, and the wife remained behind with the small child and the son whom she had given birth to in her maidenhood.

One day, when she had gone off to hoe, she was approached by Chakijana.

He said to her, "Mother, let me watch the child for you! I can see that the sun is too much for him."

The woman refused. She said, "No, I don't want you to watch my child! I'm satisfied with the baby strapped to my back."

She hoed on, then she went home.

The next day, the sun was very hot. Again, Chakijana came along; he said, "Mother, Mother, let me watch your child for you. Can't you hear that the child is crying?"

Date of Performance: February 7, 1968. Place: In the shade of a tree in Mahlabatini District, kwaZulu. Performer: Sondoda Ngcobo, a Zulu man, about forty-five years old. Audience: Fifteen women, one man, ten children. Collected and translated by Harold Scheub.

The mother said, "Well, you began all this by asking me to allow you to watch my child. Just sit nearby, and carry the child."

The mother gave the child to Chakijana, and Chakijana played with him. The mother hoed on. She finished, then prepared to go home when the cattle were returning from the pasture.

Chakijana said, "Will you come back, Mother, when the cattle return to the pasture?"

The woman said, "Yes, I'll come back—but only when it's cooler."

So Chakijana remained there, waiting for the mother to return to this field. She did come back in time, she came as the cattle spread in the pasture. Then Chakijana said, "Mother! Mother, let me watch the child for you."

The mother gave the child to him, she had no suspicions anymore. No more did she wonder "what sort of person this is who offers to watch my child," anxious lest he be some kind of monster who might bewitch the child.

Chakijana watched the child, and the mother went on hoeing. At sunset, she thanked him. She thanked Chakijana, and said, "I thank you, my child, for watching my child for me." And she said, "Well, I'll bring you some boiled mealies from home next time, so that you can munch on something as you look after the child."

Chakijana expressed his thanks, and said, "Well, Mother, I'll return in the morning."

The woman did not think to ask, "Just tell me, my child, where have you come from? Where do you live? You're so generous, all this time looking after my child in this way!"

The woman departed.

On the third day, Chakijana came. He came in the company of an animal—a duiker. He drove it ahead. As this woman hoed, he suddenly appeared.

"Mother, I'm here already! Isn't the baby crying?"

She said, "Are you already here, my child?"

He said, "Yes, I'm already here. Isn't the baby crying, Mother? Give it to me, I'll look after it." Then he said, "I want to teach him some games. I even brought something for him to play with."

"What have you brought, my child?"

"I've brought him this beautiful thing—he can throw it in front of himself, he can throw it in front. While you're hoeing, the child will not be crying!"

So the mother gave him the child.

Then Chakijana said, "Well, Mother, we'll just sit down under that tree, over there in the middle of the field."

Then he pointed to his duiker, and said, "There! The child can ride on the duiker!" he said, "Say, Mother! Say, Mother! Look how I play with the child!"

So indeed this mother was happy.

Then the mother said that she thought it was time for her to return to her home, to go and prepare food for that boy who was at home. So she said to Chakijana, "Chakijana, where's my child? Bring him back! Why don't I hear you talking to the child?"

He said, "Here he is, Mother! He's still here! He merely followed the duiker, that's all! The duiker went into the thicket there."

She said, "When did the child learn to walk? Come now, Chakijana, I know that the child can't walk! My child can't walk yet!"

He said, "The duiker's teaching him to walk, Mother. That animal! It's a very beautiful animal. He's very resourceful and wise. He's teaching the child. He'll bring the child back any minute now. He's gone to the stream with the child, they went to get a drink."

The mother was silent, she stared at Chakijana.

"Chakijana! It's time for me to go! Just look! You can see that it's about time for the cattle to come home. I must go and prepare food for my son at home!"

Chakijana said, "Well, Mother, I'll bring the child when he cries. You're in a hurry. Go on! Or don't you trust me, Mother? I'm not distrustful of you! You're my real mother!"

The woman said, "Chakijana, I really cannot leave my child behind! What will my neighbors think when they see me return without my child? And I'm still nursing the infant!"

Chakijana said, "Well, Mother, trust me. I'm sure the duiker won't harm the child. He's just gone down to the stream for a little while, to get some water to drink."

But the mother would not be persuaded. She persisted, "No! I can't trust you, I want my child!"

Then Chakijana said, "Well, Mother, I'll go and look for the duiker. He disappeared just as we started to talk, you and I. He was here just now. They went away for a short time, he and the infant. They were playing here together."

The mother said, "No, let's go together, Chakijana! Let's go together and find them!"

When they set out, Chakijana made certain that he walked in front. He said, "Follow me then, Mother! Follow me! I'm the one who knows where they've gone, where they've disappeared to."

So the mother followed, walking behind Chakijana. As he went along, Chakijana devised all sorts of schemes, thinking, "I've already transported the child, he's no longer here! He's gone! Ee! Now how can I shake this woman from my back, this woman here?"

He went down to the thicket at the edge of the field, then Chakijana caused himself to fall.

He said, "Oh! I stumbled, Mother! I'm hurt, I'm really hurt! I'm badly injured, Mother!"

She said, "Oh no, Chakijana! Get on your feet! Give me my child! You must realize that it's getting very late! The boy will soon be driving the cattle home, and he won't find anything to eat there."

Chakijana said, "Mother, I'm really hurt! I'm really hurt! I'm unable to walk further!"

The mother caught hold of him then, and said, "Get up, Chakijana!"

Chakijana refused to get up, he went limp.

The mother said, "No, no! Get up! Show me my child, Chakijana!"

Chakijana refused.

The woman loosened her cape now, and she began to hit him with it. Chakijana endured it all. She hit him harder, Chakijana endured the beating.

She said, "I beat you on the shins, I beat you on the waist, but it makes no impression on you! I'll beat you on the ears with the strings of his garment! See if that won't make you get up!"

And the woman did that—she beat him on the ears. But Chakijana persevered.

She said, "Well, he doesn't feel any pain. I'll push him!"

So the woman pushed him, she pushed him and shook him by the ears, she pinched him. Well then! Chakijana burst out crying.

Then the duiker arrived.

He said, "Duiker! Duiker, turn back! The day has not yet arrived for us to go off with the child!"

Well, the duiker realized that Chakijana was crying here under the tree.

Then he said, "Mother, I told you that the duiker had gone down to drink! And here's the child, he's come with the duiker!"

The woman looked back and saw the child riding on the duiker's back. The duiker had the child on its back.

"Oh!" the mother said, "Chakijana! What you almost did to me! What is this?"

He said, "Well, Mother I told you that the duiker had gone for a drink. But you acted as if I had killed the child!"

The mother took the child then, and said, "Well, Chakijana, today I don't see how I can come back. You've given me a fright! But I do appreciate your looking after my child, I appreciate your keeping my child occupied so that he doesn't cry as I hoe these weeds. But after today, I won't be able to come back. I've already delayed too long."

So saying, the woman departed. Chakijana also departed, he went to some ogres. As it turned out, Chakijana had been acting out all this craftiness because he had previously deceived the ogres. He had tricked the ogres, he had taken their cattle. Now the ogres were demanding that he bring them a small game animal, their favorite meat—something like a human being. Chakijana had agreed to do this, and had said, "All right, I will bring it to you! I'll bring you young game, tender soft meat, not meat that has become tough."

They said, "Well, you bring it to us, Chakijana! Bring tender meat."

He said, "Another person would fail! But not me!"

That is why Chakijana had attempted to trick the mother. He was about the business of getting the meat that he had promised the ogres, in payment for those cattle that he had consumed, that he had taken away, that the ogres had then sought and could not reclaim.

The next day, the mother came back. When she got there, Chakijana was waiting for her in the field.

No sooner had she arrived than he said, "Mother, I've been here a long time, waiting for you! Now then, Mother, I left my bucket right here. I brought the bucket with me this time so that I can dip water with it. I thought you would be in the field already, I thought you would come early. But you had not yet arrived when I got here. So I've been waiting and waiting. I thought that I would be insulting you if I just went away."

The mother said, "Well, you did well to bring the bucket along, to dip water. When your throat is dry, you'll be able to drink. I should have brought a scoop from home, but I forgot it. You do help me, Chakijana."

Well, Chakijana remained quiet.

Then he said, "Just give me the child, Mother."

The mother was happy to do so, she did not have the slightest suspicion because of Chakijana's actions the day before. Here he was once again, Chakijana had again appeared to watch her child.

So it happened that Chakijana and the mother both returned on the day after the duiker and the child had been missed. Today, Chakijana had left the duiker behind, at the stream. When he was speaking of the bucket, he actually meant the duiker itself. Now he was asking for the back strap from the child's mother.

He said, "Well, Mother, give me the back strap. Untie it from your body. Give it to me, I'll carry the child on my back. I'll take the child to the stream, all right? Then I'll come back with some water, so that I can drink as well as the child. And you too, you'll become thirsty. The sun will be hot soon, you'll also be dry. And you too can drink some of this water, it'll be right here!"

Well, this mother said, "That'll be very good indeed, my child. I can see that the sun's getting hot. And I know that I'll get dry too. Go, get the water."

Then he said, "Well, Mother, I'll go with the child. I'll carry him on my back."

And she said, "It's still early. Let me get to work, it's still early. I can't go back just now, it's not yet time for the cattle to return."

Chakijana was pleased in his heart. He said, "Today, I'll get that tender meat, and I'll deliver it to the ogres! The ogres are pushing me now because of the debt regarding their cattle!"

So Chakijana departed, cooing to the child: "Oya! Oya! Oya! Oya! Oya!"

Then Chakijana disappeared, going to the stream. When he got to the stream, Chakijana took the child and gave him to the duiker. Then he took a stone from the stream, and he tied that to his back. He took the scoop, which he had been carrying all the time, which he had left here with the duiker. He took the scoop, and as he took it in his hand and carried it in the proper manner, he returned to the fields, all the time pretending to coo to the child: "Oya! Oya! Iya! Oya! O—"

Then the mother asked, "Oh! Is the child crying, Chakijana?"

He said, "Not at all, Mother! He's not crying yet! He's still quiet. I'm cooing so that he sleeps well, Mother, so that you won't be bothered by the child."

But the duiker was then going off with the child, right up the stream, going up the stream! There were some bushes on the river bed. The duiker went on.

Chakijana remained here. But all this while, he was calming and cajoling a stone! There was no longer a child with Chakijana. The child had gone off with the duiker.

When it was about time for the mother to return to her home, when the cattle were returning, she asked for the child.

She said, "Well, Chakijana, would you give me the child so that I can nurse him? I do trust you very much, but it's time for me to hurry home. I'll only nurse the child, then I'll leave him here with you. I'll come back quickly. I'll get home, prepare some ground boiled maize over there at home, so that my son can eat and take the cattle to the pasture. Then I'll rush back."

Chakijana said, "Oh! You may go. I'm very happy that you trust me so much." Then he said, "Mother, do wait a minute. Have patience with me. Just let me go and relieve myself. I'll come back presently. But actually, you can go right now, Mother. The child hasn't cried yet. And there's plenty of water here. As you say, you won't be long. You're going to prepare some boiled maize at home, that won't take long, Mother. You'll hurry and return. And you'll find me here. Today, I'm determined to leave when you return in the later afternoon."

The mother said, "Well, Chakijana, I'll not let you down this time, I really do trust you, my child. You're a very good person, you watch my child well for me. And you get along very well with my child."

So the mother hurried; she took big strides, hurrying to prepare food for the boy who was herding cattle. She got there and made the preparations.

The boy asked, "Mother, where's the baby? Why have you come home alone? Where have you left the child?"

Then she said, "There's my boy, over there! I left the child with him over there in the field."

"Oh! What could he possibly be eating, the child is still—"

"Well, there's a little food that I took with me this morning. I left instructions that he should continue to feed it to the child."

"Oh!" The boy was startled. He said, "How could Mother leave the child behind and just say, 'There's a boy who's staying with him'? It's not even a girl who is a relative of some kind!"

The boy began to think about this, and he said, "Mh! Mh! My mother's child is no more! But she refuses to tell me where he is! I'm certain that the child is no more! Perhaps he's been hurt by wild animals, perhaps he's been eaten by the wild animals!"

The boy remained quiet. Soon, his mother departed. When she appeared in the fields again, Chakijana went out to meet her.

"Oh, Mother! The child hasn't cried yet, he's very still. Listen yourself! He hasn't cried since you left! Not a sound! Your child—"

["—will soon appear!" says a member of the audience].

But the son of this woman had an idea. He decided to leave the cattle over there in the pasture, and he turned back with the dogs. He went off like a person who was hunting wild game. He walked on and on, silently. Then he saw this person here in the field—with his mother. He approached stealthily, little by little, edging closer. The dogs were chafing to go after him. But the boy restrained them, saying, "I want to observe this person very carefully. There are certain people who are said to go about with an animal. And I want to catch this creature with my dogs."

Quietly, the boy came closer, little by little, restraining his dogs. They came closer and closer. Suddenly, his mother heard: "Say, Mother! Say, Mother! The child—Is this the one who looks after the child?"

"Yes, my child!"

Then Chakijana said, "Well, Mother, just let me go and get a drink of water over there at the stream!"

She said, "Go quickly, Chakijana! I should go back at once, my child, because here's the boy who herds the cattle—he's here already. I'll be going back soon too, I must get some water for home."

Chakijana departed immediately, carrying his scoop. As soon as Chakijana had left the field, the boy let the dogs loose, saying, "Mother, this is not the child!"

As Chakijana was leaving, the boy was examining whether or not this was actually the child, because he could not see the child's head—and he knew that when the child is strapped to the back by its mother, with the back strap, one can usually see the child's head clearly, and the feet and the arms as well. Now the boy was looking closely, but he could not see the feet, he could not see the head, he could not see the hands! All he could find was a hump on Chakijana's back!

So the boy loosed his dogs. And Chakijana then opened the hump on his back, and began to run.

[Audience laughs.]

Chakijana ran away from the dogs!

The boy said, "Mother, look! You said the child is being carried on Chakijana's back. Where is the child now? There's Chakijana, and he's dropping a stone!"

"Oh!"

[Audience laughs.]

The woman and her child!

[Audience laughs.]

"Oh, my child! Chakijana has deceived me! Chakijana has deceived me!"

The boy gave chase with his dogs. And the woman seized her hoe, and she ran too. The woman ran! She came to the stream, and when she got there, she realized that—well, she had no stone with which to hit him.

The dogs also lost the trail. As they ran, the dogs did not look carefully. But Chakijana knew this river well, he had purposely lured them there. And when he got there, he moved to one side of the river. As the dogs came straight ahead, they reached a dead-end at the river's bank.

And as the boy moved along, he remembered that he should be with the cattle—the sun was setting, and the cattle would stray into the fields of other people.

But the mother rushed on. She said, "Well now, I'll go right here, to the place where he went in. I'll get there and catch him, wherever he is, this Chakijana!"

So she ran, the mother ran. She said, "Chakijana! Give me my child! Chakijana! Give me my child!"

But Chakijana kept running. They approached a second stream, and this stream was overflowing its banks. It had been raining further up, and the rain caused these streams to be full. Then the mother arrived.

Chakijana then turned himself into a stone. When he realized that there was no way to cross this stream, he changed himself into a stone.

When the mother got there, "Oh! I thought he stopped here! I thought he stopped here."

Well, all she could see was stones. There were three beautiful stones there, with very pleasing shapes. She looked across the stream, she looked downstream to see if perhaps Chakijana had thrown himself into the water, and the water had then swept him downstream. But she could see nothing. Then she looked upstream. No, the mother saw nothing. She looked on the banks of the stream, perhaps he had submerged his body and was holding to a root on the river bank. But no, Chakijana was not to be seen.

So the mother just stood there, and she cried. She said, "You did deceive me regarding my child, Chakijana! Where will I get another child? because I no longer have a husband, I don't have anything!"

The mother went on thinking in this way. Now and then, she would look across the river, but she did not see Chakijana. Suddenly, she took one of the stones, and said, "Oh! If I had him here, I would strike him with this stone! I would do this to him!"

Saying this, she took the stone and threw it across the river.

Then Chakijana said, "Pepe! You helped me to cross!"

[Member of audience: "Oh! My God!"]

"Pepe! You helped me to cross! Pepe! You helped me to cross!"

The mother now broke down and cried. Oh! She could see that "Now I've helped him to cross the river! And here's all this water, blocking my way!"

The mother fainted, she passed out. But Chakijana went on his way, and soon he met that animal of his, the duiker.

The plan now was to take this child to the ogres. Chakijana caught up with the duiker.

"Now then, Duiker, where's the child of—Oh, here he is! Let's go then. Now you, Duiker, you must stay over there. I'll go in with this little game animal of the ogres!"

As it turned out, while Chakijana was saying that, he had already deceived the duiker as well, that very duiker had been betrayed to these ogres.

So Chakijana went on, and when he got to the place of the ogres, he went in. As soon as he had appeared, as soon as the ogres saw him, they were glad. They danced and danced.

They said, "Here's Chakijana!"

[Audience responds.]

"He's arrived!"

"Surely he's bringing with him the game animal that has tender meat!"

Well, Chakijana came along, and said, "Don't you see? I told you I would bring some beautiful game animal for you! Don't cause me any more trouble now because I robbed you of your livestock! Besides, you stole that stock too! It didn't belong to you, you didn't work for it! You didn't fight for it like the rest of mankind! After all, livestock is obtained only by acts of daring and heroism!" Then he said, "Well, I'll give you another game animal to make up for the cattle that I took."

The ogres said, "You'll have discharged your obligation to us then, Chakijana!"

"Because here you are, you've brought this game animal of ours!"

"The one we've craved so much!"

Chakijana went outside.

He said, "Give me a rope! The animal's here, I'll drive it by myself. I won't carry it."

So the ogres gave him a rope, and he went away.

When he got to the duiker, he said, "Now Duiker, come here. I want to tie you up. Then I'll go back with you, I want to take you back all tied up."

[Audience laughs.]

He said, "You'll be jumping around and struggling in the courtyard all the time, struggling, struggling, and just keep on struggling when I've tied you to the posts of the house. Keep on jumping around." He did not tell the duiker that "I have betrayed you!" He only said, "Duiker, just say that you've come there to play and dance!"

The duiker cooperated, it did everything that Chakijana told it to do. The duiker did it, and Chakijana tied it to the posts of the house. And the duiker jumped around, round and round. They speared it, that was the end of the duiker.

Then Chakijana moved on. He walked along, carrying his scoop. He came to some boys. Chakijana found these boys just sitting around, herding livestock in the pasture.

He went to the boys, and said, "How could you just be sitting around here without water? Where do you get water when you're dry?"

"Well, we just go down to the stream when we're thirsty."

He said, "I could give you a fine container! Look, here's my scoop! Who wants to go and drink? Who wants to go and drink?"

One boy said, "I do."

Chakijana made a quick trip to the stream. He scooped up some water, then returned with it. He put the water down, and said, "Don't you see how clever I am? But you don't carry scoops for water for yourselves! Just look now! I've brought you something useful. Now you can drink water."

The boys said, "Well, Chakijana, make some scoops for us too, because there are no drinking vessels at our homes."

He said, "Well, I could make some scoops for you. But today, we'll just sit around a little, and you can drink from my scoop."

As the boys sat there, they said, "Let's parry a bit!"

"Let's parry a little!"

"Here are the sticks, they're here!"

"We'll spar gently with them!"

"We won't hit one another hard!"

So Chakijana took a stock, and they parried.

Then he said, "Why don't you spar among yourselves? You see now, I don't want to take unfair advantage of you. This scoop—It would be a good idea to have a contest, to determine who among you is the champion, who is the hero!"

The boys, because boys are always ready to fight one another, were easily deceived. They took their sticks and fought. They fought each other just above Chakijana's scoop.

And the scoop was broken!

[Members of the audience snicker.]

Chakijana was enraged over the broken scoop. He said,

> "I want my scoop, my scoop!
> The scoop that I took from the ogres!
> The ogres took my game animal,
> The animal that I got from the woman!"

The boys wondered what had happened.

"Chakijana, take our sticks in return for the broken scoop. Because you walk with no stick."

Chakijana said, "No, I don't want these sticks of yours. They're not attractive! Ee! Get me some beautiful sticks!" Then he said, "Look here! Tomorrow morning, I'll be here to collect these sticks!" So saying, Chakijana turned around and departed. He said, "I really want those sticks! I shall not take this scoop!"

The boys said, "All right, Chakijana, but take it! And try to get another. As for the sticks, we'll bring them for you in the morning."

So the boys left, they looked for the sticks. They returned with some really fine sticks. And Chakijana also returned.

They said, "Here are your sticks, Chakijana. We've brought them for you."

Chakijana took them and examined them closely, admiring them. He looked at them carefully. He satisfied himself that they were indeed fine sticks. Then he said, "Stay well!" and he left those boys there.

He went on. And when he had gone on, Chakijana came to a forest.

He found two men fighting and wrestling with their hands.

Chakijana said, "I've never seen such fools! Big fellows like you! When you have a misunderstanding, you hit each other with your bare hands! Here are sticks! Take them, you'll get what you want out of each other!"

He took two sticks, and gave them to one of the men. He took two more, and gave them to the other. So these young men went at each other with these sticks. When they had been hitting each other with the sticks, the sticks snapped—they broke!

Chakijana became very upset about the broken sticks. He said,

> "I want my sticks, my sticks!
> Given to me by the boys!
> The boys destroyed my scoop,
> My scoop! My scoop!
> The scoop I took from the ogres!
> The ogres took my game animal,
> The animal I got from the woman!"

"Before Chakijana came, we were fighting in our own way. You gave us the sticks to fight with!"

"Well, Fellow, there's not much we can do. We'll replace your sticks."

"You just say how you want your sticks paid back to you, what will satisfy you."

Chakijana said, "I want clothes that are nicely decorated with splendid buttons or beads."

The young men said, "We'll bring them for you, Chakijana, because you did help us."

"We had contemptuous attitudes for each other all this time. Now, all that has changed."

"Our animosity toward each other has cooled."

Chakijana said, "Well, I'll come tomorrow morning. I'm going back there for a while, then I'll pass by here again. You'll find me right here, and I should find you here too!"

The young men said, "It's all right. We concede to you, Chakijana."

So Chakijana departed. He came back the next morning, and, true enough, he found the young men waiting for him.

They said, "Well, Chakijana, here we are. We're very happy to see you."

Chakijana, for all his craftiness, did not realize that the youth who was the brother of the child he had given to the cannibals had gone ahead of him. And now, Chakijana went on with his booty.

But he was going straight to this boy. The boy was just ahead of him, on this very road. When Chakijana got to a certain place, he found that he was moving towards a festive gathering. He encountered some young men who had no weapons.

Chakijana said, "Just look here! Here are weapons—you're not armed! I could supply you with weapons—beautiful ones, weapons that surpass those!"

Then he saw this boy.

The boy thought, "Here's the person who abducted the child of my home!" But he said nothing. He thought, "I don't want to strike him, I want to catch him. Then I'll kill him in a very painful way, because he killed the child of my home in a painful way. I don't have a sibling anymore because of this Chakijana."

The boy then attempted to persuade the other boys of his homestead—the homestead where the festivities were taking place.

The boy said, "Well, please give me two fasteners. I want two fasteners. I'll return with them in the morning. There's a little creature of mine that I want to go out and drive this way. I want to go and make it crawl, because I'm here by myself. I don't think I can drive it by myself. I'll just have to bind it, then make it crawl! And when it's too tired to run, it'll raise its head."

Well, the young men waited for him.

They said, "Well, hurry, turn it around, Fellow."

"The others will kill us when they demand their fasteners and don't find them!"

"I'll hurry, and then return them!"

The boy took these fasteners, and he made a lasso. Then he moved about like the other people who were bumping into each other in the dance. That is how he behaved. As he approached Chakijana, the other did not recognize him; Chakijana did not know that this was the brother of the infant he had sold to the ogres. The boy came with these fasteners and things. Before he knew what was happening, Chakijana was trapped.

The others wondered, "Where has this young man come from?"

Because this Chakijana was a very crafty person, he could perform all kinds of tricks.

The young men were quiet, then they said, "Where is this young man from?"

Others said, "Don't you see that it's Chakijana? It seems to be Chakijana!"

Someone said, "Ho! He seems to be dallying with the boys! What's he doing? Now he's been caught by the boys! They seem to be playing."

In the meantime, the boy pulled the lasso, and tightened his hold on Chakijana.

Chakijana struggled, and said, "Let go of me! Let go of me! Pulling me like this—where are you taking me?"

The boy said, "Come here! There's something for us to talk about!"

The boy tied Chakijana's hands, and dragged him. Chakijana did not know what to do. Because there were so many people here and because there was such a commotion because of the dancing, no one at the party took any notice. There were many people here, and they were minding their own business. They thought only of participating in the dancing. They took no notice of this activity that was occurring to the side of them and behind. They were observing only what they had come here for.

So the boy dragged Chakijana, pulling the ropes tighter and tighter.

And these other boys were watching him, and following. When he was out of the sight of the mass of people, he was joined by the others.

He explained, "This Chakijana is the one who killed my mother's child! Now I'm left alone because of this person!"

"Is that so?"

"Yes!"

Then the boys said, "Well, we won't kill him by ourselves! Let's go and call our brothers."

"Our brothers will beat him and kill him."

"We can't find it in ourselves to kill him."

The boy said, "Well, I won't find it hard to kill him! I have the same nerve he has, the one who killed the child of my home, an only child!"

Chakijana now began to go soft, then he turned himself into various things. He changed himself into all sorts of things, whatever the boys desired.

He changed himself into a goat.

Then he turned himself into a cow.

The boy said, "I won't let you go, no matter what you change yourself into! I'll never let you go, you! I'll take you with me, Chakijana!"

When the boy got to a tree, he thought of tying Chakijana to it. Then he thought, "No, he'll just untie himself."

So the boy dragged him on. He went on, going now to his mother at his home. He dragged Chakijana, and when his prisoner resisted the boy would flog him. Then Chakijana would cooperate. And when he changed himself into all manner of things, the boy beat him up. So Chakijana stopped changing himself.

The boy said, "Don't change yourself anymore! I want to do to you what you did to my mother's child!"

So the boy went on, dragging him along. And when they were close to his home, when it had come into view, the boy called out loudly, and said, "Mother! Come outside! And see! Here's the one who killed the child of my home! I'm coming with him! Burn that house at the side!"

Chakijana now began to beg him. "But young man, you're determined to kill me, ee? But I can bring the child back!"

He said, "Oh no! I'm not interested in that anymore! My mother's child is not here anymore! He's not alive anymore, Chakijana! You killed him long ago! We've already heard that he's been devoured by the ogres, that he was devoured long ago. But you're still alive! And you must die also!"

Well, the mother came outside. At first, she did not know who was calling out so loudly.

Again, the boy said, "Mother, ignite that house on the side. By the time I arrive, I want to be able to throw him into the fire!"

The mother was perplexed as to why she should burn that house.

Then she saw that the youth was getting close, and he was saying, "Here's Chakijana, the one who abducted your child!"

The boy dragged him along, and he said, "Mother, I've been telling you to ignite that house!"

The woman said, "No, my child, wait a little. Let's just wait before we kill him. Let us beat him, let's beat him to satisfy our hearts. We've lost everything because of Chakijana."

Then the woman took the handle of the hoe, and she tried to remove the hoe from the handle. It was not easy to do, because in the beginning hoes were attached in a certain way. The boy took one end, and said, "Hold it here!" He realized that he too would be pulled. He pulled on the hoe, and pulled his mother. He said, "Well, hit it against this—like this. Mother, hit it here!" So the mother hit it, and it came loose.

Then the boy caught hold of Chakijana, and said, "Hit him, hit him, Mother! I'm holding him down!"

So she hit him, she hit him, she hit him.

And Chakijana said, "I'm as good as dead!"

Then Chakijana turned himself into a snake—a snake long dead.

The boy said, "Under no circumstances will I release you—no matter what you do! I'll never let you loose, no matter what you turn into, Chakijana! I just won't let go of you!" Then he said, "Mother, bring flaming firewood! I'll burn him! He will come out—here he is, he's turned himself into this!"

The mother said, "Wait a little, my child. There's firewood here in the wood pile."

The mother took it. Her son piled the wood on top of Chakijana.

Then Chakijana said, "Forgive me! Don't burn me, I've changed again. I'm a human being again!" Chakijana said, "Oh! Do forgive me. I'll give you many cattle! Right now! Cattle, and many other things! Goats! Because I've sold your child!"

The young man said, "Yes, I understand all that, Chakijana. However, I am demanding your soul, I want your soul to become like that of my mother's child, the child who is gone now!"

Chakijana said, "Well, they ate the child long ago, they finished it."

The boy said, "You agree then, Chakijana, that they ate the child long ago."

He said, "Yes! I handed it over, together with the duiker that carried the child on its back. I'm telling everything now, so that you may pardon me, so that I may give you everything! everything! oxen! goats! to pacify you regarding the child of your homestead. I am pleading with you."

The boy said, "No, my one demand is that you allow me to take your life, and do to it what you did to the child of our homestead." Then the boy said, "Mother, get up early in the morning. I won't sleep, I'll tie him here until the break of day. I'll rope him here, I'll watch him."

The boy took his shield and his spear, and he tied Chakijana. He said, "If you but move, I'll stab you! Mother, you go and fetch the ogres! I want them to eat him up right here before my eyes!"

The mother got up and went out, and when she had done so, she met a duiker. It said, "Hello, Mother."

The woman responded.

It said, "Mother, you travel as if you're troubled by something. And you seem to be in a hurry. Where are you rushing to?"

The mother said, "Oh, my child, I'm rushing to the land of the ogres."

"Hurry, Mother, the day is all but gone!"

So the woman traveled on and on. Along the way, she met an old woman.

The old woman said, "Hello, my child."

The woman said, "Hello, Mother."

She said, "Where are you hurrying to? Where are you rushing to? You walk as if you're troubled."

She said, "Well, I am hurrying, I'm going a great distance—to the land of the ogres."

"What business do you have in the land of the ogres?"

"Well, there is certain business that takes me to the land of the ogres."

"Well, you'll never find the ogres!"

"Oh!"

"Go down this way. Go down this way, down there. I met them going down this way!"

The mother said, "I see, Mother."

Then the mother went on her way. She went up a ridge, then she came to a snake.

The snake said, "Madam, why is it you walk as if you're troubled? Are you sad?"

The mother said, "Yes, I am indeed troubled, Snake, at this time! I don't know whether my disease can be cured. My destination is the land of the ogres. But a short time ago, I met a very old woman over there, and she said that the ogres are not to be found in this direction, that they went up over this ridge."

It said, "Indeed, I too met them in this direction. But this distress of yours, Mother—do you think I can help you?"

The mother said, "I don't know, Snake. Could you help me to find the land of the ogres?"

The snake said, "I'll find out for myself. You keep going forward. But if you can't find the land of the ogres, come back. You'll find me right here on the road."

But this was one of Chakijana's tricks.

The woman passed on. And soon enough, she saw the dust of the ogres, as they moved along.

The woman called out, she clapped her hands, and said, "Hello there! Ogres, come this way!"

The ogres stopped.

They said, "What is this? What is this that has spoken?"

"What's this that has spoken on this side?"

"She seems to be saying, 'Say, you of the land of the ogres, come this way!'"

Well, the ogres remained silent. Then they looked this way.

The woman called out and said, "Say, Ogres! Come this way!"

The ogres mumbled and said, "It seems to be an animal that has become tough!" They said, "Speak up!" They were drawing nearer to her, and they said, "Speak up, speak up, speak up, speak up!" Repeatedly, they said, "What is it? What is your trouble?"

"Well, I have been sent to you! I have been told to come to you. We caught Chakijana, and now I have been sent here by my son. He says, 'Come on and take him!'"

"Really? Have you actually caught Chakijana?"

"Well, Chakijana deceived us also, he ate up our cattle, then brought us an animal in return, an animal that was quite small."

She said, "That animal that he brought to you was my child!"

They said, "Mother, was that indeed your child?"

"Yes!"

"There is nothing we can do about that. We place the blame on Chakijana."

"But we do mourn with you."

So the ogres went along with the mother all that day, the mother showing them the way.

When the ogres arrived, Chakijana again turned himself into an old snake, a snake that had long since rotted.

The ogres remained silent. They said, "Mother, but where is Chakijana?"

She said, "He is here." Then she said, "Point him out to them, my child."

The boy told them to approach. They should come close so that he could talk seriously to them.

The ogres came, and he said, "Do you indeed want me to produce Chakijana for you? Do you want to see him?"

They said, "Yes! We do want to see him!"

"Do you really know what Chakijana is like?"

They said, "Yes, we do know Chakijana."

"But Chakijana is capable of changing himself into all sorts of creatures here on earth." Then he said, "I'll show you that I have apprehended Chakijana."

He said, "Mother, let me have that burning wood."

Chakijana immediately changed himself into whatever he turned himself into, and the mother came with the burning wood. She put the wood on Chakijana.

He said, "Forgive me! Don't kill me with fire!"

He said, "You can see what they are saying."

"Yes!"

Then he said, "You see, I don't want to drive him away. If you'll eat him here, while I watch you, I'll give you these two oxen—to thank you. And you can sing my praises as I praise you."

The ogres said, "Now what shall we do to him?"

He said, "Well, I'll ignite this house, and we'll burn him in it. But we don't know if you want to cook him."

The ogres said, "Well, we do want to roast him."

The boy remained quiet, and then he said, "Now, when you roast him, will he come out of the pot?"

[Member of audience: "Yes! He'll come out!"]

They said, "No! Never!"

He said, "Wait! It turns out that you are in league with Chakijana! You mean to let him go!"

The ogres said, "Not at all! We would never let him go!"

"Chakijana has given us a lot of trouble too!"

"He has been slipping out of our hands all this time because of his cunning!"

"Now that you've caught him, we want to finish Chakijana off—so that anything by the name of Chakijana should perish!"

"Because Chakijana is responsible for the bad reputation that we have among humans and animals!"

Then the boy said, "Well, I'll show you a plan whereby we can kill Chakijana. Make a fire here. Here's a large pot, take it."

Well, the ogres took this large pot, and they put it on supports.

He said, "Kindle a fire!"

A fire was made, the fire was kindled. Then the boy got large stones. He placed the pot on them.

Then he caught Chakijana, and said, "Let's put him inside."

The ogres said, "Has water been put into the pot?"

The boy said, "No, you dare not! If you should put water into the pot, Chakijana will escape! No water should be put in!"

The ogres remained silent. Chakijana cried now, realizing that the sun was setting for him. His last day had come.

"Are you really killing me, young man? Do you actually refuse the cattle that I would give to you?"

The boy said, "I am only making you feel what you made the child of my homestead feel!"

Meanwhile, the ogres were saying, "Chakijana, you're making us angry!"

[Laughter in the audience.]

"We're hungry!"

[Performer also laughs.]

"We're hungry! We're anxious, we can't wait to eat, Chakijana!"

[Members of audience: "Don't make us angry!"]

"Don't make us angry! Don't try us!"

There was silence for a time, and then he said, "Mother, make a fire."

Immediately, the ogres kindled a fire just beneath the pot.

[Audience: "He feels it!"]

They made the fire. Some were holding Chakijana. The pot began to heat up. It got hotter and hotter. Chakijana began to burn.

He said, "I'm dying! I'm dying!"

The boy said, "When you see him cry aloud, bring all the vessels of water."

Water was brought. Then oh! the ogres came close. They were in a hurry to eat.

[Member of audience: "A hurry to eat!"]

So the ogres were made to come close to the pot. And they began to share the parts.

"Chakijana is gone! If you don't claim these parts, I'll kill you!"

The ogres then regarded the various parts. They also heard the word about killing, that "We might be killed, and such nice food has been offered to us!"

The ogres then became serious about eating. The boy poured on the water. After a time, after he had poured on the water and Chakijana was boiling, Chakijana tried to come out! The boy beat him back with a club, and Chakijana went back into the pot. When he became agitated, the boy beat him with the club, and Chakijana went back inside.

So Chakijana boiled, he was cooked, and there was a meal for the ogres.

When the ogres had eaten Chakijana, the boy offered them the two oxen that he had promised them. He gave the oxen to the ogres as a thanksgiving.

The ogres thanked him, and they departed, driving the cattle.

The story ends here.

Commentary

One Zulu storyteller thought that Chakijana is a meercat. Another said it is simply a cat. Others suggested that Chakijana is the same as *isalukazi* (an old woman). A Zulu woman suggested that Chakijana is "like a cat," though larger, a cat that kills other animals. Another said that it is a very small animal, smaller than a cat, and that it eats other animals. But, unlike the *unogwaja* (hare), which people do eat, Chakijana is not eaten by humans.

Comments by Ellen Biyela (February, 1968, in the Yanguye section of Ntonjaneni District, the Biyela area, kwaZulu): "The *chakide* [slender mongoose, *herpestes gracilis;* weasel; *ubuchakide* means cunning] is an animal that is small and low to the ground. It is similar in shape to the cat, yellowish-brown. It has a rather bushy tail which it is able to curl into a bundle (*mfuku-mfuku*) when it sits upright (or when it is excited or looking for something—hence, perhaps, the suggestion that it is a wise creature). When it runs, its tail extends straight back behind it. Its praises are *uChakijana bogcololo umphepheti wezinduku zabafo*" (Chakijana, the clever one, medicator of the fighting sticks of the men). Ellen Biyela also said that the *chakide,* apparently like a mongoose, eats fowl, rats, and snakes. And there are many *chakide* around Zululand now. It is a fact, she says, that the *chakide* will study a snake, its habitat and its habits. The *chakide* watches the snake and waits for it. It sleeps near the its hole until it comes out. When it leaves, the *chakide* burrows the hole bigger. It goes into the hole. Then it comes out and goes to find this same snake. When the *chakide* finds the snake, it antagonizes it, frightens it, and the snake goes to its hole for shelter from the *chakide.* But the *chakide* runs to the hole also and gets there first and waits for it. The *chakide* is inside the hole. As the snake enters, the *chakide* grabs it and bites its head off. The *chakide* also eats only the head of the fowl that it catches, leaving the rest. It is equally at home in trees as on the ground. It lives in burrowed-out areas under rocks.

(Many narratives reveal this character's wonderful and often outrageous activities, describing the untamed force of this Chakijana, his amorality, his seemingly endless energy, uncontrolled and unchanneled at times, magnificently focused at other times. And this trickster is always akin to the hero, as indeed was the case with the historical Chakijana, the trickster and hero who effectively fought the white man, then survived to fight once more. This historical Chakijana was one of the authentic heroes of Zulu history, one of many rebels who through the years engaged in guerrilla activities against the encroaching Europeans. Chakijana is unique in that he has an existence both in history and in oral imaginative tradition. It is said that he harassed both sides during the Anglo-Boer War, that he was a double-agent effectively working both sides. Some tell of how he lived at Nhlazatsha Mountain, near Ndlebe: it was a mountain held by the Boers during one battle, while the British held another mountain not far away. As they fired on each other, this agent provocateur was staying at a mission at the foot of the Nhlazatsha Mountain.)

There are two patterns in this trickster tale. Pattern one has to do with the relationship between trickster and mother, as the trickster takes over the mother's child-rearing functions, as the trickster becomes the mother. Associated with this pattern is the conflict of the story: the trickster owes the ogres a living being. This attaches the trickster and the ogres, giving the trickster his chief death-dealing characteristics: he is like the ogres. The presence of the duiker is to further show the trickster's negative traits: he is as opposed to nature (the killing of the duiker) as he is opposed to culture (the killing of the human child). The second pattern has to do with the purging of what the trickster represents within the mother, cleansing her of evil (represented graphically in her callous attitude towards her child). This purging is dramatized by her illegitimate son, who orchestrates this grisly pattern, as the trickster flees, transforms himself, begs for mercy, and is in the end consumed by the very ogres he represents. He is now eternally a part of the ogres who live forever, a symbol of eternal evil, sometimes, as here, masquerading as decent beings, but there is no decency here.

Pattern one involves the trickster and the mother. Trickster baby-sits for the human woman, and slowly becomes identified with her. The mother's initial suspicions of Chakijana are allayed by him. This is a typical trickster motif, one of illusion. Trickster Chakijana is in debt to the ogres: he has tricked them and taken their cattle, now they want a small animal—like a human being—in return. Hence, the tricking of the human mother out of her child.

Pattern two also has to do with the trickster and the mother. Chakijana, again building his actions on a motif of illusion, substitutes a rock for the child, gives the child to the duiker to take to the ogres, and baby-sits a rock, cooing to it. The mother, now totally under Chakijana's influence, goes home without the child, and her older son becomes suspicious. The youth discovers the truth, Chakijana drops the stone. There is a chase by mother and son; she throws the stone and it becomes Chakijana. Chakijana gives the child to the ogres, his debt is paid. He and the ogres become one in their functions.

The resolution of the story begins with a cumulative pattern, emphasizing the trickster's greed: Chakijana gets a scoop, sticks, weapon, a typical trickster set of activities. But this routine pattern of trickery is interrupted when he encounters the youth who has been seeking him. Chakijana is trapped, and made captive by the youth and his mother. In a pattern built on a transformation motif, he transforms himself into various things, a goat, cow, etc., but he cannot escape. The mother beats Chakijana, and wants to burn him. The youth wants his very soul.

Chakijana is given by them to the ogres who boil him, then eat him. The illegitimate son, by virtue of his birth, is liminal; it is as a boundary character that he manipulates events and Chakijana, in the end helping to purge the society of what that trickster represents.

Chakijana takes over the role of the mother, becomes the mother. And the trickster is death-dealing: he is equated with ogres. The story is a working-out of a drama. The humans, having allowed evil to take over their world, are now in the process of cleansing their world of evil. The trickster is death-dealing in his tricks, and the people are in the process of purging themselves of him. Trickster's characteristic ambiguity and androgyny are exposed as he becomes the mother. But he is a dualistic mother: life-giving and death-dealing; he is a fantasy character, mirroring the conflict within the real-life mother.

To emphasize his lack of harmony, he kills a duiker as well, the equivalent in nature of the human mother's child. Chakijana is equated in his death-dealing, anti-social activities with the ogres. In the end, he is pursued and destroyed, but not before he works all his wiles. Finally, he is fed to the ogres, the two becoming one. Trickster exists between the human and ogre worlds. He preys on both, cheating both humans and nature, even attempting to deceive the essence of evil, the cannibals. He is destroyed, but he remains in the guise of the ogres, who are not destroyed. He becomes literally a part of them and what they represent. Evil and death linger, the trickster has not been destroyed. He and what he stands for are here forever. We must deal with that. This story suggests that what the trickster represents is a part of us all.

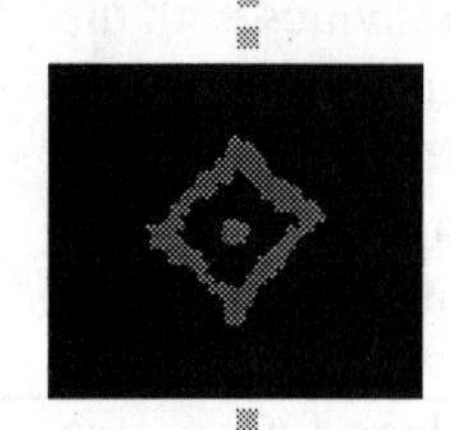

Stories are told and riddles are asked on any occasion, particularly after a marriage ceremony. After a death, however, it may not be indulged in for four days.

Mervyn W. H. Beech, *The Suk* (Oxford: Clarendon Press, 1911), p. 38.

Tigre

Beiho Tricks His Uncles

The Tigre live in Ethiopia.

It is not known who Beiho was. Some say he was a human being, others say he was an animal, perhaps of the family of the jackal.

When Beiho was in his mother's womb, his mother went down to the water. When she had filled her water-skin, she had nobody to help her to load it on her back. So Beiho came out of his mother's womb and loaded it on her back. Having done so, he returned into his mother's womb.

After she had gone home, she labored to give birth. When the women came to assist her in childbirth, Beiho said to them, "I shall be born by myself. Do not go near my mother." And he was born by himself.

When Beiho became older, he had a quarrel with the wives of his uncles. One day, when his uncles came into the house of his mother, he filled an esophagus with blood, fastened both of its ends together, and tied it around his mother's neck. But his uncles had not seen what he had done.

When his uncles entered the house, Beiho said to his mother, "Quickly, make a meal for my uncles!" But then, he said, "You are slow," and, in rage against her, he put her on the ground, and it seemed as if he were killing her. He took the knife and put it against his mother's throat. Then he cut the esophagus spread over her neck.

His uncles said, "You have done us evil! You have killed our sister!"

They were very frightened.

From Enno Littmann, *Publications of the Princeton Expedition to Abyssinia,* Vol. II, *Tales, Customs, Names and Dirges of the Tigre Tribes* (Leyden: E. J. Brill, 1910), pp. 19–25.

But he said to them, "If one does not treat women in this way, they will finish nothing quickly. And if you do not do this to your wives, they will not make a meal quickly for your guests." After that, he said to them, "We have a remedy for her." And he spoke to his mother, "Saria Maria! [Cure her, Mary!] Saria Maria! Saria Maria!" and he made her stand up.

When his uncles saw this, they asked him, "If we kill our wives in this way, will they rise for us again?"

Beiho said to them, "Just kill them, I guarantee you!"

When the uncles returned home, each of them killed his wife.

Then they said to their wives, "Saria Maria!"

But their wives were unable to rise.

The uncles went to Beiho, and said, "We killed our wives, but they are unable to rise!"

He replied, "You have cut through the vein of their lives, you killed them too much. How could I make them rise for you?"

They buried their wives.

The uncles now thought of revenge against Beiho, and they intended to kill him.

They made a plan: "When he sleeps at night at his house, let us burn his house and him."

But Beiho heard of their plan, and he took his things out and slept in another house.

The uncles set fire to his house at night, to burn it down, thinking that he was in it.

But Beiho put the ashes of his house into two leather bags, and, as he went along carrying them, he met the uncles on the road.

They asked him, "What is this?"

He answered, "These are the ashes of my home. They say that these ashes can be sold in such-and-such a country."

Moving on, he came to the village of a rich man. There, he said to the people, "Put these things of mine in a good and safe place for me. They are very costly."

They told him to put the things in a place where their money and their treasure were kept.

After that, Beiho came to them at night, and said to them, "Give me my things, so that I may go."

But they replied, "Go in yourself, and take the things from where you put them."

Beiho left the ashes there, but of their money and precious garments he took as much as he could, and came out. Then he went away.

When he came to his village, his uncles asked him, "Beiho, where did you find this?"

He answered them, "I have sold the ashes of my house for it."

They asked him, "Can ashes be sold?"

He replied, "If a man burns down his house with all its belongings, the ashes are much coveted in the country of so-and-so."

Now, the uncles burned down their houses, filled their vessels with the ashes, and went to the country that Beiho had named to them.

When they got there, they hawked the ashes, crying, "Ashes! Ashes!"

And whoever heard them laughed at them. They said, "Ashes? How is that?"

"May you turn to ashes!"

"Can ashes be sold?"

So the uncles knew that Beiho had cheated them.

When they returned, they held a council: "What shall we do?"

"How shall we deal with this Beiho?"

They decided to kill his cattle, and they did that.

Beiho ate the meat of his cattle, but the hides he dried in the sun. When the hides were dry, he took them and went to a hillside along a road. While he was sitting there, he saw traveling merchants, camel-drivers, coming. When they were near, he made the hides slide down to them. The merchants thought that an army was raiding them, so they left their camels with their loads, and fled.

Beiho came down from the hillside, took the camels with their loads, and returned to his country.

His uncles asked him, "Where did you find these camels with their loads?"

He replied, "I bought them for the hides of my camels."

They asked him, "Are hides so highly valued?"

And after he had said "Yes" to them, the uncles went and killed their cattle, then left to sell their hides.

They hawked the hides, crying, "Hides! Hides!"

But when the people heard them, they were angry, and said, "Hides? How is that?"

"May you turn to hides!"

"Take them away!"

"Why should an owner of living cattle buy hides?" [The presence of many such hides indicated that the cattle had died or had been killed because of some disease, and the other people do not wish to have hides of diseased animals near their own stock.]

The uncles returned sadly to their village.

But now they planned to throw Beiho into a large pond. They seized him and, binding him, they set him on a beast of burden. While they were going along with him, they turned aside on some business.

While Beiho was on the back of the beast of burden, a cow-driver came along. He asked him, "Who bound you?"

"My family told me to become chief, and because I refused to be chief they are now taking me to forcibly make me chief."

But the man said, "Who refuses the chieftainship? If you'll put me in your place, I'll give you cattle!"

Beiho said, "Untie me."

Then he tied the man up in his place. So that his uncles would not recognize him, he clothed the man in a large garment, and added, "Be silent while they go along with you, until they make you chief!"

Taking the cattle, Beiho departed on another road.

The uncles who had turned aside came back. Taking the man who was on the animal, they went on, then threw him into the pond.

"Now then," they said, "we have got rid of him!" and they returned to their village.

But along the way, Beiho met them with his cattle.

They asked him, "How did you find these cattle?"

He replied, "I got them from the pond you threw me into! But because I was alone, I took only these cattle. There are many more cattle in the pond! It is full of them!"

When they heard this, the uncles took their children, their wives whom they had married after the others had been killed, and all their relatives, and they went down into the pond. They were drowned in it, thinking that they would become very rich.

After Beiho had done this, he coveted and desired the daughter of a village chief, because she was very beautiful. He was planning how he might win her. She was living alone in a loft, and her brother let no men come near her.

Now, Beiho, unfolding his plan, went to his mother and said to her, "Braid my hair like that of a girl."

His mother braided his hair like that of a girl, and clothed him in the garment of a girl. When he had been made to look like a girl, he went to the son of the village chief, and said to him, "My brother, Beiho, speaks to you: 'Let this, my sister, be with your sister in the loft. I am afraid for her sake: people will not leave her alone.'"

But the chief's son answered him, "This is not possible for me."

Beiho went back, waited a little while, and then returned to the chief's son again, and said, "My brother, Beiho, speaks to you: 'Won't you do this for me? If you want money, I myself shall give it to you.'"

The chief's son replied, "Be a companion to her, talk with her, be with her. Go up, then."

While they were together, Beiho rendered the daughter of the village chief pregnant.

When the family of the daughter of the village chief decided on her wedding day, they noticed her pregnancy. They wondered how she had become with child.

Then they resolved to marry the sister of Beiho in her stead. When the members of the nuptial cortege came to them, they gave them Beiho's sister. The members of the cortege took their bride, and went away. When the bride arrived at the village of her father-in-law, she was in a bad state.

So her father-in-law asked her, "What has happened to you, my daughter-in-law? And what do you want us to do for you?"

She answered, "I have not received my dowry."

Her father-in-law said, "What is your dowry?"

She answered, "My dowry is a full-bred Arab horse clothed in gold and silver and silk. Let me ride on its back so that I might pass on him through every open space of the village."

Her father-in-law said to her, "This is easy. We shall do it for you."

The next morning, they clothed the horse as she wished, and let her ride on it. But after she had gone about a little in the village, she found a wide open place, and there she made the horse gallop, and she disappeared towards her country.

When Beiho came to his mother, he said to her, "Unbraid my hair!"

He left the hair on the top of his head and on the hind part, and was braided like a man.

He hid his treasure and his horse.

Then he went to the son of the village chief, and said to him, "Give me my sister!"

The son of the village chief replied, "Our sister became pregnant, and the family of her future father-in-law requested the wedding. We gave them your sister in marriage, counting you as our kinsman."

Beiho said to him, "You have done well. My sister is your sister. Now then, give me your sister who is with child. I must marry her."

The chief's son was glad, and he gave Beiho his sister.

So Beiho married his wife, and went away with her.

But those people who had married their son said, "They have betrayed us, and given us a man in marriage!"

They therefore went to war, destroyed each other, and both sides ceased to be known.

Commentary

An opening comment stresses Trickster's ambiguity: "It is not known who Beiho was. Some say he was a human being, others say he was an animal. . . ." Trickster is an extraordinary being: while he is still in his mother's womb, he helps her with her chores.

In the pattern created by the first four tricks, those having to do with the esophagus filled with blood, the ashes of the burnt house, the hides of cattle, and the drowning in a pond, Trickster sets up a model which is repeated by the uncles but with fatal consequences.

In this tale, the trickster's activities seem more acceptable than usual, because the uncles are villainous and Trickster cuts down the mighty. But he remains profane, never to be trusted.

Trickster's androgyny is revealed by a final intricate trick, when he transforms himself into a woman, gains access to the chief's daughter, and gets her pregnant, replacing the chief's daughter with Beiho's "sister." The motif is obviously one of transformation, illusion, and identity. And the result is not untypical of tricksters antics; war is declared, and "both sides ceased to be known."

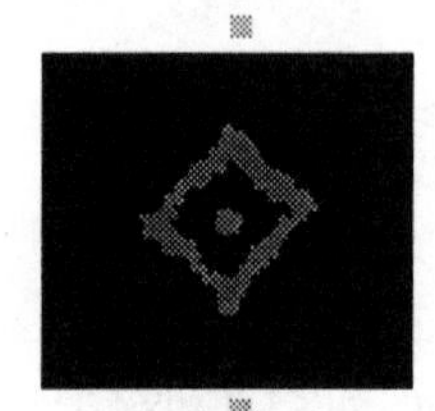

Musa al-Tahir . . . was Sultan Maiwurno's singer; and his only musical instrument was a tin drum. Hence he was nicknamed Maitanaka (literally, the possessor of a tin). Musa claims that he is 104 years of age. He was born in Nega in northern Nigeria. His father was a malam of a Qur'anic school, and Musa therefore had the opportunity of learning by heart a part of the Qur'an. His father gave him a fahami (literally, quickness at grasping details; retentiveness of memory) charm to make his memory retentive and facilitate his learning the entire Holy Book by heart, and to help him to become a malam. A year after taking the charm, any words Musa heard or read were thought to stick in his mind. Before the end of the year, however, Musa left the school and became an apprentice singer, which induced his father to expel him from home. Musa sang in Nega for some time without receiving any recompense. He later became a professional singer, and traveled widely, though he interrupted his career by serving as a soldier under the British for several years.

Ahmad Abd-al-Rahim M. Nasr, "Maiwurno of the Blue Nile: A Study of an Oral Biography," Diss., University of Wisconsin-Madison, 1977, p. 2.

Two Tar Baby Stories

Vai

The Wax Doll

The Vai live in Liberia.

It was the farm season, and everybody was making plantations, first in the low marshes and then on the highland or in the mountainous regions—all except Spider, who was said to have been at the time very ill. Everybody in the town turned out to work but Spider. From the time the bushes were cut down and burnt to the time when the rice began to ripen, Spider lay in bed ailing.

When the rice was fully ripe and the people started to gather it, Spider's case became serious. It was thought he would die. But just before dying, he asked the people, when he was dead, to bury his body in some large rice farm.

Spider then died, and his body was accordingly interred in his uncle's largest farm.

Every morning after the burial, when the people came out to the farm, they found that either rice or some other article had been stolen during the previous night. This went on every night for a week. Several attempts were made to lay hands on the thief, but without success. There was no one who could guess who the thief was.

The people then went to a diviner to seek his priestly advice, or, if possible, to have the culprit described to them. The priest, however, told them to go and make a wax

From Harry Johnston, *Liberia* (London: Hutchinson, 1906), vol. 2, pp. 1087–1089.

doll in the shape of a young girl, and to place it near the corner of the kitchen. In the morning, on their return, they would find that the burglar had been caught.

As the shades of night gradually fell, the disheartened laborers began to retire from their daily toil. There was a perfect stillness—all the farmers had gone home—and, when it was nearly midnight, Spider crept out easily from his grave, and went into the kitchen on a hunt for rice. His search was a quick one, he got everything he needed, and he commenced cooking some food. When the blaze became brighter, he looked around for a spoon with which to stir the rice, and his eyes suddenly fell on the beautiful young initiate [the doll is meant to resemble a girl in puberty school] standing in the corner.

Spider laughed, and said, "Are you watching me burn my hands without coming to my assistance?"

Spider was puzzled because the initiate did not reply. He dropped the spoon on the ground, and stepped up boldly to her and put his left hand on her shoulder.

The pots began to boil, and Spider made several attempts to go and look at his food, but the initiate refused to let him go—he was stuck to the wax.

Spider got vexed, and started to curse and swear. He told the initiate that if she did not speak or allow him to go and look after his pots, he would slap, kick, and knock her all over her face.

A deep silence ensued for a quarter of an hour. The initiate did not speak, nor did she release him.

It was now almost day—the rice in the pot had burned to cinders—and there was Spider, hanging with his hands, feet, and teeth stuck on to the beeswax coating of the initiate. When it was day, and the people came to their farms, they found old Spider hanging. They yelled and shouted at him, and some of them poured oil on him and set his body on fire. Spider was burned to cinders, and his ashes were thrown into his old grave.

Commentary

Trickster is not always successful in his activities; as in this tale, he can often become the victim of his own trickery.

In the opening trick of this tale, Trickster Spider feigns death while everyone else is working in the fields. The pattern that results: Someone is stealing food from the farm. This gives rise to the main pattern of the tale, built on the motif of the tar baby, which is, in this case, a wax doll. The spider loses this game, and he is burned to death.

≋≋≋≋≋

Ikom

The Cunning Hare

≋≋≋≋≋

by Abassi

The Ikom live in southern Nigeria.

The hare was known to everyone as a very cunning animal. He was very fond of meat, although he was unable to kill anything himself. He therefore thought out a scheme by which be would be able to obtain meat without any trouble.

The first thing the hare did was to call all the animals together, and, when they arrived, he said, "We ought to have a king over us."

The animals agreed, and, after some discussion, the elephant was chosen.

A law was also passed, at the hare's suggestion, that a piece of ground at the roadside should be set aside for the king's own private use, and that if anyone was caught defiling this piece of ground in any way he should be killed and eaten.

In the night time the hare went to the king's private piece of ground and made a mess there.

When the morning came he hid himself in the bush near the place in order to see who might be the first animal to pass the piece of ground, so that he could give false information against him.

After he had been waiting for a short time, a bush cat passed on his way to the farm, whereupon the hare jumped up and said, "Have you visited the king's piece of ground this morning?"

The bush cat said, "No," and the hare ordered him to go there at once. He did so, and returned saying that the place was very dirty.

The hare said, "How is that possible? I visited the place myself this morning, and it was quite clean then. You must have defiled it yourself. I shall report you."

From Elphinstone Dayrell, *Ikom Folk Stories from Southern Nigeria* (London: Royal Anthropological Institute of Great Britain and Ireland, 1913), pp. 3–7.

The hare then ran into the town and told the people what he had seen. The big wooden drum was then beaten, and when all the animals had come together the bush cat was put on his defense.

The bush cat told the people what had happened, and that he had nothing to do with the matter. But the hare stood up as the accuser, and the people decided that the bush cat was guilty. The king ordered him to be killed, and said that the meat was to be dried by Keroho and brought to him in the morning.

Now, Keroho is a fruit-eating animal, who is very lazy and sleeps most of the day. He always seems tired, and after he has taken a few steps he lies down and sleeps for a time.

The hare had suggested to the king that Keroho should be told to dry and guard the meat. He told the king that, as Keroho only ate fruit, he would not be likely to steal any of the meat.

In reality the hare suggested Keroho for a very different reason, and that reason was that Keroho was a fat animal in good condition, and far too lazy and sleepy to guard the meat properly.

When the evening came, Keroho made a fire and cut up the body of the bush cat and set it out to dry. He then went to sleep.

The hare was very greedy and fond of meat; he wanted to have it all to himself, so, when all the people had gone to bed, he slipped out of his house by the back way and very soon had taken the dried meat out of Keroho's yard and returned to his house, where he made a good meal. He buried what he could not eat.

Early in the morning the hare went and beat the big drum to call the animals together at the king's house.

Keroho, hearing the drum, got up and went to the fire in his back yard, where he had left the meat drying, and, to his intense astonishment, found that it had vanished. He was very frightened at this, and went to the meeting trembling in every limb. He tried to explain that he had left the meat before the fire when he went to bed, but the hare got up at once and said, "Do not believe him. Most likely he has sold the meat to get some money. I propose that Keroho be killed so that we shall not lose our meat."

All the people agreed to this, so Keroho was killed and cut up, the meat being given to the bush cow to keep.

The hare, in order to make himself acquainted with the bush cow's house, waited until sundown, and then went to the bush cow's house with a large calabash of strong tombo. The hare was careful to drink only a little himself, and very soon the bush cow had finished the whole calabash.

That night the bush cow slept very soundly, and at midnight, when nothing could be heard but the occasional hoot of an owl or the croaking of the frogs in the marsh, the hare went very quietly and stole the meat from the bush cow's fire and took it home with him, as before.

The following morning, he beat the drum as usual, and the people met together. The bush cow, failing to produce the meat, was killed by the king's order and his meat given to another animal to dry.

As usual, the hare stole the meat at night and the animal was killed the next day. This went on until there were only seven animals left.

The meat of the last animal that was killed was handed over to the tortoise. The tortoise at once placed his wife on guard over the meat, and went off into the bush to cut rubber.

Now, the tortoise was looked upon as one of the wisest of all animals. For some time it had seemed to him very curious that every night the meat should disappear and another animal should be killed. He therefore determined that, when it became his turn to dry and guard the meat, he would take every precaution possible, and would try to catch whoever it was who always removed the meat at night, as he had no intention that his body should supply food for the remaining six animals.

Before going into the bush, he gave his wife strict instructions not to let the meat out of her sight.

When he returned in the evening, he cut up the meat, saying as he did so, "Ah, there goes another poor animal. I wonder whose turn it will be tomorrow, but it shall not be mine if I can help it."

So he made a big fire and put the meat on, and then covered it all over with the rubber he had brought back with him from the bush.

The tortoise then told his wife that he was tired, and went to bed pretending to be asleep, but he had one eye open all the time, and that eye he kept fixed upon the meat, as he was not going to take any risks, knowing full well that if the meat disappeared, as it had a habit of doing, he himself would be the next victim.

When all was quiet, and the hare thought everybody had gone to sleep, he went round to the back of the tortoise's house and put his right hand out to take the meat, but when his hand closed on the rubber, he found that he could not remove it because the rubber was so sticky. He tried his hardest to get his hand away, but without success. He then called out softly, because he was afraid of waking the tortoise, "Let me go! Let me go!" but the rubber never answered, and held on tighter than ever. This made the hare angry, so he whispered to the rubber, "Look here, if you don't let my right hand go at once I will hit you very hard with my left hand, and then you will be sorry." He got no reply, but thought he heard a laugh somewhere. The hare then hit the rubber with his disengaged hand as hard as he was able, and that hand also stuck fast.

Then the hare heard the tortoise murmur, "Yes, tomorrow I will discover that rat who is always stealing the king's meat."

At length the hare became absolutely terrified, and kicked the rubber hard with one of his feet, which became as fast as his hands were, and very shortly the other foot also became caught up, so that he was held quite securely.

When the morning came, the tortoise called his wife to help him, and together they put the meat and rubber into a basket with the hare on top, and carried them all to the king's house.

When the drum was beaten, the people assembled as usual, and discussed among themselves to whom the meat of the tortoise should be given when he was killed. In the middle of the discussion, the tortoise appeared carrying the meat with the hare on top.

The tortoise then charged the hare with attempting to steal the king's meat, and told the people of the trap he had set. The hare was found guilty, and was ordered to pay a large number of brass rods, and he was told that if they were not forthcoming, he would be killed, and that his mother and sister would be killed with him, as he had been the cause of the death of so many animals.

The hare begged for a little time to enable him to get the rods, which was allowed to him.

He then ran home and got his mother and sister to come with him at once to the foot of a big cotton tree, and, having got a rope around the lowest branch, he very soon got to the top of the tree, where be built a small house for himself and his people.

The hare then went down to the lowest branch where the rope was, and hauled his mother and sister up. He put them in the house at the top of the tree, and sat down himself next to the rope with a sharp knife in his hand.

As the hare did not appear at the appointed time to pay the rods, the people went to his house, and found that they had all disappeared. It did not take long, however, to discover that he had taken refuge in the cotton tree, so they all went there and found the rope hanging down.

Then they all began to climb the rope together, leaving the tortoise on the ground, and just as be was about to commence to climb, the others having already reached halfway, the hare cut the rope with one cut of his sharp knife, and all the animals fell down upon the tortoise, smashing his smooth shell into small pieces, and hurting themselves very much. No one was killed, however, and they limped home one after the other.

On the way, they passed the tortoise's house, so they told his wife that they had fallen on her husband from a great height, and that his shell was broken into pieces.

On hearing this, the tortoise's wife got her basket and went off to the cotton tree. Having picked up all the pieces of her husband's shell, and having placed them in the basket, she lifted the tortoise and carried them all home.

When she got inside, she put all the little pieces of the shell together and placed them on her husband's back, where they grew quite strongly, but the marks showed where the pieces were joined together, and that is why you always find that the shell of a tortoise is covered in patches, and not smooth as it was formerly.

Commentary

In this Nigerian story, the trickster hare survives by means of a rope trick. The main pattern is built around the trick: Hare, through deception, gets the meat that he wants by putting someone else in his place. As long as he is able to sustain the illusion, he has all the food he wants and others take the responsibility and the punishment for his trickery. It is a mask: the shadowy trickster brings other creatures into fatal union with himself. He is all of the animals that he dupes, but these other selves take on the punishment for his misdeeds and are, simultaneously, his reward for his subterfuge.

A Xhosa storyteller (photo by Harold Scheub)

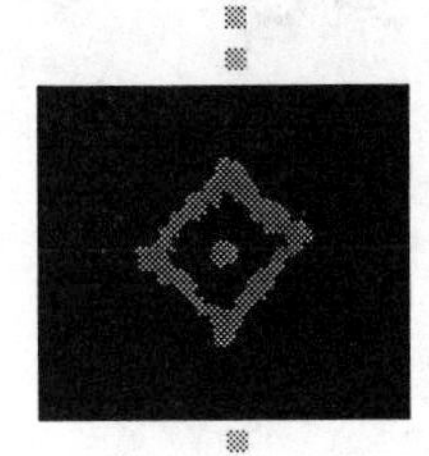

[T]here is no way to determine which interpretation is the correct one, nor does it matter as long as individuals infuse new meaning into old customs to keep them current.

Laura Davidson Tanna, "The Art of Jamaican Oral Narrative Performance," Diss., University of Wisconsin-Madison, 1980, p. 254.

Nuer

Turning the Tables on Trickster

The Nuer live in Sudan.

One day, when Rill the jackal was very hungry, he met Quoing the turtle, and suggested that they should go to the cattle kraal to get some milk.

When they got there, Rill volunteered to take the cattle out to graze. During the day, he suddenly returned, driving in front of him a black cow called Ashol which was the property of Quoing.

"Come quick," said Rill, "and spear this buffalo that is attacking me!"

Quoing hurried up, spear in hand, and, because his eyesight was bad, he killed his own cow.

"What have you done?" said Rill. "You've killed your own cow."

"But you told me it was a buffalo," said Quoing with indignation.

"I did nothing of the sort! I told you to go and get the cattle rope in order to tie it up."

Rill then took a water pot and, boring some holes in the bottom of it, ordered Quoing to go and get some sweet water from a far away pool.

While Quoing was thus employed, Rill skinned the cow, and, after hiding the meat in the grass, buried the horns in the ground, leaving only the tips sticking out.

After a lengthy absence, Quoing returned, complaining that he had made several trips to the water, but the pot seemed to be a bad one as the water always leaked out.

"Never mind about the pot," said Rill, who was now holding on to the top of the horns with apparent difficulty. "My back is nearly broken, and if you don't come and help me quickly, the cow will disappear altogether, and we shall lose all the meat."

From V. Fergusson, "Nuer Beast Tales," *Sudan Notes and Records* 7 (1924): 111–112.

When Quoing caught hold of the horns, they came away in his hands.

"I told you so! Now we've lost the cow altogether because you were so slow in getting the water," said Rill.

Rill next had to get rid of Quoing so that he could get the meat to his house unobserved.

Giving one horn to him, Rill told Quoing to give it to his wife with instructions to boil it continuously in a pot of water. On the second day, they would find the pot to be full of meat. If this did not come to pass, it was certain proof that Quoing's wife was a bad one and should be killed.

Quoing then departed, and proceeded to make his wife boil the horn. In the meantime, Rill collected his meat and went home, filling all the pots with what he could not eat himself.

At the end of the second day, Rill visited Quoing, and inquired about the meat. Quoing admitted failure, while Rill boasted of the success that he had had, and he urged Quoing to kill his wife. This Quoing did, and Rill returned to his home.

When Quoing's mother-in-law heard the bad news, she was very angry, and explained to Quoing that Rill had deceived him.

Quoing thought for a long time of how to repay such a terrible act. Knowing Rill's weakness for women, Quoing wandered along until he reached a path leading to the jackal's house. Here he sat down, and proceeded to turn himself into a portion of a woman. It was not long before Rill passed by, and seeing the object on the ground placed it on the end of his spear and walked home.

When he arrived there, he called together his wife, mother, sister, and cousin, and asked them if they had dropped anything on the path. After due inspection, nothing was found to be missing, and Rill produced his find amidst the rejoicing of his family, and he hung it up on the roof of his house. Then he left with his relations to spear fish in a neighboring pool.

On his return, he found a beautiful young woman in place of the object he had picked up on the path, and he hurried off to make known the good news. That night was spent in dancing and general hilarity.

The following morning, his newly acquired wife ordered him to go to the river to catch fish. This he did, but she was nowhere to be found upon his return, and exhaustive inquiries did not help to solve the matter.

Because he was hungry, Rill turned to the pots that held the meat of the black cow. To his astonishment, he found all of the pots empty except the last one, which still had a little fat in it. While he was licking around the edge of the pot, his tongue was suddenly seized by some unseen object. It turned out to be Quoing, who had turned himself into a turtle once again, having got his revenge. Rill implored him to let go of his tongue, but this Quoing would not do until Rill had taken him down to the river and left him there.

Rill never attempted to molest Quoing again.

Commentary

This is another trickster tale in which the trickster is himself defeated, this time by a rival trickster. The impact of the story is derived from the motif, the tables turned.

There is a pattern of three tricks in which Rill, a jackal, gets the best of Quoing, a turtle: (a) Quoing spears a "buffalo," which turns out to be his cow, (b) Quoing pulls away the horns of his cow, and (c) Quoing's wife boils the horn. Then the tables are turned, and the dupe becomes a trickster: Quoing gets even with Rill, by creating a ruse using a part of a woman which is transformed into a beautiful woman. She sends Rill to get fish, then disappears along with all the cow meat. Only a bit of fat remains. As the ravenous Rill licks it, Quoing, the turtle, seizes his tongue.

There is a playful etiological ending: Rill does not bother Quoing again, and the molester is properly punished.

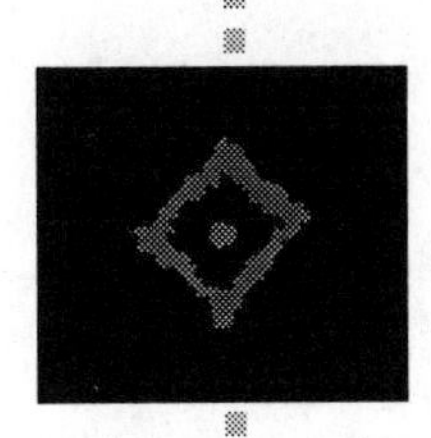

[M]asks and costumes abound in the saga of Ozidi. Apart from adding color and spectacle, they help to delineate individual characters, from Tortoise, who takes his house with him wherever he goes, to legendary Bouezeremeze, a figure so tall that Ozidi has to seek his face in the sky at their terrible encounter.

Another device serving to underline individual traits in this great gallery of character is color. Dress shades and make-up are therefore chosen and worn with particular care. The storyteller, because he represents the hero beloved by everybody, appears always in white, denoting purity and innocence. In contrast, intractable roles demand blue and indigo, and really sinister ones charcoal.

John Pepper Clark, *The Ozidi Saga* (Ibadan: Ibadan University Press, 1977), p. xxiv.

Benga

The Magic Drum

The Benga live in Gabon.

In the ancient days, mankind and all the animals lived together in one country. They built their towns, and they dwelled together in one place.

In the country of King Maseni, Tortoise and Leopard lived in the same town, the one at one end of the street, the other at the other end of the street.

Leopard married two women, Tortoise also his two.

It happened that a time of famine came, and a very great hunger fell on the people of that whole region of country. So King Maseni issued a law: "Any person who shall be found having a piece of food, he shall be brought to me"—that is, for the equal distribution of that food. And he appointed police as watchmen to look after that whole region.

The famine got worse. People sat down hopelessly, and died of hunger, just as even today it destroys the poor, not only of Africa but also in the lands of Manga-Manene, the white man's land. And, as the days passed, people continued sitting in their hopelessness.

One day, Tortoise went out early, going into the forests to seek his special food, mushrooms. He had said to his wife, "I am going to stroll on the beach down toward the south."

He journeyed and journeyed, and came to a river. It was a large river, several hundred feet wide. He saw a coconut tree growing on the river bank. When he reached the foot of the tree, and looked up at its top, he discovered that it was full of nuts.

He said to himself, "I'm going up there to gather nuts, I'm hungry!"

From Robert Hamill Nassau, *Where Animals Talk* (Boston: Gorham Press, 1912), pp. 113–120.

He put aside his traveling bag, leaving it on the ground, and at once climbed the tree, expecting to gather many nuts. He plucked two and threw them to the ground. He plucked another, but when he attempted to throw it, it slipped from his hand and fell into the stream below.

He exclaimed, "I've come here in hunger, and does my coconut fall into the water to be lost?" He said to himself, "I'll just climb down, and drop into the water and follow that nut!"

So he plunged down, splash! into the water. He dove down to where the nut had sunk, to get it. And he was carried away by the current. He followed the nut where the current had carried it, and he came to the landing place of a strange town in which there was a large house. People were in it. And other people were outside, playing.

They called to him. From the house, he heard a voice saying, "Take me! Take me! Take me!"

It was a drum that spoke.

At the landing place was a woman washing a child. The woman said to Tortoise, "What has brought you here? And where are you going?"

He replied, "There is great hunger in our town. So I came seeking mushrooms. I saw a coconut tree, and because I am hungry and have nothing to eat I climbed it. I threw down some nuts, and one fell into the river. I followed it, and came here."

The woman said, "Now you're saved." And she added, "Tortoise, go to that house over there. You'll see something there, a drum. Go at once to where the drums are."

Other people called out to him, "There are many drums there. But the kind that says, 'Take me! Take me!'—don't take those! You must take the drum that is silent and does not speak, it only echoes, 'Wo wo wo,' without any real words. Take that one, carry it with you, and tie it to that coconut tree. Then you must say to the drum, 'Ngama! Speak as they told you!'"

So Tortoise went to that house and took the drum. He carried it, and came back to the river bank where the woman was.

She said to him, "You must first learn how to use it. Beat it!"

Tortoise beat the drum—and a table appeared with all kinds of food! And when he had eaten the food, he said to the drum, "Put it back!"—and the table disappeared!

He carried the drum with him back to the foot of the coconut tree. He tied it with a rattan vine to the tree, and then said to the drum, "Ngama! Do as they said!"

Instantly, the drum set out a long table and put all sorts of food on it. Tortoise was very happy for his abundance of food. He ate and ate, and was satisfied.

Again, he turned to the drum, and said, "Ngama! Do as they said!"

And Drum took the table and food back to itself up the tree, leaving a little food at the foot. Then it came back to the hand of Tortoise.

Tortoise put the little food into his traveling bag, and gathered from the ground the coconuts he had left lying there in the morning. And he started to go back to his town.

He stopped at a place a short distance from the town. He was so delighted with the drum that he tested it again. He stood it up, and with the palm of his hand he struck it—tomu! A table at once stood there, with all kinds of food on it. Again Tortoise ate, and he also filled his traveling bag with food. Then he said to a tree that was standing nearby, "Bend down!" The tree bowed, and Tortoise tied the drum to a branch, and went off into the town.

He handed the coconuts and the mushrooms to his women and children.

After he had entered the house, his chief wife said to him, "Where have you been all this time? You've been gone since morning."

Tortoise replied, "I went wandering down to the beach to gather coconuts. And this day I saw a very fine thing. You, my wife, shall see it!"

Then he drew the food out of his bag—potatoes and rice and beef.

And he said, "When we eat this food, no one must show any of it to Leopard!"

So those two, and his other wife, and their family of children ate.

Soon, day darkened, and they all went to sleep. Soon another day began to break.

At daybreak, Tortoise went off to the place where the drum was. He arrived there and went to the tree, and he said to the drum, " Ngama, do as they said!"

The drum rapidly came down to the ground, and set out the table all covered with food. Tortoise took some of it and ate it, and was satisfied. He also filled his bag. Then he said to the drum, "Do as you did before!" And Drum took back the things, and returned to the tree.

On another day, at daybreak, Tortoise went to the tree and did the same.

On another day, as he was going there, his eldest son, curious to find out where his father obtained so much food, secretly followed him. Tortoise went to where the drum was. The child hid himself, and was still. He heard his father say to the tree, "Bend!" And the top of the tree bent down. The child saw the entire thing, he saw Tortoise take the drum, he saw him stand it up and with the palm of his hand strike it, ve! saying, "Do as you have been told to do!" At once a table stood prepared, and Tortoise sat down and ate. Then, when he had finished, he said, "Tree! Bend down!" And the tree bent over so that Drum could be tied to it. Tortoise returned Drum to the tree, and the tree stood erect.

On other days, Tortoise came to the tree and did the same thing, eating, then returning to his house, on all such occasions bringing food for his family.

One day, the son, who had seen how to do all these things, came to the tree and said to it, "Bow down." It bowed, and he did as his father had done. So Drum spread the table. The child ate, and was satisfied. Then he said to Drum, "Put them away!" And the table disappeared. Then the child took the drum, and instead of fastening it to the tree he secretly carried it to town to his own house. He went and privately called his brothers and his father's wives and other members of the family. When they had come together in his house at his command, he had the drum do what it usually did, and they ate. And when he said to the drum, "Put the things away!" it put them away.

Tortoise came that day from the forest where he had been searching for the loved mushrooms for his family. He said to himself, "Before going to town, I'll first go to the tree to eat. "As he approached the tree, when he was a short distance from it, he could see the tree standing as usual—but the drum was not there.

He exclaimed, "Truly now, what is this joke of the tree?"

As he neared the foot of the tree, he still saw no drum.

He said to the tree, "Bow down!"

There was no response.

He went on to the town. He took his axe, then returned at once to the tree, angry, saying, "Bend, or I'll cut you down!"

The tree stood still.

Tortoise at once began with his axe, he chopped ko ko! The tree fell, toppling to the ground, tomu!

Tortoise said to the tree, "Produce the drum, or I'll cut you into pieces!"

He split the tree into pieces, but he did not see the drum.

He returned to the town, and as he walked he anxiously said to himself, "Who has done this?"

When he reached his house, he was so displeased that he refused to speak.

His eldest son came to him then and said, "Oh, my father, why are you so silent? What have you done in the forest? What is it?"

He replied, "I don't want to talk!"

The son said, "Ah, my father, you were satisfied when you used to come and eat, and you brought us mushrooms. I'm the one who took the drum."

Tortoise said to him, "My child, bring the drum out to us."

The son brought it out of an inner room.

Then Tortoise and the son called all their people together privately, and assembled them in the house.

They commanded the drum, and it did as it usually did. They ate. Their little children took their scraps of potatoes and meat of wild animals, and in their excitement they forgot the orders, and went out eating their food. They went out into the street, and other children saw them, and begged them for food. They gave the food to them. Among them were children of Leopard, who went and showed the meat to their father.

At once Leopard came to the house of Tortoise, and found him and his family feasting.

Leopard said, "Ah, Friend! You have done evil to me! You are eating, and I and my family are dying of hunger!"

Tortoise replied, "Yes, not today, but tomorrow you shall eat."

So Leopard returned to his house.

Then the day darkened, and they all went to lie down to sleep.

The next day broke. Early in the morning, Tortoise, out in the street, announced, "From my house to Leopard's, there will be no strolling into the forest today! Today, only food!"

Tortoise then went off by himself to the coconut tree—where he had secretly carried the drum during the night. He arrived at the foot of the tree, and desired to test it to see if its power had been lost by its use in the town. So he gave the usual orders, and they were obeyed as usual.

Tortoise then went off with the drum, carrying it openly on his shoulder. He went into the town, and directly to the house of Leopard. He said to him, "Call all your people! Let them come!"

They all came into the house, along with the people of Tortoise. And Tortoise gave the usual commands. At once, Drum provided an abundance of food, and a table for it. They all ate, and were satisfied. Then Drum took the table back to itself.

Drum remained in Leopard's house for about two weeks. It ended its supply of food, because it was displeased at the rough way Leopard treated it—and there was no more food.

Leopard went to Tortoise and told him, "Drum has no more food. Go, and get another."

Tortoise was provoked at the abuse of his drum, but he took it and hung it up in his house.

At this time, the king's watchmen heard of the supply of food at Leopard's house, and they asked him about it.

He denied having any.

They asked him, "Where then did you get this food that we saw your children eating?"

He said, "From Tortoise's children."

The officers went at once to King Maseni, and reported, "We saw a person who has food."

The king asked, "Who is he?"

They replied, "Tortoise."

The king ordered, "Go and summon Tortoise."

They went to Tortoise: "The king summons you."

Tortoise asked, "What have I done to the king? All the time the king and I have been living in this country, he has not summoned me once."

Nevertheless, he obeyed, and journeyed to the king's house.

The king said to him, "You are keeping food while all the people are dying of hunger? Bring those foods here!"

Tortoise replied, "Please excuse me! I will not come today with them. But tomorrow, you must call all of the people to come here."

The next morning, the king had his bell rung, and an order was given: "All people, old and young, come to eat!"

The entire community assembled at the king's house. Tortoise also came from his town, carrying his drum in his hand. The distant members of the kingdom, not having heard what that drum had been doing, twitted him, "Is it for a dance?"

Tortoise entered the king's house, and stood the drum up. With his palm, he struck it, ve! saying, "Let every kind of food appear!"

And food appeared. The town was like a table, covered with every variety of food. The entire community ate, and were satisfied, and then they dispersed.

Tortoise took the drum and journeyed back to his town. He spoke to his hungry family, "Come!"

They came. They struck the drum. But it was motionless, nothing came from it.

They struck it again. Silence!

It was indignant at having been used by hands other than those of Tortoise.

So they sat down hungry.

The next day, Tortoise went hurriedly off to the coconut tree. He climbed the tree, gathered two nuts, threw one into the river, then dropped into the stream himself and followed the nut as he had done before. As before, he came to that landing place, and to the woman. And he told her about the failure of the drum.

She told him that she knew about it, and directed him to go and take another.

He went to that house, and to those people.

And, as before, they asked him, "Tortoise, where are you going?"

He replied, "You know that I have come to take my coconut."

But they said, "No, leave the nut, and take a drum."

And, as before, they advised him to take a silent one.

So he went to the house of drums.

The drums called to him, "Take me! Take me!"

Then Tortoise thought to himself, "Yes, I'll take one of those drums that talk! Perhaps they'll have even better things than the other!"

So he took one of the drums, and came out of the house. He told those people, "I have taken one. And now I must leave."

He started from the landing place, went on up the river, to the foot of the coconut tree. He tied the drum to the tree with a cord as before, set it up, and gave it a slap, ve! And a table stood there!

He said, "Ngama! Do as you usually do!"

Instantly, there were thrown down on the table—mbwa! whips instead of food!

Tortoise, surprised, said, "As usual!"

The drum picked up one of the whips and beat Tortoise, ve! He cried out in pain, and said to the drum, "But now do what you usually do. Take these things away!" And Drum took the table and whips to itself. Tortoise regretfully said to himself, "Those people told me not to take a drum that talked, but my heart deceived me."

But a plan occurred to him, whereby he might obtain revenge on Leopard and the king for the trouble he had been put to.

He took the drum and went to his own town. At once he went to the house of Leopard. He said, "Tomorrow, come with your people and mine to the town of King Maseni."

Leopard rejoiced, and thought, "This is the drum of food!"

Then Tortoise journeyed to the king's town, and said, "I have found food, according to your order. Call the people together tomorrow."

In the morning, the king's bell was rung, and his people, accompanied by those of Tortoise and Leopard, came to the king's house. Tortoise privately spoke to his own people, "No one of you should follow me into the king's house. Remain outside by the window."

Tortoise said to the king, "The food that we shall receive today must be eaten only inside your house."

So the king's people, with those of Leopard, entered the house. And Tortoise said, "We shall eat this food only if all doors and windows are fastened." So they were fastened, excepting one that Tortoise kept open near where he stood.

Then the drum was sounded, and Tortoise commanded it, "Do as you usually do!"

And the tables appeared.

But instead of food, there were whips.

The people wondered, "Ah! What do these mean? Where do they come from?"

Tortoise stationed himself by the open window, and commanded the drum, "As usual!"

Instantly, the whips flew about the room, lashing everyone, even the king, and especially Leopard. The thrashing was great, and Leopard and his people were crying in pain. Their bodies were injured, covered with cuts.

But Tortoise had promptly jumped out of the window. And, standing outside, he ordered, "Ngama! Do as you usually go!" And the whips and tables returned to the drum, and the whipping ceased.

But Tortoise knew that the angry crowd would try to seize him and kill him. So he took advantage of the confusion in the house, and he and his people fled to the river, then scattered, hiding among the logs and roots in the stream.

As Tortoise was disappearing, Leopard shouted after him, "You and I shall not see each other again! If we do, it will be you who will be killed!"

Commentary

There is a pattern of the drum: a drum of food, a drum of whips, with various interdictions, with the breaking and resumption of the pattern. Greed is a major theme here, and the trickster, though himself greedy, attacks greed in the king and leopard, two powerful figures.

The conflict is a famine. The king decrees that anyone with food must share it with all. Many die. There is an air of hopelessness. The main pattern has to do with the drums. Following a woman's interdiction, he does not take a drum that says, "Take me!" but takes the silent drum. The pattern is built on the motif of the magical drum that provides for Tortoise and his family. This pattern is broken by his eldest son, then is reinstituted when Tortoise again gets the drum. The pattern is again broken when Leopard is so rough in his treatment of the drum that it refuses to give any more food. The pattern is again resumed, and, with the help of the drum, the entire community is fed. But the pattern is broken when the drum, because it was used by hands other than those of Tortoise, refuses to give any more food. So he returns to the place where he got the drum, and this time he consciously violates the interdiction, and takes a drum that speaks.

A second pattern occurs when, instead of food, the drum provides whips, and the drum beats Tortoise. Now he has a plan to avenge himself on Leopard and the king. Typical of the trickster, he elaborately sets things up, so that the pattern can be utilized at its most effective: whips appear, lashing everyone, including the king, especially Leopard.

There is an etiological ending: Tortoise and his people flee to stream, "hiding among the logs and roots in the stream." And Tortoise and Leopard never see each other again. Etiological endings in profane trickster tales suggest that the profane tricksters dance gingerly on the border between the age of creation and the contemporary age; the tricksters are liminal, after all.

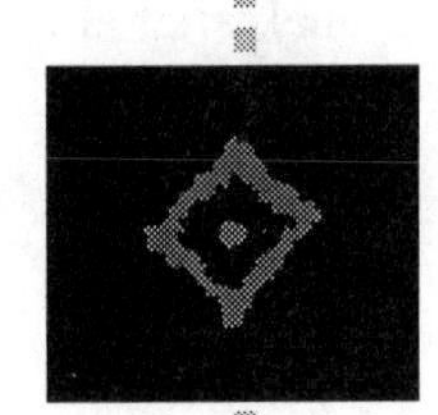

Limba stories are most frequently told in the evenings, after the sun has set. . . . The most popular time is at full moon when people go to bed late, but at other times too stories are told either under the stars, or, since people like to see as well as hear the narrator, by the light of a paraffin lamp or blazing fire. . . . [O]ne child may begin to tease a friend by asking him a riddle. . . . This may be taken up by one of the older people, and then stories proper begin to be told, often starting with the shorter and simpler ones, then gradually moving on to the long elaborate ones, which may have songs and chorus led by the teller and echoed by his listeners. . . . When one story has finished and the teller has formally brought his narration to a close, another man often comes forward to follow up the last tale with one of his own. . . . Once the session has really got going, there is even some competition in the telling and people may have to vie with each other for a hearing.

Ruth Finnegan, *Limba Stories and Story-telling* (Oxford: Clarendon Press, 1967), pp. 64–65.

Gogo

The Grasshopper and the Fiddle

The Gogo live in northeastern Tanzania.

A hare and a hyena became friends. When they had done so, they agreed to go together to a certain place to find wives. When they arrived at that place, they said, "Let us remain here until we find wives." So they began their courtship of two sisters.

The hare had food with him, but the hyena had none.

The hare tightened the string of his fiddle, then tied a grasshopper to one of the strings. He said to the hyena, "We shall see who is not able to bear hunger. I shall keep playing my fiddle."

As night drew on, food was brought to them, but they refused it, and it was taken back.

After a time, the hare started to eat the food that he had brought, but the hyena did not see him eating. They chatted with their sweethearts until they got tired, and the young women retired to their bedroom. The guests spread out their sleeping skins, and lay down to rest.

The hare resumed fiddling, and the hyena said to himself that when his companion got tired of playing his fiddle, when the hare and all the house were asleep, he would steal a goat from the courtyard. But it was not the hare playing the fiddle, it was the grasshopper. The hare was fast asleep. The hyena was deceived by this, and he dozed and woke, dozed and woke until the dawn.

At morning light, the hare took the grasshopper from the string of his fiddle until the following night, when he tied it on again.

From H. Cole, "Notes on the Wagogo of German East Africa," *Journal of the Royal Anthropological Institute* 32 (1902): 331–332.

Night after night, the hare kept his fiddle going, and so deceived his companion who thought that it was the hare who kept playing the instrument. And the hare kept secretly eating the food that he had brought with him.

Finally, the hyena, having no food, had to give in, and he called out to the hare, "Why don't you sleep?"

When he received no reply, the hyena went to the herd of his projected father-in-law, and killed a fine goat and ate it, all except the stomach which he put under a mortar turned upside down.

When it was day, the hyena sat on the mortar. The people of the house took their herd out to graze, and found that a goat was missing. They asked those who had herded them the previous day how it was that a goat was missing. The herdsmen replied that they had brought all the herd home safely the evening before, and that when they had counted the goats in the pen, they were all there.

"Where can that goat have gone?" they asked in astonishment.

Then the young woman's brothers asked the hyena, "Friend, how is it that you are so full? When did you get food?"

The hyena replied, "What do you think I have eaten? Where should I get food?"

Then the herdsmen saw traces of blood, and they went to tell their parents, who sent their two daughters, the sweethearts of the hare and hyena, to fetch the mortar. When the young women turned the mouth of the mortar upwards, they saw the stomach, and asked where it had come from. Suspecting that it was the work of the hyena, they charged him with having killed the goat. He was able to say nothing in reply.

The hyena and the hare were made prisoners.

The hare told them that his father cultivated bananas, so they tied him with strings obtained from the fibre of a banana tree.

The hyena told them that his father was a rich man, so they tied him with thongs of cow leather.

When the banana fibre got dry, the hare broke loose and made his escape. But his companion was put into a big cooking pot full of water, and the pot was put over a fire. But the people of the house, fearing that he would escape from the pot, took him out and killed him at once.

Commentary

In a typical profane trickster tale, the motif is a trick, in this case, Hare has a grasshopper attached to his fiddle. The pattern is built on that motif: Hare tricks the dupe, Hyena, into thinking that he is awake so that Hyena cannot go and steal food.

Hyena finally breaks the pattern, which leads to the capture of both trickster and dupe. But the trickster, Hare, has a final trick to play: he says that his father cultivated bananas, so they tie him with fibre of a banana tree. The more stupid dupe, Hyena, says that his father was a rich man, so his captors tie him with thongs of cow leather. Hare escapes, Hyena is killed.

[W]hen all you do is simply read a Shona folk-tale . . . you miss the firelight reflected in eager eyes, the gleam of teeth revealed by smiling lips, the hush of enjoyment of a well-loved tale and the heart-warming atmosphere of a family enjoying together a spell of restful fun at the end of a day's work.

But even if it is only by reading that you can enjoy the fable, your imagination can add to your enjoyment by creating for you the fire-side setting in which it is told . . . beneath a star-studded . . . sky. It would be a rare imagination, however, that could supply that most pleasing element of the [tale], the little solo and chorus, which are part of nearly every story. . . .

M. Hannan, "Ngano Dzokupunza. Shona Fireside Songs," *NADA, Native Affairs Department Annual,* No. 31 (1954), p. 30.

Yao

The Fox and the Hyena

The Yao live in Malawi, Mozambique, and Tanzania

The hyena made a friendship, and wanted to visit his friend.

Two days later, he set out, saying, "Let an attendant go with me."

They said, "Let him go with the mbendu."

They were going along the road and the hyena said, "If we meet women washing grains of millet, you will ask for water, and I shall ask for millet."

As they went on they met women washing millet, and the mbendu said, "Give me water." And the hyena said, "Give me millet."

The women took millet in a plate to give to the hyena, and they gave the mbendu water in a cup.

The mbendu said, "Come, let us wash the millet that it may become soft," but the hyena refused, saying, "Why did you not beg your own millet for yourself?"

And he chewed it alone without given any to his attendant.

Farther on he told him, "If we meet women cutting sugar cane, you will beg for some leaves, and I'll beg for cane. We shall tie up the cane."

They went on and met women cutting sugar cane.

The hyena said, "Give me some cane."

The mbendu said, "Give me some leaves."

The women cut four canes and gave them to the hyena, and they took leaves and gave them to the mbendu.

The mbendu said, "Let us tie the cane."

The hyena was fierce and said, "For whom?"

From Duff Macdonald, *Africana* (London: Simpkin Marshall, 1882), pp. 327–332.

And he did not give any cane to the mbendu.

They went on and came to another place and found a lake.

The hyena said, "The village we are going to is there. If we have porridge cooked for us and tie it up in a leaf [porridge was often carried wrapped in leaves], then if you hear at the nearby pool the sound, lino-lino-lino-lino-lino, you must run away, throwing down the leaf containing the porridge."

Farther on the hyena said, "This is medicine. If we get porridge, you will come back here to dig it up."

He went on and arrived at the village of his friend, who said, "My friend has come." He killed and cooked fowls; he made porridge. He said, "Let us give the food to the strangers." The porridge was put down.

The hyena said, "Go back and dig that medicine that I showed you. Bring it so that we may eat it with the porridge."

The mbendu went off running. Then the hyena cut leaves, putting them down everywhere. And he ate up all the porridge.

When the mbendu returned, the hyena said, "There came a great party of people. Look here at the leaves [the leaves were used as plates]—some of the people sat here, others sat here, others sat here. Therefore, no porridge remains for you."

Then the hyena said, "Let us go home tomorrow."

The mbendu said, "Yes, let us go." The mbendu was starving.

Next day porridge was cooked for them, and the hyena said, "Tie it all up, tie it in leaves." The mbendu tied up the porridge and carried the leaves.

Along the way, the hyena said, "I'm going to go this way. Let us meet farther on."

The mbendu kept going alone, on the path, while the hyena went to the pool and dived in, putting out his mouth, saying, "Lino-lino-lino-lino-lino."

The mbendu was afraid. He threw the leaves with the porridge into the lake.

The hyena took the leaves out and went to devour the porridge.

Then, when he came farther on, he met the mbendu who was now carrying nothing.

The hyena said, "You threw away that leaf? You did the right thing, you were wise, that wild beast would have bitten you."

When they reached their home, the villagers said, "You are thin, Mbendu, you are thin!"

He said, "Hunger!"

They stayed at home for five days.

The hyena said, "I will go to my friend's home again. Whom shall I go with today?"

The mbendu refused.

So the hyena said, "Come, Fox, let us go together."

The fox said, "Yes, chief, let us go."

So they went together.

When they came to the road, the hyena gave instructions: "Now, Fox, if we meet women, you will beg for water and I shall beg for grain."

They came to the women.

The hyena said to them, "Give me grain."

The fox said, "Give me grain and some water also."

The hyena took the grain, it was given to him on a plate.

The fox also took grain, it was given to him in his hands. And he was given water also, in a cup.

The hyena said, "Give me that water."

The fox said, "Why did you not beg your own?" And the fox refused to give it to him.

Further on, the hyena said, "Now this pool is dreadful."

The fox asked, "Why is it dreadful?"

The hyena said, "If one is carrying porridge, a wild beast can be dreadful!"

The fox said, "What does this wild beast say when it is roaring?"

The hyena said, "It says lino-lino-lino-lino."

The fox said, "Ah!"

The hyena said, "If you happen to be carrying a leaf with porridge and you hear that roaring, you should throw the leaf down."

The fox said, "Yes, I'll do that."

They went farther on, and the hyena said, "Here is medicine. If porridge is cooked for us at the village, you will come back here to dig it."

The fox secretly left his arrow there, then, when they had walked farther on, he said, "Master, I have forgotten my arrow."

The hyena said, "Where did you leave it?"

He said, "Back where you showed me the medicine."

The hyena said, "Go and get it."

The fox ran back and came to the medicine, to the place where he had left his arrow. He quickly dug up the medicine, put it in his bag, and returned.

The hyena said, "Did you find your arrow?"

The fox said, "Yes, I have it."

The hyena said, "Well, let us go on then."

They went on and arrived.

The hyena's friend said, "My friend has come. Kill a fowl for him."

They killed a fowl for him, and cooked porridge too, then came with it and set it down.

The hyena then said to the fox, "Go and dig up that medicine."

But the fox took the medicine out of his bag and said, "Master, here is that medicine."

The hyena was very fierce then, and said, "Fox, you are clever at evil!"

The hyena refused his porridge, saying, "You go on eating."

So the fox ate.

The hyena said, "Let us go away tomorrow."

In the evening, a fowl was killed, that they might eat it with their porridge.

The next day, porridge was cooked and the fowl also, and the food and was given to them. The hyena said, "Fox, tie it up."

The fox tied it, and they went along the road.

The hyena said, "You go on ahead of me, I'll go this way. We shall meet further down the road."

Then the hyena went stealthily, moving ahead, and he let himself down into the pool. He dived, then put out his mouth, wide open, and said, "Lino-lino-lino-lino!"

The fox said, "Ah! There's that wild beast Hyena told me about."

The fox sat down, took his knife, and started to cut the bark cords that tied the leaves, and he took a stone. Then he unloosed the porridge, and ate and finished it, eating it up entirely, reserving only a mouthful which he plastered on the stone. He threw the stone into the mouth that he saw in the pool.

And the hyena died.

The fox then ran and cut off his head. He made a little drum and covered it with the hyena's skin. Then he went along the road, and met women digging beans. The fox beat his drum—ti, ti, war.

The women fled, the fox picked up the baskets, and went home.

At the village they said, "Where did you leave the hyena?"

He said, "When I left him, they were brewing beer for him."

The hyena never returned.

Commentary

◈ **The storyteller develops a tables-turned pattern**—The mbendu and the fox are the intended dupes of the trickster hyena. The pattern is established by the mbendu, then repeated by the fox, the results not being the intended results as far as the trickster is concerned. The force of the story is in the alteration of the pattern established by the mbendu. Without that initial establishment of the pattern, the activities of the fox would lose their emotional force.

These women who argue with narrative, as well as performers like Goba, Dubua, and Gbomba, are the intellectuals of Mende society. Their domeisia [oral narratives] are a major source of speculation in a society which thrives on the contest of opposing ideas. They manage to entrance their audiences with song, dance, and explosions of wit, but beneath this surface glitter there is a ceaseless ordering and reordering of images into new narratives which proclaim diverse and often contradictory viewpoints. In the relationship established by the competing arguments of their narratives, a dialectical pattern which occurs over and again in Mende culture may be discerned. These performers thus manage to create in their domeisia a microcosm of the society they entertain.

Donald Cosentino, "Patterns in *Domeisia*," Diss., University of Wisconsin-Madison, 1976, p. 5.

Arabic

Mohammed with the Magic Finger

This is a Libyan tale.

Once there lived a woman who had a son and daughter.

One morning, she said to them, "I have heard of a town where there is no such thing as death. Let us go and dwell there."

So she broke up her house, and went away with her son and daughter.

When she reached the city, the first thing she did was to look about to see if there was any churchyard. When she found none, she exclaimed, "This is a delightful spot. We shall stay here for ever."

Her son grew to be a man, and he took for a wife a young woman who had been born in the town. But after a time, he grew restless, and went away on his travels, leaving his mother, his wife, and his sister behind him.

He had not been gone many weeks when, one evening, his mother said, "I am not well. My head aches dreadfully."

"What did you say?" inquired her daughter-in-law.

"My head feels ready to split," replied the old woman.

The daughter-in-law asked no more questions, but left the house and went in haste to some butchers in the next street.

"I have a woman to sell," she said. "What will you give me for her?"

The butchers answered that they must see the woman first, and they all went together to the old woman.

From Hans von Stumme, *Märchen und Gedichte aus der Stadt Tripolis in Nord-Afrika* (Leipzig: Hinrichs, 1896). Translation from Arabic, in Andrew Lang, ed., *The Grey Fairy Book* (London: Longmans, Green, 1900), pp. 178–196.

The butchers took the woman and told her that they must kill her.

"But why?" she asked.

"Because," they said, "it is our custom that when persons are ill and complain of their heads, they should be killed at once. It is much better than leaving them to die a natural death."

"Very well," the woman said. "But leave, I pray you, my lungs and my liver untouched, until my son comes back. Then give both to him."

The men took them out at once, and gave them to the daughter-in-law, saying, "Put away these things until your husband returns."

The daughter-in-law took them, and hid them in a secret place.

When the old woman's daughter, who had been in the forest, heard that her mother had been killed while she was out, she was filled with fright, and ran away as fast as she could. At last, she reached a lonely spot far from the town, where she thought she was safe, and she sat down on a stone and wept bitterly. As she was sitting, sobbing, a man passed by.

"What is the matter, young woman? Answer me. I'll be your friend."

"Oh, sir, they have killed my mother. My brother is far away, and I have nobody."

"Will you come with me?" asked the man.

"Thankfully," she said.

And he led her down, down, under the earth, until they reached a great city. Then he married her, and in the course of time she had a son. The baby was known throughout the city as Mohammed with the Magic Finger, because, whenever he stuck out his little finger, he was able to see anything that was happening for as far as two days' distance.

After a time, as the boy was growing bigger, his uncle returned from his long journey, and he went straight to his wife.

"Where are my mother and sister?" he asked.

His wife answered, "Have something to eat first, and then I will tell you."

But he said, "How can I eat until I know what has become of them?"

Then she fetched, from the upper chamber, a box full of money. She put it before him, saying, "That is the price of your mother. She sold well."

"What do you mean?" he asked.

"Your mother complained one day that her head was aching, so I brought in two butchers and they agreed to take her. However, I have got her lungs and liver hidden, until you came back, in a safe place."

"And my sister?"

"While the people were chopping up your mother, she ran away, and I heard no more of her."

"Give me my mother's liver and lungs," said the young man. She gave them to him. He put them in his pocket and went away, saying, "I can stay no longer in this horrible town. I am going to seek my sister."

One day, the little boy stretched out his finger, and said to his mother, "My uncle is coming!"

"Where is he?" his mother asked.

"He is still two days' journey off, looking for us. But he will soon be here."

In two days, as the boy had foretold, the uncle had found the hole in the earth, and arrived at the gate of the city. All his money was spent, and, not knowing where his sister lived, he began to beg of all the people he saw.

"Here comes my uncle," called out the little boy.

"Where?" asked his mother.

"Here, at the house door," and the woman ran out and embraced him, and wept over him.

When they could both speak, he said, "My sister, were you there when they killed my mother?"

"I was absent when they killed her," she said, "and, as I could do nothing, I ran away. But you, my brother, how did you get here?"

"By chance," he said, "after I had wandered far. But I did not know that I would find you!"

"My little boy told me you were coming," she explained, "when you were yet two days distant. He alone of all men has that great gift."

But she did not tell him that her husband could change himself into a serpent, a dog, or a monster, whenever he pleased. He was a very rich man; he possessed large herds of camels, goats, sheep, cattle, horses, and asses, all the best of their kind.

The next morning, the sister said, "Dear brother, go and watch our sheep. When you are thirsty, drink their milk."

"Very well," he said, and he went.

Soon after, she said, "Dear brother, go and watch our goats."

"But why? I like tending sheep better."

"It is much nicer to be a goatherd," she said.

So he took the goats out.

While he was gone, she said to her husband, "You must kill my brother, I cannot have him living here with me."

"But why should I do that? He has done me no harm."

"I want you to kill him," she said. "If you don't, I shall leave."

"All right," he said, "tomorrow, I shall change myself into a serpent, and hide myself in the date barrel. When he comes to fetch dates, I shall sting him in the hand."

"That will do very well," she said.

When the sun was up the next day, she called to her brother, "Go and mind the goats."

"Yes," he said.

But the little boy said, "Uncle, I want to go with you."

"Delighted," said the uncle, and they set out together.

After they had got out of sight of the house, the boy said to him, "Dear uncle, my father is going to kill you. He has changed himself into a serpent, and has hidden himself in the date barrel. My mother has told him to do it."

"And what am I to do?" asked the uncle.

"I will tell you. When we bring the goats back to the house, and my mother says to you, 'I am sure you must be hungry, get a few dates out of the cask,' just say to me, 'I am not feeling very well, Mohammed, you go and get them for me.'"

When they reached the house, the sister came out to meet them. She said, "Dear brother, you must certainly be hungry. Go and get a few dates."

But he said, "I am not feeling very well. Mohammed, you go and get them for me."

"Of course I will," said the little boy, and he ran at once to the cask.

"No! No!" his mother called after him. "Come here at once! Let your uncle fetch them himself!"

But the boy would not listen, and, crying out to her, "I would rather get them!" thrust his hand into the date cask.

Instead of the fruit, his hand struck against something cold and slimy, and he whispered softly, "Keep still, it is I, your son!"

Then he picked up the dates, and went away to his uncle.

"Here they are, dear uncle. Eat as many as you want."

And his uncle ate them.

When he saw that the uncle did not mean to come near the cask, the serpent crawled out and regained his proper shape.

"I am thankful I did not kill him," he said to his wife. "After all, he is my brother-in-law, and it would have been a great sin."

"Either you kill him or I will leave you!" she said.

"Well," the man said, "tomorrow I shall do it."

The woman let that night go by without doing anything further, but at daybreak she said to her brother, "Get up, brother. It is time to take the goats to pasture."

"All right," he said.

"I shall come with you, uncle," called the little boy.

"Yes, come along," he said.

But the mother ran up, and said, "The child must not go out in this cold, or he will become ill."

The boy said, "Nonsense! I am going, it is no use your talking! I am going! I am! I am!"

"Then go!" she said.

They started, driving the goats in front of them.

When they reached the pasture, the boy said to his uncle, "Dear uncle, this night my father means to kill you. While we are away, he will change into a serpent, creep into your room and hide in the straw. When we get home, my mother will say to you, 'Take that straw and give it to the sheep.' If you do that, he will bite you."

"Then what am I to do?" asked the man.

"Do not be afraid, dear uncle! I shall kill my father myself."

"All right," said the uncle.

As they drove the goats towards the house, the sister cried, "Be quick, dear brother! Go and get me some straw for the sheep!"

"Let me go!" said the boy.

"You are not big enough. Your uncle will get it," she said.

"We will both get it," said the boy. "Come, uncle, let us go and fetch that straw!"

"All right," said the uncle, and they went to the door of the room.

"It seems very dark," said the boy. "I must go and get a light." When he came back with a light, he set fire to the straw, and the serpent was burnt.

Then the mother broke into sobs and tears. "You wretched boy!" she said. "What have you done? Your father was in that straw, and you have killed him!"

"How was I to know that my father was lying in that straw, instead of in the kitchen?" asked the boy.

But his mother only wept the more, and sobbed, "From this day, you have no father. You must do without him as best you can!"

"Why did you marry a serpent?" asked the boy. "I thought he was a man. How did he learn those odd tricks?"

As the sun rose, she woke her brother, and said, "Go, and take the goats to pasture!"

"I shall come too!" said the little boy.

"Go then!" said his mother.

And they went together.

On the way, the boy said, "Dear uncle, tonight my mother means to kill both of us, by poisoning us with the bones of the serpent, which she will grind to powder and sprinkle in our food."

"And what are we to do?" asked the uncle.

"I shall kill her, dear uncle. I do not want a father or a mother like that!"

When they came home in the evening, they saw the woman preparing supper, and secretly scattering the powdered bones of the serpent on one side of the dish. On the other, where she herself meant to eat, there was no poison.

The boy whispered to his uncle, "Dear uncle, be sure that you eat from the same side of the dish as I do."

"All right," said the uncle.

So they all three sat down at the table, but before they helped themselves to the food, the boy said, "I am thirsty, Mother. Will you get me some milk?"

"Very well," she said, "but you had better begin your supper."

When she came back with the milk, they were both busily eating.

"Sit down and have something, too," said the boy.

She sat down and helped herself from the dish, but at the very first moment she sank dead on the ground.

"She has got what she meant for us," said the boy, "and now we shall sell all the sheep and cattle."

The sheep and cattle were sold, and the uncle and nephew took the money and went to see the world.

For ten days, they traveled through the desert, and they came to a place where the road forked.

"Uncle!" said the boy.

"What is it?" he said.

"You see these two roads? You must take one, and I the other. The time has come when we must part."

The uncle cried, "No, no, my boy! We shall keep together always!"

"That cannot be," said the boy. "Tell me which way you will go."

"I shall go to the west," said the uncle.

"One word before I leave you," said the boy. "Beware of any man who has red hair and blue eyes. Take no service under him."

"All right," said the uncle, and they parted.

For three days, the man wandered on without any food, until he was very hungry. Then, when he was almost fainting, a stranger met him.

The stranger said, "Will you work for me?"

"By contract?" asked the man.

"Yes, by contract," said the stranger, "and whichever of us breaks it shall have a strip of skin taken from his body."

"All right," the man said. "What must I do?"

"Every day you must take the sheep out to pasture, and carry my old mother on your shoulders, taking great care that her feet shall never touch the ground. Besides that, you must catch, every evening, seven singing birds for my seven sons."

"That is easily done," said the man.

They went back together, and the stranger said, "Here are your sheep. Now, stoop down, and let my mother climb on your back."

"Very good," said Mohammed's uncle.

The new shepherd did as he was told, and returned in the evening with the old woman on his back, and the seven singing birds in his pocket, which he gave to the seven boys when they came to meet him.

So the days passed, each one exactly like the other.

At last, one night, he began to weep. He said, "What have I done, that I should have to perform such hateful tasks?"

His nephew, Mohammed, saw him from afar, and thought to himself, "My uncle is in trouble. I must go and help him."

The next morning, he went to his master and said, "Dear master, I must go to my uncle. I wish to send him here instead of myself, while I serve under his master. So that you may know that it is he and no other man, I shall give him my staff, and put my mantle on him."

"All right," said the master.

Mohammed set out on his journey, and in two days he arrived at the place where his uncle was standing with the old woman on his back, trying to catch birds as they flew past.

Mohammed touched him on the arm, and said, "Dear uncle, did I not warn you never to take service under any blue-eyed, red-haired man?"

"But what could I do?" asked the uncle. "I was hungry, and he passed, and we signed a contract."

"Give the contract to me," said the boy.

"Here it is," said the uncle, holding it out.

"Now," said Mohammed, "let the old woman get down from your back."

"Oh no, I must not do that!" he said.

But the nephew paid no attention. He went on talking, "Do not worry yourself about the future. I see my way out of it. First, you must take my stick and my mantle, and leave this place. After two days' journey, straight before you, you will come to some tents that are inhabited by shepherds. Go in there, and wait."

"All right," said the uncle.

Then Mohammed with the Magic Finger picked up a stick and struck the old woman with it, saying, "Get down, and look after the sheep! I want to go to sleep."

"Oh, certainly!" she said.

So Mohammed lay down comfortably under a tree and slept until evening. Towards sunset, he woke up and said to the old woman, "Where are the singing birds that you have got to catch?"

"You did not tell me that I have to catch birds!" she said.

"Oh, didn't I?" he said. "Well, it is part of your business, and if you don't do it, I shall just kill you."

"Then I will catch them!" she said hurriedly, and she ran about in the bushes chasing the birds. Thorns pierced her feet, and she shrieked in pain, and exclaimed, "How unlucky I am! And how abominably this man is treating me!" At last, she managed to catch the seven birds, and she brought them to Mohammed, and said, "Here they are."

"Now, we will go back to the house," he said.

When they had gone some way, he turned to her sharply: "Be quick, and drive the sheep home, because I do not know where their fold is."

She drove the sheep before her.

Then the young man spoke: "Look here, old hag! If you say anything to your son about my having struck you, or about my not herding the sheep, I'll kill you!"

"No, I'll say nothing!"

When they got back, the son said to his mother, "That is a good shepherd I've got, isn't he?"

"A splendid shepherd," she said. "Look how fat the sheep are, and how much milk they give!"

"Yes indeed!" said the son, as he rose to get supper for his mother and the shepherd.

When Mohammed's uncle was working here, he had had nothing to eat but the scraps left by the old woman. But the new shepherd was not going to be content with that.

"You will not touch the food until I have had as much as I want," he whispered to the old woman.

"Very good," she said.

When he had had enough, he said, "Now, eat."

But she wept, and said, "That was not written in your contract. You were only to have what I left."

"If you say a word more, I'll kill you!" he said.

The next day, he took the old woman on his back, and drove the sheep in front of him until he was some distance from the house. Then he let her fall, and said, "Quick! Go and mind the sheep."

Then he took a ram, and killed it. He lit a fire and broiled some of its flesh. He called to the old woman, "Come and eat with me!"

She came to him. But instead of letting her eat, he took a large lump of meat and rammed it down her throat with his crook, so that she died.

When he saw that she was dead, he said, "That is what you get for tormenting my uncle."

He left her lying where she was, while he went after the singing birds. It took him a long time to catch them, but at length he had all seven hidden in the pockets of his tunic. Then he threw the old woman's body into some bushes, and drove the sheep in front of him, back to their fold.

When he drew near the house, the seven boys came out to meet him. He gave a bird to each.

"Why are you weeping?" the boys asked as they took their birds.

"Because your grandmother is dead!"

They ran and told their father.

The man came up to Mohammed, and said, "What was the matter? How did she die?"

Mohammed said, "I was tending the sheep when she said to me, 'Kill that ram for me. I am hungry!' So I killed it and gave her the meat. But she had no teeth, and it choked her."

"But why did you kill the ram, instead of one of the sheep?" asked the man.

"What was I do to?" said Mohammed. "I had to obey orders!"

"Well, I must see to her burial," said the man.

The next morning, Mohammed drove out the sheep as usual, thinking to himself, "I am thankful that I've got rid of the old woman. Now for the boys!"

All day long, he looked after the sheep, and towards evening he began to dig some little holes in the ground, out of which he took six scorpions. These he put in his pockets, together with one bird that he caught. Then he drove his flock home.

When he approached the house, the boys came out to meet him as before, saying, "Give me my bird!"

He put a scorpion into the hand of each boy: it stung the boy and he died. To the youngest boy, he gave only a bird.

As soon as he saw the boys lying dead on the ground, Mohammed lifted up his voice and cried loudly, "Help, help! The children are dead!"

The people came running, and said, "What has happened? How did they die?"

Mohammed said, "It was your own fault! The boys had been accustomed to birds. In this bitter cold, their fingers grew stiff and could hold nothing, so that the birds flew away, and their spirits with them. Only the youngest, who managed to keep a tight hold on his bird, is still alive."

The father groaned, and said, "I have borne enough! Bring no more birds, lest I lose the youngest as well!"

"All right," said Mohammed.

As he was driving the sheep out to grass, he said to his master, "Out there is a splendid pasture. I shall keep the sheep there for two or, perhaps, three days, so do not be surprised at our absence."

"Very good," said the man.

Mohammed started. For two days, he drove the sheep on and on, until he reached his uncle.

He said to him, "Dear uncle, take these sheep and look after them. I have killed the old woman and the boys, and the flock I have brought to you."

Mohammed then returned to his master. On the way, he took a stone and beat his own head with it until it bled. He bound his hands tightly, and began to scream.

The master came running, and asked, "What is the matter?"

Mohammed answered, "While the sheep were grazing, robbers came and drove them away. Because I tried to prevent them, they struck me on the head and bound my hands. See how bloody I am!"

"What shall we do?" asked the master. "Are the animals far away?"

"So far that you are not likely to see them again," said Mohammed. "This is the fourth day since the robbers came down. How could you overtake them?"

"Then go and herd the cows!" said the man.

"All right," said Mohammed.

For two days, he traveled. On the third day, he drove the cows to his uncle, first cutting off their tails. He left one cow behind.

"Take these cows, dear uncle," he said. "I am going to teach that man a lesson."

"I suppose you know your own business best," said the uncle. "Certainly, he almost worried me to death."

Mohammed returned to his master, carrying the cows' tails tied up in a bundle on his back. When he came to the sea-shore, he stuck all the tails in the sand, and went and buried the lone cow, whose tail he had not cut off. He buried the cow up to her neck, leaving her tail protruding. After he had got everything ready, he began to shriek and scream as before, until his master and all the servants came running to see what was the matter.

"What has happened?" they cried.

"The sea has swallowed up the cows!" said Mohammed. "Nothing remains but their tails. But if you are quick and pull hard, you may perhaps get them out again!"

Instantly, the master ordered each man to take hold of a tail, but at the first pull they nearly tumbled backwards, and the tails were left in their hands.

"Stop!" cried Mohammed. "You are doing it all wrong! You have pulled off their tails, and the cows have sunk to the bottom of the sea."

"See if you can do it any better," they said.

Mohammed ran to the cow that he had buried in the rough grass. He took hold of her tail, and dragged the animal out at once.

"There! That's the way to do it," he said. "I told you that you knew nothing about it!"

The men slunk away, much ashamed of themselves.

The master came up to Mohammed. "Go!" he said. "There is nothing more for you to do. You have killed my mother, you have slain my children, you have stolen my sheep, you have drowned my cows. I have no work to give you."

"First, give me the strip of skin that belongs to me of right, because you have broken your contract."

"That, a judge shall decide," said the master. "We shall go before him."

"Yes, we shall," said Mohammed.

They went before a judge.

"What is your case?" asked the judge of the master.

"My lord," said the man, bowing low, "my shepherd here has robbed me of everything. He has killed my children and my old mother, he has stolen my sheep, he has drowned my cows in the sea."

The shepherd answered, "He must pay me what he owes me, then I will go."

"Yes, that is the law," said the judge.

"Very well," said the master. "Let him reckon up how long he has been in my service."

"That won't do," said Mohammed. "I want my strip of skin, as we agreed in the contract."

Seeing that there was no help for it, the master cut off a bit of skin and gave it to Mohammed, who went off at once to his uncle.

"Now we are rich, dear uncle," he said. "We shall sell our cows and sheep, and go to a new country. This one is no longer the place for us."

The sheep were soon sold, and the two comrades started on their travels.

That night, they reached some bedouin tents, where they had supper with the Arabs. Before they lay down to sleep, Mohammed called the owner of the tent aside.

"Your greyhound will eat my strip of leather," he said to the Arab.

"No, do not fear."

"But supposing it does?"

"Well then, I shall give him to you in exchange," said the Arab.

Mohammed waited until everyone was asleep, then he rose softly and, tearing the bit of skin in pieces, threw it down before the greyhound, wildly shrieking as he did so.

"Oh, master, did I not say that your dog would eat my thong?"

"Be quiet, don't make such a noise! You shall have the dog."

Mohammed put a leash around the dog's neck, and led it away.

In the evening, they arrived at the tents of some more bedouin, and asked for shelter.

After supper, Mohammed said to the owner of the tent, "Your ram will kill my greyhound."

"Oh no, it won't."

"Supposing he does?"

"Then you can take the ram in exchange."

So in the night, Mohammed killed the greyhound, and laid its body across the horns of the ram. Then he shrieked and yelled, until he roused the Arab, who said, "Take the ram and go away."

Mohammed did not need to be told twice, and at sunset he reached another bedouin encampment.

He was received kindly, as usual, and after supper he said to his host, "Your daughter will kill my ram."

"Be silent. She will do nothing of the sort. My daughter does not need to steal meat, she has some every day."

"Very well, I shall go to sleep. But if anything happens to my ram, I shall call out."

"If my daughter touches anything belonging to my guest, I shall kill her," said the Arab. And he went to his bed.

When everybody was asleep, Mohammed got up, killed the ram and took out its liver, which he broiled on the fire. He placed a piece of it in the young woman's hands, and laid some more on her night-dress. She was sleeping, so knew nothing about it. After this, he began to cry out loudly.

"What is the matter? Be silent at once!" called the Arab.

"How can I be silent when my ram, which I loved like a child, has been slain by your daughter?"

"But my daughter is asleep," said the Arab.

"Go and see if she has not some of the flesh of the ram about her."

"If she has, you may take her in exchange for the ram."

As they found the flesh exactly as Mohammed had foretold, the Arab gave his daughter a beating, then told her to get out of his sight, for she was now the property of this stranger.

They wandered in the desert until, at nightfall, they came to a bedouin encampment, where they were hospitably bidden to enter.

Before lying down to sleep, Mohammed said to the owner of the tent, "Your mare will kill my wife."

"It most certainly will not."

"If it does?"

"Then you shall take the mare in exchange."

When everyone was asleep, Mohammed said softly to his wife, "Woman, I have a clever plan. I am going to bring in the mare and put it at your feet. I shall cut you, just a few flesh wounds, so that you will be covered with blood, and everyone will think that you are dead. But remember that you must not make a sound, or we shall both be lost."

This was done. Mohammed wept and wailed louder than ever.

The Arab hurried to the spot, and cried, "Cease making that terrible noise! Take the mare and go. But carry off the dead woman with you. She can lie quite easily across the mare's back."

Then Mohammed and his uncle picked up the young woman, and placed her on the mare's back. Then they led the mare away, being very careful to walk one on each side, so that the young woman might not slip down and hurt herself. After the Arab tents could be seen no longer, the young woman sat up on the saddle and looked about her. As they were all hungry, they tied up the mare, and took out some dates to eat.

When they had finished, Mohammed said to his uncle, "Dear uncle, the young woman shall be your wife. I give her to you. But the money we got for the sheep and cows, we shall divide between us. You shall have two-thirds, and I shall have one. You will have a wife, but I never mean to marry. Now, go in peace, for never again will you see me. The bond of bread and salt is at an end between us."

They wept, and fell on each other's necks, and asked forgiveness for any wrongs in the past.

Then they parted, and went their ways.

Commentary

◇ **A Review**—Consider the way storytellers work, how they construct their stories. First, motif and pattern are crucial constituents of the stories in the African oral traditions. Second, the three categories of storytelling—myth, epic, and tale—all have to do with transformation, a movement from one state to another, a betwixt and between period whether cosmological, cultural, or individual. Third, myth occurs during the age of Creation, the second of the universal ages, and tale occurs during the Contemporary Age, the third of the universal ages. Fourth, divine and profane tricksters are ambivalent characters who come represent and to embody the contending forces of those betwixt and between periods. This does not mean that every transformation story will have a trickster in it. But it does mean that every transformation story will have the two forces of creation and destruction in it, and that in some stories those forces are embodied in these tricksters. Finally, the rites of passage are transformations on an individual, or tale, level—that is, we all go through those changes or transitions in our lives. When tales have to do with the puberty ritual, the transformation from childhood into adulthood, the transition is often but not always in three stages: separation, ordeal, and reincorporation. These are some of the significant characteristics of oral stories.

◇ **The Premise**—Dualism is a characteristic of the age of creation. This dualism persists during the contemporary age: All humans are capable of destructive and creative acts. But cultural rituals and ceremonies help us to shed the destructive and shape the creative parts of ourselves. When we move from one state to another, the destructive and creative struggle and energies become evident. These energies are eternally represented in the profane trickster. We are not always tricksters, but we become like the dualistic trickster when we go through changes. The trickster represents the disorientation, the uncertainty, the amorality, the asocial state, the liminality, the boundaries when we move from one state of being to another. In "Mohammed with the Magic Finger," we see how that works. All rite of passage stories do not have tricksters, but inevitably, during the ordeal phase of the ritual, they do have that disorientation, the struggle between right and wrong, chaos and order. The trickster embodies that, and it is an echo back to the age of creation, when this chaos/order struggle was cosmological in scope. It continues microcosmically in us today.

◇ **Argument**—Keep in mind that the images in these oral stories are both fantastic and realistic: Do not attempt to read the stories literally. In this story, the uncle is a realistic character; Mohammed, the trickster, is a fantasy character. The fantasy character comments on and explores and explains the realistic character. We are in the presence of metaphor, of two images that are unlike actually perceived as the same. To put it another way, Mohammed is a mirror into the psyche of the uncle. The fantasy character, in this case, the trickster, Mohammed, becomes the energy of the uncle, as he moves to a new identity. In the case of Mohammed, that energy is positive; we have seen, in "The Story of Chakijana" (story 19), that it can also be negative. This is the language of storytelling, as a fantasy character becomes a means for understanding a realistic character: that fantasy character *becomes* the realistic character, or a part of the realistic character.

◇ **The Trickster**—Mohammed is the son of a demon. He kills his own mother and father, kills an old woman and six of seven children. The trickster, remember, is the spirit of chaos, destruction, but also of order. In this story, Trickster is a part of a human being, a force that is destructive but also creative. The trickster's force is being controlled in this story for socially acceptable ends. The killings must be seen as storytelling devices, and should not be taken literally: By destroying these various characters, Trickster is bringing order to death-dealing societies. A youth is going through his puberty rite of passage, with Trickster Mohammed being the driving force and defining part of this youth. We move from a community of death (the brutal death of the youth's mother) into the fantastic underworld where the real life society is duplicated in fantastic terms. Here is where the youth gets his mirror, a magical trickster, who immediately corrects the imbalances in his world by killing his mother and father. Then the youth confronts his nemesis, the stranger who threatens him with death, and undergoes the ordeal phase of his puberty ritual (remember that there are frequently three stages in the puberty rituals as dramatized in the tales). The youth, with the help of the trickster, his other side, overcomes this death-dealing stranger, and receives livestock, symbolic of the successful completion of the ritual. Now he can be married.

Mohammed is a trickster; this is a profane trickster story. But it is more. Here, we see the transitional trait become a part of the human character, the young uncle who is going through a puberty ritual. The two characters become the same, the trickster representing the energy as the youth moves through puberty, destroying his past (hence, all the patterns of death and destruction) and moving to marriage. At the end, when this transition is complete, the trickster goes his separate way, and the youth-become-a-man is on his own.

The story is in three parts: in part one, the storyteller describes the deaths of the youth's mother, his brother-in-law, and his sister. Death imagery is everywhere to be seen, and the youth is leaving these tainted places and people behind. It is a pattern of death, with a motif of extraordinary deaths. This is the separation phase of the puberty ritual.

Part two details the youth's life with the man with red hair and blue eyes. A pattern of impossible tasks dominates this section: he must carry an old woman on his back, get seven singing birds for the seven sons, and herd the livestock. The motif is one of impossible tasks. This is the ordeal segment of the puberty ritual. Then the trickster, Mohammed, takes over the youth's role: he gets the youth cattle and moves him through the tasks to adulthood.

In part three, the youth's life with the bedouins, the nomadic people, is depicted. The pattern is incremental, a trading-up pattern, from a strip of leather to a greyhound to a ram to a daughter to a mare. In this way, Mohammed gets the youth a wife. This is the reincorporation stage of the puberty ritual.

When it is over, Mohammed moves out of the picture, off the stage, and the youth, now a married young man, is on his own: "Then they parted, and went their ways."

It is a story of death: A woman, her son, and her daughter leave home to go to a place "where there is no such thing as death." This establishes the death theme. But the mother, ill, is killed by butchers at the behest of her daughter-in-law. The daughter, after marriage to a demon, herself becomes a death-dealer, wanting to kill her brother. The demon-husband, a transformer (serpent) and a murderer, follows the instructions of his wife who wants to kill her brother. The death pattern continues: Mohammed kills his mother and father. Later, there is a death threat by the man with red hair and blue eyes. And Mohammed kills members of the family of the man with red hair and blue eyes. Still later, there are various apparent deaths at places of the bedouins.

It is a puberty rite of passage story: A youth is moving to adulthood. He is separated from home. He goes through an ordeal, involving the various attempts to kill him—in the underworld and at the home of the white man. He is reincorporated when he is married and has the wherewithal—cattle—to build a home. The creative part of the trickster can be found here, as Mohammed orchestrates things to bring the youth to manhood.

Two characters merge into one. The youth and Mohammed are the same character. Mohammed is the fantasy part of the youth, the fantastic extension of the young man, meant to mirror graphically what happens as the youth undergoes his puberty ritual. The trickster here is a part of a human, a force that is destructive but also creative. The trickster's force is being controlled, in this tale, for socially acceptable ends. A youth is going through his puberty ritual, with Mohammed the trickster as the driving and defining part of him. But Mohammed remains a dangerous trickster with extraordinary abilities, suggested by his magical finger. He is clearly a killer. It is therefore risky to attempt to see him here as a redeemed character; he should be seen rather as a mirror of the energies that are unleashed within the youth as he moves through a betwixt and between stage, from childhood to adulthood.

The storyteller moves us from a community of death into a fantastic underworld where the realistic central character gets his magical mirror, the trickster. Then he confronts his antagonist, the force standing between him and adulthood. The results of this ordeal stage of his puberty ritual are a wife and cattle, both achieved by the trickster part of him.

Why all the death? The youth is dying to his past, is cutting himself off from his past. His past is therefore characterized as death-dealing; he cannot remain there. To do that is tantamount to death. The youth has moved into the depths of his soul, and the ensuing psychological struggle is revealed in the language of storytelling by his deadly dealings with his sister and her husband, with the white man and his family, with the roving bedouins. In the end, he emerges whole, complete. When the youth's rite is at an end, that which represented the transformation, the energy of the trickster, can go its way.

This is the meaning of the rite as it emerges from the patterns: One must cut oneself off from one's past, die to one's past, purge oneself of evil, wrest life in the form of a wife and cattle from death.

The Hero

A Xhosa storyteller (photos by Harold Scheub)

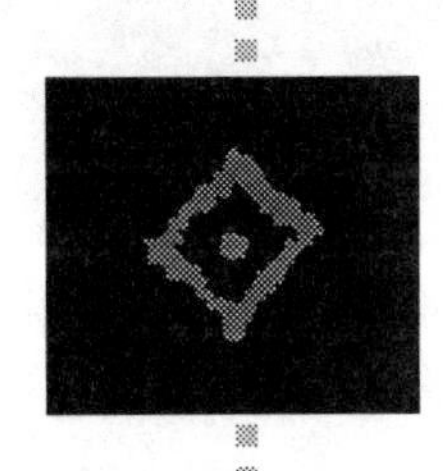

Victor Brombert: At his best the ancient hero had something of the divine in him. God, demigod, godlike, or intimate with the gods, he provided a transcendental link between the contingencies of the finite and the imagined realm of the supernatural. Time and the timeless, man's mortal state and the realm of eternal laws, were brought through him into conflict with each other. Through him also these orders overlapped.

J. R. R. Tolkien: He is a man, and that for him and many is sufficient tragedy. . . . "Life is transitory: light and life together all hasten away."

Notes on the Hero

The hero stands against an ambiguous force, and converts its destructive capability into creative energy. The epic hero contains within himself past ideals and a future vision; because of this ambiguity (the past and future both containing destructive and creative potential), he is able to lead the people from the one (the past) to the other (the future). The hero may die in the process, but not before leading the people to the brink of the new world. In the non-epic tales, the central character also contains past and future elements: the past must die as the character is transformed into the new world. But this is on an individual level; the epic hero works on a social or national level.

◇ **The heroic pattern**—Every hero follows a similar journey that takes him from the familiar to the unfamiliar, on a dangerous passage which he cannot navigate by himself, to a struggle with the forces of the underworld, to a wresting of some wonderful life-giving elixir from a death-dealing force; then there is a return to the familiar, forever changed. In the process, the earth is changed as well.

◇ **The hero**—To move the society to its new dispensation, a god/man is born who will take the society into its new form, made in the image of this god/man. The birth of the hero becomes the metaphor for the birth of the nation. The hero is a messianic figure, with ties to God and with links to humans. He must forsake oneness with the gods, as he learns that he is not a god, that he is a vulnerable human. He has godly connections, but is in the end a human like us. The heroic epic is not so much the story of the nation as the story of the personification of the nation, in the character of the hero. There is in hero stories a yearning, a sense of loss. What is being lost is the old dispensation.

The heroic epic is the grand summation of the society. It contains elements of the society: the way it was, the way it is, the way it shall be. It contains the roots of the hero and the vision, along with the struggle to bring these into a workable relationship. The hero bridges the two, past and present, to create the new world, composed of the past and the present. The activity of the epic, as of all storytelling, has to do with the chaos and order. At the center of the epic are tale and myth. Patterns are the most significant organizing devices in epics, and it is those patterns that prove the worth of the hero: they are the tests, often performed against a background of praises.

◇ **Hero and trickster**—What makes the hero of interest is the fact that trickster energy is at the heart of the heroic epic. The trickster clearly embodies, as we have seen, chaos and order. He is amoral, and therefore chaos and order are not of special significance to him—as they are, of course, to us. The hero also embodies chaos and order, but the difference is that the hero has a vision that funnels and focuses those energies, so that society is redefined in a fairly permanent way. Whatever the vision or outcome, the movement in the central part of the epic is no different from that in the central part of either the divine or profane trickster tale. All—tricksters and hero—are in the process of creating. To that extent, they are all mythic. We have defined the limits of their creative activities, but the fact remains that all are creative. The trickster embodies the essential traits of the hero, everything except vision. And the trickster often moves on the grand scale of the hero.

Tricksters are the timeless energy, the eternally liminal, the ordering and the chaotic. They are the alpha and omega, the yin and the yang, the contradictory, the ambiguous, the unending. They are primordial, and now sublime and now debased, neither the one nor the other, but a combination that emerges in strange, quirky, and unpredictable ways. We see ourselves in the trickster. It is that trickster who is the heart of the epic, the core of the tale, the soul of the creative myth. Whenever there is chaos and order, the trickster is there. And, for a time, the hero is a trickster, the tale character is a trickster, God plays the role of trickster. When considering the hero, we move into a wonderful and bizarre world, a world peopled by characters of undeniable stature and of uncertain humanity, a nether realm of cunning and unrepentant tricksters and gods. The measure of these two seemingly extreme characters has been the tale character, the everyperson of the oral tradition. The hero and trickster seem to stand on either side of the tale character, the one his shameful origins, the other his glimmering vision and promise, the one his negative option, the other his positive option.

But it is not that simple: there are other possibilities. The trickster might be seen as the obverse of the hero, the primordial trickster moving to the sublime order of the hero, in a splendid fairy-tale domestication of the trickster movement. But the most tantalizing option is neither of these. The seemingly antithetical characters are not at all contraries. The hero and trickster are the most durable of storytelling figures—ancient, unchanging, adapting to contemporary realities but ever the same. A seemingly simple brace of characters—we use the term "hero" so glibly—becomes a rather complex insight into humanity. It is the combination of the two that is the significant thing, not the movement from the one to the other, not the two as the extremes of the human condition. It is at the point that hero and trickster meet in the oral tradition—and in the lives of humans, our own lives—that the interest of the hero and trickster stories rests. It is at that point that our cosmological, cultural, and personal histories come to a focus, when creation and the gods, society and its heroes, and our own transformations are experienced as identical. That is where the interest of the hero and trickster stories rests. It is precisely at that point at which past, present, and future are sharply focused by means of storytelling that the emotions of the audience are most fully enlisted. It is at the point of tension between chaos and order that we place our emphases; we are present at a birth and a death, at a death and a birth.

There is a compelling reason that the tale is at the heart of the epic. It is not a mistake that the myth is integral to the epic. These are built one inside the other, because in the end they are not distinguishable. Myth, tale, epic, history: they move into and out of each other. We thought that we knew our heroes—but the trickster element in the hero-trickster combination gives us pause. The hero has always given us cause to wonder, has always had his Achilles heel, his vulnerability. Moses errs, Odysseus stumbles, Sunjata falters. In the movement to quintessence, the hero must navigate treacherous shoals and perilous reefs: in such an adventure is his heroism forged. That shaping, paradoxically, is at the hands of the trickster. To move to morality, one moves to one's origins, to amorality. To move to greatness, one descends to hell. To move to the embodiment of a culture, one rends the culture's foundations. To move to wholeness, to psychological fullness, one is fragmented.

The storytelling performance is therapeutic to the extent that it provides a safe laboratory for this dismantling and re-creation activity. This betwixt and between period, the time of the trickster shuffle, is a season of uncertainty and confusion, of disorientation, of psychological and cultural miasma. Heroic epics are not about heroes, any more than trickster tales are stories about scandalous con-men. Nor, in fact, are the stories about the gods meant to be histories of the heavens. Trickster, hero, God: these characters and their stories are significant only to the extent that they illuminate the lives of you and me, everyperson. Heroic stories are not a category set aside from the common person. God is not a lofty personage with no connection to humanity. Trickster is not a character so low that it is impossible to find an identification with him. The trickster tale, the godly myth, the heroic epic are reworkings of the seemingly inconsequential tale. This explains the presence of the tale in myth, in the trickster story, in the heroic epic. Nor is it simply that the godly myth reveals the god in us, the heroic epic the hero in us, the trickster story the trickster in us. That is so. But it is much more.

◇ **Performance**—It is the rich combination of these, the agony and the sublimity, the chaos and the order, the trickster and the hero, the merging of time, the universalizing of place, the linkage of the present character with the ancient past: This is the key, this explains the presence of these two seemingly antithetical characters in the same tradition. It is performance that makes this comprehensible; through performance, we become a part of the stories. In typical storytelling fashion, we are dismantled and reformed, reshaped, redefined, revitalized. We revel in the trickster story because we have secret knowledge; in the arcane and hidden niches of our experience and our psyche, we know who the trickster is. So we delight in him, we laugh at him, we understand him: He belongs to us. He is us. If we are nervous but accepting about the trickster in us, we are more sanguine about the hero in us. But we know, as the storytellers know, that the hero is not superman, not God, not perfect. In the hidden corners of our souls, we know that the hero is in large part a trickster. The storyteller takes the shards of history and places these into the dazzling emotional roller-coaster ride of the tale, and so he connects us to our past and gives us our dimension, our depths, and our possibilities.

Epic deals with the hero confronting his own limitations. To be sure, fantasy swirls on all sides of him. He is aided and mirrored by fabulous and miraculous agents, donors, and helpers, but that is the point: These exist outside of him. They are not a part of his character; he is not invulnerable. Epic occurs within the framework of fantasy, but its focus is the humanity of the hero. In all oral narrative, fantasy and realism exist side by side. Those are the two basic reservoirs of imagery. In oral narrative, there is a vision, a model, a pattern, and that guides the characters in the narrative; their world can only be based on already established models. They are therefore caught up in a pre-determined pattern, and can only pattern their own affairs and actions on it. It is vulnerability that is at the center of epic, and it is for that reason that epic often seems brooding, fatalistic, tragic. In the epic, the oral narrative character has lost his fabulous qualities; the move is towards humanity.

The stories in this section are tales, not epics. But, while the characters remain everyman and everywoman, they have the possibilities of heroic stature. And that is their essential nature.

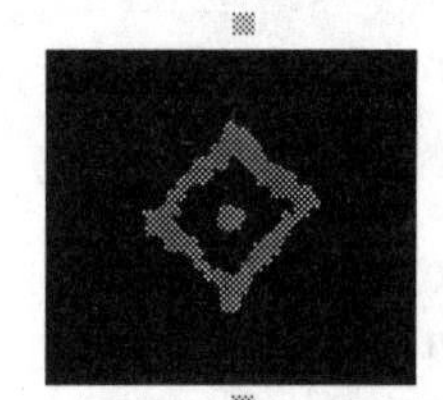

The art of composing stories is something that was undertaken by the first people—long ago, during the time of the ancestors. When those of us in my generation awakened to earliest consciousness, we were born into a tradition that was already flourishing. Stories were being composed by adults in a tradition that had been established long before we were born. And when we were born, those stories were constructed for us by old people, who argued that the tales had been created in olden times, years before. That time was ancient even to our fathers, it was ancient to our grandmothers. . . . Members of every generation have grown up under the influence of these stories.

Nongenile Masithathu Zenani, *The World and the Word* (Madison: University of Wisconsin Press, 1992), p. 7.

Nongenile Masithathu Zenani, a Xhosa storyteller (photo by Harold Scheub)

Xhosa

Sikhuluma, The Boy Who Did Not Speak

by Nongenile Masithathu Zenani

The Xhosa live in southeastern Africa.

A man and his senior wife: the wife gave birth, she bore a child who could not speak. In time, when his playmates started talking, it became clear that this child did not know how to speak.

He spoke with his hands: whenever he referred to something, he would point to it.

He spoke with his hands: he did not hear with his ears, he did not speak with his tongue.

When it was time, he was weaned.

That wife again became pregnant, and again she gave birth to a boy. That boy grew up, he learned to speak in the normal time.

He was a child who was able to speak.

The name of the child who did not know how to speak was Sikhuluma; the name of this child who knew how to speak was Sitshalotshalwana. These children grew up, they became big boys.

Date of performance: September 15, 1967. Place: At Mrs. Zenani's home in Nkanga, Transkei, South Africa. Performer: Nongenile Masithathu Zenani, a Xhosa woman, about fifty-five years old. Audience: Five women, fifteen children. Collected and translated by Harold Scheub.

1

These boys had a grandfather, the father of their father. That old man enjoyed sitting outside at the cattle kraal, relaxing in the sun, and many boys stayed there too, passing the time.

One day, some birds passed by. They appeared suddenly, moving from the left to the right side. They flew by in a thick flock. Then another flock of birds appeared from the same side, going to the other side.

When a fifth flock of birds had flown by, the old man said, "Oh! Ee! In the old days, when we were boys, those birds wouldn't have dared to do a thing like that! Passing above us like that. We boys wouldn't let those birds pass by without going after them and beating them. What's happened to these modern boys? If only I could be a lad again!"

When Sitshalotshalwana heard that, he turned to the other boys. "Did you hear grandfather? We must find sticks and throw them at those birds!"

The boys went to Sikhuluma, the youth who did not know how to speak. They gestured with their hands, they gestured as they usually did when speaking to him; they gestured until he understood what their motions meant. This boy who could not speak also took a stick, he was a good shot. The boys departed; they went after the birds, hurling their sticks at them, moving to the side that the birds were on. When one flock of birds left the boys behind, another flock appeared behind them, flying towards them, then that flock too moved to the other side. The boys went on, striking at the birds from morning until sunset. They kept moving on, they did not turn around.

When they came to a certain place, the younger boys, those who were small, were told to find firewood and to kindle a fire, "so that we can roast these birds and eat them." They had killed so many of the birds that they were weighed down by them. The boys relaxed here. A fire was built, the birds were roasted and eaten. Then they went to sleep.

They awakened in the morning, they awakened and the birds were doing the same thing they had done the day before—appearing suddenly from this side, then flying to that side.

The boys said, "Let's get started again."

They traveled with those birds once more; the boys journeyed, striking the birds, crossing river after river, passing place after place, traveling through country after country, beating those birds. But the birds seemed endless. When one flock flew by, another took its place. The sun set again, the boys were still throwing their sticks at those birds.

They said, "Let's sleep. We'll roast some of these birds. Boys, gather firewood."

The words were addressed to some of the smaller boys who then gathered the firewood. The fire was kindled, the birds were roasted and eaten. Then the boys went to sleep.

They awakened in the morning, they awakened and the birds were forming the same procession that day too.

Again, it was said, "Let's take up the chase again."

They got more sticks. They walked on, they pulled sticks from trees and added them to their arsenal. New sticks were added as the other sticks were thrown at the birds. So they moved on with the birds.

When they were far off, the sun set. At dusk, a homestead was seen glimmering a long distance away. They saw the fire, even though it was off in the distance.

"Let's go over there. To that homestead."

"It's getting tiresome, sleeping at night in the cold."

"Let's go and sleep in that homestead."

"Let's ask for a place to spend the night."

It was on that day that they first heard this boy speak—the one who did not know how to speak. In his first speech, Sikhuluma said, "No, Sitshalotshalwana, my little brother! Don't take the children to that homestead, because no one sleeps there! That homestead is not to be entered! If we go there, the children will die!"

Sitshalotshalwana stood up. As he stood, the boys said, "Yo! At last, the king has spoken!"

"Yo! My friends, has he been able to speak this well all this time that we thought he couldn't speak?"

"We did well to beat these birds. We finally heard him speak."

Sitshalotshalwana said, "Nonsense! Nonsense! What is he saying? He's telling us that we shouldn't sleep over there! He knows nothing! This is, after all, only the first time he's spoken. Now, suddenly, he's such an old man, a grown-up person! He's only beginning to speak! He doesn't know anything, he doesn't know the proper thing to say! Don't listen to him! Let's go!"

They did go. Sikhuluma was silent, he did not speak again. They walked on, they went to this homestead. They came to the homestead and found that no one was there. When they arrived, they found only some dishes, and all of the dishes contained food. These boys were twelve in number, and it turned out that there were also twelve dishes.

As they went in, Sitshalotshalwana said, "Do you realize that we almost didn't come here because of Sikhuluma—because of this Sikhuluma, who's just learning to speak, who talks about things he knows nothing about? Look! We've been provided for! We've been expected here! Look at our dishes, they're the same number as we are—twelve! Look! One, two, three, four, five, six, seven, eight, nine, ten, eleven, and twelve! Don't you see? Food has been cooked for us! Let's eat, my friends!" So said Sitshalotshalwana.

Sikhuluma spoke: "No, friend, don't tell the children to eat that food! That food is not meant for us. It belongs to the owner of the house, and she'll arrive in her own time. I've already warned you that no one should sleep in this house. The children will die!"

The boys stood up and whistled, calling each other.

"The king has spoken well!"

"It's a good thing for us that the birds came along, because we've at last heard him speak!"

Sitshalotshalwana said, "Don't be foolish! Sikhuluma doesn't know what he's talking about. He's talking nonsense again! How can he say that the food on these dishes is not meant to be eaten? These are clearly our dishes! Eat!" He said this, then took one of the dishes and ate.

The boys ate too, because they respected Sitshalotshalwana, and also because it was only Sikhuluma who spoke against him. Since this was the first day that he had spoken, what could he know?

After they had finished eating, they slept. During the night, while they were sleeping, Sikhuluma just sat there. He was not sleeping.

The others, including Sitshalotshalwana, slept.

Then he heard someone coming into the house.

When this person had entered, she said, "Yo yo yo yo! Who's this? Who has eaten my food? All of it eaten! All twelve dishes!" Then she said, "Ah, but I've got a boon here! I'll begin with this one, then I'll go to this one, then this one, then this one, then this one, then this one, then this one, then this one, and I'll finish with this juicy child!"

Sikhuluma sat there all that time, and listened. The boys were sleeping. Sikhuluma moved over to them and pinched one boy, he pulled him, he pushed him. The boy was startled.

That woman went outside, she went outside.

Sikhuluma spoke: "Get up! All of you!"

All the boys got up.

He said, "The thing that Sitshalotshalwana wanted to happen has happened. The owner of this house has come, she wants to know who has eaten her food, all twelve dishes. She said that she has got a treasure-trove: she said that she'll begin with this one, then go on to this one, then to this one, then this one. And she said that she'd finish with me! We must remain awake now, we mustn't sleep. We must stand up. Take your sticks, and let's go!"

The boys agreed.

They said, "We're thankful that you can speak!"

His little brother, Sitshalotshalwana, got up and said, "Nonsense! You always do this! Do you boys like what Sikhuluma has said? He knows nothing! He's just learning how to speak! He knows nothing! Who's this person who's supposed to have said these words? Only Sikhuluma saw her! He alone heard her speak! But we didn't see her! When this boy talks, he knows nothing. He just babbles."

The boys said, "No, let's go!"

"All right, if that's what you want."

The boys walked on then, and when they had been traveling for a time, they saw a broad road, a big white road—and a village with many homesteads. But they saw no living being. In all those homesteads, there was no one there—no dog, no ox, no sheep, nothing, only these houses.

One homestead did, however, appear to have someone in it. It was the homestead in the front, a white house. There was smoke in front of the house, it seemed that it was the only homestead with someone in it.

Sitshalotshalwana said, "Let's travel on this road. We'll pass by that homestead. We're thirsty now."

Sikhuluma spoke again: "No, Sitshalotshalwana, don't go on that road. It's dangerous. These children will all die if they travel on that road. There's some long thing there that has destroyed people. That's the reason there is no one in this village: they've been destroyed by the thing that lives over there in that house."

"We thank you, king!" the boys said. "You speak well. The things that you've said have all turned out to be so."

His little brother, Sitshalotshalwana, said, "Nonsense! Why are you thanking him? What does he know? He knows nothing! Travel on! Let's go!"

He said that, then went to that road. All the boys did the same, and Sikhuluma also traveled on that road.

They had been traveling for a short time when one of the boys died. He lay stark dead there on the road.

They walked on. No one spoke now. These boys seemed to understand that they would all die.

A short time after the death of that first boy, another died. They left him there, he lay stone dead.

They journeyed on, they continued their traveling. After a short time, another boy died.

They traveled on, and another boy died a short time later. Four of the boys were now dead.

Sitshalotshalwana was getting nervous. He seemed to understand that—well, his turn would also come. He too would die, because it was clear that any person who stepped on this road would die, no matter who he was.

They moved on, they traveled for a short time, then the fifth boy died.

They pushed on, leaving him behind, exposed there on the road. They themselves were ignorant of where this road led; they did not know if the road led to their home, because they were uncertain of the direction from which they had come. Those birds had made clear to the boys the location of their homes, but the birds were not there now, they were gone. The boys were traveling alone. They journeyed through other places, they traveled in darkness, not knowing the countryside. They did not know how to get back to their homes.

Again, they moved on, and the sixth boy died.

They walked on, and a little further along, the seventh boy died.

They were far from that house now. It was clear that it had been that house alone that had contained a person. The village was huge, but nothing had come out of it, it was empty.

They moved on, and the eighth boy died.

They went on again for a short time, and the ninth boy died. They walked sorrowfully—the ninth boy had died, and they journeyed on.

Then the tenth boy died.

Only the two of them remained now, Sikhuluma and Sitshalotshalwana. Sikhuluma and his little brother remained.

They walked on. Then Sitshalotshalwana said, "Sikhuluma, I'm going to that homestead. I want to see this thing that's killing the people, that puts something in the road to make people die. It makes no difference if I die now."

Sikhuluma answered, "No, son of my father, don't go over there. We're as good as dead, we shall die as all those children have died. It makes no difference now. We'll return alone. Let us die on this road. Don't go and bring that thing out of the house!"

He said, "You see, you're still speaking nonsense to me. You speak foolishness to me, even now that we're alone. I'm going there! You go on with your foolishness! I'm going, I want to see this thing." He said this, and went over there.

He arrived at the house. He arrived.

The thing was sleeping in a room. When Sitshalotshalwana arrived, he saw this thing and also discovered a person there who had one arm and one leg, this person was a woman.

When he entered, she said, "Oh oh oh oh! What kind of person is this? Was there ever such a person in this country?"

Sitshalotshalwana said fiercely, "Give me some water! I'm thirsty!"

This person said, "Oh worthy child, but why? I don't want to watch someone die! Well, go outside, I'll give you some water."

He said, "I won't go outside! Give me some water, I'm thirsty!"

She dipped some water. This woman gave it to him, and he drank it.

He said, "This thing that's sleeping here, is it the thing that destroys people? This thing that's sleeping here?"

He stabbed at it with a stick. The thing got up, it got up and broke his backbone. It broke his backbone in two, then it put him down. He died.

Sikhuluma knew that his brother was dead. He walked on. He did not go to that place to which Sitshalotshalwana had gone; instead, he walked on. When he was in the middle of nowhere, he turned from the road and took a footpath. He walked along that path, then became thirsty. He came to a river, he looked for water to drink but found none. As he leaned on his stick, he heard something below in the mud, saying, "Sikhuluma! Sikhuluma, you're stabbing us with that stick! Walk on, there's water on the upper side."

He was surprised: "What was talking down there in the mud?" He had not seen anything. He pulled the stick from the mud. He carried it in his hand, he did not lean on it again. Sikhuluma went to the upper side, and found water. He drank. When he had finished drinking, he stood up, then went on his way.

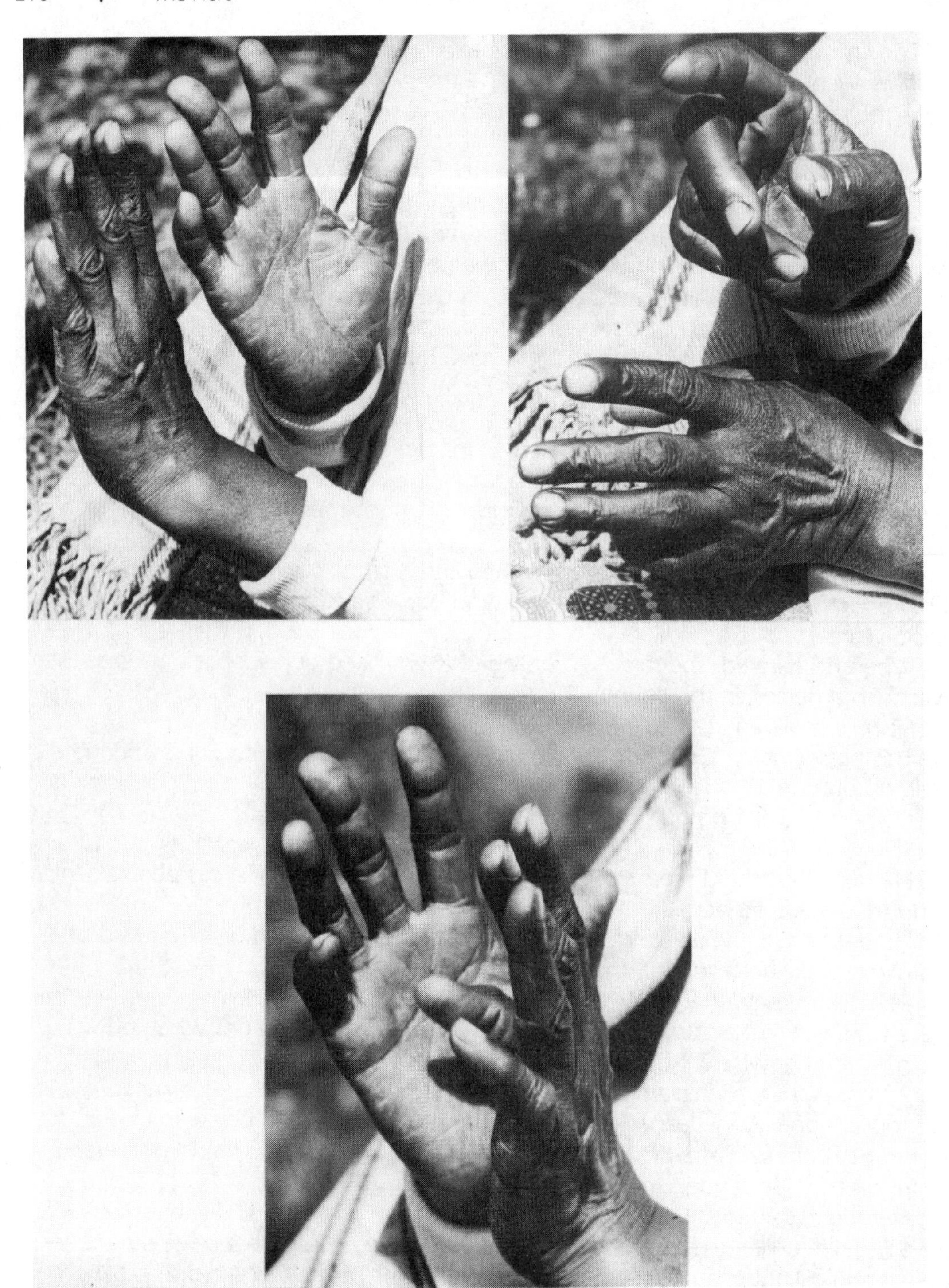

The hands of Nongenile Masithathu Zenani during performance (photos by Harold Scheub)

He was still walking when his dog suddenly appeared, the dog he had left behind at home. It suddenly appeared, wet and hungry. It trailed its tongue, panting. The dog came to Sikhuluma, wagging its tail at him. As it moved ahead, Sikhuluma followed. He knew that "If I'm going to find my home, I'll have to follow this dog. I don't know where the house is anymore." He walked behind his dog, he journeyed with that dog.

The sun set. He slept, tired. The dog slept at his side. At dawn, he trekked on with his dog; he walked and walked, he walked all day.

The sun set, and he slept. The dog slept at his side.

He traveled again at dawn, and then he saw that "This is my country! But I'm still far from home." He walked on. The dog traveled; Sikhuluma journeyed in his own land now, that was clear. This dog was leading him to his home.

Finally, he did arrive at his home. When he got there, he did not enter any house.

He cried.

While he was crying, his grandfather came to him and started to speak to him with gestures, remembering that Sikhuluma was unable to talk. He gestured, he gestured with his hands.

But Sikhuluma spoke: "Grandfather, all of those with whom I traveled have remained behind because of Sitshalotshalwana. Because of Sitshalotshalwana alone! He has remained behind also, he brought himself into the thick of it. The others are no more. I alone have returned. You should call a meeting, the fathers of those children should come and hear the reason for the absence of their children."

Sikhuluma was quiet then, he did not speak again.

The people were asked to come.

Those who were the fathers of the children arrived.

Someone said, "Let the king speak."

Sikhuluma stood and explained, "On a certain day, we departed from home, pursuing flocks of birds. There were twelve of us. Those boys, all of them, are now no longer here. This includes my brother, he was the last one.

"At the beginning of the third day, we saw the glimmer of a homestead in the distance. Sitshalotshalwana said, 'Let's go!' It was on that day that I began to speak. I said that we should not go to that homestead. If we did go there, I warned, we would all die. The boys were happy, they said that it was a good thing that those birds had come along: they finally heard me speak. But Sitshalotshalwana stood up and said, 'Nonsense! You're a fool who has never spoken before, who doesn't know what you're talking about! Let's go!' They went on then, and I remained quiet. We were going to sleep in that homestead. When we got to that place, no one was there. Some dishes were there, twelve of them, matching our number. Sitshalotshalwana said that we should eat. I spoke up again, and said that we should not eat. 'This food belongs to a person who'll be coming along,' I said. The boys thanked me for my speech, but Sitshalotshalwana insisted that I continued to speak of something I knew nothing about. Didn't I see that these dishes belonged to a person who was expecting visitors?

Those dishes were the same number as we. They went to sleep, but I didn't sleep at all that night. Then the owner of the house arrived. She said, 'Yo yo yo yo! Who has eaten the food that I prepared for myself? Who are these people? I'll start with this one, and then move to this one, then this one, then this one, and I'll finish with this little juicy one!' She was referring to me. I was awake, and I tried to awaken the boy who was next to me—I pinched him, dragged him, trying to rouse him. When he woke, I said that all the boys should get up. Then that woman, the one who had spoken, went out. I reported to the boys what I had seen. Sitshalotshalwana said that I was lying, that I was speaking of things that I knew nothing about, that I was even now speaking foolishness. 'There's no one here!' How could it be that a person was heard by me alone, while the rest of them slept? I urged that we move on. We should take our sticks and move on. He didn't agree. 'Let's stay. No one's going to move!' I said that we should go. And the boys said, 'Well, let's go!'

"We left then. We saw a road. I warned them that we should not travel on this road, that it was dangerous, that if we traveled on it the children would die. The boys thanked me, but that brother of mine said that I was delirious. 'Over there's a homestead! See the smoke?' He wanted to go to that house. We journeyed on that road then, and almost immediately after we had set foot on the road, one boy lay stone dead. He died there, we left him behind. And that is what continued to happen: dead boys formed a kind of procession, until we came to that homestead. When we neared that place, Sitshalotshalwana said that he was going over there. I said that he shouldn't go, but he insisted; he wanted to see this thing in this house, this thing that destroyed people. He went, I didn't go. When he got there, he asked for water. A certain person said that he should go outside, I was unable to hear their conversation. I did hear Sitshalotshalwana say, 'Give me some water! I'm not going out!' He drank, and when he finished drinking, he said, 'Is this the thing that destroys people?' He attacked it with his stick. The thing got up and broke his back in two, then it put him down.

"I traveled on then, I walked alone. Then I came to a river. When I jabbed at it with my stick, something below, in the mud, spoke and called me by name. It said, 'Sikhuluma! Sikhuluma, stop stabbing us! You're stabbing us with your stick! Go to the upper side, there's water on the upper side!' I pulled my stick up then, and went to the upper side and indeed found water there. I drank the water, and, as I was getting up, I saw my dog coming towards me, wagging its tail at me. The dog was wet. It helped me to find my way home."

And that is what Sikhuluma said.

The weeping of women, the weeping of the mothers of the children could be heard. There was deep mourning for the children.

The men said, "Do not blame this on a single person. All the boys together were involved in this affair when they died. They died while completing their assignments, killing the birds. They did it on their own. No one pushed them into it, they pushed themselves. We're thankful that this child of the king has returned, that he was saved, so that we might know what happened to the others, so that we might know why they aren't here."

That is what the men said, then the gathering was dispersed. That was the end of it.

2

After a brief time, Sikhuluma, the king, said, "I want to be circumcised. I want to be circumcised, I want to become a man."

"Well, all right, King."

The men were again assembled.

It was said, "The child of the great one wants to be circumcised."

"All right, but how shall it be done? The boys are not here now."

According to the custom of the Xhosa, the king is never circumcised alone. Because he is the son of a king, he must have supporters while he is in the circumcision lodge—one supporter stays on the lower side near the door, the other on the upper side, with the king between the two.

"Well, the additional boys will have to be selected from among the young boys." They would have to find the best of the younger boys to be Sikhuluma's supporters.

They assembled then, everyone was present. The people brought the boys out, so that "this child of mine might be circumcised. When my king is circumcised, he must not be left alone. He must have supporters. No matter how young the boy who is to be the supporter is, he'll do."

Finally, there were as many boys as there were fingers on the hand of the king, they were ten. And there were the two who were to be Sikhuluma's supporters.

They were circumcised. The king underwent the ritual and became an initiate. Oxen were slaughtered. The dried ox skins would be used in the circumcision lodge—the doorways of these lodges used to be closed with the skins of oxen.

There were wardens there who were men. And there was one warden who was a girl; she was in charge of the food of the king, that king who was an initiate. She remained there at the lodge.

Time passed then, time passed, time passed for the initiate. Finally, it was said that the boys must come out of the circumcision lodge.

That king spoke again. He spoke rarely, only when it was necessary that he say something. He spoke again: "I am not coming out of this circumcision lodge. I shall come out when I can put on a cloak made of the skin of a water monster. Otherwise, I am not coming out."

Someone asked, "What's that? What is this about a water monster?"

He said, "I'm speaking of a fabulous monster that lives in the river, it lives in the water. It must be drawn out from the depths, from the deep pools. I want it to be skinned, then tanned and made into a mantle for me. If I don't get the mantle, I'm not coming out, not under any circumstances!"

"But what can we do about that?"

"Who can go into those deep pools again and again to find this monster?"

"How can such a thing be?"

"Well," said Sikhuluma, "this is what you'll have to do: prepare some loaves of corn bread. Fill three baskets with loaves that have been baked, so that someone can go to these places, so that someone can find the pool that contains a water monster."

"But who can do this?"

"When this water monster comes out, won't it eat people?"

"Isn't it dangerous?"

Sikhuluma said, "If it comes out, it will attack a person, chew him up, and swallow him. And then that person is gone! But I insist, I want that water monster! I want its mantle!"

"Yo! This is a difficult matter!"

"Let's consider this carefully, from the beginning. Let's ponder it."

He said, "I don't want any pondering from any beginning! I say that I want the water monster, and that is that!"

The other boys came out of the circumcision lodge on the following day.

"That's all right," said Sikhuluma. "I'll just remain here. Even if the house is burned down, I shall remain. I shall never go home. Not until that mantle is here."

Someone said, "All right then."

They dispersed, they all went home.

They went home, then the corn was crushed. The corn was crushed, the loaves of bread were made. The baskets were filled, three baskets filled with baked corn bread. Then Sikhuluma's sister, the warden who had stayed at the circumcision lodge cooking for him, took the baskets.

She said, "I shall go. I shall find the mantle for the son of my father, the cloak that he wants to come out with. I want this thing that eats people to eat me, it must begin with me! I am going, I shall take these loaves along with me." Those were the provisions for a traveler.

So it was that this child journeyed, carrying these loaves.

When they were far off, they saw a large river. They went to this massive river, they arrived there and threw a loaf of bread into the water.

They said, "Water monster! Water monster, come out and eat me!"

There was silence. They journeyed on, beyond this river.

Someone said, "It's not in this river."

They moved on for a long time, seeking another big river. Again, they found a huge river, they sought a deep pool in this river. When they found it, they again threw a loaf of corn bread into the water, they threw another loaf into the water.

When that loaf of corn bread had been thrown, someone said, "Water monster! Water monster, come out and eat me!"

There was no water monster there.

They passed beyond that river, traveling again for a long time. They were seeking yet another large river. Little rivers were crossed, rivers having small pools that did not seem to contain the creature they were seeking.

Finally, they came to another big river, and again they stood above a deep pool. They tossed a loaf of bread into the water.

They said, "Water monster! Water monster, come out and eat me!"

The water in that pool stirred, then it roiled, it roiled, the water churned, it was brown, then red, then green.

The girl said, "Run! All of you! Take this bread with you! Make sure that you can see me at all times! Don't let me out of your sight!"

These others fled, they departed. They ran, continually looking back, constantly watching her.

The water monster came out of the water. When it came out, the girl ran. The thing that came out—it was huge in a way that she had never seen before. It was not like a horse, it was huge! It was not like anything else, this thing was gigantic! Colossal! As big as this: if it entered a kraal where cattle stay, it would fill that kraal by itself. That is how big it was.

This child ran, the water monster ran after her. It did not move with great speed, but it went steadily, moving easily. She ran, she ran and ran.

When she was far from the water monster, she sat down and rested. When it came near, she put a loaf of bread down on the ground, then she ran on again. The water monster stopped, chewed the bread, and swallowed it. Then it pursued her once more. But it did not run, it just walked.

Finally, she was a short distance from those men who were waiting for her.

When they saw what was happening, the men said, "Oh! Well, we won't stay here!"

"This thing's getting closer!"

"We're on our way, we must escape this thing!"

"You stay here with it yourself!"

"A thing so terrible!"

"A thing so big!"

"Yo yo yo yo!"

The men went on, leaving the child behind.

The child said, "You're leaving me behind, but would you please try to keep an eye on me? Please, when you're far off, watch me, so that you'll know if I've been devoured by this thing, so that you'll be able to report at home that—well, I've been eaten. Please don't let me out of your sight! Stay in a place where you can watch me."

The men agreed to do this. They hurried off, the child moved on. She waited for the water monster, and it approached. When it was a short distance away, she put a loaf of bread on the ground. Then she again went on her way. She left the water monster behind, she ran. The creature came to the loaf and chewed it. When it had finished, it again followed her. She was again resting. When it was a short distance away, she again put a loaf of bread on the ground. The loaves in her basket gradually diminished, until finally only one loaf remained. The beast came along and ate that loaf.

She ran, she hurried to these men. She replenished her supply of loaves, she poured loaves from their basket into hers. It was full again. Then the men hurried on—the thing frightened the men, they did not even want to see it. This thing was dreadful.

When the creature was near, the child again put a loaf of bread on the ground. She ran, she ran a distance, then sat down. The water monster came to the loaf and ate it. The child went on.

She came to the men and said, "Travel on now! Go home, tell them at home that they should borrow a gun. A gun should be sought, so that this thing can be shot! But no one should come near it! Shoot it from a distance! If they can get a number of guns, so much the better! We don't even know if a bullet can penetrate this thing."

The men hurried on, leaving that child behind. The girl moved on, leaving a loaf of bread on the ground. The water monster was a short distance away. She hurried on, she was not far from home.

When the men reached the homestead, they reported what the girl had asked them to say. The guns were borrowed, they were loaded, they became heavy. They were cocked. Most of the men were carrying guns now; those not carrying guns had spears.

Time passed, the sun set, and finally, a short distance from home, the girl appeared. The water monster came after her, that thing was approaching. She arrived at home, she hurried into the kraal.

She told the men to go into the houses. The water monster would enter the kraal because it wanted this girl.

"Go into the houses so that it won't see you! It will come into the kraal. When its back is turned to you and as it approaches me, come out with your weapons and go to work! I'll come out at the other end of the kraal."

The men heard; they went into the houses, all of them went into the houses. The girl arrived, the men saw her as she stood in the courtyard, just above the kraal. They were looking through some small holes, trying to see this thing.

When they saw this creature approach, the men cried out, the women cried out, the dogs howled, everything there at home fled. The dogs ran, they disappeared on the other side. Everything in this homestead ran—the cattle ran when they saw this thing coming. The water monster resembled nothing but itself, its like had never before been seen. The people in the house cried out; they were inside, they had closed the doors.

The water monster did not bother about those wailing people at all. It was face to face with this girl. It came up to her. She entered the kraal, and the thing also went in. When it had done so, the people came out, coming to assist the girl in the kraal. All of them came with their weapons. Twelve men began to shoot. They shot, they went through their ammunition. The thing stirred, it wanted to move on. Twelve other men came out and they shot until their ammunition was also finished. It was clear that the water monster was wounded. It moved there on the ground, but it was unable to stand up so that it might escape. The men with spears threw them, those men were some distance away.

The water monster would never survive this. When it collapsed, the kraal was broken down, it was shattered. The men shot repeatedly, and then the thing was dead. It had been penetrated by the men.

When they felt certain that it was dead, they skinned that thing. When the skinning was completed, the cloaks were divided. The water monster provided three cloaks, the number that they had hoped for. The boy second in rank to the initiate would put on a mantle similar to his, and the companion on the other side would also wear a cloak resembling the king's. The three mantles were tanned by the men.

The flesh of that water monster was put outside, because they did not know if it was edible. They threw the flesh away, outside. It was a windfall for the dogs and pigs, they ate that meat all month. When the second month appeared, it was still not finished; it was being eaten by all the dogs of the village and by all the hogs of the village.

After a little while, when the cloaks had been tanned, the people went to Sikhuluma. A song associated with the initiates' coming out of the circumcision lodge was composed, a song about the emergence of the initiate. He was taken out then, covered with that mantle. The mantle was turned inside out, because when the fur was on the outside it had such a fearsome appearance that nothing would approach it: everything would run, they were afraid. It was therefore necessary that he wear it so that the fur side was next to his skin. That is how all three of them wore their mantles as they came to the homestead. They arrived and remained in the yard. They sat in the yard, a mat was placed there and they sat on it. The newly initiated young man was admitted into manhood as the people presented him with gifts. All the people presented him with gifts, celebrating his transition to manhood. They acclaimed the king, they acclaimed the warden, they acclaimed the second warden, they acclaimed that one who was on the upper side. All of the twelve initiates had come here, and they were all admitted to manhood. Now it was necessary that they go to a house, that they remain in the house where something would be prepared for them to eat. They would anoint their bodies with red clay, according to the custom of the Xhosa.

3

When Sikhuluma emerged from the circumcision lodge, he spoke: "I am not going into the house. The others can go in, but I am not entering the house. I shall stay out here, I shall not go into the house. I shall go in only when I have a wife."

"Oh, what is it now?"

"Has there ever been such a thing? A person who refuses to go into the house?"

"A person who will enter only when he has a wife?"

But Sikhuluma sat there, refusing to eat. He would remain there, he would not go into the house.

He did not speak again: he would speak just one thing, then he would not speak again. He would speak again on the day that he next spoke.

"What'll we do?"

"What is this, friends? Now he won't even answer us!"

"When he speaks, he speaks!"

He did not speak again.

"Yo! This is difficult!"

It was proper that those young men entering manhood should go to the house, and the others did so. They arrived, they were anointed with red clay. Food was dished up for them, and they ate. All the things of young manhood were done for them. Songs were sung for them; they were also taught songs sung at a men's party, dancing songs.

Sikhuluma sat in the kraal.

Food was brought for him in the kraal, but Sikhuluma said, "I am not eating. I told you that I shall eat when I have a wife. I want a wife. I want one of Mangangedolo's daughters as my wife."

Someone said, "A wife from Mangangedolo's place?"

"How can anyone want to go there?"

"Men who seek brides at Mangangedolo's place are finished!"

"The bridegroom who goes there does not return!"

Sikhuluma did not speak again. He would speak in his own time. He slept here, not eating.

At dawn, the men were called.

It was said, "He says that he wants a wife. The people must go with him as always, they must go and ask for that daughter at Mangangedolo's place."

"This is only the latest of unusual happenings here at home. Now, this child wants a daughter of Mangangedolo's place!"

The men said, "When he says something, that is what must be."

"No one will forsake his king!"

"Those boys who died didn't die because of anything he did. In fact, he was warning them."

"They died because they disregarded his words."

"Well, we shall not disregard his words. We'll bring out our young men, they'll go along with him to look for a wife wherever he sees fit."

Five young men were brought out then, Sikhuluma was the sixth. The supporters also accompanied them, so that they were eight in all.

They traveled then, going to Mangangedolo's place.

Along the way, they met a mouse. The mouse crossed the road, then, when it had crossed, it returned to the other side. It stopped there on the road, and said, "Sikhuluma!"

He said, "Hmm?"

"Child of the king, slaughter me. Put my skin in your sack and travel with it. I'll advise you when you get to your destination. You can hide my flesh here in this tuft of grass."

Sikhuluma said, "I shall put you into my bag, as you have instructed. But do you know where we're going?"

"You're going to ask for a daughter of Mangangedolo's place. Now then, let me point out Mangangedolo's place to you. Do you see that hill in the distance there? On the upper side of the homestead?"

He said, "Yes."

"Those are heads over there. The heads of people who have come to ask for Mangangedolo's daughter! Your head could also be thrown onto that hill! But if you put me into your bag, I'll tell you what to do when you get there."

Sikhuluma was quiet. He took a knife, killed the mouse, and skinned it. He skinned it, then took its flesh and hid it in the grass. He took the mouse's skin and put it into the bag. Then he went on his way, he walked on.

Nongenile Masithathu Zenani performs a story (photos by Harold Scheub)

As they approached the homestead, the mouse said, "Sikhuluma, consider this. You'll be escorted to a beautiful house over there, a very attractive house. Don't agree to enter that house! Say 'We don't stay in such a beautiful house.' Tell them that you want to stay in a house in which calves are tethered, a house where the fowl sleep.

"They'll bring a new sleeping mat to you. Say that you don't use such mats, tell them that you want an old mat—the mat of a young mother, a mat that's in tatters.

"Then food will be brought to you on new plates, with new utensils. Say that you won't eat food on such plates. Say that you eat on leaky dishes, you don't want new ones.

"Now, during the time that you're over there, do not walk on mole hills, walk on the grass instead. Never walk in a place where there is no grass.

"They'll tell you over there that the bridegroom's party should assemble at the cattle kraal. Enter through the gate of the kraal, but when you're ready to come out, come out on the other side. Don't come out through the gate.

"Also, when someone over there says 'Hello' to you, say, 'Mmhmmmm.' Don't say, 'Yes,' say 'Mmhmmm.'"

"All right."

"Now put me in the bag."

Sikhuluma put that mouse into the bag, and he traveled on. He walked a great distance. When he arrived at that homestead over there, he walked on the grassy areas, he walked on the grass.

He arrived, he sat in the yard at the place where the bridegroom's party stays. The thumping steps of the owner of the homestead could be heard, Mangangedolo arrived. His knee was huge! He arrived, stomping on the ground; he stomped and stomped.

He said, "Hello, party of the bridegroom."

They said, "Mmhmmm."

"I say, 'Hello, party of the bridegroom!'"

"Mmhmmm."

"What is this? Don't you know how to say 'Yes'?"

They said nothing, they were silent.

He said, "I greet you! Hello—especially you, bridegroom!"

He said, "Mmhmmm."

Mangangedolo said, "Ah, this is a unique groom's party." He was quiet then. He chatted with them, asking, "Where have you come from?"

Sikhuluma explained, "Well, I come from my home. I have come here to seek a wife."

He said, "Select for yourself from among the daughters of my home. There are many. Let them come and greet the groom's party."

The daughters were called, they came to greet the groom's party. Sikhuluma selected a wife for himself.

He said, "It's that one. There is my wife!"

Mangangedolo laughed. He said, "Ha ha! I've never heard such a forthright groom! Well, I see how it is with you, husband. We'll meet again, we'll see each other again! Now, please tell me, on what basis are you claiming her?"

He said, "I do so with cattle. Just tell me the number you want as far as this daughter is concerned."

He said, "Do you have eighty head of cattle that you can bring here for my daughter's dowry?"

Sikhuluma said, "Even above that number! Ask whatever number of cattle you please for your daughter."

He said, "All right then, I want those eighty."

He said, "They're as good as here."

That fellow said then, "Go, women, make arrangements for the groom's party."

They went, the young women left the groom's party.

That daughter rose and grasped her groom's hand. Sikhuluma took her hand, he took her hand, not certain that he should do so—wary, not sure if this might be the cause of his death. But he took her hand anyway. Then the young woman departed.

Those young women went and prepared a house for the bridegroom. The house in which the women would sleep was beautiful. That is where the groom's party was taken. Someone told the spokesman to bring the groom's party along, and he did so, bringing the group to that house.

When Sikhuluma appeared in the doorway, he said, "No no! I'm not entering this house!"

"Why not?"

"Why won't you enter this house?"

"Are you staying outside?"

"What kind of bridegroom are you?"

He said, "No! I have never stayed in such a house! The houses at my home have pillars supporting the roof. And the houses at my home are made of mud. They have pillars, they are thatched with grass. We sleep on the floor with the calves and the fowl. Take me to the house in which the calves and fowl sleep."

They said, "Yo yo yo yo!"

"Never have we seen such a bridegroom!"

"This is an extraordinary groom."

He was quiet, he did not speak again. He was taken to a dirty house, it had manure in it, there were fleas and bedbugs in it. The calves were sleeping there, the fowl were sleeping there, hogs were coming in.

A bed mat was brought, it was new. They said that they were making the bridegroom's bed.

He said, "No! I'm not sleeping in a bed like this! I want an old mat, a young mother's mat, a tattered mat. At my home, they do not put down a mat like this. I'll not sleep on such a mat!"

"He's doing it again!"

"Really, this groom is unusual!"

"We're accustomed to groom's parties here at home, but we've never seen anything like this one!"

A tattered bed mat was brought, it was put down for him. He sat. They sat on it. They turned their mantles inside out, they turned them inside out; they turned them so that the fur was on the inside, the fur of the mantles was next to their skin—they did not wear them with the fur on the outside.

"Never have we seen such a groom's party!"

"We could see at once that they were strange—they were wearing long skin shirts!"

Sikhuluma sat, and food was brought on new dishes with fine new spoons. The food was put down there, and he said, "No! Go away with this food of yours! We don't eat from such fine dishes, we fear them! We eat from dirty dishes, leaky ones, and we eat with dirty spoons. We don't know these things, we won't eat with such things."

"Heeee! Never have we seen such a groom's party!"

"This is strange."

"What kind of groom is this?"

They went away muttering. "This is really a marvel!"

"Today, my father has come face to face with something unique!"

"Something that's really weird here in our homestead!"

"Take it! Here's the food!"

"The groom's party doesn't want this food."

"They say they want leaky dishes over there!"

"Yo!"

That is the way the groom's party became a wonder to the people in this homestead.

Leaky dishes were obtained, and the food was dished out. Dirty spoons were brought. Sikhuluma ate. From the time that he had come out of the circumcision lodge, this was the first time that he had eaten. He ate, he ate, and when Sikhuluma had finished eating, the members of the groom's party were told that they were wanted at the cattle kraal.

He said, "All right, I have heard."

He went there, he went to the kraal. They entered the kraal through the gate. They arrived, and sat.

Mangangedolo turned to Sikhuluma, and said, "Now, let's discuss our business. Because we were alone when we spoke earlier, repeat in the presence of these men what you told me earlier."

That groom answered, "Yes, all right, father. I repeat that eighty head of cattle is satisfactory to me. I want your daughter to come to my home and kindle a fire."

Well then, his words were heard.

"All right, you may go into the house."

A trap had been set at the entrance to the kraal, so that when the members of the groom's party went out, they would die there at the gate. Sikhuluma got up, he went to the other end of the kraal, he went out at that end.

Someone said, "Oh oh oh! Why don't you go out at the other end?"

He said, "This is the way we do it at home. We do not enter through the gate, then go out again through the same gate. We enter through the gate, then go out at the other end."

Someone said, "Yo! This is really a unique groom's party!"

"It's a wonder!"

"This thing's really strange!"

So it was that Mangangedolo's medicine did not work in the gateway.

Time passed. That night, they went to sleep.

The mouse said, "Sikhuluma! Take me out of the bag, hang me over there, above the door, so that I can maintain a lookout for you. While you sleep, this is going to happen: the young women will come here, to sleep with you. Each man will sleep with a woman. This is what you must do: all of the men should take the women's modesty aprons, and put them on. The men should say that they are borrowing the aprons from the young women, that it is their custom. You and your wife should remain idle. Do nothing. In case I should happen to fall asleep, just turn your mantle over, this cloak of yours, so that the fur is on the outside."

"All right."

In the night, the young women came in. When they had entered, each woman went to bed with her appropriate young man. All the young women did that, and the bride went to sleep with her groom, Sikhuluma.

A member of the groom's party said, "Women, we have a custom. We usually have a marshal. Do you know what a marshal is?"

The young women said, "No, we don't know."

"What's a marshal?"

"A marshal is a man who arranges things. He orders people about, he prepares the young women. He takes the women's aprons and puts them on the members of the groom's party." He said, "Now, one of us will play the role of the marshal."

So one of the members of the groom's party became the marshal.

The young women agreed to the arrangement, but they said, "Yo! This is really strange!"

"Never have we been in such a situation!"

"We're used to having bridegroom's parties here, but we've never seen a groom's party that takes women's aprons and wears them!"

"A wonder!"

"You're a peculiar groom's party!"

"This groom may be handsome, but he should be rejected by this woman!"

"He's made up for his strange ways because he's so handsome."

"But these habits of his!"

"No, no! We just don't understand them!"

The women unfastened their aprons, they gave them to the members of the groom's party. Then time passed for this groom's party. Sikhuluma and his wife did nothing, they slept—they chatted, then they slept.

While they were asleep, Mangangedolo came along with the weapon which he used to destroy people: a huge knife with which he cut off the heads of the members of grooms' parties. He stepped heavily, he stood at the door of the house of the groom's party.

The mouse said, "Return! Return, Mangangedolo, return with that magic! Return with it!"

"Oh!" Mangangedolo ran! He stomped as he fled, he stomped, he stomped, he stomped. He arrived at his house, and said, "Mmhmmmm! Do you know that they're awake over there in that house? Someone said, 'Return with it, Mangangedolo. Return with that magic!' We'll have to try something to make them sleep!"

They worked with their magic to put them to sleep over there, to put them to sleep. They worked with the magic, they worked with it.

"You go this time, my wife."

Well, his wife went. She threw her breasts over her shoulders, and walked with a swaying gait. She arrived and stood in the doorway.

Before she could enter, the mouse said, "Return with it, wife of Mangangedolo! Return with that magic, return with it!"

"Yo!" She ran! "Oh! oh! oh! Do you know that they're not asleep in that house? Someone said, 'Return with that magic, wife of Mangangedolo!'"

The man said, "I told you so. They're awake in that house. These are strange people. It'll soon be dawn, and they're still awake!"

"Mm."

They decided that the dog should go over there this time. There was a big dog in this homestead, and hanging from this dog were concoctions and bottles and capsules—all sorts of things.

"Please go, my dog. Go now. If they escape from this dog, they're beyond us."

This shaggy dog went then, it arrived and stood in the doorway.

It barked, "Nhu nhu!" It leapt there at the door.

The mouse said, "Return with it, dog of Mangangedolo! Return with that magic! Return with it!"

When the groom saw that this dog was going to enter the house by force, he turned his mantle around. He knew that there was nothing that the skin of a mouse could do to this dog. He turned his mantle so that the fur was on the outside. He was lying at the extreme end of the house, the others were on the upper side.

The dog barked, "Nhu!" It barked, "Nhu!" It leapt and charged at Sikhuluma, but the mantle of the water monster immediately began to maul the dog, it mauled the dog, it ripped into this dog, it tore the dog to shreds, to shreds! To shreds! It tore the dog up—all all all of it! Even the legs! It lacerated the dog. Then it took the dog and put it in front of Mangangedolo's house. The mantle returned to Sikhuluma, shook itself, then covered its owner once more.

They slept.

In the morning, the young women awakened. They awakened, took their aprons, and went out. And they saw a real wonder in their homestead, a wonder having to do with the dog.

"What could have dismembered it like this?"

"Did you see the dog come to that house?"

The young women said, "It didn't go there!" The women had been asleep, they did not see it. It must have entered the house while they were asleep.

"This dog didn't go there!"

"Why was it ripped up?"

"We were just sitting! When our father went to that house, we were still awake. We heard our father!"

"The groom's party was asleep then, but we were awake!"

"But this dog! It didn't go to that house!"

"Well, this is a mystery!"

"What kind of groom's party is this?"

"Well, we must try something else now."

"Don't bother them, let them sleep."

In the morning, the cattle kraal was about to be opened for the cattle.

A member of Mangangedolo's home said, "We've come to visit the groom's party."

"We've brought them food, so they can eat."

"Now the members of the groom's party must go out with the cattle, they must herd the cattle."

"They must herd the cattle. That is the custom in this home."

Sikhuluma said, "All right, we want to follow your customs."

"Yes."

The food was brought to them, on leaky dishes. They ate the food, they finished.

Someone said that they should move on, so they went to the kraal to take the cattle out. A trap was sprung. A trap was sprung, it was sprung on the lower side as the groom's party entered the gate. Previously, they had refused to come out through the gate, they insisted that they come out at the lower end of the kraal. So this time a trap was laid there at the lower end.

It was said, "Go into the kraal and bring the cattle out."

The groom's party entered the cattle kraal; then they brought the cattle out through the gate. When they had driven the cattle out through the gate, they also came out through the gate—on the upper side of the kraal. They did not go out on the lower side.

"Why have you come out through another place?"

"You said that you come out on the lower end!"

Sikhuluma said, "We go by our customs, you go by yours. We do it this way at home."

"Yo! This groom's party is an odd one!"

"It is a wonder!"

"Travel on, herd those cattle."

Far from this homestead was a plateau.

Someone said, "Go and herd the cattle over there on that plateau."

They traveled with those cattle, they went to herd them on the plateau. Sikhuluma had his bag with him on that plateau, the skin of the mouse was with him.

The mouse said, "Sikhuluma! You're as good as dead!"

"What must we do?"

"Do you see that cow over there? The one with the big udder?"

He said, "Yes."

"Go over there, get under that cow! All of you! All of you, all eight of you must get over there under that cow. Grab its legs! Some of you seize its tail! The others, grasp the neck! Keep it stationary. A cloud is going to appear suddenly, this cloud will thunder. That thundering will be sent by Mangangedolo. Because you triumphed over him at his home, he wants to destroy you by lightning, he wants you to be killed out here. The cloud will pass by. When it passes, you'll see some women approaching with bags. They'll want to pick up your heads."

"All right."

The cloud suddenly appeared. When the cloud had appeared, the members of the groom's party grasped that cow. They seized that cow over there. All of them. Some grabbed it by the neck, others seized its horns, others grasped it by the legs, others clung to the tail, they went beneath it. They also clutched the cow by the udder. The cow stood, and they remained there.

Then it thundered, there was a mighty thundering. The sound was engulfing, unsurpassed in volume. Other cattle were struck by the lightning.

The storm passed over. The sun came out and shone brightly. When the sun had come out, some women suddenly appeared, carrying bags.

When they got there, they said, "Heeeeeee!"

"Mmhmmmmm!"

"Such a rain!"

"Sheeeeeee! Didn't it reach you?"

"Such a great storm!"

"Ehee! You're safe!"

Sikhuluma said, "If you think that you've come here to take the heads from me, you're wrong! You'll have to take manure, you'll not be taking any heads from me!"

"Well now, what is this groom saying?"

"We've just come to gather manure, that's all."

So they said, and the women gathered manure. The groom's party went on its way, taking those cattle back to the homestead.

Yeeeeee, when the groom's party had returned, Mangangedolo said, "Well, I'm giving you your wife. Now you can travel on out of here."

He brought that wife out. When he had done so, he told her to go along with her groom's party.

Sikhuluma, the king, said, "Well, that's fine. That's all I wanted anyway. All the time that I've been here at this homestead, that's all I wanted."

"Mmmm!"

They traveled then, the wife with this groom and the party. The young women of the bride's home accompanied them, showing the groom's party the way.

After a time, they turned around: "Well, in-laws, we're going back."

"All right."

The young women turned around, the members of the groom's party traveled on with this wife of theirs.

After a time, Sikhuluma stepped on a place that had soil, even though he had been warned by the mouse that he should never tread on earth, that he should always walk on a place that had grass. If he walked on earth, he had been warned, the result would be disastrous.

Mangangedolo traveled, he went after them, seeking the groom's footprint. Finally, he found it; he came upon it by surprise at that place over there where Sikhuluma had happened to set his foot.

He said, "Yo! Thank you! I've found his footprint!"

Mangangedolo took it up, he took that footprint from the earth there. He went home where he worked his magic, he worked on this groom with his magic. He spread the earth out, he spread the footprint out.

As Mangangedolo was carrying on in that way, the groom said, "I'm hurt."

The mouse said, "Yes, you're hurt. You stepped on earth! You forgot what I told you, so you're hurt. If there's anything I can do nothing about, it has just happened. This is it. What can I possibly do about this?"

Sikhuluma said, "No, I'm the one who forgot."

The mouse felt very bad about this matter. It had helped Sikhuluma so much, and now, this close to home, he was about to die.

Sikhuluma went to that place where he had hidden the mouse's flesh. He took it, and put it into the skin of the mouse.

The mouse arose, and said, "Well, Sikhuluma, now, you're dying."

Sikhuluma said, "Yes."

The mouse went on its way.

As they traveled on, Sikhuluma said, "My body feels run down."

"What did you say, king?"

"My body is run down."

"How is it run down?" his wife asked. "How is it run down?"

"My body is run down, I'm weighed down by the mantle."

His mantle dropped to the ground.

He said, "Pick it up, pick it up, old friend."

A member of the groom's party picked it up and carried it. They walked on.

He said, "My head is in pain."

"What did you say, king?"

"I said, 'My head is in pain.'"

His stick dropped.

"Pick it up, pick it up, old friend."

Another member of the party picked it up and carried it. They traveled on.

He said, "My back is in pain, my legs hurt, my feet are aching."

His penis cover fell to the ground.

"Pick it up, pick it up, old friend."

Another picked it up and carried it.

He said, "I'm thirsty."

He was obviously giddy, feeling faint. He walked on.

"There's a pool up ahead."

He went to that pool, he went to the pool and drank. He drank and drank, then disappeared. He disappeared completely, he was not seen.

They considered the possibility of going into the water to bring him out, even if he was dead. But they did not see him. They saw some horned elands emerging from the pool.

The groom's party traveled on. His wife walked on too, crying for her dead husband.

She said, "Yo! I don't want this! I don't want to go home!" She sat down, and said, "Let's just sit down. I'll try to do some of my father's tricks. I know them. The things he does, he does in our presence. We children know all about his activities. Heeee!"

The bride took out a bottle from her bag, she opened it. She lit a fire, then heated the concoction. She threw it into the pool, when it was hot she threw it into this pool.

The elands came out, they came out. She seized one of the elands, and said, "Gather some firewood. We'll roast this eland. This eland—here's the king, in this eland! He's here, in the stomach of this eland."

"Oh really? Is that true?"

She said, "Yes, here is the king. Inside this eland."

They kindled a fire. All of these people grieved here, but they wept inside because they were men. They kindled a huge fire. Then they cut the eland's neck, they skinned it.

And the king emerged. He emerged alive. He was sick, he was not well.

She said, "Roast this eland, and eat it."

It was roasted, it was eaten here by all of them. They ate it. The wife and her groom did not eat it, however.

When all that had taken place, she took an ember from the fire. Then she opened another bottle. She blew on it, and said, "Go, Spirit! Go and scatter that earth. There it is, the earth of the king's footprint. It has been spread out by my father near the cattle kraal. When you arrive over there, become a whirlwind!"

The spirit traveled then, it was not visible, there was no wind. When it arrived over there at the side of the kraal, it became a whirlwind. It went off with the earth that Mangangedolo had spread out on a patch of cloth. It flew off with it, then scattered it and threw it away—far off, along with that patch of cloth.

In the house, Mangangedolo said, "Yo! Hasn't that wind passed by yet? Hasn't it caused me some damage?"

He stepped heavily, and went to the side of the kraal. When he got there, he could no longer find the patch of cloth or the earth.

He said, "Yo! Satan is alive, he's active wherever he is!"

Sikhuluma, the king, was now well, he was as he had been before. Now he went home with his wife. When he got to his home, he sat outside by the cattle kraal. He said that his wife should sit at the side of the house, she should not enter the house.

As for the rest of the people, they should go into the house. His second in rank would stay with him outside by the kraal; both of the seconds would remain with him.

The others went into the house, and said, "The king is outside."

They went out and asked, "King, when will you come into the house?"

He said, "I am not entering the house until I have my own house! I shall go into my own house, I cannot enter any other house!"

"King! That house—When must you have the house?"

"Your house is being built as quickly as possible! But it takes a long time to build a house."

"It takes days, months to build a house!"

He said, "My house will not take months to build. The house must be built! Then I'll go in. Speak to this wife of mine, ask her what sort of house she wants."

They went to his wife who was at the side of the house. "Woman, please tell us what sort of house you want—how big you want it to be, where you want it to be."

The bride answered, "Well, father, I want the house to be on the upper side of the sheepfold. And I want it to be big, because it's going to house a family, and because you too may stay in it when you wish. I shall build the house myself, the way I like it."

"All right then. When will you build it?"

She said, "All I need is permission, then I shall build it."

It was said, "All right then, build."

The bride opened her magical kit, she took something out that was not seen by the other people. She put it down.

She said to them, "Move over there!"

The people went to that place that she indicated. Then she put the thing down over there. She said that all the people should look to one side. The people looked to one side, in the opposite direction. When the time came for them to look back, they saw a house that had six doors. It was a wonder.

Then she said, "Let us go into the house."

They entered the house. In that house, every kind of bedding could be found, everything necessary for making a bed was there; there were things to sit on, things for standing, things for sleeping, things for clothing, things for eating, things for washing.

"Well, we've seen the house."

She said, "Tell the king that he can come into the house. His house is ready now."

They went and told the king. He got up from the side of the kraal, with those people on either side of him. He went into the house.

So it was that he sat as a king. When it was dawn, he was given his cloak; the mantle of kingship was transferred to Sikhuluma from his father, who was then pensioned. His son became the ruler.

In the morning, a huge meeting was held, and the authority was officially transferred to his son. This son was the king, he took charge.

And they all lived in happiness.

Commentary

Narratives that describe activities in the contemporary world frequently contain two themes: harmony between humans and nature, and rites of passage. Both emphasize the sustaining of unified societies. "Sikhuluma" is a tale that dramatizes the meanings of Sikhuluma's puberty and marriage rites of passage.

Rites of passage always emphasize crises in people's lives, as they move from one state of existence to another, from childhood to adulthood, from the state of being unmarried to the state of being married. The resultant change of identity is significant, suggesting as it does a reshaping and a redefining. Rites of passage are periods of transformation, of change, in individual lives.

The name of Sikhuluma, the future king, means "eloquent speaker." This name is ironic, because he does not speak at all in the early part of the tale. But later, when he does speak, it is to save lives, befitting a future king and justifying the name, Sikhuluma. And when he returns to his home after the first part of the story, he speaks splendidly; the reason for the lengthy retelling of the story there is to emphasize this eloquence, suggesting that Sikhuluma, born not speaking, has now come of age. The shift from no speech to eloquent speech suggests his movement from childhood to adulthood. The experience of the future king becomes a model for his subjects, as he moves himself, and his society, into a new dispensation: these are the hints of heroism in this tale.

◇ **Patterns and motifs**—The story is in three parts. Part one has to do with the quest for birds and dramatizes Sikhuluma's puberty ritual. The old man reveals this when he derides the boys, insisting that chasing the birds is an act of manhood. Part two centers on the quest for the fabulous river monster and signals the end of Sikhuluma's puberty, the preparation for marriage. In part three, the bride quest is central; Sikhuluma is married, and he ascends the throne.

There are three important patterns in part one of this story: (1) the bird quest, with the organizing motif of birds that strangely lure humans to their deaths; (2) Sikhuluma's speech, a pattern containing the motif of a person hitherto mute who speaks, whose speech is moreover life-giving; and (3) the deaths of the boys, presided over by a swallowing monster motif.

The second section is the pivotal part of the narrative. The cape made of the skin of the monster enables the puberty ritual to end (only then will Sikhuluma emerge from the circumcision lodge) and the marriage rite to begin. The two rituals overlap in part two. The water monster's skin becomes Sikhuluma's protection during his bride quest. The skin symbolizes the satisfactory completion of the puberty ritual and preserves the wearer in his mature life. What is being suggested here is that properly and successfully experiencing the puberty ritual sustains one as he moves into adulthood and its many dangers. In the end, Sikhuluma dies, is swallowed (a traditional symbol of death and rebirth), and is reborn a man.

In this second part of "Sikhuluma," there are two patterns, both having to do with the monster quest and both with swallowing monster motifs at their organizing center: these are the "Come and eat me!" pattern and the chase pattern.

In part three, the central activity is Sikhuluma's marriage ritual; there are three significant patterns here. The first pattern involves the mouse's advice (the motif: helpful animal); the second pattern is the murder attempts, with a reluctant father-in-law motif; and the third pattern describes the slow death of Sikhuluma, the motif being that of the dying and resurrected hero. Within the second pattern is yet another pattern, this one having to do with the comments of Mangangedolo and his people: "This is a strange, a different groom's party."

Parts one and three are connected by part two, but in a rather complex manner. The relationship between Sikhuluma and Sitshalotshalwana in part one is equivalent to that between Mangangedolo and his daughter in part three. In each case, a struggle between good and evil is dramatized, with Sikhuluma emerging victoriously in the first part, Mangangedolo's daughter in the third. As is the case with many villains in the oral tradition, Mangangedolo is both life-giving and death-dealing; he is deadly in his persistent efforts to destroy Sikhuluma, and life-giving in his daughter who is, in the language of storytelling, his extension. Father and daughter form a death-dealing and life-giving pair; similarly, Sikhuluma and Sitshalotshalwana, the brothers, are a contrasting pair, a dramatization of the struggle occurring within the initiate as he moves to manhood.

There is a parallel between parts one and three, as the storyteller moves beyond a typical male puberty ritual. Women are important here: a hero and leader like Sikhuluma does not achieve his triumphs alone. He has the active assistance of women, his sister who provides him with the life-preserving cape, his bride who gives him rebirth and who is herself undergoing a movement to adulthood.

Mangangedolo is a dualistic villain. His daughter, Sikhuluma's bride, is an extension of her father. He is the death-dealing part, she the life-giving part. Together, they form a pair. That dualistic, polar pair comments on Sikhuluma's marriage ritual: he is dying to his past and is being reborn, with Mangangedolo and his daughter the storytelling manifestations of that transformation.

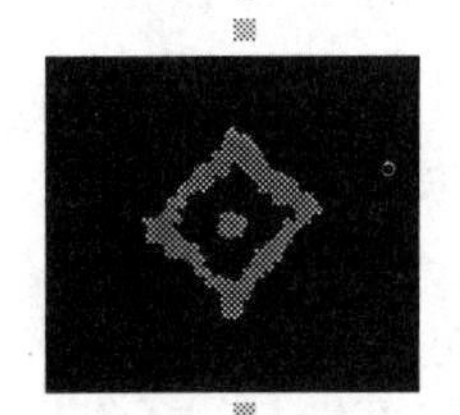

Episode by episode, the epic is first sung, then narrated. While singing and narrating, the bard dances, mimes, and dramatically represents the main peripeties of the story. In this dramatic representation, the bard takes the role of the hero. The normal musical accompaniment consists of a percussion stick . . . which, resting on a few little sticks so as to have a better resonance, is beaten with drumsticks by three young men. . . . These men regularly accompany the bard when he performs. . . . They know large fragments of the epic, and, whenever necessary, help the bard to remember and to find the thread of his story. Eventually, one of them will acquire full knowledge and mastery of the text and be the bard's successor. The narrator himself shakes the calabash rattle . . . and carries anklet bells. . . . The percussionists and members of the audience sing the refrains of the songs or repeat a whole sentence during each short pause made by the bard. . . . Members of the audience also encourage the reciter with short exclamations (including onomatopoeia) and hand clapping and whooping.

Daniel Biebuyck and Kahombo C. Mateene, *The Mwindo Epic* (Berkeley: University of California Press, 1969), p. 13.

Kimbundu

Sudika-mbambi

by Jelemía dia Sabatelu

The Mbundu live in Angola.

Let us tell of Kimanaueze kia Tumba a Ndala, favorite of friends, who fathered a son whose name was na Nzua of Kimanaueze.

Na Kimanaueze said, "Na Nzua, my son, go to Loanda. Some business has to be done there."

The son said, "But I've just brought home a wife."

The father said, "Go, I command you."

Na Nzua departed. He arrived in Loanda, and did business.

In the meantime, many-headed cannibals sacked na Kimanaueze's home; they sacked everything.

When the son who had gone to Loanda arrived at the house of his father, he found no people there.

He became hungry, and said, "What shall I do?" Then he said, "I shall go to the fields."

When he arrived in the fields, he saw a woman. He called her: she was the wife he had left behind.

She said, "Where have you come from?"

The man said, "What has done this to you?"

From Heli Chatelain, *Folk-Tales of Angola* (New York: American Folk-Lore Society, 1894), pp. 84–97.

The wife said, "The many-headed cannibals have destroyed us."

They lived together then. The woman was with child. The day came for her to give birth, and she heard someone speaking in her belly:

"Mother, my sword, here it comes.
Mother, my knife, here it comes.
Mother, my life-tree, here it comes.
Mother, my staff, here it comes.
Mother, place yourself well now,
I am coming here!"

The son emerged, and he said,

"My name is Sudika-mbambi:
On the earth, I set my staff.
In the sky, I set up an antelope."

Now the woman heard in her belly the younger child, who had remained there. The younger child said,

"Mother, my sword, here it comes.
My knife, here it comes.
My staff, here it comes.
My life-tree, here it comes.
Mother, sit well,
I am coming here."

The son emerged, and said,

"My name is Kabundungulu
Of the camwood tree.
My dog eats palm-nuts,
My kimbundu swallows a bull."

The elder son, Sudika-mbambi, said, "Plant my life-tree at the back of the house." Then he said, "Mother, what are you doing here?"

His mother said, "I wonder! I just gave birth to this child, and he is speaking already!"

The child said, "Do not wonder. You are going to see what I shall do." The child added, "Let us go to cut poles, so that we can build our parents' houses."

Sudika-mbambi and Kabundungulu took their swords, and went to the woodland.

Sudika-mbambi cut just one pole, and the poles all cut themselves.

The younger, Kabundungulu, did as his elder brother did.

Then the two bound the poles. They took them and put them outside. Then they returned to cut the grass. They brought the grass, and put it down outside.

Sudika-mbambi and Kabundungulu erected the house. Sudika-mbambi erected just one pole, and all of the house erected itself at once. He tied one cord, and all the cords tied themselves. He thatched one stalk of grass, and the house thatched itself.

Then Sudika-mbambi said, "Mother and father, come in. I have already built your house."

Later, he said, "I am going to fight the many-headed cannibals. Kabundugulu, my younger brother, stay with our parents. But if you see my life-tree wither, you'll know that, wherever I have gone, I am dead."

Sudika-mbambi set out. He arrived on a road, and heard a rustling in the grass.

He said, "Who's that?"

The person said, "I am Kipalende, I erect a house on a rock."

Sudika-mbambi said, "Come with me."

They traveled together.

Again, he heard a rustling in the grass.

He said, "Who's that?"

The person said, "I am Kipalende, I carve ten clubs in a day."

Sudika-mbambi said, "Come with me."

He arrived again on the road, and again he heard a rustling in the grass.

He said, "Who's that?"

The person said, "I am Kipalende, I gather corn-leaves in Kalunga."

Sudika-mbambi said, "Come with me."

They took to the road.

Again, he heard a rustling in the grass.

He said, "Who's that?"

The person said, "I am Kipalende, I bend the beard down to Kalunga."

Sudika-mbambi said, "Come with me."

They arrived on the road, and Sudika-mbambi saw someone coming on the other side of the river.

He asked, "Who are you?"

He said, "I am Kijandala-midi, one who eats a thousand people at once. With a hundred people, I rinse my mouth."

Sudika-mbambi said, "I am Sudika-mbambi: on the earth, I set my staff; in the sky, I set up an antelope."

When he heard this, Kijandala-midi ran away.

They arrived in the midst of the woodland. Sudika-mbambi told the four kipalende, "Let us build here, in order to fight the many-headed cannibals."

They went for the poles. Sudika-mbambi cut one pole: they all cut themselves. He tied one pole: they all tied themselves.

They prepared to erect the house. Sudika-mbambi took up one pole, and gave to to the kipalende who was able to erect a house on a rock, saying, "Take it."

The kipalende took the pole, and erected it on the rock. But it would not stand. He erected it again, and it would not stand.

Sudika-mbambi said, "You said, 'I erect a house on a rock.' Do you give it up?"

Sudika-mbambi himself then built the houses. He completed the building, and they went to sleep.

At dawn, Sudika-mbambi said, "Let us go to fight the many-headed cannibals."

The kipalende who was able to carve ten clubs a day remained behind. Sudika-mbambi took the other three kipalende along with him. They came to the many-headed cannibals, and fired their weapons.

At home, where the one kipalende remained, an old woman came along with her granddaughter.

She found the kipalende, and said, "Let's fight! If you defeat me, you shall marry my granddaughter."

They fought, and the kipalende was defeated. Then the old woman lifted a stone, and placed it on the kipalende, pinning him down. Then she went away.

Far off where the battle was taking place, Sudika-mbambi sensed that the kipalende was under a stone, and he told the other three, "Your companion is pinned under a stone."

They said, "Sudika-mbambi, you're lying! We're too far away. How can you know that he is pinned under a stone?"

Sudika-mbambi said, "What I say is the truth."

They stopped firing, and said, "Let's go home."

They arrived at home, and found the kipalende pinned under a stone.

Sudika-mbambi said, "What did I tell you?"

The kipalende said, "The truth."

They removed the stone, and said, "What happened?"

The kipalende said, "An old woman came here with her granddaughter, and she said, 'Let's fight. If you defeat me, you shall marry my granddaughter.' I fought with her, and she defeated me."

The others laughed at him, saying, "A woman has defeated you?"

They went to sleep.

In the morning, Sudika-mbambi said, "Let us go to the war."

Another of the kipalende remained behind this time. The others went off to the war, and they were firing their weapons.

At home, where the kipalende was staying, the old woman came along with her granddaughter.

She said, "Let's fight!"

The kipalende said, "Very well."

They struggled, and the old woman defeated the kipalende. She weighed him down with a stone.

Sudika-mbambi already knew that the kipalende was under a stone. He told the others, "Your companion is under a stone."

"Let's go home."

They arrived, lifted the stone off him, and said, "What happened?"

He said, "Yesterday, the old woman did the same thing to me as she did to our comrade."

They went to sleep.

At dawn, they went to war. Another of the kipalende remained behind.

At the war, they were firing their weapons.

Here at home, where the kipalende was staying, the old woman came along.

She found the kipalende, and said, "Let's fight. If you defeat me, you shall marry my granddaughter."

They fought, and the old woman defeated the kipalende. She weighed him down with a stone, and went away.

Sudika-mbambi knew this at once, and he told the others, "Let's go home. Your comrade has been weighed down by a stone."

They arrived at home. They lifted the stone off him, and said, "What happened?"

He said, "The old woman did the same thing to me that she did to our comrades."

They went to sleep.

Morning, and Sudika-mbambi said, "Let us go to the war."

Another of the kipalende remained behind.

The others went to the many-headed cannibals, and were firing their weapons.

At home, where the kipalende remained, the old woman came along, and said, "Let's fight! If you defeat me, you shall marry my granddaughter."

They fought. The old woman defeated the kipalende, and she weighed him down with a stone.

Sudika-mbambi, far off, knew what had happened at once. He said, "Let's go home. Your comrade is weighed down."

They stopped firing. Only one cannibal village remained.

They arrived at home, and freed the kipalende from the stone.

They went to sleep.

It dawned, and Sudika-mbambi said, "Yesterday, one cannibal village was left. You four kipalende go and fire the guns. Today, I shall remain behind."

The kipalende went to fire their weapons.

At home, where Sudika-mbambi remained, the old woman came along, and said, "Let's fight. If you defeat me, you shall marry my granddaughter."

They fought, and the old woman was defeated. Sudika-mbambi killed her, and he remained with her granddaughter.

The young woman said, "Today, I have life, for my grandmother always shut me up in a house of stone so that I could not get out. Today, I shall marry Sudika-mbambi."

He assented.

The kipalende came back, and said, "Today, the many-headed cannibals have been finished off."

Sudika-mbambi said, "It is well."

Time passed for them, and the kipalende made a plot to kill Sudika-mbambi, saying, "A mere child has surpassed us! How shall we kill him?"

They dug a hole in the ground, and spread mats on it. They called him.

They said, "Sit down here."

Sudika-mbambi sat down, and dropped into the hole. The kipalende covered him up.

Then they stayed with the young woman.

At home, whence Sudika-mbambi had come, his younger brother, Kabundungulu, remained. He went around to the back of the house, and found that the life-tree of his elder brother had withered.

He said, "Wherever my elder brother has gone, he is going to die."

He poured water on the life-tree, and it grew green.

Meanwhile, the elder brother, Sudika-mbambi, having dropped into the hole, found a road. He walked along that road, and came to an old woman. She was hoeing with the head part of her body, while her lower extremity was sitting in the shade.

Sudika-mbambi greeted the old woman: "My grandmother, it is warm there!"

The old woman responded, "It is hot indeed, my grandson."

Sudika-mbambi said, "Show me the way."

The old woman said, "Hoe a little for me, my grandson, and then I'll show you the way."

Sudika-mbambi took the hoe, and hoed for her.

The old woman said, "I thank you. Come, let me show you the way. Take this narrow path, don't take the wide path or you'll go astray. When you arrive outside of na Kalunga-ngombe's place, carry with you a jug of red pepper and a jug of wisdom."

Sudika-mbambi agreed. He took to the road, and arrived outside of na Kalunga-ngombe's place.

Na Kalunga-ngombe's dog barked at him. Sudika-mbambi scolded the dog, and it went into the house.

They spread a bed for Sudika-mbambi in the great house.

The sun set.

They had saluted him.

He said, "I have come to marry the daughter of na Kalunga-ngombe."

Na Kalunga-ngombe said, "You shall marry my daughter if you have a jug of red pepper and a jug of wisdom."

They cooked food for Sudika-mbambi in the evening. He uncovered it and looked: a cock and a basket of mush. He took out the cock and kept it under the bed. He took his own meat, and ate that with the mush.

In the middle of the night, he heard this in the village: "Who has killed the cock? Who has killed na Kalunga-ngombe's cock?"

Under the bed, the cock answered, "Kokolokue!"

Day broke.

Sudika-mbambi said, "Na Kalunga-ngombe, give me your daughter now."

Na Kalunga-ngombe said, "My daughter was carried away by the many-headed Kinioka kia Tumba. Go and rescue her."

Sudika-mbambi departed, and arrived outside Kinioka's place. He said, "Where is Kinioka?"

Kinioka's wife said, "He has gone shooting."

Sudika-mbambi waited for a while.

He saw some driver ants: they came towards him. He beat them off.

The red ants came towards him. He beat them off.

And bees came towards him. He beat them off.

Wasps came towards him. He beat them off.

A head of Kinioka came towards him. He cut it off.

Another head came, and he cut that off too.

Then another head came, and he cut Kinioka's palm tree, and cut off the head.

Another head came towards him, and he cut off the head of Kinioka's dog, and cut off the head of Kinioka.

Then came another head, and Sudika-mbambi cut Kinioka's banana tree, and cut off the head.

Kinioka was dead.

Sudika-mbambi entered Kinioka's house. He found na Kalunga-ngombe's daughter, and said, "Let's go! Your father has sent for you."

They arrived outside na Kalunga-ngombe's place, and Sudika-mbambi said, "Your daughter is here."

Na Kalunga-ngombe said, "Kimbiji kia Malenda a Ngandu, the crocodile, keeps catching my goats and pigs. Kill him for me."

Sudika-mbambi said, "Bring me a suckling pig." [When hunting crocodiles, the people make a hook of crossed pieces of hard wood, with both ends sharply pointed, and on this they stick a suckling pig as bait. When it swallows the pig, the crocodile gets the sharp pieces of wood stuck in its throat or stomach, and can then be pulled ashore, provided the rope and the men are strong enough. A single man would naturally have to let go or follow the beast into the water, as Sudika-mbambi does.]

They gave him the suckling pig. He put the pig on a hook, and cast it into the water.

Kimbiji came to take it, and he swallowed the pig. Sudika-mbambi began to pull, but he tumbled into the water, and Kimbiji kia Malenda a Ngandu swallowed him.

At home, his younger brother, Kabundungulu, went around to the back of the house to see the life-tree. It was dry.

He said, "My elder brother is dead. I shall go where he went."

Kabundungulu went to the road that his elder brother traveled on. He arrived at his elder brother's house, and found the kipalende there.

He said, "Where did my elder brother go?"

The kipalende said, "We don't know."

Kabundungulu said, "You have killed him! Uncover the grave!"

They uncovered it. Kabundungulu got in, and he arrived on the road on which his elder brother had traveled.

He found the old woman who was hoeing with the upper body, the lower was in the shade.

He said, "You, old woman, show me the way my elder brother took."

The old woman showed him the way.

Kabundungulu arrived outside na Kalunga-ngombe's place, and said, "Where is my elder brother?"

Na Kalunga-ngombe said, "Kimbiji has swallowed him."

Kabundungulu said, "Kimbiji has swallowed him." He said, "Give me a pig."

They gave the pig to him. He put it on a hook, and cast it into the water. Kimbiji swallowed the hook.

Kabundungulu called the people, telling them to pull Kimbiji out of the water. They pulled the crocodile onto dry land.

Kabundungulu took his knife, and cut Kimbiji open. He found the bones of his elder brother, and he gathered them.

He said, "My elder, arise!"

Sudika-mbambi arose.

The younger brother said, "Let us go now, my elder."

Na Kalunga-ngombe gave Sudika-mbambi his daughter.

They took the path, and arrived at the hole where Sudika-mbambi had died. The ground cracked, and they emerged on the earth. There, they found the four kipalende. They drove them away.

Time passed for Sudika-mbambi and Kabundungulu.

Then the younger brother said, "My elder, give me one woman, for you have two."

The elder said, "No. You, my brother, cannot marry my wife."

But when the elder brother went hunting, his younger brother went into his house to entertain Sudika-mbambi's elders.

When Sudika-mbambi returned from his hunting trip, his wife told him, "Your younger brother keeps coming here to make love to us."

When he heard this, Sudika-mbambi was displeased. He and his younger brother began to quarrel. They struck each other, they wanted to kill each other. But neither one could kill the other. They thrust at each other with their swords, but neither succeeded in cutting the other.

Finally, they got tired of fighting.

So it was that the elder—Sudika-mbambi: on the earth, he sets his staff; in the sky, he sets up an antelope—went to the east.

His younger—Kabundungulu of the camwood tree: his dog eats palm nuts, his kimbundu swallows a bull—went to the west.

The elder brother and the younger quarreled about women, and then parted. And so it has remained: when the storm thunders, it is the elder, who went to the *east; the other thunder, the thunder that responds, is the younger, who went to the west.*

We have told our story.

Commentary

This story dramatizes the puberty rite of passage of Sudika-mbambi. It is also an etiological story, combining tale and myth. But it is primarily the narrative of an extraordinary person who is both mortal and supernatural: not God now, more human. We have moved from the age of creation into the contemporary age, but there are still ties to myth-time, to the world of the gods, and there are suggestions of the hero here.

In the introduction, Kimanaueze's home has been destroyed by cannibals. This is followed by two patterns: the births of Sudika-mbambi and Kabundungulu, twins, prodigies, and a pattern fashioned of the wonderful things done by the brothers, revealing their unique abilities.

The story largely dramatizes the stages of Sudika-mbambi's puberty ritual, with emphasis placed on the second stage, his ordeal or initiation into manhood. The conflict is established as Sudika-mbambi goes to fight the cannibals who destroyed his home; it is a journey of vengeance. This is the separation stage of his puberty ritual. The storyteller plants an embedded image: the life-tree, that Sudika-mbambi leaves behind. A pattern reveals Sudika-mbambi's amazing abilities. This is the ordeal or initiation stage of the puberty rite. His abilities are shown as he measures his strength against that of the supernatural kipalende. In a patterned war against the cannibals, the kipalende remain behind, one at a time, and each is overcome by an old woman, the grandmother of a potential bride. This pattern is a development of the preceding pattern, because when Sudika-mbambi breaks the pattern, he shows his amazing abilities. He wins the granddaughter, but is then betrayed by the kipalende; they are not helpful after all. And, for the moment, he loses her.

During this transition in the story, the life-tree at home withers, but becomes green again. Sudika-mbambi, now in the underworld, goes on a quest for the daughter of the king of the underworld, Kalunga-ngombe, and the ordeal pattern deepens. Sudika-mbambi helps an old woman, who then shows him the way. A pattern of tasks follows; before Kalunga-ngombe agrees to the marriage, he sets impossible tasks for Sudika-mbambi. Task one involves Kalunga-ngombe himself and has to do with the cock substitution; he is victorious. Task two involves Kinioka, including the pattern of ants, bees, wasps, and Kinioka himself; Sudika-mbambi is victorious. Task three includes the major confrontation with Kimbiji, a crocodile; there is a struggle, and Sudika-mbambi is swallowed.

The swallowing monster motif, a common motif in the oral tradition, is a useful image that suggests change from one state of being to another. One goes into the belly of the beast one way, comes out transformed. It is a symbol, often suggesting, as it does here, the shift from childhood to adulthood. Sometimes, the suggestion of a swallowing monster, without the actual presence of a swallowing monster, is substituted.

Sudika-mbambi's ordeal is now over. He has struggled with the kipalende and won; he has struggled with Kalunga-ngombe and has won two battles and lost the one against Kimbiji. But he has not really lost. His swallowing by the crocodile is simply symbolic of the change that he has undergone, thanks to his various ordeals. What remains is his emergence from the belly of the crocodile, that is, his return.

This is the purpose of Kabundungulu's quest; it is the return stage of Sudika-mbambi's puberty rite. Kabundungulu, Sudika-mbambi's twin brother—in the language of storytelling, the two are the same—sets out to rescue his brother when the kilembe withers. A pattern establishes their identical nature: Kabundungulu has the same experiences, essentially, as Sudika-mbambi. He finds Sudika-mbambi, and brings him back to life.

There is an etiological ending, suggesting the hero as a model for humankind. The brothers quarrel, and then become subsumed into nature. Sudika-mbambi becomes the thunder; his brother echoes that thunder, echoing the basic structure of this tale. The reason for this mythic touch to what is essentially a tale is to give heavenly sanction to the ritual that the man-god, Sudika-mbambi, has just experienced.

Sudika-mbambi, god-like and heroic, undertakes to move through the stages of the puberty ritual, establishing a model for all humans. Kabundungulu, his brother, the stand-in for all of the rest of humanity, follows in Sudika-mbambi's footsteps, repeating the stages of the ritual laid down by this god-like, heroic forbear. In the end, when Sudika-mbambi becomes a part of the universe, Kabundungulu, and the rest of us, continue to echo the experience of that ideal character.

Notes

Jelemia dia Sabatelu lived in Malange. His father was a shoemaker from Mbaka who had settled at the court of Bangu, the head chief of the Mbamba people. He married a daughter of the chief's elder sister. Jelemia dia Sabatelu learned his father's trade, and became his successor in Bangu's village. Some of the narratives performed by Jelemia dia Sabatelu were transcribed in Angola, others in the United States (in 1890, Chatelain brought the artist with him to America for a visit). Kimanaueze kia Tumba a Ndala is a purely mythical figure. Sudika-mbambi: Sudika means "to hitch, or hang on or in a high place"; Mbambi is "antelope." The name suggests a thunderbolt "up on high, in the clouds, leaping to and fro like a deer."

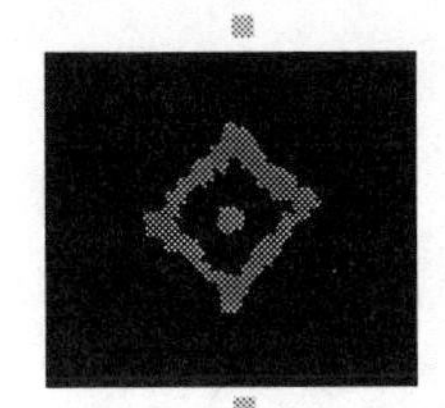

The training of a griot [oral bard] begins in boyhood, and like other craft training it takes place within the family. A griot boy will normally be trained by his father or by an older brother. . . . After a young griot has attained some proficiency, he will spend a lot of time going around with his father or older brother or other experienced griot and listening to his performance. The learner may contribute to the performance, perhaps just by playing his instrument, but also by taking some part in the narration, such as singing some songs or reciting some of the praises. For griots, learning their craft is a continuing process, since griots travel extensively and hear other griots performing.

Gordon Innes, *Sunjata, Three Mandinka Versions* (London: SOAS, 1974), p. 6.

Swahili

Liongo

The Swahili live in eastern Africa.

In the times when Shanga was a flourishing city, there was a man whose name was Liongo. He had great strength, and was a very great man in the city. He oppressed the people exceedingly, until one day they made a plan, to go to him at his house and bind him.

A great number of people went. They came upon him suddenly in his house, and seized him and bound him. Then they took him to prison, and put him into it.

Liongo stayed in the prison many days, and he made a plot and escaped.

Then he went outside the town, and for many days harassed the people in the same way. People could not go into the country, neither to cut wood nor to draw water. They were in much trouble.

The people said, "What stratagem can we resort to, to get him and kill him?"

One said, "Let us go against him while he is sleeping, and kill him."

Others said, "If you get him, then bind him and bring him."

They went and made a plan to take him. They bound him, and took him to the town. They bound him with chains and fetters, with a post between his legs.

They left him there for many days, and his mother sent him food every day. Before the door where he was bound, soldiers were placed. They watched him, they never went away except by turns.

Many days and many months passed.

Night after night, he sang beautiful songs. Everyone who heard the songs was delighted.

From Edward Steere, *Swahili Tales* (London: Bell and Daldy, 1870), pp. 440–453.

They would say to their friends, "Let us go and listen to Liongo's songs which he sings in his room."

And they would go and listen.

When night came, people would regularly go and say to him, "We have come to hear your songs."

And Liongo would sing the songs, he could not refuse. The people in the town were delighted with the songs.

Every day, through his grief at being bound, Liongo composed different songs. The people, in time, knew those songs little by little, but he and his mother and her slave knew them well. His mother knew the meanings of those songs, and the people in the town did not.

One day, their slave girl brought some food. The soldiers took the food from her and ate it. Some scraps were left, and those they gave to her.

The slave girl told Liongo, "I brought food, and these soldiers have taken it from me and eaten it. These scraps remain."

He said to her, "Give them to me."

And he received them and ate them, and thanked God for what he had got.

He was inside and the slave girl outside the door, and Liongo said to her,

> "You, slave girl, shall be sent
> To tell my mother I am a simpleton.
> I have not yet learned the ways of the world.
> Let her make me a cake, in the middle of which
> Let her put files, that I may cut my fetters,
> And the chains be opened,
> That I may enter the road,
> That I may glide like a snake,
> That I may mount the roofs and walls,
> That I may look this way and that."

And he said, "Greet my mother well. Tell her what I have told you."

She went and told his mother, and said, "Your son greets you, he has given me a message to come and deliver to you."

Liongo's mother said, "What is the message?"

And the slave girl reported to her what she had been told.

Liongo's mother understood the message, and went to a shop and got grain. She gave the grain to her slave to clean.

Then she went and bought many files, and brought those home.

She took the flour and made many fine cakes. Then she took bran and made a large cake, and took the files and put them into that cake. She gave it to the slave to take to Liongo.

The slave took the cakes, and arrived at the door. The soldiers robbed her, choosing the fine cakes, and ate those themselves. As for the bran cake, they told her to take that one to her master. She took the cake to Liongo. He broke the cake open, took out the files, and put them away. Then he ate the cake and drank water, and was comforted.

The people of the town wanted Liongo to be killed. He himself heard it said, "You shall be killed."

He said to the soldiers, "When shall I be killed?"

They told him, "Tomorrow."

He said, "Call my mother and the chief man in the town, and call all the townspeople. I shall take leave of them."

The soldiers went and called them, and many people came together, along with his mother and her slave.

Liongo asked them, "Have you all assembled?"

They answered, "We are assembled."

He said, "I want a horn and cymbals and a gong."

They brought them.

He said, "I have an entertainment today, I want to take leave of you."

They said to him, "Very well. Go on, play."

He said, "Let someone take the horn, someone take the cymbals, someone take the gong."

They said, "How shall we play them?"

He taught them to play, and they played.

There on the inside where he was imprisoned, Liongo himself sang, until the music was in full swing. Then he took a file and cut off his fetters. When the music dropped, he stopped filing and sang, and when they played he cut the fetters.

The people knew nothing of what was going on inside until Liongo's fetters were divided. Then he cut the chains until they were divided. The people knew nothing of this because of their delight in the music.

When they looked up, he had broken the door down and come outside to them. The people threw their instruments way, preparing to run, but they were not quick enough. Liongo caught them, he knocked their heads together and killed them. Then he went outside the town and took leave of his mother, so that they might "see one another again."

Liongo went away into the forest, and stayed many days, harassing people as before, and killing people.

They sent crafty people, and told them, "Go and make Liongo your friend, in order to kill him."

They went, fearfully.

When they came to him, they made a friendship with him.

Then, one day, they said to him, "Sultan, let us entertain one another."

Liongo answered them, "If I eat of an entertainment, what shall I, who am excessively poor, give in return?"

They said to him, "Let us entertain one another with palm fruit."

He asked them, "How shall we eat the fruit?"

They said, "One shall climb the palm tree, and throw the fruit down for us to eat. When we have done that, let another person climb up, and so on, until we have finished."

He said to them, "Very well."

The first person climbed up the tree, and they ate.

The second climbed up, and they ate.

And the third climbed up, and they ate.

They had plotted that when Liongo climbed up, "Let us shoot him with arrows there, while he's up in the tree."

But the intelligent Liongo saw through the plot. When all had finished, they said to him, "Come, it's your turn."

He said, "Very well."

He took his bow and arrows in his hand, and said,

"I shall strike the ripe fruit above,
And we shall eat in the midst of it."

Liongo shot his arrow, and a bough was broken off.

He shot again, and a second bough was broken.

He gave them an entire palm tree, the ground was covered with fruit.

They ate.

When they were finished eating, the men said among themselves, "He saw through our plot. What are we to do?"

They said, "Let's go away."

So they took leave of Liongo, saying,

"Liongo, the chief, you were not taken in;
You are not a man.
You got out of it like a devil."

They went away and gave their report to the headman there in the town. They said, "We could do nothing."

They advised together. "Who will be able to kill him?"

"Perhaps his nephew will do it."

They went and called Liongo's nephew.

He came.

They said to him, "Go, ask your father what will kill him. When you find out, come and tell us, and when he is dead we'll give you the kingdom."

He said, "Very well."

He went. When he arrived, Liongo welcomed him, and asked, "What have you come to do?"

He said, "I have come to see you."

Liongo said, "I know that you have come to kill me. They have deceived you."

The nephew asked, "Father, what is it that can kill you?"

He said, "A copper needle. If anyone stabs me in the navel with a copper needle, I shall die."

Then the nephew went away into the town, and told the conspirators, "A copper needle will kill him."

They gave him a needle, and he went back to his father.

When he saw him, his father sang,

> "I, who am bad, am he who is good to you,
> Do me no evil.
> I, who am bad, am he that is good to you."

And he welcomed him, knowing that "He has come to kill me."

Two days passed, Liongo was asleep in the evening, and the nephew stabbed him in the navel with the needle.

Liongo awoke because of the pain, and he took his bow and arrows, and went to a place near the wells. He knelt down there, putting himself ready with his bow.

And there he died.

In the morning, the people who came to the wells to draw water saw Liongo, and they thought he was alive. They ran back to the town, reporting the news, "No water is to be had today!"

Everyone who went came back running.

Many people set out, and when they saw him they came back, unable to get near.

For three days, the people were in distress, getting no water.

Then they called his mother, and said to her, "Go and speak to your son. If he doesn't go away so that we can get water, we shall kill you."

Liongo's mother went to him. She took hold of him to soothe him with songs, and he fell down. His mother wept, she knew that her son was dead.

She went to tell the townspeople that he was dead, and they all went to look at him. They saw that he was dead.

They buried him. His grave is to be seen at Ozi to this day.

Then they seized that young man, Liongo's nephew, and they killed him, they did not give him the kingdom.

Commentary

In the opening conflict and pattern of this story, Liongo, great in strength, oppresses the people. The second pattern has to do with the capturing of Liongo, who, when bound, sings beautiful songs. The songs are loved by the people, but to his mother and her slave, the songs have a coded meaning. He sings to the slave, telling her to tell his mother to send cake with files in its center. He is to be killed the following day, so requests full orchestration for his songs: during the orchestration, he files his fetters, and escapes, killing his captors.

The opening pattern is repeated, as Liongo again oppresses the people. The second pattern is also repeated, as the people attempt to capture Liongo. When a palm fruit ruse fails, they conclude that he is a devil, and send his nephew to him to find out what will kill him. Liongo reveals his weakness: if anyone stabs him in the navel with a copper needle, he will die. The conspirators give the nephew the needle, and he stabs Liongo. Liongo dies near the wells where the people get their water; they fear to approach, thinking he is still alive. The nephew is killed.

Liongo is a creator of song, of ritual: "And he taught them to play, and they played." The life-death struggle in Liongo has to do with his own death and life, and also the way he deals with his enemies, destroying them. Out of this comes life, in the form of poetry, song.

A Xhosa storyteller (photo by Harold Scheub)

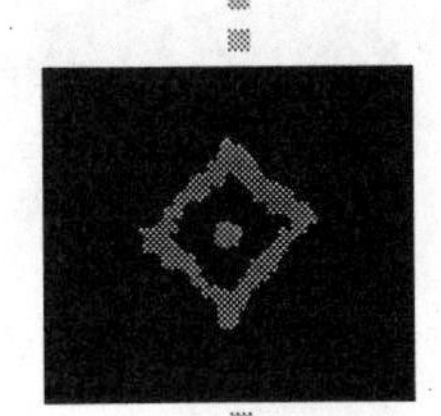

The tales were told in the evening, sometimes as a climax to other activities such as dances and plays. Evening was appropriate because everyone would be home from their diverse duties. . . . The first convention that had to be observed related to the prohibition of telling tales during the day. It was generally believed that if this convention was violated, all the cattle, sheep, and goats would mysteriously disappear and a particular society, clan or family become irredeemably poor. This convention was intended to prevent people from forsaking hard work during the day in favor of tale-telling. . . . The actual tale-telling was done systematically so that if a group was sitting in a circle, a clock-wise or an anticlockwise system was followed and everybody present had to tell one. . . .

R. N. Gecau, *Kikuyu Folktales, Their Nature and Value* (Nairobi: East African Publishing House, 1970), pp. 6–7.

Malagasy

Ibonia

The Malagasy live on the island of Madagascar, off the southeastern coast of Africa.

Once, there were two sisters who had no children, so they went to work the divination at the house of Ratoboboka.

As soon as they came in, she asked, "Why have you come here?"

The sisters replied, "We are childless, and so have come to inquire by divination here of you."

Then Ratoboboka said, "Look into my hair."

The elder one looked and saw only a bit of grass. She said, "I saw nothing, Mother, but this bit of grass."

Ratoboboka replied, "Give it to me, that is it."

Then the younger woman searched, and saw only a little bit of broken charm, red in color.

She said, "I saw nothing, Mother, but this little bit of a red charm."

Ratoboboka replied, "Give it to me, that is it."

Then Ratoboboka said, "Go alone to yonder forest to the east. When you have arrived there the trees will all speak and say, 'I am the sacred child-charm.' But do not speak for all that. Take the single tree that does not speak there, last of all. Take its root that lies to the east."

So the two sisters went away. They came to the forest, and each of the trees said, "I am the sacred child-charm [i.e., that causes the barren to give birth]."

Nevertheless, the sisters passed them all by.

From James Sibree, Jr., "Magalasy Folk-tales," *Folk-Lore Journal*, 2 (1884), 49–55.

When they came to the single tree that did not speak, they dug around the tree, and saw one of the roots that struck eastwards, and they took it away.

When they were on the road, the sisters vowed, saying, "If we should bear boy and girl [i.e., if one have a boy and the other a girl], they shall marry each other."

When they came home, they each drank of the charm.

Accordingly, the elder one became pregnant, and after a half year had passed the younger was also with child. When the time came for her to be delivered, the elder sister bore a daughter, and she game it the name Rampelasoamananoro.

In time came the day for her younger sister to be delivered, so she went to the south of the hearth to bring forth her child. But the child in her womb, they say, spoke, and said, "I am not a slave, to be taken here to the south of the hearth," so his mother went north of the hearth. But the child spoke again, "I am not a prince, to be taken to the north of the hearth." Then his mother took him to the box, but the child said, "I do not like to be smoked." After some time, the child said, "Make me a big fire of wood." So they made it. Then it said again, "Swallow a knife for me, and take me to the west of the hearth." So he was taken there. Then, at that place, with the knife his mother had swallowed he ripped open his mother's womb, then leaped into the fire that burned brightly there—after having patted the wound that he had made by tearing open his mother, so that it was healed. His father and mother endeavored to save him, lest he should be killed when he went into the fire, but when they put out their hands to take him, their hands were broken and they were unable to take him. And so it happened with their feet as well.

After a while, the child spoke: "Give me a name."

His mother said, "Perhaps you should be called Fozanatokondrilahy, for I hear that he was a strong man."

But the child did not like it.

So his mother mentioned another name, and said, "Perhaps Ravatovolovoay then, for he, I understand, was famous for his strength."

But he did not like that either. So the child gave himself a name. He said,

> "I am Iboniamasy, Iboniamanoro:
> Breaking in pieces the earth and the kingdom;
> At the point of its horn, not gored;
> Beneath its hoofs, not trampled on;
> On its molar teeth, not crushed.
> Rising up, I break the heavens;
> And when I bow down the earth yawns open.
> My robe, when folded up, but a span long;
> But when spread out, it covers the heavens,
> And when it is shaken it is like the lightning.
> My loin-cloth, when rolled together,
> Is but the size of a fist,

But when unfolded, it surrounds the ocean;
Its tongue, when girded, causes the dew to descend,
And its tail sweeps away the rocks.
Ah! I am indeed Iboniamasy, Iboniamanoro."

Having spoken thus, he came out from the fire and went to his mother's lap.

After he had grown up, he had a dog called Rampelamahavatra.

One day, while Ibonia was hunting in the fields, that famous man called Fozanatokondrilahy came seeking him.

He inquired of his parents, "Where is Ibonia?"

They replied, "He has gone for pleasure into the forest."

Then Fozanatokondrilahy took Ibonia's dog, and the parents could not prevent it.

When Ibonia returned from hunting, he asked his parents, "Where has my dog gone?"

They replied, "Fozanatokondrilahy has taken it."

Ibonia said, "I am going to fetch my dog, Father."

But his father would not let him do so. He said, "Why, child, even the crocodiles in the water are sought by Fozanatokondrilahy, and found. How can you fight with him without coming to harm?" But seeing that he would not be warned, his father made him fetch a great stone. He wanted to test the strength of his son. He said, "Since I cannot persuade you, fetch me yonder big stone to make me a seat." Ibonia went to the stone and brought it. Then his father let him go.

So off he went, and caught up with Fozanatokondrilahy.

When Fozanatokondrilahy saw Ibonia, he said, "What are you seeking here?"

Ibonia replied, "I want my dog!"

Fozanatokondrilahy asked him, "Are you strong?"

"Yes," Ibonia replied, "I am strong."

No sooner had he said that than Fozanatokondrilahy seized him and threw him more than the length of a house.

Ibonia, in his turn, seized Fozanatokondrilahy and threw him also as far as the length of a house.

So they went on, first one and then the other, until each had thrown his opponent as far as ten house lengths.

Then Fozanatokondrilahy said, "Let's not throw each other any more. Instead, let us cast each other down."

So he lifted Ibonia up and cast him down. But Ibonia did not descend fully: he stuck in the ground as far as his ankles.

Then Ibonia, in his turn, cast down Fozanatokondrilahy, who descended as far as his knees.

So they went on with each other, until Fozanatokondrilahy was forced completely into the ground, into the rock on which they were contending, and Ibonia then pressed the stones down upon him so that he was fully covered up.

Ibonia then called together Fozanatokondrilahy's subjects and asked them, "Will you obey the living or the dead?"

Fozanatokondrilahy's wife and people replied, "We will obey the living."

They became Ibonia's subjects, and he departed with all his spoils.

On his way back, a number of people met him. They were skilled in various ways: some were swimmers in deep waters, others were able to tie firmly, still others were able to see great distances, others were able to give life. Ibonia showed kindness to all these, and gave them a share of the spoils that he had obtained.

He returned to his village. When he arrived, he could not find Rampelasoamananoro, his betrothed wife, because she had been taken by Ravatovolovoay.

He asked his parents, "Where is my wife?"

They replied, "She has been taken by Ravatovolovoay."

So he said, "I am going to fetch my wife."

When they heard that, his parents warned him: "Don't do that, Child. Ravatovolovoay is extremely powerful!"

But he would not stay.

At last, his father became angry, and he took gun and spear to kill Ibonia. But he could no nothing to harm him, for the spear bent double when he hurled it.

Then Ibonia planted some arums and plantain trees, and said to his parents, "If these wither, then I am ill. If they die, that is a sign that I also am dead."

That being done, he went away, and came to an old man who took care of Ravatovolovoay's plaintain trees. He asked him, "What is it that you take with you when you go to visit your master?"

The old man replied, "A few plantains and some rice with honey, my lad."

Ibonia slept there that night. In the morning, he plucked off the old man's hair from his head, so that the whole skin from his body came away with it. Then Ibonia covered himself with that skin, and he fetched some plantains and prepared rice and honey to take to Ravatovolovoay.

He came to Ravatovolovoay's village, and when the people there saw him they said, "The old man has come." They did not know it was Ibonia because he was covered with the old man's skin.

He said, "I have come, children, to visit you."

So they took the plantains and the rice that he had brought to the prince—for Ravatovolovoay was a prince. They cooked rice for the old man, and gave it to him in the servants' plate. But Ibonia would not eat from that. He said, "Fetch me a plantain leaf on which to eat. You know well enough how well my wife and I live, so why do you give me a plate like that?"

On the day following his arrival, it was announced that the prince would engage in a sport, throwing at a mark with a cross-piece of wood. So the old man went with the rest. When they came to the place where the mark was set up, the prince aimed at the mark but not one of the people could hit it.

Then the old man said, "Just give me a cord, let me catch hold of it."

They gave him one, and he was successful with the one the prince had missed.

The prince said, "This is not the old man, but someone altogether different. Give me a spear and gun so that I may attack him."

But the old man said, "Who else is it but I, my son? I am only revealing the strength that I used to possess."

As they went on with the game, the old man pressed in with the rest, but did not obtain what he had aimed at—the cross-piece went into the earth and brought up a hedgehog, then dipped into the water and brought out a crocodile.

Ravatovolovoay said, "Did I not tell you that this is not the old man, but someone else?"

Again, he sought to kill him, but the old man spoke as before, and Ravatovolovoay again refrained.

On the next day, the prince's orders came: "Today, we shall try the tempers of the oxen. Therefore, make ropes to catch the stubborn ones."

When they began the game, many of the stronger oxen could not be caught.

Then the old man said, "Just give me a rope."

They gave him a rope, and he caught the strong oxen and held them.

When the people saw this, they wondered.

When the prince saw it, he said again, "This cannot be the old man! It must be someone else."

But the people replied, "But who else can it be?"

The old man answered again as he had done before, that he was no one else, that he was merely revealing his strength.

So the players dispersed.

The following night, Ravatovolovoay went to his other wife.

Then the old man went to the house where Rampelasoamananoro was, and said, "Let me lie here by the side of your feet."

But she said, "What a wretch you must be, old man, to say such a thing to me! To speak of lying at my side!"

But when the people were fast asleep, Ibonia took off the skin of the old man with which he had covered himself, and there was a blaze of light in the house because of his shining skin.

Then his wife knew him, and said, "Is it you who have come?"

"Yes," he said, "I have come to fetch you."

He told the people to go out of the house. When they had gone out, he bolted and barred the doors, then sat down to wait for the morning, so that he might show some marvelous things to the people of the village.

Then Rampelasoamananoro said to Ibonia, "How shall we free ourselves from this place?"

He replied, "Don't be afraid! We'll get out all right. But listen to what I say: do not speak to me or beckon to me, because if you do either they will kill me."

In the morning, when Ravatovolovoay awoke, he found that the door of the house where Rampelasoamananoro was was locked.

He said to the people, "Isn't it just as I told you? That this is not the old man, but another person?"

When he tried to break open the door, the door became like a rock, and he could not force it. Then he set fire to the thatch of the roof; it would not burn, but also became as rock.

All attempts were unavailing, and at last Ibonia and Rampelasoamananoro prepared to go out. Ibonia caused a profound sleep to fall on all the people outside the house. Everyone slept.

Then he said to her, "Let's go, but remember, do not speak to me or beckon to me."

They went out, and stepped over all the people who slept along the road they traveled. When they came to the gateway, Ibonia beckoned to a lad and told him to awaken the people. So the lad awoke and roused all the people, including Ravatovolovoay.

The prince said, "Quickly, bring guns and spears! And come, let us pursue them!"

Away they went, shooting at them with their guns. But when the smoke rolled away, there was the pair, going along without any harm. They went on without any mischance, until they arrived at a waterside. When they got there, the wife beckoned to him, to ask him where to ford the water. The moment she did that, Ibonia was struck by a bullet. He fell back into the water, he was dead.

Then Ravatovolovoay came up to Rampelasoamananoro and asked what she wished to do, to follow the living or the dead?

She said, "I shall follow the living, sir," at the same time excusing herself to him.

So Ibonia met his death, and his parents looked at the arums and the plantain trees which he had left with them as a token. When they saw that they had dried up, they lamented him, because the things that he had given them as a sign about himself were dead.

But the friends to whom he had given presents when he came from conquering Fozanatokondrilahy had by no means forgotten him. One day, Joiner-together and his companions said to Far-off-seer, "Look out for Ibonia, lest some harm should have befallen him."

He looked, and said, "Ibonia is dead. A stream is carrying away his bones."

Then Far-off-seer and Joiner-together and Life-giver said to Strong-swimmer, "Go and gather those bones."

So he went and gathered all of Ibonia's bones.

Then Joiner-together united the bones, so that they all came together again.

And Life-giver made them live.

They continued invoking blessings until flesh grew and a little breath came, until he could eat a little rice, until at length he could eat as he had formerly been used to do.

When he was alive again, Ibonia prepared to go and fetch his wife away from Ravatovolovoay. He went off, and when he came to the village there was the prince playing a game above the gateway.

When he saw Ibonia, he asked, "Where are you going?"

Ibonia said, "To get my wife."

Then Ibonia struck him with the palm of his hand, and Ravatovolovoay became like grease in his hand.

So Ibonia got everything that had belonged to Ravatovolovoay.

Commentary

This story is in five parts: the first part depicts Ibonia's marvelous birth; in part two, Ibonia is given a name; part three pairs Ibonia against Fozanatokondrilahy; and, in part four, Ibonia fights Ravatovolovoay; part five dramatizes Ibonia's resurrection.

The opening conflict of the story has to do with two barren women who go to a diviner, Ratoboboka, for advice; she gives them charms with the interdiction that they should go to a tree that does not speak, and follow its root. The women make a pact: if they bear a daughter and son, their offspring will marry. It turns out that one of them bears a girl, Rampelasoamananoro, and the other gives birth to a boy, Ibonia.

Ibonia has a supernatural birth. He speaks in his mother's womb, telling where he is to be born. He cuts himself out of his mother's womb, then heals her. He moves into the hearth fire; when his parents attempt to save him, their hands and feet are broken.

In an identity pattern, Ibonia is named. In his song, he names himself, singing his praises. He claims that he is the earth, the universe.

Now he moves to manhood. His first task involves his dog and Fozanatokondrilahy. Ibonia's father tests him to assure that his son is prepared for this challenge. Then Ibonia and Fozanatokondrilahy throw each other, and push each other into the ground. Ibonia wins, and takes the subjects of the vanquished.

In an embedded image, Ibonia helps people who are skilled in various ways: a swimmer, one who can tie firmly, one who is able to see great distances, one who gives life. That is not the only embedded image; there is also a life-tree.

The struggle with Fozanatokondrilahy was only a preliminary to the major confrontation, that with Ravatovolovoay, a battle over Ibonia's wife. Again, his father tests him.

Ibonia disguises himself, emphasizing the identity theme that is at the heart of transformation stories like this one. He takes the hair and skin of an old man who works for Ravatovolovoay, and goes to his enemy. They engage in contests. When the "old man" wins a throwing match, Ravatovolovoay's suspicions deepen. And when the "old man" wins a competition having to do with roping oxen, Ravatovolovoay's suspicions deepen the more. This contest pattern is intensified by Ravatovolovoay's patterned death-threats. After revealing his identity in a blaze of light, Ibonia and his wife are reunited, and then escape.

Ibonia tells his wife not to speak or beckon to him, or he will die. The house will not burn or be broken into. Then Ibonia causes all his enemy to sleep, and he and his wife leave. He awakens them, and they give chase. But his wife breaks the interdiction and he dies. Ravatovolovoay takes her again. Now the image embedded earlier comes to fruition: Far-seer sees what has happened, Strong-swimmer gathers Ibonia's bones, Joiner-together unites the bones, Life-giver gives them life. Ibonia is reborn, his identity as a man and a leader revealed. He gets his wife, destroys Ravatovolovoay, takes everything that belonged to his enemy, and establishes his kingdom.

This is the story of Ibonia's transformation to manhood, but there is an etiological element as well, having to do with the origin of marriage. Ibonia's experience is not his alone: he charts the way for all humanity.

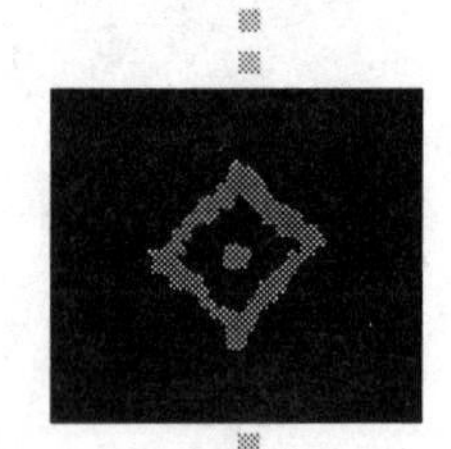

Only the king . . . has an official storyteller. Anyone with a gift for storytelling is encouraged.

Agnes C. L. Donohugh and Priscilla Berry, "A Luba Tribe in Katanga, Customs and Folklore," *Africa* 5 (1932): 80.

Shilluk

Nyikang and the Sun

(Two versions)

The Shilluk live in Sudan.

Version One

In ancient times, the people came to the country of Kerau. This is the country into which Nyikang came.

Here, Nyikang and Duwat, his brother, separated.

Duwat said, "Nyikang, where are you going?"

He replied, "I am going to that place there."

Duwat said, "Nyikang, look behind!"

Nyikang turned around. He looked back, and saw a stick for planting dura. Duwat had thrown the stick to him.

Nyikang went back to get the stick, and he asked, "What is that?"

Duwat said, "That is a thing with which to dig the ground of your village."

Nyikang went then and settled in the country of Turo. This is the country of his son, Dak.

Dak used to sit on the ashes of the village and play the tom, a stringed instrument.

But his uncles, Nyikang's brothers, said, "Is the country to be ruled by Dak alone?" They were jealous of him. They went to sharpen their spears.

Version One, from Diedrich Westermann, *The Shilluk People, Their Language and Folklore* (Philadelphia: Board of Foreign Missions of the United Presbyterian Church of N.A., 1912), pp. 158–161.

But Dak was told about them: "You are going to be killed by your uncles!"

Nyikang went to get an ambach. He hewed it, and made hands for it, so that it looked like the statue of a man.

Then Dak went and sat down in the same place again, and began to play his instrument.

His uncles came and stabbed him—that is, the ambach statue.

Dak went to his home, unhurt.

Nyikang came and said, "My son has been killed by his uncles."

The uncles were afraid, and they said, "Let every man stay at home for four days. When four days have passed, we may mourn him."

On the morning after the four days had passed, all the people came to mourn. There were many of them.

Suddenly, Dak came out of his home, and went to dance.

When his uncles saw this, they fled, and the mourning ended.

Nyikang said, "Now, I shall go."

And he went along a certain river called Faloko. The people settled on this river.

Then Nyikang's cow ran away. This was because her calves used to be speared by Nyikang: whenever he came to a new place, he killed a calf.

The cow went and came to the country of the sun.

Ojul, the grey hawk, went to search for her, and he found the cow among the cows of the sun.

Garo, the son of the sun, said, "Man, what are you seeking?"

He said, "I am seeking a cow."

He asked, "What cow?"

Ojul said, "Nyikang's cow."

Garo asked, "Where did it come from?"

He answered, "From the country of Nyikang."

Garo said, "No, there is no cow of Nyikang here."

Ojul returned and told Nyikang, "Nyikang, we have found the cow. It is among the cows of a certain man. He is very tall, just like Dak. He wears silver bracelets on his hands."

Nyikang said, "Raise an army, and find the cow."

Dak went and attacked Garo.

He threw him on the ground. He cut off his hands, pulled the bracelets off, then chased the enemy's army.

And he came to the sun.

There, the army of Nyikang was pursued, and it was utterly destroyed.

Then Nyikang himself came. He took an adze and aimed it at the sun. He hit the sun, and it returned to the sky.

Then Nyikang went and took the bracelet, and with it he touched the dead of his army. They returned to life.

The people came to the source of a river. They approached the junction of the river in their boats. They found the river full of sudd.

Nyikang said, "Where does this come from? What shall we do?"

Their way was barred.

Then a man named Obogo got up, and said, "Nyikang, I have finished eating. Spear me under the sudd. In that way, I shall part the sudd."

So Obogo was stabbed under the sudd, and the sudd parted.

Nyikang settled with his people in Achyete-guok, but he found the country occupied by white people. So his people returned to this side of the river. They settled at the head of the Pijo, and Dak passed on to Wij-Palo.

The army went home. It scattered, because the war was over.

Nyikang built villages: Nyelwal, Pepwojo, Adwelo, Tedigo, Palo. The people went on and built Wau, Oshoro, Penyikang, Otego, Akuruwar, Moro, Oryang. These are the villages of Nyikang. He said, "Ah, there are still Shilluk left."

Dak ruled, and then he died.

After him, his son, Odak, ruled. He died while he was hunting game.

Nyikang returned, and said, "Bring a cow, that we may make a bier."

When that was finished, Duwat ruled, and then Bwoch ruled, and after him Dokot ruled, then Tugo, then Okwon, then Kudit, then Nyakwacho.

Version Two

Nyikang heard of a country in which in which all ornaments and even the tools were made of silver. He made up his mind to go into this country with his sons and numerous armed people. The name of this country was Wang Garo: the country where the sun sets and sleeps, where the sun is so near it may be seized with the fingers.

Nyikang arrived in the miraculous country. Numerous cattle herds were grazing here, and the young people were richly adorned with silver rings and silver sticks.

Nyikang and Dak entered a house where a young woman was working. She was exceedingly beautiful. The Shilluk heroes had never seen her equal.

Dak asked the woman if she would like to marry him and go with him to his country.

The woman was frightened. She leapt up, cursing the black men.

Dak replied, "Though we are black and are without silver ornaments, we shall show you that our arms are stronger than those of your men, and that we may well venture to ask you for marriage."

Then the woman showed them the place where her husband and his servants herded the cattle.

Version Two, from W. Hofmayer, "Zur Geschichte und sozialen und politischen Gliederung des Stammes der Schillukneger," *Anthropos* 5 (1910), 332.

Nyikang and Dak went there.

It was just growing dark and the herds were coming from the bushes, the men with their costly ornaments following.

Dak at once rose, and went to meet them. A great fight resulted. The man who wore the heavy silver rings was defeated, and Dak stripped the ornaments off him.

In the heat of the fight and because of the scorching sun, all the Shilluk fell down. Nyikang ordered that water be brought. He sprinkled his fallen warriors with the water, and they all came to life again. He also sprinkled the sun so that it would not burn so hotly, and presently it ceased burning.

Finally, the Shilluk were victorious. They drove away the cattle and the men of the enemies. These people are the Quadshal.

When they had arrived in Shilluk country, Dak once more proposed to the woman to marry her, but he was again rejected.

Nyikang offered the prisoners in his country cattle, but they declined. He offered them Shilluk women, but again they declined. So he gave them the privilege to seize and keep a number of Shilluk women and to collect spears, sheep, and fat in the entire Shilluk country, as often as a new king would be elected. As this was a lasting privilege, they consented to accept it.

Commentary

All Shilluk kings are descended from Nyikang, a mythic ancestor, the leader of the Shilluk in their heroic age. Nyikang led the Shilluk into their present homeland. The spirit of Nyikang is believed to be in every king, embodying the timeless kingship. Nyikang is the main intermediary between the people and God. In the first version of this particular story of Nyikang, he brings his people into the country of Kerau. The story is not only that of the founding of the nation, but it has mythic connection as well, as Nyikang brings his soldiers back to life, struggles with the sun, and parts the waters of the Nile River. In the second version of the story, the struggle is also mythic, in the place "where the sun sets and sleeps, where the sun is so near it may be seized with the fingers." Again, Nyikang restores his followers to life and puts the sun in its present place. These are stories of origins, of a time when the world is coming into its present form, and the death and resurrection of the people by this intermediary with God suggest their rebirth into a new form of national identity, tied to the heavens.

Rites of Passage

A Xhosa storyteller (photo by Harold Scheub)

Arnold van Gennep: . . . an individual is placed in various sections of society, synchronically and in succession; in order to pass from one category to another and to join individuals in other sections, he must submit, from the day of his birth to that of his death, to ceremonies whose forms often vary but whose function is similar. . . . These are the constants of social life, to which have been added particular and temporary events such as pregnancy, illnesses, dangers, journeys, etc. And always the same purpose has resulted in the same form of activity. For groups, as well as for individuals, life itself means to separate and to be reunited, to change form and condition, to die and to be reborn. It is to act and to cease, to wait and rest, and then to begin acting again, but in a different way. And there are always new thresholds to cross: the thresholds of summer and winter, of a season or a year, or a month or a night; the thresholds of birth, adolescence, maturity, and old age; the threshold of death and that of the afterlife–for those who believe in it.

Franz Boas: It would seem that mythological worlds have been built up only to be shattered again, and that new worlds were built from the fragments.

Notes on the Rites of Passage

The study of the oral tradition teaches us that we are never alone, that our lives have meaning, a meaning that was laid down in the earliest of times. We progress in some respects, we change, we go through transitional periods, and these are frightening at times. These are the transformational rites of passage.

Tradition keeps us constant, gives us the companionship and familiar wisdom of the past. It is a steadying influence: no matter how unsettling the experience of transition may be, no matter how confusing and disorienting the times, our lives are punctuated by these stories, these rituals, these recurring crises and accompanying crossings, which put down emotional conduits to antiquity. We thereby become one with our ancestral past, and we are confident that, while we may be moving through turbulent times, the stabilizing authority of the past assures us, gives us meaning, keeps us balanced and secure: life remains the same, we are convinced, no matter what the evanescent details.

The rites of passage move one to a new birth. In the puberty ritual, the child dies and the adult begins life anew. As he passes through puberty, the young man becomes a fully qualified member of society. He must now learn which laws and rules are valid and, especially, how they are sanctioned. A central theme in a heroic life is redolent of both a god's first work of creation and its imitation in the initiation ritual.

The initiation is a passage through death to a new life. But how is new life acquired? The basic model for this is found in the lives of the gods. A god become human moves to the earth and journeys through the primordial rite of passage before being wafted into the heavens or metamorphosed into the cosmological spheres. It is far from accidental that the heroic pattern can also apply in many respects to the gods. The mythological world is shattered, as Franz Boas observed, and "new worlds" are "built from the fragments."

The creation is significant, the gods are important, and we keep reliving through ritual the myths of creation because these are the prototypes of our own movement to fulfillment and maturity, of our own triumph over chaos as we move through the rites of passage and are reborn.

Humans struggle to reproduce the golden age, but succeed only vaguely. Their cultural rituals and institutions are meant to help them in this regard. As people attempt to achieve this original oneness, they go through cultural rituals. During these rituals, they are adapting new identities, and this means casting off the old identities. During this betwixt and between period, they are marginalized, moved to the boundaries. The movement to the new identity is characterized by chaos and order, just as in myth, and, in the tales, the trickster is sometimes the embodiment of this chaos-order betwixt and between state.

There are three stages in these rites of passage, dramatized in the stories: (a) separation or isolation, (b) ordeal or initiation, and (c) return or reincorporation. Separation is the movement into adventure, the migration to the liminal state. The ordeal dominates the pilgrimage, and involves tests and helpers and a singular struggle. This ordeal stage is the initiation into the new state of being; it is the betwixt and between area, the region of enormous energy which is initially undifferentiated: it is the area of the trickster that lurks within all humans, and for the moment of change and transformation it is unleashed. The trickster is the force unbound when we move to the periphery. That force is not, however, outside us: it is the energy within us, forever masked (it is not a surprise that the trickster is a master of the mask), ready to erupt whenever our guard is down. When we move into a new part of our lives, that force is released. Then we behave in extraordinary ways. This is the fantasy part of the tale, the part when the central character, having moved to the boundaries, is in a dangerous and unpredictable state. But he learns, and it is his wisdom that channels these forces, that gives them the shape that will lead to the third stage of the ritual, the return, the movement back to the real world, as a new being. Equilibrium has been attained, but the world is never the same.

In the betwixt and between state, the liminal state, we are back to what we were in the ancient time, undifferentiated initially and a new age of creation is about to occur. The tale becomes myth for the intervening period. As the world is in the process of re-creation in myth, so the individual is being re-created in the tale. The world is being reformed and redefined. This period of upheaval, between two times of equilibrium, is the key: it is chaos and order, the realm of the trickster. Trickster lurks in every human, and he manifests himself during these periods of change, as the individual is transforming into someone new. That intervening moment is theater, everlasting, the eternal moment. It is a season when everything is joined, everything is disjoined, when the world is in chaos and order, when all is movement: creation is occurring. It is an exciting moment, a dangerous time, an exhilaration period, a fearful interval: change.

Most of the stories in this section fit this plan. Here are some examples:

◇ **Separation:** Ramaitsoanala, Ngomba, and Konyek's mother are all separated; they thereby become liminal:

> Ramaitsoanala is spirited away by Andriambahoaka;
> Ngomba is alone, the ogre taking her from her home;
> Konyek's mother goes to a far-off land, following the man she loves.

◇ **Ordeal:** Each goes through an ordeal, and is thereby transformed:

> Ramaitsoanala has her eyes and skin taken from her and then must do impossible tasks;
> Ngomba must live in the forest with a monster who will kill her, his suspicions deepening as she makes the getaway basket;
> Konyek's mother must live with the demons who will kill her if she attempts to escape.

◇ **Reincorporation:** Each returns, and is reborn:

> Ramaitsoanala receives her skin and eyes back, is beautiful, is taught to be a proper woman;
> Ngomba, her sores cleansed by the ogre, flies home in the basket to safety;
> Konyek's mother, by means of her own cunning and through the efforts of the nephews she saved and nurtured, destroys the demons and returns.

All of these stories have to do with rebirth:

In "Ramaitsoanala" (story 34), the child grows into womanhood (secondary theme: the mother does not want to let her go). Her "death" is being bereft of skin and eyes: her mother makes possible her rebirth. The child moves from her bird/nest past.

In "Ngomba's Basket" (story 32), the child grows into womanhood. Her death is the movement into the forest and her "swallowing" by the ogre. Her rebirths: her sores are cleansed, so that she is later not recognized (identity); she emerges from the basket a new person.

In "Konyek" (story 38), the death of the central character has to do with her movement into the land of the demons: death is on every hand, and Konyek is a killer. Her rebirth occurs with the help of the boys, and she returns from the land of the dead a new woman.

The moment of transition is crucial, because during that interlude we move out of ourselves. We are broken into parts, and all of the great possibilities of life are present. We select from among them, and thereby participate in our own re-creation. We are taken apart and rebuilt. It is for that reason that this moment of transformation, celebrated and commemorated in these tales, revitalizes us, renews us. This is a reason for our love of storytelling: it enables us to relive the transitional moment, allowing it to dissect and to remodel us all over again.

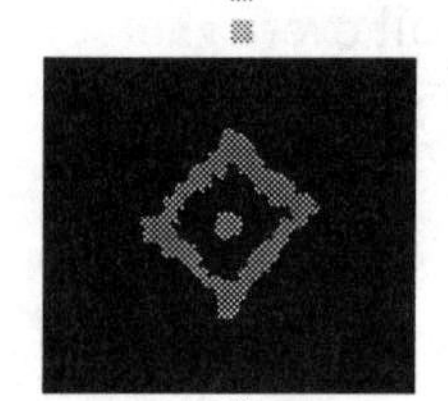

Perhaps it may interest you to know how a story is told.

Imagine, then, a village in a grove of graceful palm trees. The full moon is shining upon a small crowd of Africans seated round a fire in an open space in the center of the village. One of them has just told a story, and his delighted audience demands another. Thus, he begins:

> "Let us tell another story, let us be off!"
> All then shout, "Pull away!"
> "Let us be off!" he repeats.
> And they answer again. "Pull away!"
> Then the storyteller commences. . . .

R. E. Dennett, *Notes on the Folklore of the Fjort* (London: David Nutt, 1898), p. 25.

Fiote

Ngomba's Basket

The Fiote live in Zaire and Congo.

Four young women one day started to go out fishing. One of them was suffering sadly from sores, which covered her from head to foot. Her name was Ngomba. The other three, after a little consultation, agreed that Ngomba should not accompany them, and so they told her to go back.

"No," said Ngomba, "I will do no such thing. I mean to catch fish for mother as well as you."

Then the three women beat Ngomba until she was glad to walk away. But she was determined to catch fish also, so she walked and walked, she hardly knew where, until at last she came to a large lake.

Here, she started fishing and singing:

> "If my mother
> (She catches a fish and puts it in her basket.)
> Had taken care of me,
> (She catches another fish and puts it in her basket.)
> I should have been with them,
> (She catches another fish and puts it in her basket.)
> And not here alone."
> (She catches another fish and puts it in her basket.)

From Richard E. Dennett, *Notes on the Folklore of the Fjort* (London: David Nutt, 1898), pp. 49–53.

But an ogre had been watching her for some time, and now he came up to her and accosted her: "What are you doing here?"

"Fishing. Please, don't kill me! See, I am full of sores, but I can catch plenty of fish." The ogre watched her as she fished and sang:

> "Oh, I shall surely die!
> (She catches a fish and puts it in her basket.)
> Mother, you will never see me!
> (She catches another fish and puts it in her basket.)
> But I don't care,
> (She catches another fish and puts it in her basket.)
> For no one cares for me."
> (She catches another fish and puts it in her basket.)

"Come with me," said the ogre.

"No, this fish is for mother, and I must take it to her."

"If you do not come with me, I will kill you."

> "Oh! Am I to die
> (She catches a fish and puts it in her basket.)
> On the top of my fish?
> (She catches another fish and puts it in her basket.)
> If Mother had loved me,
> (She catches another fish and puts it in her basket.)
> To live I should wish.
> (She catches another fish and puts it in her basket.)

Take me and cure me, dear ogre, and I will serve you."

The ogre took her to his home in the woods, and cured her. Then he placed her in the paint-house and married her.

Now the ogre was very fond of dancing, and Ngomba danced beautifully, so that he loved her very much, and made her mistress over all his prisoners and goods.

"When I go out for a walk," he said to her, "I will tie this string around my waist, and that you may know when I am still going away from you, or returning, the string will be stretched tight as I depart, and will hang loose as I return."

Ngomba pined for her mother, and therefore entered into a conspiracy with her people to escape. She sent them every day to cut the leaves of the mateva-pine, and ordered them to put them in the sun to dry. Then she set them to work to make a huge basket. And when the ogre returned, he remarked to her that the air was heavy with the smell of mateva.

Now she had made all her people put on clean clothes, and when they knew that he was returning, she ordered them to come to him and flatter him. So now they approached him, and some called him "Father" and others "Uncle," and others told him how he was a father and a mother to them. And he was very pleased, and danced with them.

The next day when he returned, he said he smelled mateva.

Then Ngomba cried, and told him that he was both father and mother to her, and that if he accused her of smelling of mateva, she would kill herself.

He could not stand this sadness, so he kissed her and danced with her until all was forgotten.

The next day, Ngomba determined to try her basket, to see if it would float in the air. Four women lifted it on high, and gave it a start upwards, and it floated beautifully.

Now the ogre happened to be up a tree, and he espied this great basket floating in the air, and he danced and sang for joy, and wished to call Ngomba that she might dance with him.

That night, he smelled mateva again, and his suspicions were aroused, and when he thought how easily his wife might escape him, he determined to kill her.

Accordingly, he gave her to drink some palm-wine that he had drugged. She drank it, and slept as he put a red hot iron (for burning the hole through the stem of a pipe) into the fire. He meant to kill her by pushing this red hot wire up her nose.

But as he was almost ready, Ngomba's little sister, who had changed herself into a cricket and hidden herself under her bed, began to sing. The ogre heard her and felt forced to join in and dance, and thus he forgot to kill his wife.

But after a time, she ceased singing, and then he began to heat the wire again. The cricket then sang again, and again he danced and danced, and in his excitement tried to wake Ngomba to dance also. But she refused to awake, telling him that the medicine he had given her made her feel sleepy. Then he went out and got some palm-wine, and as he went she drowsily asked him if he had made the string fast. He called all his people, dressed himself, and made them all dance.

The cock crew.

The iron wire was still in the fire. The ogre made his wife get up and fetch some palm-wine.

Then the cock crew again, and it was daylight.

When the ogre had left her for the day, Ngomba determined to escape that very day. So she called her people and made them try the basket again, and when she was certain that it would float, she put all her people, and all the ogre's ornaments, into it. Then she got in, and the basket began to float away over the tree-tops in the direction of her mother's town.

When the ogre, who was up in a tree, saw it coming towards him, he danced and sang for joy, and only wished that his wife had been there to see this huge basket flying through the air. It passed just over his head, and then he knew that the people in it were his. So he ran after the balloon in the tops of the trees, until he saw it drop in Ngomba's town. And he determined to go there also and claim his wife.

The basket floated round the house of Ngomba's mother, and astonished all the people there, and finally settled down in front of the house. Ngomba cried to the people to come and let them out. But they were afraid and did not dare, so she came out herself and presented herself to her mother.

Her relations at first did not recognize her, but after a little while they fell upon her and welcomed her as their long lost Ngomba.

Then the ogre entered the town and claimed Ngomba as his wife.

"Yes," her relations said, "she is your wife, and you must be thanked for curing her of her sickness."

And while some of her relations were entertaining the ogre others were preparing a place for him and his wife to be seated. They made a large fire, and boiled a great quantity of water, and dug a deep hole in the ground. This hole they covered over with sticks and a mat, and when all was ready they led the ogre and his wife to it, and requested them to be seated. Ngomba sat near her husband, who, as he sat down, fell into the hole. The relations then brought boiling water and fire, and threw it over him until he died.

Commentary

This Fiote story effectively dramatizes the three stages of the puberty ritual, separation or isolation, ordeal or initiation, and return or reincorporation.

◈ **Separation**—Pattern one dramatizes this separation or isolation phase of the puberty rite. Associated with this pattern that describes Ngomba's movement away from home is the least likely hero motif. Her song emphasizes that motif.

◈ **Ordeal**—Pattern two is more complex: it has to do with the ordeal or initiation phase of the rite, and emphasizes the unhappiness of Ngomba in her life with the ogre (motif: swallowing monster), and her efforts to escape, by building a basket (motif: magical basket).

At the beginning of this ordeal phase, the ogre clears up Ngomba's sores, a physical reflection of the change she is undergoing as she moves to adulthood. Also included in this second pattern are the swallowing monster's deepening suspicions and his efforts to kill Ngomba, images of the girl's ordeal. Her sister becomes a cricket (motif: magical transformation) and sings to make the ogre dance (motif: ogre cannot stop dancing).

◈ **Return**—In the dramatization of the third phase of the puberty rite, the return or reincorporation, Ngomba flies through the air in her basket (motif: magical basket). There is no pattern associated with this third phase. She returns to her home with a new identity, emerging from the basket as if from the belly of a swallowing monster, transformed, a young adult woman.

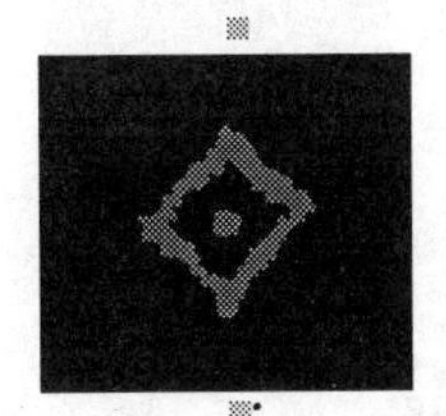

Amongst the Lamba people . . . are numbers of very clever storytellers, the most renowned being a man named Mulekelela from the village of Kawunda Chiwele. . . . [O]n being questioned as to the origin of these tales, he denied having invented a single one himself, and asserted that they have been handed down for generations from one to the other, the women especially perpetuating them. The story suffers from being put into cold print, and still more does it suffer in being translated into the tongue of a people so different in thought and life.

Overhead is an inky-black sky dotted with brilliant stars, a slight breeze is moving the tops of the trees, and all is silent save the regular gurgling noise of the calabash pipes, as the men sit or lie around the numerous camp fires within the stockade. Then the narrator will refill his pipe, and start his story: "Mwe wame!" ("Mates!"), and at once they are all attention. After each sentence he pauses automatically for the last few words to be repeated or filled in by his audience, and as the story mounts to its climax, so does the excitement of the speaker rise with gesture and pitch of voice. A good storyteller will tell over again a story, well-known to all, in such a way that they will leave their pipes and crowd nearer to him around his fire, so as not to miss a single detail.

Clement M. Doke, *Lamba Folk-Lore* (New York: G. W. Stechert, 1927), pp. xii–xiii.

Lamba

Lion-child and Cow-child

The Lamba live in Zambia.

This is what the lioness did, she went to a village of people.

She said, "Whose village is this?"

They said, "The village of the queen!"

The queen said, "Not I! I won't make friends with a lion!"

Then the lioness went back to the cow.

She said, "Let us cross countless rivers far from people, let us travel five nights and five days!"

They reached the wilderness, and built a stockade, the cow to the west, the lioness to the east.

When night came, the lioness said, "My friend, I have given birth in here, I have given birth to a man-child. Let us go hunting on the veld, and kill an animal, and let this child of mine that I have given birth to eat."

When evening came, the cow said, "My friend, I also have given birth, I have given birth to a man-child."

Where the lioness had given birth, she said, "My friend, let us go hunting on the veld, and kill some animals and give them to our children!"

Then the cow told her child, "I'm afraid that the lion will eat me when traveling on the veld. When you hear her roar, you will know that she has eaten me!"

Indeed, later on the lioness came roaring, the cow did not come. Thereupon Cow-child went out, and journeyed on and on where the lioness had gone, and found where the cow had died; and took down from where they had been hung up his

From Clement M. Doke, ed., *Lamba Folk-Lore* (New York: American Folk-Lore Society, 1927), pp. 15–23.

mother's entrails and tied them in a bundle, and returned to the stockade, and entered.

Then Lion-child said, "Mate, are you asleep?"

Cow-child was silent, he was angry.

Then Lion-child opened the door where his mate was, and said, "Mate!"

He said, "Why do you rouse me? Your mother has eaten my mother, and I am mourning my mother."

Then Lion-child said, "Mate, my mother is fierce, she has eaten your mother; and, what is more, we two are alike, we have the scent of people, indeed she will come and eat us also."

Then Cow-child said, "Don't accuse me! You will say later on that it was Cow-child who suggested killing your mother."

Lion-child said, "Come, let us go to the blacksmiths, let them forge us knives, lest my mother should kill us."

They entered, and took axes, and went to the blacksmiths.

On their return from the blacksmiths, Lion-child said, "Let us hide, me here and you there by the doorway."

And so it was, when the lioness entered, they killed her by cutting off her head, the head in the stockade, the trunk outside.

Thereupon Lion-child said, "Come, mate, let us cross five rivers, let us travel five nights and five days, let us build far, far away."

So it was that where they went they built a stockade.

One said, "Let us go to the river and look for water, we're dead with thirst!"

They traveled and reached a village of people.

They said, "Chief, give us some water, let us drink."

He said, "We don't drink water, we don't know it. The chief's son will carry a man to the water tomorrow, in the evening he will return. Then when another five days pass, they will go again to draw water."

In the morning, the drum was sounding. The headman of the village said, "Listen, they are taking the chief's son to draw water!"

Cow-child said in a whisper, "Let us go too!"

The people were going through the bush, and those two children were following them through the bush, through the bush, through the bush. They arrived at a great expansive lake, and they saw that the people had arrived to kill (i.e., to sacrifice a man to the lake-dwellers) in the water.

They said, "Let us hide, let us see!"

Then creatures with long white beards were sitting on the water and floating and gazing about.

They said, "Why are you hiding over there?"

Then Cow-child said, "They've seen us, let us come out of hiding and stand up."

Then those creatures came to kill them, but Lion-child took his knife, and cut off their heads—how many? Eight.

Then he took the calico in which the chief's son was arrayed, and tied the heads in it, and sent the chief's son, saying, "Go to the village, and tell the people, 'Today go and draw water, today it may be drunk, it may be drawn in any way!'"

The chief entered the house, and took the drum, and beat that all the people in the district hear this business. The chief said, "You people who are gathered here, did you not leave any strangers in the village?"

They answered, "No, only guards, there are no strangers."

One said, "At my village two strangers have remained."

He said, "Send a man to call them."

The chief's nephew was sent. He said, "The chief has called you."

They said, "First let us wash our faces."

When he had returned to the chief, he said, "Two of you, go tell them to come!"

So others went, and said, "Friends, they have called you to the chief, come!"

They said, "Say, 'Let them first eat their porridge.'"

They sent others saying, "The chief says let them come right now!"

They said, "Let us first load our guns."

Yet again they said, "Let us first rest."

Then the chief himself arose. When he had drawn near, they said, "Let us get up, the chief has come!"

When they say that the chief had come, they both hastened to rise.

The chief said, "Why haven't you come? I am tired of sending people, and you won't come!"

Then he set them in single-file rank, and they went to the village.

On their arrival, he said, "Which is the elder, my friends?"

Then Mr. Cow-child said, "My elder is this Lion-child."

He said, "This Lion-child, the elder, is the one who will marry this daughter of mine."

Then Lion-child undid the bundle of heads. He took out a ring, threw it up, put out his finger, and the ring slipped on. He took it off, and put it down.

Then Cow-child did the same.

The chief said, "This Lion-child is my son-in-law."

Cow-child conjured with porridge in a cooking-pot, and covered it over with leaves, and gave it to his sister-in-law, and said, "Now I am going far five nights and five days; so if my charm dries, you will know that Cow-child is dead."

So it was that he traveled that great distance, and arrived at where the clouds reach the earth, and they had put up a ladder. He climbed up and reached a small house, and saw the daughter of God.

He entered the house and said, "Now I too am going to marry."

The child of God said to a youngster, "Go to my father, and tell him saying, 'An enemy is with your child!'"

She sped to her master.

He said, "Why do you come so quickly?"

She said, "An enemy is with your child over there where you hid her!"

In the morning soldiers arose.

The God-child said, "You Cow-child, are you asleep? Wake up! There are people below!"

He said, "Why do you rouse me? Put on some porridge for me, let me eat!"

Then he ate and ate and ate, and put on his calico and took his knife, and went out. He saw two crowds of people, one on either side, and said, "Return to one side, lest you should kill one another when you throw the weapons."

They all said, "Indeed, indeed, let us return! Why have we done this, people here and people there too?"

And they returned to one side.

He said, "Now you have done well."

He took his knife and cut off the arm of one man, and said, "Go to the chief, let him bring water, and let us put it into the calabash-pipe that we may smoke hemp through it!"

He went to the chief, and said that to the chief, to God.

Cow-child killed all his companions.

Again in the morning there was a swarm of soldiers at the little house.

She said, "Wake up, man, wake up, there are people below!"

He said, "Stop waking me like that, first you put on the porridge, then I'll go outside."

Then he ate and went out; and met two crowds of people, and said, "Return to one crowd. Don't you see how your companions died yesterday because they killed one another?"

They all agreed, and returned to one side.

Then he killed them all. He took one and sent him to the chief, saying, "Go and bring tobacco and hemp, let us smoke it in our calabash-pipe."

The chief said, "All the people have died, now let us just send and call him."

Cow-child heard the dogs eating the stomach and intestines of the cow.

He said, "Ah! Today I die!"

In the morning the God-child woke and stirred the porridge, and woke him up saying, "Wake up! Eat the porridge, people are below."

He ate and ate and ate.

When he had gone out, he said, "All of you put down your weapons, just take two sticks, and just kill me, today I am no good!"

So it was that they took two sticks, and killed him.

When they had thus killed him, his sister-in-law returned to the magic preparation and found it dried up. She told his brother, "Cow-child is dead!"

Lion-child said, "Give me too some flour, let me go after my brother!"

She gave him flour, and he traveled five nights and five days.

He arrived, and carried together the corpses, and went to sleep.

Again in the morning he went and searched for his brother, and again lay down.

The next morning he searched and searched and searched, but he did not find his brother.

And again in the morning he went counting over the corpses over and over again, he did not find him, the sun went down.

Then the following morning he found his brother dead, the sticks leaning against him like this.

He struck his brother with an animal's tail, and raised him up. They shook hands, and his brother came to life again.

He said, "Now we have become two!"

They climbed the steps, and reached the God-child.

She said, "Go and say to my father that today they are two."

The girl went. She said, "Today two have come."

In the morning, God-child said, "You! Wake up, there are people below."

Lion-child said, "Stop saying that, you first make the porridge!"

They ate the porridge, they ate and ate, and went out. They saw two crowds of people. They killed them all with the knives—Lion-child there and Cow-child over there.

They left one alive, and said to him, "Say, 'Today they are two!'"

He reached the chief, and said, "They are two!"

When it was morning, more soldiers. She put on porridge for them both, her brother-in-law and her husband, and they ate. When they went out, they killed them all.

The chief said, "Let us just call them both."

He sent a man saying, "You men, they have called you to the chief, saying, 'Let them come here!'"

They both arose, and set the wife between them, and reached the chief.

The chief said, "Which is the elder?"

He said, "This one, Lion-child!"

He said, "You Lion-child, are you married?"

He said, "I am married over there where I come from, the unmarried one is Mr. Cow-child."

The chief said, "Now I am moving out of this village, so those who come to settle cases let them talk with Cow-child, not I!"

The chief left the village, and goes away to a garden-house to hide.

Cow-child married.

Lion-child said, "Now I am going."

Cow-child promised, "If soldiers attack your home, I too shall rise and fight for you."

In the morning he is left, his brother has gone home.

From that time, every case came to be settled by that same Cow-child.

Lion-child returned home.

His wife said, "Where you went did you find your brother dead?"

He said, "I found countless people dead, and I got tired of searching: on the Saturday I found him."

Commentary

This tale is constructed on a triangular relationship involving a villain, a victim, and a set of helpers in each of the three parts. The three parts of the story represent a progression, from the animal world, to the human world, to the celestial realm. Simultaneously, there is a progression in the two central characters, as they move from their animal state to a human state: Lion-child and Cow-child are going through their puberty rites of passage.

The *helpers* are constant throughout the tale: they are Lion-child and cow-child. The *victims* change, from the cow, deprived of life; to the humans in the village, deprived of life-sustaining water; to all humans who would approach God, a harsh god, destroying any who would come to him. The *villains* also change, from the lioness, to the eight old men, to God. But while the characters change, their functions remain the same, and so the three parts of the story are, in effect, identical.

◊ **Meaning and pattern**—The theme of the tale is established in the brief introduction: the lioness goes to a village of humans and attempts to make friends with the human chief. But she, the human chief, will have nothing to do with the lioness because she is an animal. The animal-human polarity is thereby revealed at the beginning of the story, and that is the theme in each of the three parts that follow: the lioness, following the law of the jungle, destroys the cow; the eight old men also follow a vicious law in their outrageous insistence that human sacrifice is necessary to obtain water; and God himself follows a similar law in his attitude toward those who would petition him. In each case, order and humaneness are established by Lion-child and Cow-child: they set things right, in the animal world, by destroying the lioness; in the human world, by destroying the eight old tyrants; and in the celestial realm, by deposing God.

◊ **Rebirth**—The entrails of the cow, carried about by the cow-child, link the cow-child to his past, to his mother. As long as he carries the entrails, that link will remain. But if he is to escape his animal past, he must also rid himself of the ties to his animal mother. In the end, when the dogs eat the entrails, the tie with the past is finally gone, and he can die. This is the end of Cow-child's rite of passage; the links with the past must necessarily be cut, so that the initiate can move into his new state of full humanity with the responsibility of an adult. When the dogs eat the entrails, he dies to his past. He can now be reborn.

But note the way he is reborn. In the animal world where the law of the jungle prevails, lions are more powerful than cows, so, according to the primal law of might is right, they kill and eat cows. And that is just what the lioness did to the cow in part one. If the lion-child and cow-child were still living according to the code of the jungle, then Lion-child would kill Cow-child, as his mother killed Cow-child's mother. In fact, just the opposite occurs: instead of killing Cow-child, Lion-child brings him back to life, is responsible for his rebirth. And, in that way, Lion-child has severed his ties with his past.

◊ **Transformation**—This means that change has occurred, as the creatures, Lion-child and Cow-child, move from the animal world into the human world and to the world of God. Even as these two central characters move through each of these worlds, taming the villains and making the three worlds more humane, they are at the same time purifying themselves, by eliminating the animal parts of themselves moving into new identities. They are shedding their pasts, sloughing off their primal forms, moving from animal to human, from one state into a new state. They are simultaneously moving the world from a world in which beings destroy one another like animals, or where humans exploit one another, or where God is a being with destructive attitudes towards humans, into a more enlightened dispensation.

The two themes are parallel: the rite of passage transformations of Lion-child and Cow-child, the transitions of the three parts of the world, from disorder to order.

In the end, Cow-child moves into his new state when the entrails are destroyed, and Lion-child moves into his new state when he brings Cow-child to life, rather than kill him. But in fact they have been moving into these new states all along, when they destroy Lioness, when they destroy the eight old men, when they depose God.

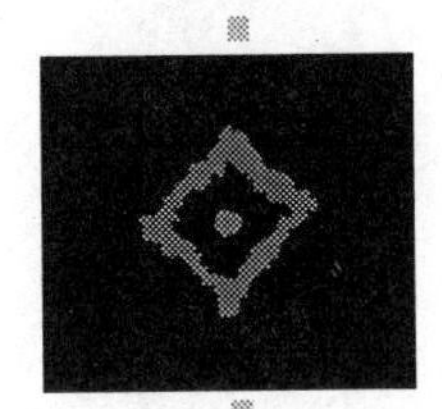

Ngano was essentially an oral art. The printed word—the medium of ngano—is only a shadow of the full actualization of the ngano as an aesthetic experience of the storyteller and her audience. These tales naturally suffer when they are reduced to writing. It is a common and excusable error these days to think of the written model as the primary, most fundamental one, even in the case of ngano. There is a tendency to concentrate on the written word to the exclusion of the vital and essential aspects, such as the performance and the situation. It must be emphasized that the actual enactment of the ngano involved the emotional situation. All the aspects which we think of as contributing to the effectiveness of the performance in the case of more literary forms, may also play their part in the delivery of unwritten pieces in addition to expressiveness of tone, gestures, facial expression, dramatic use of pause, receptivity to the reaction of the audience, etc.—all made use of to produce an effect or naturally betraying the narrator's emotional involvement.

K. G. Mkanganwi, *Ngano* (Harari: University of Rhodesia, 1973), pp. ii–iii.

Malagasy

Ramaitsoanala

The Malagasy live on the island of Madagascar, off the southeastern coast of Africa.

Once, Ravorombe, Big Bird, arose and built a house in the midst of the water. And when she had finished the house, she brought Iketaka to be housekeeper. And after Iketaka had remained there a long time, Ravorombe went away to seek prey, and, thus occupied, she swept up everything that she saw that belonged to men, and brought it to her dwelling.

After some time, she laid eggs and sat on them, and after she had sat some time the eggs were hatched, and the young birds went off to fly. But one egg alone remained unhatched, so she thought it addled, and removed it, placing it in the cover of a basket.

After Ravorombe had forgotten where it was, Iketaka said, "The addled egg is there in the basket, and we have forgotten to cook it."

Ravorombe replied, "Let it be until tomorrow, for the rice is all finished." So she stopped Iketaka.

On the next day, they forgot it again, and the same on the following day. And after a little time longer, Iketaka looked, and found that it was hatched, and had produced a human creature! She was astonished, and called to Ravorombe, "Come quickly! The egg is hatched, and has produced a human!"

She came and looked, and saw that it was really so. Then she said, "This is my offspring, her name shall be Ramaitsoanala, Green in the Forest. But there is no one to nurse it, so I'll go and steal a cow for milking, so that the child can feed on milk."

From James Sibree, Jr., "Malagasy Folk-Tales," *Folk-Lore Journal* 2 (1884): 161–166.

So Ravorombe went and swept off a cow in milk, and got it for her child's sustenance, for she, being a bird, had no breasts. Then she made a little box for the child and placed it there, telling Iketaka to mind it.

Then Ravorombe went away again seeking prey, and whenever she saw anything beautiful belonging to people she swept off with it and brought it to her child.

And when she came to her house, she cried out, "Ramaitsoanala there! Ramaitsoanala there! Why, say I, don't you peep out? Why don't you look about?"

But there was no answer, for the child was still an infant, and how could she speak and stand up?

So Ravorombe came in, and said again, "I smell humans! I smell humans!"

And Iketaka said, "Why do you say, 'I smell humans,' when we're the only ones here?"

The bird replied, "I thought that someone had come here and taken the two of you away!" Then she spoke again, "But have you given the child her milk?"

"Yes," replied Iketaka.

So Ravorombe stopped there for a time. But after a while, she went away again to seek prey, and again brought precious things belonging to people, and gave them to her child.

When she came home, she again called out, "Ramaitsoanala there! Ramaitsoanala there! Why, say I, don't you peep out, and why don't you look about?"

Again there was no reply, for the child was little, and how could she answer?

So the bird came in, and said, "I smell humans! I smell humans!"

Iketaka said, "Why do you say, 'I smell humans!' when we're the only ones here?"

The bird replied, "I thought that someone had come here and taken the two of you away!"

Then she stopped there, and said, "But how is my child? Is she getting big or not?"

Iketaka answered, "She's getting rather big now, and in a little time she'll be able to walk."

Then Ravorombe went off again, and the child began to learn how to walk.

Ravorombe returned, and called according to her custom, but no one answered for the child was still little.

After a time, Andriambahoaka came from the north, and he looked from the water's edge. He said, "Something very wonderful is over there on that island! Come, let's get a canoe and go there and see what it is." When he arrived there, he asked Iketaka, "Whose child is this? I want her for a wife!"

Iketaka replied, "This is Ravorombe's child—its mother is a bird, the child is still little. But please, sir, go away, for the day is windy and her mother will be here shortly. Please go away for a time, the mother will devour you all. Please go, and come again another time, for the child is still little."

So Andriambahoaka got up, and when he had gone only a little way, Ravorombe returned. She called the child as she usually did, but as there was no reply, she said, "I smell humans! I smell humans!"

And Iketaka, coming in, said, "What person can have been here? Every time you come in, you say that!"

Ravorombe replied, "I thought that someone had come here and taken the two of you away!" At the same time, she opened the box and looked at her child whom she saw to be getting big.

She said, "You remain here. I'm going to look for ornaments for Ramaitsoanala, she's growing up!"

So she went away.

In the meantime, Andriambahoaka spoke to his two wives and to his people: "There's a beautiful young woman, I'm going to take her for a wife because we've been most unfortunate in having no children. I'll be back after a fortnight. Tell the servants to fatten fowl and pound rice in abundance, for when I return I shall marry her. Make all preparations."

He set off, and, coming to the edge of the water, he sent for canoes, then crossed over. When he arrived there, he was welcomed by Iketaka, and he spoke to Ramaitsoanala: "What do you say, miss? If I take you for my wife, will you be willing?"

She replied, "Nonsense, sir, you can't manage me. So let it alone, sir."

He said, "Tell me why I could not manage you."

She replied, "This is why you could not: my mother is a bird!"

Andriambahoaka said, "If that is all, miss, I am equal to it. So come now, let us go."

Then Iketaka said, "But if you marry her, sir, will you not let her wait first for her mother?"

He said, "Let us go. When she comes, she can follow."

When the two could no longer resist him, Ramaitsoanala went away, and Iketaka was left to keep the house.

They took white rice and Indian corn and beans with them, in order to deceive the mother on the road until Andriambahoaka reached his home—in case the girl should be overtaken by her mother along the way and brought back.

After a while, back came the mother, and she called again as she was accustomed to.

Iketaka replied from the house, "Ramaitsoanala is not here, she's been taken away by someone."

"Who has taken her? Where has she gone?" asked Ravorombe.

"Andriambahoaka from the north has taken her, and northwards has she gone."

So Ravorombe went to the north. As she was getting near to them, the child Ramaitsoanala said, "Here comes my mother! That's why the day has become stormy. Just scatter some of the rice."

So they scattered it about, and went on their way.

When the mother came up, she said, "Here is rice that she has scattered, I'm forsaken by her!" So she sat down to gather the rice, then returned to take it back to the house.

After that, she went back to pursue her child.

But again, Ramaitsoanala knew by the wind that blew that her mother was following her, so the Indian corn was scattered on the road. The corn was also gathered up and taken back by Ravorombe, and so it happened with the beans.

By this time, her child was near Andriambahoaka's village. He sent people ahead, and said, "Tell the people to get ready, for Andriambahoaka is now just south of the village."

So the people made preparations, and the couple arrived. As the people sat there, Andriambahoaka's wives would not look into the house, saying, "How should a bird's offspring come in?"

As the couple was sitting comfortably there, up came the mother, and she said, "How is it, child, you have got a husband, and did not wait for me at all? did not even consult me?"

Her child did not answer.

Then Ravorombe arose, and took the child's eyes, she stripped off the child's skin, and she departed.

The child stood there stripped, and spoke to Andriambahoaka: "It's for this reason that I asked you if you could be bear with me, a person whose mother is a bird."

But Andriambahoaka replied, "I can still bear with you!"

When his wives heard that, they said, "Nonsense! What sort of wife is this, with nothing but bones and without eyes? We do not consent! Let the household property be divided!"

Then the wives brought Ramaitsoanala some hisatra (the strong tough peel of the papyrus) to make a mat.

So Ravorombe's child sat down.

Now when Ravorombe was going to cook rice, the eyes of her child dropped down tears from above the hearth—for it was there she had placed the eyeballs. And because of this, the mother could not by any means light the fire.

When she saw that, she said, "Come, let me go, for indeed grave trouble has befallen my child, because this falling down of her eyes is extraordinary!"

So she went off, and, coming in, she said, "What has happened to you, that I cannot light my fire?"

Her child answered, "Why, mother, the people are dividing the household goods, but I have no eyes, and that is why I am weeping."

So the mother said, "Where is it. I'll do it!"

Then Ravorombe plaited the mat quickly, and it was finished. Then she went away.

After that, Andriambahoaka's wives said, "Come, work away, and give her some silk" (for spinning or weaving).

And again, Ramaitsoanala wept, and her mother could not light the fire.

So she came again, and said, "What's the matter with you now, child, that I cannot light the fire?"

She answered, "Why, mother, they have brought me silk."

Then her mother finished the silk for her, and when it was finished she went off again to tend the fire on her hearth.

After a little while, Andriambahoaka's wives brought clothes and dresses for Ramaitsoanala to sew, and said, "Will she be able to finish these? And if we bring many other things, won't she run away?" But they were certain that she would not be able to finish them.

Then Ramaitsoanala wept again, and said, "This is too difficult!"

So her tears flowed again on the hearth, and again her mother arose, saying, "What can be happening to my child?" And away she went. She came to her daughter, and Ramaitsoanala showed her the clothes and dresses—which the mother finished, then went away as before.

After waiting a little, Andriambahoaka's wives said, "Now, let the three of us be compared, for we two are put to shame by this child of a bird! for people called her very beautiful, even though she had her eyes put out and has only bones!"

But Andriambahoaka said, "Enough of that, Ramatoa! What will you do, say I, to shame her? Enough of that!"

But she would not be quiet, she spoke all the more. As Andriambahoaka could not prevent the two women from speaking, he said, "When do you wish to be compared then?"

The two answered, "On Thursday."

He went to Ramaitsoanala and told her that she would be compared with the other two on Thursday.

Ramaitsoanala wept then, and again her mother was unable to light a fire. She rose up and came to her daughter. When she was told about it all, she said, "If that is all, don't be sorrowful. I'll go and bring ornaments for you, and then you'll be able to stand comparison with the others."

So Ravorombe went away, and brought her daughter's eyes and skin, and coral beads, and gold and silks, and all kinds of beautiful ornaments, and she also brought a golden chair for her to sit on.

When the appointed time came, Ravorombe adorned her daughter, restoring her eyes and replacing her skin, and she allowed no one to see her.

Then the three women were fetched to go in the open space to be compared, for the people were gathered together.

The two wives did not adorn themselves at all: "This woman without eyes is coming, and what of her?" They got up and stood on the eastern side.

Then Ramaitsoanala came, and she went to the northern side. But as soon as she showed her face, the two other women fled. They ran off into the fosse in their shame and died there.

So Andriambahoaka took Ramaitsoanala home, and wedded her.

And she bore a child, she had a son whom they called Andriambahoaka, for he succeeded his father at his death. And the father rejoiced, for he had obtained what he had desired.

Commentary

Ravorombe, a cannibalistic bird, gives birth to Ramaitsoanala, a human: she is betwixt and between, both human and a bird. Ramaitsoanala's moves from her home of birth, through a betwixt and between area, to her home of marriage.

◈ **Pattern and meaning**—There are three significant patterns in this tale. In the first pattern, which takes place at the house of Ramaitsoanala's birth, the mother brings the daughter things from her expeditions, things that progressively transform the child into a human, moving her from her animal past (her mother is a bird, the child hatched from an egg) to full humanity, that is, from childhood to adulthood. The motif has to do with a child borne of a bird-mother.

To emphasize her daughter's transformational state, Ravorombe, the mother, complains that she smells humans in her home. Of course a human *is* in her home: it is her daughter. This fact, along with the mother's fear that a suitor may come and take her daughter away, give these suspicions a sharper edge.

◈ **Ravorombe**—The mother's bird-ness represents the childhood of Ramaitsoanala, which she must give up to move into adulthood. At the same time, there are clear contradictions in the mother: these contradictions both suggest this betwixt stage and the mother's inner turmoil, as she resists giving up her daughter to adulthood and simultaneously prepares her for this state. The first pattern simultaneously shows the mother preparing her daughter for womanhood, yet resisting this, wishing to keep it from happening.

The second pattern involves the flight of the bride, Ramaitsoanala, and her groom, Andriambahoaka. It takes place on the veld, the land between the two houses. As the prince spirits Ramaitsoanala away, the mother, in furious pursuit, is delayed when rice and then corn are thrown to the ground. The pattern reveals the mother's anger, her determination to keep her daughter to herself, and it also moves her child into the isolation stage of her puberty ritual. As with the first pattern, this pattern simultaneously shows a part of the puberty initiation *and* the mother's determination not to allow it to progress. Motifs include bride quest and a reluctant in-law.

The third pattern, the ordeal or initiation stage of Ramaitsoanala's puberty ritual, consists of the impossible tasks assigned by the jealous co-wives and the continued reluctance of Ravorombe to allow her daughter to leave home. The mother's contradictions also reveal Ramaitsoanala's uncertainties as she moves from one state to another.

At her home of marriage, Ramaitsoanala is reborn. The mother has robbed her daughter of her identity, yet she regularly returns, when the girl's eyes tear, to assist her, which means, in the language of storytelling, that she is teaching her daughter to be a worthy woman. She teaches her by doing her tasks, making mats and weaving silk, sewing clothes, and finally restoring her daughter's beauty, a mark that the child has an identity, that she has become a full woman, that she can now take her proper place in her home of marriage as a complete woman and a knowledgeable wife. This is the re-incorporation stage of her puberty ritual.

Ramaitsoanala's liminal state is her incomplete state. The ordeal is the move from incompleteness to completeness, with the ambiguous aid of the mother. She is leaving her bird-ness behind, as she emerges into full womanhood.

If this is the story of Ramaitsoanala's puberty rite of passage, it is also the story of her mother's contradictory feelings as she prepares her daughter for adulthood. And those mother's feelings are mirrors of the internal struggle of Ramaitsoanala.

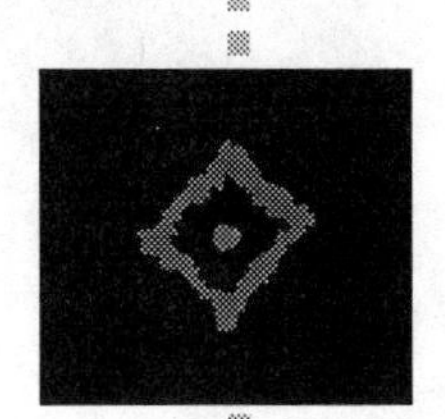

"Put your money on this sheepskin," said the old man, "and if, by the time I finish my tale, there is one of you awake, that man shall claim everything we have collected."

Young men, old men, children, women, they all put some money on the sheepskin beside the storyteller. He waited till they sat down. He himself settled comfortably on the catifa and smiled.

"It is a long tale of vengeance, adventure, and love. We shall sit here until the moon pales and still it will not have been told. It is enough entertainment for a whole night: an African night's entertainment."

Cyprian Ekwensi, *An African Night's Entertainment* (Lagos: African Universities Press, 1962), p. 7.

Chaga

Mrile

The Chaga live in Tanzania.

A man had three children. Good. And Mrile, the eldest of the children, went with his mother to dig arrowroot.

He found a bean. He said, "Ah, the bean is beautiful, like my younger brother."

His mother said to him, "How can a bean be as beautiful as a human child?"

The boy hid the bean, and his mother tied up the arrowroot. He put the bean in the hollow of a tree. He said to it, "Msura, ripen like Kambingu and Kasanga!"

The next day, he went back. He found that the bean had become a child. When his mother cooked food, Mrile carried it there. He brought the food there every day, and he became thin.

His mother and father saw that he was getting thin, and asked him, "Child, what is making you so thin? The food that we cook—where does it go? Have your brothers become so thin?"

Then his brothers watched when the food was cooked. Mrile put his food aside, he did not eat it. Then he carried it to the place where he had been hiding it.

His brothers followed him, spying on him. They saw him put the food into the hollow of the tree. Then they went home and told his mother, they told her, "We saw him put that food into the hollow of a tree, then he took it to a child there."

She said to them, "That's not true! Whose child lives in a hollow tree?"

They said, "All right, we'll show you, mother!"

From Johannes William Raum, *Versuch einer Grammatik der Dschaggasprache (Moschi-dialekt)* (Berlin: Archiv fur die Stud. dtsch. Kolonialspr. 11 [1909], 307–318). Translated from Chaga by Patrick R. Bennett, 1982.

They took their mother to that place, and showed her. And the child was in that hollow. His mother went up to the child, and killed it.

When the mother had killed the child, Mrile brought some food there, but he did not find the child there. He found that it had been killed. He went home, and started to cry.

They asked him, "Mrile, why are you crying?"

He said, "It's the smoke."

They said to him, "Sit here, lower down."

He continued to cry.

They said to him, "Why do you keep on crying?"

He said , "It's just the smoke."

They told him, "Take your father's chair outside, and sit on it there."

He took the chair, and went and sat on it outside. And he continued to cry there.

Then he said, "Chair, become as high as my father's rope when he hangs the beehive in the forest and on the plain."

The chair went up, then it caught on a tree.

He said a second time, "Chair, become as high as my father's rope when he hangs the beehive in the forest and on the plain."

Then his brothers came outside. They found Mrile climbing into the sky.

They told his mother, "Mrile has gone into the sky!"

She said, "Why do you tell me that your brother has gone into the sky? What way is there for him to climb up?"

They told her, "Come and look, Mother!"

Then Mrile's mother came and looked, and she found him climbing into the sky.

His mother called,

> "Mrile, come back!
> Come back, my child,
> Come back!"

And Mrile answered,

> "I won't come back again,
> I won't come back again,
> My mother, not I!
> I won't come back again,
> I won't come back again."

His brothers called,

> "Mrile, come back!
> Come back, brother,

Come back!
Come back home!
Come back home!"

And he said,

"Me, I won't come back again,
I won't come back again,
My brothers,
I won't come back again,
I won't come back again."

Then his father came, and said,

"Mrile, take your food,
Take your food!
Mrile, take it!
Mrile, take your food,
Take your food!"

And he answered, and said,

"I don't want it anymore,
I don't want it anymore,
My father, not I!
I don't want it any more,
I don't want it anymore."

His relations came then, and sang,

"Mrile, come back home,
Come back home!
Mrile, come back,
Come back home!
Come back home!"

His uncle came, and sang,

"Mrile, come back!
Come back!
Mrile, come back,
Come back,
Come back!"

He answered, singing,

> "Me, I won't come back again,
> I won't come back again,
> Uncle, not I!
> I won't come back again,
> I won't come back again!"

He vanished, they did not see him anymore.

Then he found people gathering firewood. He greeted them, "Firewood-gatherers, greetings! Show me the way to the King of the Moon!"

They told him, "Gather some firewood, and we'll show you."

He gathered firewood for them.

Then they told him, "Go on higher, you'll find some people cutting grass."

Mrile went on, and found the people cutting grass. "Grass-cutters, greetings!"

They returned his greetings

"Show me the way to the King of the Moon!"

They told him, "Cut some grass, and we'll show you."

He cut some grass.

Then they told him, "Go on higher, you'll find some people cultivating."

He went on, and found people cultivating. "Cultivators, greetings!"

They said to him, "Greetings."

"Show me the way to the King of the Moon!"

They told him, "Cultivate a bit, and we'll show you."

So he cultivated a bit.

Then they told him, "Go on higher, you'll find some people herding,"

Mrile went on, and found people herding. "Herders, greetings!"

"Greetings."

"Show me the way to the King of the Moon."

They told him, "Herd, a while, and we'll show you."

He helped them herd for a while.

Then they told him, "Go on higher, to the people picking beans."

"Bean-pickers, greetings! Show me the way to the King of the Moon!"

"Help us pick for a while, and we'll show you."

He picked for a while.

Then they said, "Go on higher, to the people harvesting sorghum."

He found them harvesting. "Harvesters, greetings! Show me the way to the King of the Moon!"

"Help us harvest some sorghum, and we'll show you."

"Go on higher, to the people looking for banana stalks."

He greeted them, "People looking for banana stalks, greetings! Show me the way to the King of the Moon!"

"Look for banana stalks for a while, and we'll show you."

He helped them look for a while.

Then they told him, "Go on higher, you'll find people fetching water."

"Water fetchers, greetings! Show me the way to the King of the Moon!"

"Go on higher, to the people who are eating at home."

"People of the homestead, greetings! Show me the way to the King of the Moon!"

"Eat a little, and we'll show you."

Good, he found people eating raw food. He said to them, "Why don't you cook with fire?"

They said to him, "What is fire?"

He told them, "You cook food with it, until it is done."

They told him, "We don't know about fire, sir!"

He told them, "If I help you prepare your food with fire so that it is good, what will you give me?"

Then the King of the Moon told him, "We will pay you cattle and goats."

Mrile told them, "Gather a lot of firewood, and I'll bring fire."

Then they gathered firewood. They went to a place on the far side of the house so that they would not be seen by anyone. Mrile took out a fire stick, and he made fire there on the far side of the house. They lit the wood, and Mrile put bananas into it.

He said to the King of the Moon, "Try a bit of this banana that I have cooked with fire."

The King of the Moon ate the banana. He found that it tasted good.

Then Mrile cooked some meat, and told him, "Eat some cooked meat as well."

And the King of the Moon found that it tasted good.

Mrile then cooked all edible things, until they were done.

And the King of the Moon called the people, and said to them, "A true diviner has come." And the King of the Moon said, "This man should be given something, to pay for his fire."

They asked him, "What should he be given?"

He said, "Someone should bring cattle, another should bring goats, another should bring grain from the granary."

They brought everything. Mrile distributed the fire to them, and they went and cooked their food.

Mrile thought, "Now, how can I go home, without sending a message there?"

He called all the birds, and they came to that place where he was.

He asked the crow, "If I send you there to my house, what will you go and say?"

The crow said to him, "I would say, 'Kuru kuru kuru.'"

He drove the crow away.

Then the rhinoceros bird came. "You, Rhinoceros Bird, if I send you, what will you go and say?"

It said, "I would say, 'Ng 'a ng'a ng'a.'"

He drove it away.

The hawk came. "You, Hawk, if I send you there to my home, what will you go and say?"

It said, "Chiri-i-i-o."

Mrile drove it away.

He said to the buzzard, "If I send you, what will you say?"

The buzzard said, "I would go and say, 'Cheng' cheng' cheng'.'"

He drove it away.

He tested all the birds in turn, and did not find a bird that understood anything.

Then he called the thrush. "You, Thrush, if I send you, what will you go and say?"

It said,

> "Mrile will come the day after tomorrow,
> The day after tomorrow.
> Mrile will come the day after tomorrow,
> After tomorrow,
> After tomorrow.
> Dip some fat for him with a spoon,
> Dip some fat for him with a spoon!"

He said to the thrush, "Go!"

The thrush went off. It arrived at the gate of Mrile's father, and said, "Mrile says to you,

> He will come the day after tomorrow,
> After tomorrow.
> He will come the day after tomorrow,
> After tomorrow.
> Dip some fat for him with a spoon!"

Mrile's father got up and went outside, and said, "What is this thing that has come crying here, telling me that Mrile will come the day after tomorrow? He is lost!"

He drove the bird away, and it vanished. It returned, and told Mrile, "I have been there."

Mrile said to the bird, "It is a lie. You have not been there. If you did actually go there, what was there at my home?" He said to it, "Go again, and when you arrive be certain to snatch my father's walking stick. Come back with it, so that I'll know that you have been there."

The bird went back a second time, and snatched the walking stick and took it away. The children there at home saw this, but they could not get the stick away from the bird.

It took the stick to Mrile, and then Mrile knew it had really been there.

Mrile said, "I will go home."

He was allowed to go with his cattle. He went with his cattle, and along the way he became tired.

He had a bull, and the bull said to him, "Since you are so tired, if I put you on my back what will you do to me? If I carry you and when I arrive I am butchered, will you eat me?"

Mrile said to the bull, "No, I won't eat you."

Then he got on to the back of the bull, and the bull carried him. Mrile went along singing,

"Not a seed is missing,
The cattle are mine, he!
Not a seed is missing,
The cattle are mine, he!
Not a seed is missing,
The goats are mine, he!
Not a seed is missing,
Mrile is coming, he!
Not a seed is missing!"

He arrived at home. And when he got home, his father and mother anointed him with oil.

He said to them, "This bull, feed it, let it get fat until it grows old. And when it has gotten old, I will not eat its meat."

When the bull grew old, Mrile's father slaughtered it.

Then his mother said, "This bull that my son has had so much trouble with, will it be completely finished without his eating it?"

She hid a piece of fat, she hid it in a honey-pot. When she knew that the meat was finished, she ground some flour. She took the piece of fat, and put it into the flour. Then she gave it to her son, and Mrile ate it.

When Mrile had put the food into his mouth, the meat spoke to him: "Are you going to eat me, the one who carried you?" And it told him, "Be eaten, as you are eating me!"

Mrile sang,

"My mother, I told you,
Don't give me the meat of the bull!"

When he took a second bite, his feet sank into the earth.

He sang,

"My mother, I told you,
Don't give me the meat of the bull!"

He finished the flour, and he sank completely out of sight.
Here is where the story ends.

Commentary

This is a typical puberty rite of passage story: Mrile leaves home, has an ordeal, and is reincorporated. His fantastic journey takes him to the heavens, a mythic touch in this tale that suggests that the puberty ritual is one of the means whereby humans living in the contemporary age can recapture something of the sublime purity of the perfect age. But there is another and more disturbing theme in this tale, revealed by the story's frame. That frame has to do with the relationship between Mrile and his mother. The storyteller is emphasizing the traditional view of the mother: the life-giver, the essence of human goodness. The irony here is that this life-giving mother, in an effort to give life to Mrile, her offspring, is thereby responsible for death: to preserve her son, at the opening of the story she kills the seed-bulb child; at the close, she kills Mrile even as she seeks to nourish him. This is the storyteller's way of emphasizing the flaw of the contemporary age: death is present, and no matter how we attempt to approximate the sublimity of the perfect age, it can never be wholly obtained. The fact of life is death, and the life-giving mother is also a death-dealer. That is a frame that is constructed around this story: it begins and ends with this mother who is dualistic, both life-giver and death-dealer. At the beginning, to save her child from starvation, she kills the seed-bulb child; at the end, to feed her child, she gives him the forbidden flesh of a bull.

Between these life and death images is a celebration of life, the continuity of Chaga tradition. There are five patterns that constitute this part of the tale. Spatially, the movement is from the earth to the heavens and under the earth. The storyteller thereby links life and death to height and depth, heaven and earth, eternal God and dualistic mother.

The first pattern becomes the motivation for Mrile's separation from his home of birth. He brings a seed-bulb to life, regularly feeding it his own food. The motif is the supernatural transformation of the bulb into life, because of the care and sacrifice of Mrile. This pattern is broken when Mrile's mother, fearful for Mrile's life, destroys the seed-bulb child.

Mrile, upset about what his mother has done, sits on his father's chair and rises into the sky. The second pattern: members of his family, from his mother to his uncle, beseech him to return. But he disappears into the sky. The motif is magical ascension.

The third pattern is the crucial one; it is the ordeal or initiation stage of Mrile's movement to manhood. This pattern dominates the story; as he moves closer and closer to God, which is the effect of going through the puberty ritual, Mrile encounters various people who are doing Chaga life sustaining chores: wood-gathering, grass-cutting, tilling the soil, herding, bean-harvesting, millet-reaping, banana-harvesting, water-carrying. They agree to direct him to God if he assists them in their work; in other words, once he masters these tasks, which sustain Chaga society from one generation to the next, he will touch God. So it is that Mrile arrives at the place of God, the Moon-king, and there is a heavenly exchange; Mrile gives God fire, God and his people present Mrile with livestock. Mrile has arrived at manhood, but he cannot live in heaven; he must return to reality, to earth, which is not as perfect as heaven. On the earth, life, in the form of the life-giving mother, is also death. That is the human condition.

The fourth pattern has to do with Mrile's return to the earth. The pattern: he asks various birds if they will carry a message to earth. He asks the raven, the rhinoceros-bird, hawk, buzzard. Because such a gap has grown between heaven and earth, most of the birds are not able to make the connection. Finally, the mocking-bird agrees to make the trip. Mrile's father does not believe the bird when it announces Mrile's imminent arrival; Mrile, says the father, is dead. And, indeed, Mrile is dead; he has died to his childhood past.

Mrile then goes to earth, on the back of a bull given to him by God. This bull is a symbol of the solemn pact made between God and Mrile when the mortal completed his puberty ritual. Mrile must not, therefore, eat its flesh when the bull is slaughtered.

Nevertheless, Mrile's mother, because she desires to nourish her son, feeds him that forbidden flesh, and the fifth pattern reveals Mrile's descent into the earth, singing, until he disappears.

This is a starkly realistic appraisal of the puberty ritual. The reality of life on earth is not the perfection of the realm of God. That realm is the ideal, and the ritual, like all cultural rituals, seeks to duplicate that ideal, but the reality is a mother who is a symbol of life but who is also a death-dealer. That dualism, the fact that the obverse of life is death, is the reality of the human condition. Rituals and traditions can move us closer to godly perfection, but there is no assurance of such perfection.

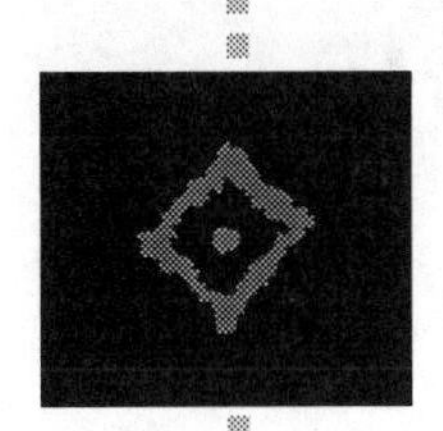

The narrator of Gbaya tales, like an actor, performs and interprets his piece before his audience. By up-dating the setting and introducing details from contemporary life he makes his story alive and meaningful for his listeners. The audience also participates in the performance by breaking in with questions and comments and by singing the chorus that accompanies the song. When the tale ends another performer takes the stage with a new tale, for nearly every member of the community from little children to old men and women have their own favorite tales to repeat.

Philip A. Noss, "Gbaya Traditional Literature," *Abbia*, Nos. 17–18 (1967), p. 35.

Swahili

The Girl with One Hand

The Swahili live in eastern Africa.

A man and his wife prayed to God to get a child, and they got first a son and next a daughter. Their father's employment was to cut firewood. The parents remained until the children were grown up. Then their father was seized by a disease. He called his children, and asked them, "Will you have blessing or property?"

The son said, "I will have property."

The daughter said, "I will have blessing."

The father gave her much blessing.

And he died.

They mourned, and when the mourning came to an end their mother fell sick. She called her children, and said to them, "Will you have blessing or property?"

The son said, "I will have property."

The daughter said, "I will have blessing."

Her mother gave her blessing.

And their mother died.

They mourned, and when the mourning came to an end it was the seventh day.

The son went and told his sister, "Bring out all my father's and mother's things."

The sister went and brought them out, leaving nothing for herself. The son took them all away.

The people said to him, "Will you leave nothing, not even a little thing, for your sister?"

He said, "I shall not. I asked for the property, she asked for a blessing."

From Edward Steere, *Swahili Tales* (London: Society for Promoting Christian Knowledge, 1869), pp. 390–407.

He left her a cooking pot and a mortar for cleaning corn. He did not even leave her a little food.

Her neighbors would come and borrow the mortar and clean their corn; then they gave her a little grain, and she cooked and ate it. Others would come and borrow her cooking pots and cook with them; then they gave her a little food. This was what she did every day.

She searched about in her father's and mother's house, but found nothing except a pumpkin seed. She took the seed, and went and planted it under the well. A plant sprang up, and it bore many pumpkins.

Her brother had no news of her, and he asked people, "Where does my sister get food?"

They told him, "People borrow her mortar and they clean their corn, then they give her a little food. People borrow her cooking pots, and cook with them, then they give her a little food."

Her brother rose, and went and robbed her of the mortar and cooking pots.

When she awoke in the morning, she sought food and could not get any. She stayed there until nine o'clock, then she said, "I will go and look at my pumpkin, to see if it has grown."

She went, and saw that many pumpkins had come. She was comforted.

She gathered the pumpkins, and went and sold them and got food. She did this every day: she gathered pumpkins, then went and sold them.

Three days passed.

Everyone who ate those pumpkins found them very sweet. So they took grain and went to her place to buy pumpkins.

Many days passed, and the young woman got property.

Her brother's wife heard about this, and she sent her slave with grain to go and buy a pumpkin.

The young woman said, "They're finished." But when she found that it was her brother's wife's slave, she told him, "Take this pumpkin, and take back your grain."

The brother's wife went and cooked it, and found it very sweet.

The next day, she again sent someone.

The young woman said, "There are none at all today."

The slave went and told his mistress, and she was very upset.

Her husband came and asked, "What is the matter with you, my wife?"

She said, "I sent someone to your sister with my grain, to go and ask for pumpkins. She did not send them, she said, 'There are none.' Other people all buy pumpkins from her."

He said to his wife, "Let's sleep until tomorrow. I'll go and pull up her pumpkin plant."

When the morning dawned, he went to his sister and said to her, "When my wife sent grain to you, you refused to sell her a pumpkin."

She said, "They are finished. The day before yesterday, she sent someone, and I gave a pumpkin to him for nothing."

He said, "Why are you selling to other people?"

She said, "The pumpkins are finished, there are no more. They have not yet come."

Her brother said to her, "I shall go and cut up your pumpkin plant."

She said, "You dare not! You'll have to cut my hand off first! Then you may cut up the pumpkin plant!"

Her brother took her right hand and cut it off. Then he went and cut up her pumpkin plant—every bit of it.

The young woman heated some water, she put her arm into it. Then she put medicine on it, and bound it with a cloth.

Her brother took everything away from her, and put her out of the house.

His sister wandered about in the forest.

This brother sold the house. He gathered much property, and continued to spent it.

The sister wandered in the forest until, on the seventh day, she came out and found herself in another town. She climbed up a great tree, and ate the fruit of the tree. She slept there in the tree.

On the next day, the son of the king and his people came out into the forest to shoot birds. At about twelve o'clock, he became tired, and said, "I'll go there by the tree and rest. You continue to shoot birds." He and his slave sat under the tree.

The young woman cried until her tears fell on the king's son below.

He said to his slave, "Look outside. Is it raining?"

The slave said, "It is not, master."

The king's son said, "Then climb into the tree, see what bird is casting its droppings on me."

His slave climbed the tree, and he saw a very beautiful woman crying. Without saying a word, he came down. He told his master, "There is a very beautiful young woman up there. I didn't say anything to her."

His master asked him, "Why?"

The slave said, "She was crying. Perhaps you should go yourself."

His master climbed the tree. He climbed, and saw her. He said to her, "What is the matter with you, my woman? Are you a person or a spirit?"

She said, "I am a person."

He said, "Why are you crying?"

She said, "I am thinking of things. I am a person, as you are."

He said, "Come down, let us go to our home."

She said to him, "Where is your home?"

He said, "With my father and mother. I am a king's son."

She said, "What did you come here to do?"

He said, "I come to shoot birds every month. This is what we do. I came here with my companions."

She said, "I do not like to be seen by anyone."

The king's son said, "We shall not be seen by anyone."

She came down from the tree.

The king's son said to his slave, "Go into the town quickly. Bring me a litter."

His slave went at once. He returned with a litter and four people. He put the woman into the litter, and told his slave, "Fire a gun, so that all the company may know."

The slave fired a gun, and the companions of the king's son came to him.

They said, "What is the matter, son of the king?"

He said, "I am cold. I want to go to town."

They carried the game they had caught, and went away.

The king's son got into the litter with the young woman. Because she was in the litter, his companions knew nothing about her.

They went to their city, and reached the house of the king.

The king's son said to a man, "Go and tell my mother and father that I have a fever today. I want some porridge at once. Let them send me some porridge."

His mother and father were worried, and the porridge was cooked and sent to him.

His father went with his advisors to see his son.

At night, his mother went with her people to see him.

The next day, the king's son went out, he went and told his mother and father, "I have picked up a young woman. I want you to marry me to her, but she has lost one hand."

They said, "Why?"

He said, "I wish to marry her as she is."

The king loved his only son very much, so he organized a wedding and married his son to the young woman.

The townspeople heard that "The king's son has married a young woman who has lost one of her hands."

Time passed, and his wife became pregnant. She bore a son, and his parents rejoiced greatly.

The king's son went on a journey, he went to travel to the various towns in his father's kingdom.

The young woman's brother, in the meantime, had no money, he was begging. One day, he heard people conversing: "The king's son has married a woman who has lost one hand."

Her brother asked, "Where did this child of the king get the young woman?"

They told him, "He found her in the forest."

And he knew that she was his sister.

He went to the king. He said, "Your child has married a woman who has lost a hand. She runs run out of town because she was a witch! She kills every man she marries!"

The king went and told this to his wife.

They said, "What shall we do?"

They loved their only child very much.

They said, "Let us run her out of town."

Her brother said to them, "Kill her. At home, they cut off her hand. Here, you should kill her."

They said, "We cannot kill her. We'll run her out of town."

So they put her and her son out of town. And she was comforted.

She went out with a little earthen pot. She went on her way into the forest, she did not know where she was going or where she came from. She sat down, looking at her child. Then she looked and saw a snake coming rapidly towards her. She said, "Today, I am dead."

The snake said to her, "Child of Adam, open your earthen pot so that I may go in. Save me from the sun, I shall save you from the rain."

She opened the pot, and the snake went in. She covered the pot.

Then she saw another snake rapidly coming towards her.

It said to her, "Has my companion passed by?"

She said, "It went that way."

The snake passed by quickly.

The snake that was in the pot said, "Uncover me."

She uncovered it.

The snake was comforted, and it said to that child of Adam, "Where are you going?"

She said, "I don't know where I am going. I am wandering in the forest."

The snake said to her, "Follow me, let's go home."

They went along together until they saw a great lake near the road.

The snake said to her, "Child of Adam, let us sit here and rest. The sun is fierce. Go and bathe in the lake with your child."

She carried the boy, and went to wash him. The boy fell into the lake, she lost him in the lake.

The snake asked her, "What is the matter, child of Adam?"

She said, "My child is lost in the water!"

The snake said, "Look for him carefully."

She sought the boy a full hour, but did not find him.

The snake said, "Put your other hand into the water."

She said, "Snake, are you making fun of me?"

It asked, "How?"

She said, "I have put my sound hand into the water, and I have not found my child. What is the use of this spoiled hand?"

The snake said, "Put in both of your hands."

The child of Adam put her hands in, and found her son. She held him. And she drew out her hand: it was sound again.

The snake said, "Have you found him?"

She said, "I have found him! And I have my hand, it is sound again!"

She was very happy.

The snake said, "Now, let's go to my elders, and let me repay your kindness."

She said, "Getting my hand back is enough!"

The snake said, "Not yet. Let us go to my elders."

They went, and arrived, and the snake's elders rejoiced, and they loved that young woman.

She remained there for many days, eating and drinking.

Her husband, the son of the king, returned from his journey. His elders had caused two tombs to be built, one for his wife and the other for his child.

And her brother had become an important man with the king.

The young woman's husband, the king's son, arrived.

He asked, "Where is my wife?"

They said to him, "She is dead."

"And where is my child?"

They answered, "He is dead."

He asked, "Where are their graves?"

They took him to the graves.

When he saw them, he wept much. He mourned for them, and he was comforted.

Many days passed.

In the forest, the young woman said to her friend, the snake, "I want to leave home."

The snake said, "Take leave of my mother and father. When they give you leave to go, and if they give you gifts, accept only my father's ring and my mother's casket."

The young woman went and took leave of them. They gave her much wealth, but she refused, saying, "How shall I, one person, carry all this wealth?"

They said, "What will you have?"

She said, "Father, I want your ring. Mother, I want your casket."

They were saddened, and asked her, "Who told you about this?"

She said, "I know it myself."

They said, "Not so! Your brother told you."

The father took the ring and gave it to her, and said, "I give you this ring. If you want food, if you want clothes, if you want a house to sleep in, just tell the ring. It will produce these for you by the blessing of God and of me, your father."

The mother gave her the casket, and told her various things.

And they gave her their blessing.

The young woman went out, she went away until she arrived at the town of her husband—but she did not go to her husband's house. When she reached the outskirts of the town, she said to the ring, "I want you to produce a great house for me."

The ring produced a house, along with furniture and slaves.

Time passed for her and her son. Her son had become a strapping lad.

The king learned that there was a large house on the town's outskirts. He sent people to go and look.

They said to the king, "It is true."

Then the king went there with his advisors and his son.

They went there, they drew near, and the woman watched them through a telescope. She saw her husband, she saw her husband's father and many people, her brother among them.

She told the slaves, "Quickly! Prepare food!"

They prepared food, and laid the table.

The people arrived, they were invited to enter. They went inside, and asked her for the news.

She said, "Good." She said to them, "Eat the food. I have come a long distance. When you are finished with the food, let me give you my news."

They ate the food until they had finished.

Then she told them everything—she told them of the time she was born, she told them about her and her brother. She told them everything, until her story was completed.

The king's son went to embrace his wife. They wept much, and everyone who was there wept.

And they knew that her brother was not good.

The king asked her, "What shall we do to your brother?"

She said, "Just put him out of town."

And she lived with her husband in joy, until the end.

Comments on "The Armless Bride" Stories

"The Armless Bride" is a puberty rite of passage tale, dramatically depicting the puberty ritual and, frequently, the marriage ritual of a woman. The story of the armless bride is told in oral societies around the world. Versions have been recorded in Germany, Brazil, Chile, Egypt, India, Puerto Rico, New Mexico, Finland, Sweden, Denmark, Ireland, Spain, France, Belgium, Italy, Iceland, Japan, Scotland, Russia. The major motif is called "the armless woman" or "the woman without arms."

In some versions of the story, the opening pattern has to do with a father's incestuous advances towards his daughter. The pattern of his intensifying incestuous demands and her adamant refusals leads to the separation of the girl from her home of birth.

The main pattern usually dramatizes the girl's ordeal or initiation: her movement into womanhood. This pattern has to do with her miserable experiences in the forest where, after her father has cut off her arms, she becomes animal-like in her desperate quest for food and survival. She loses her identity as a human in the process, and is compared to a pig, a hog, a cow. The pattern: her many efforts to fend for herself, to survive. There is a return to this pattern when she leaves her in-laws' home, when once again she must provide for herself, this time with her child strapped to her back. It is a lengthy struggle, an ordeal, a move to womanhood.

She is incomplete, she is not a whole person, and this physical state (her armlessness) is a reflection of her mental and spiritual states: she is not yet a woman. She must show her independence not only from her childhood past but also from her husband, in-laws, and children.

A letter-writing pattern sometimes reinforces the main pattern. In this letter-writing pattern, the parents write a letter to their son, pretending to be the wife; and the incestuous father writes a letter to his daughter, pretending to be the husband. These letter-writing ruses are meant to place the husband-wife relationship at risk, to compromise it, to break the marriage tie. This pattern fortifies the main pattern by adding to the young woman's isolation and ordeal.

The closing pattern occurs when a bird, or some other nurturing figure, restores the girl's arms to her, thereby giving her physical completeness (which reflects her spiritual and mental fullness, her coming of age), and the father's earlier act of removing her arms is responded to. The father's act and the bird's act make up a pattern: the arms removed, the arms restored. With the restoration of the arms, the young woman is reincorporated into human society.

Notes

Even though she marries the young man earlier, the marriage is incomplete, suggested by the fact that she remains armless. Her puberty rite of passage is not complete; her ordeal or initiation is not over. She struggles with her father, she struggles with her in-laws: these make up the main pattern. The struggle with her father is a suggestion that she must leave her home of birth to become a woman; to remain there is tantamount to incest. That is the purpose of the powerful incest motif in the first part of the tale. The struggle with the in-laws suggests that her rite of passage is still not complete: she is victimized by them, and she would not be so victimized were she a full woman. This story is a graphic, painful revelation of the ordeal part of the puberty ritual. In the end, appropriately, it is nature, in the form of the bird, that gives her an adult identity.

There are two brief African versions of this story in this collection, a Swahili version and a Somali.

In the Swahili version, "The Girl with One Hand," the first pattern involves the receiving of the father's blessing. The son takes his property, the daughter takes his blessing. In the second pattern, the brother takes all of his sister's belongings including her hand. When he departs, he leaves his sister nothing. Neighbors must lend her utensils and pots. The purpose of these two patterns is to render the girl incomplete, cut off from her past, in a state of betwixt and between. Her brother is the cruel agent of this state.

There are two central motifs in this story, the girl's hand and a magical pumpkin seed that produces many pumpkins.

The brother continues to divest his sister of everything, to the point of taking the utensils and pots given her by her neighbors. When she makes her living selling the pumpkins, he comes to destroy her plant. She tells him that he will have to cut off her hand first, and he does that, then cuts up the pumpkin plant. He takes everything from her.

She wanders, alone, in a forest seven days, sleeping in a tree. A prince comes hunting. She cries; he thinks it is raining. They are married. Now the second pattern reasserts itself, as the brother tells the king that the prince has married a witch: "She kills every man she marries." He urges the king to kill her. They run her and her son out of town.

◇ **Assistance from nature**—Once again alone in the wilderness, the girl helps a snake. This harmony with nature is repaid: when her son falls into a lake and she cannot find him for an hour, the snake causes her hand to be restored. She receives from the snake and its parents a magical ring and casket. The ring, a common folklore motif, is a cornucopia that will provide all that she ever requires.

On the outskirts of the kingdom, the ring produces a great house for her. When the king and his entourage come to visit her, she tells them her story, and they run her brother out of town.

It is the story of a girl moving to womanhood, from incompleteness to fullness.

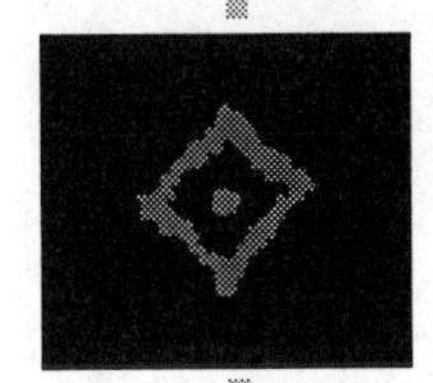

Each person will tell the same story differently, since he has to make it personal and not simply a mechanical repetition of what he had heard or narrated before. He becomes not only a "repeater" but also a "creative" originator of each story; and if listeners have already heard it from a different person, it will have its own freshness and originality through the telling of another narrator, if he is good. The plot of the story and the sequence of its main parts remain the same, but the narrator has to supply the meat to this skeleton. This he will do in the choice of words, the speed of reciting, the imagery he uses, the varying of his voice, the gestures he makes with his face and hands, and the manner in which he will sing or merely recite the poetical portions. . . .

John S. Mbiti, *Akamba Stories* (Oxford: Clarendon Press, 1966), p. 26.

Somali

The Girl without Legs

by Mohammed Jibril

The Somali live in the country of Somalia.

A sultan had a daughter. The daughter was taught the Qur'an.

One day, the sultan went on a pilgrimage, and he entrusted his daughter to a priest. He said, "Continue to teach this girl the Qur'an."

The priest coveted the girl, wishing to lie with her, but the girl refused.

Then one day, she said, "Come to me tomorrow."

The next day, she removed from the house the ladder by which the priest was accustomed to ascend, so that he could not get to her.

The priest then sent a letter to her father. He wrote, "Your daughter has become a whore."

When the sultan returned from his pilgrimage, he was angry with the girl, and he handed her over to some slaves, saying, "Cut the girl's throat."

The slaves took the girl and brought her to a wooded place. They cut off her legs while they dug her grave.

While they were digging the grave, she crawled away, and went among some trees and hid.

When the slaves had dug the grave, they looked in the place where they had lain the girl, and could not find her. Then they killed a gazelle, and they poured the gazelle's blood into a bottle. They brought the blood to the sultan, and said, "We have killed the girl."

From J. W. C. Kirk, "Specimens of Somali Tales," *Folk-Lore* 15 (1904), 319–321.

One day later, a caravan passed by the place, and camped where the girl lay. In the afternoon, as the members of the party were loading up the camels, they saw the girl sitting under a tree.

A man took the girl, put her on a camel, and brought her to the next town that they came to. Then the man who had taken the girl put her into a house to live.

Later, the son of the sultan saw the girl's face, and the young man saw that she was beautiful. He said to the man in whose house she dwelt, "Let me marry that girl."

The man said, "The girl has no legs."

The sultan's son said, "I shall marry her. Give her to me."

So the man said, "Well and good."

And the sultan's son married her.

She bore two children.

While she was with child, the young man said, "I am going on a pilgrimage."

He left her a ram, and went on the pilgrimage.

While he was away on the pilgrimage, his wife had a dream. She dreamed that two birds sat on her two legs, and her legs had grown out, and that she made the pilgrimage.

In the morning, at the break of day, she saw the two birds sitting on her two legs, and the legs had grown out.

After daylight, she took her two children and the ram and the two birds, and went on the pilgrimage. She came to a building when she was half way there, and along came her father and her brother and the priest and her husband. None of them knew her.

She told stories to her children, and in the stories she related everything that had happened to her. And her father heard, and so did the priest.

Then the priest tried to run away, but the sultan said, "Sit down until the story is finished."

When the story was finished, the sultan, the girl's father, cut the priest's throat, and the girl and her father and her husband went on together, and made the pilgrimage.

So the girl and her father were reconciled.

Commentary

In this version of "The Armless Bride" tale, the girl loses her legs: a priest, her teacher, tries to seduce her. When she refuses him, he accuses her of being a prostitute, and her father, a sultan, has her legs cut off.

This represents her separation from her childhood past. Now, in an incomplete state, living with no legs, she undergoes her ordeal or initiation. She is married, and becomes the mother of two children. When her husband goes on pilgrimage, there is a dream pattern: birds sit on her legs, and restore them. The pattern: as depicted in her dreams, so it happens in reality.

The return stage of her puberty ritual occurs when she goes to her father, brother, husband, and the priest, and, in their presence, tells her children stories: in the stories, she tells of what happened. The sultan cuts the priest's throat.

Noplani Gxavu, a Xhosa storyteller (photos by Harold Scheub)

When one deals with oral narratives when they are written down, one has to remember that a lot has been lost in the process of transcription and translation. The narrator's voice is not there and it is the voice that often helps the audience to make a value judgment. The artist, for instance, laughs when he says that Simbi was looking for a man who didn't shit, a man without an anus. The laughter however is not recorded. The artist changes the voice depending on whether he/she was imitating the ogre or a bird. In this way, he/she can shape the audience's emotions.

Wanjiku Mukabi Kabira and Kavetsa Adagala, *Kenyan Oral Narratives* (Nairobi: Heinemann, 1985), p. xvi.

Masai

Konyek

The Masai live in Kenya

A big dance was once held. Many warriors and young women were present. Towards evening, the dancers dispersed. Each warrior selected one or more young women to accompany him home.

One of the men, a particularly handsome and well-built fellow, went away with three sisters. As they departed, he asked the young women where they would like to go.

They told him that they wished to accompany him to his homestead.

He said that it was a long way off.

They replied that that did not matter.

They started off, and, after walking some distance, they approached the kraal.

The young women noticed some white things scattered about on the ground, and they asked the warrior what they were.

He said that they were his sheep and goats.

But when they reached their destination, they saw that they were human bones.

They entered the warrior's house, and the young women were surprised to find that he lived alone.

It happened that this warrior was really a demon who ate people, but the young women did not know this because he concealed his tail under his garment. The demon had even eaten his mother, and had thrown her bones into the heap of grass that formed the bed.

From Alfred Claud Hollis, *The Masai, Their Language and Folklore* (Oxford: Oxford University Press, 1905), pp. 143–147.

Shortly after their arrival at the house, the warrior went outside, leaving the young women alone.

A voice that came from the bed startled the young women by asking them who had brought them there.

They replied that the warrior had brought them.

The voice then told them to open the mattress. The young women threw off the top layer of grass exposing the bones to view. The voice that came from the bones then related that she had been the warrior's mother, that he had become a demon and had eaten her.

The young women asked the bones what they should do, and the voice said, "The warrior will come presently and bring you a sheep. Accept it. He will then go outside again, and, having shut the door, sit down there. Make a hole in the wall, and go out. If he asks you what the knocking is, say that you are killing the sheep."

Everything took place as the voice had predicted, and the women made a hole in the wall of the house through which they passed and escaped.

When they reached the road, however, one of them suddenly remembered that she had left her beads behind. Her sisters told her to go and get them while they waited for her. She returned to the house, but met the warrior. He gave her a choice: should he eat her, or make her his wife?

She thanked him for giving her the choice, and said that she preferred the latter.

They lived together for a considerable period, and after a time the woman presented the demon with a son whom they named Konyek. From the day of his birth, Konyek accompanied his father on his journeys to the forest in quest of people to devour. The man and the boy ate human beings, but they took with them for the woman goats and sheep to eat and cows to milk.

One day, one of the woman's sisters came to the kraal to visit her. Konyek and his father were both absent when she arrived, so the two women sat and talked until it was time for the visitor to depart. The weather looked threatening as she rose to take her leave, and Konyek's mother cried out to her not to go to the baobab tree in the middle of the plain, should it rain, for it was her husband's and son's custom to rest there on their way home. But the woman hurried away without paying attention to her sister's warning, and when it started to rain a little later, she ran to the baobab tree in the middle of the plain, and climbed into it.

She had not been there long before Konyek and his father arrived there, and stood under the tree to get shelter from the rain. Their appearance recalled to the woman her sister's words, and she was greatly alarmed.

Konyek gazed up into the tree, and remarked that there was something peculiar about it.

But his father said that it was only because it was raining hard.

Shortly afterwards, however, Konyek saw the woman, and called out, "There is my meat!"

The woman was forced to descend, and she gave birth to twins.

Konyek picked up the children, and said, "I shall take these kidneys to mother to roast for me."

When it stopped raining, the two returned home, and Konyek asked his mother to roast the kidneys for him.

But the woman knew at once that her sister had been put to death, and she hid the children in a hole in the earth, roasting instead two rats.

When they were ready, Konyek went to the fire, picked them up off the stones, and ate them, grumbling at the same time because they were so small.

His mother pretended to be very annoyed at this, and, turning to her husband, complained of what their son had said.

The old man told her not to mind the boy, as he was a liar.

The woman fed and tended the children, who were both boys, and gradually they grew.

One day, she asked her husband to bring her an ox which, she said, she wished to slaughter and eat.

Konyek, on hearing this request, at once pricked up his ears, and remarked, "It really amuses me to hear of a woman who wants to eat an ox all by herself. I think these kidneys of mine have something to do with this matter."

However, the two men searched for an ox. They procured one, and brought it back with them. They slaughtered the animal, and left the meat with the woman, after which they went for a walk in the forest.

As soon as they had departed, the woman let the children come out of their hole, and gave them the ox to eat. They ate until sunset, when she sent them back again to their hiding place.

Konyek and his father returned shortly afterwards, and Konyek, being very sharp, at once noticed the small foot marks on the ground.

"I wonder," he said, "what those small and numerous foot marks are. They are certainly not mine."

His mother, however, insisted that the marks had been made by herself or by the two men, and her husband supported her.

Because he was annoyed with the way Konyek treated his mother, the old man killed him and ate him. But Konyek immediately came to life again, and cried out, "There, I have come back again!"

As time passed, the children grew up, and their aunt asked them one day if they knew that the people who lived in the same kraal with them were really demons and cannibals. She also asked them if, were she able to obtain weapons from her husband, they could put Konyek and his father to death.

The boys replied that they could, but asked the woman what she would say if her husband wanted to know why she required the weapons.

She told them that she would say she wanted them to protect herself against any enemies who might come.

When Konyek and his father next returned home, the woman asked her husband if he would procure for her two spears, two shields, and two swords, "because," she said, "I am always here alone, and, if enemies come, I wish to be able to fight with them."

Konyek said that he had never before heard of a woman who wanted men's weapons, he said that he thought that those kidneys that he had brought his mother to roast for him must have something to do with this request.

Notwithstanding Konyek's protest, the old man obtained for his wife the weapons that she asked for.

When he had given them to her, she got an ox hide, and asked the two men to lie down on the ground while she stretched the hide over them and pegged it down. She told them that when she was ready she would cry out. She wanted to see if, were an enemy to come, they would be able to assist her. She pegged the ox hide down securely, and asked them if they could get out. Konyek found a hole and began to crawl out, but his mother told him to get in again, and she pegged the hide down once more. Then she raised her voice and called to the two youths, who came from their hiding place and killed Konyek and his father.

As Konyek was dying, he said to his father, "Did I not tell you so? And you said I lied!"

After killing the two demons, the youths took their aunt away to their father's home.

Commentary

This story has to do with death and resurrection, a dramatization of the ordeal stage of the puberty ritual when, in some way, the central character is reborn as an adult, a new member of human society. In the initial situation, women follow a handsome demon lover to his home. This is the separation phase of the puberty rite. One girl returns for her beads. The demon captures her, gives her a choice. She marries him; this is the ordeal stage of her ritual. Pattern one, not developed in great detail, has to do with this ordeal; the demon husband and the demon son, Konyek, regularly kill humans for themselves, bringing back animals for her. The mother is a prisoner in their land (the demon husband is the deadly side of the swallower, the land does the actual swallowing; together, they make up the swallowing monster motif). Pattern two is the major pattern; it has to do with the return or reincorporation phase of the ritual. Her pregnant sister brings her the wherewithal for her escape. In this pattern, the wife brings up her sister's children, feeding them, rearing them into men. Associated with this are the growing suspicions of her demon son. In the end, the youths help her to escape from this swallowing monster.

['Abdille 'Ali Siigo] was a venerable elder who almost every evening after the camels had been milked and secured in the kraal would, by the fireside, chant the poetry of Sayyid Mahammad late into the night before a captivated audience of men, women, and children. He was a dramatic chanter who seemed to command even the attention of the camels which sat nearby, lazily chewing their cuds. So the fire crackled, its red flames casting a hazy glow over his silvery beard, giving the elder's expression a pale, ghostly aspect. Outside the kraal fence the winds howled monotonously, pierced by the occasional roar of a hungry lion. Every now and then this would stir the camels from their dreamy drowsing, causing them to stop chewing and prick their ears, alarmed by the danger outside. Meantime, elder 'Abdille chanted ecstatically, seemingly oblivious of everything but his rhymes.

Said S. Samatar, *Oral Poetry and Somali Nationalism* (Cambridge: Cambridge University Press, 1982), p. x.

Swati

The Pregnant Boy

by Albertine Nxumalo

The Swati live in Swaziland.

There was once a woman who lived in a house with her children.

One day, she told one of her children, a boy, to go and get some medicine for her from a certain man.

Before the boy departed, his mother told him, "Now if you do get the medicine, you must not touch it, don't eat it! It is not meant to be eaten! You might get sick. Don't touch it, don't touch it even a little!"

The boy agreed, and set out. He went to the home of the man who had the medicine.

When he got there, he said, "My mother told me to come here to get a certain medicine."

This man gave it to him, and the boy went away.

As he walked home, he wondered why his mother had given him this injunction, that he should not eat this medicine. "What is it for?" he wondered. "Let me just taste it a little." But he restrained himself. "But if I eat it, maybe I'll die!" Then he changed his mind: "No, I won't taste it!" He continued walking. Then he looked at the medicine again, and said, "Well, let me just taste it and see what it's like." So the boy uncovered

Date of Performance: October 24, 1972. Place: In a home in Zombodze, Shiselweni District, Swaziland. Performer: Albertine Nxumalo, a Swati woman, about twenty-one years old. Audience: Twenty children and teen-agers, two men, two women. Collected and translated by Harold Scheub.

the medicine, and tasted it. Then he continued walking, going to his home. He said, "That is strange. I feel nothing. Nothing's happening to me. But why, then, did my mother say that I shouldn't eat it?"

Finally, he reached his home, and he gave the medicine to his mother.

She said, "Are you sure that you didn't touch it?"

He said, "No, I didn't touch it."

"Are you sure that you didn't take even a little bite?"

"No, not at all!"

Then she said, "I'll find out if you did touch it. There'll be evidence."

Time passed for them, time passed, and this boy took the cattle to the pasture to herd them. When he was out in the pasture, he noticed as time passed that his knee was swelling.

He said, "What's the matter? My knee has swelled. It's infected!"

Time passed for him, time passed, and at length he returned to his home with the cattle.

When he reached home, he told his mother, "My knee hurts."

She said, "What's the matter with it?"

He said, "It's swelling up."

He sat down.

"Well, there's nothing to it. It'll heal soon."

Time passed for them, and then they went to sleep.

In the morning, the boy got up, and again he took the cattle to the pasture. His knee continued to swell during this time.

When he had returned and closed the cattle in the kraal, his mother asked, "How is your knee?"

He said, "It continues to swell."

She said, "Are you certain you didn't eat the medicine?"

He said, "No, I didn't touch it."

She said, "If you didn't touch it, the swelling will soon go down."

Time passed, and the boy continued to take the cattle out to the pasture.

One day, when he had reached the mountain, he gave birth to a child. The infant came out of his knee!

He took the child, and said, "Here's a child! Is this the way children are born?" He took the baby, and said, "My child! Oh, my people! Isn't it beautiful? Oh my God!"

Time passed for the boy and his child in the pasture. He wrapped his child, and said, "My child is so beautiful! I must take it home and show it to my mother." But he changed his mind: "No! I must never show her to my mother, because then she'll know that I ate her medicine."

So he remained there with his child. And he returned the cattle to the kraal. When he returned the cattle, he put the child at the side of the kraal, in a certain place. That place was sheltered, he covered the child with clothes. He wrapped the child, and put it there, and then he went into the house. Then he sat with his mother.

She said, "How is your knee?"

"Well, it's much better now."

Time passed, and he played with his mother's other child.

Time passed there at home: the boy would get up early, he would take the cattle to pasture, he would pass by the place where he kept his child and suckle her. Then he would leave her there. When he came back in the evening, he would suckle the child again, then shut the cattle in the kraal and go to the house. In the morning, he would suckle the child, then open the kraal for the cattle, and go out to the pasture.

He said, "I'll give the child a name. What shall I call her?" He said, "I'll call her Matinci." Then he went on his way.

The next day, as he was going to open the kraal for his cattle, he went to the child and said, "Matinci!" He spoke lovingly to the child—"Ayi tobho tinci!"—and then called her by name: "Matinci! Matinci!"

The child began to cry. When he saw that she was still in her proper place, he took her out and suckled her, then put her back again. And she remained there in the shelter.

The boy went out to herd the cattle. In the afternoon, he returned to shut the cattle in the kraal. When he had finished doing that, he passed by the child again.

He said, "Matinci! Matinci! Ayi tobho tinci! Matinci, Matinci, ayi tobho tinci! Matinci, Matinci, ayi tobho tinci!"

As usual, the child cried. The boy took her out and suckled her, then he returned to the house and sat down.

One day, his mother noticed that, when he went to close the cattle in the kraal, he passed by that shelter of his.

She said, "Why do you pass by that same spot every day? What did you put there?"

He said, "Nothing, Mother!"

So it went on: the boy would go to bed and get up in the morning, then stealthily go over to his child. If he saw that his mother was watching him, he would not go there. Then, when she was not looking, he would hurry to that sheltered spot. When he got to the shelter, he would say, "Matinci, Matinci, ayi tobho tinci! Matinci, Matinci, ayi tobho tinci!" And the infant would cry, and the boy would suckle her. Then he would go to open the kraal for the cattle.

One day, his mother said to herself, "Let me just go and look into this. I want to see what this is all about. I'll just go out there before he brings the cattle back to the kraal. What, I wonder, is out there?"

When the boy had gone to the pasture that day, his mother went out. She said, "There is a child here!" She said, "Who can it belong to? Who owns it? Where did he get this child?"

Time passed, the mother remained silent.

The boy returned, he inspected the shelter. When he got there, he said, "Matinci, Matinci, ayi tobho tinci! Matinci, Matinci, ayi tobho tinci!"

The child cried, and the boy suckled her. Then he went to the house.

Time passed, his mother said nothing. She acted as if she knew nothing about this matter.

The next morning, the mother picked up the infant when this boy had gone, after he had breast fed the child and gone out to the pasture. His mother took the child, and she hid her.

When the boy returned from the pasture in the late afternoon, he went to the shelter, and said, "Matinci, Matinci, ayi tobho tinci! Matinci, Matinci, ayi tobho tinci!"

There was no response. There was no child! It did not cry!

Then he said again, "Matinci, Matinci, ayi tobho tinci! Matinci, Matinci, ayi tobho tinci!"

But no child cried. There was only silence.

The boy wondered what had happened. "Could my child have died? What has happened? Why isn't she crying? Matinci, Matinci, ayi tobho tinci!" he said, his voice tremulous now. He realized that his child was not there. "Matinci, Matinci, ayi tobho tinci! Matinci, Matinci. . . ."

No response.

The boy went into the house. He sat by the ashes, he sat there and cried near the ashes in the hearth. He cried and cried.

His mother said, "Why are you crying?"

He said, "I'm not crying. The smoke is making me my eyes water. The ashes are suffocating me!"

"Then why are you sitting there?"

But he continued to sit there. He stayed there, he even ate his food by the ashes.

Whenever he left his place near the ashes, his mother would say, "What's wrong? Why do you keep rubbing your eyes?"

He said, "The ashes are bothering me."

She said, "But why don't you move? Will you keep crying for no reason? Merely saying that the ashes are causing you to cry?"

He said, "The ashes are bothering me."

"But why don't you move?"

He remained silent.

Time passed, and they went to sleep.

The boy got up early the next morning, and he said to himself, "Maybe today I'll find the child." Then he said again, "Matinci, Matinci, ayi tobho tinci!"

Silence.

He said, "Could my child have died? What could have gone wrong?"

He opened the shelter again, but found no child. Then he went out to the pasture. In the pasture, he cried and cried. He returned again, then went to look for the child, but he found nothing. He returned to the house. He sat there by the ashes, and cried.

His mother said, "But what has happened?"

He said, "I'm bothered by the ashes."

She said, "What are you constantly looking for over there by the kraal?"
He said, "I don't go there."
She said, "What is it that you seek in the shelter over there?"
He said, "I don't go there!"
She said, "The day I asked you to go over there and get some medicine for me, when I told you not to eat it—what happened?"
He said, "I didn't eat it."
His mother said, "What is this thing that you're always looking for?"
He said, "There's nothing!"
She said, "So you won't tell me why you keep going over there to the shelter! I can see that you're crying about something, and I can tell you why you're crying. But, since you won't tell me that you did in fact eat my medicine, I won't tell you why you keep crying. I won't show you that thing of yours. But if you tell me the truth about the medicine, I'll show it to you!"
The boy remained quiet. He thought, and finally he said, "Well, on the way home, I did think that I would taste that medicine, to see if I would die. I didn't know what the medicine was for."
His mother said, "But why did you deny everything and insist that you had not eaten the medicine?"
He said, "I was afraid that you'd beat me!"
She said, "Now, why are you crying? On the day that you said that your knee was hurting—what caused it to stop hurting?"
He said, "I don't know! It stopped hurting by itself!"
She said, "In that case, I won't show you! Since you won't tell me the truth, I won't show you where your thing is—the thing that makes you cry, the thing you're crying for."
So he said, "When I was out in the pasture with the cattle, I gave birth to a child. It came out of my knee, the one that had been hurting."
She said, "But why did you hide it from me? What did you expect me to do?"
The boy kept quiet, and continued to weep.
Then his mother produced his child.
She said, "Take her, feed her. When she stops suckling, how will you nourish her? I don't know why you behaved so badly with the medicine. Well, I'll see if you know how to bring a child up."
The boy smiled broadly as soon as he saw his child. He took her, and hurried and returned her to the sheltered place. He became happy again, he did not return to the ashes.
Things went on normally again: he would take the cattle out.
He was happy, he began to eat normally—because, until now, he had not been eating well at all.
The tale has ended.

Commentary

This is a whimsical and very popular southern African story about a boy's movement to manhood, and the consequent sorting out of gender roles.

The boy, going against a parental interdiction not to drink a medicine meant to cure barrenness, gives birth to a child. He loves the child, and hides it at the side of the kraal where he suckles it as a mother would. The pattern is the improbable image of a boy nursing his child. This pattern is intensified as the boy's mother becomes suspicious and by the later quest for the child. The motif is the pregnant boy.

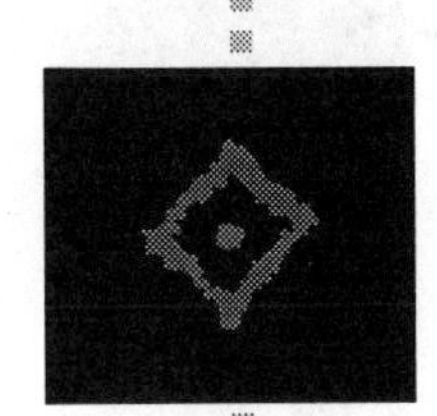

. . . African folklore possesses a greater and more philosophical value than would appear at first sight. . . . It can no longer be classed merely as an amusement for old women during the long evenings, or as a more or less intellectual parlor-game: it is a monument upon which the soul of the race has recorded, unconsciously perhaps, its ideas and its aspirations.

Henri Junod, *The Life of a South African Tribe* (New York: University Books, 1962), vol. II, p. 225.

Sotho

Thakane and Her Father

The Sotho live in Lesotho and South Africa.

There was a boy called Hlabakoane. His sister was Thakane, daughter of Mahlabakoane.

Her father and mother hoed in the gardens; she stayed at home, Hlabakoane herded the cattle.

One day, Hlabakoane said, "Thakane, give me Kumonngoe."

Kumonngoe was a tree that Thakane's father and mother were in the habit of eating. When the tree was chopped with an axe, milk would come out of it. But the children did not eat of that tree.

The boy said, "Thakane, give me Kumonngoe."

She said, "My brother, we cannot eat the food of that tree. Only father and mother do so.

"All right then, I won't herd! Let the cattle stay in the kraal!"

Thakane thought about it, and her brother remained in the reed enclosure. Presently, she said, "When will you be going to herd?"

He said, "I shall not go to herd!"

Then Thakane took a pot, she took an axe, and chopped Kumonngoe. Only a little piece was broken off. She gave it to him, but he refused it. He said it was a small thing, it would not be enough for him. She took more of the tree, she cut a large portion from it. Now thick milk poured out in a flood. It came out in a flood, it went into the house like a river.

From Edouard Jacottet, *The Treasury of Ba-Suto Lore* (Morija: Sesuto Book Depot, 1908), pp. 112–125.

Thakane cried to Hlabakoane for help, saying, "Hlabakoane, help me! The property of father and mother is coming out in a flood! It's filling the house!"

They vainly tried to stop the thick milk. But it came out in a flood, it flowed like a river.

Presently it flowed outside. And it went to the gardens, it kept following the path to the gardens. And the father, Rahlabakoane, saw it.

He said, "Mahlabakoane, there is Kumonngoe coming to the gardens. The children have been up to mischief at home."

They threw their hoes aside, and went to meet the milk. The husband took some in his hand and ate it. The woman took some in her hand and ate it. Kumonngoe was gathered, and it went back home. And the father and mother went behind it.

They arrived at home.

They said, "Thakane, what have you done to make the tree that your father and mother eat flow so to the gardens?"

She said, "It is Hlabakoane's fault, not mine! He left the cattle in the kraal, he refused to herd! He wanted Kumonngoe, so I gave him some of it."

Now the father sent them to bring back the sheep from the veld.

He slaughtered two of the sheep and cooked them. The mother ground grain and made some bread. The father took clothes, anointed them, and went to fetch a smith to fasten rings on his daughter. The smith fastened them on her legs, her arms, and around her neck. The father then took the clothes and put them on her. He made her a fine petticoat and put that on her.

He was going to accompany her, and cast her off.

He called the men of his court, and said, "I am going to get rid of Thakane."

They said, "But she is your only daughter! How can you get rid of her, seeing that she is your only daughter?"

He said, "She has eaten of the tree which was not be eaten."

He accompanied her then, taking her to an ogre who would eat her.

As they were journeying below the gardens, a steenbok came along.

The steenbok asked Rahlabakoane, "Where are you taking this beautiful daughter of yours?"

He said, "You may ask her. She's old enough to answer."

Thakane said,

> "I have given to Hlabakoane Kumonngoe.
> To the herd of our cattle Kumonngoe.
> I thought our cattle were going to stay in the kraal, Kumonngoe,
> So I gave him my father's Kumonngoe."

The steenbok said, "I hope they will eat you, Rahlabakoane, and leave the child alone."

Rahlabakoane then met some elands, and they asked, "Where are you taking this beautiful child of yours?"

He said, "You may ask her. She's old enough to answer. She has done great damage to me over there at my home."

Then the young woman said,

> "I have given to Hlabakoane Kumonngoe.
> To the herd of our cattle Kumonngoe.
> I thought our cattle were going to stay in the kraal, Kumonngoe,
> So I gave him my father's Kumonngoe."

One of the elands said, "I hope it is you who will die, Rahlabakoane."

Rahlabakoane passed on, he slept in the open country. He met with some springbucks.

"Rahlabakoane, where are you taking this beautiful child of yours?"

He said, "You may ask her. She's old enough to answer. She has done great damage to me over there at my home."

His daughter said,

> "I have given to Hlabakoane Kumonngoe.
> To the herd of our cattle Kumonngoe.
> I thought our cattle were going to stay in the kraal, Kumonngoe,
> So I gave him my father's Kumonngoe."

One of the springbucks said, "I hope it is you they will eat, Rahlabakoane."

At last, Rahlabakoane arrived at the ogres' village. He found that the court of Masilo, the chief's son, was full of people. It was Masilo's father who ate people. Masilo himself did not eat them.

Rahlabakoane sat down in the court with the young woman. They took a skin and spread it, and the young woman sat on it. The father sat on the ground.

The chief, Masilo, asked him, "Rahlabakoane, where are you taking this beautiful child of yours?"

He said, "You may ask her. She's old enough to answer."

His daughter said,

> "I have given to Hlabakoane Kumonngoe.
> To the herd of our cattle Kumonngoe.
> I thought our cattle were going to stay in the kraal, Kumonngoe,
> So I gave him my father's Kumonngoe."

She told her tale in the men's court.

Then Masilo, the chief of this group of ogres, sent his court messenger, and said, "Take that man and the young woman to the court yard of my mother, and tell her to take that man to my father but to keep the young woman in her court yard. That man must go and salute my father."

The mother took that man, then, and sent him to the ogre on the mountain. She sent the court messenger along, saying, "Masilo says that I must bring you this man so that he can salute you."

Masilo's father took Rahlabakoane, put a piece of broken pot on the fire, and threw him down into it. Rahlabakoane was burned, he was well roasted, and became meat.

Masilo's father then ate him.

The court messenger came down from the mountain and returned to the village.

Masilo then took Thakane as his wife. He had not yet married, he had refused all young women, but now he married this daughter of Rahlabakoane.

After a time, she became pregnant and gave birth to a girl.

Her mother-in-law said, "My child! You have suffered to no purpose!"

When girls were born, they were taken to the ogre to be eaten by him. That ogre was like a grave.

Thakane was silent.

Then the people told Masilo, "A child has been born. A girl!"

He said, "Take her to my father, so that he can take care of her."

Thakane said, "Oh! Oh! With us, humans are never eaten! When they die, they are buried. I refuse to give up my child!"

Her mother-in-law said, "Here, no girls are to be born. Only boys are to be born."

Thakane's husband, Masilo, came, and he said, "My wife, give up this child to my father, so that he can take care of her."

The mother refused. She said, "I'll bury her myself. I refuse to allow my child to be eaten by your father, the ogre who ate my father!"

She took her child, and went to the river. There she found a pool where reeds were growing. She arrived there and sat down near the pool. She cried, she was afraid to bury her child.

Presently an old woman came out of the reeds. She came out of the pool, and said, "Woman, why are you crying?"

She said, "I'm crying because of my child, because I must throw my child into the water!"

The old woman said, "Yes, at your place no girls are to be born. Only boys are to be born. Give the child to me, I'll take care of her for you. Name the days when you will come to see your child here in the pool."

Thakane consented, and gave the old woman the child.

Then she went home. She remained there some days, and then went to the pool to see her child.

When she arrived at the pool, she said,

> "Give me Lilahloane, that I may see her,
> Lilahloane who has been cast off by Masilo."

Now the old woman brought the child out. The mother found that she was already grown up, and she rejoiced. She remained with that old woman, she stayed there, she stayed, she stayed, she stayed, she stayed, she stayed, she stayed there.

Then the old woman took the child and went back with her into the water. Thakane returned home.

She usually would remain at home for many days, then would go to see her child. And the old woman would bring the child out of the water.

In one year, the child grew up, and became a young woman. The old woman took the child through the initiation ceremony there in the water.

On a certain day when Thakane went to the river, they came out of the water—and the mother saw that her daughter was now a girl just out of initiation.

It happened that a man from the village had come to cut some branches near this river, and he saw that young woman. As he looked at her, he concluded that her style of beauty was like Masilo's. The man got up and went home. Masilo's wife also went home.

The man told Masilo in secret, "I have seen your child with her mother by the river. It was the child she said she was going to bury!"

Masilo said, "Has it not been drowned in the water?"

He said, "No, and she is now a young woman, she has been initiated, she has just come out of the initiation."

Masilo said, "What must I do?"

"When your wife says that she is going to bathe in the river, get there ahead of her. Doesn't she usually tell you when she is going?"

Masilo said, "She usually tells me."

The man said, "Go there before her and sit down in the bush. When your wife arrives, you must already have hidden yourself in the bush."

One day she told Masilo, "I am going to bathe in the river."

He gave her leave to do so. But Masilo got there before her. He arrived, and sat down in the bush and hid himself.

Thakane came afterwards. She arrived, stood by the pool and said,

"Give me Lilahloane, that I may see her,
Lilahloane who has been cast off by Masilo."

The old woman brought Lilahloane out of the water. When Masilo looked at the young woman, he saw that she was his child, the one Thakane had said she was going to bury. He wondered, he wept when he saw that his child was already grown up.

Presently, the old woman said, "I'm afraid, it's as if someone were here spying!"

She took Lilahloane and went into the water with her. Thakane went home. Masilo also went home, by another way.

He arrived and went into his house, it was still noon. His mother was sitting in the reed enclosure. Masilo was crying all this time because he had seen his child.

MaMasilo said, "Why are you crying, Masilo?"

He said, "My head aches, I am ill."

At dusk, he said to his wife, "I've seen my child at the place where you said you were going to bury her. You buried her in the pool. I have seen that she is already a young woman."

Thakane said, "I do not know about that! I buried her in the sand!"

He implored his wife, saying, "Let me see my child!"

She said, "You'll just tell me to take her to your father to be eaten!"

He said, "I will not say any more than she should be eaten, because she's grown up now."

Next morning, Thakane went to the old woman, and said, "Masilo saw us. He says that I must come and beg you to give him his daughter, he wants to see her."

The old woman said, "You must give me a thousand head of cattle."

Thakane went home to her husband, and said, "The old woman said that you must give her a thousand head of cattle."

He said, "It is a small matter, only a thousand head of cattle. If it were two thousand, I would still give them to her, because without her my child would be dead."

Next morning, he went to one of the men of his court with the order that messengers should go to all the people, telling them to bring all the cattle. They brought the cattle, a thousand head of cattle.

The cattle went to the water, to that pool with reeds. They stood outside the pool.

Then Thakane came up, and said,

> "Give me Lilahloane, that I may see her,
> Lilahloane who has been cast off by Masilo."

Presently the old woman brought Lilahloane out. Before she came out of the water, the sun had ceased to shine, the sky was darkened. Now, when Lilahloane stood outside, the sun shone again. Masilo saw this child. All the people saw the child of Masilo, already a young woman, at the place where her mother had buried her.

Then the cattle were thrown into the water. But it was water on the surface only. Underneath, it was where the people of that old woman were living.

They went home. Masilo's mother said that Thakane should be sent home so that her mother and brother might see her. As for her father, he was dead.

A court messenger was sent, he gave orders to the people. They came with all their cattle, they were told that Thakane was going to be married.

Thakane and Masilo and Lilahloane went, going to Thakane's home. As they were journeying, they approached the mountain neck through which Thakane and her father had passed, on the high road. And they found that a rock had grown in the middle of the neck.

Thakane said to Masilo, "What does that rock mean there in the way, in the mountain neck?" Masilo said, "Perhaps you did not notice it when you came with your father." She said, "No, it was merely a neck then, that rock was not there."

They were journeying with the people and the cattle. Thakane was going in front, because she was the one who knew the way to her village.

When they came to the neck and were near that rock, the rock began to speak. It said,

> "Rue le, le rue, I shall eat you, Thakane, my child,
> You who lead the way! I shall eat the people afterwards."

That rock was Rahlabakoane. His heart had become a rock.

Now his daughter said, "All right, you may eat the cattle." She said to Masilo, "It is my father. He has come to lie in ambush for me in the neck."

They took many cattle, and gave them to that rock. The rock swallowed all these cattle, opening a huge mouth.

Presently Rahlabakoane spoke again. He said,

> "Rue le, le rue, I shall eat you, Thakane, my child,
> You who lead the way! I shall eat the people afterwards."

They took all the rest of the cattle, and gave them to him. He swallowed them.

Then that rock that blocked the neck again said,

> "Rue le, le rue, I shall eat you, Thakane, my child,
> You who lead the way! I shall eat the people afterwards."

The daughter said, "You may eat the people too."

Her father ate the people.

As they were trying to pass on, he stopped them again. He said,

> "Rue le, le rue, I shall eat you, Thakane, my child,
> You who lead the way! I shall eat the people afterwards."

She took all the rest of the unfortunate people. and gave them to her father, and all were eaten.

There now remained only Thakane and Masilo and their two children, Lilahloane and a younger one.

As they were trying to pass, the rock stopped them. It said again,

> "Rue le, le rue, I shall eat you, Thakane, my child,
> You who lead the way! I shall eat the people afterwards."

She gave herself up to her father, along with her husband and her children. All of them were eaten, they all went into her father's belly.

Inside was a cavern. They found a boy there, already a young man. He was cutting the belly, making a hole in it.

The people were vainly telling him, "You'll bring harm on us!"

But he went on cutting pieces of flesh. He cut it, he cut it, he cut it, and he opened a door. And then that rock died, it fell down.

Now the people came out of it, many people came out. There only remained the rotten ones, whom it had eaten long ago. The people who had just entered it came out, and others too, and also the cattle—still living and walking in the belly of that rock. The people went home, so did Ndebele people carrying their medicines. All, all these people went to their homes.

Then that woman and her husband went to her mother's village. When they arrived, it was like a miracle, because her mother and brother knew nothing about her. They sat down and wept, they were sorrowful. Cattle were slaughtered, and that woman and her husband were well received.

Commentary

This tale incorporates the simple puberty rite of passage tale, but also points to reasons as to why the ritual is necessary: the flawed world, including the deadly father, the deadly cannibals, the deadly rock which is the calcified heart of the father.

◇ **Mirroring**—Two themes co-exist here, the one showing the wretchedness of life on the earth, the other showing the way to triumph, at least partially, over it. The three parts are the same in revealing this theme: In part one, the father wishes to destroy the daughter for cutting into the milk tree, a punishment that does not fit the crime, emphasized by the pattern of animals. In part two, the ogres have a law that all girl-children must be destroyed, a ridiculous law directed against innocent girl-children. In part three, the calcified heart of Thakane's father devours all living beings, the logical and absurd extreme of what the father does in part one. Parts two and three are mirrors, exaggerated fantasy comments on what the father does in part one.

The theme of triumph is the typical rite of passage theme. Thakane's ritual separation occurs as the father takes her far from home; the ordeal, in the father's determination to kill his daughter and in her life with the ogres; the return, as Thakane goes home with her family after getting past the rock. There is a second puberty ritual, that of the daughter, Lilahloane; she is taken far from home, the cannibals desire to kill her and she lives in a pool; she emerges from the pool and is reunited with her parents. Two rites of passage stand against the anti-social acts of the father. Part one takes place, largely, in the real world. Parts two and three are meant to mirror part one, to comment on it. In each of the three parts, the punishment does not fit the crime: each part successively exaggerates this theme.

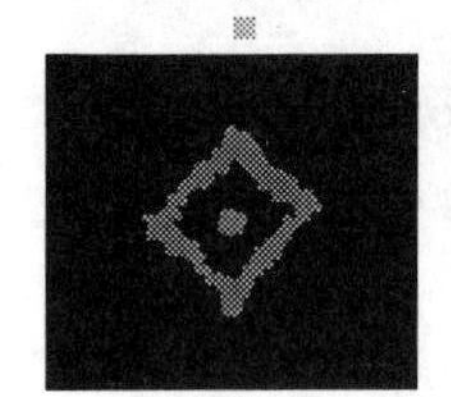

It is in performance that a storyteller makes a tale his or her own. Even if there is little in the verbal text that is new or surprising, the fleshing out of imagery depends on ingenuity in performance. Here, though most tales are seemingly told again and again, the individual is able to place a personal stamp on the narrative. . . . The coloring of character can be a complex operation, with voice and gesture giving depth to what is often predictable dialogue or declaration. The use of descriptive detail, even in obvious digressions, can add texture and vividness to any basic plot. Is the storyteller expressive in voice and gesture? What is the teller's relationship to the specific audience during that session? Is the tone of the tale humorous or seriously didactic? How does the teller's personality shape the performance in context? When the performer is not only in command of his or her stage presence but also an inventive embellisher of narratives, the results can be both entertaining and transforming.

Robert Cancel, *Allegorical Speculation in an Oral Society* (Berkeley: University of California Press, 1989), pp. 19–20.

Hausa

Yarima, Atafa, and the King

The Hausa live in northern Nigeria and in Niger.

There was once a girl called Atafa. Her mother and father possessed slaves, cattle, camels, horses, donkeys, mules, sheep, and household goods in plenty.

But the day came when her mother died, leaving her and her father. Not long after, her father also died.

As for Atafa, she took the cattle and swallowed them. She took the horses and swallowed them. She took the donkeys and swallowed them. She took the camels and swallowed them. In fact, she swallowed every beast that there was in their compound. Then she turned on the household goods, and swallowed them too.

Then she rose and, having arrived in another town, she lay down at the mouth of the well. Presently, there came a slave girl from the king's compound. She belonged to the king's senior wife, and she said to herself, "This is one of those poor unfortunate creatures that our mistress says we should take to her if we come across them." When she had drawn her water, she said to Atafa, "Get up and come along."

Obediently, Atafa got up and followed the girl to the king's compound. They went right in and to the senior wife's house.

The slave girl said, "Lady, here is a girl I found at the well-head. I've brought her along, for that is what you said you wanted."

"Where is she?" asked her mistress.

"There she is."

From Frank Edgar, *Litafina Tatsuniyoyi Na Hausa* (Belfast: W. Erskine Mayne, 1911-1913). Translated from Hausa by Neil Skinner: *Hausa Tales and Traditions* (Madison, Wisconsin: University of Wisconsin Press, 1977), pp. 269–279.

"That's fine." Turning to Atafa, she said, "What is your name?"

"Atafa," she said.

The king's senior wife said, "Well, Atafa, now you are my daughter."

So she stayed there.

Now, the senior wife had a son called Yarima. Whenever he came in to eat, he would order them to hide Atafa, saying that if they did not hide her, he would hit her. So they would take Atafa and hide her. Yarima would come in, eat his food, drink his porridge, help himself to kola nuts, then go out through the compound entrance. Atafa would then come out of hiding.

Things continued in that way until the day of the festival arrived.

The senior wife said to the other women of the king's compound, "Each of you help by bringing me a strip of cloth, so that I can make a cloth and give it as a gift to Atafa."

They put the strips together and sewed them up into a cloth, and they presented it to her.

Next day was the festival, and in the morning the usual mounted procession to and from the place of prayer took place.

Atafa said, "Mother, may I go and get wood?"

"What!" said the other. "Atafa, who is going for wood today? It's the festival, and everyone's dancing."

But Atafa said, "No, mother. You know that the dancing is for Yarima and I must hide from him whenever he comes home. What would happen if I went to his dance? No, I'll go to the bush and bring you some wood."

"All right," said the senior wife.

Atafa went to the bush and went into a thicket where she vomited up the slaves, the cattle, the horses, and the mules—in fact, all the wealth that she had swallowed, all of it she vomited up. She became slim again, she washed herself and put on armlets and anklets. Taking several cloths to wear, she stood up and said to the slaves, "Round up those cattle, and the camels, the horses, the mules, the donkeys, all the animals." Then she ordered the slaves to guard them. They did so.

From there, she set off to go to where the dancing was. Yarima had had his couch carried there, and had come and sat down.

Along came Atafa, and Yarima said to the young men with him, "Look at that young woman coming along there! Go and bring her here. Don't let her go to where the other women are. Bring her to sit on my couch here."

So they fetched her. She sat down, and she and Yarima chatted until the dance was over. Then she said that she must go home, and he went with her some of the way. When the time came that he had to turn back, he said goodbye, sending his compliments to her family.

Yarima returned home, and Atafa went on to the thicket. She entered the thicket, again swallowed all the animals and slaves and household goods. Then she again took up the cloth that the senior wife had made for her, and, collecting some wood, she set off.

Yarima was already home, in the compound, when Atafa came along with her wood.

The same thing happened daily for the seven days that the dancing went on. Atafa went into the bush and vomited up all that wealth, and she dressed herself as she had on the other days. Again, she came to the dance.

The king's son said, "There she is! Atafa is coming. I shall go and meet her." And he got up and went to her and said, "I've come to meet you."

"That's very nice, Yarima," she said.

Then they both went and sat down on the couch. The dancing continued, and came to an end. Then he brought kola nuts and gave them to her, and money and cloths.

But she said that she did not want any of them. "Just give me those rings of yours," she said. "They are all I want."

"Very well," he answered. "But what town are you from?"

"My town is a long way off, Yarima," she answered.

"Is that so?"

"Yes. If a man were to go to our town, he would go to where they eat beans, and pass by. Then he would go to where they eat guinea corn, and pass by. Then he would go to where they eat rice, and pass by. Then to where they eat wheat, and pass by. Then to where they eat bulrush millet, and pass by. Then he would reach a town where they don't have corn, only bran, and even that is brought from another town. Well, he would pass by there, then travel for three more days, and then he would reach our town."

"Very well," he said. "Goodbye."

"Goodbye, Yarima," she said.

Atafa returned to the bushes and, picking up all her animals, she swallowed them, along with her slaves and all her household goods, swallowed the lot. Then she collected some wood, and she went home. She threw down her load of wood.

Presently, Yarima came in, and Atafa was duly taken off and hidden.

Not long after, Yarima asked his mother to have some guinea corn pounded up for him. When she agreed, he went and asked his father too, and he too agreed. They set about pounding the guinea corn. When the sweetmeat had been made and dried out, Yarima's mother called, "Go and pound some more guinea corn. You haven't given my daughter, Atafa, any!" Then she went and took a slab of sweetmeats and gave it to Atafa, saying, "Here, this is for you to eat."

"Thank you," said Atafa.

Atafa divided her sweetmeats into two, and put one ring in one half and one ring in the other half. Then she pressed the two pieces into a ball again, and kept it drying on the thatch of her house until it was dry.

Yarima came to take his leave of his mother before setting off on his journey. He sent his attendant to fetch the sweetmeats from his aunt's house. Obediently, the attendant went and asked for it and, on being given it, went out again.

But Atafa went after him and called out, "Attendant, please wait. Look, here's something for both of you to eat on the road. But don't give it to Yarima until your own provisions are all finished. Then you can give it to him. Do you understand?"

"Yes," he said, and she gave it to him, and he departed as she went back.

Yarima traveled and traveled, day after day, until his sweetmeats were all finished. Then, very hungry, he said, "Attendant."

"Yes," said the other.

"Have we no provisions left?"

"Our provisions are finished, Yarima," answered his attendant, "except for the piece that Atafa gave me."

"Ugh! I'm not having that!"

The night came and went, and another day, and still they traveled. Then, when the day was nearly spent and it was evening, he again asked, "Attendant, are there no provisions left?"

Indignantly, the attendant answered, "Do you think there are provisions that I'm hiding from you?"

Then his horse stalled, and Yarima said, "Attendant, catch the horse's urine and mix that with Atafa's piece of sweetmeat."

"Very well," said the attendant, and he caught the urine.

He took the piece of sweetmeat and was about to break it, when Yarima said, "Bring it here. Let me see."

Yarima broke the piece, and there was a ring.

He said to the attendant, "How many pieces of this sweetmeat are there?"

"Two," said the attendant.

"Give me the other one."

He took it and gave it to him, and he broke it—and there was another ring.

"Attendant," he said.

"Yes."

"It is at home that victory awaits us!"

"Are you sure of that, Yarima?"

"Yes," said Yarima. "We shall turn back."

"All right," said the attendant.

They turned back and traveled day and night without pause until they reached home.

When he got there, as soon as he had dismounted, Yarima went straight to his mother's house.

"Where is Atafa, mother?" he said.

"Over there, where she hid," she answered.

He himself went and took hold of Atafa.

"Atafa," he said, "you must stop running away, do you hear?"

"Well," she said, "whenever you come in, you tell them to move me out of the way."

"Stop running away from me," he insisted.

When he had been there four days, he went and sought out his aunt, and asked her to arrange his marriage to Atafa.

But his aunt said, "Yarima, has that journey made you mad?" For it had been arranged that Yarima should marry the daughter of the galadima of the town. Now he was saying that he did not want her, he wanted Atafa.

Next, Yarima went and told the king that he wanted to marry Atafa.

The king said, "Get out of here, you damned good for nothing boy! You have been given as a wife the daughter of the galadima of the town, and now you say you don't want her but you want this ragged creature. Get out! For I shall not even give you a place to live in when you marry."

Yarima obediently departed.

He and Atafa were married.

Atafa's foster-mother said to the other women of the compound, "My daughter is to be married—a love match between her and Yarima. So we must all escort her there."

All the women said, "Let's rally round and help her. Let's each give her four strips of cloth."

When they had done that, they sewed up two cloths for her. And they escorted her to Yarima's place.

On the fourth night after they were married, Atafa said to Yarima, "Go and sleep in your own private room tonight."

"All right," he said, and he went and slept in his own room.

That night, Atafa rose and vomited up all the beasts, the horses, the camels, the cattle, the mules, the donkeys, the slaves, the household goods, the sheep, and the goats, and she filled the compound so that it overflowed with wealth. Then she put on her bracelets and anklets.

All the visitors to Yarima's place were amazed to hear cattle lowing, to see the camels and to hear the din of all the other beasts. Word was quickly brought to Yarima's mother, and she sent for Atafa.

Atafa made her preparations, putting on all her finery, and she made her way to the entrance to the king's compound. The king and all his courtiers were in the entrance house. Atafa arrived, and passed through.

The king said, "That woman—whose wife is she?"

"That is Atafa," they said, "the one who lived in your senior wife's house, whom Yarima married."

"Call her back," said the king, and they called her.

The king said to her, "Atafa, your big belly was nothing but wealth all along! And you are a handsome slip of a woman. Go along now, and greet your mother."

When she went in, the king's senior wife embraced her, saying again and again, "Greetings, greetings, Atafa, my daughter! God bless you!"

The women of the compound came and crowded around her.

Presently, she asked leave to return to her own home, which was granted. She went home.

Now the king, Yarima's father, having seen the young woman, desired her. He schemed with his chief slave, saying, "I want all of you to go with Yarima. I shall tell him that we are at war, that I am not going and am appointing him in my place to command the army."

He had Yarima sent for, and said, "Yarima, the enemy has collected in the bush near a certain well, and I want you to go there. Here are two hundred horses. Mount, and my chief slaves will follow you. Go, and drive the enemy away. Do you understand?"

"Yes," said Yarima. The horses were saddled, and they mounted.

Just before Yarima set out, Atafa brought him a date and put it in a plait of his hair. Then they went into the bush, they traveled right through the bush, but saw no enemy.

At length, they came to a well and stopped to water their horses. When they reached it, they dismounted. But each slave, when he was told by Yarima to go into the well to fetch up water for the horses, answered that he would not do it because they were not his father's horses. Each slave he called said the same, that he would not go into the well to get water for the horses, as the horses were not his father's horses. In the end, they had all, in turn, made the same excuse.

Then Yarima said that he would go into the well. He took off his gowns and, wearing only his trousers, which he hitched up, he went down into the well, and passed up the water. They watered all the horses, and all drank until they had had enough.

Then the chief slave, who had plotted with the king, said, "Come, let us carry out the king's orders!"

They picked up stones and began throwing them into the well.

Yarima found a hollow in the well shaft and took refuge there.

They went on throwing stones into the well, and then mounted their horses and went home.

When they got home, they said that the enemy had killed Yarima. When Atafa heard that, she fell to the ground. The king left his home and moved into Yarima's compound.

Meanwhile, Yarima had taken the date from the plait of hair, and, putting his hand to the ground, felt that it was damp, and he planted the date there. The date sprouted and grew and presently emerged from the mouth of the well. From time to time, Yarima took hold of the date tree and shook it to test it.

Finally, the day came when the date tree was strong enough, and, getting on to it, Yarima climbed out, and squatted there above the ground in the tree.

Atafa had had her cattle sent along the path towards this well. Her slave girls followed the path, and came and milked the cattle. One of them was late. The others had all come and gone, but she came along on her own.

Yarima hailed her. "Won't you spare a little milk for me to drink?"

"I shall give you some for the sake of charity," she said. "Just wait a minute."

"Thank you," he said.

When she came to him, she saw him squatting there, a fair skinned youth, and she gave him some milk.

He drank it, and said, "Please tell me, in the town where you are going, whose compound do you live in?"

"Atafa is my mistress," she said, "and she is the wife of Yarima, who they said was killed by the enemy in this area."

"And is she, Atafa, still alive?"

"Yes."

"And she has not married again?"

"Oh," she answered, "she took to her bed when Yarima was killed, and has not risen since. But the king moved from his own compound into ours, for the sake of our mistress."

Then Yarima took the rings from his fingers, and gave them to the girl, saying, "Wash them well. When they are clean, put them in the milk. Then go home and ask her, by God, the Prophet, and by Yarima, who was killed, to get up and help you put your load down."

"Very well," she said.

"And when she has done that," he went on, "say to her, 'Madam, for the sake of Yarima who was killed, pour out the milk for me.' Do you understand?"

"Yes," she said.

The girl went home. When she got there, she said, "Get up, madam, and help me put my load down."

But Atafa answered, "In all the times that you have gone milking, have you ever seen me help anyone take her load down? Since Yarima died, have you seen me rise to my feet?"

But the girl said, "For the sake of Yarima who was killed, help me put my load down."

Atafa rose and helped her put the load down.

Then the girl said, "Pour it out for me."

"Well," said Atafa, "there is a shameless girl!"

The girl said, "For the sake of Yarima who was killed, pour it out for me."

Atafa rose, picked up the milk, and poured it out—and saw the rings. She swiftly picked them up and embraced the girl, saying, "Where did you find these rings?"

"I got them out in the bush, near the place where Yarima was killed. I saw a man there, up in a date tree, squatting there. His head was unshaven and he was very thin."

Atafa rose and told them to summon the king to her. Now, the king was sitting, surrounded by his courtiers. Ever since Yarima had died, he had not entered the compound, nor did he speak with Atafa. When the girl entered among all the courtiers and said, "King, my mistress wishes to speak to you," he said, "Certainly." He rose, and went to her.

As soon as he was out of sight of the courtiers, he ran until he reached Atafa, and he said, "Who do you wish to be killed in the town?"

"No one," she said. "That is not what I want. Rather, I want you to have Yarima's horse saddled—the horse that he usually rides. And I want all his clothes, his sword, his retainers, his trumpeters, his drummers, his horn-blowers."

The horse was therefore saddled, and so was her horse. Atafa mounted Yarima's horse, and sent for a barber. They brought a brass basin and a metal pot and soap. The slave girl led the way, and they all followed her until they came to the date tree.

Atafa had Yarima brought down from the tree and had his head shaved. Then they took him behind a bush and bathed him, then washed him well with hot water and soap, until he was as clean as a new pin.

Atafa gave him gowns and trousers, turban and cap, and he put them on. He wound on his turban, and, taking his sword, he slung it over his shoulder.

After that, Atafa went home, leaving Yarima there.

The king was thinking that she must be pining for Yarima, not having seen him for so long. "And she won't see him on this side of the world either," he said to himself.

But presently Yarima came within hearing, drumming and trumpeting.

One of the king's courtiers said, "I can hear trumpeting that sounds like Yarima's."

"Slay that courtier," said the king, and he was slain.

But after a while, as they sat there, another courtier said, "But—that trumpeting is Yarima's."

"Kill him," said the king, and the courtier was killed.

Then a third courtier said, "Whether they kill me or not, those are Yarima's trumpets."

"Seize him," said the king.

But the courtier fled and ran in the direction of Yarima.

"Seize him! Seize him!" everyone was shouting, but the courtier reached Yarima safely.

Yarima reached the compound and dismounted.

The king, when he saw him, hung his head.

But all his courtiers said, "May your life be prolonged, it is Yarima."

Yarima stopped some way off, and stood there, saying, "Good people, how does one treat an enemy?"

They were silent.

Again, he asked.

Again, they were silent.

They were asked seven times in all.

Then one among them came forward and said, "Death is the treatment for an enemy."

And Yarima took his sword, and took off the king's head.

After this, they made Yarima the king of the town.

That's all.

Commentary

This Nigerian story contains two puberty rituals, those of Atafa and Yarima, and an added theme: when one has completed her ritual, she must help someone else to complete his. So it is that the society is assured continuity.

The first part of the story dramatizes Atafa's ritual, the second Yarima's. Part one is dominated by the first pattern; Atafa swallows slaves, cattle, camels, horses, donkeys, mules, sheep, household goods. She becomes very fat, and her identity is ambiguous, as is appropriate during this betwixt and between stage of her transformation. During the Seven-Day Festival, there is a second pattern. When Yarima, the queen's son, comes to eat, Atafa must hide. Similarly, during the seven-day-festival, she cannot go to the festival and dance, or Yarima will hit her.

The transformation of Atafa is suggested by the first pattern, as she regularly moves from one state to another, with the reactions of Yarima calling attention to this shift in identity.

In a Cinderella variant, Yarima falls in love with the transformed Atafa, and, in a third pattern, he offers her many things. Atafa will take only two rings, an embedded image which will later be used twice to call attention to identity.

On a bride quest, Yarima is sent by Atafa on a fool's errand. Loaves are prepared for his journey, the fourth pattern in the story. Atafa puts the rings in them. On his journey, he has an epiphany, guided to that insight by Atafa: he now knows the true identity of the beautiful woman.

Yarima's marriage to Atafa, against his father's wishes, ends part one of the story and sets up part two, Yarima's puberty ritual. When Atafa vomits a final time, it is to create a homestead for her and her newly indigent spouse. Her transformation is complete.

When the king learns of Atafa's true identity, he wants her for himself, and so sends his son to fight a war. In a fifth pattern, a second embedded image is introduced; Atafa gives Yarima a date. Following the king's directions, slaves cast Yarima into a well. Now that fifth pattern is continued. The date grows into a tree, and he climbs out of the well. The first of the embedded images returns, the ring pattern, establishing identity, the essence of the puberty ritual. Now Yarima's transformation can occur. Atafa goes to him and prepares him for his entry as a man: rebirth. She shaves him, bathes him, and clothes him; she is fulfilling her proper role as one who has gone through the ritual.

Yarima cuts himself off from his childhood past, represented by his father. This is the purpose of the sixth pattern; when courtiers announce Yarima's approach, the king has the courtiers killed. And it is the purpose, too, of the seventh pattern; Yarima asks the people seven times: "How does one treat an enemy?" They finally answer him: "Death." The king is beheaded, Yarima is a man.

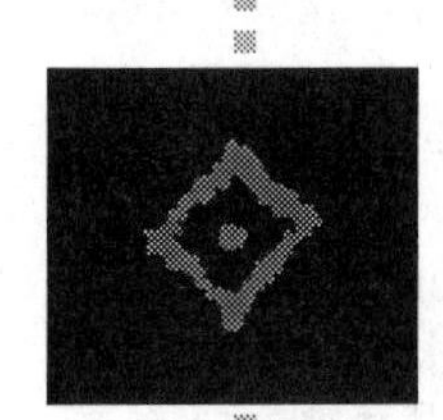

Storytelling is an art whose expression depends on subtlety in gesture and tone as well as a constant interchange between performer and audience. This calls for an intimate theater where the actual distance between the participants is like that in ordinary conversation. But, on the other hand, storytelling "play," as a collective event, also needs to attract an audience. Its setting is normally a public space: an empluvium, parlor, or open air. At first, this arrangement would seem to go against a spirit of person-to-person contact among the players. The modest story competes for audience in a communal space given over to children's games, women preparing food, people parceling goods for sale, domestic conversations, or individuals passing by. Amidst this activity the story survives by promoting a mutual willingness among the players to blot out distraction.

Deirdre LaPin, "Story, Medium, and Masque: The Idea and Art of Yoruba Storytelling," Diss., University of Wisconsin-Madison, 1977, pp. 284–285.

Adégbóyègún Fáàdójútìmí, a Yoruba storyteller (photos by Deirdre LaPin)

Yoruba

The Romance of the Fox

by Adébóyègún Fáàdójútìmí

The Yoruba live in Nigeria.

Once there were three boys who had the same mother and the same father, just the three of them. But before they had any real understanding of themselves and their world, their father died and their mother died, leaving them all alone. Only the Great Head was left to look after them until they grew up.

When at last they were grown, they consulted among themselves, "What shall we do now?" and decided they would set out on a journey to find what lay ahead. The eldest announced that he was going his own way and that if they ever saw him again, it would be by a chance meeting in a far off town. He took to the road and was gone.

When he was some distance from his hometown, he reached a place where people did nothing but dance madly every day of their lives—just dance—as if dancing were their life work. One person at a time, you see, prepared the feast for the dance. One person. He would gather his life's saving and spend it all on the feast, and then face financial ruin for the rest of his life. Meanwhile, the whole town was fed at his expense for three whole months, and the feasting stopped only when his money ran out. Thereafter, he was impoverished until he died.

Date of performance: June 2, 1973. Place: In Mr. Adébóyègún Fáàdójútìmí's home in the town of Ilé-Olú'jí. Performer: Adégbóyègún Fáàdójútìmí. Audience: Seven peers and several dozen children. Collected and translated by Deirdre LaPin.

Friends, when the eldest brother got there, he joined in their feasting and dancing, and forgot completely about his purpose in leaving home. He stayed and went no further. Instead, he reveled with the townspeople and indulged in fun and dance to the exclusion of everything else.

Not long after, the next boy followed. When he got to the town and saw his brother dancing, he called out, "Have you forgotten what you came here to do?" but his brother snapped back that he should go off and make his own life, that he had found a place where he wanted to stay, that he had no wish to go anywhere else. So the second brother left, and went to another town. He was never heard from again.

Meanwhile, the youngest brother stayed and played at home with a friend, and folks, this friend was none other than a fox. When the boy began his journey, this fox accompanied him everywhere he went. Whenever they came to a town, the fox would hide on the outskirts in the bush. The youngest brother soon came to the town of feasting and dancing, and when he saw how his brother had taken on their ways, he passed by with little more than a greeting.

Further on, he came to another town, and went straight to the king's palace.

"What do you want?" asked the king.

"Money," the boy replied.

Then the king agreed to set him a task, and if the boy fulfilled it, he would be given a rare and beautiful bird. There was a tree in the town, so mighty that it cast a shadow over the whole area. "If you can uproot that tree, we shall sing your praises and dance for joy. The sun will fill the whole outdoors, and as soon as the sun shines on the town once more, you will have many gifts for letting me see sunlight before I die."

Well, friends, he stared hard at that tree for such a long time that the fox finally asked, "Why so forlorn? There's nothing to be afraid of. You only need to start digging around the foot of the tree, right around the base."

The boy answered, "All right," and attacked the foot of the tree with his hoe. As the earth began to loosen, he hacked with redoubled effort. Chop, chop chop. He had only seven days in which to fell the tree, and so he dug and dug and dug, chop, chop, chop. Then, two days. He couldn't unearth a single rootlet!

"Don't worry," said the fox. "You've nothing to worry about. The tree will be down tomorrow."

Lickety-split, he scurried off, his tail flying up and down. Then he called all the forest animals to gather round.

Friends, to cut a long story short, when Láayé the elephant arrived, Spirit-of-the-forest, Òrìsà-with-one-arm-who-wakes-and-bathes-himself-in-dew, and, friends, when he struck fen his foot against the side of the tree and kicked it fèén, like that, and then stepped on the trunk, it snapped and crashed to the ground, pàn, right over the path. Everyone scattered in all directions. Just before daybreak, Elephant, the Àjànàkú, yanked out the stump and roots that remained.

At dawn, everyone came to look, and, friends, there was a great shout, "Look at this! Look at this! What do you know? The boy has uprooted the tree, true!"

The king cried, "He's a scoundrel, a thief! Imagine what he might have done if he had chosen to wage war against us! It took real brains to uproot a tree like that." To the boy, he declared, "This has finished me! You will have to pass another test before I give up the bird you want to take away from here. Go to the next town up the road. A certain woman lives there, and when you see her you will think you have seen Olórun himself. All you need do is to bring the woman back here. Then you may take the bird and go on your way."

"All right. I understand."

How was he going to kidnap a woman who was not a relative? Here was a real problem! But the king had promised to give him the bird. He had said the bird would be his. And so the boy got ready to go.

"Let's go," said the fox, "and don't worry. On the way you will come upon

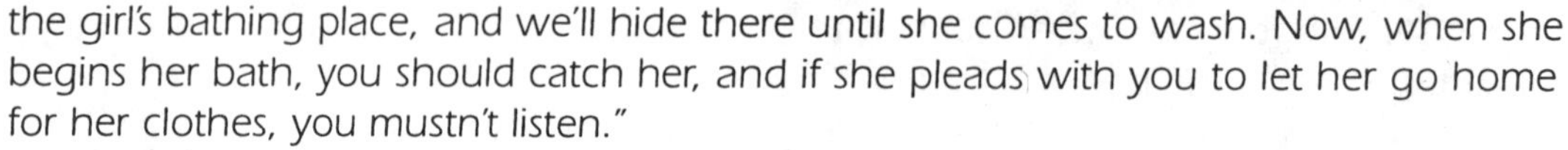

the girl's bathing place, and we'll hide there until she comes to wash. Now, when she begins her bath, you should catch her, and if she pleads with you to let her go home for her clothes, you mustn't listen."

"I see."

"Don't listen if she starts to beg," the fox said again.

"I understand."

Well, they got to the spot and hid. A short while later, the girl got ready to take a bath. Nobody went with her: she always went in the bath shelter alone. Now, as soon as she went in to wash, the boy burst inside and grabbed hold of her.

"Auntie," he said, "the king has asked me to come get you."

Ah! She was astonished.

"Please, sir, let me go home and get my clothes!"

He refused.

"Oh, please! Turn your head and let me get a cloth to cover my body. Don't let me go there completely naked!"

Her begging reached such a passionate pitch that he finally agreed to go along with her to get a wrapping cloth. My father! You see, the very moment the girl turned to enter the house, he was noticed. Father of birds! Oh, Lord, they beat him with sticks and shouted, "You scoundrel!" Well, Lord in heaven, they threw him down and tied him up. You know, you should have seen his two eyes when they began to tie him up.

The king expressed his surprise, "You are an impudent fellow to come in here like this to carry my wife off. Have you seen him before?"

Mmmmm. The girl didn't say a word. She just sat there gawking at the boy who had tried to take her away.

Then the king said, "All right, now you've come to carry her off. Never mind. Please accept my greetings. You may take her, you may take the girl if you like, but on the condition that you perform this task for me. You must go to the seventh town from here. In that town is a horse sheathed in gold and diamonds. Go there, and if you succeed in bringing the horse back to me—and quickly—there will be no problem about taking the girl away with you."

Ha! The boy muttered to himself, "So, it looks like more trouble than before."

And then the king continued, "But if you fail to bring the horse back and you return empty-handed, it will be your head."

"Yes sir," the boy replied, and got ready for the journey.

As soon as the boy crossed the edge of town, the fox appeared.

"Greetings. Why did you let her go in her room when I told you she shouldn't get her clothes? You've just made more trouble for yourself."

The boy admitted that he had indeed been warned.

Then the fox offered to help him fulfill his next task. "But if you again fail to heed my advice, you will meet your end. Don't ignore my warnings this time."

The boy agreed.

Well, friends, if you could only have seen him here. Lord in heaven! His poor abused body. . . . Here was a person who had been beaten, beaten and beaten again until he was covered everywhere with bruises. Friends, the eye pays for what it sees.

The fox moved nearer and commanded, "Take hold of my tail, and we'll fly."

As the boy grabbed hold of the tail, they sped through the air faster than a car. One, two: they reached the town in a flash. As soon as they neared the town gate, the fox set the boy down.

"Look, this is what you should do. When you find the horse, tie this rag around it for a bridle, and lead the horse back. Don't use the gold bridle chain you see hanging from his mouth. If he comes back with gold, I will not be able to help you."

The boy said, "All right."

Well, he set off, and when he got there, he came upon the groom who tended the horse. Yes, indeed! Good Lord, there were at least three thousand and two hundred people there armed with guns and cudgels, and were those blades sharp! Lord protect me. You see, when he got there, they were all dead asleep. Olórun had planned well. Friends, he took the rag rope and draped it over the horse's neck.

"How am I going to lead a horse out quickly enough when all I have is a rag rope? It's impossible."

So, he stretched out his hand and slipped the gold chain between his fingers.

My father! The grasshopper in the fire had burst through its tail, *pam*! *pam*! When it burst, it sizzled and popped *gìrìrìrì* and was answered by thundering footsteps *gbáágìì*. My father! They grabbed the boy and beat him. Hey friends, there he was shitting in his pants, and then things went from bad to worse. They tied him up and called for the king. Well, the king arrived and asked what the man had done, and they answered that he had tried to take his horse away, that he had come to take the horse away and was leading him off with the gold chain.

Ha! The king said, "All right. Sit down over there and rest a bit."

And he rested until the next day.

Then the king greeted him and asked, "What did you want with this horse?"

The boy pleaded for mercy, but the king said there was nothing he could do. His hands were tied. Whatever will be, will be.

But then the king thought again, and said, "Blessings on you, boy. Do you see that hill in the town there?"

It was exactly the size of Ùróró mountain here in Ilé-Olú'jí. Its rocky mass spread so far and wide that it shaded the whole town and blocked out Olórun's face in the sky. You couldn't see the sun, and you would never know whether it was light or dark. It cast a pall over everything.

"My son."

"Yes, sir."

"If you can remove this hill before seven days are up, I will give you the horse to take along."

"Your highness, it shall be done."

The boy gazed at the mountain for a long while and then burst into bitter tears. "My life will soon be over. I've reached my end." How was he going to level the mountain? So he asked the king, "Can you suggest a way to remove this mountain?"

"Wait," said the king, "I will bring you a digger."

Friends, the king went in his house and brought out his wife's hairpin. "Here, use this tool to dig your mountain."

Ah! "Is *this* what I am to use?"

"If you want to level the mountain in seven days, you will have to try this hairpin."

"Ha!" thought the boy. "With my life at stake, what else can I do?"

For a long while, he gazed upwards at the sky in deep reflection, and then set out on the mountain path, walking briskly *kè kè kè kè*.

The moment he passed the town, the fox appeared.

"Hi. Didn't I tell you to use the rag to lead the horse? You have disobeyed me. Depend on your own resources for digging the mountain. I'm going my own way."

Well, the boy burst into a flood of tears. He cried bitterly. You know, friends, that eyes weep water, but out of this boy's eyes came a torrent of blood *pòrò pòrò*. Friends, night fell over the forest, and the boy grew afraid. He had no father or mother to appeal to for help. Lord, preserve me from misfortune.

You see, when he reached the foot of the mountain, he began digging, and before nightfall he had dug no more than a spoonful. It seemed likely to him that, before it was all over, his corpse would be buried at the foot of the mountain, and he was almost dead from hunger besides. No words could describe how hungry he felt! Friends, the fox had gone away, and the boy didn't have a single soul to lend him a hand. He knelt down and set to work, pulling out dirt and stone, and when five days were passed, he had still unearthed little more than a spoonful. Meanwhile, the king let it be known that a human sacrifice to the mountain had been found and that he was as good as in their hands.

Now listen. On the evening of the same day, the fox appeared. "Hello there. I admire your effort. No one has come to assist your Head? Your destiny hasn't found a helpmate?"

"Father, I have no one."

"So what brilliant system are you applying to your task?"

"None. I've done all I can."

"All right then," said the fox. "With the blessing of Olórun, I will help you this once, but after this you are on your own."

"Oh, father, if you could only help me!"

Blood poured from his eyes as he wept tears of relief.

The fox picked up the hairpin and shoved it into the ground. It brought up no earth at all.

"Look," he said to the boy, "I'm going now. Keep working."

At daybreak—oh Lord, only one day left!—the whole town woke and saw the hill.

"Still there. Shall we sacrifice him now?"

A messenger was sent to have a closer look.

"You've worked hard."

"Thank you," the boy replied.

You know, by the sixth day, the entire center of town was filled with delicious food cooked for their victim. But by evening, you see, the fox had gathered together all the bush animals, and by nightfall, when everyone was asleep, they began to work. They worked on and worked on, and by cockcrow the next morning they had leveled the mountain. Meanwhile, they sent the boy to go to sleep, and lo and behold when he woke up at dawn he looked up and saw the mountain had disappeared! The day's first ray of sunshine glistened on his body, and it likewise woke the whole town. People gawked at the bright sky above in utter amazement.

Well, friends, the king looked up and began to bite his fingers nervously. Things had not turned out as planned, but he couldn't go back on his promise, even though everyone urged him to kill the boy anyway.

Meanwhile, the fox turned to the boy and said, "The rest is up to you. With Olórun's hand, I have helped you all I can." Then he left.

The boy went to the king and said, "Your highness, I have finished the work you asked me to do."

The king replied, "All right." He removed the gold and diamonds from around the horse's neck and secured the rag rope for the boy to lead him away. Everyone in town gathered round to give him gifts in two's. They shouted his praises.

Since the king had removed the horse's gold chain and diamonds, the boy finally said, "Your highness, the work I have done warrants a better reward. Return the gold and diamonds so that, when I ride round the town, everyone will know who has done this mighty deed."

The king agreed, took the heavy and shining gold chain, and briskly fastened it around the horse's neck. Then he took one of the diamonds and secured it around his belly. Friends, you should have seen how brightly they glistened! The king then took his costliest clothes and dressed him in indigo.

The boy dressed and mounted the horse. Lo and behold! You know, there wasn't a place where that horse didn't go. Climb up, give a kick, and you'll be flying through the air faster than a bird, féeèn. He could take off and fly across the face of the sky just like a plane, but the king didn't know about it. As the boy went clippety clopping along, the king sent some people to follow to be sure he wouldn't run away.

Well! The boy gave a smart kick to the horses's flanks pèén, and he leapt into the air, waving goodbye to everyone. As soon as the fox saw the boy take off, he too sprang into the air fé.

When the boy landed in the town of the beautiful girl, the fox approached, "I've come."

"How did you get here?"

"Ha!" replied the fox. "You are not as fast as I am."

Then the boy stopped the horses before the king, and said, "Your highness, I have come back."

"This is a disaster!" the king thought to himself. "He has come back on horseback. My wife! The boy has come to take my wife away."

Despite his distress, what could he do? Well, he gathered up all the cloths he had bought for his wife, took his foot-cleaning rag, and told her to put it on in their place.

"Your husband will dress you when you get to his house."

Ha! "Your highness," said the boy, "this is not the way to behave. You know quite well that since I succeeded at what you've asked me to do, you ought to return her wardrobe—all two hundred cloths—as a departing gift. After we've paraded through the streets, I'll bring your wife by to say farewell and we'll be off."

The king had to admit that he was telling the truth. The boy had been a long time carrying out his orders. Friends, then he went into his room and brought out a cloth, and listen, it was of spun gold. Next, he adorned it with silver and diamonds and then gave it to the girl to put on. . . . By Olórun, I hope my tale isn't making your cheek swell? Completely dressed, she was so beautiful that words couldn't describe it. Her teeth gleamed so brightly that it looked as if they might utter her name on their own power.

Then the girl mounted the horse and the boy swung behind. They rode through the town and were showered with gifts in two's, and they were all fastened onto the horse. The boy gave the animal a kick and pèén it leapt into the air.

"Hey!" the king shouted. "I'm done for, I've been cruelly wronged! All that effort for nothing."

Lord, do not let us labor in vain. (Amen.) But friends, there is not a sufferer who does not recover in time.

Now, the boy rode and flew and finally reached the town where the bird was. Arriving there, he met the fox once again.

"Welcome," said the fox. "You have done well, you have done very well. Now, when you reach your destination, you should ask to let your wife hold the bird. Then both of you should mount the horse and prance round and round the town. When you've done that, don't walk the horse back to the palace. Keep the girl, the horse and the bird, and go."

"All right."

He did just as the fox instructed. When they arrived at the palace, the king exclaimed, "Thank you! You have brought precisely the woman I wanted, and, along with her, you have brought a horse! Splendid! Lord in heaven, a woman and a horse and all the woman's property. Here, have the bird."

The boy thanked him and added, "Your highness, there is just one thing. You see, you should let the girl carry the bird so we—she, myself, and her property—can show off all round the town. As soon as it gets dark, I will bring them back and take the bird away."

The king said, "Fine," and ordered a lavish feast. Olórun, don't let us spend our money in vain. (Amen.)

Now, look. The boy took the bird and set it in the woman's lap and then mounted the horse behind her. He ordered his slaves to load up all the gifts collected from the other towns and to carry them home. So, they rode off, and when they got to the town gate, he looked to the left, he looked to the right, gave the horse a sharp kick and flew peun right over the palace.

"Ha!" the king said. "I'm finished! Such a loss! They've gone."

But friends, the grasshopper in the fire hadn't burst open yet. The town was in a clamor.

"He's gone! He's gone! He's flown away!"

You know, he landed right in the dancing town where he had found his brother years before.

The fox greeted him, "You have done well by not disobeying me as you have in the past."

The boy vowed that he would never make that mistake again. His heart had grown wise, and the wisdom had served him well. Lord, spare us from trouble on the road of life.

You see, by evening he was riding his horse out of town, when he came upon his brother right at the gate. His hands were tied behind his back like an àyàkú. Do you know what àyàkú means in Yorùbá? It's a person whose chest has been exposed to the sun. He was lying directly in the sun with his back flat against the ground, oh Lord.

"What has happened to you?"

The brother replied that he was done for, it had come his turn to prepare the feast, and the whole town had descended on him búbùbú their footsteps going like mad. Friends, the miserable wretch had nothing to offer, and so they tied him down, declaring they would kill and eat him that very day.

The boy, who was a grown man by now, started down from his horse and studied his brother for a long while. "Didn't I tell you, the day I came, to leave this place?"

He averred that his brother had told him so.

"Thank the Lord I've come back in time. Look at me: I chose the path of hard work. Look at you: you chose the gay life. Olórun has given you his due." Lord, don't have us reap our due. (Amen.) Friends, he heaped curses on his brother, and when he had done that, the fox spoke.

"Don't let him go. Don't let him go."

After some reflection, the boy spoke in reply, "This is my brother who has no mother and no father."

"Don't let him go."

"But I must look after him."

"No, you cannot help him."

"Then the boy took three bags of money—the amount for the feast—and paid it, and his brother was untied. While the brother was praising Olórun for his release, the boy suggested they return home to their town.

"All right," the senior brother agreed, "but first, come along and see my beautiful things. You should come and see, they are worth the sum you spent on me. Let's go."

The junior brother told his wife to wait, and went with his senior to see his property. The unfortunate fellow! Friends, in this town was a huge ditch where they threw the corpses of people who had been beheaded, and as soon as they reached the spot, the senior brother called to the younger and threw him into the pit.

"You told me you are rich. Now all your property belongs to me, and the effort of all these years is now mine."

Lord, spare us from paying our benefactor in bad coins.

Then the older brother went back to the wife. "Let's go."

She protested, "Where is my husband? Where's my husband?"

"Why ask for someone else? Don't bother me with all your talk. I am your husband."

"I'm finished!" she lamented. "Look who I have for a husband."

The man quickly swung onto the horse. Friends, you know the horse had fairly flown in high spirits before, but now he clopped along kéte kéte, with his head bowed in a sour mood. The wife began to weep, and the bird—ah!—he tucked his head under his wing. Then the brother started beating the horse and threatened loudly to kill him and leave his corpse along the road if he didn't improve his plodding pace ghón ghón ghón. He raised his cudgel in the air and ranted and raved the whole way home.

When the horse reached the center of town, they were greeted with joyous shouts, "Hey! Hey! Hey! Look who's come back loaded down with beautiful things."

Friends, as they unloaded all his belongings and carried them into the house, people from town and the nearby villages came to have a look. Now, as soon as the slaves and bondsmen saw the older brother close up, they whispered among themselves, "This is not our master. What has gone wrong?" They frowned and starred at him suspiciously.

Three days later, the fox came to the ditch and scampered up to the edge.

"Friend?" he said.

The boy answered, "Sir?"

"There is no need to use 'Sir.' I am your friend, the fox."

But the boy told him that his head was ablaze with shame for not having done as he was told.

"Yes," said the fox. "I'm afraid it is all over for you. You have brought these flames on your own head. Goodbye, friend."

"Ah!" pleaded the boy. "Help me this once, please!"

But the fox turned away, "Oh, no!"

Friends, the boy began to weep. Tears of blood poured from his eyes. What poured on the ground that day became a lagoon—the world's first.

Friends, after long and bitter weeping, he called to his friend, and the fox returned.

"Blessings on you. Stop your crying. You should heed the advice that is given to you. Didn't I tell you not to do what you have done?"

"Yes, friend, you did indeed. My head led me into trouble."

"No," said the fox, "it was your belly that did it."

Lord, keep our bellies from leading us into trouble. Your belly brings misfortune, and you think it is your head.

So the fox agreed to help him once more. He stuck his backside over the hole, dropped down his tail, and pulled the boy up. The boy came out to face his most difficult decision thus far.

"Friend!" he said. "I am so happy! I've been granted a new lease on life."

"There is just one thing in the whole world you must help me do," answered the fox. "When we reach your home, I'll tell you what it is. I trust you realize that I have served you ever since you left home, but I am only going to ask you this one thing."

The boy assured him that he would do it.

He and the fox set out, and when they reached the backyard of the boy's father's house, the fox hid himself again in the bush. You see, when he got home and was being greeted and the bird saw him and his wife saw him and the horse saw him—his wife smiled so broadly that her teeth gleamed—it was as if Sàngó in heaven had sent down a thunderbolt! Friends, the bird cooed ghenrenrenren and preened his feathers, flapping his wings with joy. His tail was waving up and down yéghe yéghe yéghe. The crowd roared louder and the horse reared into the air, prancing madly gòjò gòjò gòjò. Everyone was drunk with joy. When the slaves and bondsmen saw their master, they cried in a swell of voices, "Welcome, sir! Welcome, sir! Welcome, sir! Welcome!"

Well, friends, he walked into his house and took the elder brother by surprise.

"He's come back! How did he do it? How did this happen?"

Inside the house, the boy untied the goods he had sent and brought out some food. Then he led his wife and the bird and the horse to the house and gave them some yam and plantain to eat. All—the bird, the wife, and the horse—had grown thin because there was no one to give them the right food. Friends, he took his wife's food and gave it to her, and she was satisfied. He gave the horse his and the bird his. Friends, everyone in town noticed.

"What does this mean?"

So the king called for him and asked for an explanation.

In the evening, he went and told his story. When he left the town, he had taken a road to a place where he found his brother dancing and drinking.

"Brother," he said, "let's be going."

But the brother refused to leave.

Quitting the town, he found nothing but trials and tribulations ahead. He reached the first town and suffered horribly: that was the town where he got the bird. When he arrived in the next town, he suffered in the same degree: in that town, he was given the girl. He came to the third town, cast in darkness by a dreadful mountain: he dug it up, and they gave him the horse. With his wife and the horse and the bird, he returned to his brother's town and found him tied down in the sun: he saved his brother. After that, his brother tossed him into a pit for executed criminals and left him for dead. But in time, he was saved by a fox. That was the gist of what had happened.

The listeners said they had suspected his brother was not the owner of what he had brought because, ever since his arrival, they had been very unhappy.

Then the king ordered the elder brother to be brought and tied up. He was thrown to the ground and killed on the spot. The sword unsheathed in his presence was returned to its sheath in his absence.

His junior brother said, "You are the one who brought this upon yourself. It is not my doing."

His head was buried at the threshold of his house, and every morning before dawn, he would chew his stick slowly and spit on his brother's head.

"You are the one who brought yourself to this unhappy pass."

One day, after the boy had begun to enjoy his new life, he rose very early and went to the backyard to relieve himself. As he bent down, the fox took him by the foot.

"Friend, is that you?"

They embraced tearfully.

"Friend," said the fox, "you should not be happy. Today is a sad day."

"What's the matter?"

He told the boy to go back to his house and fetch a cutlass.

"A cutlass?"

"That's right."

So he went home, got his cutlass, and came back.

Then the fox said, "I beg you in the name of Olórun to take your sword and cut my head off in a single stroke."

"Never," replied the boy, "to the time when I draw my last breath will I ever use my sword to cut off your head."

The fox insisted. "If you refuse to cut off my head, both our lives will end today."

"I must repay all the good will you have shown me by cutting off your head? I cannot."

"Ah! You must do so right away."

The two friends huddled close to one another, and began to weep sad tears.

"Weep or not," said the fox, "you must take up your sword."

So, in a word, his companion made a brave effort: he raised his cutlass . . . tears poured down his face . . . he closed his eyes . . . and in one stroke beheaded the fox.

As blood began to trickle onto the ground from the wound, the fox began swaying back and forth, then suddenly rose up in human form.

The boy opened his eyes. "Friend, what kind of miracle is this?"

"It's because you did me a good turn." He told him he had once been a human being and his mother's only child. But his mother died when he was young, and the senior wife had changed him into a fox. From that moment, he was condemned to live in the bush because he was helpless against human beings. "I told you that you would do me a favor some day."

"Now," said the boy, "you are rightfully a member of humankind. All of your work has been repaid, friend. The accounts are settled. From now on, there will be no misunderstandings between us."

They entered the town center.

"So, friend, you are now one of us. Olórun has brought you a good life. Why didn't you ask me to do this deed sooner?"

Friends, then the fox turned and went inside the boy's house. Praise the Lord, may we find someone to reverse our ill fortune. (Amen.)

So they grew rich and lived happily for the rest of their lives. And this is as far as I went with them before coming home.

(Welcome.)

Commentary

Known to his friends as Ekun or "Leopard," Adébóyègún Fáàdójútìmí enjoys a reputation as a specialist in children's remedies and as a member of the local hunters' guild. No false modesty rings through his own account of his skill, and he often punctuates his performances with self-praise: "He who tells tales without falling into error, Son of Slender Neck" (i.e., Leopard). Many features of his personal style reflect his background and personality. He is a Christian, as his invocations to God or Olórun suggest; he is a strong male advocate, fond of sexual and scatological references. He is above all a buoyant, fun-loving man who seeks to absorb his audience into his vision with comic appeals, such as "Friends. . ." or "You should have seen him there!" or "But the grasshopper in the fire hadn't burst through its tail yet!" meaning that there is still more of the story to come. (Note by Deirdre LaPin)

There is a framing pattern in this Yoruba puberty rite of passage tale: it is based on the organization of the good girl/bad girl story (see the analysis of "The Pauper's Daughter," story 48). It has to do with the contrast between the good and bad brothers at the opening of the story and at the closing.

There are three significant patterns in this tale. Pattern one has to do with the journeying of the brothers, each setting out on his quest. The motif is least likely hero, since the youngest brother will become the positive character. Pattern two is the major pattern, composed of the impossible tasks that the youngest brother must complete. He is assisted by a magical animal, the fox. Motifs include impossible tasks, helpful animal, transformation, identity. This pattern describes the relationship between the boy and the helpful fox, his mentor. Associated with this pattern is the advice that the fox regularly gives to the boy; this wisdom is usually given in the form of interdictions. The boy learns that if the fox's recommendations are followed, all will be well; if the advice is ignored, the boy is captured and punished. This pattern of the fox's advice and the impossible tasks clearly dramatize the education of the boy as he grows up, as he passes through the ordeal phase of his puberty ritual. The separation stage of the ritual occurs when the boy leaves home (and his rite is compared to that of his older brother); the ordeal stage is composed of the impossible tasks and the fox's education of the boy; the reincorporation takes place when the boy, now a man, emerges from the pit, a kind of swallowing monster, and destroys his brother, meaning that he severs his ties with his past. Pattern three is a false hero pattern. The oldest brother, having cast his youngest brother into a pit, takes credit for what that brother did. This pattern includes the reactions of the woman, the bird, and the horse; they establish the identity of the true hero. Motifs include false hero, identity.

◇ **Mirroring**—With the aid of the fox, the boy proves himself equal to the kings. Now that the boy has learned his lesson, he will heed the fox's instructions when his companion tells him to kill it. The fox's transformation (a physical transformation of animal into human) mirrors the boy's change from childhood to adulthood. The fox's metamorphosis depends on that of the boy.

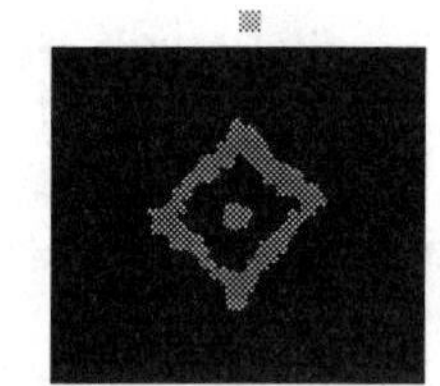

In addition to the plot and its denouement, the story is also rich with other artistic expositions such as gestures, movements, imitation of voices, music and other types of vividness. It is very difficult to sever the plot from this chain of activities. . . . [D]ue to his genius as a storyteller as well as a gifted musician, Fashir (Abbakar Hassan of Maiurno, Sudan) is always able to attract the admiration of his audience. He has certain devices with which he keeps the story constantly vivid and interesting. These include: 1. Music. Being a talented musician, he makes use of his two-stringed musical instrument. . . . 2. Imitation. Fashir is not only a musician but an actor as well. The bulk of the story is based on direct speech. . . . 3. Onomatopoeia and Ideophone. Onomatopoeia in the story is used to describe the marching of the warriors and the walking of the heavily loaded horse of the young man. . . . Ideophones are used when describing some parts of Dija's body. . . . 4. Proverbs and Epithets. One could not help admitting Fashir's ability to use the proper proverbs and epithets in their proper places. . . . 5. Modernization: Use of Current Expressions. The performer tries . . . to link fictitious events with his people's day to day life.

Al-Amin Abu-Manga, "Baakankaro, A Fulani Epic from Sudan," *Africana Marburgensia* 9 (1985), 9–11.

Egyptian

The Two Brothers

Once, there were two brothers, of one mother and one father. Anpu was the name of the elder, and Bata was the name of the younger.

Anpu had a house and a wife. His younger brother was to him, as it were, a son. Bata made his clothes for Anpu, he followed behind Anpu's oxen to the fields, he did the plowing, he harvested the corn, he did for Anpu all of the work connected with the field. Anpu's younger brother grew to be an excellent worker; there was not his equal in the whole land. The spirit of a god was in him.

Now, this younger brother followed Anpu's oxen in his daily manner, and every evening he returned to the house laden with all the herbs of the field, with milk and with wood, and with all the things of the field. And he put these down before his elder brother, who was sitting with his wife. And Bata drank and ate, then he lay down in his stable with the cattle.

At the dawn of day, he took bread that he had baked, and put it before his elder brother. And he took bread with him to the field, and he drove his cattle to pasture in the fields. As he walked behind his cattle, they said to him, "The herbage in that place is good." Bata listened to all that the cattle said, and he took them to the good place that they desired. The cattle that he was responsible for developed into excellent animals, and they multiplied greatly.

At the time of plowing, Bata's elder brother said to him, "Let us make ready for ourselves a good yoke of oxen for plowing. The land has come out from the water, it is fit for plowing. Bring corn to the field, we shall begin the plowing tomorrow morning."

From W. M. Flinders Petrie, ed., *Egyptian Tales* (London: Methuen, 1895), pp. 36–65.

That is what Anpu said to him, and Bata did all the things as his elder brother had instructed.

When the morning came, they went to the fields with their things, and their hearts were exceedingly pleased as they began their work.

As they worked in the field, they stopped for the corn. Anpu sent his younger brother, saying, "Hurry, bring corn from the farm."

When Bata returned to the home, he found the wife of his elder brother sitting, adorning her hair.

He said to her, "Get up and give some corn to me, so that I may hurry back to the field. My elder brother has told me to hasten. Do not delay."

She said to him, "You go and open the bin, and take what you will, because I don't want to drop my locks of hair while I am dressing them."

The youth went into the stable. He took a large measure, because he wanted to take much corn, and he loaded it with wheat and barley. He went out, carrying it.

She said to him, "How much of corn is on your shoulder?"

"Three bushels of barley and two of wheat, in all, five bushels. That is what is on my shoulder." That is what he said to her.

She conversed with him, saying, "There is great strength in you, I see your might every day."

And her heart knew him with the knowledge of youth.

She arose and came to him, and conversed with him, saying, "Come, stay with me, and it shall be well for you. I shall make for you beautiful garments."

Then Bata became like a panther of the south with fury at the evil speech that she had made to him, and she feared greatly.

He said to her, "You are to me as a mother, your husband is to me as a father, for he who is elder than I has brought me up. What is this wickedness that you have said to me? Don't say it to me again! For I shall not tell it to any man, and I shall not let it be uttered by the mouth of any man."

He lifted up his burden, and he went to the field. He came to his elder brother. They took up their work, laboring at their task.

Afterwards, in the evening, Anpu, the elder brother, returned to his house. The younger brother was following his oxen, and he loaded himself with all the things of the field. He brought his oxen before him, to make them lie down in the stable that was in the farm.

The wife of the elder brother was afraid because of what she had said. She took a parcel of fat, she became like one who is evilly beaten. She desired to say to her husband, "It is your younger brother who has done this wrong." Her husband returned in the evening, as was his habit every day. He came into his house, and found his wife ill of violence. She did not pour water on his hands as she usually did, she did not make a light for him and the house was in darkness, and she was lying very sick.

Anpu said to her, "Who has spoken with you?"

She said, "No one has spoken with me except your younger brother. When he came to get corn for you, he found me sitting alone. He said to me, 'Come, let us stay together. Tie up your hair.' That is what he said to me. I did not listen to him, but I said to him, 'Am I not your mother? Is not your elder brother a father to you?' He was afraid, and he beat me to keep me from reporting his behavior to you. If you let him live, I shall die. He is coming in the evening, and I complain of these wicked words, because he would have done this even in the daylight."

The elder brother became like a panther of the south. He sharpened his knife, he took it in his hand, and he stood behind the door of his stable to kill his young brother as he came in the evening to bring his cattle into the stable.

Now the sun went down, and he loaded himself with herbs in his daily manner. He came, and his foremost cow entered the stable, and she said to her keeper, "Your elder brother is standing here with his knife, to kill you. Flee from him!"

Bata heard what his first cow had said, and the next cow that entered said the same thing. He looked beneath the door of the stable, and saw the feet of his elder brother; he was standing behind the door, and his knife was in his hand.

Then the younger brother cried out to Ra Harakhti, saying, "My good Lord, you are the one who divides evil from good."

Ra stood and heard Bata's cry, and Ra made a wide body of water between him and his elder brother, and it was full of crocodiles. One brother was on one bank, and the other was on the other bank. The elder brother struck his hands twice because he had not killed Bata.

The younger brother called to the elder on the bank, saying, "Stand still until dawn. When Ra rises, we shall be judged before him, he discerns between good and evil. I shall not be with you anymore, I shall not be in a place where you are. I shall go to the valley of the acacia."

When the land was lightened and the next day appeared, Ra Harakhti arose, and one brother looked to the other.

Bata spoke with his elder brother, saying, "Why did you come after me to kill me in craftiness, without hearing what I had to say? For I am your brother in truth, and you are to me as a father, and your wife is like a mother to me. Is that not so? Truly, when I was sent to bring us corn, your wife said to me, 'Come, stay with me.' But this has been turned over into something else for you."

And Bata caused Anpu to understand all that had happened between him and Anpu's wife. Bata swore an oath by Ra Harakhti, saying, "Your coming to kill me with your knife was an abomination."

Then the youth took a knife and cut off his phallus, and threw it into the water where a fish swallowed it.

He faltered, he became faint, and his elder brother cursed his own heart greatly. He stood weeping for Bata afar off; because of the crocodiles, he did not know how to pass over to where his younger brother was.

Bata called to Anpu, saying, "Whereas you have done an evil thing, will you also do a good thing, like that which I would do for you? When you go to your house, look to your cattle, for I shall not remain in the place where you are. I am going to the valley of the acacia.

"Now, as to what you shall do for me: you should come to seek me if you see that something has happened to me. This is what will happen: I shall draw out my soul and put it on the top of the flowers of the acacia. When the acacia is cut down and it falls to the ground, you must come to look for it. If you search for it for seven years, do not let your heart become weary. For you will find it, and you must put it into a cup of cold water and expect that I shall live again, that I may exact revenge on the one who has done me wrong. You shall know that things are happening to me when someone gives you a cup of beer and the beer is troubled. Don't wait when this happens to you."

Bata then went to the valley of the acacia, and Anpu went back to his house. His hand was on his head, and he cast dust on his head. He came to his house, and he killed his wife. He cast her body to the dogs, and he sat in mourning for his younger brother.

Many days after these events, the younger brother was in the valley of the acacia. No one was with him. He spent his time hunting the beasts of the desert, and he came back in the evening to lie down under the acacia tree that bore his soul on the uppermost flower. After this, he built a tower in the valley of the acacia with his own hands; it was full of all good things that would enable him to provide for himself a home.

He went out of his tower, and met the nine gods who were going forth to survey the entire land.

The nine gods talked with one another, and they said to him, "Ho, Bata, Bull of the nine gods! Are you staying by yourself? You have left your village because of the wife of Anpu, your elder brother. His wife has been killed. You have been avenged." Their hearts were exceedingly pained for Bata.

Ra Harakhti said to Khnumu, "Create a woman for Bata, so that he does not remain alone."

And Khnumu made for Bata a mate who would dwell with him. She was more beautiful in body than any other woman in the land. The essence of every god was in her.

The seven Hathors came to see her, and they said with one voice, "She will die by the knife."

Bata loved her greatly, and she lived in his house. He passed his time hunting the beasts, and he brought and laid them before her.

He said, "Do not go outside, for the sea might seize you. I cannot rescue you from the sea, because I am a woman like you. My soul is in the flower at the top of the acacia. If someone else finds it, I must fight with him." So it was that he revealed to her all of his thoughts.

Later, Bata went to hunt in his usual manner. And the young woman went out to walk under the acacia that was at the side of her house.

The sea saw her and cast its waves up after her. She fled from the waves, and went into the house. The sea called to the acacia, "I wish that I could seize her!"

The acacia brought a lock of her hair, and the sea carried it to Egypt and dropped it at the place where the royal clothes-washers cleansed the pharaoh's linen.

The smell of the lock got into the clothes of the pharaoh, and they were angry with the pharaoh's washers, saying, "The smell of ointment is in the clothes of the pharaoh."

The washers were rebuked every day, and they did not know what they should do. The pharaoh's chief clothes-washer walked along the sea-shore, his heart pained by the daily quarrels with him. He stood still, he stood on the sand opposite to the lock of hair, which was in the water, and he had someone go into the water and bring the lock of hair to him. The scent of the hair was found to be exceedingly sweet, and he took it to the pharaoh.

The scribes and wise men were summoned, and they said, "This lock of hair belongs to a daughter of Ra Harakhti. The essence of every god is in her. It is a tribute to you from another land. Let messengers go to every alien land to seek her. The messenger who goes to the valley of the acacia should be accompanied by many men to bring her here."

The pharaoh said, "Excellent! What you have said is excellent!"

The messengers were sent.

Many days later, the people who had been sent to the strange lands returned to give their report to the pharaoh. But those who had come to the valley of the acacia did not return, because Bata had killed them, allowing one of them to return to give a report to the pharaoh.

Then the pharaoh sent many men and soldiers, including horsemen, to bring her back. With them was a woman; she had been given beautiful women's jewelry.

And the young woman came back to Egypt with her, and they rejoiced over her throughout the land.

The pharaoh loved her very much, and he raised her to a high state. He asked her to tell him about her husband.

She said, "Let the acacia be cut down, and have it chopped up."

The pharaoh sent men and soldiers with their weapons to cut down the acacia. They came to the acacia tree, and they cut down the flower on which the soul of Bata rested.

And Bata suddenly fell dead.

Meanwhile, Anpu, the elder brother of Bata, entered his house and washed his hands. Someone gave him a cup of beer, and it became troubled. Someone gave him a cup of wine, and the smell of it was foul.

Anpu took his staff, his sandals, and his clothes, along with his weapons of war, and he set off to the valley of the acacia. He entered the tower of his younger brother, and found him lying on his mat. He was dead. Anpu wept when he saw his younger brother truly lying dead, and he went out to seek the soul of Bata under the acacia tree under which his younger brother lay in the evening.

He spent three years seeking it, but did not find it. When he began the fourth year, he desired in his heart to return to Egypt. He said, "I shall go tomorrow morning." That is what he said in his heart.

When the land lightened and the next day appeared, Anpu was walking under the acacia. He spent the day seeking Bata's soul. He returned in the evening, and continued to look for it.

He found a seed. He returned with it. This was the soul of Bata. Anpu got a cup of cold water, and he put the seed into it. Then, as was his habit, he sat down.

When night came, Bata's soul sucked up the water: he shuddered in all his limbs, and he looked on his elder brother, while his soul was still in the cup.

Anpu took the cup of cold water which contained the soul of his younger brother. Bata drank it, and his soul again stood in its place, and he became as he had been.

They embraced each other, and they conversed.

Bata said to his elder brother, "I shall transform into a great ox that is beautifully marked, an ox not hitherto known to mankind, and you must sit on my back. When the sun rises, I shall be where my wife is, and I shall avenge myself on her. You shall take me to the place where the pharaoh is. All good things will be done for you. You will be rewarded with silver and gold because you brought me to the pharaoh. I shall become a great marvel, and they shall rejoice for me throughout the land. Then you shall return to your village."

When the land had lightened and the next day appeared, Bata transformed himself into an ox. And Anpu sat on his back. At dawn, they came to the place where the pharaoh was, and they made themselves known to him. He saw the ox, and was very pleased with him. He made great offerings for him, saying, "This is a great wonder!" They rejoiced over him throughout the land. They presented Anpu with silver and gold, and he went and stayed in his village. The pharaoh gave the ox many men and many things, and loved him more than all that was in the land.

After many days, the ox entered the purified place, and stood where the princess was.

"I am alive," he said to her.

She said to him, "And who are you?"

He said, "I am Bata. I am aware that when you caused the acacia tree to be felled for the pharaoh, which was the abode of my soul, you did it to destroy me. But I am indeed alive, I am an ox."

The princess became very frightened when she heard the words her husband had spoken to her.

And the ox went out of the purified place.

The pharaoh was sitting at the table with her, exceedingly pleased with her.

She said to him, "Swear to me by God, saying, 'Whatever you say, I shall do it, for your sake!'"

He agreed to listen to her.

"I want to eat the liver of the ox, because he is not fit for anything." That is what she said to him.

The pharaoh was very sad when he heard her words, his heart was greatly pained.

After the land had lightened and the next day appeared, the pharaoh proclaimed that there would be a great feast with offerings to the ox. Then he sent one of his royal butchers to sacrifice the ox.

When the ox was sacrificed, as he was carried on the shoulders of the people, he shook his neck and threw two drops of blood against the two doors of the pharaoh, one drop of blood on one side of the great door of the pharaoh, and the other on the other side.

They grew into two great Persea trees, each of them excellent.

Someone went to tell the pharaoh, "Two great Persea trees, a great marvel for the pharaoh, have grown up during the night by the side of the great gate of his majesty."

There was rejoicing throughout the land for the trees, and offerings were made to them.

A long time after this, the pharaoh was adorned with the blue crown, with garlands of flowers on his neck, and he was in his chariot of pale gold. He went out from the palace to see the Persea trees. The princess went out, following the pharaoh, on her own horses. As the pharaoh sat under one of the Persea trees, it spoke with his wife: "You deceitful one, I am Bata! I am alive, although I have been treated in an evil way. I know who caused the acacia tree to be cut down by the pharaoh at my home. I became an ox, and you caused me to be killed."

Many days later, the princess stood at the pharaoh's table, and the king was pleased with her.

She said to him, "Swear to me by God, saying, 'Whatever the princess shall say to me, I shall grant it.'"

He listened to what she said.

And he commanded, "Let these two Persea trees be cut down, let them be made into fine wood."

He listened to all she said.

He sent skilled craftsmen, and they cut down the Persea trees of the pharaoh while the princess, his royal wife, was standing there looking on. They did to the trees all that was in the princess's heart.

But as they did so, a chip flew up, and it entered the mouth of the princess. She swallowed it, and after many days she bore a son.

Someone went to tell the pharaoh, "A son has been born to you."

They gave to the child a nurse and servants, and there was rejoicing throughout the land. The pharaoh had a merry day as they set about naming the child, and he loved the child very much. He raised the child to be the royal son of Kush. After a long time, the pharaoh made him crown prince of all the land, and later Bata became the heir of the pharaoh.

Then the pharaoh died, he flew up to heaven.

And Bata, the heir, said, "Let my great nobles be brought before me, so that I can acquaint them with all that has happened to me."

They also brought his wife before him, and Bata judged her in the presence of the nobles, and they agreed with his judgement.

Anpu, his elder brother, was brought to him, and Bata made him hereditary prince in all his land.

Bata was pharaoh of Egypt for thirty years, and his elder brother took his place on the day that Bata died.

Commentary

"The Two Brothers" is a puberty rite of passage tale, in which Bata dies to his past and is reborn. It is one of the oldest stories known to humanity, from the eighteenth dynasty of the New Kingdom of Egypt, 1575–1085 BC.

The opening pattern in this story reveals Bata's harmony with nature (the cattle that he herds) and culture (his relations with his brother). This pattern results in the first stage of Bata's puberty rite, his separation. At the center of the pattern is the motif of a woman who seduces a man and, when her efforts fail, accuses him of raping her. It is the motif of the rejected lover (in Greek mythology, the story of Phaedra and Hippolytus; in the Hebrew oral traditions, the story of Joseph and Potiphar's wife).

This leads to Bata's banishment and flight. He signals the identity and movement to sexual maturity themes when he cuts off his penis; he is no longer a man. He must now move to adulthood, the state of being a male.

The second stage of Bata's puberty ritual, the initiation or ordeal, dominates the story, and emphasizes his transformation. He lives in the deep acacia forest, swallowed up by that fantasy place. His ordeal: his wife, made for him by the gods with the nine gods in her, tests him. His godly wife has become his tormentor and the means to his transformation. The main pattern has to do with the various changes experienced by Bata, and the motif in this section of the story is transformation.

◇ **He dies**—his heart is in a tree, and he is betrayed by his wife when she reveals where it is. And he is reborn—thanks to his repentant brother, Anpu. Now Bata begins a series of transformations, the heart of his ritual; he changes into an ox, which is a castrated bull, the bull being a symbol of maleness. When he is again killed by his wife, he is metamorphosed into a pair of erect Persea trees; these are chopped down by his wife and made into furniture. The series of transformations suggests change in him: each time he makes his identity known to his wife, she has him killed.

The third stage is Bata's return or reincorporation. He becomes a splinter, flies into the mouth of his wife, and she becomes his swallowing monster and his mother; Bata is reborn physically by means of this woman, his wife and his mother. He is now a complete man.

◇ **Male and female**—This is the story of a male's puberty ritual with various symbols of maleness. And, while the two women are meant to move Bata through his puberty ritual, they are also images of women who castrate men. He is guided through it by a woman created by the gods. So the story moves on various levels: the one level informs and defines the other. On one level, it is a simple puberty ritual. On another level, it has to do with the women who are destroyers. There is also a touch of myth in this tale; the woman who guides Bata through his ritual is created by the gods and is carrying out their will. And when Bata becomes a man, he also becomes a pharaoh, part god and part human. The storyteller is emphasizing the heavenly origins of cultural tradition.

[S]cholars and students of "Oral Literature". . . sometimes fail to account for the qualities of the oral medium by reducing its characteristics to merely printed words frozen on a page. In the process, the dynamic relationship existing between performer and audience engaged in the manipulation of emotions and in the creation of suspense, the vital non-verbal features such as the rhythmic swaying of the body during the rendition of a song, a subtle facial expression to convey sorrow, joy, or surprise, or the imitation of the movement of stock characters, all these elements, indispensable for an appreciation of the art-form, become obliterated.

Modupe Broderick, *Go Ta Nan,* 1 (1980), 7–8.

Ijo

The King's Twelve Sons and One Daughter

by Donald Mangite

The Ijo live in Nigeria.

Storyteller: The story.
Listeners: Yes.
Storyteller. The town was in the land of stories. There was a big town, a big town, called Big Town.
Listener: Ho!
Storyteller: Now, there was a king. He had twelve children. One followed the other, one followed the other, with two years between each of them. Now, this town was very bad. They made a law saying: "Other rulers who have been ruling, up to the time of their father, were all males."
Listener: The story.
Listeners: Yes.
Listener: It is.
Listeners: Yes.
Storyteller: "Because only males should be rulers in this town, if a person has been ruling, the last child, the last child the person will bear will rule the town.

Collected and translated by Joel Alagoa.

Therefore, if it happens that a female is born, all the children who came first will be killed."

Storyteller: The story.

Listeners: Yes.

Storyteller: There was such a law. So, as they were staying, look, the wife conceived. "The wife has become pregnant!" All the town started to shake, ha, before long a story had passed round quickly.

As it was coming, as it was coming, thinking that she had stopped delivering: "So, there is another again? Will it be a male?" They were very very anxious about it till it came to the ears of the king. The wife—as it was in those days, husband and wife did not see each other often.

He sent to call the wife, and asked, "How is it? Are you all right?"

Listener: The story.

Listeners: Yes.

Listener: It is.

Listeners: Yes.

Storyteller: She said, "I have passed a place."

"Yes, but is it from outside that I am hearing it? It is good. If it will be good, it is good," he said.

The time was just passing, the nights were just passing, till one day, the thought of it was with him continually, his dreams too became different dreams. He had had twelve children, but as it was coming, if a female came, these children would just suffer, they could not stay any longer, he would have the name of not having any children—his thoughts ran on this.

At last, the time for the woman to deliver came near. He came and looked at his things, and he said, "Ha!" and called her. "My wife, I want to speak my mind to you. As it is being done in this town, if it happens that you deliver a female, this woman will rule the town. Then, you have changed the custom of the town. You and I have changed it. As we do not want this, if this girl is delivered and does not die, I will kill all these children. I will kill the girl too."

When she heard that, she became afraid. He said, "Now go."

Not long after she went down, he called his five young men: "Make coffins, make twelve coffins very very quickly."

Listener: The story.

Listeners: Yes.

Storyteller: "In this big town, what has not happened before is about to happen. My dreams are different. I have borne children and have never before dreamt such dreams. Make the boxes and tell the blacksmith to make swords, shining ones, and put one on top of each of the boxes. Then make rooms for them, and call me to see them."

They came and did that. The workers were hurrying and hurrying till they finished making them. When they called him to see them, he said, "All correct."

He called the wife at daybreak. When she went, there were just coffins. Made very very cleanly. On top of each one was a sword. She began to cry.

She said, "My soul, please save me, God shall decide with me."

As she said so, her mind was not happy in the house any more. Now, these children were very lively. Some of them were grown-up too. As she was doing this: "Ha, our mother is doing this, doing this, doing this," but how it was, the story, it began to go round in the town. This story. He did not make it known to any of them, he did not frown at them, because he did not quarrel with them either, they did not know what had happened. But as it was, the story, it was going round in the town.

Listener: The story.

Listeners: Yes.

Listener: It is.

Listeners: Yes.

Storyteller: As it is, the time came near. The mother—

Listener: The time for her to deliver?

Storyteller: The mother could not be patient any more. She called the children. "Your father told me something like this. When the day becomes dark, at seven o'clock you come, I will take you and show you these coffins."

When the time came, she took them there. As they saw them, all of them, she only stood there crying, they stood there gazing at the coffins that they would enter, till the group went back.

Storyteller: The story.

Listeners: Yes.

Storyteller: The day was coming till when it was early morning, they called one another, those children. They all had a room each. As it is said of a king, he had a big place fenced round; therefore, each of them had a place. Some of them were grown-up too.

Listener: Indeed.

Storyteller: They gathered together. "We cannot remain to suffer on account of a woman," the middle one said. He stood up and said, "I am deciding like this, all of us should run in a group to one place, and we shall listen till if a man is born let us return, if it is a woman let us scatter from the place. Instead of suffering on account of a woman." So all of them agreed. When they had agreed, they wanted to make this thing known to their mother. When they called their mother and told her, she cried. She cried for as long as we have been here. As she did so—

Listener: Didn't she sing a song?

Storyteller: She did not sing a song. She did like that. Then, as she stayed in their house, there was a tree which grew up in the middle of the forest. It was just the tallest tree in the forest, and she pointed it out to them.

"If you will hear me, my children, I am begging you sincerely, you should go to the depths of that forest, I will give you whatever you want, and you run in the night and stay in the depths of that forest. But look this way after climbing and climbing.

When you have climbed up, if the white flag should go up, you come out, I have delivered a male child. But if the black one should go up, something has gone wrong."

Listener: The story is in the field of stories.

Listeners: Yes.

Storyteller: "Something has gone wrong in this big town."

They said, "It is all right, we shall go as you have said, it is finished."

So they went slowly and sadly and got to the depths of that tree. They quickly cut open a place. They did not go with things. But alive and living at the place, in a small house. The last one among them was the housekeeper. Because they went with guns, they went to the bush. If they killed an animal, they brought it and made themselves very happy. One by one climbed each day. The eldest came and climbed, he came down, there was nothing. The second one climbed, they went on till it came to the last one. When it came time for the housekeeper to climb, he stayed at the top quietly till they asked him, "How is it? Come down now."

He said, "I will not be able to tell."

"Ha, what is it that is troubling you? Come down and say what has happened."

Listener: The story.

Listeners: Yes.

Storyteller: He was coming down with difficulty till when he reached the ground, he said, "Young man, we are lost in the forest. The black flag has gone up. We are lost in the forest, our mother has given birth to a female. So, now what shall we do?"

Then the group arranged: "Let us not go away from the place, but as we have to suffer on account of a woman, as we are here, we are in the mouth of wild animals, we are in the mouth of evildoers too, we have come here to suffer different kinds of sufferings, so if a woman comes our way, we shall kill her." They passed it. "You are the housekeeper, you are the last one, you are the cook, we shall go and kill and come and eat. If we bring anything, cook it so that we eat and stay with happiness and watch the door which God shall decide for us."

Storyteller: The story.

Listeners: Yes.

Storyteller: There they stayed. Many, many years had passed since the time they had come there. Then, with what they planted, the place looked very nice indeed. Very small trees grew up at the place, at the back of their house. Little trees, big ones followed the others, one followed the other, they grew up like that; little tiny flowers came out at the tips, twelve grew up like that.

But one day, the smallest one went and saw them. He said, "You come and let us go and look at something, the thing which I have seen."

So as they went, these things had grown up like that. "Ha, who is the person who came to plant this thing?" They all began to wonder till they left it.

Storyteller: The story.

Listener: Yes.

Storyteller: These years passed. This girl had grown up yonder. The king had entered into great mourning too. As he turned to kill the children, he did not see them any more. As there was no way to turn and challenge the wife, and so, with that female child, he had gone into mourning. She had grown up in the house too. As it happened, the mother brought out their clothes, of those who were not full grown, brought them out and was drying them, she saw that they were clothes for men.

"My mother, since I have grown up, there has been no man in this house yet, so why is it that you are bringing out these clothes, bringing men's clothes out from your box to dry?"

She cried. She worried her, she refused to tell her. Till at last, she came and told her. "As it is, you . . ."

Listener: It is.

Listeners: Yes.

Storyteller: ". . . are a female child that came out among twelve men, strong, strong men. As it was being done in such and such a way in the town, it was forbidden to bear a woman as the last one, then you were born. Therefore, your father said they would be killed, so they have run. But the bottom of that tree, that is the place I pointed out to them. Perhaps wild animals have killed them, or else they have scattered. If they have not scattered, they will be there at the place."

When this was said, the girl remained silent and thought deeply. At last, she said, "Oh, I did not know that I came out with other people as the only girl, and instead of being called an only child, I will go too. And you stay in your town."

She said so, they—she did not consult her mother before she turned her head in that direction, toward the bottom of that tree. Dressed in royal dresses, she went out. She went on till she came to the bottom of the tree, the grass began to make a noise. When someone was coming, this boy was cooking something. He was full grown, if she was a grown-up too, as it was when the elders you knew when you were small have got grey hair. But he was still bearing the name of a child, so he took the gun and came out.

"You should speak, or else I will shoot!"

One, two, and as he was saying three, she came out. With the royal dresses.

He was silent, then: "What do you want?"

She said, "Kill me, kill me, I am looking for something. My mother told me that my twelve brothers were under this tree so I have come here to look for them. So if you are the one who killed them, kill me too."

She was quiet, he looked at her quietly, and as he went back tears came from his eyes. The resemblance had come out. God had carved and brought her exactly like the mother, the girl too.

Storyteller: The story.

Listeners: Yes.

Storyteller: It is.

Listeners: Yes.

Storyteller: He saw the mother at once. So he came and took her, and went inside the house first. And he returned to the other room, he shut himself up and wept. The life which he had forgotten, he began to cry. He cried till after that he came back to her.

"Greetings, woman, I am one of your brothers. I am revealing myself to you, I am your immediate senior, but we have made a law. I am here with my brothers, and they have gone to bush, the eleven men. When they return and see you, without asking they will kill you before it is known you are our sister. Therefore, I want to hide you. I will hide you and when they come I shall wangle it with them before we bring you out."

She said, "Look, any way you want it. Are you really my brother?"

"Ha," he said. "Be patient."

He said so, and put her in a big barrel which they had rolled, whether for biscuits, whether it was a beef barrel which they had finished eating, and closed her inside it.

Storyteller: The story.

Listeners: Yes.

First Listener: It may be they brought it in order to store water.

Second Listener: Yes.

Storyteller: Yes. Then, soon after she was inside, there was a noise in the bush, they had come.

They were chattering: "Brother, what has happened today?"

He said, "Nothing has happened." He was not happy at all. He was thinking of how to tell the story in respect of the law which they had made, till after they had finished eating: "What is it?"

He said, "If you will tear the book which we have written, I will say something."

"Oh, you have brought women here to marry. You have brought a woman here to marry. Yes, we put you in the house, and you have married a woman! If not, why should you say that we should tear the agreement which we wrote about a woman?"

He said, "Not at all."

They argued till they agreed, and the book was torn.

So he told them the story, and as he brought her out, instead of rejoicing there was crying. When the crying began, it was very much. They were doing like that till they stopped themselves. Then the group of brothers and sister was complete, so the one who had been keeping the house would now begin to go to bush with them.

"You now watch the house, our sister, we are happy that you have come. Our suffering is because of you, you did this, but you were not the person responsible for it. You should keep the house."

So they went to the bush.

Storyteller: The story.

Listeners: Yes.

Storyteller: They were going and coming, going and coming. Then, when it came to a certain day, as they loved their brothers, in the old times, they used to play with their brothers with little things, so when she went to the back of the house, these little trees as they began to grow, one did not grow more than another. She went and plucked the little flowers that were there. As she went and plucked them, she kept them so that when they came, she would pin them on one by one and to tell them a story, so she kept them till when they came, she was happy and ran quickly to them, and as she threw the flowers against them her twelve brothers just turned into doves and flew away.

Listener: The story.

Listeners: Yes.

Listener: It is.

Listeners: Yes.

Storyteller: She did not see them any more, all of them turned into doves and flew to her and beat her, flapping their wings, and flew away into the sky. She alone remained.

Listener: Yes, it was marvelous.

Storyteller: The story.

Listeners: Yes.

Storyteller: She tried to cry, but she was unable. She wanted to shed her blood too, but she was unable. She wanted to kill herself by going without food, but hunger was unable to kill her. The suffering that had come to her, there was no way to say it. She was like that, thinking, till at last the voice of a dog barked in the middle of the forest. A thing which had never happened before. Since they had been there, a dog had never barked. She went up a tree and was on a branch like this, and cried till she was tired. She wanted to tear herself with her fingers, but she was unable to do so, and as she was like that, a dog barked again. He came on, smelling, till when he came to the place, he began to look for one way or the other to get her, get her, get her, get her, while she was trying to climb up in order to escape from him, but there was no way.

At last, someone in the forest started to look for the dog, the dog must have come with someone. The forest was shaking till at last a man came out—animal—holding a gun.

He said, "A woman like this? But the girl is very beautiful. Even if you are a fairy, I will marry you."

So he immediately put her on his shoulder, as if he had killed an animal, he went out with her. He walked on to another country, day and night, before coming out to the town. No—as she was going on the road, she began to shout till he left her quietly.

He said, "This is a fairy." Ha, he began to think until he said, "All right, I will go first. If I go and come back and you are still here, you will not have escaped," so he went away.

When he had gone, that night she was still at that place. If she was to run away, where would she run to? She must stay at the place of their house. So when it was night, the place started to shake again. As it was making a light noise, an old woman came to her.

"You, girl, be at rest now. These children came here on account of you, I am keeping their souls like this, no wild animal touched them, nothing at all touched them, and when you came, it is these flowers that you plucked to show them. Now, what will you do?"

She had just seen the person who will deliver her. So she began to shout, the shout became stronger.

"Look, crying will not do anything for you. There is work for you to do before your brothers come, you will be dumb, for three years."

Listener: Ho!

Storyteller: "If these three years pass, then I will tell you the thing you must do. If not, your brothers are lost. As they have turned to these birds, they are lost. I changed their souls into these trees. I am the one caring for them. I am a fairy."

As she said that, she vanished.

Storyteller: The story.

Listeners: Yes.

Storyteller: As she was thinking of this thing, this man came back again.

He said, "Ha, so you are still here? So you are a person. Come, let us go out, let us go out."

So she went out with him.

"Come, let us go out. Please follow me."

She refused.

As he carried her, it was on the shoulder. So he carried her hurriedly and went on for day and night . . .

Listener: The story.

Listeners: Yes.

Listener: It is.

Listeners: Yes.

Storyteller: . . . until after three days' time, they came out. They came out into the town. He spread the news around the town. It happened that he was a king. The king of another country, but as kings do nowadays, going hunting with dog and gun, that is how he went into the bush to hunt with dog and gun till he found her. He had not married since he became ruler of the town. He said he had not seen the woman he would marry. It was this girl that he wanted to marry, so the story went.

Immediately, he sent a message to other countries. He sent to Big Town, her father's town, too, calling him too, "I want to marry, come."

Since she went, they wanted to make her laugh, but she refused to laugh. They wanted to make her talk, she refused to talk. Whatever they did, he said, "Whatever you do, I will marry you," so they were engaged.

They came to the presence of the person who would marry them, and he was asked, "Will you marry this woman?"

He said, "I will marry her, so I have brought her, so now do the things according to how it is done in the town."

"Woman, is this your husband?"

No answer.

However she was asked, no reply.

"Ha, burn her to death!"

So they carried her, and went out. When they took her there, they prepared fire. They stood her there.

Listener: It is.

Listeners: Yes.

Storyteller: They stood her there. The fire was burning towards her, burning towards her, burning towards her, till at once the sky was covered, the twelve doves appeared. When they came, when they came, they came and put out the fire by beating the fire fiercely. They came and beat the fire out. At last, when this king returned, when he got home, he started to think.

He said, "This, truly this woman—"

Listener: The story.

Listeners: Yes.

Listener: It is.

Listeners: Yes.

Storyteller: "It is a fairy. If not, doves, the holy birds of God, would not have come to beat these fires out, it is good. I must find out about her." He said so, and he went away. After he had said this, some years passed. About a year remained for her. So, when it was midnight, this old woman came to her at the place where she was sleeping. The woman who had come to her in the forest.

"Little girl, you have worked, but I will come and give you the last work. I have cut short the days. Look, you now go into the place where they bury bad people in the middle of the night."

Listener: Where bad people are buried? Ho!

Storyteller: "You will go to the place where bad people are buried. You will go and remove thorns. If you remove these thorns, you will make thread with the bark, and you will weave twelve sets of clothes down to the wrist like this. . . ."

Listener: The story.

Listeners: Yes.

Storyteller: "But these brothers of yours, when they come to burn you at last, they will never look back. As they come like that, if you throw these things to them, these twelve brothers of yours, they will come."

All right, she began to think of it in the night till she left off. Then, the day broke. When the day broke, she started to think about how she would go to this place due to the work of God, when it was midnight, they gave a time, those who were watching her, the group that was to make her laugh began to go toward the house, so she went out. When she got to the waterside, there was a canoe. She entered it. There was nothing to terrify her. She went and removed the thorns very well, got everything, and returned with them. When the day broke, they looked at her, and she was doing work.

The husband became more afraid. He said, "This woman, when did she go to remove these things?"

One group said, "The town is divided. Send back the woman you have brought. You have come to destroy the town. Take the woman you have brought, we are saying."

One group said, "It is a lie, if she is a fairy we will know. We shall go and die, we have even gone to war."

Storyteller: The story.

Listeners: Yes.

Storyteller: It is.

Listeners: Yes.

Storyteller: Then when she looked, they did not come to trouble her, so she began to weave. She wove on till she had woven about nine of them. No one troubled her. When it came to the last time, he said, "This last time, this woman, even though she is a fairy, I will do something to her. Therefore, you now, the person who will marry us, today, if she does not come to talk in front of you, this woman will be burnt totally."

He came to tell his people to make the fire, make it very high properly.

Then, she wove on till she had woven eleven. She was making the last one, the small one, the one of the small brother, and as she was doing it, they took her out, so as to marry her.

They asked her, she did not say anything. Whatever they did, she did not say anything, so the town said, "Take her there."

They had told all the people with medicine, "Now, your medicines. . . ."

They had gone to all the oracles, and they said, "Look, this woman is not a fairy but a human being."

Anywhere they went said that.

But there was something else that was worrying her. So it was said, and she was brought, and the fires began to make a noise. When she had woven the last one up to this place, the fire began to be very very hot.

At that time, the doves came to beat, but the fire was not quenched. They were doing so till when they were tired, they came and stood on her. They were standing there till the fire was too much and they were flying upward, she could not withstand it so as she threw that half one, there were her twelve brothers, stoutly built.

Listener: It is.

Listeners: Yes.

Storyteller: It was there they came, and the father narrated how it happened, and then they held a feast.

Now, the person who told this story is Donald Mangite, the son of Itabara, who told it at Abobiri. The story has ended.

Listeners: It is all right.

Commentary

A girl leaves home, questing after her brothers; she endures an ordeal, set up by an old woman (she is not allowed to speak for three years: to do so will result in the deaths of her twelve brothers, but to do so also means that she will not be able to marry a king). She is reincorporated when she has satisfactorily completed the tasks set by the old woman; then she and the brothers come to life.

The story focuses on the girl's puberty rite of passage, with the boys' fantasy rite of passage reflecting and thereby commenting on the girl's ritual. The mirroring suggests that the puberty ritual means breaking with the past, characterized here as an animal past. As the brothers move from dove to human, so the girl moves from childhood to adulthood.

In the story's major pattern, the girl transforms her brothers into doves, then from doves into humans. The motif: transformation and identity.

There is also an ordeal pattern: the girl dare not speak, the transformation of the boys into doves, the fire and trousers ordeals. Together, these make up her ordeal. The motifs include transformation, helpful animals, impossible tasks. Her ordeal pattern largely has to do with transformation: transforming the boys into doves, the doves into men. This mirrors her own transformation from girlhood into a betwixt and between stage (suggested by the doves), then from girlhood into womanhood (dramatized by the change of the doves into men).

The brothers' fantasy experiences comment on the girl's puberty rite. She is leaving her childhood, her animal-ness, her dove-ness behind, and moving into a new identity. The boys' fantasy transformations (trees, doves, men) comment on the girl's more realistic struggle as she moves to adulthood. Their dramatic transformation is a fantasy view of her real-life transformation.

The brothers' transformations become her means for transformation. When they become birds, she too "dies." When they are reborn, she too is "reborn." The old woman, controlling all of this, leads the girl to maturity by using the boys as the tests, and also using the boys to mirror the progress of the girl. When the boys "die" (become birds), the girl "dies" (her girlhood is being lost). She is now betwixt and between—neither girl nor woman. It is an agonizing period; she is alone, separated from all loved ones. And she is confused, even wanting to take her own life.

Notes

The forest is a motif, suggesting fantasy, danger, change, fairies. It is a twilight zone, where changes occur.

The old woman, a fairy, is a magical helper: she is orchestrating the girl's ordeal. She also becomes a symbol: the old woman is testing the girl. It is the old generation assuring the continuity of the culture by preparing the young generation to take its place.

The girl is a least likely hero: no woman, the men insist, will take over the kingship; no mere woman, the boys assert, will cause our suffering. But the fact is that it is a world that is controlled by women, by the girl and the old woman. And, in the end, it must be assumed that the girl will take the leadership, will become the queen.

The death and resurrection motif includes these images—the twelve coffins, the brothers' law: death to females; the "deaths" of the brothers (doves); the threatened fire death of the girl; the cemetery. Why all the life and death images? The king will kill the girl and the sons. The sons "die." The daughter is to be burned twice. She gets thorns from the burial place of the bad dead. The images of death symbolizes death on two levels: the death of childhood, the death of a suffocating law.

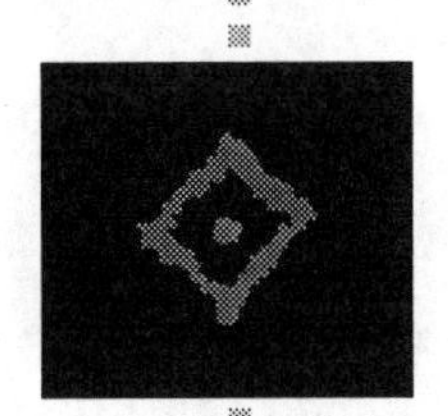

A final outstanding feature of many of these narratives is one or more series of songs which are interspersed at fixed intervals in the account. . . . By adding a poetic and musical aspect to the overall aesthetic quality of a performance, these songs greatly increase its dramatic potential and emotive impact.

But perhaps the most important function of these poetic sections is to provide an opportunity for the audience to actively participate in the creation of a tale, which is a very satisfying and enjoyable experience for every member of the group. Along with the other forms of audience participation—such as the stylized responses interjected at phrase or clause boundaries during the introduction and initial stages of a tale . . . ; spontaneous exclamations of dismay, joy, fear, anger, surprise, rebuke, etc. (including laughter, cries, whistles, ululations) in response to sudden changes and emphatic confrontations in the plot; rhetorical questions and repetitions reflecting upon what the narrator has just spoken; the clapping of hands, and verbal comments, promptings and expressions of encouragement—songs allow the listener to play a significant role in the performance of a narrative, which is in effect a joint activity whose success or failure in many cases depends equally upon the ability of both artist and audience.

Ernest Wendland, *Nthano za kwa Kawaza* (Lusaka: U of Zambia, 1976) p. v.

Fulbe

The Two Hammadis

by Malick Secka

The Fulbe (also called Fulani, Fula, and Peul) live throughout western Africa, from Senegal to Cameroon. This story was performed in the Gambia.

At one time, there was a woman living with her husband. They lived together for a long time. Finally, the husband went to look for a second wife. From that time, two co-wives lived there. By the grace of God, both of them gave birth at exactly the same time. They both had boys, and they were both named Hammadi.

All lived together in this way for a long time, until the babies were old enough to be weaned. When the children had been weaned, the second wife died, leaving only the first wife who now had to care for both children. She took care of the two of them until they had grown up, until they had been circumcised.

At this time, however, she began to worry. She said to herself, "Only one of these children is actually mine. The other is the child of my co-wife. But I can't tell the difference between them. I can't even say which one is really mine. I don't know what to do. But I should make a plan that I can tell which child is my own."

She traveled a long way, until she met an old woman called Debbo Jaawando (the name literally means "the woman who gives advice").

Date of performance: June 19, 1977. Place: In Malick Secka's compound in Basse, Gambia. Performer: Malick Secka, a thirty year old griot (bard), a member of the Tukulor griot caste. His home is in Basse, Gambia. Audience: Seven family members. Collected and translated by Sonja Fagerberg.

She said, "I'm troubled about my two children. One of them is my child, the other is the child of my co-wife. But I can't tell them apart. I don't know which of them is my child. I would like you to help me. Perhaps you can do something special so that I can recognize my own son."

Debbo Jaawando said, "This is what you must do. While you are taking a bath, call both of them. Call them, and tell them to come because you will wash them. You'll be able to recognize your own child, because he'll be the only one who will not be afraid to come. The one who is not your child will be ashamed and won't dare to come. Then you'll be able to mark your child in some way so that you'll know him."

The woman said, "All right, I'll do that."

She went home. The next day she emptied the water storage pot, took off her clothing, and began to wash. She called the two boys, saying, "Come here. I want to wash the two of you. Because you cannot be separated, both of you should come. I'll wash you."

Both of them came running. One of them ran in to his mother, but the other one couldn't. He turned away.

The woman seized the child, and said, "So you are my child! It's the other one who is not mine, that's the child of my co-wife. You're the one who is really mine!"

Then she took a bracelet and put it on his arm. She would be able to recognize him in that way. From that time, the one wearing the bracelet would be her child, and the one without the bracelet she would recognize as her co-wife's child. When she was finished, both of the boys ran off.

Later, she prepared a meal, and when she was finished she called them both to come to eat. But one of the children was unhappy. He said that he was full, that he did not want to eat.

The other child said, "Tokora, why don't you eat?"

He replied, "It's nothing. I'm just full. I don't know why, but I can't eat."

The other said, "I know what is keeping you from eating. It's our mother who has hurt you. She wants to separate the two of us. But she can't do it. We won't be separated. Come on, let's go."

They got up and left the house to go to the blacksmith.

The first child asked, "Blacksmith, do you see this bracelet?"

He replied, "Yes."

The child said, "I want you to make one exactly like it for my tokora. I will pay you for it."

He went and took some money from his mother. (You know that this child could get anything he wanted because he was the true child.) He took the money, and went back to pay the blacksmith who was making the bracelet. Then he took the bracelet and put it on his tokora's wrist. From that time, both of them had identical bracelets.

They returned home and stood in front of their mother. She stared at them, and said, "Hey kaay, this one has a bracelet, and the other one also has a bracelet."

Now they were the same again, and she could not tell which was which.

She said, "So this is how you treat me! He went and had a bracelet and put it on?"

Then she began to curse and shout loudly.

Then one child said, "We cannot be separated. No one shall ever be able to tell the difference between us. That's how it is. We are tokoras of each other. He is Hammadi, and I am Hammadi. That's all there is to it."

The woman sat quietly for a long time, until she finally decided to go back to Debbo Jaawando.

She told her, "I was able to mark my child so that I could tell which one he was. Then I gave him a bracelet. For a couple of days, I could tell which one was my son. But now they have gone and had an identical bracelet made. Now I can't tell them apart anymore."

Debbo Jaawando replied, "Now, do exactly as I tell you. Go into your room and pretend to fall asleep, throwing off all your clothing. Have the children called. But only your child will enter. The other will be ashamed."

She answered, "All right, I'll do that. And when I've done it, I'll give my own child a white horse."

She went home again. She went to lie down, she threw off all her clothing.

She called them, "Hammadi, come inside!"

Both of them came, but only one of them came inside.

She said, "This is what I was looking for. You are my child! You're the one who tricked me by having another bracelet made. Now I'm going to give you a horse. It's the horse that your father left to you before he died. He left two horses, a white horse for you and a brown horse for the other Hammadi. One horse is white, the other is brown. Now each of you will have his own horse."

The first Hammadi called the second, and explained this to him.

He said, "All right, I'll accept that."

Time passed. But now the second Hammadi knew that his stepmother wanted to separate the two of them. He knew because she was always making plans so that she could tell them apart. He therefore decided to make a plan of his own. He waited until it was night, then he got up and saddled his horse. In this way, he departed.

He traveled a long distance. Whenever he stopped, he would be given food, and he would eat some and put a portion aside, saying, "This is for my tokora. I know that he will come. When he comes, he should eat this." He explained this to his hosts. He said, "My tokora is coming. When he comes, give him this food to eat." And whenever his horse ate, he would leave a little, saying, "This is for the horse of my tokora. When he comes, he should eat it."

Then he hurried on, doing this same thing everywhere until he finally arrived at one particular village. This village could get water only once a year. The old people would look for a beautiful young girl once a year to give to the snake living in the river. When he would take the young girl, he would say, "Indeed, this is an innocent young girl who knows nothing about men." It was only then that the people could draw water from the river. If this did not happen, no one would dare to touch the water in the river.

This is how things were when Hammadi came. Everyone was bustling about, preparing for something. Hammadi went on, then stopped by an old woman.

She said to him, "There's not water here for me to offer to you."

He said, "But I want to drink, so does my horse. What am I supposed to do?"

She said, "Well, really, we don't have water here. It's only once a year that we can get water. However, I do have a little water stored away. If you really want it, I'll give it to you."

She brought the water. There were worms in it, all sorts of kirip-karap. Hammadi took one look, and said, "I can't drink that! I can't possibly drink it! Isn't there a river here?"

She said to him, "There is a river, but no one can touch it. Only once a year can we get water from it. That's when we take a beautiful young virgin and give her to the snake. When he takes her, if he finds that she is indeed a virgin, then we can have some water. That's the only way we can drink."

He said, "Well, I'm going to get a drink. I'm going to go there and I'm going to drink. Furthermore, my horse is going to drink. And I'm going to wash. And my horse is going to be washed."

The old woman said, "Do you want to die? As soon as you reach the river, you will die. Take it easy. I don't want to see you die because you are a beautiful young man, a good young man. I don't want to see that happen. That's why I've explained it to you."

But he said, "No, I'm going."

He saddled his horse, and went down to the river. When he arrived, he started to draw water.

The snake said, "Who's there?"

He replied, "It is I, a stranger here."

The snake asked, "You've never been here before?"

He answered, "No."

He said, "All right, then go ahead and drink."

And he drank until he had quenched his thirst.

Then he said, "My horse would also like to drink."

The snake said, "All right, but only because you are a stranger here."

The horse drank.

Then he said, "I'd like to wash up."

The snake said, "Even that is no problem, because you are a guest and don't know this place. You can wash if you want."

He washed, and then he asked, "Can my horse also be washed?"

The snake replied, "No, absolutely not. You, you can drink. You can wash. Your horse can drink. But your horse cannot be washed here. Absolutely not."

He said, "Oh yes, my horse is going to be washed here! I'll do it myself."

The snake said, "That's your business. Your horse can be washed—but not here in this river! If your horse even touches the water, I will kill it."

Hammadi took his horse and drove it into the water. He started to wash it. The snake jumped up and came after him. They grabbed each other, they whirled around, they whirled around and whirled around. Hammadi took out his gun and shot the snake. And when he was shot, he died. When the snake had died, Hammadi dragged him over to the edge of the river. He cut him into little pieces, then he left him in the water. He did not even bother to pull him out. He left the snake in pieces in the river. He took out a trophy of the event, and left it on the river bank; he took off his right shoe, and left it there. Then he returned to the old woman.

He brought the old woman much water. He called to her, "Grandmother!"

She replied.

He said, "Here's some water. Go on and drink. And wash."

She said, "How did you get that water?"

He said, "Well, I killed the snake. Now whenever you want, you can drink as you like. You can wash, you can do everything! You can wash your clothes. You can do everything, because I have killed the snake."

The old woman said, "I don't believe it. Not at all!"

He said, "Here's some water. If you want more when you've finished with this, I'll go and draw more for you."

She said, "All right, here's the bucket. Take it, bring me some more water for drinking!"

He went and filled the bucket. He brought it back, and said, "Grandmother, here's the water. It's just as I told you. I have killed the snake!"

She said, "Now I believe that it's true! And now, even though I am an old woman, I will do something special for you. The most beautiful woman in Africa is living here. I will take you to her room, the place where she stays. You can stay with her there until morning. Then I'll come and get you so that the king won't see you. That's what I'll do for you!"

He said, "That's fine!"

She took him and put him into a big box which she then locked. She looked for some young men to carry it, since she was an old woman who could not carry much weight on her head. She found two young men, and they carried it.

Then she started crying and moaning.

The ruler said to her, "Why are you crying?"

She said, "You know that tomorrow they are going to take this young woman to the river for the snake. Everyone will come to attempt to get drinking water. Don't let them take this box. Please, don't let them take it! My clothes are in it, everything I own is in it. I should leave it inside until morning."

He replied, "Is that all you're crying about?"

She said, "You know the value of such possessions. Take this box into the room. The young woman is there—Faatumata—the one who is so beautiful. Let me leave this with Faatumata."

They carried the box into the room and left it with Faatumata. Then they locked the room. No one could enter the room until the next morning when they would take Faatumata to the snake at the river.

Then the young man came out of the box. When he opened it and came out, Faatumata saw him and began to cry.

She said, "What brings you here?" She said, "You're creating trouble for me! From the time I was born, I have never seen a man. Anything male in this world, I have not seen. And today, I see a man. Because of that, the snake will not accept me when I am carried to the river. He will say that I know everything about men. I am truly ashamed. And I will die today, because he will kill me. The village will not have water. You have created nothing but trouble for me. I don't know what I shall do. I don't know why this old woman made trouble for me, she has ruined everything! I will die, and nobody will have water! They will curse my mother, they will say her child was no good! They will do nothing but gossip until it destroys my mother."

Then the young man said, "Oh, come now. Don't be afraid of the snake. I killed him! Tomorrow, when you go to the water, nothing will happen. Absolutely nothing will kill you!"

She said that she did not believe him. She said, "The old woman, she just wants some evil thing to happen to me!"

Hammadi pleaded with her. He explained and explained, he explained to her, until she finally believed that what he said was true.

They stayed together there until early morning. Then he got back into the box, hiding himself completely.

The old woman arrived, and said, "Because Faatumata will leave shortly, I'll take my box back. I'll take it out of the room. I'm afraid that once Faatumata leaves, everyone will enter the room, and someone might take the box. I want to take it now."

The ruler said, "You want the box? All right, go ahead and take it! It's none of my business, take it if you want. But don't bring anything else!"

She said, "No, I won't, bring anything again. But now, I'll take my box."

They took the box, and still no one knew anything about what was in it. They carried it to her room and put it down there.

When the box was opened, Hammadi came out. She brought him water for washing and everything else he needed. She cooked for him and he ate.

Then she said, "Lie down here."

She brought out a good mat, and he lay down.

In the meantime, they had brought Faatumata down to the river to the snake. There were drums all around, griots [poets] were singing. The griots were shouting praises and reciting Faatumata's genealogy. They told how last year they had taken her older sister and carried her to the river. And because she had been truly innocent, the entire village had been able to drink, and wash, and draw water.

They cried, "Next year, it will be your younger sister. But now, it is you who will be sacrificed. You—innocent as a child. We will carry you there and see what happens. Today, we are praying to God and his Prophet that we will have water."

At this point, Faatumata began to cry. She knew that she had been with a man, that she was no longer a child. She did not know what to do, so she began to cry.

Everyone came to her and said, "Don't dare shame us now!"

All the old women came to her and said, "I'm sure she will be shamed. She has known men for a long time! If that is the case, no one will be able to drink. Everyone will know that she is not a child. No one will have water this year! All of us will die here without water to drink!"

They did nothing but gossip in this way.

"We don't believe that she is still innocent! I'll bet she knows things!"

And Faatumata heard all this.

Finally, they reached the river and lowered her into it. The water remained very still. Normally, when they arrived at the river, the water would turn red and then yellow and then white. But this day, it did nothing. It merely remained calm. No one dared touch the water.

They lowered her into the water, saying, "We're afraid! The water is not changing! Perhaps she is not really a young girl, perhaps she has known men a long time! Faatumata, you will die here. It's certain that you will be killed."

They lowered her again into the water. Still, the water did nothing, even though they waited and waited.

Suddenly, she touched something, and she cried out, "I've touched something!" She seized it, she pulled it out and found that it was a piece of the snake. She said, "It's a part of the snake!" She threw the piece to the others, and they found that it was true.

They told her to come out, then they dragged out the pieces of the snake. They began beating all the drums, saying, "Who killed the snake?"

At that point, a young man named Hammadi Boyelen came striding up, and he said, "I'm the one who killed it. I killed it last night. I just came here last night and killed it."

They said, "So it was you who killed it!"

And he said, "Yes."

They said, "Do you see this shoe? Put it on, we'll see."

But when he put the shoe on, it was much too big for his foot.

They said, "You don't own this shoe! If it was your shoe, it would fit your foot! But you're not the one who owns it."

So he departed.

Then another young man came, and said, "I'm the one who killed it."

They said, "All right, try this shoe. Put it on, we'll see."

But when he tried it on, it was too small. His foot was much bigger than the shoe.

They said, "You're not the one. Get out of here!"

Then the old woman said, "I have a stranger staying at my house. He came here last night. When he arrived, he begged for water from me. I gave him what I had, but he refused to drink it. He said that he could not drink it. Then he asked me if there was a river nearby. I told him that there is a river, but that no one dared go near it. Anybody who touched it would die. But he said that he would dare to touch it. He went away, and when he returned he brought water with him. He gave me some water to drink. I'm sure he was the one who went to the river last night. Now, he is sleeping in my room."

The ruler said, "Call him."

They went to awaken him.

He got up, and they said, "The ruler says that he wants to see you right away at the river bank."

He said, "All right."

He mounted his horse. He put on his one shoe, leaving the other foot with nothing on it.

When he arrived, he dismounted.

They said, "Today, we found the snake dead. But we don't know who killed it. Right now, we're seeking the killer."

He replied, "I'm the one who killed it last night."

He went and put the shoe on, and it fit him perfectly. They saw the shoe on his other foot, and knew that he was the owner.

The ruler said, "All right. Because you're the one who did this, you will have the honor of marrying Faatumata. Furthermore, I'll split the rule of this country in two. You will take half, and I will take half. You will rule one side, and I will rule one side."

Hammadi said, "As you wish."

They went and showed him the boundaries, where the country was split. The old ruler took one part, and Hammadi the other. Then he settled down with his wife, Faatumata.

They lived there, for a long time. All this time, his tokora was coming nearer.

When he had prepared for his departure, he had said, "My mother will die alone here because I must go. My tokora has gone off to see the world, and I must find him."

She said, "Is that so?"

And he said, "Yes."

As he was leaving, he said, "Now you alone will be left here, because you planned to separate me and my tokora. But no one can separate us. Now I will see him. I'm going, and I am leaving you here all alone."

So he set off on his journey, leaving his mother behind. And from this time, her life became hard and she suffered. She had no food, or anything.

As for the first Hammadi, he departed. Wherever he went, people told him, "Someone passed by here, and he said that after a time his tokora by the name of Hammadi would also pass by. He told us to give that tokora a portion of the food."

He replied, "That's true. He was my tokora."

Then he would eat, and his horse would eat.

They said, "This straw is what was left after his horse ate. He said that we should give you the rest when you arrived with your horse."

Then he would eat and continue his journey.

That is how it was, until one day he arrived at Hammadi's village.

At the time he arrived, everyone had gone into the bush to hunt and trap animals. They had gone off to burn the bush, then trap the squirrels and birds, seizing everything. As they had prepared for this hunt, the Hammadi who lived there said that he would join them.

They said, "Do you want to go?"

He said, "Yes."

They said, "Well, all right. But you know that there is a baobab tree in the bush. if you go near it, you'll find a great wind that will come looking for handsome young men. The wind will seize you and take you inside the baobab. A jinni lives there. Now the problem is that you don't know where this tree is, so it would be better if you did not go."

But he insisted. "I have to go. All my age-mates are going. I'm a strong young man. I have to go!"

He got ready to leave. They ran and hunted in the bush. He ran and ran and ran, until a wind came up, and it seized him. It carried both him and his horse into the baobab tree. He was trapped in the tree, and could not get out.

The rest of the men went back home. Faatumata saw them and said, "Where is my husband?"

They said, "We haven't seen your husband. We all went together, but we haven't seen him."

She said, "My God! The baobab has caught him!"

She went around to everyone, asking where he was.

They all said, "Well, we haven't seen him."

Two days passed, then three, and no one saw him.

They said, "It must be the baobab that has caught him. Your husband is very stubborn. We told him not to go, because he is a stranger here, but he refused our advice. He said that he had to go. But now, it was all a waste."

She said, "That's the way it is."

As for his tokora, he arrived at this village in the morning. As soon as he arrived, Faatumata saw him and ran toward him. She seized him, and said, "My husband has returned! He didn't get caught in the baobab after all! Here is my husband!"

You see, she didn't know. But Hammadi realized that this was the wife of his tokora.

He went to sit down while she drew some water for him and gave it to him. She said, "Go and wash." He went and washed. When he came back, it was evening. She said, " Come to bed."

He said, "No. Spread a mat for me here on the ground. You see, my body is sore, it hurts all over! I can't lie down on a bed."

So she spread out a mat and covered it with cloth, and he spent the night there. He refused to sleep with the woman, because he knew that she was the wife of his tokora.

He said, "If you agree, you should allow me to sleep over there with my age-mates, because I'm not feeling well tonight."

She said, "No, I'll spread the mat here for you if you want."

So she spread the mat, and he spent one night there, then another. All this time, she did not realize who he was. They would walk together, but he would not sleep with her. He kept refusing to go inside and sleep in her bed.

She said, "Huh, my husband has returned, but I think he is not feeling well. He refuses to sleep in my bed. Is it that you don't want me?"

He said, "Of course I want you, but I prefer to lie here. I don't feel well, that's all. When someone isn't feeling well, what can he do? That's all, that's why I'm sleeping on the ground."

She said, "All right."

One week passed, and everyone decided to go hunting again. They would burn the bush and catch the animals in a trap.

Faatumata said to Hammadi, "But you will not go."

He said, "Of course I will go."

She said, "No! Last time, I told you not to go and you went anyway. Then you disappeared. Every year the baobab seizes someone who never gets out but dies in the tree. I told you not to go, but you refused to listen, and you went. Only by the grace of God did you return. But don't push your luck!"

He said, "No, I'm going!"

Now he knew that his tokora was in the baobab tree. He understood this. He said, "This is the wife of my tokora. Now I know where he is—inside the baobab. But his wife doesn't realize that he is there!"

So he said that he would definitely go.

The woman said, "Don't go!"

But he insisted.

He got ready. He saddled his horse tightly, and mounted. He said that he was ready to go along with his friends. They chased, they chased and chased and chased, but he was also listening to everything they said. They said that if the wind came up, it would seize someone and take him into the tree. Then he started to dawdle behind the rest.

Suddenly the wind came up, it pushed him to the tree! It pushed him wiririririri to a hole in the tree; he suddenly stuck out his foot and hit the tree. The baobab fell over. And as soon as it fell, his tokora came out. They greeted each other, then returned to the village.

They came to the village, and both stood in front of Hammadi's compound. Faatumata came out, not knowing who was her husband. She stared at the two of them, and said, "My husband has returned. But he has become two people now. Me, I'm only one, and I have two husbands! I don't know where they both came from!" She was confused. She said, "But he has become two!"

Finally, her husband said, "Come here. This is my tokora. We were born together, and we grew up together. But our mother made a plan to attempt to separate us."

The other Hammadi said, "It is he who is your husband."

As for the ruler, when he heard that the baobab had been felled, he realized that now people would go into the bush whenever they wanted and nothing would threaten them or seize them. The tree had been chopped up.

He asked, "Who chopped the baobab down?"

Hammadi answered, "It was my tokora. We have grown up together, from the time we were born. It is he who cut down the tree."

He said, "It was your tokora?"

He said, "Yes."

The ruler said, "All right, from now on I will leave the business of ruling. Now I am only going to rest, because I am an old man. First, the younger sister of your wife should be given to your tokora. Then, one Hammadi should rule one half of the country, and the other Hammadi should rule the other half."

From that time, both of them lived in the same compound. That is how they lived. And this is where the story ends.

Commentary

This is a puberty ritual story; its theme is revealed by a mirroring process. The storyteller first establishes that the two boys are identical, then places one into a fantasy struggle and the other into an analogous realistic struggle: in the language of storytelling, the latter comments on the former.

The storyteller creates two patterns that establish the identical nature of the two Hammadis; the surviving mother of Hammadi One cannot tell the two apart, and when, in the first pattern of the story, she attempts to distinguish them, she fails. But Hammadi Two, understanding that he is not loved, leaves home; it is the separation phase of the puberty ritual. A second pattern is created as Hammadi Two, knowing that Hammadi One will undertake the same journey, leaves food at his various stops for his namesake.

With their identical natures now made plain, the mirroring process can commence. Hammadi Two arrives at a village the members of which can get water only once a year when they sacrifice a virgin to a tyrannical snake. This regular sacrifice to the snake is the third pattern, a pattern that is broken when Hammadi Two kills the snake. He leaves a shoe behind, an embedded image that will later identify him, identity being at the heart of these puberty ritual stories.

The fourth pattern is a complex one. Hammadi Two and the snake are the same, except that Hammadi Two will be a benevolent ruler.

Hammadi Two is the savior of the people; they can now get life-sustaining water. He has triumphed over his ordeal, and is now a man. But the people do not know this yet, and there is an elaborate scene in which he is taken, encased in a box, into the room of Faatumata, the virgin who is to be this year's sacrifice to the snake. But if the snake determines that she is no longer a virgin, it will kill her and give the villagers no water. The purpose of this scene is to establish that Hammadi Two and the snake are the same, that Hammadi Two has taken on the power and the perquisites of the snake, but for positive rather than negative reasons. The snake kept water from the people: Hammadi Two provides water to the people. But Faatumata is afraid; if she spends the night with Hammadi Two, her mission will be a failure. When she is taken to the snake, however, it does not emerge from the water: Hammadi Two was right.

Now a fifth pattern is developed. Who is the hero? Who killed the snake? Various false heroes attempt to take the credit, but the embedded image, the shoe, identifies the real hero. Hammadi Two marries Faatumata, and rules over one-half of the kingdom.

The second pattern is now revisited, as Hammadi One leaves his mother behind, and repeats the journey of Hammadi Two. In the meantime, a sixth pattern is initiated, as Hammadi Two, against an interdiction, goes hunting near a villainous baobab tree. He is swallowed up by the tree. When Hammadi One arrives in the village, Faatumata assumes that he is Hammadi Two, and insists that they live together.

This is the seventh pattern of the story, the ordeal of Hammadi One; he must continue to refuse to sleep with Faatumata. To do so would be to break the marriage covenant. Then, in a repetition of the sixth pattern, Hammadi One goes on the hunt, and he rescues Hammadi Two. As the snake was destroyed by Hammadi Two, so the baobab tree is felled by Hammadi One. He now marries Faatumata's sister, and rules the other half of the kingdom.

Are the two Hammadis the same character? From the point of view of the confused mother of Hammadi One, they are the same. And the patterns establish their sameness as well. It is in the ordeals of the two Hammadis that the purpose of this confusion becomes evident. Hammadi Two has a fantasy ordeal with the snake; he overcomes the monster and thereby attains manhood. Hammadi One has a realistic ordeal with Faatumata, which he overcomes and thereby attains manhood. The ordeals are the same: the fantasy ordeal with the snake, the real-life ordeal with Faatumata: these are the ordeals that move the youth to manhood. The fantasy struggle becomes a means of comprehending the real-life psychological ordeal of Hammadi One as he struggles within himself to curb his biological instincts and obey cultural law, which is one of the purposes of the puberty ritual. In the language of storytelling, fantasy (the experiences of Hammadi Two with the snake) comments on reality (the experiences of Hammadi One with Faatumata).

Note

tokora means "namesake." When two people are named after each other, or when they have the same name, they refer to each other as tokora.

A Xhosa storyteller (photo by Harold Scheub)

Once there was a king who sent out summons through the whole country, saying, "All of my people! Come to me! Come and hear what I have to tell you of my wish."

When the people had assembled, the king spoke to them, telling them that he was very fond of stories and wished to have someone tell him a story without an end. And he said to them, "If anyone starts a story which finally comes to an end, I will cut off his head." Then he added, "But he who can tell a story that does not come to an end may cut off my head and become a king in my stead."

"The King's Endless Story," in Merlin Ennis, *Umbundu, Folktales from Angola* (Boston: Beacon Press, 1962), p. 1.

Arabic

Ma'aruf the Cobbler and His Wife

This is one of the stories in the collection that came from Egypt.

And Shahrazad saw the dawn of day and stopped her storytelling. Then Dunyazad said, "My sister, how pleasant your tale is, and how tasteful, how sweet, how generous!" Shahrazad replied, "And what is this compared to what I could tell you in the night to come, if I live and if the king spare me?" The king thought, "By Allah, I shall not kill her until I hear the rest of her tale, for it is truly wonderful." So they rested that night in mutual embrace until the dawn. After this, the king went to his court, and the minister and the troops came in and the court was crowded. The king gave orders and judged and appointed and deposed, bidding and forbidding during the rest of the day. Then the council broke up, and the king entered his palace. When it was the third night, and the king had had his will of Shahrazad, Dunyazad, her sister, said to her, "Finish for us that tale of yours," and Shahrazad continued her story. . . .

Once there lived in the God-guarded city of Cairo a cobbler who made his living by patching old shoes. His name was Ma'aruf. He had a wife named Fatimah, whom the people had nicknamed "The Dung," because she was a whorish, worthless wretch, without shame and given to mischief. She ruled her spouse and abused him. He feared her maliciousness and dreaded her misdoings, because he was a sensible if poorly conditioned man. When he earned a considerable amount of money, he spent

From *The Book of the Thousand Nights and a Night* (London: Burton Club, 1886), vol. 10, pp. 1–50.

it on her; and when he earned only a small amount of money, she avenged herself on his body that night, giving him no peace and making his night as black as her Doomsday book. She was like the woman in the poem:

> How many nights have I passed with my wife
> In the saddest plight with all misery rife:
> Would Heaven when first I went in to her
> With a cup of cold poison I'd taken her life.

One day, she said to him, "Ma'aruf, I want you to bring me, this night, a vermicelli cake dressed with bees' honey."

He replied, "If Allah the Almighty helps me with its price, I shall bring it to you. By Allah, I have no money today, but our Lord will make things easy to me!"

She rejoined, "I know nothing of these words. Be certain that you do not return to me without the vermicelli and bees' honey, or I shall make your night as black as your fortune when you fell into my hands!"

He said, "Allah is bountiful!"

And he went out with grief scattering itself from his body. He prayed the dawn-prayer, and opened his shop.

He sat there until noon, but no work came to him, and his fear of his wife redoubled.

Then he arose and went out perplexed as to what he should do about the vermicelli cake, considering that he did not even have the wherewithal to buy bread.

Presently he came to the shop of the vermicelli cake seller and stood in front of it while his eyes brimmed with tears.

The pastry cook glanced at him and said, "Master Ma'aruf, why are you weeping? Tell me what's happened to you."

Ma'aruf told the pastry cook about his case, saying, "My wife wants me to bring her a vermicelli cake. But I sat in my shop until past midday, and did not even get the price of bread. I'm afraid of her."

The cook laughed and said, "No harm shall come to you. How many pounds of cake do you want?"

"Five pounds," answered Ma'aruf.

So the cook weighed him out five pounds of vermicelli cake, and said to him, "I have clarified butter but no bees' honey. Here is some drip honey, however, that is better than bees' honey. What harm can there be if it is drip honey?"

Ma'aruf was ashamed to object because the pastry cook was going to have patience with him for the price of the cake, and said, "Give it to me with drip honey."

So the cook fried a vermicelli cake for him with butter, and he drenched it with drip honey until it was fit to present to kings.

He asked him, "Do you want bread and cheese?"

Ma'aruf answered, "Yes."

So the cook gave him four half dirhams [silver pieces] worth of bread and one of cheese. The vermicelli cost ten nusfs [half dirhams].

Then the cook said, "Ma'aruf, you owe me fifteen nusfs. Go to your wife and make merry, and take this nusf for the Hammam. You will have credit for a day or two or three, until Allah provides you with daily bread. Don't distress your wife, because I'll have patience with you until such time as you have dirhams to spare."

So Ma'aruf took the vermicelli cake and bread and cheese, and he went away with a heart at ease, blessing the pastry cook, saying, "Extolled be thy perfection, O my Lord! How bountiful art thou!"

When he came home, his wife asked him, "Have you brought the vermicelli cake?"

He replied, "Yes." And he set it before her.

She looked at it, and saw that it was dressed with drip honey.

She said, "Didn't I tell you to bring it with bees' honey? Will you go contrary to my wish and bring it dressed with drip honey?"

He excused himself, saying, "I had to buy it on credit."

She said, "This talk is idle. I shall not eat vermicelli cake unless it has been dressed with bees' honey."

She was angry about the cake, and she threw it in her husband's face, saying, "Get out, you pimp, and bring me another cake!"

Then she hit him on the cheek and knocked out one of his teeth. The blood ran down on his chest, and in anger he struck her a single blow on the head. She seized his beard, and shouted, "Help, Muslims!"

The neighbors came in and freed his beard from her grip. Then they reproved and reproached her, saying, "We are all content to eat vermicelli cake with drip honey. Why, then, do you oppress this poor man in this way? This is disgraceful of you!"

Then they soothed her until they made peace between her and him.

But when these neighbors were gone, the wife swore that she would not eat that vermicelli cake.

Ma'aruf, burning with hunger, said to himself, "She swears that she will not eat, so I will eat."

Then he ate, and when she saw him eating, she said, "Inshallah, may the eating of it be poison to destroy your body!"

He said, "It shall not be as you say," and he went on eating, laughing, and saying, "You swear that you will not eat this. But Allah is bountiful, and tomorrow night, if the Lord decrees, I shall bring you vermicelli cake dressed with bees' honey, and you shall eat it alone."

He attempted to appease her, while she called down curses on him. She did not stop railing at him and reviling him with gross abuse until morning, when she bared her forearm to beat him.

He said, "Give me time, and I shall bring you another vermicelli cake."

He went to the mosque and prayed, then he went to his shop and opened it. He sat down, but hardly had he done so when up came two runners from the [religious] judge's court, and they said to him, "Come, you must speak to the judge, because your wife has complained to him about you."

He recognized her by their description, and said, "May Allah Almighty torment her!"

He walked with them to the judge's presence, and he found Fatimah standing there with her arm bound up and her face-veil smeared with blood. She was weeping and wiping away her tears.

The judge said, "Ho, man, have you no fear of Allah, the Most High? Why have you beaten this good woman, broken her forearm, knocked out her tooth, and treated her in this way?"

Ma'aruf said, "If I beat her or put out her tooth, sentence me to what you will. But the truth is, what happened was this and this, and the neighbors made peace between me and her." And he told him the story from first to last.

Now, this judge was a benevolent man, so be brought out to him a quarter dinar [gold piece], saying, "Man, take this and get her a vermicelli cake with bees' honey, and the two of you make peace with each other."

Ma'aruf said, "Give it to her."

So she took it, and the judge made peace between them, saying, "Wife, obey your husband. And you, man, deal kindly with her."

They left the court, reconciled at the hands of the judge. The woman went one way, and her husband returned by another way to his shop.

As he was sitting there, the runners came to him and said, "Give us our fee."

He said, "The judge took no money from me. On the contrary, he gave me a quarter dinar."

But they said, "It is no concern of ours whether the judge took money from you or gave money to you. If you do not give us our fee, we shall exact it in spite of you."

Then they dragged him about the market.

So he sold his tools and gave the runners half a dinar. They let him go and went away. He put his hand on his cheek and sat sorrowfully, because now he had no tools with which to work.

Presently, two ill-favored fellows came up and said to him, "Come, man, and speak to the judge, because your wife has complained to him of you."

He said, "He made peace between us just now."

But they said, "We come from another judge, and your wife has complained of you to our judge."

So he got up and went with them to their judge, calling on Allah for aid against her.

When he saw her, he said to her, "Did we not make peace, good woman?"

And she cried, "There is no peace between you and me."

He came forward and told the judge his story, adding, "And such-and-such a judge made peace between us this very hour."

The judge said to her, "Strumpet, since you have made peace with each other, why have you come complaining to me?"

She said, "He beat me after that."

But the judge said, "Make peace with each other. Don't beat her again, and she will cross you no more."

So they made their peace, and the judge said to Ma'aruf, "Give the runners their fee."

He gave them their fee. Then he went back to his shop, opened it, and, because of the chagrin he felt, he sat down as if he were a drunken man.

While he was still sitting there, a man came to him and said, "Ma'aruf, get up and hide yourself, because your wife has complained of you to the high court and Abu Tabak, the father of whipping [Abu Tabak is an officer who arrests at the order of the judge], is after you!"

He shut his shop and fled towards the Gate of Victory. He had five nusfs of silver left of the price of the lasts and gear, and with these he bought four worth of bread and one of cheese, as he fled from her.

It was winter and the hour of mid-afternoon prayer. When he came out among the rubbish mounds, the rain descended on him like water from the mouths of water-skins, and his clothes were drenched. He therefore entered a mosque, where he saw a ruined place. Inside this ruined place was a deserted cell without a door. He took refuge in that cell, he found shelter there from the rain. Tears streamed from his eyes, and he started to complain about what had happened to him. He said, "Where shall I flee from this whore? I ask thee, O Lord, to give me someone who shall conduct me to a far country where she shall not know how to find me!"

While he sat weeping, the wall parted, and there came toward him a tall man whose appearance caused Ma'aruf's body hair to bristle and his flesh to creep. This man said to him, "Man, what ails you, that you disturb me tonight? I have lived here two hundred years and have never seen anyone enter this place and do what you have done. Tell me what you want, and I shall do it for you, because my compassion for you has taken hold of my heart."

Ma'aruf said, "Who are you? What are you?"

He said, "I am the haunter of this place."

So Ma'aruf told him all that had happened to him with his wife.

He said, "Do you want me to convey you to a country where your wife will know no way to get to you?"

"Yes," said Ma'aruf.

The other said, "Get on my back."

So Ma'aruf got on his back, and he flew with him from supper-time to daybreak, and set him down on the top of a high mountain.

He said, "Now, mortal, descend from this mountain, and you will see the gate of a city. Enter it, because your wife cannot come at you there."

He left Ma'aruf and went on his way, and Ma'aruf remained in amazement and perplexity until the sun rose. Then he said to himself, "I shall get up and go down into the city. I have nothing to gain staying up on this highland."

He descended to the foot of the mountain and saw a city surrounded by towering walls, full of lofty palaces and gold-adorned buildings, a delight to behold. He entered through the gate, and found a place that lightened his grieving heart. But, as he walked through the streets, the townsfolk stared at him as a curiosity; they gathered around him, marveling at his clothes, because they were unlike theirs.

Presently, one of them said to him, "Man, are you a stranger?"

"Yes."

"What country have you come from?"

"I am from the city of Cairo the Auspicious."

"When did you leave Cairo?"

"I left it yesterday, at the hour of afternoon prayer."

The man laughed at him, and cried out, "Come and look, folk, at this man! Hear what he says!"

They said, "What does he say?"

The townsman said, "He pretends that he has come from Cairo, that he left it yesterday at the hour of afternoon prayer!"

They all laughed. They gathered around Ma'aruf, and said to him, "Man, are you mad to talk like this?"

"How can you pretend that you left Cairo yesterday at mid-afternoon and found yourself here this morning, when the truth is that it is a full year's journey between our city and Cairo?"

He said, "No one is mad but you! I speak the truth. Here is bread that I brought with me from Cairo! You can see that it is still fresh." He showed them the bread, and they stared at it because it was not like their country's bread.

The crowd around Ma'aruf grew, and the people said to one another, "This is Cairo bread! Look at it!"

Ma'aruf became a subject of interest in the city. Some believed him, others thought him a liar and they mocked him.

While this was going on, a merchant came up, riding on a she-mule and followed by two black slaves. He made a way through the crowd, and said, "Folk, aren't you ashamed to mob this stranger and mock him and scoff at him?"

He went on berating the people until he drove them away from Ma'aruf and no one could respond to him.

Then the merchant said to the stranger, "Come, my brother, no harm shall come to you from these people. They have no shame."

He took Ma'aruf, and carried him to a spacious and richly adorned house. He seated him in a room fit for a king, while he gave an order to his slaves who opened a chest and brought out to him clothing worth a thousand, clothing that might be worn by a merchant. The merchant clothed him, and Ma'aruf, being a handsome man, appeared to be the consul of the merchants. Then his host called for food, and the slaves set before them a tray of all manner of exquisite viands. The two ate and drank, and the merchant said to Ma'aruf, "My brother, what is your name?"

"My name is Ma'aruf. I am a cobbler by trade, I patch old shoes."

"What country are you from?"

"I am from Cairo."

"What quarter?"

"Do you know Cairo?"

"I am a Cairene. I come from Red Street. Do you know anyone who lives on Red Street?"

"I know such-and-such a person," answered Ma'aruf, and he named several people.

The other said, "Do you know Sheikh Ahmad, the druggist?"

"He was my next neighbor, wall to wall."

"Is he well?"

"Yes."

"How many sons has he?"

"Three. Mustafa, Mohammed, and Ali."

"And what has Allah done with them?"

"Mustafa is well, he is a learned man, a professor. Mohammed is a druggist. After he married and his wife had borne a son named Hasan, he opened a shop next to that of his father."

"Allah gladden you with good news," said the merchant.

Ma'aruf continued, "As for Ali, he was my friend when we were boys. We always played together, he and I. We used to go about in the guise of the children of the Nazarenes. We would enter the church, steal the books of the Christians, and sell them and buy food with the money. Once, the Nazarenes caught us with a book, and they complained of us to our parents. They said to Ali's father, 'If you do not keep your son from troubling us, we shall complain of you to the king.' So Ali's father appeased them, and he gave Ali a thrashing. Ali ran away. No one knew where he went, and he has now been absent for twenty years. No one has brought news of him."

The host said, "I am that very Ali, son of Sheikh Ahmad, the druggist, and you are my playmate, Ma'aruf."

Then they saluted each other, and after the salutations, Ali said, "Tell me why, Ma'aruf, you came from Cairo to this city."

Ma'aruf told him all of the bad things that had happened to him with his wife, Fatimah the Dung, and said, "When her annoyance grew on me, I fled from her towards the Gate of Victory, and went to the city. After a while, the rain fell heavily on me, so I entered a ruined cell in a mosque and sat there, weeping. Then the haunter of the place, a jinni, came to me and questioned me. I acquainted him with my case, and he took me on his back and flew with me all night between heaven and earth, until he set me down on yonder mountain and told me of this city. So I came down from the mountain and entered the city, and the people crowded around me and questioned me. I told them that I had left Cairo yesterday, but they didn't believe me. After a time, you came along and, after driving the people away from me, carried me to this house. That is the cause of my departure from Cairo. And you, what brought you here?"

Ali said, "The giddiness of folly turned my head when I was seven years old. From that time, I wandered from land to land and city to city, until I came to this city, the name of which is Ikhtiyan al-Khatan. I found its people to be hospitable and kindly. They had compassion for the poor man and sold to him on credit, believing everything he said. So I said to them, 'I am a merchant, I have preceded my packs and need a place in which to stow my baggage.' They believed me, and assigned me a lodging. Then I said to them, 'Will any of you lend me a thousand dinars until my loads arrive, because I am in need of certain things before my goods come. When the loads get here, I shall repay the money.' They gave me what I asked, and I went to the merchant's bazaar where I saw goods and bought them. Then I sold them the next day at a profit of fifty gold pieces and bought others. I consorted with the people and behaved liberally to them so that they loved me. And I continued to sell and buy until I grew rich. Know, my brother, that the proverb says, 'The world is show and trickery: and the land where no one knows you, do there whatever you like.'

"Now you, if you say to everyone who asks you, 'I'm a cobbler by trade and poor. I fled from my wife and left Cairo yesterday,' they will not believe you and you'll be a laughing stock among them as long as you stay in the city. But if you tell them, 'A spirit brought me here,' they will be frightened of you and no one will come near you, because they will say, 'This man is possessed by a spirit, and harm will come to anyone who comes near him.' Such public report will dishonor both you and me, because they know that I come from Cairo."

Ma'aruf asked, "What shall I do then?"

Ali answered, "I'll tell you what you should do, Inshallah! Tomorrow, I'll give you a thousand dinars, a she-mule to ride, and a black slave who will walk before you and guide you to the gate of the merchants' bazaar. Go in to them. I shall be there, sitting among them, and when I see you, I shall get up and salute you with the salaam. I shall kiss your hand and make a great man of you. Whenever I ask you about any kind of stuff, saying, 'Have you brought along any of such-and-such a thing,' you answer, 'Plenty.' And if they question me about you, I shall praise you and magnify you in their eyes, and say to them, 'Get him a store-house and a shop.' I shall let it be known that you are a man of great wealth and generosity. If a beggar comes to you, give him what you can, so they will put faith in what I say and believe in your greatness and generosity, and love you. Then I shall invite you to my house, and I shall invite all the merchants on your account, and bring you and them together, so that all may know you and you know them. Then you shall sell and buy and take and give with them, and it will not be long before you become a man of money."

The next day, the merchant gave Ma'aruf a thousand dinars, a suit of clothes, a black slave, and, mounting him on a she-mule, said to him, "May Allah enable you soon to repay me, but in the meantime I give it to you for your own free use. You are my friend, and it is incumbent on me to deal generously with you. Have no care, and put away any thought of your wife's misdeeds and give her name to no one."

"Allah repay you with good!" replied Ma'aruf, and he rode on, preceded by his slave, until the slave brought him to the gate of the merchants' bazaar. The merchants were all seated, and among them was Ali. When he saw Ma'aruf, Ali rose and threw himself on him, crying, "A blessed day, Merchant Ma'aruf, Man of good works and kindness!" He kissed his hand in front of the merchants, and said to them, "Brothers, you are honored by knowing the merchant, Ma'aruf."

So they saluted him, and Ali signed to them to make much of him, and he was therefore magnified in their eyes.

Then Ali helped him to dismount from his she-mule and saluted him with his salaam. Then he took the merchants to one side, one after the other, and extolled Ma'aruf to them.

They asked, "Is this man a merchant?"

He answered, "Yes, he is the chiefest of merchants. There lives no wealthier man than he. His wealth and the riches of his father and forefathers are famous among the merchants of Cairo. He has partners in Hind and Sind and Al-Yaman, and is well known for his generosity. So know his rank, exalt his degree, and do him service. Know also that his coming to your city is not for the sake of traffic, but to divert himself with the sight of other folks' countries. He has no need of strangerhood for the sake of grain and profit, because he has wealth that fires cannot consume, and I am one of his servants."

He did not stop extolling Ma'aruf, until the merchants set him above their heads and began to tell one another of his qualities. They gathered around Ma'aruf, and offered him breakfast and sherbets. Even the consul of merchants came to him and saluted him, while Ali proceeded to ask him, in the presence of the traders, "My lord, perhaps you have brought with you some of your goods?"

Ma'aruf answered, "Plenty."

That day, Ali had shown him various kinds of costly clothes and had taught him the names of the different goods, dear and cheap.

One of the merchants said, "My lord, have you brought yellow broadcloth with you?"

Ma'aruf said, "Plenty!"

Another said, "And gazelles' blood red dye?"

The cobbler said, "Plenty."

No matter what the merchant asked him, he gave the same answer.

So the merchant said, "Merchant Ali, if your countryman wanted to transport a thousand loads of costly goods, he could do so."

Ali said, "He would take them from a single one of his store-houses, and not miss a thing."

While they were sitting there, a beggar came up and went the round of the merchants. One gave him a half dirham and another a copper, but most of them gave him nothing. Then the beggar came to Ma'aruf, who pulled out a handful of gold and gave it to him, whereupon the beggar blessed him and went on his way.

The merchants marveled at this, and said, "Truly, this is a king's gift, because he gave the beggar gold without counting it. Were he not a man of vast wealth and money without end, he would not have given a beggar a handful of gold."

After a while, a poor woman came to him, and he gave her a handful of gold. She went away, blessing him, and told the other beggars who then came to him, one after the other, and he gave them each a handful of gold, until he had disbursed the thousand dinars. Then he struck hand upon hand, and said, "Allah is our sufficient aid and excellent is the agent!"

The consul said, "What ails you, Merchant Ma'aruf?"

He said, "It seems that most of the people of this city are poor and needy. Had I known their misery, I would have brought with me a large sum of money in my saddle-bags and given it to the poor. I fear that I may be abroad for a long time, and it is not in my nature to turn down a beggar. But I have no gold left. If a pauper were to come to me, what would I say to him?"

The consul said, "Say, Allah will send you your daily bread!"

But Ma'aruf replied, "That is not my practice, and I am care-ridden because of this. I wish I had another thousand dinars with which to give alms until my baggage comes!"

"Don't worry about that," said the consul. He sent one of his dependents to get a thousand dinars, and gave them to Ma'aruf, who went on giving them to every beggar who passed until the call to noon-prayer.

Then they entered the cathedral-mosque and prayed the noon-prayers, and what was left of the thousand gold pieces Ma'aruf scattered on the heads of the worshipers. This drew the people's attention to him and they blessed him, while the merchants marveled at the abundance of his generosity and openhandedness.

Then Ma'aruf turned to another trader and, borrowing from him another thousand ducats [gold coins], also gave these away, while Merchant Ali looked on at what he did but could not speak. Ma'aruf did not stop doing this until the call to mid-afternoon prayer when he entered the mosque and prayed and distributed the rest of the money.

By the time they locked the doors of the bazaar, he had borrowed five thousand sequins [gold coins] and given them away, saying to everyone from whom he borrowed, "Wait until my baggage comes. Then, if you want gold, I shall give you gold. And if you want goods, you shall have goods. For I have no end of them."

At eventide, Merchant Ali invited Ma'aruf and the rest of the traders to an entertainment. He seated Ma'aruf at the upper end, the place of honor, where he talked of nothing but cloths and jewels, and whenever they mentioned anything to him, he said, "I have plenty of it."

Next day, he again repaired to the market street where he showed a friendly bias towards the merchants and borrowed more money from them, which he distributed to the poor. He did not stop doing this for twenty days, he had borrowed sixty thousand dinars. And still no baggage came—no, not a burning plague.

At last, people began to clamor for their money, and say, "The merchant Ma'aruf's baggage has not come. How long will he take people's money and give it to the poor?"

One of them said, "My advice is that we speak to Merchant Ali."

So they went to Ali, and said, "Merchant Ali, Merchant Ma'aruf's baggage has not come."

He said, "Have patience, it cannot fail to come soon."

Then Ali took Ma'aruf aside, and said to him, "Ma'aruf, what fashion is this? Did I tell you to brown the bread or burn it? The merchants clamor for their money and tell me that you owe them sixty thousand dinars, which you have borrowed and given away to the poor. How will you satisfy the folk, seeing that you neither sell nor buy?"

Ma'aruf said, "What does it matter? What are sixty thousand dinars? When my baggage comes, I shall pay them in goods or in gold and silver—as they wish."

Merchant Ali said, "Allah is most great! Have you any baggage?"

He said, "Plenty!"

The other cried, "Allah and the Hallows repay you your impudence! Did I teach you to say that, that you should repeat it to me? But I will acquaint the folk with you."

Ma'aruf rejoined, "Go, and prate no more! Am I a poor man? I have endless wealth in my baggage. As soon as it comes, they shall have their money's worth, two for one. I have no need of them."

At this, Merchant Ali became angry, and said, "Unmannerly person that you are, I'll teach you to lie to me and not be ashamed!"

Ma'aruf said, "Do your worst! They must wait until my baggage comes, and then they shall have their due and more."

So Ali left him and went away, saying to himself, "I praised him once, and if I accuse him now, I shall make myself out to be a liar, I shall become one of those of whom it is said, 'Whoever praises and then blames, lies twice.'"

He did not know what to do.

Presently, the traders came to him and said, "Merchant Ali, have you spoken to him?"

He said, "Folk, I am ashamed. Though he owes me a thousand dinars, I cannot speak to him. When you lent him money, you did not consult me, so you have no claim on me. Dun him yourselves, and if he does not pay you, complain of him to the king of the city, saying, 'He is an impostor who has imposed on us.' And the king will deliver you from the plague that he is."

So they went to the king and told him what had happened. "King of the age, we are perplexed about the merchant, whose generosity is excessive. He does thus and thus, and all that he borrows he gives away to the poor by handfuls. Were he a man with nothing, his sense would not allow him to lavish gold in this way; were he a man of wealth, his good faith would have been made clear to us by the coming of his baggage. But we have seen none of his luggage, although he assures us that he has a baggage train and that he has preceded it. Now some time has passed, but there appears no sign of his baggage train, and he owes us sixty thousand gold pieces, all of which he has given away in alms."

Then they went on to praise him and extol his generosity.

Now this king was a very covetous man, more covetous than Ash'ab [a Medinite servant of Caliph Osman, known for greed], and when he heard of Ma'aruf's generosity and openhandedness, his desire for gain got the better of him, and he said to his minister, "If this merchant a man of immense wealth, he would not have shown all of this munificence. His baggage train shall assuredly come, and these merchants will then flock to him and he will scatter among them riches galore. Now, I have more right to this money than they. I therefore have a mind to make friends with him and profess affection for him, so that when his baggage comes whatever the merchants would have had I shall get from him. And I shall give him my daughter to wife and join his wealth to my wealth."

The minister said, "King of the age, I think he is nothing but an impostor. It is the impostor who ruins the house of the covetous."

The king said, "Minister, I shall test him and soon learn if he is an impostor or a true man and whether he is a rearling of fortune or not."

The minister asked, "And how will you test him?"

The king answered, "I shall send for him to the presence, and treat him with honor. I shall give him a jewel that I have. If he knows the jewel and its price, he is a man of worth and wealth; but if he does not know it, he is an upstart and an impostor and I shall have him die by the foulest fashion of deaths."

So he sent for Ma'aruf, who came and saluted him.

The king returned his salaam and, seating him beside himself, said to him, "Are you the merchant Ma'aruf?"

He said, "Yes."

The king said, "The merchants say that you owe them sixty thousand ducats. Is this true?"

"Yes," he said.

The king asked, "Why don't you give them their money?"

He answered, "Let them wait until my baggage comes, and I shall pay them twofold. If they want gold, they shall have gold; should they want silver, they shall have silver. If they prefer merchandise, I shall give them merchandise. The one to whom I owe a thousand, I shall give two thousand in repayment of that with which he has veiled my face before the poor, for I have plenty."

Then the king said, "Merchant, take this and explain its kind and value." He gave Ma'aruf a jewel the size of a hazelnut, which he had bought for a thousand sequins. Because he had nothing else like it, the king prized it highly. Ma'aruf took it and, pressing it between his thumb and forefinger, broke it, for it was brittle and would not tolerate the squeeze.

The king said, "Why have you broken the jewel?"

Ma'aruf laughed and said, "King of the age, this is no jewel. This is just a bit of mineral worth a thousand dinars. Why do you call it a jewel? What I call a jewel is worth seventy thousand gold pieces, but this is just a piece of stone. A jewel that is not the size of a walnut has no worth in my eyes, and I pay no attention to it. How can it be that you, the king, calls this thing a jewel when it is but a bit of mineral worth a thousand dinars? Still, it is excusable, considering that you are poor folk and do not possess things of value."

The king asked, "Merchant, do you have jewels such as those of which you speak?"

He answered, "Plenty."

Then avarice overcame the king, and he said, "Will you give me real jewels?"

Ma'aruf said, "When my baggage train comes, I shall give you no end of jewels. All that you desire, I have in plenty, and I shall give it to you without price."

When he heard this, the king rejoiced, and he said to the traders, "Go your ways, have patience with him until his baggage arrives. Then come to me and receive your money from me."

So they went on their way, and the king turned to his minister and said to him, "Pay court to Ma'aruf, converse with him and tell him of my daughter, Princess Dunya, so that he marries her and so that we get these riches of his."

The minister said, "King of the age, I do not like this man's demeanor. I think he is an impostor and a liar. Don't go forward with these plans, or you'll lose your daughter for nothing."

Now this minister had some time before requested that the king give him his daughter in marriage. The king was willing to do this, but when his daughter heard about it she refused to consent to marry him.

The king therefore said to him, "Traitor, you desire no good for me, because in the past you wanted my daughter in marriage, but she would have none of you. So now you would cut off the possibility of her marriage, you would have the princess lie fallow, so that you might take her. But hear from me one word. You have no concern in this matter. How can he be an impostor and a liar, seeing that he knew the price of the jewel, he even knew why I bought it, and he broke it because it did not please him? He has jewels in plenty, and when he goes in to my daughter and finds that she is beautiful, she will captivate his reason, and he will love her and give her jewels and objects of price. But you, you would forbid my daughter and myself these good things."

So the minister was silent, fearing the king's anger, and he said to himself, "Set the curs on the cattle! [i.e., "Show a miser money and hold him back, if you can"]."

Then, with a show of friendly bias, he went to Ma'aruf and said to him, "His Highness the King loves you. He has a daughter, a beautiful woman and amorous. He wants to marry you to her. What is your response?"

He said, "There is no harm in that. But let him wait until my baggage comes, for marriage settlements on king's daughters are large, and their rank demands that they not be endowed except with a dowry befitting their degree. At the present, I have no money with me, and will have none until my baggage comes. I have wealth in plenty, and I must make her marriage portion five thousand purses. Then I shall need a thousand purses to distribute among the poor and needy on my wedding night, another thousand to give to those who walk in the bridal procession, and yet another thousand for provisions for the troops and others. And I shall require a hundred jewels to give to the princess on the wedding morning, and another hundred gems to distribute among the slave girls and eunuchs, for I must give each of them a jewel in honor of the bride. And I need money to clothe a thousand naked paupers. Alms too need to be given. All this cannot be done until my baggage arrives. But I have plenty and, once it is here, I shall make no account of all this outlay."

The minister returned to the king and told him what Ma'aruf said.

The king said, "Since this is his wish, how can you style him an impostor and a liar?"

The minister replied, "And I do not stop saying this."

The kind berated him angrily and threatened him, saying, "By the life of my head, if you do not stop this talk, I shall kill you! Go back to him, bring him to me and I shall manage matters with him myself."

So the minister returned to Ma'aruf, and said to him, "Come and speak with the king."

Ma'aruf said, "I hear and obey."

He went to the king.

The king said to him, "You shall not put me off with these excuses, because my treasury is full. Take the keys and spend all that you need to spend, give what you will, clothe the poor, fulfill your desire and have no care for the girl and the servants. When your baggage comes, do what you will with your wife by way of generosity. We shall have patience with you regarding the marriage portion until then, because there are no differences between you and me, none at all."

Then he sent for the Sheikh al-Islam [the chief of the olema, or learned of the law], and told him to write out the marriage contract between his daughter and Merchant Ma'aruf, and he did so. The king then gave the signal for beginning the wedding festivities and gave orders that the city be decorated. Kettledrums were beaten, tables were spread with meats of all kinds, performers came and paraded their tricks.

Merchant Ma'aruf sat on a throne in a parlor, and the players, the gymnasts, the female impersonators, dancing men of wondrous movements, and posture-makers of marvelous cunning came before him, while he called out to the treasurer and said to him, "Bring gold and silver." The treasurer brought gold and silver, and Ma'aruf went round among the spectators and gave liberally, by the handful, to each of the performers. He gave alms to the poor and needy, he gave clothes to the naked. It was a clamorous festival and a very merry one. The treasurer could not bring money fast enough from the treasury. The minister's heart almost burst from rage, but he dared not say a word. Merchant Ali marveled at this waste of wealth, and he said to Merchant Ma'aruf, "May Allah and the Hallows retaliate upon the sides of your head! Wasn't it enough to squander the traders' money? Must you squander the king's money to boot?"

Ma'aruf replied, "It's none of your concern. When my baggage comes, I shall repay the king manifold."

And Ma'aruf went on lavishing money, saying to himself, "A burning plague! What will happen will happen, and there is no flight from that which has been foreordained."

The festivals went on without stop for forty days. On the forty-first day, they organized the bride's procession, and all the emirs and troops walked before her. When they brought her in before Ma'aruf, he began scattering gold on the heads of the people, and they made a splendid procession for her while Ma'aruf expended in her honor vast sums of money.

Then they brought him in to Princess Dunya, and he sat down on the high divan. They let the curtains fall, and shut the doors and withdrew, leaving him alone with his bride. Then he struck hand against hand, and sat sorrowfully for a time, saying, "There is no majesty and no might except in Allah, the Glorious, the Great!"

The princess said, "My lord, Allah preserve you! What ails you that you are so troubled?"

He said, "How can I be anything but troubled, seeing that your father has embarrassed me and done to me a deed that is like the burning of green corn?"

She asked, "And what has my father done to you? Tell me."

He answered, "He has brought me in to you before my baggage has arrived, and I wanted at least a hundred jewels to distribute among your servants, to each a jewel, so that she might rejoice and say, 'My lord gave me a jewel on the night of his going in to my lady.' I would have done this good deed in honor of your station and for the increase of your dignity. I have no need to stint myself in lavishing jewels, because I have a great plenty of them."

She said, "Don't be concerned about that. Do not trouble yourself about me, for I will have patience with you until your baggage arrives. As for my women, don't worry about them. Rise, take off your clothes, and take your pleasure. And when the baggage comes, we shall get the jewels and the rest."

So he arose and, having removed his clothes, sat down on the bed and sought to make love to her. They fell to toying with each other. He laid a hand on her knee, and she sat down in his lap and thrust her lip like a tidbit of meat into his mouth. That hour was enough to make a man forget his father and his mother. He clasped her in his arms and held her close to his chest, and he sucked her lip until the honeydew ran out into his mouth. He laid his hand under her left armpit, and his vitals and her vitals yearned for coition. Then he clapped her between the breasts, and his hand slipped down between her thighs. She girded him with her legs, and he made of the two parts proof amain, crying out, "O sire of the chin-veils twain!" [addressing his member, "O you who can take her maidenhead while my tongue does away with the virginity of her mouth"], he applied the priming and kindled the match and set it to the touchhole, and gave fire, and breached the citadel in its four corners, so there occurred the mystery concerning which there is no inquiry, and she cried the cry that must be cried. While she did so, Merchant Ma'aruf abated her maidenhead. That night was not one to be counted among lives for that which it comprised of the enjoyment of the fair, clipping and dallying langue fourrée and futtering until the dawn of day.

Then he arose and entered the bath. Then, having put on clothing suitable for sovereigns, he went to the king's room.

All who were there rose to him, and received him with honor and worship, giving him joy and invoking blessings on him.

He sat down at the king's side, and asked, "Where is the treasurer?"

They answered, "Here he is, in front of you."

He said to him, "Bring robes of honor for all the ministers and emirs and dignitaries, and clothe them with the robes."

The treasurer brought all he asked for, and he sat, giving the robes to all who came to him, lavishing largess on every man according to his station.

In this way, he lived for twenty days. No baggage or anything else arrived for him, until the treasurer was straitened by him to the utmost. He went in to the king and, in Ma'aruf's absence, sat alone with the minister.

He kissed the ground between his hands, and said, "King of the age, I must tell you something, lest by chance you blame me for not acquainting you with this matter. Know that the treasury is being exhausted. There is only a little money left in it. In ten days, we shall shut the treasury upon emptiness."

The king said, "Minister, truly, my son-in-law's baggage train has been long delayed, and there is no news regarding it."

The minister laughed and said, "Allah be gracious to you, King of the age! You are heedless with respect to this impostor, this liar. As your head lives, there is no baggage for him—no, nor a burning plague to rid us of him! No, he has only imposed on you without ceasing, so that he has wasted your treasures and married your daughter for nothing. How long will you continue to be heedless of this liar?"

Then the king said, "Minister, what shall we do to learn the truth of his case?"

The minister said, "King of the age, no one may discover a man's secret but his wife. So send for your daughter and let her come behind the curtain, so that I may question her regarding the truth of his estate, so that she may question him and inform us about his case."

The king cried, "There is no harm in that! As my head lives, if it is proved that he is a liar and an impostor, I shall truly have him die the foulest of deaths!"

Then he took the minister into the sitting chamber, and sent for his daughter. She came behind the curtain, her husband being absent, and said, "What do you want, my father?"

He said, "Speak with the minister."

She asked, "Minister, what is your will?"

He said, "My lady, you must know that your husband has squandered your father's substance and married you without a dowry. He continues to promise us and then break his promises. No news comes regarding his baggage. In short, we want you to inform us regarding him."

She said, "His words are indeed many, and he still comes and promises me jewels and treasures and costly things. But I see nothing."

The minister said, "My lady, can you tonight converse with him, and whisper to him, 'Tell me truly and don't fear me, for you have become my husband and I shall not transgress against you. So tell me the truth, and I shall devise you a means whereby you shall be set at rest.' Play fast and loose with him in words, profess love to him, win his confession, then tell us the facts of his case."

She answered, "My papa, I know how I shall find out about him."

She went away then, and after supper her husband came in to her, as he usually did. Then Princess Dunya rose, and took him under the armpit and wheedled him with winsome wheedling (and all sufficient are woman's wiles when she wants something from men). She did not stop caressing him and beguiling him with speech sweeter than honey, until she stole his reason. When she saw that he altogether inclined to her, she said to him, "My beloved, coolness of my eyes and fruit of my vitals, Allah never desolate me by giving me less of you, and may time never separate us! Love of you has settled in my heart, and the fire of passion has consumed my liver. I will never forsake you or transgress against you. But I want you to tell me the truth, because the sleights of falsehood give no profit, nor do they secure credit at all seasons. How long will you impose on my father and lie to him? I am afraid that, before we can devise some plan, your affair will be discovered by him and he shall lay violent hands on you. So acquaint me with the facts of the case, for nothing shall happen to you except that which will gladden you. And when you have spoken truth, do not be afraid: no harm shall come to you. How often will you declare that you are a merchant and a man of money and that you have a luggage train? For a long time, you have been saying, 'My baggage! My baggage!' but no sign of your baggage has appeared, and there is anxiety in your face because of this. If there is no truth in your words, tell me, and I shall devise a contrivance by which you shall come off safely, Inshallah!"

He replied, "I shall tell you the truth, and then you do what you will."

She said, "Speak, and make certain that you speak the truth, for truth is the ark of safety. Beware of lying, it dishonors the liar. He is God-gifted who said,

> 'Beware that you speak truth, though truth when said
> Shall cause you to fall into threatened fire:
> And seek Allah's approval, for he is most foolish
> Who shall anger his Lord to make friends with thrall.'"

Ma'aruf said, "Know then, Lady, that I am no merchant and have no baggage, no, nor a burning plague. I was but a cobbler in my own country and had a wife called Fatimah the Dung, with whom this and that befell me." And he told her his story from beginning to end.

She laughed then, and said, "Truly, you are clever in the art of lying and imposture!"

He answered, "My lady, may Allah Almighty preserve you to veil sins and counterveil chagrins!"

She said, "Know this, that you imposed on my father and deceived him by means of your deluding boasts, so that out of greed he married me to you. Then you squandered his wealth, and the minister bears you a grudge for this. How many times he has spoken against you to my father, saying, 'Indeed, he is an impostor, a liar!' But my father did not listen to his words because the minister had wanted to marry me and I did not consent that he be baron and I his wife. But my father was becoming conscious of the lengthening time and he became straitened, and he said to me, 'Make him confess.' So I have made you confess, and that which was covered is discovered. Now my father has mischief in mind for you because of this. But you have become my husband, and I shall never transgress against you. If I told my father what I have learned from you, he would be assured of your falsehood and imposture, that you have imposed upon kings' daughters and squandered royal wealth, so that your offence would find no pardon from him, and he would kill you without a doubt. Then it would be said among the folk that I had married a man who was a liar, an impostor, and that would smirch my honor. Furthermore, if he were to kill you, most likely he would require me to marry someone else, and to that I would never consent—no, even if I were to die. So get up now and put on slave's clothing and take these fifty thousand dinars of my money, mount a swift steed, and get to a land where the rule of my father does not reach. Then make yourself a merchant and send a letter to me by a courier, who shall bring it secretly to me, so that I know what land you are in, and I shall send you everything that my hand can attain. Your wealth shall thereby grow, and, if my father dies, I shall send for you, and you shall return in respect and honor. If we die, you or I, and go to the mercy of God the Most Great, the resurrection shall unite us. This, then, is the advice that is right. While we are both alive and well, I shall not stop sending you letters and money. Arise before the day gets bright and you be in a difficult plight and perdition comes down on your head!"

He said, "My lady, I beg you to favor me and bid me farewell with an embrace."

She said, "There is no harm in that."

So he embraced her and knew her carnally. After that, he made a complete ablution. Then he put on the dress of a white slave, and told the grooms to saddle him a thoroughbred steed. They prepared a courser for him, and he mounted. Bidding his wife farewell, he rode out of the city at the end of the night, and all who saw him assumed that he was one of the slaves of the sultan going abroad on some business.

Next morning, the king and his minister went to the sitting chamber and sent for Princess Dunya, who came behind the curtain.

Her father said to her, "My daughter, what do you say?"

She said, "I say, Allah should blacken the minister's face, because he would have blackened my face in my husband's eyes!"

The king asked, "How so?"

She answered, "He came in to me yesterday, but before I could mention the matter to him, in walked Faraj, the chief eunuch, letter in hand, and he said, 'Ten white slaves standing under the palace window have given me this letter, saying, "Kiss for us the hands of our lord, Merchant Ma'aruf, and give him this letter, for we are his slaves with the baggage. The news has reached us that he has married the king's daughter, so we are to acquaint him with what happened to us along the way."' I took the letter and read as follows: 'From the five hundred slaves to his highness, our lord, Merchant Ma'aruf. We want you to know that, after you left us, plundering nomads came out upon us and attacked us. They were two thousand horses and we five hundred mounted slaves, and there followed a mightily sore fight between us and them. They kept us from the road for thirty days, doing battle with them, and this is the cause of our being behind time. They also took from us two hundred loads of cloth and killed of us fifty slaves.' When the news reached my husband, he cried, 'Allah disappoint them! What caused them to wage war with the nomads for the sake of two hundred loads of merchandise? What are two hundred loads? They should not have tarried on that account, for truly the value of the two hundred loads is only some seven thousand dinars. But I must go to them and hurry them. As for the merchandise taken by the nomads, it will not be missed from the baggage, nor does it mean anything at all to me, for I regard it as if I had given it to them as alms.' Then he went down from me, laughing and showing no concern for the waste of his wealth nor the slaughter of his slaves. As soon as he was gone, I looked out of the lattice and saw the ten slaves who had brought him the letter—they were like moons, each dressed in a suit of clothes worth two thousand dinars. There is not among my father's chattel anyone to match one of them. He went with them to bring his baggage, and hallowed be Allah who hindered me from saying to him anything that you asked me to say, for he would have mocked me and you, and perhaps he would have looked at me in a disparaging way and hated me. But the fault is all with the minister, who speaks words against my husband that are untrue."

The king replied, "My daughter, your husband's wealth is indeed endless and he pays no heed to it, for from the day he entered our city he has done nothing but give alms to the poor. Inshallah, he will speedily return with the baggage, and good in plenty from him shall befall us."

The king, duped by her scheme, went on to appease her and menace the minister.

So it went with the king, but as regards Merchant Ma'aruf, he rode on into waste lands, perplexed and not knowing where he should go. And, in the anguish of parting, he lamented, and in the pangs of passion and love-longing, he recited these couplets:

"Time falsed our union and divided who were one in two,
And the sore tyranny of time melts my heart away.
My eyes never cease to shed tears for parting with my dear.
When shall disunion come to an end, and dawn the union-day?
O favor like the full moon's face of sheen, indeed I'm he

Whom you left with vitals torn when faring on your way.
Would I had never seen your sight, or met you for an hour,
Since after sweetest taste of you I'm a prey to bitters.
Ma'aruf will never cease to be enthralled by Dunya's charms,
And long may she live although he die whom love and longing slay.
O brilliance, like resplendent sun of noontide, deign them heal
His heart for kindness and the fire of longing love allay!
Would heaven I knew if ever the days shall conjoin our lots,
Join us in pleasant talk of nights, in union glad and gay:
Shall my love's palace hold two hearts that savor joy, and I
Strain to my breast the branch I saw on the sand-hill sway?
O favor of full moon in sheen, never may sun of thee
Stop rising from the eastern rim with all-enlightening ray!
I'm well content with passion-pine and all its bane and bate,
For luck in love is evermore the butt of jealous fate."

And when he ended his verses, he wept with sore weeping, for, indeed, the ways were walled up before his face, and death seemed to him better than enduring life, and he walked on like a drunken man because of the stress of distraction, and before noon he came to a little town and saw a ploughman nearby ploughing with a yoke of bulls. Now he was very hungry, and he went up to the ploughman and said to him, "Peace be with you!"

The ploughman returned his salaam, and said to him, "Welcome, my lord! Are you one of the sultan's slaves?"

Ma'aruf said, "Yes."

The other said, "Stay with me for a guest-meal."

Then Ma'aruf knew him to be liberal, and said to him, "My brother, I don't see anything with you that you might feed me. How is it, then, that you invite me?"

The husbandman said, "My lord, good fortune is at hand. Dismount here. The town is nearby, and I shall go and fetch you dinner and fodder for your stallion."

Ma'aruf rejoined, "Since the town is nearby, I can go there as quickly as you can and buy what I have a mind to in the bazaar and eat."

The peasant replied, "My lord, the place is but a little village, and there is no bazaar there, neither selling nor buying. So I appeal to you, by Allah, stay here with me and cheer up my heart, and I will run there and return to you in haste."

So Ma'aruf dismounted, and the fellow left him and went off to the village to fetch dinner for him, while Ma'aruf sat awaiting him.

After a time, he said to himself, "I have taken this poor man away from his work. To make up for having hindered him from his work, I shall get up and plough in his stead, until he comes back."

Ma'aruf took the plough, then, and, starting the bulls, he ploughed a little, until the ploughshare struck against something and the beasts stopped. He looked at the share and, finding it caught in a ring of gold, he cleared away the soil and saw that the ploughshare was caught in the middle of a slab of alabaster the size of the lower millstone. He worked at the stone until he pulled it from its place, and there appeared beneath it an underground passage with a stair.

Presently, he descended the flight of steps and came to a place like a bath, with four platforms, the first full of gold, from floor to roof; the second full of emeralds and pearls and coral, also from ground to ceiling; the third, of jacinths and rubies and turquoises; and the fourth, of diamonds and all manner of other precious stones. At the upper end of the place stood a coffer of clearest crystal, full of union-gems each the size of a walnut, and on the coffer was a casket of gold, as large as a lemon.

When he saw this, Ma'aruf marveled and rejoiced with exceeding joy. He said to himself, "I wonder what is in this casket?" He opened it and found inside a seal-ring of gold on which were engraved names and talismans, as if they were the tracks of creeping ants.

He rubbed the ring and a voice said, "Adsum! Here I am, at your service, my lord! Ask and it shall be given to you. Will you build a city or ruin a capital or kill a king or dig a river-channel or anything of the kind? Whatever you seek, it shall come to pass, by leave of the king of all might, creator of day and night."

Ma'aruf asked, "Creature of my lord, who and what are you?"

The other answered, "I am the slave of this seal-ring, standing in the service of the person who possesses it. Whatever he seeks, that I do for him, and I have no excuse in neglecting what he asks me to do, because I am sultan over seventy-two divisions of the jinn, each seventy-two thousand in number, every one of these thousands rules over a thousand marids, each marid over a thousand ifrits, each ifrit over a thousand satans, and each satan over a thousand jinn—and they are all under the command of me and may not deny me. As for me, I am spelled to this seal-ring, and may not thwart whoever holds it. Now you have gotten hold of it and I have become your slave, so ask what you will, for I listen to your word and obey your bidding. If you have need of me at any time, by land or by sea, rub the signet-ring and you will find me with you. But beware of rubbing it twice in succession, or you will consume me with the fire of the names that are engraved on the ring, and you would then lose me and regret that. Now, I have acquainted you with my case and—the peace!"

The merchant, Ma'aruf, asked him, "What is your name?"

The jinni answered, "My name is Abu al-Sa'adat."

Ma'aruf said, "Abu al-Sa'adat, what is this place, and who enchanted you in this casket?"

He said, "My lord, this is a treasure called the Hoard of Shaddad, son of Ad, the one who laid the base of many-columned Iram, the like of which was never made in the lands. I was his slave in his lifetime and this is his seal-ring that he laid up in his treasure. But now, it has fallen to you."

Ma'aruf asked, "Can you transport what is in this hoard to the surface of the earth?"

The jinni replied, "Yes! Nothing could be easier."

Ma'aruf said, "Bring it there, and leave nothing behind."

So the jinni signed with his hand to the ground, and the ground broke open, and he sank and was absent for a while. Presently, there emerged young boys full of grace and fair of face, bearing golden baskets filled with gold; they emptied these, then went away and returned with more. They did not stop transporting the gold and jewels until an hour had sped by, and then they said, "Nothing is left in the hoard."

Then Abu al-Sa'adat came out, and he said to Ma'aruf, "My lord, you see that we have brought out all that was in the hoard."

Ma'aruf asked, "Who are these beautiful boys?"

The jinni answered, "They are my sons. This matter was not such that I should have the marids do it, so my sons have fulfilled your desire and they are honored by such service. Ask me what you wish beside this."

Ma'aruf said, "Can you bring me he-mules with chests, and fill the chests with the treasure, and load them on the mules?"

Abu al-Sa'adat said, "Nothing easier."

He cried a great cry, and his sons, eight hundred of them, presented themselves before him. He said to them, "Let some of you take the form of he-mules and others of muleteers and handsome slaves, and others of you be changed to muleteers, and the rest to menials."

So seven hundred of them changed themselves into pack mules, and another hundred took the form of slaves. Then Abu al-Sa'adat called upon his marids, who presented themselves between his hands, and he commanded some of them to assume the aspect of horses girded with saddles of gold crusted with jewels.

When Ma'aruf saw them do as he asked, he cried, "Where are the chests?"

They brought the chests before him, and he said, "Pack the gold and the stones, each sort by itself."

So they packed them, and loaded three hundred he-mules with them.

Then Ma'aruf asked, "Abu al-Sa'adat, can you bring me some loads of costly goods?"

The jinni answered, "Will you have Egyptian goods or Syrian or Persian or Indian or Greek?"

Ma'aruf said, "Bring me a hundred loads of each kind, on five hundred mules."

Abu al-Sa'adat said, "My lord, allow me some time so that I may send my marids to do this. I shall send a company of them to each country to fetch a hundred loads of its goods and then take the form of he-mules and return, carrying the goods."

Ma'aruf asked, "How much time do you want?"

Abu al-Sa-adat replied, "The time of the blackness of the night. Day shall not dawn before you have all that you desire."

Ma'aruf said, "I grant you this time," and he asked them to pitch him a pavilion.

They pitched it; he sat down in it and they brought him a table of food.

Then Abu al-Sa'adat said to him, "My lord, tarry in this tent, my sons shall guard you. Fear nothing. I am going to muster my marids and despatch them to do your desire."

So saying, he departed, leaving Ma'aruf sitting in the pavilion with the table before him and the jinni's sons attending him in the guise of slaves and servants and suite. While he sat in this state, up came the husbandman with a great porringer of lentils and a nose-bag full of barley. Seeing the pavilion pitched and the slaves standing, hands on breasts, he thought that the sultan had come and he therefore halted. He stood open-mouthed, and said to himself, "I wish I had killed a couple of chickens and fried them red with clarified cow-butter for the sultan!"

He would have turned back to kill the chickens as a feast for the sultan, but Ma'aruf saw him and cried out to him, and said to the slaves, "Bring him here."

So they brought him and his porringer of lentils before Ma'aruf, who said to him, "What is this?"

The peasant said, "This is your dinner and your horse's fodder. Excuse me, for I did not think that the sultan would come here. Had I known that, I would have killed a couple of chickens and entertained him properly."

Ma'aruf said, "The sultan has not come. I am his son-in-law, and I was vexed with him. However, he has sent his officers to make his peace with me, and now I am minded to return to the city. But you have made me this guest-meal without knowing me, and I accept it from you, lentils though it be, and will not eat save of your cheer."

Accordingly, he told him to place the porringer in the middle of the table, and he ate his full of it, while the fellow filled his belly with those rich meats. Then Ma'aruf washed his hands and gave the slaves leave to eat. They fell on the remains of the meal and ate. When the porringer was empty, Ma'aruf filled it with gold and gave it to the peasant, saying, "Carry this to your dwelling and come to me in the city, and I will treat you with honor."

The peasant then took the porringer full of gold and returned to his village, driving the bulls before him and considering himself akin to the king.

Meanwhile, they brought Ma'aruf girls of the Brides of the Treasure [the beautiful girls who guard the hoard], who beat on instruments of music and danced before him, and he passed that night joyfully and with delight, a night not to be reckoned among lives.

Hardly had the day dawned when there arose a great cloud of dust. When it lifted, seven hundred mules were discovered laden with goods and attended by muleteers and baggage tenders and torch bearers. With them came Abu al-Sa'adat, riding on a she-mule, in the guise of a caravan leader. Before him was a traveling litter, with four corner terminals of glittering red gold, set with gems.

When Abu al-Sa'adat came up to the tent, he dismounted and, kissing the earth, said to Ma'aruf, "My lord, your desire has been done to the uttermost, and in the litter is a treasure suit that does not have its match among the king's raiment. So don it and mount the litter, and bid us do what you will."

Ma'aruf said, "Abu al-Sa'adat, I want you to go to the city of Ikhtiyan al-Khatan and present yourself to my father-in-law, the king. Go in to him only in the guise of a mortal courtier."

He said, "To hear is to obey."

Ma'aruf wrote a letter to the sultan and sealed it, and Abu al-Sa'adat took it and set out with it.

When he arrived, he found the king saying, "Minister, my heart is indeed concerned for my son-in-law. I am afraid that the nomads might slay him. I wish to heaven I knew where he was going, so that I might have followed him with the troops! I wish he had told me his destination!"

The minister said, "Allah be merciful to you for your heedlessness! As your head lives, the person saw that we were awake to him, and he feared dishonor and fled, because he is nothing but an impostor, a liar."

At this moment, the courier came in. Kissing the ground before the king, he wished him permanent glory and prosperity and length of life.

The king asked, "Who are you, and what is your business?"

"I am a courier," answered the jinni, "and your son-in-law who has come with the baggage sends me to you with a letter. Here it is."

He took the letter and read these words, "After salutations galore to our uncle, the glorious king! Know that I am at hand with the baggage train, so come to meet me with your troops."

The king cried, "Allah blacken your brow, Minister! How often will you defame my son-in-law's name and call him liar and impostor? Look, he has come with the baggage train, and you are nothing but a traitor."

The minister hung his head groundwards in shame and confusion, and replied, "King of the age, I said this only because of the long delay of the baggage and because I feared the loss of the wealth that he has wasted."

The king exclaimed, "Traitor, what are my riches! Now that his baggage has come, he will give me great plenty in their stead."

Then he gave orders to decorate the city and, going to his daughter, he said to her, "Good news for you! Your husband will be here shortly with his baggage, for he has sent me a letter to that effect. I am now going out to meet him."

Princess Dunya marveled at this, and said to herself, "This is a wonderful thing! Was he laughing at me and mocking me, or did he want to try me when he told me that he was a pauper? But glory to God that I did not fail in my duty to him!"

This is what was going on in the palace.

Regarding Merchant Ali, the Cairene, when he saw the decoration of the city and asked the cause for it, they said to him, "The baggage train of Merchant Ma'aruf, the king's son-in-law, has arrived."

He said, "Allah is almighty! What a calamity is this man! He came to me, fleeing from his wife, and he was a poor man. How, then, could he get a baggage train? Perhaps this is a scheme that the king's daughter has contrived for him, fearing his disgrace, and kings are not unable to do anything. May Allah the most high veil his fame and not bring him to public shame!"

All the merchants rejoiced and were glad, because they would get their money.

Then the king assembled his troops and rode forth, while Abu al-Sa'adat returned to Ma'aruf and told him about the delivery of the letter.

Ma'aruf said, "Tie on the loads."

When they had done that, he put on the treasure suit and, mounting the litter, became a thousand times greater and more majestic than the king. Then he set forward.

When he had gone half way, the king met him with the troops. Seeing him riding in the moving throne and clad in the splendid clothing, the king threw himself on him and saluted him, and, giving him joy of his safety, he greeted him with the greeting of peace.

Then all the lords of the land saluted him, and it was clear that he had spoken the truth, that in him there was no lie.

Presently, he entered the city in such a state procession as would have caused the gall bladder of the lion to burst for envy, and the traders pressed up to him and kissed his hands, while Merchant Ali said to him, "You have played out this trick, and it has prospered to your hand, Sheikh of Impostors! But you deserve it, and may Allah the most high increase you of his bounty!"

Ma'aruf laughed. Then he entered the palace and, sitting down on the throne, said, "Carry the loads of gold into the treasury of my uncle, the king, and bring me the bales of cloth."

They brought the bales to him and opened them before him, bale after bale, until they had unpacked the seven hundred loads. Out of these, he chose the best, and said, "Take these to Princess Dunya so that she may distribute them among her slave girls. Carry her also this coffer of jewels so that she may divide them among her servants and eunuchs."

Then he proceeded to make over to the merchants, whose debt he was in, goods by way of payment for their arrears, giving him whose due was a thousand goods worth two thousand or more. After that, he fell to distributing to the poor and needy, while the king looked on with greedy eyes and could not hinder him. Nor did Ma'aruf cease largess until he had exhausted the seven hundred loads. He then turned to the troops and proceeded to apportion among them emeralds and rubies and pearls and coral and other jewels by handfuls, without count, until the king said to him, "Enough of this giving, my son! There is but little left of the baggage."

But he said, "I have plenty."

Then, indeed, his good faith having become clear, no one could call him a liar. He had come to the point at which he was heedless about giving, because the slave of the seal-ring brought him whatever he wanted.

Presently, the treasurer came in to the king, and said, "King of the age, the treasury is truly full, it will not hold the rest of the loads. Where shall we put what remains of the gold and jewels?"

The king assigned him another place.

When Princess Dunya saw this, her joy redoubled, and she marveled and said to herself, "I wish I knew how he came to have all this wealth!"

The merchants similarly rejoiced in what he had given them, and they blessed him.

Merchant Ali marveled, and said to himself, "I wonder how he lied and swindled to get all of these treasures? Had they come from the king's daughter, he would not waste them like this! But how excellent is the saying,

> When the king's king gives, pause in reverence
> And do not venture to inquire into the cause:
> Allah gives his gifts to whom he will,
> So respect and abide by his holy laws!"

So far concerning Merchant Ali.

Regarding the king, he also marveled with passing marvel at what he saw of Ma'aruf's generosity and openhandedness in the largess of wealth.

Then Merchant Ma'aruf went in to his wife, who met him, smiling and laughing-lipped, and she kissed his hand, saying, "Did you mock me or did you want to test me when you said, 'I am a poor man and a fugitive from my wife'? Praise be Allah that I did not fail in my duty to you! For you are my beloved, and there is no one dearer to me than you, whether you be rich or poor. But I would have you tell me what your intention was by those words."

Ma'aruf said, "I wished to test you and see if your love was sincere or for the sake of wealth and greed of worldly goods. It has become clear to me that your affection is sincere and, as you are a true woman, welcome to you! I know your worth."

Then he parted and went into a place by himself and rubbed the seal-ring.

Abu al-Sa'adat presented himself and said to him, "Adsum, at your service! Ask what you will."

Ma'aruf said, "I want a treasure suit and treasure trinkets for my wife, including a necklace made of forty unique jewels."

The jinni said, "To hear is to obey," and he brought Ma'aruf what he asked for.

Ma'aruf dismissed him then, and, carrying the dress and ornaments to his wife, laid them before her, and said, "Take these and put them on, and welcome!"

When she saw this, her wits fled for joy, and she found among the ornaments a pair of anklets of gold set with jewels of the handiwork of the magicians, and bracelets and earrings and a belt such as no money could buy. She donned the dress and ornaments, and said to Ma'aruf, "My lord, I will save these for holidays and festivals."

But he said, "Wear them always, I have others in plenty."

When she put them on and her women looked at her, they rejoiced and kissed his hands.

Then he left them and, going apart by himself, rubbed the seal-ring. Its slave appeared, and he said to him, "Bring me a hundred suits of apparel, with their ornaments of gold."

"Hearing and obeying," answered Abu al-Sa'adat, and he brought him the hundred suits, each with its ornaments wrapped up within it.

Ma'aruf took them and called aloud to the slave girls. When they came to him, he gave each a suit. They donned them and became like the black-eyed girls of paradise, while Princess Dunya shone among them as the moon among the stars. One of the servants told the king of this, and he came in to his daughter and saw her and her women dazzling all who beheld them. He wondered with passing wonderment.

He went out and called his minister. He said to him, "Minister, such and such things have happened. What do you say now of this affair?"

He said, "King of the age, this is no merchant's fashion, because a merchant keeps a piece of linen for years and will not sell it except at a profit. How can a merchant have generosity like this generosity, and where can he get the likes of this money and jewels, which is generally found with the kings? Why should such loads be found with merchants? There must be a reason for this. If you will listen to me, I shall make the truth of this case clear to you."

The king answered, "Minister, I shall do you bidding."

The minister rejoined, "Get together with your son-in-law, make a show of affection to him, talk with him and say, 'My son-in-law, I have a mind to go, just you and I and the minister, to a flower garden where we might take our pleasure.' When we come to the garden, we shall put wine on the table, and I shall ply him with the wine and compel him to drink it. When he shall have drunk, he will lose his reason, his judgement will forsake him. Then we will question him regarding the truth of his case, and he will reveal to us his secrets, for wine is a traitor and Allah-gifted is he who said,

> When we drank the wine, and it crept its way
> To the place of secrets, I cried, 'O stay!'
> In my fear lest its influence stint my wits
> And my friends spy matters that hidden lay.

When he has told us the truth, we shall know his case and may then deal with him as we may, because I fear the consequences for you of what he is doing at present: perhaps he covets the kingship, and hopes to win over the troops by generosity and lavishing money, and so will depose you and take the kingdom from you."

"True," answered the king. "You have spoken truth."

And they passed the night on this agreement.

When morning came, the king went forth and sat in the guest chamber when the grooms and serving men came in to him in dismay.

He said, "What has happened to you?"

They said, "King of the age, the grooms curried the horses and foddered them and the he-mules that brought the baggage, but when we arose this morning we found that your son-in-law's slaves have stolen the horses and mules. We searched the stables, but found neither horse nor mule, so we entered the lodging of the slaves and found no one there, nor do we know how they fled."

The king marveled at this, not knowing that the horses and slaves were all ifrits, the subjects of the slave of the spell. He asked the grooms, "Accursed ones, how could a thousand beasts and five hundred slaves flee without your knowledge?"

They answered, "We do not know how it happened."

He cried, "Go, and when your lord comes out of the harem, tell him what has happened."

So they went out from before the king and sat down bewildered, until Ma'aruf came out. Seeing that they were chagrined, he asked, "What is the matter?"

They told him all that had happened, and he said, "What is their worth, that you are so concerned about them? Go on your ways."

And he sat laughing and was neither angry nor grieved about it.

Then the king looked in the minister's face, and said to him, "What kind of man is this for whom wealth is of no worth? There must be a reason for this."

They talked with Ma'aruf for a while, then the king said to him, "My son-in-law, I have a mind to go, you and I and the minister, to a garden, where we may divert ourselves."

"No harm in that," said Ma'aruf.

So they went to a flower garden in which every sort of fruit was of two kinds and its waters were flowing and its trees towering and its birds caroling. There they entered a pavilion, the sight of which did away with sorrow from the soul, and they sat talking while the minister entertained them the rare tales and quoted merry quips and mirth-provoking sayings. Ma'aruf listened attentively, until the time of dinner came. They set a tray of meats and a flagon of wine. When they had eaten and washed their hands, the minister filled the cup and gave it to the king, who drank it off. Then he filled a second and handed it to Ma'aruf, saying, "Take the cup of the drink to which reason bows its neck in reverence."

Ma'aruf said, "What is this, Minister?"

He said, "This is the grizzled virgin and the old maid long kept at home, the giver of joy to hearts, of which the poet has written in the following couplets:

> The feet of sturdy miscreants went trampling heavy tread,
> And she has taken a vengeance dire on every Arab's head.
> A kafir youth like fullest moon in darkness hands her round
> Whose eyes are strongest cause of sin by him inspirited.

And Allah-gifted is the one who said:

> 'Tis as if wine and he who bears the bowl
> Rising to show her charms for man to see,
> Were dancing undurn-sun whose face the moon
> Of night adorned with stars of Gemini.

So subtle is her essence it would seem
Through every limb like course of soul runs she.

And how excellent is the saying of the poet:

Slept in my arms full moon of brightest blee
Nor did that sun eclipse in goblet see:
I nighted spying fire whereto bow down
Magicians, which bowed from ewer's lip to me.

And that of another:

It runs through every joint of them as runs
The surge of health returning to the sick.

And yet another:

I marvel at its pressers, how they died
And left us aqua vitae—lymph of life!

Yet goodlier is the saying of Abu Nowas:

Cease them to blame me, for your blame does anger bring
And with the draught that maddened me come medicining
A yellow girl whose court cures every carking care;
Were a stone to touch it would with joy and glee upspring:
She rises in her ewer during darkest night,
The house with brightest, sheeniest light illumining:
And going round of youths to whom the world inclines
Never, save in whatso way they please, their hearts shall wring.
From hand of coynted lass begarbed like yarded lad,
Wencher and people of Lot alike enamoring,
She comes: and say to him who dares claim lore of love
Something has learned but still there's many another thing.

But bets of all is the saying of Ibn al-Mu'tazz:

On the shady woody island his showers Allah deign
Shed on Convent called Abdun drop and drip of railing rain:
Often the breezes of the morning have awakened me therein
When the dawn shows her blaze, before the bird of flight was fain;
And the voices of the monks that with chants awoke the walls

Black-frocked shavelings ever wont the cup amorn to drain.
Amid the throng how many fair with languor-kohled eyes
And lids unfolding lovely orbs where black on white was lain,
In secret came to see me by shirt of night disguised,
In terror and in caution hurrying amain!
Then I rose and spread my cheek like a carpet on his path
In homage, and with skirts wiped his trail from off the plain.
But threatening disgrace rose the crescent in the sky
Like the paring of a nail, yet the light would never wane:
Then happened whatso happened: I disdain to kiss and tell;
So deem of us your best and with queries never mell.

And gifted of God is he who says,

In the morn I am richest of men
And in joy at good news I start up,
For I look on the liquid gold
And I measure it out by the cup.

And how fine is the saying of the poet:

By Allah, this is the only alchemy;
All said of other science false we see!
Carat of wine on hundredweight of woe
Transmutes gloomiest grief to joy and glee.

And that of another:

The glasses are heavy when empty brought
Till we charge them all with unmixed wine.
Then so light are they that to fly they're fain
As bodies lightened by soul divine.

And yet another:

Wine-cup and ruby wine high worship claim;
Dishonor it were to see their honor waste:
Bury me, when I'm dead, by side of vine
Whose veins shall moisten bones in clay misplaced;
Nor bury me in wold and wild, for I
Dread only after death no wine to taste."

The minister did not stop egging Ma'aruf on to drink, naming to him such of the virtues of wine as he thought well and reciting to him what occurred to him of poetry and pleasantries on the subject, until Ma'aruf addressed himself to sucking the cup-lips and cared no longer for anything else.

The minister did not stop filling Ma'aruf's cup, and Ma'aruf did not stop enjoying himself and making merry, until his wits wandered and he could not distinguish right from wrong.

When the minister saw that drunkenness in him was complete and transgressed the bounds, he said to him, "By Allah, Merchant Ma'aruf, I admire the way you got these jewels the likes of which the kings of the Chosroes do not possess! In all our lives, we have not seen a merchant who has heaped up riches like yours, or has been more generous than you. Your doings are the doings of kings, not merchants' doings. Allah upon you, tell me about this, so that I may know your rank and condition."

And he went on to test him with questions and to cajole him, until Ma'aruf, bereft of reason, said to him, "I am neither merchant nor king," and he told the minister his whole story from first to last.

Then the minister said, "I appeal to you by Allah, my lord, show us the ring, let us see its make."

In his drunkenness, Ma'aruf pulled the ring off, and said, "Take it and look at it."

The minister took it and, turning it over, said, "If I rub it, will its slaves appear?"

Ma'aruf replied, "Yes. Rub it, and he will appear to you. Divert yourself with the sight of him."

The minister rubbed the ring then, and the jinni appeared at once, and said, "Adsum, at your service, my lord! Ask and it shall be given to you. Will you ruin a city or raise a capital or kill a king? Whatever you seek, I shall do for you, without fail."

The minister pointed to Ma'aruf and said, "Take this wretch and cast him down in the most desolate of desert lands, where he shall find nothing to eat or drink, so that he may die of hunger and perish miserably, and no one know of him."

The jinni snatched him up and flew with him between heaven and earth. When Ma'aruf saw this, he was certain of his destruction, and he wept and said, "Abu al-Sa'adat, where are you going with me?"

The jinni replied, "I am going to cast you down in the desert quarter, you ill-bred person of gross wits. Shall one have the likes of this talisman and give it to folk to look at? Truly, you deserve what has befallen you, and were it not that I fear Allah, I would let you fall from a height of a thousand fathoms, and you would not reach the earth until the winds had torn you to shreds."

Ma'aruf was silent and did not speak again until he reached the desert quarter. The slave of the seal-ring cast him down there, went away, and left him in that horrible place.

So much concerning him.

Returning to the minister, who was now in possession of the talisman: he said to the king, "What do you think now? Did I not tell you that this fellow was a liar, an impostor, but you would not believe me?"

The king replied, "You were in the right, my minister, Allah grant you prosperity! But give me the ring, so that I may solace myself with the sight."

The minister looked at him angrily, and spat in his face, saying. "Lack-wits, how shall I give it to you and remain your servant after I have become your master? But I shall spare your life no more."

Then he rubbed the seal-ring, and said to the slave, "Take up this ill-mannered churl and cast him down by his son-in-law, the swindler."

So the jinni took the king and flew off with him.

The king said to him, "Creature of my lord, what is my crime?"

Abu al-Sa'adat said, "I do not know, but my master has commanded me, and I cannot cross the person who has the enchanted ring."

He flew on with him until he came to the desert quarter and, casting him down where he had cast Ma'aruf, he left him and returned.

The king, hearing Ma'aruf weeping, went to him and acquainted him with his case. They sat weeping over what had befallen them, and found neither meat nor drink.

Meanwhile, the minister, after driving father-in-law and son-in-law from the country, went forth from the garden and, summoning all the troops, held a council of state, and told them what he had done with the king and Ma'aruf, and acquainted them with the affair of the talisman, adding, "Unless you make me sultan over you, I will tell the slave of the seal-ring to take you up, one and all, and cast you down in the desert quarter where you shall die of hunger and thirst."

They replied, "Do us no damage, for we accept you as sultan over us, and will not in any way deny your commands."

They agreed, in their own despite, to his being sultan over them, and he bestowed on them robes of honor, seeking everything that he wanted from Abu al-Sa'adat, who brought it to him at once. Then he sat down on the throne and the troops did homage to him.

He sent to Princess Dunya, the king's daughter, saying, "Make yourself ready. I mean to come in to you tonight, because I long for you with love."

When she heard this, she wept, for the cases of her husband and father were grievous to her. She sent to the minister, saying, "Have patience with me until my period of widowhood [four months and ten days] is ended. Then draw up your contract of marriage with me, and go in to me according to law."

But he sent back to say to her, "I know neither period of widowhood nor to delay when I have a mood. I do not need a contract nor do I know lawful from unlawful. But I must go in to you tonight!"

She answered him, "So be it, then, and welcome to you!" But this was a trick on her part.

When her answer reached the minister, he rejoiced and his breast was broadened, because he was passionately in love with her.

He ordered that food be set before all the folk, saying, "Eat, this is my bride-feast, for I propose to go in to Princess Dunya tonight."

Sheikh al-Islam said, "It is not lawful for you to go in to her until her days of widowhood are ended and you have drawn up your contract of marriage with her."

But he answered, "I know neither days of widowhood nor any other period, so don't multiply words on me."

Sheikh al-Islam was silent, fearing the minister's mischief, and he said to the troops, "Truly, this man is an infidel, a miscreant. He has neither creed nor religious conduct."

As soon as it was evening, the minister went in to her and found her robed in her richest raiment and decked with her finest adornments.

When she saw him, she came to meet him, laughing. She said, "A blessed night! But it would have been more to my liking had you slain my father and my husband."

He said, "There is no help but I slay them."

She made him sit down, and began to jest with him and make a show of love, caressing him and smiling in his face, so that his reason fled. But she cajoled him with her coaxing and cunning only so that she might get possession of the ring and change his joy into calamity on the mother [crown] of his forehead. She dealt with him in this way, following the advice of him who said,

> I attained by my wits
> What no sword had obtained,
> And returned with the spoils
> Whose sweet pluckings I gained.

When he saw her caress him and smile upon him, desire surged up in him and he sought carnal knowledge of her.

But when he approached her, she drew away from him and burst into tears, saying, "My lord, do you not see the man looking at us? I appeal to you, by Allah, screen me from his eyes! How can you know me while he looks at us?"

When he heard this, the minister was angry, and he asked, "Where is the man?"

She answered, "There he is, in the bezel of the ring, putting out his head and staring at us!"

He thought that the jinni was looking at them, and said, laughing, "Don't be afraid. This is the slave of the seal-ring, and he is subject to me."

She said, "I am afraid of ifrits. Pull it off and throw it far from me."

So he took the ring off and, putting it on a cushion, drew near to her. But she kicked him, her foot striking him in the stomach, and he fell over on his back senseless.

She cried to her attendants, who came to her in haste. She said to them, "Seize him!"

Forty slave girls took hold of him while Princess Dunya hurriedly snatched up the ring from the cushion, and rubbed it.

Abu al-Sa'adat presented himself, saying, "Adsum, at your service, my mistress."

She cried, "Take up that infidel and clap him in jail, shackle him heavily."

So he took the minister and, having thrown him into the Prison of Wrath, returned, and reported, "I have put him in limbo."

She said, "Where did you go with my father and my husband?"

He said, "I cast them down in the desert quarter."

She said, "I command you to fetch them to me at once."

He replied, "I hear and I obey."

He flew off at once, and did not stop until he reached the desert quarter, where he came down on them and found them sitting, weeping and complaining to each other.

He said, "Do not fear, relief has come to you." And he told them what the minister had done, adding, "I indeed imprisoned him with my own hands, in obedience to her, and she has instructed me to carry you back."

They rejoiced in his news. He took them both up and flew home with them. It was no more than an hour before be brought them in to Princess Dunya, who rose and saluted her father and spouse. Then she made them sit down, she brought them food and sweetmeats, and they passed the rest of the night with her.

On the next day, she clad them in rich clothing, and said to the king, "My papa, sit on your throne and be king as before, and make my husband your minister of the right. Tell the troops what has happened. Then send to have the minister taken out of prison and have him die, then burn him, because he is a miscreant. He would have gone in to me in the way of lewdness, without the rites of marriage, and he has testified against himself that he is an infidel and believes in no religion. Treat your son-in-law tenderly, the one you make your minister of the right."

He replied, "Hearing and obeying, my daughter. But give me the ring, or give it to your husband."

She said, "It is not fitting that either you or he have the ring. I shall keep the ring myself, I shall likely be more careful of it than you. Whatever you want, ask me for it and I will demand it for you of the slave of the seal-ring. Fear no harm as long as I live. And, after my death, do what you two will with the ring."

The king said, "This is the right advice, my daughter." Taking his son-in-law, he went to the council.

The troops had passed the night in sore chagrin for Princess Dunya and what the minister had done with her, going in to her in that lewd way, without marriage rites, and for his poor treatment of the king and Ma'aruf. They were afraid lest the law of Islam be dishonored, because it was clear to them that he was an infidel. So they assembled in the council chamber and started to reproach Sheikh al-Islam, saying, "Why did you not forbid him from going in to the princess in a lewd way?"

He said, "Folk, the man is a miscreant and has gotten possession of the ring, and you and I may not prevail against him. But almighty Allah will punish him for his deed. Be silent, lest he kill you."

As the host was engaged in this discussion, the king and Ma'aruf entered the council.

Then the king gave orders that the city be decorated, and he sent to get the minister from the place of duress. They brought him, and, as he passed by the troops, they cursed him, abused him, and menaced him, until he came to the king, who commanded that he die by the vilest of deaths. So they killed him and then burned his body, and he went to hell after the foulest of plights. It is correctly said of him:

The Compassionate show no ruth to the tomb where his bones shall lie,
And Munkar and also Nakir never cease to abide there!

The king made Ma'aruf his minister of the right, and the times were pleasant to him and their joys were untroubled.

They lived in that way for five years until, in the sixth year, the king died and Princess Dunya made Ma'aruf sultan in her father's stead. But she did not give him the seal-ring.

During this time, she had conceived by him and borne him a boy of passing loveliness, excelling in beauty and perfection, who continued to be reared in the laps of nurses until he reached the age of five. Then his mother fell sick of a deadly sickness and, calling her husband to her, said to him, "I am ill."

He said, "Allah preserve you, darling of my heart!"

But she said, "Perhaps I shall die and I do not need to tell you to care for my son. Therefore, I charge you only be careful of the ring, for your own sake and for the sake of this your boy."

He answered, "No harm shall befall him whom Allah preserves!"

Then she pulled off the ring and gave it to him, and the next day she was admitted to the mercy of Allah the most high, while Ma'aruf lived in possession of the kingship and applied himself to the business of governing.

Now it happened one day, as he shook the handkerchief [in sign of dismissal] and the troops withdrew to their places, that he went to the sitting chamber where he sat until the day was gone and the night advanced with thick darkness. Then his cup-companions of the notables came in to him, as was their custom, and sat with him for his solace and diversion until midnight, when they asked permission to withdraw. He gave them leave, and they retired to their houses. After that, there came in to him a slave girl whose task was the service of his bed. She spread the mattress for him, and, removing his apparel, she clad him in his sleeping gown. Then he lay down and she kneaded his feet until sleep overpowered him. Then she withdrew to her own chamber and slept.

Suddenly, he felt something beside him in the bed. Awaking, he started up in alarm, and cried, "I seek refuge with Allah from Satan the stoned!"

He opened his eyes and, seeing by his side a woman foul of favor, he said to her, "Who are you?"

She said, "Fear not, I am your wife, Fatimah al-Urrah."

Then he looked in her face and knew her by her loathly form and the length of her dog-teeth.

He asked her, "When did you come in to me, and who brought you to this country?"

"In what country are you right now?"

"In the city of Ikhtiyan al-Khatan. But you, when did you leave Cairo?"

"But now."

"How can that be?"

"Know," she said, "that when I fell out with you and Satan prompted me to do you a damage, I complained of you to the magistrates, who looked for you, and the judges inquired of you, but did not find you. When two days had passed, I repented what I had done, and knew that the fault was with me. But patience did not help me, and I stayed for some days weeping because of your loss, until what was in my hand failed and I was obliged to beg for my bread. So I fell to begging from everyone, from the courted rich to the despised poor. Since you left me, I have eaten of the bitterness of beggary and have been in the sorriest of conditions. Every night, I sat weeping over our separation and what the sufferings that I endured since your departure, of humiliation and ignominy, of abjection and misery." She went on to tell him what had happened to her, while he stared at her in amazement, until she said, "Yesterday, I went around begging all day, but no one gave me a thing. As often as I accosted anyone and asked of him a crust of bread, he reviled me, and gave me nothing. When night came, I went to bed without supper, and hunger burned me, and sore on me was that which I have suffered.

"I sat weeping when one appeared to me and said, 'Woman, why are you weeping?'

"I said, 'I once had a husband who provided for me and fulfilled my wishes, but he is lost to me and I do not know where he has gone. I have been in sore straits since he left me.'

"He asked, 'What is your husband's name?'

"I answered, 'His name is Ma'aruf.'

"He said, 'I know him. Know that your husband is now sultan in a certain city. If you want, I shall carry you to him.'

"I cried, 'I am under your protection. Of your bounty, bring me to him!'

"So he took me up and flew with me between heaven and earth, until he brought me to this pavilion and said to me, 'Enter that chamber, and you shall see your husband asleep on the couch.'

"So I entered and found you in this state of lordship. I did not think that you would forsake me, your mate, and praised be Allah who has united you with me!"

Ma'aruf said, "Did I forsake you or you me? You complained of me from judge to judge, and ended by denouncing me to the high court and bringing down on me Abu Tabak from the citadel. So I fled in my own despite."

He went on to tell her all that had befallen him, and how he had become sultan and had married the king's daughter, and how his beloved Dunya had died, leaving him a son who was then seven years old.

She said, "What happened was foreordained of Allah. But I repent, and I place myself under your protection, beseeching you not to abandon me, but allow me to eat bread with you by way of alms."

She did not stop humbling herself to him and supplicating him until his heart relented towards her, and he said, "Repent from mischief, and stay with me. Nothing shall happen to you except what gives you pleasure. But if you work any wickedness, I shall kill you and fear no one. Do not think that you can complain of me to the high court and that Abu Tabak will come down on me from the citadel, for I have become sultan and the folk dread me. But I fear no one save Allah almighty, because I have a talismanic ring. When I rub it, the slave of the signet appears to me. His name is Abu al-Sa'adat, and whatever I demand of him he beings to me. So, if you want to return to your own country, I shall give you what shall suffice you for the rest of your life, and will send you there speedily. But, if you desire to remain with me, I shall clear for you a palace, and furnish it with the choicest of silks, and appoint you twenty slave girls to serve you, and provide you with dainty dishes and sumptuous clothing, and you shall be a queen and live in delight until you die or I die. What do you say of this?"

"I wish to stay with you," she answered, and kissed his hand and vowed repentance from her frowardness.

Accordingly, Ma'aruf set aside a palace for her sole use, and gave her slave girls and eunuchs, and she became a queen.

The young prince visited her as he visited his father, but she hated him because he was not her son. When the boy saw that she looked at him with the eye of aversion and anger, he shunned her and took a dislike to her.

As for Ma'aruf, he occupied himself with the love of fair handmaidens and did not think of his wife, Fatimah the Dung, because she had grown into a grizzled old fright, foul-favored to the sight, a baldheaded blight, loathlier than the snake speckled black and white, the moreso because she had had acted towards him in an evil way beyond measure in the past. As the old adage says, "Ill-usage the root of desire divides and sows hate in the soil of hearts." And God-gifted is he who says:

> Beware of losing hearts of men by your injurious deed;
> For when aversion takes his place none may dear love restore:
> Hearts, when affection flies from them, are like glass
> Which, broken, cannot be made whole—it is breached forevermore.

And indeed, Ma'aruf had not given her shelter because of any praiseworthy quality in her, but he dealt with her generously only out of desire for the approval of almighty Allah. He would have nothing to do with his wife by way of conjugal duty.

When she saw that he held aloof from her bed and occupied himself with other women, she hated him, and jealousy mastered her, and Iblis prompted her to take the seal-ring from him, slay him, and make herself queen in his stead.

So she went forth one night from her pavilion, going to the pavilion of her husband, King Ma'aruf. It chanced by decree of the Decreer and his written destiny that Ma'aruf lay that night with one of his concubines, a woman endowed with beauty and loveliness, symmetry, and a stature all grace. It was his custom, out of the excellence of his piety, that when he was minded to lie with a woman, he would take off the enchanted seal-ring from his finger, in reverence to the holy names engraved on it, and lay it on the pillow. He would not put it on again until he had purified himself by the complete ablution. Moreover, when he had lain with a woman, he was used to order her to leave him before daybreak, out of fear for the seal-ring. When he went to the bath, he locked the door of the pavilion until his return, after which he put on his ring. Then all were free to enter, according to custom.

His wife, Fatimah the Dung, knew of all this, and did not go forth from her place until she had made certain of the case. So she sallied out, when the night was dark, proposing to go in to him while he was drowned in sleep and steal the ring, unseen by him.

Now it chanced at this time that the king's son had gone out, without light, to the chapel of ease for an occasion, and sat down over the marble slab of the jakes in the dark, leaving the door open.

Presently, he saw Fatimah come out of her pavilion and move stealthily to that of his father.

He said to himself, "What ails this witch to leave her lodging in the dead of the night and make for my father's pavilion? There must be some reason for this."

So he went out after her, following in her steps, unseen by her. Now he had a short sword of watered steel that he held so dear that he did not go to his father's council unless he had it on. His father used to laugh at him, and exclaim, "Mahallah! This is a mighty fine sword of yours, my son! But you have not gone down with it to battle or cut off a head with it." The boy would reply, "I shall not fail to cut off with it some head that deserves cutting." And Ma'aruf would laugh at his words. Now, treading in her track, he drew the sword from its sheath, and he followed her until she came to his father's pavilion and entered, while he stood and watched her from the door.

He saw her searching about, and heard her say to herself, "Where has he laid the seal-ring?"

Then he knew that she was looking for the ring, and he waited until she found it and said, "Here it is." Then she picked it up and turned to go out. But he hid behind the door.

As she came out, she looked at the ring and turned it about in her hand. But when she was about to rub it, he raised his hand with the sword and hit her on the neck. She cried a single cry, and fell down dead.

With this, Ma'aruf awoke and, seeing his wife strewn on the ground with her blood flowing and his son standing with the drawn sword in his hand, said to him, "What is this, my son?"

He replied, "My father, how often have you said to me, 'You have a mighty fine sword, but you have not gone down with it to battle or cut off a head.' And I have answered you, saying, 'I shall not fail to cut off with it a head that deserves cutting.' Now, look, I have cut off a head for you, a head well worth the cutting!"

He told Ma'aruf what had happened. Ma'aruf sought the seal-ring, but did not find it. So he searched the dead woman's body until he saw her hand closed upon it.

He took it from her grasp, and said to the boy, "You are indeed my very son, without doubt or dispute. Allah ease you in this world and the next, as you have eased me of this vile woman! Her attempt led only to her own destruction, and Allah-gifted is he who said:

> When forwards Allah's aid a man's intent,
> His wish in every case shall find consent:
> But if that aid of Allah be refused,
> His first attempt shall do him damagement."

Then King Ma'aruf called to some of his attendants, who came in haste, and he told them what his wife, Fatimah the Dung, had done. He told them to take her and lay her in a place until morning. They did his bidding.

The next day, Ma'aruf gave her in charge to a number of eunuchs, who washed her, shrouded her, made her a tomb, and buried her. Her coming from Cairo was but to her grave, and Allah-gifted is he who said:

> We trod the steps appointed for us:
> and he whose steps are appointed must tread them.
> He whose death is decreed to take place in our land
> shall not die in any land but that.

And how excellent is the saying of the poet:

> I know not, when to a land I fare,
> Good luck pursuing, what my lot shall be:
> Whether the fortune I perforce pursue
> Or the misfortune that pursues me.

After this, King Ma'aruf sent for the husbandman, whose guest he had been when he was a fugitive, and made him his minister of the right and his chief councillor. Then, learning that this husbandman had a daughter of passing beauty and loveliness, of qualities ennobled at birth and exalted of worth, he married her, and in due time he married his son.

So they lived a while in all solace of life and its delight, and their days were serene and their joys untroubled, until there came to them the destroyer of delights and the sunderer of societies, the depopulator of populous places and the ophaner of sons and daughters.

And glory be to the Living who does not die and in whose hands are the keys of the seen and the unseen.

Commentary

Alf Layla wa Layla, A Thousand and One Nights, is a collection composed of Persian stories that were adapted into Arabic in about the ninth century AD. The Persian stories contained influences from India. Later, between the tenth and twelfth centuries, a new layer of stories was added to the collection from in and around Baghdad. Between the eleventh and fourteen centuries, stories composed in Egypt were appended. The modern form of the collection dates from the fifteenth century. For one thousand years, from the ninth century to the eighteenth century, the collection was altered, modernized, and expanded. There is much variation in the various manuscripts and in the early Arabic editions of the work. The different versions did not necessarily contain one thousand and one nights, although modern compilers, in their efforts to bring it to that number, added stories from other sources.

◇ **The structure of A Thousand and One Nights**—It is a frame story: a series of stories is told within the frame of a larger story. The idea is to keep the audience in a state of continual suspense. This is the frame of the story: King Shahryar has been betrayed by his wife. He discovers that he has been cuckolded by his wife and by his ten favorite concubines. He therefore beheads them. To assure that his future wives are faithful, he marries a new queen every night, beheading her at the end of the night. This goes on for three years, until finally the people rise up in protest, and King Shahryar's wazir, the state minister, can find no young women willing to give up their lives to be queen for one night. The wazir then offers his own daughter, Shahrazad (Sheherazade). She develops the stratagem of entertaining the king with a different, unfinished story every night, so that his curiosity about hearing the ending delays his ordering her death. Shahrazad is successful. Three years pass, she bears Shahryar three children and entertains him for a thousand and one nights, and she is accepted as the new and permanent queen.

"Ma'aruf the Cobbler and His Wife" is one of the Egyptian contributions to the collection of stories. The main patterns are as follows. In pattern one, Fatimah complains that Ma'aruf has beaten her. In pattern two, Ma'aruf, a trickster, pretends to be a merchant, and borrows much money from merchants and the king, eventually turning his friend, Ali, against him. The king and the merchants are duped by him. Pattern three is built on the minister's suspicions and his jealousy of Ma'aruf. He arouses the king's suspicions, but the greedy king wants to believe Ma'aruf. Pattern four has to do with truth. Ma'aruf tells Dunya the truth, tells the minister the truth, tells Fatimah the truth. Pattern five involves the ring of gold and the jinni, and much wealth. Ma'aruf makes an honest man of himself. The pattern becomes more complex as Ma'aruf, the minister, Dunya, Fatimah all get control of the ring. Pattern six is the pattern of wives that controls the theme of the story: Fatimah (negative) and Dunya (positive).

◇ **Fantasy and reality**—Ma'aruf tells the big lie, then the jinni (fantasy) makes the lie reality. But this is largely a story of greed: the minister wants Dunya, the king and merchants want wealth, with Ma'aruf, a bright trickster kind of character, walking among them; he is honest (the pattern of truth) and therefore vulnerable, but he wins. Fatimah, the king, the merchants, the minister: all are arrayed against him. Ma'aruf is characterized by honesty and by generosity especially to the needy, he pays his debts. He is also a trickster and a liar.

Notes

The storyteller attaches a theme to motifs and patterns: The pattern of wives, Fatimah (negative) to Dunya (positive), is the route taken by Ma'aruf, as he moves from dreams, deception, and trickery to reality. The movement of the story: Ma'aruf leaves home, a tainted society. In a far-off land, he is swallowed by a splendid city. His ordeal is dealing with greed, to survive becoming a trickster. His return has to do with overcoming greed.

The ring symbolism attests to Ma'aruf's honesty, goodness. Others, greedy, attempt to take it. Finally, it is in the control of his wife. The first wife must be seen as villainous, greedy, and is a real-life version of the king, the minister, the merchants.

Ma'aruf moves from one tainted society to another, but he controls the second with his trickery. That is his ordeal. The return is his ability now to cope with his situation.

The climax: what he did to the merchants and king and minister, his son now does to the wife. It is the passing of the torch from one generation to the next.

The Igbo . . . have a great fondness for fairy tales. They have a big stock of legends and folklore. . . . On paper, expression and gesture are lost, and these are just the elements that make the stories live. The Igbo is a good storyteller, with a faculty of putting reality into fables. He uses as illustrations animals and birds in such a way that they seem to be endowed with human powers. He can conjure up an atmosphere, and carry his audience with him, and thus provide a thrilling entertainment. Some are good mimics and add to the enjoyment by emulating the sounds of the animals and birds they impersonate.

George Thomas Basden, *Niger Ibos* (London: Cass, 1938), p. 424.

Ndau

The Sky Princess and the Poor Youth

The Ndau live in Mozambique.

It happened, it happened. . . .

There was a chief who lived in heaven. He had a child, a very beautiful girl. This princess had as attendants a nurse and other girls, with whom she played. The girls who were with the princess were very beautiful. All were supremely beautiful.

Every day, the princess and her nurse and the other girls came down from the sky to bathe in a lake which was nice. The lake was near a forest. The princess and her girls came down and went up to the sky by means of plumes which they had.

When the sky girls came to bathe in the lake, and the young men of earth saw them, they wanted to court them, but when these girls saw the men coming to the lake, they came out of the water, took their plumes, and flew away, going up to the sky.

Many youths, the sons of chiefs and noblemen, wanted to marry the princess. They wanted to take her plume. Some of the youths would take the plume of the girls. When a youth took the plume of the girl, she could not go with the other girls to the sky, but she would follow the youth, singing and playing her reed rattle. If the youth looked back, the plume would fly away from him and go to the girl, and the girl would fly away, going to the sky. These young men would take the plume, and, when they heard the girl singing and playing her reed rattle, would look back, and the plume would go to its owner.

From Franz Boas and C. Kamba Simango, "Tales and Proverbs of the Vandau of Portuguese South Africa," *Journal of American Folk-Lore* 35 (1922): 200–201.

When the sons of royalty and of nobility had failed to take the sky girls, a youth, the son of a poor man, said that he would go and try to take the plume of the sky princess.

Those youths who had failed to take the plume laughed heartily at him, but he persisted, saying that he would go and try to take the plume of the sky princess.

He hid himself in the forest.

The sky girls arrived, and, after they had gone into the water, this youth took the plume of the princess. When the girls saw that he had taken the plume, they came out of the water. They took their own plumes and flew away.

The princess remained.

She began to play her reed rattle, singing,

> "Dear young man, ndekande!
> Listen to my rattle, ndekande!"

Audience: Keep still!
Storyteller: "Just look, ndekande!"
Audience: Keep still!
Storyteller: "Dear young man, ndekande!
I want to go, ndekande!"
Audience: Keep still!
Storyteller: "Dear young man, ndekande!
Child, look now, ndekande!"
Audience: Keep still!
Storyteller: "Dear young man, ndekande!"
Audience: Keep still!
Storyteller: "I want to go, ndekande!"

But the youth did not look back. When he had walked a long way, the princess spoke to the young man, saying, "Wait, you shall marry me!"

The youth stopped, and the princess said, "You shall go with me to my home in the sky."

The sky princess and the young man went to the sky.

Commentary

In a story that has mythic echoes of the story of Nambi and Kintu (story 9), a love tale and a story of the heavens are joined by a "Cinderella" image. The poor youth, laughed at by his wealthy and powerful counterparts, breaks the pattern that his more privileged peers earlier established: They did not have the strength to avoid looking back when the sky girl sang her song. He breaks that pattern, and so marries the sky princess, joining heaven and earth.

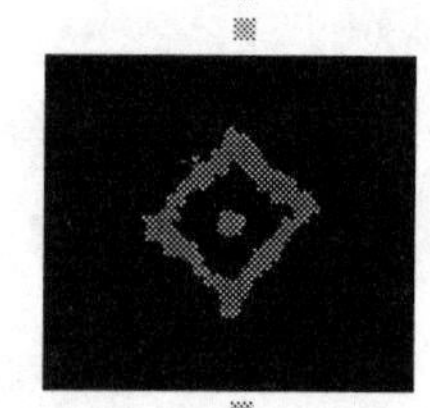

The sequence of a narrative is unique and has a specific beginning and end. Its seemingly random and unpredictable progression through time, the end of which is not known until it is over, is like the life of an individual. Narrative patterns, which give a sense of order that exists because of, and yet apart from, sequence, is like society, timeless and eternal. The experience of the fusion of these two dimensions—sequence and form, diachrony and synchrony, time and timelessness, individual and social existence—mediates the most basic of human contradictions. In this way, art makes sense of life whose parts we can never see in relation to the whole. Once the form of a life can be known to itself, it no longer exists. We do with our art forms that which we cannot do with our lives.

Deborah Foster, "Structure and Performance of Swahili Oral Narrative," Diss., University of Wisconsin-Madison, 1984, p. 197.

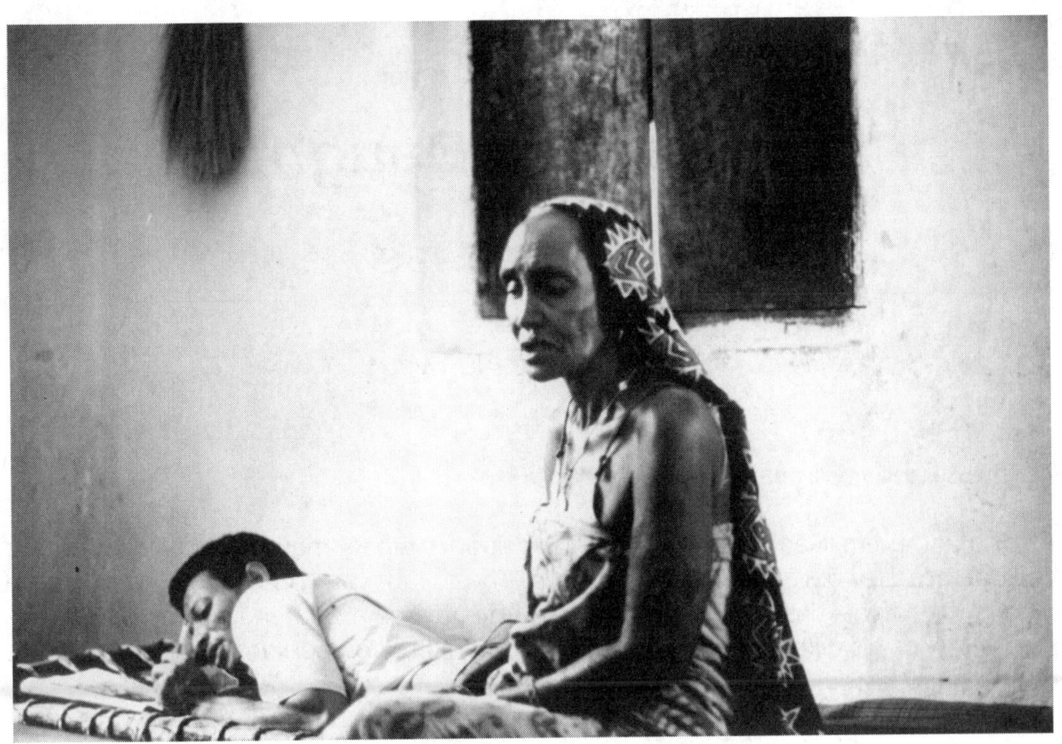

Mwaziza Jugwe, a Swahili storyteller (photo by Deborah Foster)

Swahili

The Pauper's Daughter

by Mwaziza Jugwe

The Swahili live in eastern Africa.

Long ago there lived a rich man, his advisor, an ordinary man and a pauper of God. Together they built a town. Time passed. The sultan, with his relatives and children, lived in the town—the sultan, the rich man, the advisor, and their relatives. The pauper lived with his wife far from the center of town, at Kifombani (the poor section of town). Time passed.

One day, the sultan married, the rich man married, the advisor married. The wife of the rich man, God granting, became pregnant. She bore a child, a girl, the daughter of the rich man. The wife of the sultan became pregnant. She was in her eighth month when the sultan went to call Memwandazi: "Memwandazi, Memwandazi, come home with me to help my wife who is in her eighth month now."

Memwandazi said, "No, I can't go. Go call Mzungu-wa-ngia [lit., 'European of the road,' a nickname of the narrator]." And Mzungu-wa-ngia is me. I was called to stay at the sultan's house until the ninth month.

The wife of the sultan gave birth. She gave birth to a boy, the son of the sultan.

The wife of the pauper became pregnant. The pauper had no work, he only fished. He would go to the seashore and catch only one fish, which he would cut in half. Half he would sell and half he would use for sauce. His wife remained pregnant

Date of performance: March, 1977. Place: The town of Vanga in Kenya. Performer: Mwaziza Jugwe, a Swahili woman. Collected and translated from Swahili by Deborah Foster.

until the time arrived, the ninth month. She had labor pains. The pauper went out at night, calling in the town, "You Muslims, help me! My wife is having labor pains, and I am alone in the house. I have no witness. So, Muslims, who will follow me and look after my wife?"

He was told, "There at Ulaya (another section of town) is a woman called Memwandazi."

The pauper went running. He called, "Memwandazi, Memwandazi!"

She replied, "I am unable. Go to Mwaziza Hamadi's house. There is a woman there called Mzungu-wa-ngia, Mwaziza Jugwe."

He went to Mwaziza Hamadi, and knocked. She asked him, "What do you want?"

He asked her, "Is there a person here called Mzungu-wa-ngia?"

I said, "I'm here."

The pauper told her, "I have been sent here by Memwandazi. My wife is in labor, and I am a poor man. I want you to come with me."

She said, "All right, let's go."

When we reached the pauper's house, his wife was alone and having labor pains. God granting, we stayed with her until she gave birth. She gave birth. As for me, I became the midwife. I stayed there until the pauper's wife reached the fortieth day. But the pauper had nothing to give me. For the hakisalama (gift given to the nurse or midwife of the new mother), the pauper gave me four rupees (at the time of rupees). He said to me, "Ndugu [a term of familiarity or fondness], take it. I am a poor man only."

I told him, "All right," and I returned home.

The sultan's wife had already borne her first child, Kibwana. She became pregnant again, the sultan's wife. Her pregnancy continued until it reached its months. The sultan's wife! And I was her midwife! Memwandazi was again unable to go. I stayed in the house until the sultan's wife gave birth. She bore a male child, Mohamedi, the sultan's son. She closed the book (an idiom indicating the termination of further child bearing). After Kibwana and Mohamedi, no more child bearing for the sultan. The pauper's child, Kibibi, was very pretty, like me. The pauper's work was the same, fishing.

The sultan raised his child, Mohamedi. And the pauper raised his child, his daughter. Time passed. The pauper's work was the same, fishing. He would go to the seashore, get one fish, cut it in half, sell one piece, and eat the other. Time passed until the pauper's child had milk in her chest (i.e., attained puberty).

The pauper's wife became ill with a serious fever. Her husband could not leave her side to go to the seashore. He stayed home with his child and his wife. One day, the fever became very bad.

She said, "My husband, come nearer, come nearer." She said, "The healthy person can die and the sick person can survive, but I see myself with this fever. I am not well, perhaps I will journey. One thing I ask of you. When I die, for the sake of my child, don't marry, pauper, until my child gets a husband. Even if a Mnyamwezi [a Tanzanian people] comes, or a Mduruma [a Kenyan people] comes, marry her to him. Then if you want a wife, marry her."

The pauper's wife died. The pauper was alone in the house, only he and his child. He ran to the sultan's house, his hands holding his head.

"Say, pauper, what is it?"

He replied, "My wife has died and I am alone with my child. Now what am I to do?"

"And this only is the reason you are crying, pauper?"

He answered, "This only."

The sultan said, "All right, stay here." He called the people from Kiungani and Magaoni (sections of the town). He said to them. "Go help the pauper. Women, wash his wife. Men, dig the grave."

We went to Kofumbani to help the pauper. We women washed his wife, the men dug the grave. God granting, it was finished. She was wrapped in a shroud. The pauper's wife went to be buried.

"So, people, the pauper is alone here. Let us sit with him, even if we sit three days. We shall help the poor man."

We sat there until the mourning period had ended. At the end of the third day, we all went our own ways. We left the pauper with his child. The pauper's work was the same, fishing. He caught only one fish. The child stayed in the house. She had become a grown woman with full breasts on her chest. She had become a woman, and yet a man had not yet come to ask for her in marriage.

Now I return to the house of the sultan and his two children, Kibwana and Mohamedi.

Now Kibwana told his father, "I want a wife."

"Which wife?"

He told him. "The daughter of the rich man."

That small child of the rich man became betrothed.

Now the pauper's work was the same, fishing. He had no other work and still he caught only one fish, neither more nor less. In the house it was the daughter who cooked, it was she who served, it was indeed she who did everything. I return to that place now.

There was a woman whose husband passed away. She had one child. One morning, two or three months after the death of her husband, she left her house at dawn.

"Today I am going to the pauper's house. I haven't been there to visit since his wife died. Today I am going to greet him." She went there, she knocked on the door. "Hello, daughter of the pauper. Hello."

"Yes?"

"Why do you remain silent?" the woman asked the girl.

She answered, "What am I to do?"

"Wake up, and open the door!"

"Who are you?"

"Just me, open the door for me!"

The child went and opened the door for her. The woman entered the house.

"Mh, where is your father?"

The daughter told her, "Father has gone to the seashore."

"Ah, poor thing. He is surely in trouble to leave such a small child alone here in the house without even a friend. She has no one. Someone might come to do her harm "

The child asked her, "What am I to do? I have no father, my father is at the seashore. And here in the house, mama has died. Here in the house, I have no friend. I want to cat, and father wants to eat—so should he just stay here in the house to guard me? How would it be if he didn't go to the sea?"

The woman took a broom and swept. She finished. She went to the well and drew water. She filled the birika (a cistern in the house for all the household water). There was corn—she pounded it, she ground it, she finished.

"So, mama [title often used affectionately for women or girls, regardless of age or relationship], goodbye. I'm going home. When your father returns, greet him for me."

She went home, that woman, the first day.

The second day, the woman performed the same tasks. She continued doing that for a month.

Finally, she said, "Today, I'm waiting for the pauper to come home. I have a craving for fish relish."

What was the fish relish the pauper was going to give her when he caught only one fish?

"Well, Mamie Fulani [lit., Mother of So-and-so], how are you?"

"I'm fine. Mh, pauper, my brother, I have a craving, and my craving is for fish relish."

He told her, "And I, I have a problem, and my problem is fish relish. Since I began fishing, the fish I catch every day is only this one. I cut one piece to sell and with the other piece I make our relish. Now what can I give you? Oh well, this is today's piece—you take it." He gave it to the woman.

She took it and went home. Now that woman had what she wanted from the pauper.

One day, the woman told the pauper, "I have a question. If a man is widowed by his wife, is it surprising?"

"What do you mean?"

She told him. "Why don't you marry me? Your child will be getting a companion."

He said, "That's a thought." The pauper thought to himself, "My wife told me not to marry. If I do marry, what will happen to my child?"

That woman stuck to her point with the pauper. You know, "That which is sharpened must become sharp, even if it is wood."

The pauper told his child, "My child, I want to marry this woman. What do you say?"

She told him, "Marry her. That is your right. If you marry, is it I who will pay the dowry? Marry her. What would be wrong if I get a companion? Marry her."

The pauper married the woman. He married her, he finished. He took his wife and her child and came to the house. Now how many people are there? There are four—the wife and her child, the pauper and his child. They lived that way. Time passed.

The pauper and his fishing were the same, only one fish. One piece he sells, and one piece he uses for relish.

Later, the child of the sultan had finished becoming betrothed to the daughter of the rich man. A wedding was being prepared for. An announcement was made (when the horn sounds, there is something important): "You are called to the house of the sultan. Men only."

People went. They were told, "Listen, I want a house built for a wedding. My child wants to marry the daughter of the rich man."

So the men entered—he who breaks stones, he who whitewashes, he who cuts trees. At the end of a month, the house was finished. Everything was ready.

Those like Mwaziza Hamadi were called: "You people, this announcement is for women. You are called to the house of the sultan."

People went. The pauper's wife went also. A bag of flour was cut. It was said, "Bakora [special wedding cakes, very sweet] must be made."

Mwaziza Hamadi said, "That's the work I want."

People made those wedding cakes until all the flour was used up. No one ate at his own house, no one drank at his own house, no one took snuff at his own house, everything was done at the house of the sultan. Those who had husbands ate there, and those who had no husbands ate there. They kneaded that flour until it was finished.

When is the wedding? The ninth month (in the Arabic calendar). It was prepared in that way. And the pauper was also at the sultan's. He was not going to the seashore now. When he received food, he sent it to his child. The pauper's wife was also there. There in the house were the child of the husband and the child of the wife.

So it went. Time passed. On the ninth month, the crescent moon was seen. A letter was written to all the towns. The people came to see the dancing. Santana was there, Stafu was there, Chembe was there (locally known dance groups). All the dance groups met in the town. The sultan brought soap for us, and we were wrapped in new cloth (according to custom). The dancers met each other. Mama Mzungu-wa-ngia became involved the way she wanted to. And so it went until the twenty-seventh day of the month, when they wanted the wedding to take place.

The pauper's wife told her child, "Do you know, pauper's daughter, that I shall be leaving this house. The wedding is Friday."

The daughter of the pauper now became annoyed with her stepmother. She wanted to beat her with a stick. Ah! She wanted to beat her with a stick, but she saw that it wasn't right. The stepmother's daughter didn't do any work, she didn't cook, she didn't prepare food—she did nothing at all. All the work was done by the daughter of the pauper. And his daughter did not say a word, she was silent, she was becoming thin. She remembered the words of her mother: "Pauper, don't get married. If you marry, you are going to trouble my child." But the father had not listened to these words, he had married.

Time passed.

One day, when the pauper went to the seashore, God granting it, he got fish. Even the dhow was about to sink! He lowered himself out of the dhow, and pushed the boat with his legs.

He went that day to sell all those fish. He bought new clothes for his child, he bought clothes for his wife, he got a basket full of sugar, he bought rice and oil. He went home.

The next day, when he went to the sea, the fish were the same as the day before yesterday. The third day the pauper went fishing, he caught two changu (a type of scaled fish) and one chafi (a type of scaleless fish), that big chafi with a tiny head.

He said, "Today, even if the sultan appears from nowhere to give me a bag of money, I don't want it. I will eat these three fish. Today I will rid myself of this craving for fish!"

He hid the fish in the bottom of the boat. After selling one fish, he went home, and called, "Daughter, come and scale these fish!"

The stepmother laughed derisively. "Heh! Today we will satisfy our craving for fish! Mh! Today many fish are available—fat ones, fat ones! Take them, go prepare them at the sea front."

She gave them to the pauper's daughter. The child took the fish to the seashore. She prepared them. She scaled the changu, and she was about to pierce the chafi when it said, "Stop! You have no manners! Nor do your father and mother! That father of yours comes and takes me from my place in the sea, and then you come and stab me and eat me! Now throw me back! I should go home, my children are crying."

Umh! The poor child was puzzled. Should she keep the fish or throw it back? She was confused. She realized that if she threw the fish back she would be beaten at home by her stepmother. But, mh! She slowly tipped the plate and let the fish slip into the water, chubwi!

The pauper's daughter was puzzled. "Mh! You, fish, are going your own way in the water. But what am I going to tell that devil?"

The fish came up and said, "Daughter of the pauper, why aren't you going home?"

She said, "I'm not going. If I go home with only these two fish, mama will beat me."

The fish told her, "You go. Let her beat you, let her kill you, but you go! As for me, goodbye. But, child of the pauper. I will tell you one thing: if you are pushed to the breaking point, come here. If someone does something to you, make haste until you come here." The chafi said these words to the child of the pauper. He continued, "So goodbye, go home, daughter of the pauper." The fish entered the water, and went home.

And the pauper's daughter went home, weak.

When she arrived, "Dohsalala Muhamedi [an all-purpose exclamation], do you mean to tell me that you have been preparing that fish ever since you left? Do you have a basket full of fish, or just those two? And explain to me where the chafi is!"

"The fish was taken by a hawk."

She was slapped right there.

She went outside to cry. With bitterness, she thought of her mother and father—her father who was told by her mother not to marry. "Father has married like this, and I am killed." The child cried until she licked salt.

Her father found her, and asked, "Why are you crying?"

She replied, "I have been beaten by mama."

"For what reason?"

"I went to the seashore to scale the fish, and one fish was stolen by a hawk. When I told this to mama, she beat me."

Her father grieved. He said, "This is the way it is. I was told by my wife not to marry, but I went against those words and married. Nevertheless, what's done is done. All right, be quiet, my child. You will grow up."

The pauper went to ask his wife, "Why has that child been crying?"

"I beat her."

"What for?"

"She took the fish and bribed a hawk with it."

"Mh, my wife, the fish was taken by the hawk, isn't that so?"

"I have beaten her. What do you want me to do now?"

"Just stop." The words were finished.

The pauper's daughter was hungry, but she was not given food. Again, it was because of her stepmother. The stepmother and her own daughter ate together and were satisfied. The pauper's daughter was given only the crumbs, she had to scrape the pot for her dinner. But cooking, sweeping, and all the work were hers. The stepmother's daughter did nothing.

The child ran quickly like a bird to the seashore to find her friend. When she arrived, the chafi was right there. He was waiting for her. He took her with him into the water, and they went to eat. Her hunger was satisfied. Then he sent her back home.

Time passed.

The wedding was bring held at the home of the sultan. People were rushing around, people like Mwaziza Hamadi, like Fatuma Seif [both are members of the audience]. They were all running around like chickens all over the town. Everyone was involved. If you had been pregnant, you would have had a miscarriage.

Now, when is the wedding? It is Friday. Today is Tuesday, tomorrow is Wednesday, day after tomorrow is Thursday, that day Friday is indeed the day of the wedding. At six o-clock on Friday, the sultan will be marrying his son Kibwana to Fatuma, the daughter of the rich man.

Now on that day, Tuesday, the mother of the daughter of the pauper, that stepmother, said, "Today, God granting, I am going to the wedding with my child. You stay here and guard the house of your father. You don't come to the wedding!"

The child said, "Mh, I am not going anywhere. You go your own way."

They left, the stepmother and her daughter. The pauper's daughter remained alone there in the little house. She stayed there alone. Even her father was at the wedding. The sultan was having a wedding, the pauper would stay there. He stayed there, and the child stayed at home. "Ah, a huge ceremony there in town, But I am not going. I will go to the place of my friend, the chafi."

The chafi arrived, "Well, daughter of the pauper?" She told him, "Mama has gone to the wedding, father has gone to the wedding, even my stepsister has gone to the wedding. I was told not to go."

"Well, what is it you want?"

"I want to go to see that ceremony!"

He told her, "Well then, today is Tuesday, tomorrow Wednesday, Thursday, Friday is the wedding. Friday morning let me see you here." The chafi told her, "Go home now."

Time passed, until Thursday. She swept in the morning, she washed the dishes, she prepared, she prepared. She slept soundly until dawn. She awoke, she opened the door for the chickens. While it was still dark, they went outside. She swept, she finished. At five a.m., the pauper's daughter went out.

In town, Mwaziza Jugwe came at the head of Santana.

The child passed her on her way to the seashore.

The chafi was there waiting. "Well, daughter of the pauper, you have come."

She said, "Uhuh."

He told her, "Enter." Chubwi! into the sea. There was a very small horse there. The chafi said, "Quickly, put the horse in your womb, daughter of the pauper."

She put the horse in, she shook it and shook it. She took it out, and the chafi told her, "Not yet." The third time she took it out, the daughter of the pauper looked stunning—like that European daughter-in-law of mine who is sitting there (referring to the collector). She was wearing bracelets, a woven necklace, earrings of gold, tremendous! Golden sandals were put on her feet. A horse was prepared and given to her. It was five o'clock.

In town, dohsalala, things were bustling. People were bumping into each other, I swear, like that. Money was just thrown by the sultan.

The daughter of the pauper was brought out from the seashore. The daughter of the pauper was loaded with clothes, completely—beautiful clothes, not like these of mine. She was put on the horse and given an umbrella which opened quickly—ga. She was covered. On either side of the horse rested a sandal of gold.

The horse said, "Um-hu, there you are. Very well."

And off he flew with the daughter of the pauper, up and up. The horse went as far as Jimbo, then as far as Ngoa (nearby towns). He went as far as that slowly, slowly.

It was six o'clock.

Kibwana went to the lavatory to wash. He put on his finery, and went to the mosque. The dance groups gathered. The trumpeters gathered. Chaos was everywhere, we were rushing about. People gathered. Kibwana went to the mosque, he was married, finished. "God is great. Keba hoo keba [a song sung when a groom is going to the house of his bride]," until he entered the house. Kibwana appeared.

Ululation. Women were running in the streets. Chaos all around the house. Kibwana entered the house. The attendant of the bride, who was Mwaziza Hamadi, entered.

He extended his hand to her, and said, "I was warmed by my mother" (a euphemism meaning that he will not be impotent).

Mwaziza reported that he had fired the cannon, "Dohsalala!"

He gave his bride her reward (a gift is given to the bride if she is a virgin).

Then the pilau was cooked, it was eaten, it was thrown. There was plenty of food, nobody could finish it. A pit was dug for it, and the remains were thrown in. All those like the pauper of God picked at it.

The pauper's daughter did not eat. She did not bother. She just walked with the horse, she just walked. And so it went until the wedding was finished. People went home then. Those like Mwaziza Jugwe stayed there. They swept, they scraped the dishes. Money was just wasted.

Later, the servant of the sultan was sweeping around the mats when he saw something glittering in the doorway.

"Mh! What's that?"

He went closer. My god, it was a gold sandal.

"Prophet!" He started to pant. "I should go to the master, Chibwana" (the narrator imitates his accent in a derogatory way).

"Wait! I'll tell him." Mwaziza Hamadi went. "Sir, your servant wants to tell you something."

He sat there on the chair with his fan, fanning himself. He said, "Let him come, that servant. What word does he have for me?"

He came. "Sir, I found something by chance."

The sultan asked, "What thing?"

He talks through his nose: "The shoe, have you seen it?"

The sultan told him, "Sleep until morning. When you wake, go to every house and measure the foot of every person—even if he is a one-eyed person, measure him also. If it happens that the shoe fits someone exactly, put it on that person and bring him here. Begin at the edge of town, and go to its other end. If you fail in this town, then go to another town!"

The servant said, "Praise be to God, that which I wanted I have received."

The pauper and his wife had entered their house, they were resting there. The people from the sultan's place had not yet come. They were waiting.

That child, after she had dropped her sandal, returned to the water of the fish, and was changed back to the way she had been. She went to her small house.

The servant searched and searched with the sandal. He went one way, he met people sitting, he measured feet. Alas, one was too short, the others were too thin. The servant continued for half a month until he had searched the entire town. What remained?

The servant said, "I want to finish this town. If I hit, if I miss, I will be sent to another town."

Papapapa (a sound to indicate traveling) until four o'clock. He went to Kifombani to the home of the pauper. The pauper's child was in the house, the pauper had gone to the seashore. So there were the pauper's wife, the pauper's daughter, and the daughter of the wife.

The wife, seeing the servant coming, told the child of the pauper, "Quickly, leave! Go hide yourself!"

"Mh!"

"Leave quickly, go hide yourself!"

The children of long ago were fools. The pauper's daughter left, she hid under the bed. The wife and her daughter remained there.

The servant arrived, and said, "Greetings, madam."

"Delighted."

"How are you?"

"Very well."

He told her, "I saw three people. Why are there only two now? The pauper's daughter, where is she?"

She replied, "How do I know where she went, father? She was here, I don't know where she is now."

"Mh. All right." The servant prepared a cloth and took out the sandal. The daughter of the wife extended her foot. Alas, it didn't fit. The mother tried next—same results. "Now that friend of yours, where is she?"

"We don't know, damn it, where she went! How are we supposed to know?"

"Mh!" The servant said, "That person annoys me. I'm going, eh!" He left.

He slept until five in the morning. Then he went out, he walked to Kifombani and hid behind the house. You know that that is the hour that chickens go out.

The pauper's daughter opened the door, and said, "I am going to the toilet." She went around to the back.

The servant grabbed her leg.

"You, be quiet!"

"Who are you? It is this Nokoa, the servant of the sultan, who has seized my leg! Well! This Nokoa this night, where is he coming from?"

He replied, "Hold still, and don't annoy me! You want to give me trouble for nothing. Hold still while I measure this foot!"

She put the sandal on. That mother of a person stood by and watched her. The pauper's daughter tried the sandal on, and her foot went in—oh! her stepmother was furious!

She cursed her stepdaughter, she wanted to slap her.

Nokoa, the servant, said, "Now why do you curse her? I measured your foot and it didn't fit, and your daughter also and it didn't fit her. Now it fits this one perfectly, so what is the matter? Woman, you are not good, you! He who is not good is the devil of God!"

Nokoa, the servant, took the sandal and went away. He arrived at the house of the sultan, and said, "I have looked throughout the town. I was unsuccessful until I went to the pauper's house in Kifombani. That is where things went well."

Kibwana took the sandal and put it into a box.

He told Nokoa, "Tell my father I am coming to see him."

When Kibwana arrived there, his father asked, "What is it that you want?"

He told him, "I want a wife."

"Which wife, apart from the one you already have?"

He said, "I want the pauper's daughter. Betroth her to me today."

Nokoa, the servant, was sent to Kifombani. The pauper was still at the seashore.

When she saw Nokoa, the stepmother was angry. She wanted to beat him with a stick.

"Wife of the pauper?"

"Uh huh? What do you say? What have you heard? What news do you have?"

"I have been sent by the sultan."

"What does he want?"

She was told, "The pauper is summoned by the sultan."

"Well, he's not here. He went to the seashore, and I don't know if he will come or if he won't come, if he will die there or what."

The child remained silent, listening to her stepmother.

"I will be at the sultan's. If he comes, I will return and tell him." Nokoa left, parrrrr (a sound to indicate quick movement), up to Kibwana's place. He told him, "Sir, watch the sea. If he comes, I will be told."

The woman waited for the pauper to return. When he reached the doorway, she told him, "Quick, you are summoned by the sultan right now! Don't pause even to drink water! Don't bother to change those clothes of the sea." That wife of his told him that, just like that. "You have been summoned by the sultan! Quickly! I don't know what you have done. Just go there!"

The man dropped his nets in the doorway, the fishing basket he dropped there also. He said, "It's your own business whether or not you cook these fish." And wearing those very same sea clothes, he went to the place of the sultan.

"Peace be with you, sir."

"And with you peace. Ah, pauper, why have you come in such a state?"

He replied, "What should I do, sir, when I have been told to come immediately? You have summoned me, yet I don't know what offense I have committed or what I have done."

The sultan asked, "Who told you these words?"

"That wife of mine."

Now the sultan's wife spoke: "Don't you know that woman is bad? If you were to be killed, why didn't she at least detain you for a cup of porridge?"

He said, "Anything that happens is my fate."

The sultan told him, "Well, you didn't kill a person, nor did you steal from anyone, so relax. Fatuma wa Seifu?"

"Yes?"

"See if there is tea in the kettle."

"There is."

"Is there bread remaining?"

"Uh huh, there is some remaining."

"Well, bring it to the pauper."

First, the pauper went to the lavatory to wash. He went to the lavatory, but he still had no confidence. When he finished washing, he was given a spare kikoi (the cloth that men wear wrapped around their waists) and a spare shirt.

"Hang your fishing clothes there to dry."

The pauper ate, but he had no hope. He said, "Today I will be killed here." He drank his tea, he took his snuff, he was satisfied. "Now sir, tell me why you have summoned me here."

"I have summoned you, pauper. You didn't beat anyone, nor did you kill anyone. Yet I have summoned you. Kibwana, that devil, has said that he wants a wife."

"Which wife?"

"Your child, the daughter of a pauper."

"Well, sir, I—ah—the daughter of a pauper, mnh mnh. Is there a need to wait for me? I am a person who goes to the seashore. The wife is there, why not just come and take her?"

The sultan replied, "Truly, it is my son and it is your daughter. Why, doesn't a pauper have a child? Seeing that you bore the child, should I just come and take her? Is she a cow? Even a cow needs a guardian. When shall I come to get her?"

The pauper said, "Sir, just come and get her, even if you come immediately."

"Very well, pauper, this is what I have summoned you for. You may go now."

The pauper returned home. When she saw him, his wife said, "So now, explain what happened to you."

He said, "I have killed a man. I have been told to come to say farewell to my child." He is fed up with her ways.

She asked him, "Do you want porridge?"

He said, "I don't want any."

"How about washing?"

He said, "Also, I don't want it."

"Mh! After going out, you've been adorned! Mh! Look at your father now, he's been adorned, that one. He's been decked out! He's been given a shirt, he's been given a kikoi. He's eaten, he's been satisfied."

The child said nothing. The pauper sat down and took out his pipe. He sat weaving and weaving. Suddenly, up came Noti (a local donkey herdsman) with his donkey. The donkey walks by farting, pfe, pfe, pfe. When they arrived at the palm trees Noti tied up the donkey.

"Now I'm asking you, pauper, how is it that seeing me come with the donkey, you don't help me, you just sit there?"

The pauper asked him, "Now what am I supposed to do for you? This is a big road. A cow passes, a donkey passes, and now you pass with your donkey. What am I supposed to do for you?"

"Get up and take your bags," Noti told the pauper. The pauper got up. He took down the bag of rice, he took down the lamp oil, he took down cooking oil, he took down everything that was offered. He took the small cow that was sent for slaughtering.

"Those things are yours, pauper. They have been sent by the sultan. The sultan's son wants a wife, and the wife that he wants is your child. This wealth is for her father, for the child, and also for her mother."

The bags were full to the brim.

That mother of a person let out a raucous laugh. "Heee-hee-heh, we will satisfy our cravings, we will eat, we will dress! You know that money goes where money is. And my child will be wanted by whom? Why should she be wanted? He will not want the child of a pauper. She will have to become rich for someone to come looking for my child."

The pauper was minding his own business. He took his bundles, set them inside and tied his cow near some grass. Noti left with his donkey. The pauper sat until the sun had set in the west. He finished eating his meal and then called his daughter.

"Come here to see the things that have been brought by Noti. To whom do you think these things belong?"

"I don't know."

"Well, they are yours. You have been proposed to by the son of the sultan. I don't know if the wedding is today or tomorrow. Only God knows. Your clothes are here in this box. All these things are yours."

Her stepmother became angry. She was about to burst.

Time passed.

"Ah, that friend of mine, when will I tell him of my news?" At dawn she awoke, she went out and found her way to the place of her friend, the chafi. When she arrived, the chafi was waiting for her.

"Explain, child of the pauper, why have you come running?"

"I have been proposed to by the child of the sultan, Kibwana!"

He said, "Humph! Go away from me! I don't want to hear nonsense! You are saying words to, me and I know these words. You are not telling me anything that I don't know. So go away and rest peacefully. But first, today is Wednesday. A person will come on Thursday to take you to the sultan's place. And Thursday your stepmother will look for the chaff of some leaves that she will cook for you. You eat it. Don't worry, you eat. Don't be afraid, just eat. Now then, go and rest peacefully. From now on, you should not come here again."

The daughter of the pauper returned home.

Nokoa came and reported, "I have been sent by the sultan. He tells you this: Thursday night, when people are coming from the mosque, the pauper's daughter will be taken. The wedding is Friday."

The father said, "Even if he wants to come today, let him come and take her. I don't want any problems."

On Wednesday, the stepmother went to fetch the chaff of millet, corn, and rice, a full basket. She went to Mwakifukuwa (an area of the town where garbage is dumped and weeds grow) to get mnukauvundo and mchakari (inedible plants), both very bad leaves, a full basket. Afterwards, she went to Sanuri's shop (a local shop).

"Sanuri, lend me a cooking pot that can hold three pishi (about two and one-half kilos)."

"Ah! Today the wife of the pauper is having such a huge feast?"

"Eh."

So that Wednesday the woman boiled the leaves until they were done. She took the chaff and put it into the pot, stirring, stirring, stirring, stirring until those things were done.

The daughter of the pauper was in the other room, covered with a veil by her father, peaceful.

The mixture was dumped onto a huge plate, phuuu. The woman smoothed it out and carried it over to her stepdaughter. She was bent over with the weight of it.

"What's this, mama?"

"It's food."

"Mama, since this morning I've been hungry. I waited, but didn't see you."

"All right, eat."

"Bring me water." She brought it to her. In the time it took the wife of the pauper to open and close her eyes, the plate was white—empty. She said, "Not yet, mama, I'm still not satisfied. Bring me more!"

Her stepmother exclaimed, "Dohsalala Mohamedi, a person, you? This food that I have put before you—you've finished it?"

"Yes, and I'm not full at all! My stomach is completely empty. If you want to cook for me again, all right cook for me."

"You have defeated me. Your funeral. Bad luck, you! Dohsalala Mohamedi. Did the pauper conceive a child or a devil? Mh! You have defeated me. I'm not cooking again."

"Who told you to cook? If you cook, it's your own decision."

It was Wednesday. She slept the whole day.

Thursday evening, young women and adults like Mwasiti Abdullah (a woman from a nearby island) were sent. People were coming with their noise and their ululation and their big pressure lamp. The pauper had bought and prepared coffee and cakes. His daughter was covered with a veil. He spread out mats. People entered the house hooting and shouting. The songs of Santana went sung. Mwaziza wa Jugwe had come out, she was there. The people entered the house.

"So, pauper, how are you?"

"I'm fine."

"We are sent by the sultan. We want the bride."

"She is here. But wait, drink some coffee."

Mwaziza Jugwe was right where she wanted to be. She quaffed her coffee. The bride was carried off, ngwa (indicated the speed with which she was taken away). She was covered with a large piece of cloth. Rejoicing, noise, the journey. We went rejoicing all the way. At the sultan's house, the bride was put into a room. Mama Mwankaramu (an old woman who lives in the town) was called to cover her with a veil. Who was the bride's attendant? It was Fatuma wa Seifu (a young woman who was in the audience). She was stuck to the daughter of the pauper. So they stayed that way through the night.

In the morning, it was the wedding. Time passed until the people were praying on Friday. Kibwana was married to the daughter of the pauper.

The pauper rejoiced. He said, "Poor me, this wedding by myself. If my wife were here, we would be rejoicing together."

He was told, "Hush, father, that's the way the world is."

The pauper shouted, 'Hurrah!" Kibwana was coming. "Hurrah! Hurrah!" until Kibwana arrived at the house and slipped in. He gave the daughter of the pauper his hand.

He said, "I want my property."

Fatuma said, "Here is your bundle."

It has been torn. He has shot the cannon! People rejoiced! The pauper rejoiced until he cried! He had raised his child well. The people feasted and then returned home.

Which day did he marry? Friday. Saturday, Sunday, Monday night the bride wakened Fatuma wa Seifu, "Sister Fatuma, quickly, wake up, wake up quickly, wake up!"

"What is it?"

"Wake up, my stomach is hurting me. I want to go to the lavatory, I have diarrhea."

Fatuma hastened to help her. She tightened her cloth. "All right, get out." The husband was sleeping. She took her to the lavatory. She squatted down and started grunting. Fatuma told her, "Leave that place, leave, leave, leave." She took her to the washing area. Mother! She poured silver and gold! Look at the heap! Mh! Mama Seifu exclaimed, "Since I was born of my mother and father, I have not yet seen a bride like this one! Let's go, mama." She returned her to a room. "Where am I going to get a bag?" Fatuma tied her cloth, she stuffed it with gold. She put it in the room of her mother. Oph! Now the husband felt the need to urinate. He looked for his wife on the bed.

"Ah, where did my wife go?" He got down from the bed. He saw only blinking eyes. "Fatuma?"

"Yes?"

"Where is my wife?"

She told him, "She is there, squatting."

"What is she doing?"

"I don't know. Step down yourself, and come and look at her."

Kibwana came down. "Mtume! (Messenger of God!) This is no wife! This is a spirit! What's going on here?"

Fatuma told him, "Take a look at the rest in the lavatory."

Kibwana jumped. He wrapped his kikoi around his waist, took the flashlight, and headed for his father's house.

"Father! Father! Father!"

"Eh? Who is it?"

"It's me, Kibwana."

"Of whom?"

"Of the sultan."

"What do you want?"

"Wake up!"

The sultan woke up. "Toba ya rabi (Lord help me), now what? The old man of Kibwana wakes, what is it?"

"Ah, father, there is nothing to worry about. Come!"

He took his cane in his hand, "Toba ya rabi, now what?" He washed his face to wake up. A fit man, that sultan.

"Let's go to my house."

"What for? Is there sickness?"

"No, no, no! Let's just go!"

He walked with his father until they reached the house.

"Father, look at this work."

"Where did these things come from?"

"Your daughter-in-law, the daughter of the pauper! It is that shit that she shat!"

"Laila-haila-lah! Kibwana, have you married a person or have you married a spirit? Since when have these things happened? Nokoa, quickly, take a sack."

Fatuma had already filled a bag full, and had hidden it.

Time passed.

The people finished taking their money and hiding it. The day was Monday. Tuesday it was the same. Wednesday she closed there (i.e., she stopped defecating gold and silver). Fatuma had hidden four or five bags.

Time passed.

The brother of Kibwana, Mohamedi of the sultan, said, "Father, I too want a wife. And the wife that I want is the daughter of the pauper, the child of his wife. Do you understand?"

He and his father went to propose to her. He sent Nokoa the same way.

He said, "I have been sent by the sultan to call the father of the child of the pauper."

"Why?"

"I don't know."

"Very well, he went to the sea. If he comes I will tell him."

The pauper returned.

"Listen, Father, you have been summoned by the sultan!"

"What for?"

"I don't know."

"Mh! The sultan doesn't even give me time to drink water. If I get restless at all, the sultan summons me. Well!"

"Go, Ndugu, to listen to what he has to say to you."

"Sultan, sir, what now?"

"I want nothing except another wife. And the wife that I want is at your house. It is he, Mohamedi, who wants your child, the daughter of your wife."

"All right, I will tell her." He returned home.

"Well, Bibi (an equivalent to Mrs.), the good news increases. It is security. The sultan summoned me to say that his son, Mohamedi, wants a wife."

"Which wife?"

"It is your child."

"Mh! Pauper, are you telling the truth or lies?"

"Wait and see if I am telling lies."

As before, a donkey loaded with things came with Noti to the house of the pauper. The mother was laughing, laughing, her back tooth was visible. She took her daughter's things down from the donkey and set them inside. They slept until morning.

Then Nokoa came and said, "The same Thursday night your child will be taken."

The woman asks, "Why doesn't the sultan come and take her himself, it's his wife."

On Wednesday, she went searching for the same leaves that she had collected before. She cooked them in a pot. She dressed her daughter and covered her with a veil. When she finished, she put her in a separate room.

The child asked her, "What is this now? Ah! Myself, I can't eat this food!"

"Mh! Your mother's vagina, why can't you eat? What a fool! Haven't you heard that when your sister ate this food she defecated silver and gold? What is the reason that you don't want it?"

"Mama, I am not able to eat that!"

But the child stuffed her stomach full. She felt that she had the stomach of eight months (i.e., eight months pregnant).

Time passed until Thursday evening. Her mother went to buy cakes. She prepared coffee. She spread out mats and covered her daughter with a veil. We went there, those like Mwaziza wa Jugwe, and said, "Give us the bride."

"Wait and drink coffee first."

We drank coffee and said again, "Give us the bride."

Because of her full stomach, the bride could not be carried. She was covered with a veil. The people were gossiping, "What kind of stomach does this bride have?"

"Mh! You gossips! What kind of talk is that? Just let it alone. Let's go!"

They arrived. The bride was put into a room and covered with a veil. Mama Mwankaramu was called.

"Say, this bride! Why is she like this? She has such a stomach!"

"Mh! Mind your own business."

Mwanasha wa Ulili is selected as the bride's attendant.

Time passed until morning. People came out of the mosque, Mohamedi ya Sultan had been married. There was dancing and celebration. The mother was rejoicing, the pauper was silent.

"Rejoice?" he asked her. "When I married my child, why didn't you rejoice? Rejoice by yourself."

So the bride came with her drums—boom, boom, boom, up to the house.

The groom gave her his hand and said, "I want my wife."

Peace! The people rejoiced.

Time passed until the wedding was over, they had married that woman.

Friday, she stayed inside all day. She slept.

Monday at the same time that the stomach of her friend had started troubling her, hers also began to give her pain. Her stomach began rumbling.

"Mama Mwanasha wa Ulili?"

"Eh?"

"My stomach is hurting me."

"How is it hurting you?"

"I have diarrhea."

"Mh!"

There was someone else's new mat in the room. She took it, and placed it on the floor. There was someone else's prayer mat which she also spread out on the floor.

"I want to go to the lavatory."

"Shit here. Do you want to just throw money away? Don't you remember your sister? She defecated silver, and you, you want the labor of throwing money away! Shit right here."

The child squatted and relieved herself. Wee! The diarrhea piled up! The leaves had rotted inside her stomach to the extent that one would think a rat had died there. Mh! Such vehemence here. It came out until the empty space beneath the bed was full. Those leaves came out of her stomach. The cramps! They were coming out, plop, plop!

Ah, Mwanasha wa Ulili said, "Stay there! I don't want to faint!"

And so she left that place, and headed home. She hit the road to Ngoa.

The husband was still asleep. The child was dropping that shit. The house was permeated with the smell, a continuous stench. The smell began to invade the man's nose, it beat upon his nose without interruption.

"My God! What is that smell?"

The husband started. The child remained where she was, it was burning her. You know, a stomach beset with diarrhea seizes you with tremendous cramps, whole pots are dropped!

Mwanasha wa Ulili had by this time reached Ngoa. Mohamedi had now awakened completely. He called, "Eh, Mwanasha wa Ulili?" Will he see her soon? "Ah! What's going on here?"

"I'm shitting."

"You're shitting! Is there no lavatory any more?"

"It was that sister. When I told her I needed to go, she rolled out this mat and told me to shit here."

"Where is she?"

"I don't know."

He yelled, "Eh! Mwanasha wa Ulili-ee! Mwanasha wa Ulili—ee!" He didn't see her. Mohamedi was annoyed. He lost his temper. He was unable to remain in the house because of a smell like shark oil all over the house. Ah! he was irritated! His eye was changing to a red color. He went to awaken his father.

"Father! Father! Father!"

"What is it now? Who is it?"

"It is I, Mohamedi ya Sultan!"

"What do you want?"

"Open!"

His father took his kikoi and wrapped himself in it.

"All right, what is it?"

"Father, today at my house there is something surprising! I don't know how to describe it."

"What has been done to you?"

"That dog, that Mwanasha wa Ulili! The bride whom she was given expressed a desire to defecate, and asked her to take her to the lavatory. Instead, she rolled out a mat for her. Now the house cannot be entered. I have no place to stay. If I see Mwanasha wa Ulili, I'll beat her with a stick and pay the fine for it! Mh! Aha, father, wouldn't you lose your temper? Let's go."

The sultan arrived in the doorway.

"Salala! Muhamedi! You are unable to enter, doh!"

"That's the shit, Father, go and see!"

My child, when he went, she was there. She was doing her work.

"God forbid! Who has committed this outrage? Is she here, that Mwanasha wa Ulili?"

She was there? She had slipped out to Ngoa silently. Mohamedi was fuming.

"Today, if I see Mwanasha, I'll beat her with a cane until she's dead! and pay the fine for it! You'll see her as a fool now!"

Well now, a plan was made to have the mother come and collect her daughter and her shit. That woman was sleeping in Kifombani, sleep had entered her! Nokoa lit the large pressure lamp. He was told to go quickly and fetch that mother of a person. Nokoa went off grumbling. "What sort of distress is this? Even if a man goes to bed, he doesn't get any sleep! This is the shit of what? Ah!"

He went. The mother of a person saw the light approaching.

"Father of the girl?" (She is addressing her husband, the pauper.)

"What is it?"

"A large pressure lamp is coming."

"You, woman, why are you worried? That light isn't coming here. People are passing by, not coming—like people going home or to work."

The woman went out and sat. "Why is it coming here?"

"Ah, you, woman, why are you troubled? I will allow passage, I'm going to sleep."

The pressure lamp was placed firmly in the doorway, it sputtered.

"Machikini?"

"Yes?"

"Is your wife sleeping, or is she awake?"

"I'm awake!"

"Mh! You are awake, you are awake, go outside!"

"Father of the daughter, you are called. Wake up!"

"What is it?"

"You are summoned in town. Your child has put shit in someone else's house. It is uninhabitable. The bridal attendant has disappeared. The bride had the urge to go to the lavatory because of diarrhea, and Mwanasha wa Ulili rolled out the mats for her. So Mohamedi is fuming. He wants you to take your child!"

"Mh! Nokoa, are you telling the truth?"

"Let's go."

"What you're saying—is it true?"

"There's no need for you to wear out my patience. Let's just go and you can see for yourself."

They went to the house.

"What is it, Babu (lit., Grandfather, but used affectionately for others)?"

"Please, my father-in-law, I say this to you: go there to the house. Take your mats, take your rugs, and take your shit! The mats I don't want, the rugs I don't want—and your daughter, from today I have left her! I have given her back the dowry. And scour my house until the smell of shit has been removed. Mwanasha wa Ulili has done me a grave injustice. She knew there was a lavatory, but she put that dog there to shit! God is great! Today I have no place to sleep."

"Eh, child, what's this?"

"Child? Child? I have been outraged, that's what! I am now going to my father's place to sleep!"

The bride's mother entered. "Oh child, what have you done?"

"It was that attendant! She told me to shit on the carpets that she rolled out."

"Today, that which you wanted, you got. Your sister has become wealthy, but you? Well, anyway, let's go with our shit."

The young girl dragged her mats behind her to the seashore. The whole night passed. Then she and her mother returned to scrub the other person's house. They brought rose water and incense. They fumigated. For three days, Mohamedi did not sleep in his house.

The child was divorced, the child of the wife of the pauper.

When the pauper's wife returned, he told her, "At this time I am going to live with my daughter. And you can stay with your bad ways and your daughter. That house I have left to you. Whether or not you get married again is your own choice."

The pauper left and went to stay in town.

One day the chafi came to visit the wife of Kibwana in her sleep. He asked her, "Have you been married?"

"Eh."

"Peace."

"Peace."

"Have you seen my gift?"

She replied, "Yes, I have seen it."

"Tomorrow night, I want you to come with my brother-in-law. I want to see him."

"All right."

She slept until twelve midnight. Then she woke her husband. "Wake up. Let's take a walk."

"Mh! You woman, walk where?"

She said, "Let's go."

They went to the landing place. Her friend was waiting there to take her and her husband into the water. They stayed until one o'clock, and then returned home. The husband asked his wife nothing.

Two days later, the fish told her, "Thank you very much for your respect. I have seen it. You have fulfilled your share, and I have seen it. But forgive me, my state is now that of a sick person. I don't know myself whether I am well or sick. You see me how I am, I am sick. But, pauper's daughter, it is your last hand whether I live or die. Tomorrow morning when you awaken, your last hand will be in the doorway. So we will give each other the last farewell, my friend. Let us forgive each other. I will not see you, and you will not see me anymore."

The daughter fell into a deep sleep until morning. She awoke.

"That friend of mine, I wonder what words he told me."

She slept until morning. She awoke.

Kibwana also woke up, and went out to wash his face. He opened the door. There was a huge house there—very long, it reached from here to there!

"Mh! Daughter of the pauper?"

"What do you want?"

"Come here."

"Ah, go and pray."

"How can I pray with a house in the doorway? Have you seen it? Come!"

The wife came to look. "Ah, go and pray, you have a devil inside."

"When was this house built?"

"Ah, go and pray."

The husband went away to pray, but he was disturbed in his mind.

When people awakened, they were astonished. "Dohsalala! When was this built? My God!" Every person was surprised.

After praying, Kibwana came home running. He said, "My wife, you will tell me, where did this house come from?"

Again the woman remained as she was. She explained to her husband from beginning to end. She said, "Listen, my husband, we will live in this new house. The other one we will leave for father, the pauper. We will shift to the other house."

When the house was opened, there were crowds inside. Indeed, this was the source of these water taps coming into being (she is referring to the few houses in the town that have piped water)—that house, it was the origin of these taps. Radios were in the house, bought for the daughter of the pauper by the chafi her friend. My! That huge house, the storage space and extra things, my! If you went inside you couldn't be seen. Crowds were in there, cows were there inside, everything. If you coughed, the house coughed. If you spoke, the house spoke. If you were careless, you would fall. That house! The door was even sufficient for you, Mwaziza (Mwaziza was a rather plump member of the audience)! Well!

She moved, the wife. Afterward, Kibwana of the sultan, Mohamedi of the sultan, the daughter of the rich man, the daughter of the poor man, their workers, a whole group lived inside.

The other house was left for the pauper. My, there were young women inside, some were virgins, some were ripe, some were flirting. Women were arranged for the pauper. A wife was stuck to him. He was rejuvenated.

Now the daughter of the pauper said, "At this moment I want to do work. I have not yet done work. I want to do it now."

The pauper had not even taken a step, the stomach was up. The daughter of the rich man coughed, the stomach came up. They bore their children. After the child was dropped, he was taken—it wasn't known where he was, he went to be brought up. So the daughter of the pauper and the daughter of the rich man were bearing children. The pauper of God, he and his wife, remained until he finished his years. And the sultan spent his years until he was taken by death. Then the son, Kibwana, took the sultanship. The rich man was walking feebly. He who dies, he who survives, that is the way it is.

Time passed. They thanked God. Praise be to God.

That grandmother there, I don't know where she went.

The story, my friends, is finished here. The pauper lived with his children, and Kibwana lived with his children. The sultan died, Kibwana took over. Mohamedi was given a wife, he was married.

The story and the tale have finished here. If it's good, take it. If it's bad, give it to me, myself, The European-of-the-road, my lies.

Commentary

This is a "Cinderella" story that incorporates, for thematic reasons, a popular story of a good girl and a bad girl. Notes regarding the "Cinderella" story and a version of the good girl and bad girl story follow this discussion.

Wives of a rich man, a sultan, and a pauper give birth: the rich man's wife bears a girl (Fatuma); the sultan's wife bears a boy (Kibwana) and later another boy (Mohamedi); the pauper's wife bears a girl (Kibibi).

Running through much of the story is a pattern having to do with the pauper's work, fishing. He typically catches one fish, then sells a piece and eats the other.

The pauper's wife dies, and Kibibi grows into womanhood; no man asks for her hand in marriage. In the meantime, Kibwana, the son of the sultan, wants to marry the daughter of the rich man. A widow now goes to the pauper with the intention of marrying him. There is a pattern: she cleans the man's house daily for a month, leaving each day before he comes home. In the end, the pauper marries the widow, and brings her and her child to his home.

The ingredients for the "Cinderella" story are now in place. There will be a ball, at the marriage of Kibwana, the sultan's son. And the pauper and his wife will go to the wedding. The stepmother's daughter does no work; everything is done by the pauper's daughter.

One day, the pauper catches a chafi fish. At its insistence, the pauper's daughter releases it, and it becomes her benefactor. It makes it possible for the pauper's daughter to attend the wedding. She is transformed, her identity changed. At the great festival, the pauper's daughter leaves a gold sandal behind. A pattern follows; the sultan sends his servant to try the sandal on all feet. Now Kibwana wants to marry the pauper's daughter.

The good girl and bad girl story (for an example of this story, see "Nobubele and Yoliswa, below) is attached to the tale. In this Swahili story, that good girl/bad girl theme begins with the furious and jealous stepmother, who, in an effort to spoil the celebration, gives Kibibi food to upset her stomach. She therefore has diarrhea, and on her wedding night, she defecates silver and gold, bags full. Mohamedi, Kibwana's brother, wants to marry the pauper's other daughter. The pauper's wife finds the same awful leaves, etc., makes food for her daughter so that she will defecate silver and gold also. Her stomach is so full the bride cannot be carried. Everyone is amazed at the size of her stomach. At the wedding, her stomach is pained, she has diarrhea. But unlike her stepsister, she defecates feces, pots full, in the middle of the room.

Nobubele and Yoliswa, the Good Girl and the Bad Girl

A Xhosa story

Now for a story:

There was an old woman, very old, very sick. Her husband was dead.

This woman, little and old, lived with Nobubele and Yoliswa, her two grandchildren. But there was a famine, and the old woman was anxious because they were not able to find any food to eat. Day after day, the children got up and went to the fields to glean corn. What corn they found, they boiled.

One day, Nobubele said to the old woman, "Grandmother, we are dying of hunger. I am going to go and seek work."

Her grandmother asked, "But where will you find work, my child?"

She said, "I do not know, Grandmother, but I shall try."

The old woman said, "All right then."

So it was that Nobubele traveled, and when she was entering a forest she came upon a dog that was carrying a huge bundle of wood.

This dog said to her, "Nobubele! Please help me to carry this bundle of wood. I'm tired!"

Nobubele helped the dog carry its wood.

Then she journeyed on; she walked on, passing through that forest.

As she walked, she met a woman who was very old, very old, exceedingly forbidding in appearance, extremely dirty.

And her eyes were filled with dirt.

She said, "Nobubele, my child. Please help me, come here and wipe my eyes clean."

Nobubele, with great solicitude, cleaned the aged woman's eyes.

Then the little old woman went on her way, saying, "Remain the way you are, my child, wherever you go."

Nobubele journeyed on then, walking, seeking work.

Then she came to a cat.

The cat said, "Nobubele, please give me some milk."

She said, "But where shall I get milk?"

Suddenly, unexpectedly, milk appeared a short distance from the cat. Nobubele took the milk and brought it to the cat, and the cat drank it.

Then the cat said, "Listen, as you travel on, you're going to encounter an old woman. Heed this woman's words."

Nobubele agreed to do that, and she was again on her way.

After some time, she met this old woman, who said to her, "Nobubele, I know that you are journeying and that you are anxious because of the famine that you left behind at your home."

The child said that the old woman spoke truth.

The woman said, "Now, my child, do you see that homestead, over there, in the forest? When you get there and enter that homestead, you'll be given red corn. But do not grind the red corn! Grind white corn instead. And when you are given a new sleeping mat, do not agree to sit on it. Agree only to sit on an old mat."

Nobubele walked on then, and she arrived at this homestead. She came to some people who were very kind. They gave her an old mat, and she sat. But when they gave her some red corn, she refused it, taking white corn instead. They instructed her to prepare porridge, and put it at the upper side of her head when she went to sleep.

She ground this corn then, and made a thick porridge. She put the porridge down, poured some milk over it, and placed it near her head, as she had been instructed.

She went to sleep.

In the depths of the night, as she lay sleeping, an enormous snake came into the room where she slept. When it saw her, it hurled itself at her head: it was going to eat her. Then the snake saw the porridge, and it moved into this bowl of food, and ate it. When it emerged, it was satisfied.

The snake returned to the forest.

The next morning, when they saw that this child was healthy and well, the people of this homestead rejoiced. They lavished her with splendid gifts; they gave her food, and, so that she might return to her home, they presented her with money.

Nobubele traveled on then, and in time she arrived at her grandmother's home. She told her what had happened.

Her grandmother celebrated Nobubele's return, was pleased that her granddaughter had returned with much money, that she had come home with such beautiful things.

And her sister, Yoliswa, when she saw that Nobubele had returned with such fine things, also wanted to go to find work.

"But my sister," said Nobubele, "you are so obstinate, how will you find work?"

But Yoliswa said, "I'll find out for myself! I don't want any advice from you!"

So it was that Yoliswa also journeyed, she traveled a great distance, walking along the same way that Nobubele had walked.

She met the same dog that Nobubele had come upon.

The dog said to Yoliswa, "Please help me carry this load."

She said, "You're mad! Am I a servant of dogs?"

The dog said, "May you be treated in the same way wherever you go."

She journeyed on, walking, irritated, speaking to herself: "The dog is mad!" She conjectured about how that dog should bark at houses rather than come to gather firewood in the forests.

Yoliswa walked on, and then she came to a little old woman.

The old woman said to her, "Please help me, child of my child. I am dying. I can no longer see because of the dirt that is in my eyes. Just wipe my eyes."

Yoliswa said, "You're a mystery, you are! You just sit around, you don't wash your face, and then you think that I am going to wash it for you?"

The woman said, "Child of my child, you shall be what you are wherever you go. Travel on then."

So Yoliswa moved on, walking, talking to herself: "This old woman is really silly! She sits around, not washing, thinking that I should be the one who cleans up old women!"

She met the cat.

"Please help me," said the cat. "There's the milk, bring it near me."

Yoliswa said, "What's this? Am I one who hands milk to cats?"

The cat said, "May it be the same for you wherever you go."

Yoliswa traveled on, again walking and talking to herself: "This is really a day of misfortunes! Even cats have learned to speak to me!"

She walked on, annoyed, and came to the same homestead that Nobubele had come to. Yoliswa arrived there, and was given some red corn. She ground it, not even bothering to pick the stones out of it. Then she was given a sleeping mat, and she sat on it, paying no attention to the kind of mat it was.

In the evening, she did not even ask for milk so that she might prepare some palatable food. Instead, she made some mediocre porridge with that corn that had stones in it.

In the depths of the night, the snake arrived. When it was about to heave itself at her head, it saw the food. And when it moved into that food, it discovered that the porridge was disgusting.

The snake lashed her then, it flailed her with its tail until she was swollen. Then it left, returning to the forest.

At dawn, she was still swollen, she would remain so for a full week.

When the people of this homestead came to the house in which Yoliswa slept, they could not awaken her: her eyes were shut tightly.

Then the people gave her some things, ugly things, grotesque things, and they told her, "Go! Go home! We don't know why you came to us here. You did not heed the instructions you were given along the way."

Yoliswa traveled then, she returned to her grandmother.

When she got home, her grandmother said, "Child of my child, I told you so."

The story ends there.

The "Cinderella" Story

"Cinderella" is one of the world's enduring stories, a familiar and indispensable part of raconteurs' repertories from Asia to Africa, from Europe to the Americas, and continually refurbished and revitalized whatever the medium, from oral storytelling to literature, motion pictures to television soap operas. Whatever the milieu, the ash-girl remains the same: she is Aschenputtel and Aschenbrodl in Germany, Centrillon in France, Cenerentola in Italy; she is Mityi in southern Africa, Yeh-hsien in China; she is Catskin, she is Cap o' Rushes. She is all of these, but she is forever the ragged child who moves to adult splendor.

The earliest known version is Chinese, dating from the 9th century AD, but the part of the story having to do with the slipper test is even older, occurring, according to the Greek geographer, Strabo, in ancient Egypt. The most popular European versions appeared in the early fairy tale collections of Giovanni Basile (*Il Pentamerone* [1674]) and Charles Perrault (*Contes de ma Mere l'Oye* [1697]).

In 1893, Marian Roalfe Cox published 345 variants of "Cinderella." And, in 1951, Anna Birgitta Rooth published a study of the story, *Cinderella Cycle,* based on 700 versions of the story. More than 500 versions have been found in Europe alone. Throughout the world, the story is told in basically the same way; it typically involves a persecuted heroine, magical help of some kind, a meeting with a prince, some proof of identity, and marriage to the prince. Common motifs in the various versions of the story include a cruel stepmother, an abused youngest daughter, a dead mother returning from the grave to aid her persecuted daughter, a fairy godmother, clothes and carriage produced by magic, a prince enamored of the heroine at a ball, remaining too long at the ball, a slipper test, and the lowly heroine's marriage to the prince.

The Chinese version, found in a Chinese book published about 850–860 AD, was written down by Tuan Ch'eng-shih, whose father was controller of a large district in Szechwan. The story was told to him by Li Shih-yuan, a servant in his family, who said that it took place before the Han and Ch'in dynasties. It is the tale of Yeh-hsien, ill-treated by her stepmother, befriended by a huge fish that she regularly feeds until it is beheaded and eaten by her stepmother. A man comes down from the sky to tell Yeh-hsien to take the fish's bones and hide them in her room; the bones provide her with gold, dresses, and food whenever she wants them. She goes in brilliant attire provided by the fish's bones to a cave festival, but leaves behind a shoe of gold. The shoe finds its way to an island kingdom, the ruler of which launches an extensive quest for the owner of the shoe. He finally finds Yeh-hsien, "as beautiful as a heavenly being." In the end, after providing the ruler with treasures and jade without limit, the bones are washed into the sea.

In a Xhosa story from South Africa, a child named Mityi is badly treated by her stepmother. Her dead mother, in the form of a fish, comes to the grieving Mityi, tells her that she will be fished from the sea, that she should take the bones and bury them at a certain kraal. Mityi does this, and over night a huge tree grows up in the kraal which happens to be the home of a wealthy, unmarried man. No one can touch the tree, so the man has a contest: if a man touches the tree, he will be given wealth; if a woman touches it, and if she is unmarried, he will marry her. All try, none succeeds. But her mother, in the form of a bird, comes to Mityi, and transforms her: a gloriously beautiful Mityi goes to the tree, and touches it. She leaves without identifying herself, with the man gazing longingly after her. Then there is a ring contest, with the same results. And finally there is the quest for the shoe, and Mityi identifies herself, and is married.

This Xhosa version has a second half, in which the stepsister of Mityi becomes, at her own request, the servant of Mityi and her husband. The jealous stepmother invites Mityi to come home for a reconciliation, but while massaging Mityi's hair slides a long pin into her head and kills her. A bird thereupon soars from the dead Mityi's head, and it flies home to her husband where it flutters about the mourning man until, in the end, he takes it in his hands, ruffles through the feathers, finds the head of the pin, withdraws it, and Mityi magnificently returns to life. The husband hides Mityi, invites the stepsister to return to him, pretending that he loves her. He strips her naked, suspends her in a tree, then burns her. He cuts up her body and sends all but the hands, feet, and head back to her parents. They, thinking it is the flesh of a cow, eat it, and only then does Mityi's husband send them the head, feet, and hands, so that they are aware of the terrible thing they have done. The husband and Mityi then live happily.

In this Xhosa story, the young girls, in the language of storytelling, become two contrasting parts of the same person, the performer dramatizing the puberty ritual of a girl as she moves into adulthood, purging herself of anti-social behavior, represented by her sinister stepsister.

A Zuni version of the story was collected by Frank Hamilton Cushing and published in 1901. At a place called Matsaki, a very poor girl herds turkeys for a living. She is kind to the turkeys, and they become attached to her. As she is herding the turkeys, she learns that the Dance of the Sacred Bird is to occur in four days. She would love to go, but knows that she cannot, "ugly and ill-clad as I am." Every day, she sees others preparing for the great dance. After the people have gone toward Zuni to the dance, the turkeys speak to the girl: Would she like to go to the dance? The turkeys will make it possible, but they warn her not to forget them in the excess of her enjoyment. The girl throws off her clothing, and the turkeys triumphantly dance on it until it is transformed into resplendent dresses. She goes to the dance, forgets the time, and returns to her home late. The turkeys, having given up on her, have moved away. The girl pursues them, calling; as she runs after them, her clothing slowly reverts to its former raggedness. "Weary, grieving, and despairing, she returned to Matsaki."

It should not be surprising that there are as many interpretations of this fairy tale as there are audiences. Bruno Bettelheim argued that "No other fairy tale renders so well as the 'Cinderella' stories the inner experiences of the young child in the throes of sibling rivalry, when he feels hopelessly outclassed by his brothers and sisters." He noted that it is "Not just sibling rivalry but sexual rivalry, too," that "The prince receives from Cinderella the assurance he needed most: that while all along she had a wish for a penis, she accepts that only he can satisfy it." He concluded that "'Cinderella' guides the child from his greatest disappointments—oedipal disillusionment, castration anxiety, low opinion of himself because of the imagined low opinion of others—toward developing his autonomy, becoming industrious, and gaining a positive identity of his own. Cinderella, at the story's end, is indeed ready for a happy marriage."

P. Saintyves thought that "Cinderella" represented a ritual having to do with the end of winter and the onset of spring. In an ancient custom, a girl could divine the man she was to marry by putting ashes on her clothes, going to sleep without uttering a word: she would then see her future husband in a dream. The contrast between ashy clothing and the transformed Cinderella's bright dresses represents the contrast between winter and spring.

The Cinderella figure, pathetic and humbled, is the badly treated least likely hero in all of us, and we cherish her for that. We know that she will rise above her wretched circumstances, made the worst by the relentless pattern of viciousness indulged in by her stepmother and stepsisters. It is as if some storytellers could not bear to have the child's biological mother treat her child in such a callous way: distance had to be found, so that in some versions of the story a stepmother, unrelated to the child, was chosen, an outsider with a jealous disposition and an ugly vanity and selfishness.

The fairy godmother affects the transformation, but not without a cost. The fairy initiates and orchestrates the tests of the child as she moves through her puberty ritual, transforming her but testing her at the same time: she must return to her former circumstances, as tempting as it may be for her to live in her dream. This emphasis on the relationship between the child's reality and her dream is a common image in these "Cinderella" tales. The story helps the child to adjust the relationship between her dream world, the world of her unconscious, on the one hand, and the conscious world, the world that exists outside of her, on the other. Storytelling is one of humanity's means of assuring a harmonious relationship between our inner, spiritual lives and the world that exists outside us. We cannot live in art, we cannot live in our dreams, but art and our dreams become the means for a successful integration of our selves into our world.

Identity is at the heart of "Cinderella" stories, a child growing into womanhood, leaving her ragged childhood identity behind, exquisite and magical clothing and conveyances along with a tiny slipper or a jewel of some kind to attest to her new sense of self, along with a smart young man to pursue her, the combination of these calling attention to her new status, her new singularity. She will now rise from the ashes, the phoenix incarnate, everyone's mythic and magical transformation from innocence to experience, from degradation to exaltation: Cinderella is a universal dream-come-true. There is also the exhilarating sense of being present at a splendid occasion with all of one's acquaintances, including one's enemies, in attendance; and to have all of these, including and especially one's enemies, express awe at the splendor of a person whom they routinely disparage. It again emphasizes identity: people finding an attractiveness in the person they most debase.

"Cinderella" is the story of a loss of innocence, of a break with the past, a movement into a new state of being. The ragged child gives way to the refulgent adult, as the young person sloughs off her past and moves boldly into her future. It is an rejuvenating story of transformation, a celebration of adulthood, a drab moth transmuted into a luminous butterfly.

These ancient motifs having to do with transformation and identity—the rags to riches motif, the slipper or jewel imagery, the magical fairy or turkey or fish—go deep in the culture, each capable of eliciting strong emotional responses. In the "Cinderella" story, the fairy godmother and the slipper are the connections between present and past, with the dream constantly faced with the real—majesty alongside rags. Cinderella will not be allowed to forget the circumstances on either side of the great puberty transformation that she is experiencing. The images having to do with "Cinderella" do not so much shape us as reflect our most deeply felt hopes and fears. Her dreams are ours, and when, in the end, La Cenerentola sings, "No longer sad beside the fire/shall I sit alone, singing./Ah, my long years of heartache/were but a streak of lightning, a dream, a game," her grand transformation is also ours. "Cinderella" is the enchanted embodiment of our inner lives, drawn in bold and cardinal colors as folklore characters are, and raised in grand opera to the highest emotional pitch; the fairy tale and the opera become the theater of our souls. Cinderella is not human beings in all of our complexities and nuances: she is our finest instincts raised to the level of myth, and her fabulous transformation is our apotheosis.

The story is the distillate of the experiences and dreams of peoples in diverse geographical, linguistic, and ethnic contexts, a tale told around hearth-fires throughout the world. That upward mobile young girl sparks a passion and a yearning in peoples from Asia and Africa, Europe and America. Cinderella charms her way into our lives, assuring us that we too have worth, that we can escape our cheerless worlds.

At night, the usual time for storytelling, the people gather around the fire to listen and watch, to perform and enjoy the tales. Children, even babes in arms, are permitted to stay up for the occasion. Anyone may tell a story, but there is usually one, noted for his skill as a raconteur and for his wide repertory of tales, who carries much of the performance. There are also special times when stories are told during the day in the market-places—as when a noted teller of tales comes to a Hausa village. The usual market activities slow down or cease altogether while the storyteller performs in much the same way as did the European jongleur and troubadour of medieval times.

Alta Jablow, *Yes and No, The Intimate Folklore of Africa* (New York: Horizon Press, 1961), pp. 29–30.

Duala

The Old Woman and the Eggs

The Duala live in Cameroon.

Two women whom a man married quarreled very often. One day, one of the women went to the house of an old woman, which lay behind the wood.

She said to her, "My mother, I am a poor woman. Help me out of all my sorrows."

But the old woman had smallpox.

She said to the woman, "Stay here until my smallpox is cured."

The wife gave the old woman her medicine until the smallpox was cured.

One day, the wife got very hungry. She said to the old woman, "I am now very hungry."

The old woman said to her, "Go, take cow dung and sand, and put both into a pot."

The wife did as the old woman had told her to do. She put the things into a pot. The cow dung became beef and the sand became rice. They both began to eat.

When they had finished their meal, the wife said to the old woman, "My mother, your smallpox is cured. Now I will go home."

The old woman said, "Yes, I will give you the blessing that you wanted."

She sent the wife to a place where she had put her eggs, and said to her, "When you get there, all the eggs will talk a lot. Now, the egg that says, 'Take me! Take me!' that one do not take. But if an egg says, 'Take me not! Take me not!' then take it."

The wife went there.

All the eggs began to talk.

The eggs in one part said, "Take me!"

From Wilhelm Lederbogen, "Duala Fables," tr. M. Huber, *Journal of the African Society* 4 (1904): 65–68.

The eggs in the other part said, "Take me!"

She took an egg that said, "Take me not!"

She went back to the old woman and said to her, "I took the egg that said, 'Take me not!'"

The old woman said, "Take this egg and go home. When you come to your house, tell your husband to clear a space from bushes and grass. And when he has cleared it, throw this egg on the ground. A big house will then come out of this space."

The wife got home and did exactly as she was told. A big house came out of the egg. Now the husband began to love this woman very much.

But when the other wife saw this, she went to the house of the old woman, too, and said to her, "I want a house from you, too."

The old woman said, "Yes, but you must first wash the smallpox that I have on my body."

But the wife did not want to do what the old woman told her. She was astonished that she should have to do such work. She did it, but she did not wash the pustules clean. And while she was washing them, she spat continually.

The old woman saw how the young woman did everything, but she kept silent.

When the young woman had finished washing the smallpox, she said, "I am hungry."

The old woman said to her, "Go, take cow dung and sand, and put both in a pot."

The woman had to force herself when she put the cow dung and sand in the pot. The cow dung disgusted her. She took banana leaves, and with these put the cow dung and the sand into the pot.

The old woman did not like the way the wife worked, but in no way did she let her see that she was unhappy.

When the food was ready, the wife would not partake of it. She said to the old woman, "I will go home now. I shall not stop here, where the hunger is killing me."

The old woman said to her, "Yes, but go first to the place where my eggs are. When you get there, take the egg that says, 'Take me not! Take me not!' But the egg that says, 'Take me! Take me!' that one do not take on any account."

When the wife came to the place where the eggs were, she heard an egg that said, "Take me not! Take me not!" But she listened to another egg that said, "Take me! Take me!" She took this egg that said "Take me!"

When she came back to the old woman, the wife would not show her the egg.

The old woman asked, "Will you not show me the egg?"

The young woman did not answer her.

The old woman said, "As you did your things badly, precisely so will you be recompensed."

Now the wife went home. When she got home, she said to her husband, "I think that from now you will love me as much as you do that other woman, because I bring you the same things that she brought you." Then she added, "Call many people, and have them clear a space from bushes and grass."

After the people had cleared a place, the wife took the egg and threw it on the ground.

No house came out of it, but warriors emerged. When the warriors had come out, they beat the woman. Then they went into the village, shooting their guns. After the shooting, they returned into the egg.

The wife threw the egg on the ground once again.

The warriors came out of the egg, and again began to shoot with their guns. They did this for seven days, killing many people.

The few people they spared went to the house of the old woman.

They said to her, "What kind of egg did you give this woman?"

The old woman answered, "This woman came into my house and was impertinent and bold. She did not listen at all to my words. I sent her to my eggs, saying to her, 'The egg that says, "Take me!" that one do not take, and the old that says, "Take me not!" that one take.' But she took the egg that said, 'Take me!'"

To the people, the old woman said, "Go now! When the warriors want to fight you, just say to them, 'Old woman!' They will not do anything to you then."

Commentary

The structure of this story is identical to the good girl-bad girl story (see "The Pauper's Daughter," story 48) and it has echoes of "The Magic Drum" (story 23). It is constructed on the establishment of a pattern by the first wife. The force of the story, its emotional resonance, is achieved with the repetition of the pattern by the second wife, and the alterations in the pattern. The story has an obvious didactic element, but the real message is in the emotional contrast.

Children's tales now; but not the invention of a child's intellect. . . .

Henry Callaway, *Nursery Tales, Traditions, and Histories of the Zulus* (London: John A. Blair, 1868), preface.

Zulu

Umxakaza-wakogingqwayo

by Lydia Umkasethemba

The Zulu live in southeastern Africa.

A certain king had a child whose name was Umxakaza-wakogingqwayo (Rattler-of-weapons-of-the-place-of-the-rolling-of-the-slain). That name was given to her because when she was born an army went out to battle rattling its weapons—and so she was named Umxakaza. The name Wakogingqwayo was given because this army killed many men, and their bodies rolled on the ground. The king had another child who was called Ubalatusi (brass-colored-one), so called because she resembled brass.

As Umxakaza was growing up, her father said, "On the day that you come of age, we shall collect many cattle for the purpose of bringing you home! And these cattle that are brought to you shall be taken at the point of the spear, cattle-raids will be made into distant nations, and when the cattle come to you they will darken the sun!"

After a time, Umxakaza came to maturity. She was out with others in the open country, and she said to them, "I have come of age."

The other girls rejoiced when they heard this, and they ran to all the villages, telling other girls. They all came and remained with Umxakaza for a time. Then they left her, and went home, plundering the entire village.

The town was huge, the rows of its houses could not be counted. If a man standing in the middle of a cattle-enclosure shouted, people standing on the other side

From Henry Callaway, *Nursery Tales, Traditions, and Histories of the Zulus* (London: John A. Blair, 1868), pp. 181–216.

could not hear that there was anyone shouting at all. A man standing on the top of a hill would conclude that there were many villages, but in fact it was one.

The girls returned to Umxakaza. The people in the town had watched in wonder when they saw the girls coming to plunder. They shouted, "The king's child is of age!"

The king selected twenty head of cattle, and sent them to bring Umxakaza back from the open country.

But Umxakaza, remembering her father's pledge, said, "I do not see anything."

The cattle were taken home, and the father selected forty. They were taken to Umxakaza.

She said, "I do not see anything."

And these cattle were also taken home. Her father selected a hundred, and said, "Take those."

They took the cattle to Umxakaza, but she said, "I can see the sun."

They took the cattle home.

All the men belonging to her father's society came running with cattle, shouting, "Umxakaza-wakogingqwayo is of age!" There were now two hundred head of cattle, and these were taken to Umxakaza.

She said, "I still see the sun. Until the sun is darkened, as my father promised, I'll not return!"

They returned to the king. Men ran through the entire nation, taking the cattle from Umxakaza's father's people. When these cattle were collected and brought to her, Umxakaza said, "I still see the sun." They returned home.

An army was levied. It went to spoil foreign nations of their cattle, and came back with them. They were brought to Umxakaza.

She said, "I still see the sun!"

Another army was levied, and it returned with many thousand head of cattle.

But Umxakaza said that she still saw the sun.

Again an army was levied. The soldiers set out, and after a time they saw some cattle feeding in a large valley. They could not count how many hundred there were, but there were cattle white and dun, brown, black, red; the horns of some were directed downwards, the horns of others were moveable, others had only one horn. And there was a huge beast sitting on the hills overhanging that valley where the cattle were. The name of this beast was Usilosimaphundu (the rugose-nodulated-beast). It was called Usilosimaphundu because there were hills on it, and little hills, and on one side of it were many rivers, on another side were great forests, on another side precipices, on another side there was open high land.

And amidst all the trees that were on the beast were two trees much higher than all the rest. They were both named Imidoni (Water-boom-tree). They were the officers of Usilosimaphundu.

When Usilosimaphundu saw the army driving the cattle away, he said, "Those cattle that you're driving away, who do they belong to?"

The soldiers replied, "Get away! Let the wrinkled beast get out of the way!"

He replied, "All right, go off with them then."

But about this beast: there were only a mouth and eyes—his face was a rock, his mouth was very large and broad, but it was red. In some of the countries that were located on his body it was winter; and in others it was early harvest. But all these countries were in him.

The soldiers drove off the cattle of Usilosimaphundu. And as they approached their town, the sky clouded—it was as if it were going to rain, neither sun nor heaven could be seen, they were concealed by the dust raised by these cattle. They said, "The sky was clear! Where does this mist come from? It's impossible to see!" Then they saw that it was caused by the dust. When they came near to their homes, it was dark and they could no longer see the cattle.

They took the cattle to Umxakaza.

She said, "Here are the cattle that darken the sun."

So they went home with her. When she arrived, the umgongo (a small house or chamber in which a girl is placed when she comes of age) was already built, and the incapha (a soft kind of grass for putting under girls menstruating for the first time) spread on the ground. She entered the umgongo with the girls, and remained there.

And now all the men who had gone out with the army killed bullocks: everyone in the town killed his own bullock. But because there were so many slaughtered cattle, many were not even skinned. The crow skinned for itself; the vultures skinned for themselves; and the dogs skinned for themselves. Throughout the entire nation, there was no smell but that of meat.

But the cattle of Usilosimaphundu were not slaughtered, because those belonged to Umxakaza's father.

She remained uncounted years in the umgongo. The people no longer knew her; she was known only by the girls who were in the umgongo with her, for they would allow no one to enter the house. Those who were allowed to come in merely sat down without actually seeing her, and she remained inside the umgongo.

After a long time, the people said, "Before Umxakaza comes out, let all the people go to the royal-garden" (in which the people assembled to dig and sow for the king).

The people agreed: "It will be painful to harvest after she has come out, because beer will be made throughout the whole kingdom."

So it happened that, when she was about to leave the umgongo, all the people rose very early in the morning. In her father's village, there was beer everywhere—in one place, it was strained; in another, it was mixed with malt; in another, it was soaking. In the morning, all the people set out for the royal garden. The garden was very far off, and the people thought that by getting an early start they would be able to return early in the evening.

Only Umxakaza and her sister remained at home.

Some time after the departure of the people, Umxakaza and her sister heard the heaven thundering, and the earth moved even in the very house where they were sitting.

Umxakaza said, "Just go out and see what this is, Ubalatusi. Why should the heaven thunder when it is so bright?"

Ubalatusi went out, and she saw a forest standing at the entrance of the village! And she could no longer see where the entrance had been!

She came into the house, and said, "You will see, child of the king. There's some thing huge at the gateway! The fence has been broken down on one side, and is now just lying on the ground."

As they were speaking, two leaves broke off from the Imidoni and entered the house where they were sitting.

On their arrival, the leaves said, "Take a water-vessel, Ubalatusi, and go fetch water from the river."

She took the water-vessel and went to the river. They sat waiting for Ubalatusi. But at the river, she dipped water into the water-vessel—and when it was full, she was unable to leave the place.

After a time, the leaves said, "Go out, Umxakaza, and look for some water here at home."

She said, "I am of age, and it's not yet time for me to leave the umgonqo."

They replied, "We already knew that you were of age. But we say, Go and get water!"

She went and brought water from another house, and came back with it.

The leaves said, "Light a fire."

She replied, "I cannot light a fire."

They said, "We already knew that you could not light a fire. But we say, Light a fire!"

She lit the fire.

The leaves said, "Take a cooking-pot and place it on the hearth."

Umxakaza said, "I can't cook."

The leaves replied, "We already knew that you could not cook. But we say, Cook!"

She put the pot on the fire, and poured water into it.

The leaves said, "Go and bring some corn from your corn-basket. Then pour it into the pot."

She went and fetched some corn, and put it on the fire. They sat, and the corn was boiled.

They said, "Turn up the millstone, and grind the boiled corn."

But she said, "I cannot grind, I am the king's child. Look here—" showing them her hands, for her nails were very long. (Kings and great men allowed their nails to grow long. Such long nails were regarded as honorable. But women were not allowed to have long nails, as they would interfere with their work. Umxakaza, being the king's child, had allowed her nails to grow.)

One of the leaves took a knife, and said, "Give me your hand." The leaf cut the nails with the knife, and said, "Now grind!"

Umxakaza said, "I cannot grind! I'm the king's child!"

The leaves said, "We already knew that you could not grind, and that you are the king's child."

One of the leaves arose and turned up the millstone, then took the upper stone and, putting the boiled com on it, ground it. It said, "See, that is called grinding." Then it left the stone, and said, "Grind!"

She ground a large mass of corn.

They said, "Take your pot of amasi (curdled milk), and put it here."

She did so.

The leaves said, "Take a large pot and put it here."

She did so.

The leaves said, "Wash it."

She washed it.

The leaves said, "Go and pick out the milk calabash from your calabashes, and bring it here."

Umxakaza said, "Our milk calabash is large. I can't carry it alone! It takes three men to carry it!"

The leaves said, "Go, and we'll go with you."

They went and brought the calabash back.

The leaves said, "Empty it."

She brought the pot near, and they poured the amasi into it. They also poured some into the large pot. Then they took a basket, and put some of the ground corn into it. They took another basket and placed it on top of the ground corn. They took yet another basket and covered the amasi that was in the pot. One of the leaves took a spoon, and put it on the top of the basket. Then he took the pot and the amasi to Usilosimaphundu.

When the leaf came to him, Usilosimaphundu took the ground corn and the basket, and also the basket that covered the ground corn, and he opened his mouth and put it in his stomach—both the two baskets and the ground corn. Then he took the amasi that was covered with the basket, and put it all into his stomach, along with the spoon.

The leaf went up and again entered the house. It said, "Take down three spoons." It said, "Look here, here is a spoon. Eat, and we'll eat with you."

Umxakaza said, "But I do not eat amasi! I'm still under the obligations of puberty! " (That is, she has not yet left the umgonqo, and is still bound by the customs that are observed on coming to puberty, one of which is that the young woman is not to eat amasi until she is called upon by her father to come out of the umgonqo. When she comes out, they slaughter a bullock for her, the caul of which is placed over her shoulders and breasts, the head is shaved, and the whole body bathed; she dances, and then she can eat amasi.)

The leaves said, "We already knew that you are of age, and that you do not yet eat amasi. But we say, Eat!"

Umxakaza-wakogingqwayo cried, and said, "Oh, my mother! Who would eat amasi before the ceremonies of puberty are completed?" She said this because when she should eat amasi many oxen would be slaughtered, because it would be given her properly by her father.

The leaves said, "Eat, at once!"

She took a spoon, and they all ate the amasi.

Then the leaves went down to the house which was near the gateway. When they got there, they took out the pots containing beer, and the pots containing the boiled meal, and mats and vessels—everything that was in the house, they took to the gateway. And, even though the village was a large one, they took out everything from the entire village, leaving nothing in a single house. When they were about to take the things from the house of Umxakaza-wakogingqwayo's mother, Umxakaza said, "Just leave the little pot for me. It's in the upper part of the house, luted down with cowdung. You'll see it, it's little."

They went and took out everything, but they left the very large pots that contained beer that was strained (i.e., already fit for use). They also left the little pot. Then they went down to the gateway.

Everything that had been taken out of the village by the leaves Usilosimaphundu ate up. He did not chew it, he merely swallowed it.

Finally, everything in that village had been removed, but Usilosimaphundu was not satisfied. The leaves went up and entered the house where they had left two pots of beer. One of the leaves threw itself into one of the pots, and the other cast itself into the other, and when the two leaves came out of the pots, both pots were empty. They took the pots and carried them to the gateway to Usilosimaphundu. He took them both, and put them in his mouth, and swallowed them.

The mouth of Usilosimaphundu moved with rapidity. He said, "Come down now, Umxakaza-wakogingqwayo."

Umxakaza went into the house, and took the little pot and uncovered it. She took out the brazen ornaments for her body, and put them on. She took out her brazen pillow, she took out her garment ornamented with brass, she took her brass walking stick, she took out her petticoat ornamented with brass beads. She dressed herself, and went outside. She stood there, holding her garment and pillow, resting on her sleeping mat and rod.

Usilosimaphundu said, "Just turn your back to me, Umxakaza-wakogingqwayo."

She turned her back to him.

He said, "Now, turn again, Umxakaza-wakogingqwayo."

She turned.

Usilosimaphundu said, "Just laugh now, Umxakaza-wakogingqwayo."

But Umxakaza did not wish to laugh, for she was in trouble. She was leaving her father and mother and her regal position.

Usilosimaphundu said, "Come down now, Umxakaza-wakogingqwayo."

She went down to Usilosimaphundu.

And when she went down, it was as if her little sister at the river felt her departure. She started up suddenly with her water-vessel, and went up to the village. And it was as if her mother felt it too, for she left all the people who were walking with her.

Umxakaza-wakogingqwayo mounted Usilosimaphundu. And as soon as she had mounted, Usilosimaphundu ran speedily off. Her sister saw him as he disappeared behind a hill, but she did not know what it was. And the mother, too, as he disappeared, saw it—but did not know what it was.

Ubalatusi and her mother arrived at home together. The mother saw that the fence had been broken down on one side.

She said, "What has been here?"

Ubalatusi said, "I say it was the beast whose cattle were taken away."

The mother said, "Where were you?"

She said, "I was sent by the leaves to fetch water with a vessel from the river. When I got to the river, I was unable to get away again."

Her mother said, "But do you say that my child is still here at home? What was it that disappeared over there, just as I reached that place?"

The mother ran then, and entered the umgongo. When she got there, she found that Umxakaza was not there. She went into another house, but she did not find Umxakaza there. She went into another, she did not find her there.

She ran swiftly back to the men, and said, "Hurry! My child has been taken away by the beast who was plundered of his cattle!"

They said, "Have you seen him?"

She replied, "Something disappeared behind the hill as I approached home. And my child is no longer there!"

The men went home, and all armed. They set out following the tracks of the beast. They saw it, they went to it—it had stood still, awaiting them. They came up to it.

Usilosimaphundu laughed and said, "Do what you're going to do! Do it quickly, so that I can go. The sun has set."

They hurled and hurled their spears. One spear was thrown into a pool, another on a rock, another fell in the grass, another fell in the forest—all were thrown, but nothing was stabbed. Not a single spear was left.

The beast said, "Go, and arm again!"

They went home to arm.

Again, they hurled their spears. It happened as before: they did not stab a thing.

Finally, they said, "We're defeated!"

Usilosimaphundu said, "Goodbye."

All the people cried, "Let her come down!"

He assented, and Umxakaza came down when he said, "Descend."

They kissed her, weeping—and she too was weeping. The army of her people put Umxakaza in the middle.

But when the beast saw this, he said, "They want to take her away!" He turned, and passed through the middle of the group. It was as though something threw Umxakaza into the air. Then Usilosimaphundu turned back with her, and went away with her.

Umxakaza's mother and sister, her father and brother followed the beast. They went on, and when the beast rested they also rested. In the morning when he awoke, they went on with him. The mother went on, weeping. But the father and brother and sister were tired, and they turned back.

Her mother continued to accompany the beast. They went some distance, then rested. Usilosimaphundu plucked some sugarcane and maize, and gave it to the mother of Umxakaza. She ate.

In the morning, when Usilosimaphundu set out, Umxakaza's mother also set out. Finally she became tired, and she asked the beast to allow Umxakaza to come down so that she might see her.

He replied, "Get down then, Umxakaza-wakogingqwayo. Get down, so that your mother may see you."

She got down. They both wept, both she and her mother.

Her mother kissed her, saying, "Go in peace, my child."

Usilosimaphundu said, "Get up, Umxakaza."

She got up. He went away with her, and put her down far off—she did not know in what direction her people's country was. Usilosimaphundu came to the site of an old village. There was a large tobacco garden in the middle of it. On the border of the garden was a beautiful cave. Its floor was smeared with fat, it was very bright inside, and there were a blanket and sleeping mat there, a pillow, and a vessel of water.

Usilosimaphundu said, "Stay here, Umxakaza-wakogingqwayo. I have ruined your father, because he would have got much cattle for you when you married. But I have ruined him, because you will never see him again, and he will never see you. Stay here. Your father ruined me by taking away my many cattle, and now I have ruined him."

So Usilosimaphundu departed. And Umxakaza remained there alone, with two sugarcane and four ears of maize given to her by Usilosimaphundu. She sat until she lay down to sleep there in the cave.

In the morning, she awoke and sat in the sun. She took a sugarcane, broke off a joint, and threw it away. She broke off another, and threw it away. Only one joint was left, and she peeled that and ate it. Then she took the ears of maize and roasted them. She rubbed off the grain, she rubbed off the grain, and ate the portion that was in the middle. The rest she threw with the sugarcane. (Great people select the middle joints of the sugarcane, rejecting the upper and lower joints. They also reject the grains of maize that are at the ends of the car, selecting only those in the middle.)

At noon, the sun now bright, she saw something coming in the distance—for the cave was on the high land. There was just one tree there, and the thing that she saw went and sat under it. Then again she saw it approaching by leaps. Umxakaza went into the cave. The thing came into the tobacco garden, and it plucked the tobacco. It saw footprints, and was frightened. It looked around, then again plucked some tobacco, and went and put it outside the garden. Then it entered the cave. When Umxakaza-wakogingqwayo saw the thing, she arose and thrust out her hand. It saw the hand and fled, leaving the tobacco behind. It went and disappeared over a hill. She remained there until it was dark.

In the morning, Umxakaza-wakogingqwayo went and sat outside. Then she saw two things approaching, proceeding by leaps. They went and sat in the shade of the tree. Then they got up and went to the tobacco garden. Umxakaza went into the cave. When they had entered the garden, they plucked the tobacco. The one she saw the day before plucked tobacco in fear.

It said, "Footprints! Footprints! Where did they come from?"

The other said, "Where are they?"

It replied, "There."

They went and put the tobacco outside. Then they entered the cave. Umxakaza got up and thrust out both hands. She saw that they were one-legged ogres. When they saw the hands, they fled and disappeared behind a hill.

When they reached their chief, they said, "There's something in the chief's cave!"

The chief of the ogres said, "What is it like?"

They said, "There are two."

Other ogres were summoned, and in the morning they went to the chief's cave.

Umxakaza saw many of them approaching, and she said, "The day has now arrived on which I shall be killed."

When they reached the tree, they sat in the shade, they sat there in the shade and took snuff. Always when they went to pluck tobacco, they sat there in the shade. Then they got up and went into the tobacco garden and plucked tobacco, putting it outside. The chief of the ogres had ordered that his cave should be swept regularly, and that the people who went to sweep the cave should first pluck some tobacco, then put it outside the garden.

The others asked the two ogres where they had seen it.

They said, "It was in the cave."

They were told to go and look in the doorway, and see if it was there. They went stealthily, afraid, and looked in. They were unable to see clearly because her body glistened.

They came back and said, "It is one, it glistens! We cannot see it clearly."

The chief of the ogres said, "Let's all say together, Is it a man or a beast?"

So everyone shouted, "Are you a man or a beast?"

Umxakaza replied, "I am a human being."

They said, "Come out so that we can see you!"

Umxakaza said, "I don't want to come out, because I'm a chief's child!"

The chief sent some ogres, telling them to run swiftly and bring a bullock—a large ox—and hurry back with it. When the ox was brought, it was slaughtered. Then Umxakaza-wakogingqwayo came out, carrying her blanket and her sleeping mat, and pillow and rod, wearing her petticoat that was ornamented with brass beads. She put the blanket and pillow down at the doorway, and rested on her rod and sleeping mat.

The chief of the ogres said, "Turn your back towards us."

Umxakaza turned her back to them.

The chief of the ogres said, "Turn round."

Umxakaza turned.

The ogre said, "Oh, the thing is pretty! But oh, the legs!"

And again they said, "It would be pretty but for the two legs!"

They told her to go into the cave, and they all went away.

Many ogres were called together.

In the morning, they went to Umxakaza. They carried a veil through which, if anyone put it on, the body could be seen. They came and sat in the shade and took snuff.

When Umxakaza saw them, she said, "They're coming now to kill me!"

They came to the tobacco garden, they plucked tobacco, and put it outside the garden. Then they entered the cave and told her to come out. She went out. They gave her the veil. She put it on while they looked at her and said, "It would be a pretty thing—but oh, the two legs!" They said this because she had two legs and two hands, unlike them: if an ox of the white man is skinned and divided into two halves, the cannibals were like one side, there not being another side.

The ogres danced for Umxakaza. And when they had finished dancing, they went home with her.

When she saw the village of the chief of the ogres, she said, "Oh, this village! It's large, just like my father's!" And it was very great. She was placed in a house at the top of the village. Many cattle were killed, and she ate meat. She was called the chief's child, because the chief of the ogres loved her very much and called her his child. Umxakaza lived in the dark palace; there was a white palace at the lower part of the village. (No visitors were allowed to enter the dark palace; the white palace was entered by those called by the chief.)

Finally, Umxakaza was very fat and unable to walk. When she left the palace and was halfway between the white and the dark palaces, she became tired and returned to the house. When she got up, a pool of fat remained where she had been sitting. The chief of the ogres would drink the pool of fat that came from Umxakaza, because the nation of the ogres used to eat humans.

The people said, "Oh, chief, let her be eaten! Let the fat be melted down, because it's being wasted on the ground!"

But the chief of the ogres loved Umxakaza-wakogingqwayo very much, and said, "When she is eaten, where shall I be?"

The ogres said, "Oh, chief, she is a mere deformity! Of what use is a thing that can no longer walk, that is wasting the fat of the chief?"

Finally the king assented—they had continued to beseech him for three months, saying, "Let the fat of the chief be melted down!"

So he assented. Many ogres were summoned, and they went and brought back much firewood. A great hole was dug, and a large fire was kindled. Then a large sherd was taken and put on the fire.

It was very bright, there was not a single cloud in the sky. Finally the sherd was red. When it was very red, Umxakaza was called. She went with them. When she got to the gateway, she looked. She saw that there were many many people.

She sang,

"Listen, heaven! Listen, listen!
Listen, heaven! It does not thunder with loud thunder,
It thunders in an undertone. What is it doing?
It thunders to produce rain and change of season."

Then the ogres saw a cloud gathering tumultuously in the sky. Umxakaza sang again,

"Listen, heaven! Listen, listen!
Listen, heaven! It does not thunder with loud thunder,
It thunders in an undertone. What is it doing?
It thunders to produce rain and change of season."

The whole heaven became covered with clouds. It thundered terribly, and it rained a great rain. The rain quenched the red hot sherd, and took the sherd and tossed it in the air. It was broken to pieces. The heaven killed the ogres who were walking with Umxakaza—but it left her uninjured. It killed some others too, but many remained with their chief.

Again, the heaven became clear and bright.

The ogres said, "Let a fire be kindled at once! Let the sherd get hot at once! And let Umxakaza be taken and raised and placed on the sherd! Then she'll not be able to sing!"

The sherd was made hot. Finally, it was red.

They went to get her, they lifted her up. When she got to the gateway, she looked up and said,

"Listen, heaven! Listen, listen!
Listen, heaven! It does not thunder with loud thunder,
It thunders in an undertone. What is it doing?
It thunders to produce rain and change of season."

It rained and thundered terribly. The chief of the ogres was killed, and many other ogres died. Only a small number remained.

The small remnant that remained were afraid, and said, "Let's not touch her again, but let's not give her food, let her get thin and die!"

Umxakaza rejoiced because they now gave her but little food. She remained there until she became thin—but she was not excessively thin, only much fat had disappeared. She took a basket then, and into it she placed the things that the king of the ogres had given her. When she had put them in the basket, she set out. She carried it on her head, and she went on her way thus burdened, for some of the garments were ornamented with brass beads. She journeyed sleeping in the open country, because she feared the ogres. She went for a long time without eating, until finally she came to a nation of humans. She traveled, sleeping among them. Sometimes at one village they would give her food, at another they would refuse her. She traveled until she was very thin.

One day, she reached the top of a hill. She saw a very large town, and said, "That town! It resembles the town of the ogres from which I have come! The town that was like my father's!"

She went down, seeing the smoke of fire coming from the houses at the top of the town, and when she came to the gateway she saw a man sitting there in the shade. But his hair was as long as a ogre's. She merely passed on, but she compared him, saying, "That man resembles my father!"

She went to the upper end of the town, and recognized it now as her father's. When she arrived at her home, he mother was making beer.

Umxakaza sat down by the wall, and said, "Queen, give me some of your beer."

They said, "Good day!"

She saluted them in return. She saw that her mother's head was deranged, and asked, "But what's the matter at this kraal? And what's the matter with the man at the gateway?"

The mother answered, "You, where do you come from?"

She replied, "From over there."

The other said, "Well, princess, death entered this place. The princess royal of my house went away. That is her father whom you saw at the gateway. Don't you also see what condition I'm in?"

She replied, "When she went away, where did she go?"

The mother said, "She went with the beast."

She said, "Where did he take her?"

The mother said, "She was of age. The beast's cattle were taken away because the princess's father had said, before she was of age, that when she came of age, the cattle that would bring her home would darken the sun. But her father did not possess that many cattle, so they went and took those belonging to the beast."

The girl said, "But why do you cry, since your child was treated badly by yourselves alone? Why did you take away the cattle of the beast? You killed her on purpose!"

The mother replied, "Let this contemptible thing go! She sees because I have given her my beer. She now laughs at me about my dead child! Does anyone exist who would be willing to give anything to the beast? From the day my child departed from the midst of her father's nation, has there been any joy here? Do we not now just exist?"

Umxakaza said, "Here I am! I am Umxakaza-wakogingqwayo! Although you left me, here I am again."

Her mother cried, and so did the others who were sitting by the door.

Her father came running, saying, "Why are you crying?"

They said, "Umxakaza has come!"

Her father said, "But she has returned! Why do you cry?"

He sent men out, telling them to go to the whole nation, summoning the people, telling them to make beer throughout the land, for Umxakaza-wakogingqwayo had come home.

Beer was made throughout the land. The people came together, bringing cattle, rejoicing because the princess had returned. Cattle were slaughtered, and her father and mother had a great festival. Her father cut his hair, and put on a head-ring; her mother cut her hair, and put on a top-knot. (The head-ring is a sign of manhood, and no one is permitted to wear it until he has received the chief's command. It is regarded as the chief's mark, and must be treated with respect. The top-knot of a woman is formed of red clay. Much attention is paid to the head-ring and top-knot, and the hair is kept shaven both inside and outside the ring, and all around the knot. When they are in trouble, this is neglected, and it can be seen at once by the head that there is some cause of affliction.)

There was rejoicing throughout the land.

It was rumored among all the nations that the princess had returned to her home, and that she was very beautiful.

A king came from another country to ask Umxakaza's father for his daughter in marriage.

He refused, saying, "She has just come home. She was carried off by the beast, and I don't want her to go away. I want to live and be glad with her."

Many kings came, but her father gave them all one answer. Finally the kings went away, without getting Umxakaza for a wife.

But there was a king of a distant country. He had heard about this young woman. He sent an old man, he said, "Let him go." And the old man went, and when he came to the entrance of Umxakaza's town, he turned into a beautiful and glistening frog. The frog entered the town leaping, and it settled on a gatepost. Umxakaza was playing with others near the gateway.

Umxakaza said, "Come and see this beautiful thing!"

All the people came out, looking at it, and saying, "What a beautiful frog!"

It leapt out of the gateway. When it had gone out, Umxakaza said, "Oh, give me my things!" She put them all into a basket, and set out with them.

They cried, "But you've just come home! Where are you going now?"

She replied, "I'm going to follow the frog, to see where it is going!"

The father selected twenty men, to carry food and her things. They all set out, following the frog as it leapt, until they were tired.

Umxakaza then traveled alone with it, and when they were alone the frog turned back into a man.

When it had turned into a man, Umxakaza wondered and said, "What happened to you, that you became a frog?"

He said, "I just became a frog."

She said, "Where are you taking me?"

He replied, "I'm taking you home to our king."

They went together until they came to another nation. When they had gone a great distance, she saw a large forest. The path went through this forest. When they reached the forest, the old man knew that they were now near home.

He said, "Hurry! The place we're going to is far off."

She came to the forest. The old man took her, left the path, and went into the middle of the forest.

He said, "No! Shall I take such a beautiful thing for another man?"

He stood still with her in an open place. Umxakaza wondered at such a beautiful place in the forest—it was as if humans dwelled there.

The old man said, "Let all beasts come here!"

Umxakaza heard the entire forest in a ferment, a crashing sound. She was afraid.

The old man departed and went into the forest, shouting and whistling, "Fiyo, fiyo! Let all the beasts come here!"

Umxakaza stood still, and said, "Open, my head, so that I may place my things inside."

Her head opened, and she put all her things in it. Then her head closed again, it was as though it had not opened. But her head was now fearfully large, and when a person looked at it, it was fearful.

Then she went up into a tree. When she was on the top of the tree, the branches came together, for she had climbed at a place where the trees were thick, and united. She turned the branches aside, and went up. The branches again closed behind her.

From the top of the tree, Umxakaza was able to see a village in front of the forest. She remained in the tree. Wild beasts came, seeking prey. They seized the old man.

He said, "No! Don't eat me! The one I called you here for is no longer here! I no longer see her!"

They tore him.

He scolded them, and said, "Leave me alone, my children! I'll give you something tomorrow!"

So the animals departed. The old man was left alone, and he set out and went home.

When Umxakaza saw that he had gone outside the forest, she quickly came down from the tree and ran out of the forest. When the old man was nearing the village, she saw him and said, "Wait for me, because we're traveling together! Why did you leave me?"

He halted. But he wondered when he saw how large her head was, for Umxakaza's head used to be small. But the old man was afraid to ask, "What happened to you?" because he had called the beasts to come to her.

They went into the village. She stood at the doorway. The old man saluted his king, and said, "I have found a wife for you. But her head is not right."

They went into the house, and sat down. All the people wondered, "Oh, she's beautiful! But the head is that of an animal!"

They said, "Let her be sent away."

But the king's sister was there, and she objected, "Leave her alone! If she's deformed, what of that?"

The bridegroom did not love her, however, and he said, "Since I am taking my first wife, and I a king, should I begin with a deformed person?"

His sister said, "It is no matter. Leave her alone, let her stay even if you do not marry her."

So she remained there, and the people called her Ukhandakhulu, Big Head.

People gathered to go to a dance, and the king's sister asked her to go with her to look at the dancing.

But Ukhandakhulu said, "Because I'm a deformed person, the people will laugh at me and they'll drive me away, saying that I came to spoil the dance. If I make an appearance there, the young women will stop dancing and flee when they see me."

She said, "No, we'll sit down at a distance if they laugh."

Ukhandakhulu said, "Won't you dance yourself?"

She replied, "No, I don't wish to dance, I wish to remain with you." For the young woman loved her very much, and she loved her in return; that is why she did not like to go to the dance and leave her alone.

They put on their ornaments, and both went to the dance.

Those who saw them fled, saying, "There's a deformed thing walking with the princess!"

Others asked, "What is it like?"

They said, "The head is frightening!"

As soon as the two had arrived at the dancing place, all the people fled, and some warned them off, saying, "Don't come here!" They went away and sat on a hill until the dance was ended. Then they returned and sat down at home.

The entire nation exclaimed in wonder, "You should see the thing the king has married!"

They remained at home many days.

Once they went to bathe. They bathed, they came out of the water and stood on sods of grass so that their body and feet might dry, because they had scraped their feet. (When they washed, they rubbed their feet with a soft sandstone, to smooth the skin.)

The young woman said, "Ukhandakhulu, what caused you to be as you are?"

She replied, "It's just natural to me."

The young woman said, "You would be beautiful, child of my parents, Ukhandakhulu. But you are spoiled by your head."

Ukhandakhulu laughed and said, "Open, my head, so that my things may come out."

Her head immediately opened, her things came out, and she placed them on the ground. Her head closed and was small again. When the young woman saw this, she threw herself on her, seizing her. They laughed, the young woman saying, "Can this be the one we call Ukhandakhulu?" They rolled each other in the mud, laughing, unable to get up.

Finally they got up and bathed again.

As they were standing, the young woman said, "What had you done?"

She replied, "I had placed my things in my head." She then told everything that had been done by the old man.

The young woman wondered, and Umxakaza said, "That's what made me have such a large head."

Then Umxakaza gave her one of her garments.

She put on her own garment which was ornamented with brass beads, and told her, "I am Umxakaza-wakogingqwayo. That is my name."

They returned home. When they arrived, they stood at the doorway.

The people went out and said, "There's a young woman come to point out her husband."

Others said, "Whose daughter is she?"

Those who saw her said, "We don't know where she comes from."

They asked, "Is she alone?"

They replied, "There are two. But the one accompanies the other."

All the people went out then and looked, asking, "Which of you has come to point out a husband?" They could not see them distinctly, because they bent their heads down, looking on the ground.

The young woman of the village raised her head, and said, "This is Ukhandakhulu."

All the people wondered, they ran and told the king, "You should see Ukhandakhulu when her head is as it is now!"

The king went out and saw her. He called for many cattle, and many were slaughtered. The whole nation was summoned.

It was said, "Let the people assemble! They are going to dance for the queen!"

All who saw Ukhandakhulu wondered.

Beer was made. The king danced, he loved Umxakaza very much.

His sister said, "What is this? You gave directions that she should be sent away!"

The old man was killed because of what he had done.

At length, she returned to her father's place with the cattle by which the bridegroom's people declared her his chosen bride. They arrived at her father's place.

They said, "Umxakaza-wakogingqwayo has come."

They killed many cattle for the bridegroom's people. The dowry was paid immediately.

She was married.

The king loved her very much. She became his wife, she reigned prosperously with her husband.

Commentary

"Umxakaza-wakogingqwayo" is a Zulu tale that dramatizes a girl's puberty rite of passage, her change of identity as she moves into womanhood, and it has as its companion themes the necessity of respect for humanity and reverence for custom. Only when Umxakaza moves away from her willfulness, her childishness and vanity, to an understanding that obedience to custom is society's best hope for establishing peaceful relations among themselves is she prepared to move into womanhood.

This new knowledge and the consequent move from childhood into adulthood is accomplished in and by the three parts of the story and by the primary pattern of the story. Keep in mind that the themes of these stories are to be found by means of an analysis of the language of poetry, the language of storytelling, in the fantasy images and the way these are constructed or patterned.

Part One

Umxakaza prepares for her puberty ritual. She comes of age, and is placed in the purification lodge: she goes in a girl, she will presumably emerge a woman. But something goes sour here: she is not prepared for womanhood. This is made clear by the first pattern in part one: "I can still see the sun," she stubbornly protests each time her father brings more cattle to fulfill his pledge that on the day that she comes of age he will darken the sun with cattle. His ravaging of the countryside to get more and more cattle, and her belligerent insistence that he continue to do so, make of them kindred spirits: her very name reflects her father's martial exploits, his assaults on humankind and on nature. Father and daughter are equally responsible, equally guilty.

When, therefore, she is ready to come out of her purification lodge a woman, Usilosimaphundu, symbol of nature, interferes; he removes her from the lodge. The second pattern in part one: When she protests that she is a princess, the emissaries of Usilosimaphundu insist that she nevertheless do their bidding, and so she is humbled; she loses her identity as a princess.

To emphasize this retaliation of nature against human excess, Usilosimaphundu, in the third pattern of part one, ravages the king's realm, doing to the king what the king had earlier done to nature.

As the first part of the story comes to an end, the fourth pattern in part one, the attempts to stop Usilosimaphundu from taking Umxakaza away, reveals the futility of interfering with nature.

Part Two

This part has to do with Umxakaza's life with the cannibals. This part of the story is a stark reflection, a mirror, of part one; the cannibal chief is equivalent to Umxakaza's father. He pampers and spoils the child much as her father did in part one. As the father's indulgent treatment of his daughter resulted in her moral grotesqueness in part one, so the cannibal chief's indulgence in part two results in her physical grotesqueness. They are the same. Part two is a dramatic reflection, a mirroring, of part one.

In the first pattern of part two, Umxakaza is established as a bizarre curiosity in the eyes of the cannibals, a further reflection of her loss of identity. Not a princess, not even human: she is a quaint monstrosity. In the second pattern of part two, she becomes enormous. And the third pattern of part two has to do with her cries to nature for assistance. And Usilosimaphundu returns, this time in the form of thunder and rain, and he helps her again. His help in this third pattern of part two reveals that his actions in part one are to be seen as positive. He is not an ogre, a negative swallower.

Part Three

In this section, Umxakaza's life in the prince's village is depicted. There is an elaborate transition, in which she is enticed from her home by the wizard who transforms himself into a frog. Again, there is an identity problem; she loses her identity as the beautiful princess when she puts her jewelry, things of her vanity, into her head; she is again transformed, again ugly, as she was morally ugly in part one and physically ugly in part two. Now she has an enormous head. There is a frame pattern, the first pattern in part three in this part of the story: she begins with a big head, will end with a normal head. In the second pattern of part three, she is alienated from the prince's people. She again loses her identity; no longer Umxakaza, she is called Big Head. The prince, though he had her kidnaped so that he could marry her, will now have nothing to do with her.

But in the second section of part three, this changes; she transforms into a beautiful woman, her big head gone. She gives the prince's sister a gift, the first evidence in the tale of a selfless act on Umxakaza's part. Her identity restored, she has moved to womanhood. •

Note

"When a princess royal comes of age, she quits her father's home, and goes out into the wilds, from which she is brought back by having a bullock slaughtered on her account. Other girls tell her parents where she is; and all law and order are at an end; and each man, woman, and child lays hold of any article of property which may be at hand, assegais [spears], shields, mats, pots, etc. The king says nothing, it being a day of such general rejoicing that it is regarded as improper to find fault with anyone. If during this reign of misrule, anything is taken which the chief really values, he can obtain it again only by paying a fine." (Notes by Henry Callaway. Other notes by Callaway are placed in brackets in the text of the narrative.)

BIBLIOGRAPHY

Abrahamsson, Hans. *The Origin of Death, Studies in African Mythology.* Uppsala: Studia Ethnographica Upsaliensia, 1951.

Abu-Manga, Al-Amin. "Baakankaro, A Fulani Epic from Sudan." *Africana Marburgensia* 9 (1985): 9–11.

Barrett, W. E. H. "A'Kikuyu Fairy Tales (Rogano)." *Man* 12 (1912): 112–114.

Basden, George Thomas. *Niger Ibos.* London: Cass, 1938.

Beech, Mervyn W. H. *The Suk.* Oxford: Clarendon Press, 1911.

Biebuyck, Daniel, and Kahombo C. Mateene. *The Mwindo Epic.* Berkeley: University of California Press, 1969.

Bleek, Dorothea F., ed. *The Mantis and His Friends.* Cape Town: T. Maskew Miller, [1923].

Bleek, W. H. I. *Reynard the Fox in South Africa.* London: Trübner and Co., 1864.

Bleek, W. H. I., and Lucy C. Lloyd. *Specimens of Bushman Folklore.* London: George Allen and Co., 1911.

Boaz, Franz, and C. Kamba Simango. "Tales and Proverbs of the Vandau of Portuguese S. Africa." *Journal of American Folk-Lore* 35 (1922): 151–204.

Broderick, Modupe. "Foreword." *Ga Ta Nan* 1 (1980): 7–8.

Brown, John Tom. *Among the Bantu Nomads.* London: Seeley, Service, 1926.

Burton, Richard F., tr. *The Book of the Thousand Nights and a Night.* London: Burton Club, 1886.

Butcher, H. L. M. "Four Edo Fables." *Africa* 10 (1937): 342.

Callaway, Henry. *Nursery Tales, Traditions, and Histories of the Zulus.* London: John A. Blair, 1868.

Cancel, Robert. *Allegorical Speculation in an Oral Society.* Berkeley: University of California Press, 1989.

Casati, Gaetano. *Ten Years in Equatoria.* New York: F. Warne and Co., 1891.

Chatelain, Heli. *Folk-Tales of Angola.* New York: American Folk-Lore Society, 1894.

Chimenti, Elisa. *Tales and Legends from Morocco.* New York: Ivan Obolensky, 1965.

Clark, John Pepper. *The Ozidi Saga.* Ibadan: Ibadan University Press, 1977.

Cole, H. "Notes on the Wagogo of German East Africa." *Journal of the Royal Anthropological Institute* 32 (1902): 331–332.

Cosentino, Donald. "Patterns in *Domeisia.*" Diss. U. of Wisconsin-Madison, 1976.

Cummins, A. G. "Annuak Fable." *Man* 15 (1915): 34–35.

Dayrell, Elphinstone. *Ikom Folk Stories from Southern Nigeria.* London: Royal Anthropological Institute of Great Britain and Ireland, 1913.

Dennett, R. E. *Notes on the Folklore of the Fjort.* London: David Nutt, 1898.

Doke, Clement M. *Lamba Folk-Lore.* New York: G. E. Stechert, 1927.

Donohugh, Agnes C. L., and Priscilla Berry. "A Luba Tribe in Katanka, Customs and Folklore." *Africa* 5 (1932): 181.

Edgar, Frank. *Litafina Tatsuniyoyi Na Hausa.* Belfast: W. Erskine Mayne, 1911–1913. Tr. from Hausa by Neil Skinner. *Hausa Tales and Traditions.* Madison, Wisconsin: University of Wisconsin Press, 1977.

Ekwensi, Cyprian. *An African Night's Entertainment.* Lagos: African Universities Press, 1962.

Elliot, Geraldine. *The Long Grass Whispers.* New York: Schocken Books, 1968.

Ellis, A. B. *The Ewe-speaking Peoples of the Slave Coast of West Africa.* London: Chapman and Hall, 1890.

Ennis, Merlin. *Umbundu, Folktales from Angola.* Boston: Beacon Press, 1962.

Evans-Pritchard, E. E. *The Zande Trickster.* Oxford: Clarendon Press, 1967.

Fáàdójútìmí, Adégbóyègún. "The Romance of the Fox." Unpublished.

Fergusson, V. "Nuer Beast Tales." *Sudan Notes and Records* 7 (1924): 111–112.

Finnegan, Ruth. *Limba Stories and Story-telling.* Oxford: Clarendon Press, 1967.

Foster, Deborah. "Structure and Performance of Swahili Oral Narrative." Diss. U. of Wisconsin-Madison, 1984.

Freeman, Richard Austin. *Travels and Life in Ashanti and Jaman.* New York: Frederick A. Stokes, 1898.

Frobenius, Leo. *Volksmärchen der Kabylen.* Vol. 3, *Das Fabelhafte*. Jena: Eugen Diederichs, 1921.

Gecau, R. N. *Kikuyu Folktales, Their Nature and Value.* Nairobi: East African Publishing House, 1970.

Green, Feridah Kirby. "Folklore from Tangier." *Folklore* 19 (1908): 453–455.

Hannan, M. "Ngano Dzokupunza, Shona Fireside Songs." *NADA, Native Affairs Deaprtment Annual* No. 31 (1954): 30.

Helser, Albert D. *African Stories.* New York: Fleming H. Revell, 1930.

Hobley, Charles William. *Ethnology of A-Kamba and Other East African Tribes.* Cambridge: Cambridge University Press, 1910.

Hofmayer, W. "Zur Geshichte und sozialen und politischen Gliederung des Stammes der Schillukneger." *Anthropos* 5 (1910): 332.

Hollis, Alfred Claud. *The Masai, Their Language and Folklore.* Oxford: Oxford University Press, 1905.

Huffman, Ray. *Nuer Customs and Folklore.* Oxford: Oxford University Press, 1931.

Innes, Gordon. *Sunjata, Three Mandinka Versions.* London: School of Oriental and African Studies, 1974.

Jablow, Alta. *Yes and No, The Intimate Folklore of Africa.* New York: Horizon Press, 1961.

Jacottet, Edouard. *The Treasury of Ba-Suto Lore.* Morija: Sesuto Book Depot, 1908.

Jalla, Ad. *History, Traditions and Legends of Barotseland.* London: Colonial Office, 1921.

Johnston, Harry. *Liberia.* London: Hutchinson, 1906.

Johnston, Harry. *The Uganda Protectorate.* London: Hutchinson, 1904.

Jordan, A. C. *Towards an African Literature.* Berkeley: University of California Press, 1973.

Jugwe, Mwaziza. "The Pauper's Daughter." Unpublished.

Junod, Henri A. *Les Ba-Rongas.* Neuchâtel: Paul Attinger, 1898.

Junod, Henri A. *The Life of a South African Tribe.* New York: University Books, Inc., 1962.

Kabira, Wanjiku Mukabi, and Kavetsa Adagala. *Kenyan Oral Narratives.* Nairobi: Heinemann, 1985.

Kirk, J. W. C. "Specimens of Somali Tales." *Folk-Lore* 15 (1904): 319–321.

Lang, Andrews. *The Grey Fairy Book.* London: Longmans, Green, 1900.

LaPin, Deirdre. "Story, Medium, and Masque: The Idea and Art of Yoruba Storytelling." Diss. U. of Wisconsin-Madison, 1977.

Lederbogen, William. "Duala Fables." *Journal of the African Society* 4 (1904): 56–77.

Littmann, Enno. *Publications of the Princeton Expedition to Abyssinia.* Leyden: E. J. Brill, 1910.

Macdonald, Duff. *Africana.* London: Simkin Marshall, 1882.

Mangite, Donald. "The King's Twelve Sons and One Daughter." Unpublished.

Maugham, Reginald Charles F. *Zambezia.* London: J. Murray, 1910.

Mbiti, John S. *Akamba Stories.* Oxford: Clarendon Press, 1966.

Mkanganwi, K. G. *Ngano.* Harari: University of Rhodesia, 1973.

Nasr, Ahmad Abd-al-Rahim M. "Maiwurno of the Blue Nile: A Study of an Oral Biography." Diss. U. of Wisconsin-Madison, 1977.

Nassau, Robert Hamill. *Where Animals Talk, West African Folk Lore Tales.* Boston: Gorham Press, 1912.

Ngcobo, Sondoda. "The Story of Chakijana." Unpublished.

Nkonki, Garvey. "The Traditional Prose Literature of the Ngqika." Diss. U. of South Africa, n.d.

Norris, H. T. *Shinqiti Folk Literature and Song.* Oxford: Clarendon Press, 1968.

Noss, Philip A. "Gbaya Traditional Literature." *Abbia* Nos. 17–18 (1967): 35.

Nunn, Jessie Alford. *African Folk Tales.* New York: Funk and Wagnalls, 1969.

Nxumalo, Albertine. "The Pregnant Boy." Unpublished.

Petrie, William Matthew Flinders. *Egyptian Tales.* London: Methuen, 1895.

Plutarch's Lives. Ed. and tr., Samuel Squire. Cambridge: Cambridge University Press, 1744.

Raum, Johannes William. *Versuch einer Grammatik der Dschaggasprache (Moschi-dialekt).* Berlin: Archiv für die Stud. dtsch. Kolonialspr. 11 (1909): 307–318.

Rattray, R. S. *Akan-Ashanti Folk-tales.* Oxford: Clarendon Press, 1930.

Ross, Mabel H., and Barbara K. Walker. *"On Another Day." Tales Told among the Nkundo of Zaire.* Hamden, Conn.: Archon Books, 1979.

Samatar, Said S. *Oral Poetry and Somali Nationalism.* Cambridge: Cambridge University Press, 1982.

Scheub, Harold. *The Xhosa Ntsomi.* Oxford: Clarendon Press, 1975.

Secka, Malick. "The Two Hammadis." Unpublished.

Sibree, James, Jr. "Malagasy Folk-tales." *Folk-Lore Journal* 2 (1884) 49–55.

Sidile, Mercy. "The Conspirators." Unpublished.

Smith, Edwin E., and Andrew Murray Dale. *The Ila-speaking Peoples of Northern Rhodesia.* London: Macmillan and Co., 1920.

Steere, Edward. *Swahili Tales.* London: Society for Promoting Christian Knowledge, 1870.

Stumme, Hans von. *Märchen and Gedichte aus der Stadt Tripolis in Nord-Afrika.* Leipzig: Hinrichs, 1896.

Talbot, P. Amaury. *In the Shadow of the Bush.* London: William Heinemann, 1912.

Tanna, Laura Davidson. "The Art of Jamaican Oral Narrative Performance." Diss. U. of Wisconsin-Madison, 1980.

Torrend, J. *Specimens of Bantu Folk-lore from Northern Rhodesia.* London: Kegan Paul, Trench, Trübner, 1921.

Weeks, John H. *Among Congo Cannibals.* London: Seeley, Service, 1913.

Weeks, John H. *Congo Life and Folklore.* London: Religious Tract Society, 1911.

Wendland, Ernest. *Nthano za kwa Kawaza.* Lusaka: University of Zambia, 1976.

Westermann, Diedrich. *The Shilluk People, Their Language and Folklore.* Philadelphia: Board of Foreign Missions of the United Presbyterian Church of North America, 1912.

Williams, R. H. K. "The Konnoh People." *Journal of the African Society* 8 (1909): 136–137.

Zenani, Nongenile Masithathu. "Sikhuluma, The Boy Who Did Not Speak." Unpublished.

Zenani, Nongenile Masithathu. *The World and the Word, Tales and Observations from the Xhosa Oral Tradition.* Madison: University of Wisconsin Press, 1992.